A Gallows Set Upon A Hill

James Howard Trott

Ye are the light of the world. A city that is set on a hill cannot be hid . . . Let your light so shine before men, that they may see your good works, and glorify your Father which is in heaven. **Matthew 5:14, 16**

That God hath a Controversy with his New-England People is undeniable, the Lord having written his displeasure in dismal Characters against us. Though personal Afflictions doe oftentimes come only or chiefly for Probation yet as to publick judgements it is not wont to be so; especially when by a continued Series of Providence, the Lord doth appear and plead against his People. 2 Sam. 21. 11. As with us it hath been from year to year. Would the Lord have whetted his glitterring Sword, and his hand have taken hold on judgement? Would he have sent such a mortal Contagion like a Beesom of Destruction in the midst of us? . . . In which respect, a deep and most serious enquiry into the Causes of his Controversy ought to be attended. Nevertheless, it is sadly evident that there are visible, manifest Evils, which without doubt the Lord is provoked by.

-- *The Necessity of Reformation*, **General Court Synod (1679)**

OAK AND YEW
PRESS

A Gallows
Set Upon A Hill

James Howard Trott

First Edition	December 2002
Second Printing	March 2003
Second Edition	December 2005
Expanded Edition	July 2015

Oak and Yew Press
Philadelphia

OAK AND YEW
PRESS

Goodwife   Rebecca   Nurse   in   Gaol

. . .That you may not delay the voyage intended, for your full satisfaction know this is the place where the Lord will create a new heaven and a new earth in, new churches and a new commonwealth together. -- Edward Johnson, ***Wonder-Working Providence of Sion's Savior*** (1654)

And thou New England, which art exalted in privileges of the Gospel above many people, know thou the time of thy visitation, and consider the great things the Lord hath done for thee. . . . The Lord looks for more from thee than from other peoples: more zeal for God, more love to His truth, more justice and equity in thy ways . . . -- Peter Bulkeley (d. 1659), ***The Lesson of the Covenant, For England and New England***

And it's certain it's better to suffer all the plagues without any one sin than to commit the least sin and to be freed from all plagues. Suppose that all miseries and sorrows that ever befell all the wicked in earth and hell should meet together in one soul, as all the waters gathered together in one sea; suppose thou heardest the devil's roaring, and sawest hell gaping, and flames of everlasting burnings flashing before thine eyes? It's certain it were better for thee to be cast into those inconceivable torments than to commit the least sin against the Lord. Thou dost not think so now, but thou wilt find it so one day.
-- Thomas Hooker (d. 1647), ***A True Sight of Sin***

God is not a man that he should lie; neither the son of man, that he should repent: hath he said and shall he not do it? Or hath he spoken, and shall he not make it good? Behold I have received commandment to bless: and he hath blessed; and I cannot reverse it. . . . Surely there is no enchantment against Jacob, neither is there any divination against Israel. . .
-- ***Numbers* 23: 19, 20, 23a** (Baalam addresses King Baalak)

Learn these four lines by heart.
Have communion with few,
Be intimate with ONE,
Deal justly with all,
Speak evil of none.
-- from the ***New England Primer***

Preface — Bad Bargains

The New-Englanders are a People of God settled in those which were once the Devil's Territories; and it may easily be supposed that the Devil was extremely disturbed when he perceived such a People here accomplishing the Promise of old made unto our Blessed Jesus, That He should have the Uttermost Parts of the Earth for his Possession.
    —Cotton Mather, "Of Beelzebub and His Plot" in **Wonders of the Invisible World,** 1693.

The persecuted and holy men who founded our colony spoke often, in the words of scripture, of our "city set upon a hill". It was clear to them we sought a heavenly city, the Jerusalem above, which was the ultimate gathering place of all true children of Abraham's and heirs to his faith. But a confusion lurked in hearts and minds when the first boat touched at Plymouth, and it grew quickly thereafter. The "city set upon a hill" was openly identified with New England and Massachusetts Bay Colony. A subtle but certain bargain had been struck for the soul of the colony: *Establish us safe, prosperous, and secure and we will serve . . .* serve whom? Our fathers said, "we will serve God," but submitting to enter into such a bargain is foreign to the nature of God. To the extent we made bargain, we made a bad bargain — not with God, but with the devil.

How ironic then, that we were sure the devil was vigorously opposing us and our "city set upon a hill". We saw him in the Indian attacks, in the mysterious sicknesses and deaths, and we saw him at his fiercest and most malevolent in the witches whom we discovered all around us in 1692. Our city set upon a hill was under attack, and so we counterattacked by erecting a great engine of war to bring down the enemy's stronghold. We built a gallows and set it upon a hill.

Now many have come full circle to see that our "gallows set upon a hill" was not an engine against the devil, but an altar for his worship. Our "city set upon a hill" shone forth a message of great dishonor to God : that his people deal out lies, accusations, and death to the innocent. We made a very bad bargain, indeed.

That there have been witches in some places at dark times we do not doubt. But we know those hanged here were none. Gradually some began to doubt after the first examinations, then a few more after Martha Corey and Rebecca Nurse were arrested. Others became skeptical as ultimately hundreds were accused. Most are convinced of it now, since the courts have reversed their judgments and found the convictions and executions unlawful.

Yet there have been witches, and this is a puzzling thing. What is it in a man or woman that draws and leads to a covenant with the devil? It is not enough to say the devil does it—for he is not a free agent nor an omnipotent one. All his acts are contingent on the permission of God, as in Job's case. And his "bargains" all depend on the consent or cooperation of his human victim, as in King Saul's case.

Unfortunately and contrary to the simple formulas of our best witch-seekers, not all transactions with the devil are carried out by means of a bound contract which the "witch" signs with his or her own blood. Men submit to the devil more subtly and in myriad ways. There is something essential about us that inclines toward it.

What brings a person to submit to the devil? We might say the answer wis part of God's secret counsel and go back to cutting hay. Or in a meditative mood, we might once have said such a person was not of the elect, or else due for a sharp course of discipline before hearing his calling. But since our "troubles" many of us have come to another way of answering questions about evil. We look at hearts nearer home, and if we do not see a sure parallel in our own, we often find it in the bosoms of those we love best.

We submit to the devil for two reasons. First, we do not know who God is, and second, we do not know who the devil is. Or in terms of practical experience, we submit to evil because we feel we lack some necessary thing. We turn to an immediate though dubious source of supply for some supposed necessity, counting the expected gain more important than the less apparent loss.

These days no Villager would have the gall to mention Francis Nurse, Sr. and the devil in one breath. Nevertheless, some of those who loved that venerable man feel liberty in saying he too made a bad bargain which was only thrown out of court after long litigation.

Francis' bargain was a kind of indenture, like the articles he signed when he became an apprentice traymaker. After seven years, he was a master of that craft, and free of that servitude. He had grown to love woodworking as most men never could. But he wanted more, so he bought a small farm and for thirty years made all he could of it. He was born to hard-work and loved hard-work as few others could love that either.

His hard work accrued to buying a bigger farm, the Chickering place in Salem Village. There his status and the prosperity of his family seemed well established. He believed in labor's rewards, and in direct dealing, and was willing to be hard-headed if he thought he was in the right. Yet he had no love for dishonesty or what he called "removing of boundaries," which Bible language he used to cover any devious means toward personal ends. He was not a scholarly man. He gave less time to the Word of God or anything else than to farming and, during the winters, woodworking.

Francis' bargain with the devil was the subtle one struck by most of the best men in this new world: "I'll work hard if you'll make me comfortable. Give my family sufficient earthly means to be certain and secure throughout our days, and I will labor until I drop." He bargained not for a city, but a farm set upon a hill. And his became one of the best plantations in Salem Village. The Nurses were well on their way toward the level of respect afforded the Porters, Hutchinsons, and Endicotts. Like our founders, Francis did not imagine his bargain made with any but God. He expected to continue his own master, despite having bargained away something very like his soul. Just as those real witches out there, wherever they may be, have a wild and romantic faith in a benevolence bigger than their bargain, a power for good which will somehow break their contract at the end, Father Nurse believed in an abiding earthly justice, the foundation and frame upon which he built his hopes. How cruel was the day of his reckoning.

Tom Preston's father raised himself up much as Francis Nurse did. Roger had been a tanner in Ipswich when Tom was born. He and his sons worked among the hides and pits for seven years, until Tom was fifteen. By then Roger had accumulated enough money to give up the stink of hair and tannin, and move up, according to the customary bargain. He and his wife Martha got a nice place in Ipswich, but memories know a tanner even when noses no longer do, so they sold again and moved to what we now call Procter's Corner, where they set up a licensed ordinary or inn. Tom began to work as hard in the fields and stable as he had in the tanyard. He had four younger brothers and a sister, but he was the oldest and took seriously his responsibility.

They had just about got the Preston team settled in harness and ready for the long-pull, when Roger began to have lung trouble—an effect of years in the tannery. After but six years at the new place, he left Martha a widow, with both an inn and a farm to run, and a twenty-three year old son who might have managed it if his mother had let him. Tom felt bereft of his father and found his mother preoccupied with what she took to be solely her burden, the maintenance and care of family and business. Tom was young, strong, and knew how to work. But instead of turning the management over to him, his mother married again. The youngest boys, John and Samuel, were put under the care of new kin in Andover. Jacob was apprenticed to a foundryman and blacksmith. The inn and farm were sold. Tom's eyes and heart turned a mile and a half to the north, where he had worked and where he had begun to have feelings for Francis Nurse's daughter, Rebecca, named after her mother.

There Tom Preston found his almost paradise on earth amongst the Nurses. Even after he married Rebecca, Jr., he longed to extend his arm of protection around his brothers. He was troubled when his brother Jacob found his apprenticeship difficult. And he took his sister Mary under his wing, inviting her to stay with them, during the early years of his marriage. Mother Nurse introduced Mary Preston to one of the Village's bachelors, young Nat Ingersoll, who kept the Village ordinary in apprenticeship to his uncle of the same name. Tom's other sister, Sarah, also was welcomed by the Nurses, and Francis Nurse, Jr. became interested in her.

Tom Preston had made a somewhat different bargain from Francis, Sr. Neither he nor John Tarbell, bound to Nurse sisters though they were, loved farming as much as their father-in-law did, although they were counted good farmers. Tom's bargain was for a warm and lasting family, an abiding tribe in which he was respected and loved. The Nurse family provided him Rebecca, Jr., and a tightknit clan in which to raise his children. They received his two sisters, as well. They were a hearty people who steadfastly embraced, directed and disciplined him and his. Tom was not susceptible to Francis' idols, but he was susceptible to Francis and his family as idols.

John Tarbell's bargain was something like Tom's, yet his idolatry had more to do with his wife than the "Nurse tribe". It was a year and half after Tom's wedding that John married Mary Nurse. They built a place on an old barn foundation right on the Ipswich

Road. John's wife, Mary, was no more servant of the devil than her mother, yet his objects in marrying her were not all righteous. She is no longer young, yet it has taken him this long to properly delight in the wife of his youth. Perhaps something similar was true for her, although different temptations and different flesh dictated her bargain. But it would be fairer to say of them as of us all, that we began in motives of mixed faith and idolatry — and grow into God's will. The grace of God extends into the most benighted and bewildered places of both minds and marriages. Now John does indeed delight in her. Now his covenant appears, if not free of sin, so much closer as to be well nigh that.

A year after John and Mary Tarbell were wed, Sam Nurse married Mary Smith. Sam and Mary built a house a quarter mile south of his parent's. But Sam bargained his soul to the devil, if you will, for this: keep me from having to step out alone, from taking solitary risks, and give me the comfort of always following in the train of wiser companions. As Tom Preston became Francis Nurse's right hand man, so Sam Nurse became Tom Preston's. Tom, and until our troubles to a lesser degree, John Tarbell, were closer companions than his own brothers, John and Benjamin Nurse. Sam was never noted as a leader, or a thinker. He was strong in harness, but only as part of a team. Yet as things approached and then passed the crisis, his idolatry was gradually put off, so that by the end Sam (with John Tarbell) had taken to completion what others had grown too weary to finish. In the words of scripture they gathered where others had sown. The tears of the sowers gradually become the songs of the reapers.

The year Tom and Rebecca Nurse Jr. were wed, her sister, Sarah, married Michael Bowden and they settled in Marblehead with his people.

John Nurse, the eldest son of Francis and Rebecca, married a few years later, and his first wife died bearing little John. After that he married Elizabeth Very, and they settled on the corner of the place across the Ipswich Road, next to the boundary disputed with the Endicotts.

Elizabeth Nurse married William Russell, who had fought in King Philip's War. William worked as a fisherman out of Salem, until they moved to Reading.

At the Village ordinary, Nat Ingersoll married Mary Preston, Tom's sister. They continued to work under Nat's namesake uncle there in Salem Village.

Francis Nurse, Jr., married Sarah Preston, Tom's other sister. But both men's joy turned to sorrow when Sarah died two years later of one of those diseases that sprang up among us. Francis, Jr. was married a second time, to Sarah Craggen, and they settled in Reading — seven years before our troubles.

Benjamin Nurse, youngest son of Francis and Rebecca, married the next year. He and Thomasina were still in Salem Village during our troubles. With him were John, Sam, Tom Preston and John Tarbell, all settled on the large farm around Francis, Sr. and Rebecca Nurse. The family were faithful not only to each other, but in the Salem Village church. Only Rebecca, "Mother Nurse," retained her old membership in the church of Salem Town. This family were the furthest thing from devotees of Satan, yet all had made some bad bargains.

Those who call themselves witches or wizards or sorcerers or Satanists may be more deliberate in their evil intentions than the rest of us. They may say the Lord's Prayer backward and celebrate black masses, but they do not know what bargains they make, for what prices, or with whom, any more than we others who make bad bargains. None who knows who Satan is ever sells a soul to him. None who knows who God is ever turns away from him. Satan, himself, may be the only exception.

Not even Adam and Eve knew what they rejected or what they were to receive in return — for at the moment she went on to the second step in those infamous negotiations, Eve was already deceived, and moving actively away from the God who made her. Before the moment Adam tasted, he had made the conscious error of thinking his wife as wise or as worth keeping as God. Satan was obscurely whispering behind their backs, but their own thrusting hands blocked a clear vision of God's face.

Why does a witch make a compact with the devil? Because of an illusion of something important lacking, compounded with an illusion of something important to be gained. That much is true in the story of Dr. Faustus.

If there is any error in that tale, it is in the idea that one only realizes the illusions behind his bad bargain when it's too late – when he is beyond the power of forgiveness. Our witches taught us a different lesson — how to break the bargain with the devil.

This story then may not rightly be said to belong to Francis and Rebecca. It is not the story of Tom Preston or John Tarbell or Sam Nurse, nor of the staunch "conspirators," Daniel Andrews and

Joseph Putnam; nor of all the Nurses or even all the families of the accused. It is the story of Salem Village and Massachusetts Bay colony – the story of all of us, our bad bargains, and where they led us.

The gallows set upon a hill became the beacon of New England's bad bargains. But the memory of what went on there and the manner of those who died there, pointed many of us toward another gallows set upon another hill, and a different bargain altogether.

Elizabeth Parris

TABLE OF CONTENTS

Preface – Bad Bargains   1

Contents   8

Illustrations   11

CHAPTERS

One	—	My How They Love One Another	15
Two	--	The First Sparks	27
Three	--	The Least of These	37
Four	—	The Poor Always With You	59
Five	—	The Few Confer	65
Six	—	Enemies of Good	77
Seven	—	The Third Witch	89
Eight	—	The Two Magistrates	99
Nine	—	Courts of Injustice	105
Ten	—	Eyes Further Opened	113
Eleven	—	Hiatus – Vengeance Naps	123
Twelve	--	Warning	135
Thirteen	—	Respect No Object	141
Fourteen	--	Fifth Examination	159
Fifteen	--	The Fellowship of Suffering	177
Sixteen	—	Turnings	189
Seventeen	—	Petitioners	201
Eighteen	—	Solemn Humiliation and Fasting	217
Nineteen	—	Sarah Cloyce and the Procters	229
Twenty	—	Cold Comfort	243
Twenty-One	— Revolution or Repentance		253
Twenty-Two	— Wider Nets		265
Twenty-Three	— The Price of Contrition		279
Twenty-Four	— The Number of the Elect		291
Twenty-Five	— The Third Sister		301
Twenty-Six	— Conspiracy Fails		311
Twenty-Seven	— Forged Links		323
Twenty-Eight	— The Archangel Falls		331
Twenty-Nine	— I Bear in my Body the Marks		339
Thirty	— Conspiracy Succeeds		345

Thirty-One   -- Into Hiding   335
Thirty-Two   -- The Mystery of Christian Trask   363
Thirty-Three -- Isolation and Community   373
Thirty-Four   -- Hope Deferred Makes the Heart Sick 379
Thirty-Five   -- Toil and Trouble   385
Thirty-Six   -- Cave-Dwellers   391
Thirty-Seven -- Trial Preparations   401
Thirty-Eight -- Whither Thou Wouldest Not   409
Thirty-Nine   -- Fair Days of June   415
Forty   -- First Convicted   421

Forty-One   — The Walls Raised Higher   427
Forty-Two   — The Few Grow Faint   443
Forty-Three   — First Hanged   453
Forty-Four   — The Violent Take it by Force   459
Forty-Five   — High Places   469
Forty-Six   — The Silent Souls   475
Forty-Seven   — Determined to Go Forward   481
Forty-Eight   -- The Mare and the Pipe   485
Forty-Nine   — The Case Against Susannah Martin   491
Fifty   — The Case Against Sarah Wildes   499

Fifty-One   — Sentence of Death   503
Fifty-Two   — The Two Tables   511
Fifty-Three   — Last Throes of Justice   517
Fifty-Four   — Colony of Calvary   525
Fifty-Five   — Groans Too Deep For Words   539
Fifty-Six   — The Prayers of Boston   543
Fifty-Seven   — August Harvest   549
Fifty-Eight   — Sarah Cloyce Escape   559
Fifty-Nine   — Last of The Hellbrands   567
Sixty   — Conspirator Captured   573

Sixty-One   — October Reversals   579
Sixty-Two   — General Gaol Delivery   583
Sixty-Three   — The Apologists Divide   587
Sixty-Four   -- Schools of Thought   597
Sixty-Five   — Biblical Discipline in Salem Village   605
Sixty-Six   — Excuses and Exodus   619
Sixty-Seven   — God Smiled — Public Repentances   633
Sixty-Eight   — The Diligence of Reverend Green   641

Sixty-Nine — It's Over   643
Seventy   — The Nurse Trees   650

Afterword   652

Bibliography   657

ILLUSTRATIONS

Frontispiece . . . . Goodwife Rebecca Nurse in Gaol

Elizabeth Parris...   7

Map of Salem Village and Town...   13

Map of Massachusetts Bay...   14

Abigail Williams...   26

Justice Hathorne...   36

Anne Putnam...   64

Justice Corwin...   98

The Nurse Place (Salem Village)...   112

Ingersoll's Ordinary (Salem Village)... 122

Samuel Parris... 158

Procter's Inn 188

Cotton Mather... 216

Israel Porter's House 278

William Phips... 290

Woodcut from Wonders of the Invisible World   310

Jonathon Corwin's House (Salem Town)... 364

George Burroughs   330

William Stoughton...   384

Samuel Willard...   442

Captain John Alden   452

Sheriff George Corwin   538

Increase Mather   604

Samuel Sewall...   618

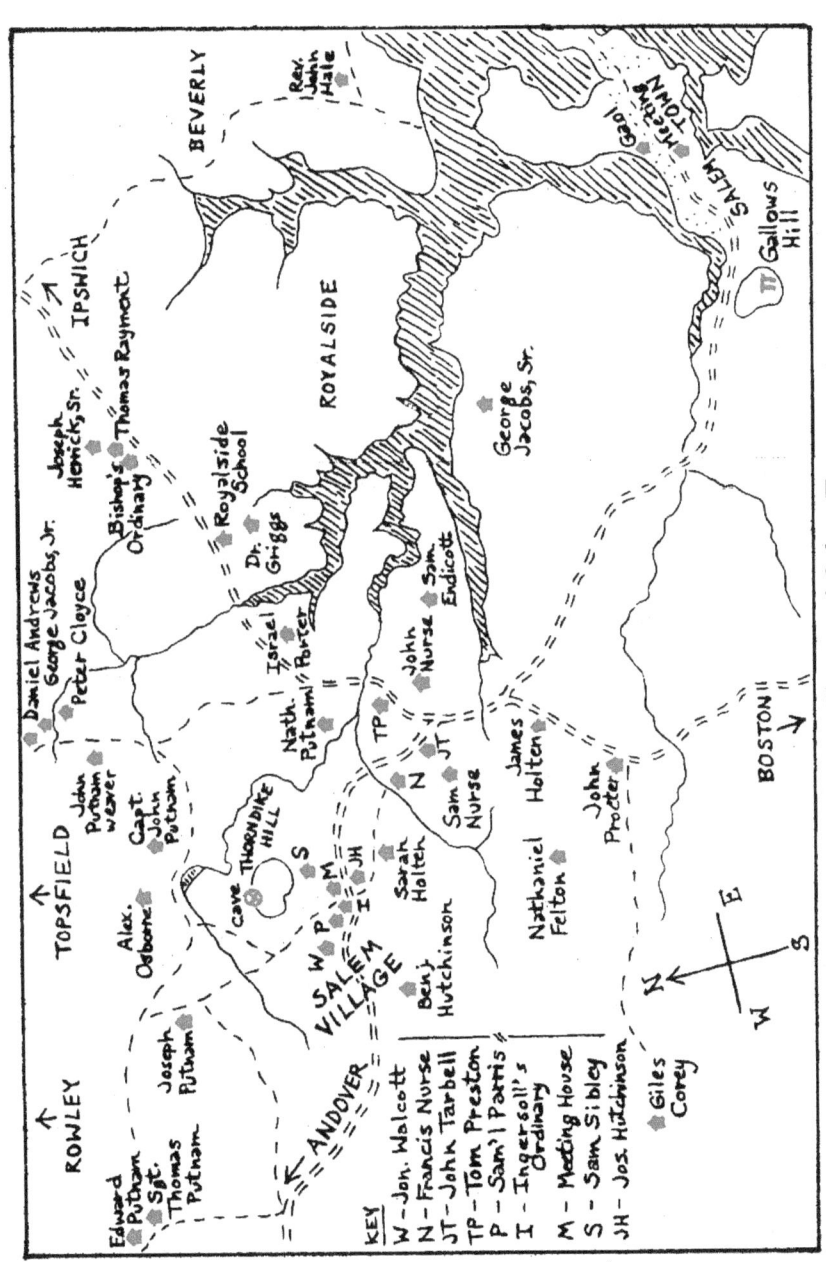

Salem Village and Salem Town

KEY

W – Jon. Walcott
N – Francis Nurse
JT – John Tarbell
TP – Tom Preston
P – Sam'l Parris
I – Ingersoll's Ordinary
M – Meeting House
S – Sam Sibley
JH – Jos. Hutchinson

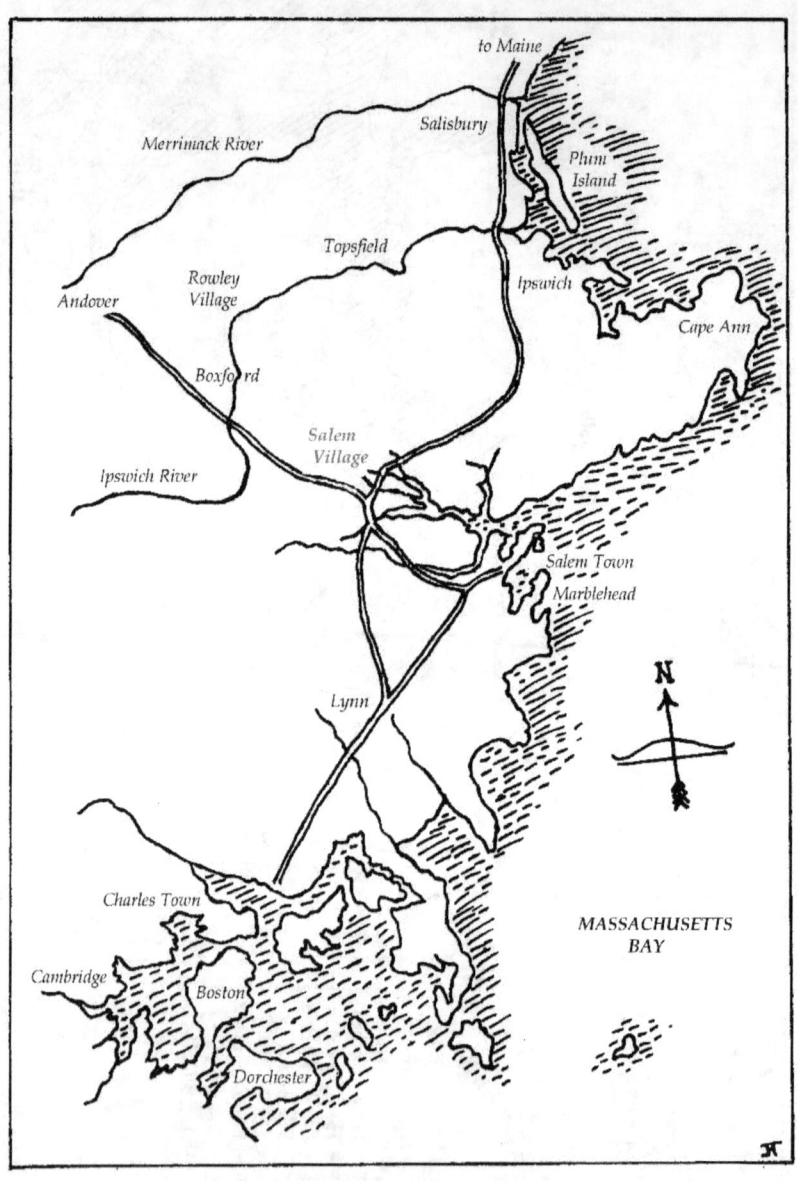

Chapter One — My How They Love One Another

. . .Uncharitable expressions and uncomly reflections tost to and fro
. . . have a tendency to make such a gap as we fear, if not timely
prevented, will lett out peace and order and let in confusion and
every evil work. -- **Committee of Salem** arbitrating dispute in
the Village church under Reverend Deodat Lawson, 1687

One might almost say Christ's claim to bring a dividing
sword was never so clearly fulfilled as in Salem Village. It is said
that during her first years, the ancient church was noted for its
rejection of the pagan gods, but also for the uncanny degree to which
its members were full of love for one another. They were also known
for their love of the disenfranchised — so as to be willing to lay down
their lives for their friends. The degree of our love for God in Salem
Village appeared in the converse.

There was an old rivalry and growing resentment among
those of Salem Village over against Salem Town. Up until 1672, the
Village people had no meeting but the one in Town — which on a icy
winter Sunday or Thursday (Lecture Day), was often an unpleasant
journey. The people of the Village made application for their own
meeting, which was at last granted by the Salem selectmen, but they
did not allow for a full-fledged congregation. We were given the
right to build our own meeting house and parsonage, but only to hire
subordinate pastors. Finally, in 1689, the Village was allowed a
separate congregation with our own ordained man. We hired
Samuel Parris.

Reverend Parris thought he was embarking on a brand new
enterprise, a fresh, new congregation in an up-and-coming town. In
fact he was plunging clumsily into a smoldering war that singed his
three predecessors. It was a war of sides and factions, involving
most of the Village. Ours was a church of which several perspicuous
observers said, "my how they contend with one another!"

Nor can primary blame for the Village ecclesiastical wars be
placed on its first three pastors. No one suggests any of them was a
particularly bad man — at least, since our troubles, none is willing to
say so publicly.

The church conflicts seem to have mirrored our other idolatries. Most particularly they seem to have concentrated about the question of who would control the church, which meant for Congregationalists such as we, who would choose and control the pastors. Directly related to that, the conflicts often burned most hotly over the pastors' compensation—real property, money, and the church tax.

The question of who would control the church and the pastors was the same as the question of who would control the community. These questions divided Europe at the Reformation, and England against Rome. In our own world at many points it divided the colonies against England, the Puritans against the Anabaptists, and Congregationalists against Episcopals, Presbyterians, Baptists and Quakers. Those, however, were at least divisions with some basis in principles.

The colonies were separated from the distant British Isles by water and by charter. The Village was separated from the Town by about four miles of road. Some of the prosperous third generation farmers of the Village found themselves separated not only by geography but from the power and respect enjoyed by the better-connected merchants and ship-owners of Salem proper—some of whom were only second or even first generation colonists. Old Governor Endicott had been a Villager. Several other Village families, such as the Porters, had both respect and office in the public life of the Town, but for the most part the importance of the Village faded as the trade of the Town attracted wealthier and younger men to its glitter and bustle.

The desire for a separate church was felt by all who had to walk the cold winter paths to Town, but it was felt most by those of us who felt a separate parish would provide a foundation for independent respect, political power, and influence.

Once the right to a separate meeting was granted, and an independent and "particular" church established, the old Town vs. Village rivalry re-emerged in the Village itself, where the factions still held to their distinctive desires and grudges. Although the Town commissioners finally granted the Village a separate meeting, they were not willing to grant a separate jurisdiction—our own town government. Indeed, Salem Village's own Porter family continued to oppose our separation into an independent jurisdiction. The Putnams, on the other hand, were very active in their efforts to bring about that object, as were Deacons Ingersoll and Walcott. Most others in the Village had mixed allegiances through marriage and business.

As in other places, there were frequent controversies in the Salem Village church over fine points of doctrine or style, lingering remnants of old debates: Anglican versus Puritan, Congregational versus Presbyterian, a whiff of Baptist, and lately more than a whiff of Quaker doctrine. With so many strong-minded women among us there was on ongoing argument over women speaking in the public worship. But the evolution of factions up to the time of our troubles continued to center about the issue of choosing and controlling the minister — and subjoined to that, who should own the minister's home.

The meeting house was built in 1672, after we were first given permission for our own meeting. Reverend James Bayley became our first pastor. He resigned his membership in Newbury and joining the Salem church in 1671. Things began well for him, with Nathaniel, Thomas, and John Putnam, together with Joseph Hutchinson and Joshua Rea, giving him 30 acres of land. He built a house, which his family still owns, on the land given him in the center of the Village, not far from the Meeting House.

Reverend Bayley's wife, Mary, brought her twelve year old sister, Anne Carr, from Salisbury to the Village. In 1678, when she was seventeen, Anne Carr married Sergeant Thomas Putnam. (During our troubles in 1692, when their own daughter, Anna, was twelve, Anne Putnam claimed a witch had caused the death of her "sister Bayley" four years earlier.) Reverend Bayley seems to have been supported as much by contribution as by "rates" (taxes), and of course a few wealthier Villagers contributed the greatest part of his income, either way.

In 1679, Nathaniel Putnam and Bray Wilkins (another patriarch) publicly charged Reverend Bayley with lacking qualifications for ministry and with being offensive in his practices. Nathaniel and John Putnam, Jr. (his son), together with several of the Wilkins wrote a petition in which they expressed discontent not only with Reverend Bayley's inexperience and lack of pastoral ability, but also with his settling so firmly among us before his abilities had been proven — while he was still "on sufferance". Joseph Hutchinson later added his voice to those of these men.

On the other side, in support of Reverend Bayley, Thomas Putnam (by then his wife's brother-in-law), Captain John Putnam, and Joseph Porter, signed a petition in which they defended

Reverend Bayley's position and performance and denied he was still "on sufferance".

Then (on the first of many such occasions) the Village church agreed to ask the Salem elders for guidance. The Salem men made several suggestions, including that the householders of the Village appoint a committee to adjust the tax rates for paying the minister's salary. Reverend Bayley offered to resign despite a petition in his favor signed by forty inhabitants. A petition was sent to the General Court asking our leaders to clarify whether the householders or only the "saints," that is the covenanted members, might vote for the minister.

The Court only pointed back to the standing law, which was by then in the midst of change and variously interpreted. More petitions and counter-petitions were sent to the court, which finally led to a court order that Reverend Bayley continue. The court also stipulated that a committee be appointed to set rates, unless there could not be found 30 householders to support the minister. His salary was set at 60 pounds per year, at least one third to be in money.

Nevertheless in 1680, partly due to non-support (which is to say those in the Village who did not like him, did not contribute) Reverend Bayley remitted his pastorate, and George Burroughs was hired. Although the men who had originally given Reverend Bayley the land confirmed it by deed of gift, he moved to Roxborough, where he began to practice as a doctor.

Reverend Burroughs had been in Maine until 1676, when our first great conflict with the Indians, King Phillips War, drove many of the those "to eastward" back to Massachusetts. He and his family had settled in Salisbury until he was called to the Village. Due to lack of a parsonage, the Burroughs lived with John Putnam, Sr. for nearly a year. As well nigh inevitable with two couples living in the same household, the Senior Putnams observed some conflicts in Reverend Burrough's marriage, to which they were to testify during his trial in 1692.

In 1681, a parsonage and barn were built on land donated by Joseph Hutchinson. All the men in the Village and Farms put in time and materials — donating labor and lumber to build it. The congregation agreed the parsonage would belong to the community perpetually for the incumbent pastor. A strongly worded stipulation was placed in the constitution of the Village church that parsonage and land would: "stand good to the inhabitants of this place and to their successors forever, for the ministry." The resolution also entailed the land, forbidding future transfer of the property "to any particular person, not for any cause, by vote or other ways." The words smelled of the smoke of the recent battle over Reverend Bayley.

Reverend Burroughs was himself a strong-minded man. He seems to have gotten along all right at first, and been adverse to favoring any faction. Partly because of his unwillingness to ingratiate himself, several community leaders nonetheless came to view him as an opponent. As they had with his predecessor, those who came to dislike him neglected to pay the support tax. He ceased to receive the patronage of many of the wealthier members. When Burroughs found himself without financial support, he simply refused to preach. Within three years, during which he lost his second wife, Reverend Burroughs was in debt and when he left there were some who held strong resentments against him. When he returned briefly to settle his affairs, Lieutenant Thomas Putnam sued him for moneys owed. If good-natured Thomas Haynes had not paid his debt, Reverend Burroughs could have been put in prison. Bailed out by Mr. Haynes he folded up the last traces of his ministry in 1683, and slipped off to "eastward" again, becoming pastor in Wells, Maine. There George Burroughs hoped to hear no more from Salem Village.

Mr. Burrough's wife's maid, Mercy Lewis, an orphan originally brought from Maine, went to live and work with William and Rachel Bradford after the Burroughs left. From the Bradford's she came to live with Sergeant Thomas Putnam's family, where she became involved in our troubles.

Deodat Lawson came in 1686, after the Village had been without a resident pastor for nearly two years. Yet by 1687, another Salem committee was asked to arbitrate in a controversy between the new pastor and the Village. This time it was over whether Reverend Lawson should be ordained or not, and was largely precipitated by his clumsy attempt to bring about reconciliation in the Village. He thought it would help to expunge the more acrimonious sections of the Village church record book.

The Salem committee appointed to arbitrate cautioned the Village people that factions and strong statements against each other had potential to work lasting damage. They agreed with Reverend Lawson in recommending the more heated passages (proposals and votes) in the Old Record Book be repealed or revised. The majority of the congregation agreed. Sergeant Thomas Putnam was hired in April to transcribe the book of records and expunge the offensive ones. Some afterward suggested he thus became the Village's leading authority on old conflicts. Many of those "offensive records" though expunged from the book, were recorded in his mind, including no doubt, a number involving Reverend Burroughs.

At the same time the Salem church granted the Village church further (although not complete) independence as a separate "body," and Peter Cloyce (Rebecca Nurse's brother-in-law) was among the members in that first "embodying".

The same year a controversy sprang up between Joseph Hutchinson and the Putnam faction. Hutchinson owned the land around the Meeting House, having given some for the Meeting House itself, and then fenced his own land. Some said he did this to spite Reverend Lawson, whose ordination he opposed. In a complaint to the courts, Captain John and Sergeant Thomas Putnam said those fences made it necessary for all the congregation to enter by one gate. Those accustomed to arrive by several paths looked upon this as persecution. But members of the congregation themselves had expanded Hutchinson's stone fences as barricades around the church, as per the model of Topsfield's meeting house, which town had turned their building into a fort during King Philip's War. Mr. Hutchinson pointed this out to the court and said he had only fenced his own lands. In fact, he said, he wished the stones of the barricades would be returned to his original fences.

Reverend Lawson's wife and daughter died in the Village. (The deaths in Village pastor's families were ominously recalled at the time of our troubles.) Unhappy with the continuing factions and the resulting parsimony of the Village, Reverend Lawson left and went to Scituate in 1689, in which year Samuel Parris was hired. After the onset of our troubles, reports that Lawson's loved ones had died by cause of witchcraft brought him back to investigate.

After growing up in a Barbadoes sugar family, Reverend Samuel Parris came to operate a warehouse and wharf in Boston. He studied but did not finish at Harvard, yet he felt called to the ministry. He came among us just at the time of the wider turmoil during which Governor Andros was imprisoned and the colony went through yet another change of government.

He was cautious in negotiating with the village committees. Nevertheless, when he finally agreed to become our minister, Reverend Parris blundered into a viper's nest. For reasons beyond our understanding the church commissioners agreed to give him the parsonage and land! They did this despite the strongly worded vote of 1681 that forbade such a gift, which was not among the matters expunged in Sergeant Putnam's new manuscript of the record book. Perhaps they intended to diminish the conflicts by thus keeping his other compensation and thus church rates lower.

At the October 1689 meeting called to approve Reverend Parris's hiring, they made the gift "legal" by revoking the congregation's prior decision that forbade both the gift and such a revocation! Finally those members present at that meeting voted to give "outright to Samuel Parris and his heirs the Village parsonage together with its barn and two acres of land." The members of the commission which hired Parris under these terms were: Nathanael Ingersoll, Nathaniel Putnam, John Putnam, Jonathon Walcott, and Thomas Flint.

Many of those not present at the meeting, along with some present but opposed, regarded this as a high-handed slap. Some in the congregation said they had not been warned of the meeting in the manner required by law. They were not only incensed by this course of events, but according to the pattern of action and reaction, set themselves in opposition to Reverend Parris from the beginning.

Nevertheless, Reverend Parris was ordained in November, 1689, with the Reverend Samuel Phillips of Rowley (one of the few local ministers soon to oppose the witch business) participating in the laying on of hands. Twenty-five Village "saints," including Peter Cloyce, entered into covenant together with the Parris's in the newly independent Church of Christ in Salem Village. Their covenant said:

> We do, in some measure of sinceritie, this day give up ourselves unto God in Christ, to be for him and not for another, at the same time renouncing all vanities and Idols of this present evil world. . .

Rebecca Nurse never moved her membership from the Salem Town meeting—at first because she had many friends there, including a few Towne relatives from Topsfield—and then out of distaste for the continual contentions in the Village meeting. But in the first year of the church many other villagers became members through transfer or profession of faith. Sarah Cloyce (Peter's wife and sister to Rebecca) joined in January 1690. In March, Sam Nurse was baptized and admitted to the church. His wife, Mary (Smith)

Nurse became a member the same month, along with John Tarbell and his wife Mary. In April, Martha (Penoyer) Corey, a widow and Bible-woman from Boston married Giles Corey of the Village and became a member, by communion of the churches, on the same day. In May, Sarah Bishop, wife of Edward, Jr., transferred to the Village church from Topsfield. In June 1691, Anne Putnam, wife of the Sergeant, was admitted to membership. All of these were to be deeply involved in the witch troubles.

Reverend Parris started out vigourously. He proposed Nathanael Ingersoll, Sr., the keeper of the inn near the meeting house, as the first Deacon. The congregation elected Deacon Ingersoll in November.

But Reverend Parris was slow to discover the temper of our congregation. By December of 1690, he was already publicly admonishing us for non-attendance, asking for better furnishing of the Lord's Table and the building, and admonishing his congregation to more giving toward those ends. By early the next winter, he was complaining about lack of firewood. When he humbled himself to broadcast this need among his exhortations, the response was disapproval, even from his sympathizers. What manner of New Englander waits until winter to prepare for it! It in no way improved his relations that he talked as though the congregation was obliged to make up his deficiency and in effect suffer the penalty of his poor stewardship.

By March 1691, Reverend Parris was attempting to use church discipline to maintain peace among the brethren. It seems Ezekiel Cheever's wife had suddenly gone into labor. Having no means of transportation close at hand by which to fetch the mid-wife, Mr. Cheever borrowed Joseph Putnam's horse out of his stable without asking.

Most of the Village men felt considerable sympathy toward the frantic father and were ready to excuse him, until, instead of properly apologizing to Putnam thereafter, Cheever took a high tone about it. Joseph Putnam, went to the pastor for advice on how to proceed and the pastor referred it to the meeting. Joseph said later, had he known it would go that way, he would have swallowed his objections, but we were all just getting to know Reverend Parris. When the minister felt Cheever was still too "mincing" in his public confession on the Lord's Day, he required him to come back with a better performance the following week. After finding that acceptable, the pastor admonished him publicly, and warned everyone in general against behavior that might offend against the unity and peace of the church.

Reverend Parris was trying hard, but should have sought counsel. At this first hint of conflict he jumped right in, authoritative and severe. It was a sadly reasoned attempt. He made the congregation wary and cool toward him, rather than raising confidence and respect or promoting peace. Just about everyone felt he made a mountain out of a molehill. Joseph Putnam, too, was chagrined by the business and never trusted the pastor after that. Ezekiel Cheever, on the other hand, in the manner of a kicked dog, seemed to take a remarkable liking for the pastor. During our troubles they were zealous witch-hunters together.

That November, Edward Putnam, Joseph's half-brother, second son of the late Lieutenant Thomas, was put forth by the pastor as a second candidate for deacon. Edward, the most melancholy of the Putnam tribe, kept putting off the matter, although the congregation voted him in the next lecture day. Edward, meticulous and habitually subordinate to his brother, Sergeant Thomas, doubted his qualifications and would not submit to being ordained even seven months later, when Deacon Ingersoll was re-ordained to office. It was perhaps his careful subordination that qualified him most for the pastor's high regard. However, Edward was still hemming and hawing about it late in the summer, and was not finally ordained until a year later.

Over the first two years of Parris' ministry, much hot talk and finally some counter-stratagems were precipitated, so that in October 1691 at the election of church commissioners, those on the other side of the fence were well-prepared. Not only did they all come to the meeting, but they elected men sympathetic with them to all the offices. These were: Joseph Porter, Francis Nurse, Joseph Putnam, Daniel Andrews, and Joseph Hutchinson. At that same meeting there was open talk of continuing opposition to the transfer of the parsonage to Reverend Parris.

This new commission never quite got around to gathering the churchtax or paying the Reverend Parris. Parris got more and more upset about this and preached about factions and enemies of the church within the church, but it did him no good.

Standing on his dignity, he sent "messengers" to the committee, to wit the two deacons and Captain John Putnam, instead of going himself and having the kind of conversation that would have at least gotten everybody's complaints on the table. The delegation relayed his message to the committee — that they ought to fix the tax rates for the pastor's pay and see to it that he got necessary supplies. The committee took careful note and then dismissed — without any further action. They, on their part, were waiting for the open discussion of what was to them the issue — namely the irregular transfer of the house and land to Reverend Parris. But since no one raised it or asked the kind of question which would allow them to raise it, no headway was made.

Everyone got more hard-headed and hard-hearted — which is also a kind of violence — a strangling of the conscientious response to keep it from interfering with other intentions or desires. If ones intentions or desires have been well-examined and proven godly, then there is a place for resisting the gentler reflexes, but if the intentions are ungodly, then that hardness buries one more deeply in bitterness and sin.

Reverend Parris's interpretation of these things — his coming to see them primarily as symptoms of the attack of Satan on Christ's Kingdom — was not peculiar to him. Our early ministers had been delivered from the persecution of papists and prelates only to suffer the persecution of new world winters. This great wilderness seemed terribly hostile compared to England's green fields. And lately the French and Indians seemed to have become the devil's agents against us. Our leaders often reverted to biblical allusions to describe our hardships. They continually spoke of our settlements as the New Jerusalem, the city set upon a hill. In scripture the old Jerusalem was often described over against the wilderness, which was sometimes described as the devil's own province. As we moved into the wilderness, our sufferings seemed counterattacks of the devil against the inroads of Light.

We believed our ancestors were righteous, and our colonies seemed to us righteous, therefore we found it easy to believe God was using us to glorify himself before his rebellious angels — as he had used the sufferings of Job. But on the other hand, we believed the devil was a liar, a deceiver, and (if we only could have remembered) an accuser of the brethren. We grew to think of him as we had come to think of the hostile Indians — a powerful enemy, out to hurt, divert, or trap us any way he could.

It was but a slight shift to conclude that the enemy had crept into the church and that the divisions among us were also of Satanic agency. Reverend Parris began to express this particular conclusion in his sermons about the time his girls began their odd behavior.

These sermons were about the Kingdom of Darkness and its attack on the Kingdom of Light — good and true texts about good and true principles — preached partly out of private motives. The best of saints can listen to such sermons and go away built up in faith. The rest of us go away angry, with divided minds and sore hearts.

     The true causes of division in the church are much clearer — "From whence come fightings and wars among you? Come they not hence, even of your lusts that war in your members?" The scripture's answer applied all too well to us, but it was difficult to hear. It is worse when one knows his enemy is unrighteous — for it makes it easy to leave aside the question of one's own sins, and to justify turning an opponent's weapons against him — especially in the heat of conflicting lusts. Thus were our church wars fought, not with shot, and with no blood shed or torture done — not yet — but for a long time before our troubles, never likely to be characterized in sentiments such as "my how they love one another!"

Abigail Williams

Chapter Two – The First Sparks

The governor shall direct the defense of the province, and may exercise martial law in case of necessity ... that the said governor shall not at any time . . . grant Commissions for exercising the law martiall upon any the inhabitants of our said province . . . without the advice and consent of the councill or assistants of the same . . . nothing herein shall extend to be taken to allow the exercise of any admirall court jurisdiction, power, or authority but that the same be and is hereby reserved to us . . .

And lastly for the better provideing and furnishing of masts for our royall navy wee do hereby reserve. . . all trees of the diameter of twenty four inches and upwards of twelve inches from the ground growing upon any soyle or tract of land within our said province . . . not heretofore granted to any private persons and wee doe restrain and forbid all persons whatsoever from felling, cutting, or destroying any such trees without the royall lycence of us. . . first had and obteyned upon penalty of forfeiting one hundred pounds sterling unto us . . . for every such tree so felled, cutt, or destroyed.
-- **Second Royal Charter of Massachusetts**, dated October 7th, 1691.

When a disaster roars or rolls in upon a community it reveals the foundations of that community. Like a forest fire or hurricano devouring a pine grove on a hill, it uncovers the bedrock and leaves little above ground, except for smoking remnants and tokens of the trees that once lived upon it. If a great wind or blaze strikes a human habitation, it leaves only stone fences, roads, walls, and fireplaces – things made of the stuff that had longest abided. If the bedrock of a community is its faith and morals, then it is crisis that reveals what these really are.

The landscape of a hilltop changes – particularly under the influence of human habitation. Our New England hilltops, rock-bound though they be, are not proof against the changes that come with roads, fields, and the tendency to level or excavate for a house, a cow-house, or a house of worship. We try to protect the bedrock of faith and morals in order that our structures be solid and lasting, but we want to accommodate other goals, as well. We build up the institutions of church and law, ministry and magistry. But we are so intent on building strong houses for ourselves that we not only break up and move the bedrock, but we bring in foreign materials, as well—not just wood, hay and stubble – but stone come ballast in alien vessels. Thus our traditions and ordinances, our common knowledge, and our practices include a great deal of ancient paganism. We do not see this until the crises come.

The devastation of a hurricano, of fire, flood or earthquake may reveal a fundamental landscape far different than what we thought was under our feet – in our civil government – and in our community and church.

A few years ago a fire swept through Perkins' barn and swallowed it up. Three men saw the fire from the edge of a meadow where they had been clearing. Although they worked together, they told three rather different stories. Being strong-minded fellows, they flared up in hot debate as quickly as the burning barn. How much more do accounts differ when a conflagration sweeps not a barn, but one's family away—when friends, neighbors and loved ones are caught up in gusts of accusation and testimony, defense and fear. And much more yet do accounts differ when the whole community and even the colony seem to be ablaze. There remain then many opinions about what began our troubles and how they went forward.

Memories of earlier witch cases in England and the colonies were fresh among us. Marblehead, Ipswich, and Salem had accused or tried witches within a score of years. Baxter's and Mather's books were well-known .

Careless words did much to fuel the fire. It seems common opinion that indisposed persons cannot understand what is said in their presence. But is it not also said that little pitchers have big ears? Reliable men heard Hannah Perley's mother and brother accuse Elizabeth Howe in Hannah's presence. In the same way, the ministers, doctors and judges, talked freely and foolishly in front of the Parris and Putnam girls. In this way the girls learned a great deal about how bewitched persons were expected to act.

But probably the first spark we can trace was struck by Mary Warren, through no fault of her own, and began to smoulder in the breast of little Betty Parris. Mary Warren was the twenty year old maid of the Procters. She appeared an ordinary, pretty young woman, except during fits, which came upon her weeks or months apart. Before our troubles she was distracted only rarely and of a sudden. Then she chattered and bit her tongue, and acted bewildered for some time after. Her "fits" seemed a kind of seizure, in which she sprawled in a daze. John Procter, her master, made no secret of the fact that he had tried beating her during these fits. (He claimed this brought her out of them, but the hard-handedness of this stern and proud man ended much the same as that of Giles Corey.)

Mary's distracted fits were genuine, unlike those of the girls who imitated her. Yet she was kin to Elizabeth Knapp, the Boston girl who was "bewitched" twenty years earlier in much the same ways as our Village girls.

Elizabeth Knapp had been "afflicted" during the time she worked for Reverend Samuel Willard of Boston. When she accused others of bewitching her, Reverend Willard would not have it. He confronted her and prayed for her over many months. After some time she was delivered out of it. But Reverend Willard, a devotee of science with many other leading divines of Boston, wrote up his observations of her case and speculated on its causes. He gave copies of his report to the Boston ministers. Reverend Willard had concluded, largely from Elizabeth Knapp's own confessions, that her primary spiritual problem was envy of the prosperity of others—that she was thus made susceptible to the devil. Perhaps Elizabeth Knapp and Mary Warren were the third and fourth generation upon whom the sins of their fathers were visited.

The first of our own "afflicted girls" was the pastor's daughter. Betty was only nine years old. It is no wonder she acted and spoke like one who had not put away childish ways. Furthermore she was the spoiled favorite of her household. Her cousin Abigail, although two years older, had learned she could gain nothing by opposing Betty. Abigail found, on the contrary, that she was surest to curry favor by imitating and submitting to her. Betty Parris and Abigail Williams began acting strange in January, a few weeks before any accusations were made.

The Procters and Mary Warren lived south of the Village, where they ran the ordinary next closest to Salem Village on the Boston road. That road leads from Topsfield and Ipswich in the north to Lynn and Boston to the south. Procter's Inn or Ordinary did a good business in bed, board, and livery. The Procters often came to church and lecture at the Village, and Mary was known among the farm families as something of a curiosity. She was ordinarily unremarkable, which made her "fits" all the more fascinating to those children privileged to witness them.

One December evening the Parris family rode back from Boston, where they had visited Mistress Parris's family, the Eldridges. As they traveled, a blowing snow came up, and began to hide the road. Reverend Parris found conditions severe enough to justify stopping short of home, so they spent the night and part of the next day at Procter's Ordinary. There Betty was fascinated to see Mary's fits close at hand.

The two of them were sitting at the kitchen table, where Mary was preparing dried apples for stewing. They talked together in the manner of a young woman and nine year old girl. Suddenly Mary's shoulders hunched as she dropped a handful of apples on the floor. She began to make panting and grunting noises, and her eyes rolled up. She slipped from her chair, then under the table, where she curled up and began to cry out. At this, Mistress Procter and Mistress Parris came running in from the parlor. They pulled Mary out from under the table and sat her on the settle before the fire, chafing her hands and rubbing her face. She seemed to respond to these things like one persecuted. She murmured "No, no," moving her head from side to side. When Mistress Procter gently slapping her, she shrieked and cried out, "No more! I'm sorry!" Then, after a few minutes, she became quiet and her eyes came down to a level, glazed stare, which gradually faded into a merely weary one.

Betty Parris, still seated at the table, had watched in wonder and admiration. She had seen Mary Warren transformed from a mere serving maid to being the center of attention for her mistress and her guest. She had gone from doing chores to enacting strange rituals. She had changed in that brief time from an insignificant factotum to a mysterious and respected stranger.

Several weeks later Betty and Abigail Williams began to exhibit unusual behavior — crawling under furniture, apparently retreating into trances, crying out as though in pain, and otherwise confounding Reverend Parris and his wife.

The fire had begun.

England has long hanged those she found to be witches. A witch could only be burned if convicted of "petty treason", that is, if she used her supposed powers to cause her husband's death. We did not burn any of those accused among us as witches. But our witch troubles kindled a kind of bonfire in Salem Village. Together we committed a kind of petty treason.

The first sparks crackled among the small tinder of the demented and the disenfranchised. Tinder is generally those scraps of wood regarded as having no value — the parings and shavings shed and left behind from what is useful. Kindling is best which has lain about ignored through a season of heat and dryness. Such were those distracted and dull-witted, those dejected and delirious souls.

But no fire rises to roar unless there is fuel of more substance than kindling. Towering above the chips and twigs are the trees of the forest, some of them young giants, best for lumber, for furniture, for fine woodwork — or for firewood. In our woods, in addition to kindling, we might be said to own four grades of human timber.

The highest grade is the men respected in London and ultimately residing in the home isles. These are the "king's trees". Not long ago such a one would have been a peer, but now he might be a wealthy merchant or an influential minister. Many of our great trees, particularly among our scholars and merchants, secretly regard themselves as but temporary transplants, brought here only to grow hardier, more fruitful, and more weather resistant while the religious and political climates at home remains hostile. When they opportunity arises these often returned to root in England where they can tower and spread in the ancient dignity for which they believe they were born.

One of the earlier pastors of Salem Town, Hugh Peter, returned to England during the Revolution and became chaplain to Oliver Cromwell. He flourished a while at the coming of the kingdom of God there. At the Restoration, this giant of the forest was hanged on another tree, drawn and quartered as a regicide. Since the greatest of all was similarly suspended and executed, no simple moral may be drawn from Reverend Peter's story. But like the king's trees, this grade of lumber is ever rarer.

The more humble or realistic among us aspire to the next grade, that of respected colonial. Such a tree is prosperous and looked up to, serving as teacher, assistant (our equivalent to a member of Parliament) deacon, law officer, or militia officer. Most of our established trees would be content to continue into moss-grown respectability this side of the Atlantic, if only the freaks of storms and lightning would allow it. The trees of this class flourish best in the bay air of Boston or Salem Town.

Third grade are the shaded trees, which at maturity may obtain some height and girth, but seldom surpass their betters, nor feel the full sun of unclouded respect. Nevertheless they may live long years and see their saplings spring around them. Their roots may be secure and go deep enough to touch good water and soil rich enough to nourish their old age. Such are our better tradesmen and small farmers, fishermen, and shopkeepers. This class of tree grows best on the edge of towns. Many of our leading families in Salem

Farms and Salem Village labored to make our own community grow into such a settlement. It seemed yet but a nursery and woodlot of Salem Town.

Last is that class of tree which creeps up low and gnarled on the borders or beneath the eaves of the forest. These are often as stunted as bushes, their roots working the hard soil to nourish healthier neighbors, their branches sacrificing nuts and fruit to deer and rodents, whose predations less often reach the more prosperous pillars around which they cluster. The successful trees gaze over the tops of these scrubs. Birches and aspen are they all, ever nursing young oaks and maples, then dying back to rot and ruin, their own seedlings arising briefly on hill or stream far from the parent's grave.

But no—contrary to the Creator's injunction, the seedlings of these last may not always be birch or aspen according to their kind, nor are any of the other grades certain to produce young of their own species. The unbounded new world with its innumerable fortuities has made it possible for one grade of lumber to become another. No more can be said than that it generally takes more than a generation for a bilberry to become an oak or an maple a thorn, but even that rule has been challenged among us. Our own governor was son of a colonial gunsmith who made as many children as guns. And little did he know that his last pistol would become such a great cannon.

This transmutability, often called a blessing for which to be most thankful, is also a curse. For there is open and active hostility in a herd which acknowledges no leader or follower. Where rank is recognized, every rank has its identity and its prerogatives, but in a place where every tree would be a mainmast on a man-o-war or be sawn and worked into an ornamented chest, any tree may also become a backlog or mere splitwood. Those descended from old "king's trees," who for many generations were branded and recognized as noble gentlemen in England, are much indignant when an upstart apprentice, through whatever means, be it happenstance or hard work, rises to an height equal to their own. And it is not always good for the one who so rises, either.

"They who will be rich. . ." saith the scripture, "fall into temptation and a snare, and into many foolish and hurtful lusts, which drown men in destruction and perdition." Nor does the desire for success and respect always accumulate in coin, any more than great pines always end as masts or carved tables. The pursuit of higher stature was sometimes cut short by blasting lightning or killing frost. Much good wood ended as winter fuel.

So the tinder did not burn alone—but found lumber of all grades ready to join it in the bonfire of our troubles. As we have said, the first sticks of kindling given deliberately to our fire were the delicate limbs of our pastor's daughter and his niece. Elizabeth "Betty" Parris and Abigail Williams flared in the first sparks which became our conflagration. These carried what might have been but a flash of tinder or an ordinary kitchen blaze to wood stacked nearby. Like cured cedar that fuel broke out in sudden heat.

The first lumber to catch was Pastor Samuel Parris, himself. He was fresh with all the resin of a Harvard education, and experienced enough through business to know something of the world's weather. He aspired to loftiness and naively thought Salem Village would prove fertile ground for him.

He had been thus sorted and stacked together with other wood, drier and harder—Sergeant Thomas Putnam, his brother Deacon Edward and their brother-in-law Captain Jonathon Walcott. These solid timbers, aspiring to power and prosperity, were stacked close to the Salem Village ordinary, or inn, presided over by two trees, an uncle and a nephew, both named Nathanael Ingersoll. Deacon (or Lieutenant) Ingersoll was a respected churchman as well as owner and operator of that ordinary. His only son had drowned in a shipwreck some years earlier, about the time his wife died. Although his daughter, Sarah, lived with him, he had brought in his nephew, "Nat" to take root alongside him in business.

Deacon Ingersoll endeavored to keep the good will of the more prosperous in the Village. He not only wished his business to flourish, but he hoped to recover some of the losses he suffered through investment in Governor Phips' Quebec expedition. In turn his young nephew hoped to attain the level of respect enjoyed by his uncle. They were allied with several of the Putnams in earlier controversies of the Village Church and laterally with Reverend Parris.

Ingersoll's Inn became not only a regular stop for officials coming and going on witchcraft business, but an official meeting place for magistrates Hathorne and Corwin. (It was sometimes to serve as an overnight gaol as well.) On every one of these occasions, Deacon Ingersoll or the younger, fastidious "Nat" made careful notation in the ledger of so many pounds, shillings, and pence owed for meat, drink, and lodging of constables and assistants, keeping of horses, keeping of prisoners, and entertaining of magistrates in the boom of "witch business".

Mr. Jonathon Corwin and Mr. John Hathorne were the Salem magistrates. As Salem ruled over the Village, these assistants ruled over matters of law in both. They were authorized to make legal judgments on all except those capital cases which required a higher court. They were lofty trees, with few lower branches, though perhaps not strongly enough rooted. Nevertheless they believed themselves among the last bulwarks against storms in the years before our troubles. In the period between the Andros government and the new commission of Governor Phips, the institutions of our community and justice were shaky and insecure, kept together under the dubious authority of the Committees for Safety. Such as held offices were afraid disaster would come if their authority were but slightly weakened. Even as the Phips government began under the new commission, and with it a general resurgence of confidence, these great ones remained cautious of the strength of our wilderness society. They had worked determinedly hitherto. During our troubles they worked even harder to withstand iniquity — so much so that they became chief agents of it.

Nat Ingersoll was married to Mary Preston, whose brother Tom was treated as an equal among the Nurses, level with John and Sam Nurse, and John Tarbell — below none but Francis. But to his terrible regret and for his deep refining, Tom signed the first witch accusations brought to law and thus contributed to the fire.

"Father" Nurse — Francis, Sr. — was a tower of a tree, one of those risen by his own hard work to a surprising eminence befitting the straightest mast on the greatest ship, and by all estimates before the troubles, invulnerable to hurricane or pestilence. But no tree is immune to lightning, nor to fire that roars around it from the brush below. Neither was he without sin, that blithe and noble sin of the best colonists. Indeed it may be with us like the Spirit — to the ends of the age.

Francis' Village farm had originally been Townsend Bishop's, then Henry Chickerings. Governor Endicott bought it of Chickering and gave it to his son, who died childless. His widow married Pastor Allen, who sold it to the Nurses. In the early days when Mr. Bishop owned it, Governor John Endicott, John Porter and John Putnam were the chief neighbors, but Francis did not come to Salem Village until 1778, and by then there were eighty families round and about. He and Rebecca, of the Towne tribe of Topsfield, worked wisely and well from the beginning. They brought in their sons, as well as sons-in-law Tom Preston and John Tarbell. Theirs was the pleasant circumstance that illness nor war struck their several bread-winners. They needed hire no help. The Nurse tribe seemed a veritable grove of towering trees.

Rebecca Nurse was no witch, yet she, with her husband, Francis, and with John Tarbell, John and Sam Nurse and their wives Mary, Elizabeth, and Mary came to recognize some contribution to the fire due to petty traitors. In the end most of them recognized their common part with the forests of New England in contributing well-grown wood to that fire that blazed up among us in February of 1692.

In Salem, when the men were sure judges could be found who were well armed, they took the risk of presenting the village accused witches in order to rid Salem of the undesirables.

Rev. Cotton Mather was a well-known writer of the time, but he has often been misjudged because of his support of the Salem witch trials. Mather was a part of the trials and played a role in defending his own writings, which would later be seen as the words of a man caught up in the hysteria that had overtaken the region.

Justice Hathorne

Chapter Three – The Least of These

*And the King shall answer and say unto them, Verily I say
unto you, Inasmuch as ye have done it unto one of the least of
these my brethren, ye have done it unto me.*
– Matthew 25:40

Many of the chief players in our tale were lowly sufferers,
whose influence or even welfare was thitherto given the least regard.
These, too, became tinder for our troubles.

    Dorcas Good had small part during our troubles, yet now she
wanders large among us. One might almost say she haunts us.
Dorcas had enough baleful drink to fill her youthful cup without that
great dollop of wormwood added when she was five. She was the
youngest to be accused. These days her ability to project spectres,
though not that of which she once was accused, is well nigh
inescapable. She is almost a young woman now, but her mind still
carries the marks of chains—marks more genuine than any of those
exhibited by the "afflicted" girls. Benjamin Putnam's family has the
keeping of her and her father. It is a fine Christian charity they show
in this, yet the wide-eyed blankness of her face must haunt them, too.
She walks in strides, facing straight ahead like a soldier on the
training ground, but her arms swing as listless as a jaded veteran's,
or as though still in chains. Should one chance to face her straight
on, her gaze comes back; seeming one moment to stare through to
eternity; the next, but an eyelash flicker between, examining one's
soul deeper than Judge Hathorne or Reverend Noyes ever could.
Never did young heart learn so thoroughly to imitate Christ in what
the scripture saith that he trusted himself to no man.

    Her father, Good Will, has sought redress from the court for
the execution of her mother. Perhaps it is chiefly due to the more
worldly-wise oversight of Goodman Putnam that his petition asks
compensation not only for his executed wife, but on behalf of Dorcas,
declaring she can not govern herself as a result of her imprisonment
and confinement in chains. Others say she governs herself too well.

    But her father is of another kind. He has long been called
"Good Will"—though not by so many now as formerly. He often

seems the fool, but a wise fool, for he speaks little and only in such cryptic words and at such pregnant moments that they sound sententious — to the particular bewilderment of those do not know him. Those of us who have worked beside him in the fields or in the workshop know he is also sometimes given to eldritch whoops and ridiculous ramblings which seem to have no purpose but a certain comfort to his own mind. Until Francis Nurse died, Good Will came regularly to watch his work in the turning shed and helped in small ways with the woodworking.

Those who deal much with him have some respect for his parables and proverbs. Those who don't know him well and are unsure whether to count him simple or sage, are apt to miss the poetical or ironical side of the man. This was true during our troubles — to his wife's hurt. But sometimes we heard the ring of wisdom in things he said beyond the ear of office.

Jacob Goodale was a true simple, who talked like a child, although able-bodied. It was he whom Giles Corey finally beat so badly that he died. That was one of the few genuine grievances brought against Corey during our troubles. A charitable master would have gotten half of the work of a whole-witted laborer from him and neither of them the worse for it, but Corey was not that.

Years earlier in late summer, John Tarbell went with Father Nurse and Tom Preston to clear stumps for Corey in exchange for a wagon load of hay. Jacob worked with them and Giles appeared angry with him from the beginning. Tom and John began to take note of the way the two affected each other. Giles would set Jacob to a job, giving him instructions, but always too many, so that Jacob did the first thing he was told, but could not remember the second or third. He would chop through a root, and then come to a kind of bewildered halt, glance furtively in the direction of Giles and finally lean on his ax, awaiting the inevitable outburst that punctuated their labors. Goodman Corey, deeply engaged in his own exertions would glance over and see Jacob at rest. He would yell out some insult, "you good-for-nothing lout" or the like, walk over and deliver a short tongue-lashing, another list of tasks, and the cycle would re-commence.

Toward the end of the day, fatigued themselves, and weakened with anticipation of each episode, Tom and John became thorns in each others flesh, winking, chuckling, then ashamedly laughing low. Finally when dusk came, they rode home on top of the load of hay with Father Nurse, bursting with laughter in recollection of the expressions recurring across the two faces. They debated who was the most simple-minded, the man born that way, or the one who could not bring himself to recognize the fact. Father Nurse said Corey couldn't admit Jacob's limitations because he felt that would be admitting to a bad bargain. Yet he paid but bed and board for Jacob whose labor was worth more than that.

Two times during the day the humorous side of it went suddenly into abeyance. On the first occasion, toward noon, Jacob struck an ill-aimed blow at a root and dinted the ax on a stone. Goodman Corey then gave him such a tongue-lashing that Jacob fell down and began to writhe on the ground, a strange and ugly sight. As he lay wriggling, he held his hands in front of his face and made whining and grunting sounds. The other men were embarrassed.

In mid-afternoon, Corey's mood was fouler. He had broken an ax handle, himself, and began to realize they weren't going to clear as much as he'd planned. Jacob, in a rare moment of independent action, had finished cutting one root, and moved to a different stump where he had begun chopping. But this was not Corey's particular instruction to him, so that Corey not only came over to belittle him in word, but struck him with the broken ax handle. Again Jacob fell to the ground writhing groaning, and protecting his face. The others suspected this form of the drama had been rehearsed often. Jacob was little the worse for the two blows, but the presence of the others seemed to restrain Corey. Though Jacob was thought to have died at Corey's hands well before our troubles began, he played a part in our tale.

There were many such people about the country of Salem — oppressed, bemused, simple-minded, or distracted. Eleazor Keyser has a daughter who is more in the latter category. (Eleazor testified against Reverend Burroughs, while Hannah, his sister, helped Surgeon Barton examine the accused women for "witch marks".) Although the daughter grew quieter in her ways as she got older, she is doubtless distracted. She comes to meeting in Salem at times. Her eyes wander independently and her head wobbles on her neck as she catches at bits of conversation, and repeats or jumbles them, then lapses back to other bits stuck in memory — animal sounds and laughter. When she walks, it is with short awkward steps like a dove and with that bird's motion from side to side.

She no longer speaks aloud in meeting. She was constantly hushed as girl, and no doubt thrashed at home when she had been particularly obstreperous. But outside meeting, she makes up for her vocal restraint, and since our troubles, she is listened to patiently.

We've already mentioned Mary Warren, whose original afflictions were genuine. She came to play more than her initial part, however. Her kinswoman, Elizabeth Knapp, contributed too, through Reverend Willard's accounts of her afflictions, which informed more than one adjudicator and more than one imitator.

Hannah Perley, afflicted daughter of Samuel of Topsfield, died nearly ten years before our troubles, but accounts of her words helped put a noose about the neck of neighbor Elizabeth Howe long after Hannah had departed. She had fits, too, apparently much like Mary Warren's. Her family testified she would call out the name of Goody Howe in these fits and claim to be afflicted by her. Other witnesses, as respectable as pastors Samuel Phillips and Edward Payson of Rowley, spoke to the contrary, saying that little Hannah didn't mention Goody Howe at all during the fits which they witnessed. They said that in ordinary conversation the girl expressed a high opinion of Goody Howe and did not think she did her any harm.

More telling than that, Reverend Phillips overheard her brother Samuel whispering to Hannah "say Goody Howe is a witch, say she is a witch." The minister rebuked him for it, and concluded Hannah had often been influenced by mother and brother to speak against Howe.

Her father, up to the time of her death, corrected Hannah whenever he heard her speak ill of their neighbor. He continued to refer to Goody Howe as a godly woman until Hannah died. But he saw his daughter's death as confirmation of witchery. When Elizabeth Howe tried to join the Ipswich church, both the Perleys led a whispering campaign, naming her witch and saying she had been the death of their daughter, so that she was not allowed to covenant with that congregation.

Many other children died in the years preceding our troubles. For example, Sergeant Thomas and Anne Putnam lost a son in December 1689. Who knows how much the pain of that loss had to do with the zeal with which they named and prosecuted witches in 1692.

There have been others among us much distracted in dreadful ways. Two years before the troubles, Christian, the wife of John Trask of Royalside, had her throat cut, apparently with a pair of sewing scissors, a thing awful to imagine and infinitely worse to have done. She was a striking young woman, with wide eyes that seemed to look too openly into one's own. She was also the mother of five, the youngest but five months born. It was said, come the troubles, she was at odds with Edward Bishop's wife, who therefore bewitched her.

At the time of Christian's death, Bridget Bishop was accused, but others including Reverend Hale defended her. He changed his opinion during our troubles, so that his and related testimony led to the arrest of Bridget in 1692. At the time of Christian's death, both Edward Bishop, Sr. and Edward, Jr. were on the coroner's jury, along with Daniel Andrew and William Rayment, Jr. What was said there about her state of mind pointed to some deep melancholy, but it had little outward show until her last desperate act—if it was her own. The nature of her injuries was such that there always lingered the strong suspicion another's hand had caused them.

Likewise Rebecca, sister of Daniel Andrew and wife of George Jacobs, Jr., was distracted and melancholy more often than not for at least ten years before our troubles. The chief things she said about her sorrows seemed connected with the loss of a child before birth. She was capable of caring for her other five children, but her melancholy weighed much on brother and husband, who nevertheless came to bear it patiently, and to encourage her daily with scripture. Some days she received the seed into good soil, but other times, she was full of wild and vain imaginings which no one and nothing alleviated. At worst she became her own accuser, claiming she had killed her child, and like Rachel of the scriptures, refused to be comforted. Her mother, brother and husband thought her guilt and fears but crazy fancies.

Sarah Good, Dorcas's mother and Will's wife, one of the three accused at the beginning of our troubles, at times seemed barely in her right mind. Death had robbed her of a wealthy uncle, and a first husband. Through the children of the first and the ineptitude of the last she lost her estate, land, and home. They say she married Will as a wrecked sailor grabs hold of a spar. She was not a fool herself, and could read the distant signals of Will's wit. But thrown on the charity of the Village, they did not well together. His style was not hers and the two voices had little harmony as a beggars' duet. Which is to say either of them alone would have found readier charity than did the two of them together. If he was enigmatic, she wore her coarser sentiments upon her sleeve—and increasingly the sentiments were dominated by bitterness and resentment. The two of them quarreled, his words the fewer and his tone the milder.

Sarah became famous for muttering, especially at parting, and those whose hearing was sharp enough, caught bits of what were not unfairly called curses, insofar as a curse is a word spoken in condemnation. She was that strange mixture, a proud beggar, capable of asking in the politest tones if she might borrow some tobacco for her pipe, but suddenly sullen and bitter where she was refused—no matter how tender or justified the refusal. She became a universal judge against the rest of the community and mankind. Her approach in seeking charity became a sort of moral ultimatum, which worked only with a few people, and then only a few times. She quickly wore out her welcomes. More than others of unusual turn of mind among us, hers was a profound anger gradually and willfully entered into. Her words and manner on the scaffold betrayed the profound vengeance she had wrested for her own, despite the Lord's words concerning the proper ownership of that commodity.

Some, of the "least," like Dorcas Good, suffer young and scarcely recover. Yet others who have suffered life-long, seem always able to adapt to new sufferings.

Tituba, Mr. Parris's Indian servant was one of those—accustomed to suffering. Some would lay much of the blame for our troubles on her, but her belabored shoulders are too narrow for that yoke. No servant, or rather slave—for such she was—can be made to bear responsibility for his actions unless those actions be isolated from the knowledge or complicity of his master. Tituba cannot be said to have had an independent or initiatory part in our troubles.

She and her husband John—often called John Indian—came with Samuel Parris from the Barbadoes, where Pastor Parris's father had brought his son up as a planter and trader in sugar. There slavery was an widespread institution. Tituba and John were captured as children by Spanish man-stealers in South America. When Mr. Parris moved to Boston before coming to Salem Village, he brought them with him as household servants, along with a young Negro lad, who was his personal servant.

Tituba and John grew up under plantation rule, as severe as Goodman Corey's over Jacob Goodale. That kind of tyranny breeds fear and cowing in a simple man like Jacob. In sharp-witted persons like Tituba and John, introduced to it as children, it produces a web of responses all designed with one end—to alleviate so far as possible the suffering that is their lifelong lot. If suffering may be distinguished into that of body and that of spirit, the defenses of the former avoid endless labor and extreme punishment. But defenses of spirit have another end—to reserve some sovereignty for the soul.

Although we have few slaves among us, most of those we have wear masks of servility and feigned stupidity which armor them against the afflictions which would otherwise accrue to them. Such was certainly the case with Tituba, and to scarcely a smaller degree with John. Both were so familiar with beatings that the act itself was no longer needed to bend them to their master's will. Servility and submission were reflexes with them, requiring no calculation.

On one occasion when the Parrises were newly arrived in the Village, the minister was invited to preside over the customary feast surrounding a hog-butchering at Ingersoll's. Tituba, John and the Negro lad had been given some fermented cider as it made the rounds among the young men. The three of them began to feel the effects and danced for a few minutes about the fire where the rendering went forward. Mr. Parris chanced to look out the door and see this. He stepped out upon the stoop and merely stared at them for half a minute, at which Tituba suddenly saw or sensed his presence and stopped so abruptly John nearly fell into the fire. Without a word being spoken, she hurried up to the steps and dropped on her knees before Reverend Parris. "Yes, master, " she said, "We do wrong master. Master please forgive us, master." Mr. Parris turned and went inside which the onlookers supposed was equivalent to clemency and perhaps the end of it.

A few months later, in March, the Negro lad died, unable to resist our severe winters.

When our troubles began, Tituba was the first named. Almost, if not quite immediately, she "confessed". With great savvy of how the depraved hearts of men work, she offered alternative objects for the wrath directed against her. She named two others — and the bull was out of the pasture.

To confess sounds an irrational thing to do, yet it was also a cunning thing. To name two other "witches" was both a clever thing and one instinctive to her in circumstances of fear. Reason and unreason travel well together in this fallen world. The rick and rack of the split rail fence that enclosed the slough of our troubles was built of both.

The chiefest movers of our troubles were a band of maids, the first three but eight, eleven and twelve years old. Soon a number of their older friends, sixteen to nineteen, were involved. What a strange thing that these should become the powerful dictators, the "little despots" as John Tarbell called them or the "benevolent ladies" as Daniel Andrews named them after the ancients' euphemism for the Furies. Their very weakness became their power—for their parents and guardians could not bring themselves to believe any evil of them. The ministers and magistrates in particular, regarded them as innocent glasses through which God was revealing the machinations of darkness.

Yet not all the weak, or distracted, or simple, or mad, or melancholy, or oppressed and subjugated minds in the colony could have brought about the terrible troubles that came upon us, without the educated, ordered, scientific, and lawyerly reasoning that sought out, established, bolstered, and confirmed the insanity.

At the same time as Giles Corey was beside himself trying to beat the simplicity out of Jacob Goodale; at the same time as Hannah Keyser's daughter and Mary Warren were gabbling in distracted fits; at the same time as Christian Trask and Rebecca Jacobs were wandering lonely in confused melancholy; great minds among us were playing another part. Sparkling with lofty learning, and vigorous with intellectual vitality, they were writing books full of marvelous records and brilliant conclusions for the edification of mankind in general and the kingdom of God in particular. A favorite arcane topic among some of these wise men was witchcraft. The wise, too, played pathetic parts in our tale—for they were laying groundwork before it happened. They, too, were distracted.

Cotton Mather had gone a few years earlier to consult with Reverend Willard. The immediate purpose of his appointment with Mr. Willard was to seek counsel in regard to the young woman, Martha Goodwin, whom Mather had taken into his household. Martha continued to have severe fits even after the execution of her purported tormenter, the washerwoman Goodwife Glover.

The older minister greeted the younger with a slight dip and twist of the head, "Mr. Mather," he said, "welcome in Christ."

The youngest graduate of Harvard replied, "Mr. Willard, God's blessing on your family and yourself. Thank you for your kindness in granting opportunity to avail myself of your wisdom. "

The visitor followed Simon Willard into the side parlor which was his office.

"Your father is well?" inquired Mr. Willard, as he directed the mild-featured young man to a chair.

"Most well, by God's grace," Mr. Mather answered, and then in proper if not heartfelt response, "And your family are also well I hope?"

"Quite well, thank you, though perhaps too active for such a heat as we have had. But you mentioned an interest in a particular matter, and I know how precious the hours can be to a young and active pastor, so let us pass over to what is on your mind."

"Oh, thank you sir. I have been most fascinated by your report of some years ago concerning the young woman of your household — and would like to clarify in my own mind some of the events and observations of which you wrote, now that I am in similar circumstance."

Mr. Willard's congenial smile had withdrawn steadily from the corners of his mouth and he replied in a less hospitable tone.

"I am surprised that you have seen my report. It was not meant for publication beyond the small number of ministers to whom I gave it for purposes of pastoral consultation."

"Among them my father, sir, and since I have been made his assistant, and a member of your Philosophical Society, he thought it not improper that I read it. In full honesty, I saw it among his papers and asked — it was not he who introduced the idea, you see — but he gave permission. Yet I heartily beg your forgiveness if in this we have transgressed against your intentions."

Mollified by the energetic young man's candor, and by the reference to Increase Mather's permission, Mr. Willard waved his hand in dismissal.

"No. One certainly has one's intentions, but I see no transgression in what you tell me. I will confess, however, that the issue of pastoral confidentiality can hardly be overemphasized. The only thing to compete with the deadly tongue for destructiveness is the deadly pen. It may be I should not have written the report at all. However since I did and you read it with your father's permission, I will be happy for any discussion of the report which would further its aims -- namely the wiser conduct of Christians in dealing with particular cases of demonic or devilish attack such as seems to have come into our households. I have heard a bit about your ministry to the Goodwin girl.

"However, I offer the further caveat that the report should be shown to no others without my explicit consent, nor it's contents further published."

"Oh, sir, I think you underestimate how important your report is. My father and many others have spoken of the particular objection our Enemy makes to these colonies and the church within them. He roars against us, lies in wait for us, and is particularly bent on deceiving the brethren herein. There are many good teachers at Harvard, but in these matters we are greatly in want of wisdom. We have wise men of grammar, logic, rhetoric, theology and science, but we are ill equipped to fight the devil on his own ground. I would almost ask that you publish the report more widely, or at least make it available to students and ministers."

"I must repeat that pastoral confidentiality is of the greatest importance. Had I been wiser, perhaps, I would have disguised the case and the identity of the young woman. Then further distribution might have been possible. However probably even then it would have been impossible to keep her secrets as we are obligated to do. However, with her identity clear as I have made it, I say again the report should be shown to no others without my explicit consent, nor it's contents further published.

"So far as I can tell from scripture the only three kinds of sinners who are to be publicly exposed are those who will not listen to the church after the steps of Matthew 18, those who are prosecuted for crimes by the civil authority, and leaders who sin publicly, as in Paul's rebuke of Peter in Galatians. Within the constraints of decency, of course, any of us may speak of his own sins in testimony of deliverance from them. But even in partial accounts of the sins or struggles of our flocks the identities and characters of those concerned should be veiled with the greatest care."

The younger man moved about on the edge of his chair, barely able to keep silent as the older one re-emphasized his point.

"But sir, would you have an army go to battle unarmed and untrained! Must not the officers, at least, be taught the tactics and strategies of their enemies! If we cannot publish the accounts of these battles which have been fought and won, how are we to learn?"

Mr. Willard was amiably amused by the younger pastor's zeal and the simple lines of his arguments. For a brief moment he remembered himself in the early days of his ministry, fiercely determined to gather in the loose ends of all practical knowledge that would make him humanely omniscient.

"We take seriously the need of an educated clergy, Mr. Mather, but we must remember that complete sanctification cannot be obtained in universities, libraries, or even in ministry — not at least before the age of thirty!"

At this warm touch of humor, Mr. Mather smiled sheepishly, then replied, "Surely sir, by your age . . ."

They both laughed.

"No," answered Mr. Willard, "We cannot learn what the devil means to do any more than we can learn what our neighbor means to do—or even what trials or blessings we ourselves will experience tomorrow. Principles may be gained from scripture and experience—even the experience of others—but neither scriptural principles nor the practical ones gained from experience are substitutes for faith and humility upon the battleground of living."

"Yet I believe we ought to prepare for Satan's especial malevolence towards us," said Mr. Mather, with a deferential tone equally allowing of refutation or assent.

"Certainly the scriptures say 'Be ready. . .'; 'be prepared. . .'; 'put on the full armor of God . . .' and so forth. It seems to me we may say two things about the devil's strategies, which seem almost contraries. On the one hand, he has no imagination at all. 'There is no temptation that has befallen us, but such as is common to man . . . ' On the other hand, he is always changing his angle of attack. As you indirectly mentioned, he seems to be crafty enough that the brethren may be well-nigh deceived by him."

"Does he not seem to work in particular ways at particular places and times?" asked Mr. Mather, "For instance, through the Egyptians, the Canaanites, the Babylonians or Persians at different points in Israel's history?"

"Different agents, certainly, yet not very different tactics, so it seems to me. At least in the cases you mention, he uses only a few tactics—hostile captivity, friendly captivity, subversion—and all with the constant pressures toward idolatry and away from the worship of the true God."

"Precisely," replied Mr. Mather," And always a desire for other or better provision and a tendency toward complaining against God. But see how the faithful men such as Job and Joseph and Daniel were attacked with particular hardship, while others like Saul and David and Solomon with particular luxuries."

"There may indeed be some science in these things. Yet as we teach and preach, we cannot limit ourselves to how the devil attacks one kind of men, since our flocks are made up of all kinds of men."

"But does not the devil have strategies as well as tactics? Does he not develop and build, modify his policy, and make particular plans against certain nations and in certains epochs? Does not the army of hell follow certain marching orders in each age of history?"

"In my opinion the devil does not so much maintain a march through history as a continual spinning about of his slaves. They are after all surrounded and hemmed in by the work of Christ. But he wheels and thus re-aligns the battlefront, causing schism along different axes and over different issues through time.

"His most effective action is this wheeling, for by it he keeps the church attacking the positions of yesterday, while he strikes where we are weakest. There, you see, is where the academy can even be his ally, for it is necessarily deliberate and analytical — and must have its reports to study and from which to draw principles before ever it can teach — all drawn from yesterday's battles. Meanwhile the devil's rag-tag army continues to march by the flank and change fronts.

"I believe the most important principles are not those found in college lectures or books, but those we gain by faith in the midst of the battle itself. Thus my report on Elizabeth Knapp was a working document, which as you will know, reaches no definite conclusions, but rather implies some lessons being learned."

"Even such lessons are of infinite value to us younger men. I would like to ask you more specifically about some of them if I may."

"Let us have a cup of tea first, and then perhaps we may speak for another half hour. After that I fear my time is not my own."

A serving maid, the successor of Elizabeth Knapp, brought tea and toast. Over the tea they spoke of things unlikely to hinder digestion, but as the tray was borne away again, Mr. Willard regarded the clock in the hall, and resumed the more serious discussion.

"I will allow you three questions, and then I'm afraid I must depart myself. I will answer as well as I am able."

"Thank you sincerely sir. Then I will waste no more time. My first question is whether any further developments ever brought any firmer conclusions as to who had bewitched Elizabeth."

"Dear, dear, Mr. Mather! You surprise me exceedingly! If you have read my report you know that there remained and, I might add, remains, a previous question as to whether there was any bewitchment at all! In my estimation, jumping to that conclusion is exceedingly dangerous and perhaps the greatest aid we can lend the devil in cases like these."

"But surely sir, despite your laudable caution, you so concluded yourself."

"Not at all! Indeed, I did not even include the possibility in my conclusion. I concluded with brief reference to four major questions in regard to her distemper. In the first I stated my conclusion that her distemper was real, due to the great and unnatural strength she exhibited during her fits and her great weakness after them.

"In the second I stated my opinion that her distemper was fundamentally diabolical, although I made two reservations which I continue to find weighty enough to keep that conclusion tentative.

"The third question had to do with whether the devil spoke in her during her fits. I offered five observations that led me to believe such was indeed the case.

"Finally, I concluded that the question of whether she had covenanted with the devil or not was unanswerable, since her own statements in this regard were so contradictory. At some points, I might add, as is made evident in my narrative, she was evidently deceitful about the cause of her fits, especially in regard to its agency. I did opine — and subsequently it proved so — that she remained a legitimate object of pity and a subject for hope. Within a year of that report her recovery seemed to be complete, and I have since found her profession of trust in Christ credible. Indeed I cannot believe she remains subject to our Enemy beyond the degree to which we ourselves are subject to him. She has, in fact, married and both she and her husband appear to prosper."

"But surely sir, if this may still be counted under my first question, it cannot be that she was subject to the devil using her voice and body unless she had given herself to that use, and if given to that use then someone must have taught her or led her to that subjection!"

"I say this for you sir," and Mr. Willard laughed good-naturedly, "no man could get more garments out of one bolt of cloth than you get out of one question!

"Yet you raise profound matters — much broader than the particulars of my account. In answer I can only say I find the essential matter of your questions to be in the realm of extreme mystery and incline to believe the answers among the secret things God alone knows.

"Job was given over to the devil to a degree beyond what any of us have known, yet he was never made agent of the devil's voice or the devil's strength. The Gaderene demoniac, on the other hand, whom we are told was possessed, seems to have been both a mouthpiece and demonically strong. The slave girl of Philippi had supernatural powers of foretelling by diabolical means. Jesus freed various demoniacs, who prior to that deliverance were cast by demons into the water and into the fire.

"I think there must be a distinction between those who are considerably plagued and those possessed by demons. Similarly there must be a distinction between those possessed and those who give themselves deliberately to the devil. But I am convinced that a Christian cannot be truly possessed or ruled by the devil, and that therefore believing the gospel is the certain cure for a demoniac. Further, I am confident repentance and faith will deliver even a witch, that is one who has deliberately given himself or herself to the devil—that nothing can prevail against the name of Christ spoken in faith."

Mr. Mather answered, "These are matters much on our minds with Martha Goodwin now in our care. Yet I am convinced that the spiritual assault of witches against the innocent is also possible. I make this my final question, then: When Elizabeth complained of a particular woman appearing in various guises and bewitching her, how was it you came to the conclusion she falsely accused that one?"

"Yes, that was the one place in my narrative where I touched on the question of affliction by witchcraft per se. Elizabeth on several occasions offered descriptions of encounters with figures whom she took to be the devil, and on a few occasions the appearance of a beast who became a woman or a particular woman herself in the motions of witchery.

"I warned her solemnly not to name the woman openly, and hastened to call the woman herself that she might face this girl who had become, in this, her accuser. The woman was of good reputation and there was no reason apart from these accusations to think her anything but a godly person.

"When she came, I minutely questioned Elizabeth in regard to her former reports, then separately questioned the woman about her activities at the times Elizabeth mentioned. Two major inconsistencies emerged: First, Elizabeth's reports varied considerably from the versions she had earlier given. Second, the woman was not only known to have been elsewhere and about other activities on the occasions Elizabeth said she had seen her, but on at least one of those, she was with church members who remembered the heartfelt prayers she offered up."

"When confronted with these inconsistencies, Elizabeth could offer no sensible explanation and became exceedingly uneasy, and finally went off into one of her fits, at which point I sharply abraded her for lying, and she not only recovered from the fit, but began to express sorrow for her deceit."

The younger man was plainly bursting with more questions, but he glanced at the clock in the hall and restrained himself. "I see time presses, or I would ask many more things, for I am convinced few things are of more moment for us in these times."

"I regret to say I must leave you, "replied Mr. Willard. "I hope you will keep me informed of your progress with the Goodwin girl."

The two of them parted at the door.

Mr. Mather, despite his respect for the older pastor and his good manners, was much dissatisfied with the discussion, not least because of a fourth question which was most central to his thoughts, and which Mr. Willard, by implication had altogether dismissed. That question was the degree to which a human agent of the devil, witch or wizard, could actively and secretly afflict an innocent and godly person, while at a distance and even while appearing innocent and godly, herself.

He had already discussed this at length with his father and with a number of his own contemporaries. His father and those contemporaries had read the accounts of English witch-hunters, and were nearly all in agreement that a witch was capable of afflicting someone at a great distance—by means of "spectres," usually having the appearance of the witch.

Later that week he spoke again with his father, rehearsing Mr. Willard's answers.

"He seemed surprised and even displeased that I should suggest Elizabeth Knapp was plagued by a witch or witches. He said that he considered the idea to be one of the most dangerous raised in regard to the subject, yet we have seen irrefutable evidence of it with Goody Glover and how many other hundreds of witch cases reported by wise and godly men!"

Mr. Mather, Sr. answered deliberately but not condescendingly, for he had a great deal of affection for his son.

"I know no minister with more love for Christ or his people than Mr. Willard, and I would not oppose him in this or anything else without considerable study, but could it be you misunderstood him? His experience with the Knapp girl led him to conclude that her fits were not a matter of being bewitched, but I'm sure he does not discount the existence or danger of witches."

"Yet , if not, he would seem to make that question the very last he would consider in a case like that of Elizabeth Knapp or Martha Goodwin. What evidence do you suppose would lead him to look for that solution to such a case?"

"Surely both you and I agree that in the ordinary course of events, we would first look for more ordinary causes of suffering, then patterns of sin, then perhaps the demonic, and only at last the agency of a human witch."

"But, forgive me, Father, in these cases we are already out of the course of ordinary events. How often have you and the other patriarchs of our colony talked of how unique this people and this country? Is it not legitimate to suppose the devil is doing all he can of an extraordinary nature to oppose the kingdom of God in the special manifestation which providence has made of it here?"

"Speaking of the general case, I would answer in the affirmative, but nonetheless, in any specific case we must progress from the more usual explanations to the less usual."

"Father, perhaps it is my impatience -- yet, being involved in an extraordinary case, I am zealous that we should be able to understand it and be armed against similar cases which are sure to arise among us."

The Mathers were by no means unique among us, but rather representative. In addition to the idols common to us all, those who lead and teach have particular little gods before which their guild bows. "The wise" are inclined to have as their chief delight the discovery of what is obscure, yet to them essential, knowledge. It is no wonder the scholars and theologians gathered so often around our troubles in Salem and the Village. There is no doubt where one may find flies in a pasture. But the desire for secret knowledge did not come upon them in fits. It became their very life-blood. Though they speak strongly against Mannichees or alchemists, they are like them. Each hoards his share, and all their common store of secret or special knowledge. It is one of the principle things that distinguishes our "educated clergy". Secret knowledge and the desire for more fed the fantasies of Baxter and Mather and continued to fuel our troubles.

Ministers Hale, Lawson, Parris, Noyes and Higginson had all tasted of the secret knowledge dispensed liberally at Harvard -- that which surpasses the understanding of ordinary mortals. A thousand years of aristocracy lay behind us, and our new formulation of it was that superiors could be raised up through education. Thus Harvard was formally described as the institution for producing our ministers and rulers. Secretly believing the principle seat of the sanctified soul to be the well-educated mind, our wise men carried on their confident cabalism. The ministers and the magistrates under their instruction (particularly that of Mr. Noyes of Salem, pastor to both magistrates) carried out their strange questionings and concludings in assurance their secret wisdom particularly qualified them for that calling.

The gnostic wisdom of our sages tossed back and forth between God and Baal (like that of Baalam, the great antetype of their prophetic school) deriving not so much from assiduous study of the scriptures as from what they delighted and delight to call "science". Though the more sceptical call our "science" a bastard of alchemy and astrology, it is hailed by others as the highest service of the Christian mind, the ultimate exercise in "thinking God's thoughts after him" and of "studying" all things. Scripture gives us some warrant to "go to the ant," and good warrant to "study" God in the sense the good man of the Psalms "meditates" in God's law both day and night. But our leading teachers had a commitment to arcane science more thorough than the purported covenant of the accused witches.

Some freethinkers have said our troubles were the result of a rigid Christianity. Certainly we have been heirs to many features of Pharisaical religion. Yet it was not Bible religion but superstition, bad precedent, and bad science upon which our pitiful proceedings were founded.

The wholesale hunting and prosecuting of witches did not begin until the last few centuries – with the rising fashion of "systematic science". Astrology and alchemy were the hobbies of many educated men of Europe and England in the last century. They had their counterparts in anti-alchemy and anti-astrology. All of these were "scientific," that is they conducted themselves according to formulas, experiments, and "proofs". Witches and the hunters of witches likewise had their formulas.

Our wise men, too, conceived of themselves as "systematic" and as scientists. The tide of science that swept Sir Isaac Newton from the country furrows to the streets of Oxford and on to a chair of Cambridge, rushed high enough to wet the dingle of every educated mind, even in the colonies. This science made a particular hobby out of observation, intuition, and analysis. In his leisure hours many a wise man might be found contemplating the stars, beasts, plants, or other creatures. This had gone on from very early in the colonies. Governor Winthrop kept a journal which included many "observations" of strange and numinous events, generally interpreted as of spiritual import. These including tales much like the "spectre" stories that provided so much of the fabric of our witch troubles. (And his son was regarded as enough of a scientist to be admitted to the Royal Academy.)

But Newton was part of a new movement -- which held the observations to more rigid standards of analysis, to the generating of laws, and to the application of those laws to all similar phenomena. He was lecturing the Royal Academy in London on what he had learned of light and color through his newly invented reflecting telescope about the time we were driving the Narragansetts from their swamp fort during King Philip's War. Later, during two years in succession, great comets passed over New England and were viewed from distinct perspectives. First men of God such as Increase Mather said they were signs of God's wrath and impending judgment against New England for our sins. But others, notably the almanac printer, John Foster, gave us detailed observations and measurements of these heavenly bodies with the aid of Newton's new telescope.

When Increase Mather preached about the second comet, he began to meld these perspectives, and to talk of God speaking to us, no longer through "prodigieus" signs, that is ones beyond natural explanation, but through "signal providences," that is natural phenomena with a message. The wise man's task, then, was to observe and pass along the message -- rather than to miraculously "interpret" it in the sense that Daniel read the writing on Nebuchnezzar's wall. Further, the wise should teach the less learned to read these natural messages through reasonable means.

Suspended between these two tasks, the wise went about their "science" -- observing, passing on the message, but where "extraordinary" or "prodigious" phenomena were seen, interpreting them for the ignorant and unlearned.

In 1684, Increase Mather's *An Essay for the Recording of Illustrious Providences, Wherein , an Account is Given of Many Remarkable and Very Memorable Events, Which Have Happened in This Last Age; Especially in New England* was printed in Boston. It was originally begun by John Davenport and supplemented not only by the elder Mather but by various New England ministers in response to a request which he sent out. It was a collection of stories taken from observation of natural phenomena for the purpose of exemplifying and illustrating spiritual truths. Mr. Mather regarded it as a "Natural History of New England" following "the rules and method described by the learned and excellent person Robert Boyle, Esq." It included a number of accounts of demons and witchcraft.

In 1689, Cotton Mather's *Memorable Providences, Relating to Witchcrafts and Possessions. A Faithful Account of the Many Wonderful and Surprising Things That Have Befallen Several Bewitched and Possessed Persons in New-England . . .* was published in Boston by Joseph Brunning "at His Shop at the Corner of Prison Lane Next the Exchange." It seems to follow consciously on his father's earlier work -- a "scientific" document full of detailed observation, although he ends it with his first attack against the Scots Quaker George Keith, with whom he and other Bostonians were to exchange volleys for some years.

Both Mathers were conscious not only of "scientific observation," but of a theological principle of the Reformation that "signs and wonders" chiefly accompany apostolic office. Both Papists and Protestants agreed the authentication of Jesus' ministry and the office of the apostles were connected with miraculous events and deeds. However Reformation doctrine held that authoritative signs and wonders had ceased with the apostles -- in refutation of Catholic authority and Catholic miracle.

Yet not only the Mathers, father and son, but other wise men among us seemed to be building a foundation for a different argument -- that since New England was a special land in a new era of God's blessing, its leaders held offices analogous to those of the apostles (some argue there is room for such a view in Luther and Calvin). Certainly put bluntly like that, it sounds a proud and dangerous point of view, but it was one that fitted well with their "observations" of new "wonders" and "providences". It also seemed to justify the rhetoric of spiritual warfare and the high-handed "justice" of our troubles in 1692.

Cotton Mather's title shows that he was still keeping the door open to Reverend Willard's more biblical approach to such cases — that is that demonic affliction or possession were at least nominally categories he was willing to include. His own account of the Goodwin children and Goody Glover, however, gave little space to those categories. It was witches, witchcraft, and witchery that fascinated him, and it was these more spectacular categories of evil upon which he concentrated his study.

He seems to have entirely rejected the possibility that ordinary flesh and mundane sin, cited by Reverend Willard as the chief causes for Elizabeth Knapp's afflictions, might also be the chief causes of evil among the afflicted "innocents" to whom he ministered.

The widening category of "innocent afflicted" would seem to be an unusual one for a Calvinist, whose principle doctrines include the depravity of every human heart. Nor was it to prove a harmless one. Perhaps it is another instance of losing the battle to one's opponents in the very fighting of it—of unconsciously picking up their weapons on the battlefield and thus implicitly bowing to their cause. For in Calvinist theology "innocent" has only a very relative meaning except as it applies to Christ. But even before the new charter made official the validity of "half-way" covenant for the churches of New England, the idea was becoming widely accepted that the children of the "saints," through the effects of the covenant , were somehow freer from original sin—and God's "innocent" grandchildren, so to speak.

Thus it was that young Mr. Mather, over against the warnings and despite the conclusions of Mr. Willard, preferred to regard Elizabeth Knapp as chiefly sinned against. He certainly treated the Goodwin children so. It is not surprising then that Reverend Parris similarly regarded his daughter and niece, and the other "afflicted girls" nor that the Salem divines so fully concurred with him.

Although they were "scientists," most of our New England sages did not like Isaac Newton and his new methods. In fact, our wise men held doggedly to what they thought of as the better "science" or "physics" of Rene Descartes. Descartes maintained the necessity of following "intuition," the ability to think God's thoughts as one made in God's image. The follower of Cartesian philosophy relies on "intuition" as the means by which he come to "first principles". By intuition Descartes seems to mean an innate knowledge of what is and what is not, what true and what false, somewhat parallel to the idea of righteous conscience or "original righteousness" as the Arminians put it. Descartes says something about intuition being the "undoubting conception of an unclouded and attentive mind, which springs from the light of reason".

Newton claimed no room for intuition. He believed that although God made the universe, dwelt throughout it and held it all together, there were created principles in operation which could be discovered by observation, measurement and calculation -- the powers of observation and reason. Newton said no intuition or "hypothesis" was necessary or legitimate to this task. To our colonial wise men, as to others of Puritan descent, this seemed almost an atheist view, for it seemed to allow for an understanding of the creation without a right knowledge of God. They all the more fiercely advocated Cartesian principles and the importance of "intuition," which they seemed to view as another word for faith. Descartes' religious principles were as far as Newton's from those of the colonial scientists, but he offered an alternative to Newton, and they fancied that his "science" and "intuition" was more consonant with scripture. Thus was Descartes' "physics" taught at Harvard.

It is difficult to see how one can believe in original sin and a reliable or pristine intuition at one and the same time. Yet Ministers Noyes, Higginson, and Cotton Mather, with many other wise men among us, seem so to do. For this was the essence of their unswerving faith in the strange and contradictory, conspiratorial and contagious "intuitions" of the afflicted girls. Did they not unerringly guide the officers to the witches among us and not only reveal their past deeds of darkness, but register their every machination? This despite the lack of perception of these things by the learned themselves! Was not another sort of "intuition" the real basis of the ministers' and judges' conclusion that in the girls contortions and cries, they were seeing witchery and "effusion" and vortexes of matter acting out their cycles and dramas? -- even when their own eyes and ears could only perceive the results in the girls words and gyrations?

The "intuition" exercised by our leaders was in fact merely a form of deduction in which the "givens" were not admitted to examination. The wise men were convinced the girls were reliable not on the basis of the Bible, but on the basis of their own pride, standing prejudices and superstitions. In other words, the witch business was carried forward by sinners, according to heretical principles and by means of heretical methods.

A few years earlier Reverend Nicholas Noyes of Salem delivered a sermon intended to discourage men from wearing periwigs. In it he appealed to "scientific" reason. Women's hair, he said, "when on their own heads is a token of subjection, and is suitable to their soft moist, cold constitution, but not to the masculine, hot and dry constitution." This sort of combination of biblical and gnostic "science" continues among our learned men.

Nor is it the simple or the distracted or the melancholy or those beside themselves with bitterness who are hardest to forgive. Rather it is the mighty fools. How hard it is to remember that the least among us are often the greatest: the generals who send their troops to senseless deaths; the merchants who fatten themselves in the day of slaughter; the scholars who know little of life, yet direct others into illusion and futility; the governors and judges who can scarcely govern or judge themselves; and the ministers of God who operate as devil's advocates with the devil's weapons, while their purported goal is to defeat him.

We can only forgive them when we have recognize these men too were kindling — the things that are nothing — the least of these, Christ's brethren.

Chapter Four — The Poor Always With You

For ye have the poor always with you, but me
ye have not always. -- **Matthew 26:11**

I will also leave in the midst of thee an afflicted and poor
people, and they shall trust in the name of the Lord. --
Zephaniah 3:12

We have no class of contented serfs or tenants, although many of our forefathers were such in England. Slaves among us are almost the only ones who are not consciously in pursuit of prosperity. We do not call it a desire to be "rich" but only a desire to be "established." But it is a state of material abundance and security which we seek, such as only the merchant gentlemen and nobility enjoy in England or Europe.

Most of us had no freehold in England. Yet here Everyman may come to own his own land, his own house, and conduct his own business. Since the first generation, it is increasingly this which has brought us to the colonies. Acquisition and accumulation are the one goal common among us. We agree more fully in these than in our religious views, which vary ever more widely. The desire to own and accumulate is a motive never questioned. Even slaves such as Parris's Tituba and Indian are lent a certain respect in that they are engaged in their master's pursuit of comfort and prosperity.

But those who accumulate nothing and seem peculiarly unsuited to accumulating anything, like Will and Sarah Good, are an insult to the claims and desires of the rest of us. They are the town-criers of failure who might as well wear badges pinned to their breasts or placards that say, "your hope is vain, riches are vain, the seeking of comfort is vain, your pursuit of happiness is vain."

Such prophets seldom seek the office they fill. As fire takes first among the kindling, those who have the least may be the most fully caught up and consumed in the pursuit of prosperity. Those who most thoroughly fail in that pursuit are liable to become most bitter. The root of all evil, saith the scriptures, is the love of money — but it is not exclusively the rich that are susceptible to that love, though they best sustain it.

The chips and twigs among us were not only those afflicted in mind or body, but also our paupers. The Lord said the poor we have with us always and that they are blessed in various ways, while the rich often wander close to spiritual peril, and pass into the kingdom with difficulty. But somehow we have set these elements of the gospel aside. Despite His words, we do all we can both to avoid being poor and to avoid having the poor near us. Thus we "warn out" any persons who settle in our townships, lest they become indigent, and but for the "warning out" our responsibility to maintain.

Yet we also require an appearance of godliness in the pursuit of security, thus disability or poverty are not the sole things which make men "poor" in our regard. In addition to those who can not attain prosperity, there are ever more who seek prosperity without the prerequisite hypocrisy which is necessary for public approval. They serve Mammon, without pretending to serve God.

Bridget Bishop, first to be tried by the high court, began making money at her ordinary (more accurately a tavern) in Salem, near the home of Reverend Noyes, who would have nothing to do with her. Later she and her second husband Edward, the sawyer, set up another ordinary in Royalside on the Ipswich Road. There drinking and gaming often went on late into the night. As she and her husband worked hard toward their own prosperity, they were oblivious to the disapproval of the respectable members of the community. Some still mention her as an example of the love of money. But one may openly seek what one barely gains, while others get what they pretend not to seek.

Sarah Osborne was "poor" chiefly in reputation. When she and her second husband began to farm her first husband's land, it was rumored she intended to disinherit her own sons. They, the Prince boys, were related to Putnams on their father's side. Her second husband was first her indentured servant, and that carried considerable opprobrium. Even before her marriage to him, Goody Osborne was regarded as eccentric, particularly in dress. She seemed to care little about reputation although she was a member of the Village church. So far as we know, Tituba was the first to accuse her. Sarah Good, with instincts of self-defense like Tituba's, also seemed to point away from herself toward Sarah Osborne. Neither Sarah had many allies. It is always the weakest of the herd the catamount waits for — always the straggler, the least of Christ's brethren.

A third class of "poor" among us, beyond those who could not attain prosperity and those who had forfeited public approval, were those who would not seek it. There remain even now some who believed, as the early Plymouth and Salem colonists did, that God had kept them as a remnant primarily for the furtherance of His Kingdom, not for inhabiting or building a paradise on earth. Some of these kept apart from idolatry, ordered their steps, and made right sacrifices. Some of them took the lonely stands of prophets against the golden calf and other new gods. Thus they, too, became, if not broken kindling, then isolated sentinels exposed on the hilltops in the midst of our storm—likely victims for the next stroke of lightning or the ax.

In the Village, we think talk of serving Mammon more appropriate to those of Salem Town or Boston. After all, we have hardly any shops, and apart from Ingersoll's and Procter's inns, no businesses but farms, smithies, tanneries and mills. We produce necessities not fripperies. We are not like the great Babylon seated on many waters, sending our ships to alien ports for luxurious goods and polluted spoils. Like our ancient father Cain, we soil our hands chiefly with good clean soil, and see little good in less strenuous or further-ranging pursuits. Like him, too, we are jealous and angry toward God when he withholds his blessing or bestows it elsewhere. We have thought and behaved more like Cain, or at the least like the elder brother of the prodigal, than ever we are likely to admit.

There is a deeper-set pride than that of the Pharisee—not that which says, "I thank you Lord that I am not like that publican," but rather, "I thank you Lord that I am not like that Pharisee."

Before our troubles, we in Salem Village justified our hatreds and greeds because they were seldom fulfilled. We said that the Salem merchants were rich and fat, and envied them with condemnation. While enumerating the many ways they broke the sabbath, we built our secret tabernacles in our high groves, where we offered our own pagan worship. While some of them went seldom to meeting, we but hurried home to put a little more corn in the ground. Therefore when the troubles came among us, the officials and ministers, except for Mr. Parris, were chiefly of Salem, but the accusers as well as the victims chiefly from the Village.

Many accusers and witnesses were poor—people for whom each new hardship was indeed a blow. Several were widows, women whose husbands had been taken away by the wars of wealthier and more powerful men. People like Widow Sheldon, whose family, living just below the Nurses, seemed to come in for more than their share of accidents, disease, and uncanny deaths. In early winter three years before our troubles, Nathaniel Sheldon, her ten year old son, was well on Monday, sick on Tuesday, quite distracted by Thursday, and died on Friday. In July of the next year, her older son Godfrey was killed by Indians. And the winter our troubles had their first glimmerings, her husband William, eighty years old, fell and hurt his knee, which became infected, which soon led to his death. Widow Sheldon and Widow Holten, with Goodwife Vibber, and old Mistress Goodale became witnesses or afflicted evidences against the accused in our troubles.

In addition, many of the accused were poor. William Buckley and his wife Sarah had worked hard – in Ipswich and then in the infant community of Marblehead. But they fell into debt and Governor Bradstreet brought suit against them for what they owed him. They moved to Salem Village where William worked as tanner and cobbler, but one of their sons pulled the family into debt again, and William lost everything, even his cobbler's bench, in the suit. The avarice and unbelief of our hearts was such we could not suffer the poor to remain in our debt, but must take him to court once the debt was due. Fearing what? That blessed providence would refuse to bless or provide? Being forgiven much, we would forgive very little. Sarah Buckley seemed fair game when the girls accused her in May.

It is true that hard years preceded our troubles. Our hardships masked our avarice. King Philip's War cost us many a life, and while we suffered less from Indian depredations than many in the Bay colony, we spent as much as any in lost soldiers, and lost time (which meant lost crops) fighting Massasoit's sons. When Philip and Alexander were killed and their warriors much subdued, most of us thought that the last war we would have to fight. But new outbreaks came on our borders, and those too were kindled by our avarice – for ever we made treaties and ever we broke them in the desire for more ground. Not even our Christian Indians could trust the word or law of their white brothers. We counted less the bond of worshipping Christ than the lust for land.

Hurricanos swept across the Connecticut Valley and over our fields, doing less damage here than further south, but doing damage enough in '83 and '84, that most of us were worse off a few years later than we had been a few years before.

In 1688, Governor Phips, still Captain Phips, outfitted an

expedition to the Barbadoes, where he salvaged gold from Spanish wrecks, and made himself and his investors rich. He was knighted, for he made the King richer, too. Sir William returned to us a great hero, a successful scaler of that prosperous height which we all longed to climb. He came back in 1690 with another scheme, which excited every Johnny-come-lately who could borrow a spare shilling.

William Phips' invited the rest of us to join in the conquest of Quebec. His promoters told investors of gold and furs for the taking, and began to raise money for a fighting fleet. Not only did much of the savings of Salem Village and Town join that of Boston in outfitting the fleet, but thousands of men enlisted. Those who joined this Armada of ships expected in return a percentage of the booty. They were to be paid, as in whaling ships, by shares. Salem Villages' own Captain William Rayment was commissioned to lead an overland expeditionary force. Pastor Hale of Beverly went as chaplain. The land force, however, was stymied by swamps and forests, and turned back before it reached its objective.

Sir William's fleet was much delayed awaiting supplies from England. They did not embark until October, and arrived late that month, where they made scarcely a dent in the walls of Quebec before running out of powder and shot. Returning, they lost three ships and were so beset by storms and sickness, that half of the men aboard died. Some of these were brothers and sons of the Village, and not a few husbands and fathers.

Plagues of smallpox and whooping cough and other diseases mysterious to the physicians crept or swept through us thrice in the ten years before the troubles, and disease lingered always. In the two winters before the troubles, strange sicknesses produced deliriums or dumbness and frequently raged unto death within a few days.

Crops were delayed, drowned and stunted. Spring and autumn rain were heavy, winters were severe and snow stayed long. Cattle, too, were struck with unnamed illnesses, and ancient rhymes were repeated against unknown enemies. The willingness of many to repeat these old spells showed the hardy paganism in our hearts. We were far from believing God to bring peaceful fruits of righteousness out of our discipline.

We did not believe ourselves idolaters, because our idolatry had not resulted in abundance. We did not think ourselves evil men, because we did not prosper like the evil man. We did not think ourselves pagans, because we were not as honest as the pagans.

But we ever ready to sacrifice, if not our firstborn, at least those "poor" who served our other gods least successfully — or were too dedicated in service to but one god or God. Our children perceived this. The "afflicted girls" found the poor made excellent playthings.   After all, if we have the poor with us always, why not make some use of them?

Anne Putnam

Chapter Five — The Few Confer

Satan and the world have least power to fasten errors upon humble souls. The God of light and truth delights to dwell with the humble; and the more light and truth dwells in the would [the will], the further off darkness and error will stand from the soul. The God of grace pours in grace into humble souls, as men pour liquor into empty vessels; and the more grace is poured into the soul, the less error shall be able to overpower the would, or to infect the soul.   From Remedy 6 to Device 11.

It is better to have a sore than a seared conscience. It is better to have no heart than a hard heart, no mind than a blind mind   Footnote 88 (Device 8, Remedy 7), Thomas Brooks, *Precious Remedies Against Satan's Devices*

Before the first formal complaints and arrests of 1692, four ministers from the Salem region gathered at the home of Reverend Noyes in Salem to discuss the afflictions manifested in the Village. After prayer, Nicholas Noyes began their discussion.

"The things that trouble us are deep and difficult. It is important to study and pray together to understand them, in order that we may lead our communities and churches without stumbling.

"While remembering that the secret things belong to God, we must also keep in mind that there is no temptation befallen us but such as is common to man, and that God is faithful, who will provide a way of escape. He has promised not to try us beyond that which we are able to resist. Since we bear the principle charge of teaching and feeding our flocks, it is right to expect that He will show us how to lead them out of these evil times and afflictions which have befallen us.

"Samuel, you have told us a great deal about the things that have come upon your household. Mr. Hale has been witness to some of them, as well as to similar things in his own parish. Mr. Higginson and I have conferred with some of the ministers in Boston concerning what goes on here.

"What do you see as the principle difficulties for which we

must seek wisdom?"

"Most of all," replied Mr. Parris, " I am troubled with identifying the causes of my daughter's and niece's afflictions. That their afflictions are supernatural is almost universally agreed. But as to what order of supernatural affliction, there is still some doubt. Secondly, if they be bewitched as increasingly seems the case, I am perplexed about how to identify those who afflict them."

"As to the affliction," asked Mr. Hale, "What remains of doubt concerning whether it is indeed witchcraft?"

"I only hesitate to so pronounce it," replied Mr. Parris, "based on my lack of knowledge how far hysteria in young women might cause bizarre behavior. Mr. Griggs, the physician, however, tells me my Betty is still far too young, and even Abigail not yet at the age where such an explanation is likely.

"There would only seem to remain demonic attack and witchery. So far as I can tell from others more learned than I, the demoniac must have some history to account for particular affliction—some moral failure that opened the door to the demonic— or at least some family history of such. Neither of their girls to the best of my knowledge fits those particulars.

"Therefore, both from the girls' behavior and from what others tell me of the difficulties the Village and the church have had, it seems most tenable to conclude we suffer from malevolent enemies in our midst."

"Does Mr. Griggs say more about the causes of the girls' afflictions?" asked Mr. Noyes.

"Indeed, he says he finds no physical cause and is inclined to point to a spiritual one."

"Does he speak of any spiritual cause beside bewitchment?"

"No, indeed it was he first used the word, although a suspicion of it had occurred to my wife and grows with me."

"Is there anything then, gentlemen, to keep us from proceeding on the basis of that diagnosis?"

"It seems the wisest course," said Mr. Higginson after a considerable pause in the conversation. "If it should prove otherwise, we would all be ready to revert to what presents itself. It can only be prudent to proceed as though it were thus the severest case until further developments either prove or disprove it."

"I am also of that mind," said Mr. Noyes, as the others murmured their assent.

"Then the next head becomes to determine the sources of this bewitchment—how to find those who practice witchcraft against these young ones," he went on. "Have you taken any steps in this direction, Samuel?"

"It is difficult to proceed. I confess confusion. As you know, some of you better than I, the congregation has been much tossed about. There would seem to be a considerable number of the members, not to mention other inhabitants of the Village, who seem hard-hearted and divisive—indeed, who seem particularly hostile toward me. I humble my heart daily to be charitable toward them, yet it occurs to me that if some are my fervent enemies, perhaps a few have gone thus far in enmity toward myself and my family."

"But you have not more narrowly investigated?"

"No, I scarce know how to proceed. I do not even like to question my daughter and niece. They behave so wildly at times. I have tried to rein them in with but limited success. I am afraid that if I question them much, it will only stir them to further fits. At times their behavior seems no more than eccentric play and I find myself wondering if I make too much of it. Then again they will fall into terrible fits and cry out strangely and act quite beside themselves."

"Perhaps several of us should come together to pray and talk with them. It is an awful thing to go against the Enemy alone."

"Yes, I would be most grateful if you of greater experience and wisdom would help me in this. Perhaps you can explain some more about this witchery business. I must confess that although I heard it spoken of during my time at Harvard, I had not thought then that it would touch me so closely, and paid too little heed."

"Well," began Mr. Noyes, "in addition to what the scriptures tell us, there has been considerable light shed on these matters by the science of Descartes. Cartesian science is founded on an acknowledgment of the spiritual essence of things."

"God is the only substance according to the Cartesians," added Mr. Higginson. "All created things hold together in him. In this they are in considerable contrast to Newton and his fellows, who argue for a mechanical "natural order". Newton seems to propose an independence of the creation over against its Maker. He views the universe as composed of voids and solids – being almost empty, one might say, containing only a smattering of things, all governed by fixed, universal, and apparently independent laws."

"In contrast, having set his storm anchor in God as the only substance," continued Mr. Noyes, "the Cartesian maintains that there are no vacuums, no 'spaces' in the universe that are not filled with created matter. Matter is of various sorts, some gross, as the great planets, and some very subtle, both in the fluids or animal spirits that run through our nerves and vessels and the very fine matter which rises to the highest heavens and gathers in vortices (focused yet mobile concentrations of matter) as suns and stars. These exert pressure back through the mediate and transparent 'second matter' (which we call air or sky). This second matter transfers that pressure down to our eyes, where it produces the further movement of our own subtle matters and causes us to 'see,' by what we call 'light'."

Mr. Hale, who seemed less familiar with these things than the two Salem ministers, interposed, "What then is the difference between vision and delusion? Could not derangement of these matters by other forces change the pressures in this second matter and distort what we see?"

"Most certainly," answered Mr. Noyes, with a scholar's fervor, "And does not scripture call Satan the Prince of the Power of the Air, and an angel of light, as well as the Great Deceiver? It would seem he can, under certain circumstances allowed by God, cause our eyes and our own subtle animal spirits to move in a manner which does not correspond with what is, but rather according to illusion.

"The eyes are not merely passive, however, but as scripture says are the lamp of the body, filling the godly with light. Cartesian physicians propose that the eyes, as well as receiving, can also eject or effuse particles, sending pressure back through the second matter to influence other beings. Where there is commitment to evil, these particles of "effluvia" may even afflict or delude. Our Lord speaks of the godly eye being clear or single, while the eye of the ungodly is evil or murky. And as the eye is, so is the whole person."

Mr. Higginson picked up the thread. It became apparent to the others that he and Mr. Noyes had discussed these things at length.

"The Cartesians maintain there is no independent action of minds and body, for these are instruments of God's causality. But they also assert that the "self" can direct at least part of its own physical activity and its own volitions—not producing "change," but determining the spiritual character manifested in its activities. This we call faith or its contrary, unbelief, in relation to God -- and charity or hatred, in relation to other men. The "self" or soul can direct the body, but not the body the soul. Pure thought and volition are the proper activities of the soul, while extension and mobility are the proper activities of matter and bodies. The spiritual being, angel, or man, wills himself to serve good or evil, the devil or God, but beyond this act of will, he is subject to forces of matter-in-motion that he cannot change or direct."

"Thus it has been found," added Mr. Noyes, "That witches are sometimes inevitably brought forward by the devil himself, it would seem. Having given themselves by their volition, there are other forces of matter and motion that work about them willy-nilly. With perseverance, it is nearly certain that we may find out such persons if they are among us!"

"Although I do not understand all you say, "replied Mr. Parris, "Yet this last gives me great encouragement, for I feared that such enemies might be able to go on deceiving us for years, and that the afflictions of innocent persons might continue indefinitely."

"No," continued Mr. Noyes, much stimulated, "there is no resisting the motions of matter. The flux has certain laws which the witch herself is subject to, although she open the machinations with her wicked will. There are many tests and proofs which have been proven effective in the discovery of witches. Cartesian principles give a scientific basis for some of the ancient tests. Once we have narrowed the field to those most likely to have operated against the girls, we need only bring them to trial and they will be shown either innocent or witches."

"Then narrowing the field and bringing them to trial must be our next object."

And toward that goal the ministers immediately made their plans.

That the Salem and Salem Village elders should be looking for the incredible was not only due to their science and heightened sense of spiritual warfare in New England, but also to many written accounts of witchcraft from respected church leaders. The venerable Richard Baxter in England and our own Cotton Mather had reported as credible many things which certainly did not happen. Although many of these reports of prodigious events were second hand, the authors wholeheartedly affirmed even the most unlikely ones. Most distracted and distractingly, they published their accounts.

What kind of distraction is it that makes one believe a person might pass hundreds of gallons of blood in a year, yet live, or that a woman could float to the ceiling of her bedroom and resist being pulled down by many persons tugging upon her? Truth subverted, be it never so small, is deception promoted, and deception accumulates always toward destruction and death. There is only one

Deceiver, who is as happy to have his methods lied about, as to have his existence denied. Since he has a monopoly on his stock-in-trade of lies, he makes profit in every exchange of them.

Mr. Baxter, in other times and circumstances, would be excused for his age, as perhaps Mr. Mather would be for his youth. However, the stature which the former had already achieved and the latter seems on his way to achieving, require that we hold them to high standards, even in more ordinary times. Given the contribution of their "scholarship" to our troubles, we must say what they wrote was evil. For the scriptures say when an elder sins publicly he ought to be rebuked publicly, and did not Paul do this very thing with him who was chief in the church of Jerusalem?

To this point then, I will say that Baxter's *Certainty of the Worlds of the Spirits: Fully Evinced by Unquestionable Histories of Apparitions and Witchcrafts . . .* and Mather's *Memorable Providences Relating to Witchcraft and Possessions . . .* spread a poison which weakened us against the plague of accusation and suspicion. By these works we were particularly disarmed and less able to resist.

What they wrote and published was already commonly supported by traditions going back to the medieval church and ancient paganism. But their two narratives together repeated and reinforced those false and unbiblical claims so that they were seldom questioned in the time of our troubles, except in muffled voices in the corners of fields and houses.

Three of those claims were: first, that the devil has extraordinary power in our times to work unnatural wonders over against and despite the prayers of the saints. Second, that there are a number of visible and experimental evidences which may be used to reveal and prove a witch. And third, that some among us have extraordinary powers to perceive invisible unnatural wonders as they are performed, as well as to identify the agents thereof -- usually at the same time as these very perceptive persons are uniquely "afflicted" victims -- able to perceive, yet (although innocent) unable to defend themselves against those same extraordinary afflictions of the devil.

The books of these two divines, among others as superstitious, rested on the shelves of pastors Parris, Lawson, Hale, Noyes, and Higginson. These teachers read them and repeated their contents over again. Through them they entered into the conversation of most of our people, and reinforced old pagan rumors. These ministers were members of a larger and reasonable "school of prophets," which means on this side of the ocean, Harvard scholars. (Harvard was chartered explicitly to provide us with wise ministers and rulers.) Our wise men were taught a great science of spiritual things, which became a foundation for our troubles.

Even Samuel Willard's report about Elizabeth Knapp, despite his own wiser conduct both then and in the time of our troubles, contributed to our over-readiness to see witchery in sad or evil deeds. We must reiterate, however, that neither the report nor Willard himself allowed "witches" to be blamed for Knapp's spiritual struggles. In 1683, Mr. Willard had joined Increase Mather and a number of other gentlemen of Boston in a scientific club which they named The Philosophical Society. Mr. Willard had published his "observations" with a "scientific" perspective similar to what the Mathers shared, though he was more careful and deductive than they.

When Cotton Mather began to "study" supernatural affliction, he ignored two salient points of wisdom a better student would have garnered from Mr. Willard's experience: first, where Willard only circulated his report among the ministers of Boston, Mather published and broadcast his report of the Goodwin children for all to read; but, second and even more significant, where Willard rebuked the accusations of witchcraft which Elizabeth Knapp made, Mather only counseled the Goodwins to keep the identity of their bewitchers private. In other words, where Willard treated the accusations as sin, Mather validated them. "Private" accusations of witchcraft, where they are validated will inevitably break out as public accusations.

Baxter's and Mather's faulty and false accounts came down to us, despite the greater, if quieter wisdom of Willard (whose active and growing opposition to the madness of our troubles eventually helped bring it to a close).

Another minister, John Hale of Beverly, was a neighbor of and principal witness against one of the accused. He was also the spiritual advisor for many in Beverly and Wenham, and knew in detail many of the earlier accusations against Bridget Bishop and Sarah Wildes. He was called in early by Reverend Parris, along with five or six other men of the cloth, to pray for Betty and for Abigail Williams. He saw their early fits firsthand and heard accusations come from their mouths. All this was prior to the official involvement of magistrates Hathorne and Corwin which raised the level of the disturbance to capital charges. If Pastor Hale had been a better scientific observer, he might have seen the more glaring facts of the cases near the outset -- that the girls were shamming or "playing games" and that the accusations were whimsical means by which enemies and rivals of the accusers were being attacked. Again, this was in contrast to Willard, who brought the accused and the accuser together and quickly discovered the lies the afflicted girl concocted.

Minister Hale not only wrote early accounts in fervent support of the trials, but bore witness in court to Bridget Bishop's supposed bewitching of little Hannah Perley and melancholy Christian Trask, despite having defended her a few years earlier against the same charges. (As a scientist may change his theory on the basis of fresh observations or, if he is a Cartesian, fresh intuitions.) He also participated in interviews of various accused persons in prison, where, with fellow ministers Noyes, and Higginson, he brought pressure to bear on such recalcitrants as Mary Warren to step back into the ranks of accusers rather than be left as lonely confessors of deception. It was not until his own wife was finally accused, late in our troubles, that Reverend Hale questioned the godless principles he had used, and then at least in his published remarks, with rambling ambivalence.

Deodat Lawson, third minister of our Village church, the last before it became a particular congregation, wrote an account of the early proceedings. He had come back to witness them because of recent rumors his own wife and daughter were slain by witchery four years earlier. His accounts have the ring of objectivity, but like those of Hale, Parris and Noyes, they ignore the hard evidence of shams and deceptions unmasked. Instead the ministers, with all the judges, treated proven fabrications and cheats as exceptional. Despite a number of clear proofs of false witness, they continued to rely on the fancies and concoctions of the accusers as sources of "fact" about the events. They trusted the intuition of the accusers and confessed witches to interpret the spiritual realities which these purported to see.

Why this blindness? Christ says the cause of blindness, especially among the correctors of the people, is something in the eye -- something worse than what is in the eye of those they would correct. What was in the eyes of our ministers? On the one hand, these men worshipped the same material gods as the rest of us, believing it only proper that Joshua and Aaron ought to have a goodly share of the milk and honey flowing through the Promised Land.

On the other hand they conceived of themselves fighting a pitched battle against the idolatries of European papistry and various Protestant heresies as well as atheism . Thus Cotton Mather wrote, after the hanging of Goody Glover in 1689, that a denial of the spiritual forces of evil would lead to a denial of the gospel: "We shall come to have no Christ but a light within and no Heaven but a frame of mind," which may have been particularly aimed against the followers of Anne Hutchinson and the Quakers, but was also directed against what nearly all our leading men saw as a wider wholesale assault upon a biblical worldview. But in seeking the means to fight back, their hands fell upon the weapons of their enemies, and in seeking to be wise, they became foolish. Thus for instance, those words of Mather seem but one step away from saying Christianity is indeed chiefly a frame of mind.

In the witch-trials we were treated to two strange (but ancient) proofs: first, observations of a witch "afflicting" the poor girls by small motions of the "witch's" own body, an instrument of her malignant will; and second, the "healing" of the bewitched when these "afflicted" were brought to touch the one who "bewitched" them. This "healing" was predicted and "understood" by our wise men. They expected it to occur not because the witch or even the devil desired it, but because of "laws" of flux and matter made it occur.

But was the obvious and damning affliction in the open court caused by the will of the witch? Did she want to send the venomous particles which tortured the accuser right there in front of the judges? If her only active part was willing submission to the devil, why did he in turn so blatantly expose his servants in the courtroom? Or is the devil himself but a passive tool worked upon by the "laws" of matter, flux and vortical return, as Mr. Noyes seemed to suggest. All of which would bring us back to a universe more thoroughly mechanical and independent than that of the Newtonians.

Virtue and righteousness are supposed by these philosophers to consist in making our volitions conform to divine reason, the expression of perfect rationality, which is "the unique love of right reason". Our divines maintain Descartes' motto, "I think, therefore I am," is stated in this context — of thinking well and rightly — thinking God's thoughts after him, as it were. If one "thinks" well or reasons well, one must be in harmony with God and divine reason. Evil, then, is opposing divine reason or hating it. But there is a much greater problem with the question of what is true appearance and what false.

Mr. Noyes maintained divine reason dwells in or is one with the only substance, that is God. The matter which we see, as well as the matter by which we see are not essential substance — are not "real" as God (or his "substance") is real.

On the other hand, for the Cartesian, "thought" is a supreme human activity, linking man with God. The Cartesian maintains we may "think of" a person and that our doing so presents his "objective presence" to our minds, even though his "local" or "physical" presence is elsewhere. Since the mind, like all else in the universe deals in somethings rather than nothings (there are no vacuums), there must be something there, the objective presence, for the mind to be thinking about it.

This explanation became an admirable justification for a third shameful feature of the witch trials: "spectre evidence," supposed proof that a person is a witch because one of the afflicted saw her image bewitching someone, albeit at a great distance from where the "witch" was locally present at the time. Since the afflicted "saw it" it must have been. (A "distracted" person might see an illusion, but the "proof" that one was distracted was thought to be obvious inconsistency. The ministers and magistrates maintained the "afflicted" were always consistent in their reports.)

Perhaps then, the witch cannot even help sending the evil matter which afflicts the poor victim. Perhaps by merely "thinking" about the girls and the devil or about particular afflictions, a witch brings them into conjunction. The girls are thus touched by the demonic and the hellish in her thoughts in the material which makes up an "objective presence," whatever that material may be. (This is not the language the judges and ministers commonly used — rather they spoke of the witch giving the devil permission to use her apparition to afflict others for his purposes. But then they were scientists addressing laymen.)

But how do we distinguish between true and false appearances — between what is a faulty "objective presence" which we have inaccurately "thought" due to some disturbance of the matter intervening between us and the truth as it is in the divine mind? How can we trust our own eyes and sensations when we see the devil has power to thoroughly disturb the eyes and sensations of others?

Yet our troubles cannot be attributed to this "science" alone. Our literature also promoted the strange combinations of gnosticism and rationalism. At the same time as Mistress Anne Bradstreet was writing her beautiful and simple poems, the most popular poetry among us was Mr. Michael Wigglesworth's *Day of Doom*, in which the poet attempts to dispel the mystery that veils God's judgment, showing the "justice" and "holiness" of God in damning the many sorts of sinners brought before his throne. That scripture which tells us God himself takes no delight in the death of the wicked seems to have been lost to Mr. Wigglesworth, for clearly he expects not only God, but fellow sinners to take delight in the damnation of the lost. Such a small movement it seems from affirming God's unrivaled holiness and justice to depicting him in the most uncharitable light possible. It is the same as Adam and Eve's great error of trying to know "as gods" what only God can know. This may indeed be the wisdom of serpents, but it lacks entirely the gentleness of doves.

And our literature had preserved ages of superstition. Robert Herrick, Cavalier vicar and poet, (1591-1674) and first cousin to our Marshall Herrick's father, wrote a number of poems about witchcraft including this bit of doggerel:

> Another [Charme] to Bring in the Witch
> To house the Hag, you must doe this;
> Commix with Meale a little Pisse
> Of him bewitcht: then forthwith make
> A little Wafer or a Cake;
> And this rawly bak't will bring
> The old Hag in. No surer thing.

Perhaps Mary Sibley got her recipe thus. In addition to bad science and tainted literature, we had many old stories and "charms" passed on by the simplest peasants, and carried forward out of pagan days from father to son and mother to daughter.

Nevertheless, it was not the simple folks who originated or most effectively perpetuated such ideas. The greatest respect was given the teachers who were called to direct us in the way of truth rather than the path of error. If the rest of us believed foolish things, yet we were most persuaded by what we were taught. A people may be "distracted" in many ways — and so we were, not only in ways variously recognized as distracted, but at the very heart of our community and in the thoughts, teaching and actions of our leaders.

Yet our wise were ultimately confounded by the foolish, including especially those they put to death. Oh that our teachers might know themselves fools. God has not chosen many wise.

Chapter Six — Enemies of Good   (late Feb - 1 March)

Thus God hath visited and scourged me for my sins and sought to wean me from this world; but I have ever found it a difficult thing to profit ever but a little by the sorest and sharpest afflictions.
    -- Thomas Shepard (1605-1649), *Autobiography.*

By the time Goodwife Nurse was arrested, four others had already been examined and were in gaol. On the Day of Solemn Humiliation in the Village (March 31) a week after her arrest, Abigail Williams said she saw the spectral witches gathered in the Village for a mock sacrament. The witches (or the girls) was celebrating a reverse holiday. The girls said they saw Sarah Good, Sarah Osborne, Martha Corey, and Rebecca Nurse, along with a mysterious dark man, the head of the coven.

Because they had paid little attention to the first four arrests and examinations, the Nurse family were unprepared for the flood of events which broke upon them at Mother Nurse's arrest. Partly because of Tom Preston's signature on the complaints against the first accused, some in the Nurse tribe were inclined to believe the first three were indeed witches. Rebecca and Francis Nurse never agreed, however, nor despite his signature, did Tom participate in the trials. In fact, he withdrew as far from Village and Church life as possible, working long hours in the fields, and changing the subject whenever the witch business came up. But the Nurses did not realize the bewildering extent of the catastrophes which had come upon the Good and Osborne families until their own came. Although they were ignorant of the nature of the deluge, the rapid flood was well in spate by the time it reached the Nurses.

The Village knows least about Tituba's arrest and the process which led up to it, because almost everything prior to her arrest and examination (March 1) occurred in the Parris home. Nor was Reverend Samuel Parris ever very forthcoming.

Nevertheless we were able to gather some idea of what happened. After Betty Parris and Abigail Williams began their games, Reverend and Mistress Parris became worried. At first they took it for the unsuitable sport it was, but having heard and read of witchery, they had growing fears. Reverend Parris borrowed more books on the subject, including one of the few copies of Samuel Willard's observations on Elizabeth Knapp. One sabbath afternoon, perhaps a week after the girls began their game, Reverend Parris read it to his wife in the privacy, as he thought, of their parlor.

The two girls, who had been outside, came in quietly, and hearing the voice of Mr. Parris in the parlor, sat down in the kitchen where they heard several episodes of the narrative, before Mr. Parris broke off.

Samuel Willard had been wiser than our own magistrates and ministers in denying some, doubting much and suspending credence to most of the things Elizabeth Knapp reported. If there is any error in his account, it is his record of the details of it. While he did not act as though her claims were true, neither did he fully discount them. Or perhaps we might say he had too much "objectivity" in recording her claims of supernatural visions and events. His account thus provides for the simple-minded an extensive narrative of demonic afflictions and symptoms of bewitchment. The young girls heard and remembered many of those elements.

Reverend Parris himself, like many other ministers, seems to have made the error of thinking Reverend Willard obtuse or simple-minded for remaining such a skeptic. They believed he missed the greater revelations within his own record.

Mistress Parris was from Boston, where she'd heard more about the Knapp and Goodwin cases than we of Salem. Boston was full of Satanic suspicions for months after Mather's report on the Goodwins. She was disturbed when she walked into the quiet kitchen and found her girls seated there. Hoping they had heard little, she sent them back outside.

Nevertheless, the two girls had heard a number of things about Elizabeth Knapp. They reviewed the new account and discussed what they could add to their game. Some of its elements included: an afflicted one hurting herself with her own hands; crying out at mysterious bodily pains in various limbs; the accusation of a neighbor as a witch and cause of her affliction; the traveling of the witch up and down a chimney; the appearance of a strange beast with a women's head which changed into a woman; the devil appearing as an animal (a black dog); and trying to compel the afflicted to sign "his book," thus making covenant with him for riches and comfort in return for her soul. In short, they had thus been taught many new details of what a bewitched person was supposed to do and see and say.

A few days later, Anna Putnam came down to the Parris's while her father met with Reverend Parris over Village church matters. Betty and Abigail invited Anna to play their game with them. They told her she could play the witch.

"I don't want to be the witch. It isn't lawful. Why don't you be the witch!" replied Anna, feeling the right as the older girl to treat the younger ones with some condescension.

"Because its our game ," said Betty, "That's why! And besides, father says we are afflicted."

"He thinks we may be bewitched," said Abigail light-heartedly. " I don't want to be the witch, either. Who do you think the witch is?"

"I don't know, I'm sure" replied Anna, "How do you suppose one can tell a witch?"

"A witch is an ugly old woman, who curses you," said Betty, "and she appears as a black dog or a hairy man or sometimes a cat."

"Why don't you ask your Tituba to be the witch?" asked Anna.

"Because Mother says she must finish the washing."

"There are lots of ugly old women about," volunteered Anna, and then looking up, "Perhaps she is the witch."

The girls followed the direction of Anna's gaze past the corner of the house. Sarah Good was coming down the Meeting House Road toward the Parris's. She carried little Dorcas in her arms, and was puffing a short discoloured pipe. They went out of sight in front of the house.

After a few minutes, Dorcas came out the back door, eating a piece of bread. "You girls look after Dorcas while we visit for a few minutes, " directed Mistress Parris.

"Hello, Dorcas," Betty greeted her, "how are you today?"

Dorcas said nothing, but looked wide-eyed at the three girls. She continued to eat her bread, which was spread with honey.

"Don't you speak to us, Dorcas?" asked Abigail, then to the other girls, "Perhaps she is also bewitched."

"You aren't bewitched are you, Dorcas?" asked Anna, confidingly. "You remember playing at my house when we slid down the hay stack?"

Dorcas nodded her head in the affirmative.

"Is your mother a witch?" inquired Abigail.

Dorcas continued to gaze at them without response.

"If her mother was a witch," said Betty, "the devil would come to her as a black dog."

"Does a big dog come to your mother?" she addressed herself to Dorcas again.

Dorcas nodded her head "yes" to this inquiry.

"And does he bring his book to her?" ask Abigail, eagerly.

Dorcas shook her head "no".

"But tell us about the dog, Dorcas. Is he very large?"

Dorcas was finishing her bread and honey. She licked her untidy fingers and wiped her hands upon her well-smudged apron, then suddenly occupied her tongue otherwise.

"A big dog come after us at Holten's," she said. "But Momma din't let it hurt me."

"No, not Holten's dog, dear Dorcas, "said Betty, "We are speaking of a dog that is not really a dog, but an evil person, only pretending to be a dog."

"The yellow birds are like people," volunteered Dorcas.

"What birds are those?" asked Anna.

"The birds eat more than they need and are mean to the hungry ones."

"Where did you see the yellow birds, Dorcas? Were they very big?"

"No, little birds. The yellow birds come to Momma's hand. She gives them food between her fingers."

"Are they very frightening?" asked Abigail.

"Yes, they frighten away," answered Dorcas, "Momma say they can eat from my hand, too."

"Betty," called Mistress Parris, "Your father and Mr. Putnam have come home and it is time for Dorcas to go."

As Sarah Good left the house with her daughter, Reverend Parris turned from his conversation with Sergeant Putnam and called a parting to her. Sarah muttered some grudging words, and went on along the road with Dorcas walking beside her.

After Anna and her father had left, Abigail asked Betty. "Do you think Goody Good is a witch then?"

"Dorcas said her mother could feed a yellow bird from her hand," answered Betty. "Perhaps the devil can make himself a yellow bird as well as a black dog."

"Then we shall play, and you shall be Goody Good, the witch, and you shall come to me and tell me I must write in the devil's book."

"No," said Betty, "You must be the witch. I don't like to be the witch."

Tituba finished the long washing, tipped up the wash kettle, and stood back to look at all the linen and woolens hanging on long withes to dry in the cold air. Sore in back and chapped of hand, she walked up to the kitchen, poured herself some tea and sat down before the fire. She had barely finished her cup before the girls came running in and begged her to come and play witches with them."

"Tituba no play witches," she said, "Witches is bad. You be bad girls to play witches. Master be angry with you."

"But we think Goody Good is a witch. Dorcas say her momma has yellow birds that come and eat from her hand. Is that the devil pretending to be a yellow bird do you think?"

"The Good Lord knows about that. They do say the devil drinks blood from people, and he can look any way he wants. But I don' want to talk 'bout that. You girls go out and play. Tituba's all tired and sore from the wash. I got to make supper pretty soon now."

The following day, Indian John had been hauling firewood to Parris's woodpile from that of their neighbor, Samuel Sibley. Toward noon, Mistress Sibley came out and talked with John, who mentioned that the Parrises were upset because the girls had lately spoken of witches. Mistress Sibley, who knew of the girls' odd behavior, told Indian John of an English charm for finding a witch. She described the making of a witchcake. Within a few days, John and Tituba made the cake to the amusement of the girls who felt quite wicked at providing the "water". John eventually succeeded in feeding it to Holten's dog as per recipe. The dog was followed around for most of one day, but John lost track of it before it led to the witch.

That night the girls made oblique reference to the "witchcake" at supper. Their mother pursued the matter until the girls were forced to tell about it. This development went far in upsetting the minister and his wife. Reverend Parris extracted the full story from John and Tituba that evening. He was sufficiently frustrated that he became angry. His was an uneasy anger which brooked no opposition. With threats largely implied, but a few explicit ones, he interrogated them about "other" magic. Desperate to make him happy, Tituba told about an egg-in-a-glass-of-water fortune-telling episode from many months earlier. Reverend Parris was so exasperated at hearing of another occult transgression in his own household, he called her a witch. Throwing out various responses in an effort to placate him, she at one point said, yes, she supposed she had been a witch. He fastened on that confession, and demanded she tell who her confederates were. Tituba, greatly troubled at his wrath said Sarah Good was a witch, and, still desperate, eventually mentioned Sarah Osborne, too.

John was questioned too, but had little to add. Although he became an "afflicted" witness in the examinations and trials, he was never publicly accused himself. He blamed Mistress Sibley and Tituba for his own involvement in the witchcake incident.

Just a few days earlier Reverend Parris had called the Village church to a day of prayer with services to be held in the Parris home. There other ministers and leaders of the community first saw the "afflicted" in their contortions and fits. While blaming Mary Sibley for the witchcake episode, Reverend Parris still believed Tituba's exposure was an answer to those prayers for unearthing the evil. He hoped his children's maladies were part of a greater revelation – that the discovery of the witches might bring an end to the mysterious afflictions and deaths in the Village and to the divisions in the church, as well.

Samuel Nurse and Tom Preston were splitting rails west of the Nurse homestead. The bitter air of late February became pleasant as they worked together, driving wedges and wielding splitting axes in a steady rhythm. The echoes of their work cracked back sharply from the edge of the woodlot from which the young trees had been cut. Distinct clouds floated out with each breath and sentence of conversation.

Someone hallooed from beyond the copse of firs off toward the Village. Tom hallooed back as Thomas Putnam, "the Sergeant," as they called him, came around the firs along the path. He was a dark man of medium build, with an energetic pace unmistakable even at a distance. As he drew near, they saw an even more determined expression on his face than the normally serious one.

Sergeant Putnam gave a few minutes to small talk after greeting the two others, but he was clearly impatient to get on to something else.

"So what's on your mind, Sergeant?" Tom asked him.

"There are worse things going on in the Village than any of

us ever imagined," He answered.

Sam and Tom stood still and silent. It was a strong statement, but the Sergeant's demeanor made it seem a reference to something too awful for words. They all knew of the Village conflicts, the church fights, the suits over land, and the Indian wars. They knew of recent disasters, diseases and mysterious deaths—so the idea that there was something much worse frightened the Nurse men.

The Sergeant spoke again, with combined horror and fervor, "We have witches among us!"

Thomas Putnam was a soldier and son of a soldier. He was a rugged-looking man intent on pursuing all things boldly. As a gruff sergeant of militia he tolerated no nonsense at musters. Both as husband and father, he was ever ready to defend the community. But as a man, he was often at war with himself, and therefore ready to enter any campaign against another enemy. Nor was he likely to turn back once such a campaign was begun. His words rang as declarations of war, more than observations.

"You know how Reverend Parris has been asking for prayer for his girls and their strange maladies? He has been to the leaders in Salem seeking counsel, and they with Dr. Griggs thought perhaps there were witches behind it. Somehow he caught his Indian woman, Tituba, acting suspicious.

"She was playing at soothsaying, as more than a few foolish persons do. Such things as predicting husbands by means of an egg dropped in a glass of water, where the shape was supposed to show the future husband, or playing at the sieve and shears.

"When talk began about witches, it seems Tituba and Indian John made a "witch cake." Somewhere they heard they should feed it to a dog, which was then supposed to lead to the witch.

"When Reverend Parris found out about this, he was beside himself, as you or I would be. But when he confronted Tituba, she not only confessed to the soothsaying, but said that she herself was a witch, and that she had been drawn into it by two other Village women.

"Reverend Parris's talked with the Salem elders again, then went to the magistrates. These told him some Village men needed to sign complaints against the women so they magistrates might bring them in for examination.

"We know who three of the witches are," the Sergeant told Sam and Tom, "but we have good reason to believe there are more. It's no wonder we have been so plagued and afflicted. We have these wretches in the midst of us calling down curses from Satan."

The Sergeant then revealed his specific business. He asked Tom Preston if he would join his signature to the complaints, and Tom said, of course. Sam could not blame Tom—he would have done it had the Sergeant asked him. But Sam was left to finish the splitting while the other two men went into the Village. There they added their signatures to those of Jonathon Walcott, and Joseph Hutchinson, as complainants against Sarah Good and Sarah Osborne.

On March 1st, since Tituba had already "confessed," she was brought in prior to the first official examination, and questioned by the magistrates and ministers—mostly in regard to the other two women. Tituba was briefly recalcitrant, but became cooperative again, admitting to being a witch, and informed the magistrates about the witchery of the other two.

Sarah Good, was primed to expect persecution from life, but she had never seen persecution like this. She was arrested by Constable George Lockyer in accordance with the complaint. Being punctual, Constable Lockyer brought her to Ingersoll's Ordinary as stipulated. He kept her sitting on a bench near the stables while he consulted with those inside. Since the magistrates were doing their first unofficial questioning of Tituba at the Meeting House, Lockyer was told he should wait to take his charge over until Tituba was brought out.

The two of them sat on the bench as Constable Joseph Herrick rode up with Sarah Osborne. The two women glanced at one another as Constable Herrick put their horses in the stable. When he came out, Goody Good asked if he could spare her some tobacco. Grudgingly he gave her a pipeful. He then took Sarah Osborne into the ordinary.

After her first and unofficial examination, Tituba was led out of the Meeting House across the way by Marshall Herrick. Several of the afflicted girls and their parents went in, as well as a number of villagers. Constable Lockyer then led Sarah Good across. Meanwhile Constable Herrick brought Sarah Osborne out of the ordinary and into the Meeting House behind them. There Constable Herrick spoke briefly with the magistrates, before he took Sarah Osborne back out again.

Inside the Meeting House, Sarah Good was made to stand near the front, her hands upon the back of a bench. The two magistrates, Reverend Parris, and Reverend Higginson of Salem, sat before her, as well as Ezekiel Cheever of the Village, who recorded the examination. Other transcripts were recorded in abbreviated forms by both Sergeant Thomas Putnam and his half-brother, Joseph Putnam. Although Joseph was unsure before that first day of examinations, he soon became a vigorous opponent of the witch business.

Four girls sat to the left of the accused, including "Betty," Abigail, and Anna Putnam. With them also was Elizabeth Hubbard, the niece of Doctor Griggs, the fourth girl to get involved as an "afflicted evidence" (and the second older girl to join in).

The girls talked among themselves. Their words and behavior were not rebuked or restrained during these first examinations -- not then and very seldom during the whole period of our troubles.

The charges against Sarah Good were read, and her face grew hard.

"Sarah Good, What evil spirit have you familiarity with?" began Magistrate Hathorne.

"None," answered Sarah, her voice sullen.

"Have you made contact with the devil?" continued Mr. Hathorne.

"No," she said.

"Why then do you hurt these children!" said Mr. Hathorne, with a strong note of accusation.

Adjusting to his change in tone, she replied nearly as strongly, "I do not hurt them. I scorn the idea."

"Who do you employ then to do it!"

"I employ nobody," she answered and there seemed to be a faint note of amusement in her voice.

"What creature do you employ, then!" shot back Mr. Hathorne.

"No creature," she said, "I am falsely accused."

"Why did you go away muttering from Mr. Parris at his house a few days ago?"

She paused and seemed to consider, then answered, "I did not mutter. I thanked him for what he gave my child."

"Have you made no contract or covenant with the devil?"

"No," she answered again.

Mr. Hathorne then turned to the four girls and told them to look at her and see if this was the person who hurt them.

The girls all looked at her some sheepishly, some boldly.

Abigail spoke, "Yes, she hurt us."

"It is one of the witches!" said Anna.

Betty said, "She is hurting us, oh, my arm!"

Then one by one, at first quietly and sheepishly, all four of the girls began to moan. Abigail began to writhe, apparently in pain, and the others joined in this motion, twisting from side to side.

The magistrates and ministers looked with horror upon what was happening before them—that this deviltry should be carried out in the open and before a court of law. They were blind to the agency by which the "waves" of "affliction" seemed to travel from one girl to the others, that is by imitation, but rather saw in it a verification of demonic activity. They did not try to restrain the girls, assuming from the beginning they were helpless victims.

After a few minutes of this, at the advice of the ministers, their parents, who stood behind the girls, led them to a bench at a greater distance.

The girls quieted down, but not before one cried out, "she hurts us!"

Mr. Hathorne was now intensely indignant and imperious as he confronted this woman who performed her malefactions in open court.

"Sarah Good, do you not see now what you have done! Why do you not tell us the truth. Why do you thus torment these poor children?"

Sarah answered, her voice smaller and tighter, "I do not torment them."

"Who do you employ then!"

"I employ nobody. I scorn it entirely."

"How came they to be thus tormented then!" he said, and his whole tone and manner implied there was no other explanation possible.

"What do I know. I have never seen them in this condition before. You bring others here and now you charge me with it."

"Why, who was it?"

"I do not know, but it was someone you brought into the Meeting House with you."

"We brought you into the Meeting House."

"But you brought two more," she insisted.

"Who was it then that tormented the children?"

"It was Osborne," she said. It was unclear whether she merely remembered and spoke the name of the woman she had seen, or whether she intended this as answer to the question. The judges and ministers took it for the latter.

The magistrates asked the girls who had tormented them, and Anna Putnam said it was Sarah Osborne that time. Abigail Williams, however, said it was Sarah Osborne that time, but that in the past both of them had hurt them.

After consulting a note given him by Reverend Parris, Judge Hathorne continued to question Sarah.

"Who is it you speak with when you walk by yourself?"

"I speak with nobody."

"What is it that you say when you go muttering away from persons' houses?"

Sarah Good seemed to become more calculating, at the same time sounding less hostile.

"If I must tell, I will tell," she said and then, "It is the commandments. I may say my commandments I hope." There was again a certain irony in her face and tone.

"What commandment is it?"

"If I must tell you, I will tell," she said, "It is a psalm."

"What psalm," asked Mr. Hathorne.

She paused as if silently saying it first to herself, then recited, "Yea, though I walk through the valley of the shadow of death, I will fear no evil. Thy rod and thy staff they comfort me. Thou preparest a table before me in the presence of mine enemies. Thou anointest my head with oil. My cup runneth over. Surely goodness and mercy shall follow me all the days of my life, and I will dwell in the house of the Lord forever."

"Who do you serve?" asked Mr. Hathorne, a bit subdued by the recitation of scripture.

"I serve God," Sarah replied.

"What God do you serve?"

"I hope the one that made heaven and earth."

"Why, then do you come so seldom to meeting?"

"I do not have proper clothes."

Turning his head in silent query toward the other men, Mr. Hathorne found none who had further questions.

The magistrates and ministers consulted together a moment, then directed Constable Lockyer to take the defendant across to Ingersoll's again, and to bring her husband in.

When William Good ("Good Will") came in, the magistrates directed him to stand before them while he was asked a number of questions.

"To your knowledge is your wife a witch?"

"No, I do not think so."

"Do you see no evil in her conduct?"

"Aye, Good has known her a good time, and there's many a time I think she is an enemy of Good."

"Why think you she is no witch, then?"

"Nay, she is not one, but if she keep on, she may well become very quickly the worse."

"Why say you this?"

"Because she scorns Good and all good. I say with tears she is an enemy of Good."

Mr. Hathorne missed any subtlety in William's answers — as he was to miss much more during the many following months, except at a number of points where he pounced upon subtleties of his own manufacture. The ministers did not know "Good Will," and therefore missed the poetry of his answers.

Mr. Corwin, alone, heard the irony in the witness's replies. Yet, at this and many other points, he was caught in his characteristic dilemma — of being the most perceptive and at the same time, the least assertive of the magistrates. He remained silent.

Chapter Seven — The Third Witch (1 March)

*Brother is against brother and neighbors against
neighbors, all quarreling and smiting one another.*
— Villager **Jeremiah Watts** on Village controversies, 1682.

After Sarah Good was taken out of the Village Meeting
House, Sarah Osborne was brought in. A large and florid woman,
she had a more cheerful countenance than Sarah Good.
Nevertheless, she was obviously nervous, the sweat standing on her
brow as the charges were read.

Sarah (Warren) Osborne had first married Robert Prince,
whose sister was the wife of Captain John Putnam. When Sarah's
husband died just before King Philip's War, he left her with two
sons. In order to keep the farm going, she bought the indenture of
Alexander Osborne, whom she eventually married. Her Putnam
relatives believed she and her former servant, turned husband, were
trying to usurp the land which was rightfully the inheritance of the
Prince boys. Although they farmed respectably, the unorthodox
change in their relationship was held against her. Furthermore, she
adopted a fashion in dress which would have gotten her arrested
under the sumptuary laws thirty years earlier.   Her clothing was
"scandalous" in being nearly as fashionable as that of the gentlefolk
of Boston. Her tailor in Salem later testified against her on the basis
of the exotic bits of cloth she bought . Her own self-respect had been
affected by all this, so that she sometimes acted as though she were
embarrassed at her own temerity. Under the suspicion cumulative of
these things she was an easy object for scorn.

"Sarah Osborne, what evil spirit have you familiarity with?"
asked Mr. Hathorne.

"None!" she said, attempting to maintain her cheerful
disposition, and looking about for a sympathetic eye — of which she
found few.

"Have you made no contract with the devil?"

"No, I never saw the devil in my life."

"Why do you hurt these children."

"I do not hurt them."

"Who do you employ to hurt them?"

"I employ nobody." She blushed here, as though she suspected an allusion to her original relationship to her husband.

"What instrument do you use?"

"I do it not, nor with any instrument."

"What familiarity do you have with Sarah Good?"

"None. I have not seen her these two years."

"Where did you see her then?"

"One day a-going to town."

"What communications had you with her?"

"I had none, only how do you do or so. I did not know her name."

"What did you call her then?"

Goodwife Osborne was at a loss at this question, and bit her lip nervously.

"I called her. . . I suppose I called her Sarah."

"Sarah Good saith that it was you that hurt the children."

Again she was at a loss for a few moments, but gathered herself to reply, "I do not know of it, if the devil goes about in my likeness to do any hurt." Thus she was the first to "admit" this dangerous possibility.

Magistrate Hathorne had all the girls stand up before her. "Do you know this woman?" he asked them.

As with Sarah Good, all said they knew her and that she hurt them.

"She wore that dress when she hurt me at our home," said Abigail. (The clothes in which an "apparition" was dressed were to become important evidence in the subsequent round of accusations.)

The girls were asked to sit again, and as they did so, they cried out they were being hurt. Anna Putnam and Abigail Williams seemed to be the loudest voices. Mistress Parris stood behind Betty and kept her two hands upon her shoulders, perhaps in consequence of which the girl was much quieter than she had been during Sarah Good's examination.

"Marshall Herrick says that when he came for you this morning you said you were more likely to be bewitched than to be a witch. What made you say that?"

"I was given a fright one time in my sleep. I either saw or dreamed someone like an Indian all covered in black, and he pinched my neck and pulled me by the hair to the door of the house."

"Did you never see anything else of this kind?"

"No," she answered.

One of the fifteen bystanders who had come into the meeting during the morning suddenly spoke. "She once said she had a lying spirit. She said she would never be tied to that lying spirit anymore."

Magistrate Hathorne went on, "What lying spirit is this? Has the devil ever deceived you and been false to you!"

Sarah Osborne was shaken by this contribution from a neighbor and confidant, and her face became even more flushed and wet with perspiration.

"I do not know the devil. I never did see him," she answered.

"What lying spirit was it then!"

"It was a voice that I thought I heard."

"What did it propound to you?"

"That I should go no more to meeting. But I said I would go and did go the next Sabbath day."

"Were you never tempted further?"

"No! I wasn't!"

Reverend Parris spoke up, "Why did you yield thus far to the devil as never to go to meeting since!"

"Alas. I have been sick and not able to go."

The magistrates conferred and she was led out. Her husband Alexander Osborne was called forward. Alexander, an Irishman and his wife's former servant, was shown little respect by Mr. Hathorne.

"Do you know your wife to be a witch?"

"Nay, I know nothin' of it."

"What know you of a lying spirit that has been tied to her?"

"I know only that some years ago she said she was tempted not t' go t' meetin', but did go anyway."

"Does she go to meeting since?"

"Sometimes she has gone."

"How long since she came to meeting?"

"I suppose some time now."

"How long?"

"It seems to me the last time was the winter before this one."

"What month?"

"I suppose 'twas the first month."

"What evil has kept her away?"

"I know nothin' of it."

Goodman Osborne was dismissed and his wife taken out.

After Sarah Osborne was led away, Tituba was brought in for

her official examination. The girls murmured, but only Anna Putnam cried out. The Parris girls seemed somewhat confused to have their playmate brought before them in this setting.

At first, for her part, Tituba was again more recalcitrant in "confessing" before the court than she had been before her master.

"Why do you hurt these poor children? What harm have they done unto you?"

"They do no harm to me. I don't hurt them none at all."

"Why have you done it?"

"I done nothing. I can't tell when the devil works."

"What doth the devil tell you? That he hurts them?"

"No, he tells me nothing."

"Do you never see something appear in some shape?"

"No, I never see any thing."

"What familiarity have you with the devil? Or what is it if you converse withal?"

"I don't know."

"Tell the truth who it is that hurts them?"

"The devil for ought I know."

"What appearance. . . how doth he appear when he hurts them? What shape or what is he like that hurts them?"

"Like a man I think. Yesterday in the lean-to (the shed addition of the Parris house) I saw something like a man. And he told me serve him and I told him no I would not do such a thing."

"Do you know anything of Sarah Good and Sarah Osborne?"

"They're the ones hurt the children and told me to do it."

The girls had murmured and Abigail and Anna cried out a few times during these early questions, but as soon as Tituba began to talk about her involvement with the witches, they grew quiet and listened raptly. They remained silent throughout the rest of her questioning. In their further consultations, the magistrates and ministers were to take this cessation of "affliction" as proof of the genuineness of Tituba's repentance — a pattern for subsequent examinations. From then on throughout our troubles Tituba steadfastly admitted she was a witch, and thus was treated as a "confessor" and reliable "friend" of the court.

"Were there other beside them?" asked Mr. Hathorne.

"I see four of them last night when I washed the room. There was Goody Osborne and Goody Good and I don't know who the other two."

"What did they say to you?"

"They told me hurt the children and want me go to Boston with them.

"How many of them were there?"

"There was five of them with the man. They told me if I don't go and hurt them, they would do the same thing to me."

"Did you hurt the children?"

"I didn't want to, but I do it so they won't hurt me, but I say I wouldn't do it no more."

"Would they have you hurt the children last night?"

"Yes, but I was sorry. I said I wouldn't do it no more, but would fear God."

"But why did not you do so before?"

"Why? They tell me I done it before and must go on."

"Who were they?"

"They was four, but I only know Goody Good and Goody Osborne. The other two from Boston."

"At first, beginning with them, what then appeared to you? What was it like that got you to do it?"

"One come to me like a man. Just as I was going to sleep, he come to me."

"When was that?"

"When the children was first hurt. He said he would kill the child and she would never be well. He said if I wouldn't serve him he'd do the same thing to me."

"Is that the same man that appeared before to you that appeared last night and told you this?"

"Yes."

"What other likenesses besides this man hath appeared to you?"

"Sometimes like a hog. Sometimes like a great black dog, four times."

"But what did they say unto you?"

"They told me serve him and that was a good way. That was the black dog."

"And what did you answer?"

"I told him I was afraid. He told me he would be worse then to me."

"What did you say to him after that?"

"I answer I will serve you no longer. He told me he would hurt me then."

"What other creatures have you seen?"

"A bird."

"What bird?"

"A little yellow bird."

"Where doth it keep?"

"With that man that has other pretty things."

"What other pretty things?"

"He hasn't showed them to me, but he said he would show me tomorrow. He told me if I served him, I should have the bird."

"What other creatures did you see?"

"I saw two cats, one red and another black as big as a little dog."

"What did these cats do?"

"I don't know. I have seen them two times."

"What did they say?"

"They say serve them."

"When did you see them?"

"I see them last night."

"Did they do any hurt to you or threaten you?"

"They did scratch me."

"When?"

"After prayer, and scratched me because I would not serve them. And when they went away I could not see how, but they stood before the fire."

"What service do they expect from you?"

"They say more hurt to the children."

"How did you pinch them when you hurt them?"

"The other pulled me and haul me to pinch the children and I am very sorry for it."

"What made you hold your arm when you were searched? What had you there?"

"I had nothing."

"Do not those cats suck you?"

"No never yet would I not let them, but they had almost throw me in the fire."

"How do you hurt those that you pinch? Do you get those cats or other thing to do it for you? Tell us how it is done?"

"The man sends the cats to me and bids me pinch them and I think I sent over to Mr. Griggs and have pinched her this day in the morning. The man brought Mr. Grigg's maid (Elizabeth Hubbard, the niece of Dr. Grigg's wife) to me and made me pinch her."

"Did you ever go with these women?"

"They are very strong and pull me and make me go with them."

"Where did you go?"

"Up to Mr. Putnam's and they make me hurt the child."

"Who did make you go?"

"A man that is very strong and these two women, Good and Osborne, but I am sorry."

"How did you go? What did you ride upon?"

"I ride upon a stick or pole and Good and Osborne behind me. We ride taking hold of one another."

"Did you go above the trees? What path did you take?"

"I don't know how we go for I see no trees nor path. We presently there when we was up."

"How long since you began to pinch Mr. Parris' children?"

"I did not pinch them at first, but he make me afterward."

"Have you seen Good and Osborne ride upon a pole?"

"Yes and they have held fast by me. I was not at Mr. Grigg's but once, but it may be they send something like me. Without would I gone, but they tell me they will hurt me. Last night they tell me I must kill somebody with the knife."

"Who were they that told you so?"

"Sarah Good and Osborne and they would have me killed Thomas Putnam's child last night."

Mr. Hathorne asked Anna if she had seen Tituba the night before.

"Yes," she said, "They all came to me and would have me cut my head off at my throat."

"Who was it?"

"It was Goody Good and Goody Osborne. They said if I did not cut my head off, they would have Tituba do it.

"Oh, oh," Anna cried out, "a knife cuts me now!"

Mr. Hathorne turned to Tituba. "Why did not you tell your master of these things?"

"I want to do it, but they told me if I tell, they cut my head off."

"Who tells you so?"

"The man and Goody Good and Osborne's wife."

"When did they tell you this?"

"Goody Good came last night when he was at prayer and wouldn't let me hear. I couldn't hear a good while. She had one of those birds."

"What bird was that?"

"A yellow bird and she would give me it but I wouldn't have it. At prayer time she stopped my ears and would not let me hear."

"What should you have done with the yellow bird?"

"Give it to the children. I saw Sarah Good have it on her hand when she came to me when master was at prayer."

"What was it doing on her hand?"

"I saw the bird suck Good between the fingers right here." She spread her forefinger and middle finger apart.

"Which hand was it?"

"On the right hand."

"Did you ever practice witchcraft in your own country?"

"No, never before now."

"Do you see them do it now?"

"Yes, today, but that was in the morning.

"But did you see them do it now while you are examining?"

"No, I did not see them but I saw them hurt at other times."

"What other things do they have beside the bird?"

"I saw Good have a cat beside the yellow bird which was with her."

"What hath Osborne got to go with her?"

"Something, I don't know what it is. I can't name it. I don't know how it looks. She has two of them. One of them has wings and two legs and a head like woman. The children saw the same but yesterday, and afterward turned into a woman."

"What is the other thing that Goody Osborne hath?"

"A thing all over hairy and a long nose and I don't know how to tell how the face looks, with two legs. It goes upright and is about two or three foot high and goes upright like a man and last night it stood before the fire in the hall."

Then Mr. Hathorne returned to the subject of the mysterious man among the witches who became so important to the examiners during the first months of our troubles.

"What clothes doth the man appear unto you in?"

"Black clothes sometimes. Sometimes he wear a serge coat another color."

"What does he look like?"

"A tall man with white hair, I think."

"What apparel doth the tall woman wear?"

"I don't know."

"What color clothes hath she?"

"I don't know what color.

"What kind of clothes hath she?"

"A black silk hood with a white silk hood under, with a top knot."

"Which woman is it?"

"Which I don't know, but I see her in Boston when I live there."

"What clothes does the little woman wear?"

"A serge coat with a white cap. That what I think."

The girls jumped about and cried out again for the first time since Tituba began to "confess".

"See, these children are having fits at this very time. Who is it that hurts them?"

"Goody Good."

Abigail cried, "Oh Goody Good, leave us alone."

At the end of this, her first examination before the magistrates, Tituba was worn out and near the end of her resources. As Elizabeth Hubbard collapsed again on the floor and rattled her heels upon it and her body trembled and grew stiff, Mr. Hathorne asked who it was that afflicted Elizabeth now. Tituba was distressed at this renewal of the afflictions.

"I can't tell, they won't let me see. I can't see and they won't let me talk."

As Tituba's voice trailed off in a wail, she too collapsed and lay rigid. They set her upon the bench, and when she began to recover, they asked who had done it, at which she again became rigid, her eyes staring wildly. It was mid-afternoon by then, and the magistrates declared the examination at a close.

Before concluding their day's investigations, the magistrates went across and asked Sarah Ingersoll to privately examine the bodies of the three witches for any strange excrescences or unusual marks. Repelled at the request, but not daring to refuse, Sarah went with the women into a closed room of the ordinary. The women were sent in one by one, after being sternly commanded by the magistrates to disrobe before Sarah, so that she might examine them. As uncomfortable with all this as the defendants, she performed but a cursory examination and pronounced them free of any such marks to the best of her knowledge.

Justice Corwin

Chapter Eight — The Two Magistrates

*The great questions which have troubled the country are
about the authority of the magistrates and the liberty of the people. .
. .being called by you, we have authority from God, in the way of an
ordinance, such as hath the image of God eminently stamped upon
it, the contempt and violation whereof hath been vindicated with
examples of divine vengeance. I entreat you to consider that when
you choose magistrates, you take them from among yourselves, men
subject to like passions as you are
   . . . But when you call one to be a magistrate, he doth not
profess nor undertake to have sufficient skill for that office, nor can
you furnish him with gifts, etc.; therefore you must run the hazard
of his skill and ability. But if he fail in faithfulness, which by his
oath he is bound unto, that he must answer for. If it fall out . . . the
error is not in the skill but in the evil of the will: it must be required
of him. But if the case be doubtful or the rule doubtful to men of
such understanding and parts as your magistrates are, if your
magistrates should err here, yourselves must bear it.*
-- John Winthrop, **Speech to the General Court** (1645)

Barratry was looked down upon in the early days of the
colony, indeed it was regarded as criminal — although it comes to be
regarded as a virtue now, just as usury and even simony are. At the
time of our troubles a "professional" lawyer was still little respected,
but those with inclinations toward that role were increasing filling
our offices. Judge Hathorne gained a knowledge of the law through
his years as justice of the peace, despite little firsthand scholarship,
either biblical or civil. Nevertheless his experience and diligence
went a long way toward making up for this deficit.
    This examiner, whose vehemence we came to know so well,
had accumulated respect and position through diligence and a kind
of doggedness that came naturally to him. He took the lead in
questioning those accused – with almost an animal relentlessness.
Yet even during our troubles, his doggedness never seemed
particularly malicious – any more than that of a dog worrying a cat,
or a cat playing with a mouse.
    Judge Hathorne's father, the Major William Hathorne, had

been a respected companion of the headstrong Governor Endicott. The two of them were credited with wise diplomacy in at least one of the crises where the colonial administration was in conflict with the royal court. On this occasion, Major Hathorne had been granted considerable land in appreciation of his services to the colony, and thus become a prosperous farmer.

Judge John Hathorne was born in 1641 in Salem. He left his father's farm and became a small merchant and local politician, then a justice of the peace, and finally reached the high office of colonial assistant. His sister Elizabeth was married to Israel Porter. Though skillful at remaining in the background, the Porters had considerable political power in Salem Town, which contributed to Judge Hathorne's advancement. A surprising number of our legal papers—licenses, tax accounts, judgments, deeds, and wills—bear his signature. He was bold to take up responsibilities that involved hard work and had little immediate reward. Thus he became active in Marblehead politics and legal matters, although it was an outlying district with little status, that nonetheless required much travel and trouble.

He had other family connections—two sisters married to Porters; his brother married to Abigail Corwin; his own wife, a Gardner; and close social and ecclesiastical connections to Ingersolls, Walcotts, Endicotts, Putnams, and Gedneys. Thus Judge Hathorne, by birth, by marriage and by his own efforts, had come to have considerable social and political standing.

He functioned more as a prosecutor than as a jurist during the examinations leading up to the trials. Perhaps for that reason, Mr. Hathorne made many enemies during our troubles – some of whom persist in unforgiveness.

We have an old saying in prediction of a hard winter "many hawes – many snawes," meaning that when the hathorne bush is laden with berries, there will be a lot of snow. During our troubles it went the other way – a hard winter preceded Mr. Hathorne's much fruit.

Fewer among the unforgiving hold a grudge against his partner, fifty-two year old Judge Jonathan Corwin of Salem. Some will argue he showed great wisdom in his habitual silence. But silence is not always virtuous.

Jonathon was second son of George Corwin and Elizabeth Herbert. Judge Corwin's parents came from Essex. They arrived at Salem about 1638, where the father, George, became a prosperous and respected merchant. Jonathon's mother died in 1668.

In 1675, Judge Corwin married Elizabeth Sheaffe, daughter of the wealthy Jacob Sheaffe and the mysterious Margaret (Webb) Sheaffe — Margaret Thacher by a later marriage. Jonathan Corwin joined in the mercantile business of his father and prospered over the next decade.

By the time George, Sr. died in 1685, he was the very epitome of a Salem merchant, at the acme of colonial prosperity. Mr. George Corwin's funeral was an event of unprecedented proportions, drawing people from all the surrounding settlements. It was one of those landmark events that people used twenty years later in calculating the date of some other incident.

The same year his father died, Jonathan had a son whom he named George. During the last week of January, 1692, little George fell ill. This coincided with the first three warrants. During the examinations of the first three accused, Mr. Hathorne asked Tituba "Did you not hurt Mr. Corwin's child?" To which she replied, "Goody Good and Goody Osborne told me that they did hurt Mr. Corwin's child and would have had me hurt him, too, but I did not."

The magistrate's older brother, Mr. John Corwin, married Margaret Winthrop, the governor's daughter. Their son, also George, was considerably older than his cousin of the same name and became Sheriff of Essex County. As such he served warrants, made arrests and executed the forfeiture of property during our troubles. It also fell to his lot to carry out the hanging of those defendants sentenced by the high court on which his uncle sat.

Judge Corwin's younger sister Abigail, married Eleazur Hathorne, older brother of the bolder Salem magistrate, John Hathorne. Thus our two judges were joined by marriage as well as by complementary temperaments.

Margaret (Sheaf) Thacher, the mother of Judge Corwin's wife, was one of the persons accused during our troubles. Although he was involved in all the examinations up to the establishment of the Court of Oyer and Terminer in late May, and although his fellow magistate, Hathorne continued on that second court, Judge Corwin was not initially appointed to the highest court — perhaps because his mother-in-law had been accused. Mr. Hathorne's active prosecution of the examinations may have made him seem better qualified than Judge Corwin.

Judge Corwin was born and raised amidst a family of considerable respect. Nor did he act in any way to diminish it. In spite of that inheritance, or because of it, he became a reflective rather than an active man.

Meditation and reflection are not productive, that is they make no product, grow no crop, manufacture no tangible merchandise. We colonists are not much interested in things so manifestly useless, for it is our essence of value to be useful. The fruit of that which is useful is tangible results — if not in a completed product, per se, then in measurable steps of progress. Reflective persons, therefore, are seldom raised to our first rank.

Which was just as Judge Corwin would have it, for from a young man he believed he was not meant to lead. It may be this was instilled in him by overly competent or careful parents, a domineering brother, or the impulses of his own soul. However it was, he was never first in command. He was always prone to turn to his parents, his teachers, or his pastors for instruction on how to proceed or decide, from his youth onward. This paradigm carried over to his business, ecclesiastical and political offices. He neither sought nor received positions which required solitary leadership. If perchance he was given such a job, he was careful to find some stolid person he could appeal to at points of doubt or decision.

Such timidity often seems the characteristic of unthinking or shallow men, but in the strange alchemy of the fallen and divided human heart, the opposite was the case with him. Jonathon Corwin thought more deeply and more coherently on the first principles and motives of everything about him. This habit seems to have been the second spring of his unwillingness to lead, for he saw always the contrary logic and suspected perverse motives, his own and others'. He was ever unwilling to hazard upon unproven ground.

The two magistrates, as different as night and day, got on well by animadversion. Judge Corwin did all the meditating and Judge Hathorne most of the talking. Judge Corwin was in charge of reservations and Judge Hathorne in charge of decisions. When one regards such a relationship, it is always the first impulse to mock the dominant member as the buffoon. Where such a pair are set in a domestic or merely social sphere, they often do provide comic relief, but where they hold life and death in their hands, where they have been given supreme or nearly supreme authority, there is little comic about it. And it is no longer the thoughtless and decisive who is the most incredible, but rather the more capable yet silent one.

Judge Corwin knew from the start that the witch examinations were not right. He heard the arguments and the old lists from the English witch jurists. He heard the ministers mention various scriptures and he already knew the Penteteuch, for he had studied it assiduously when he was made magistrate. He knew the working definitions of "witness" and of "victim," indeed of "crime" accepted as currency in our troubles, were suspect. He saw that the fancies of the girls, though approved by the ministers, and now his fellow magistrate, did not stand up to biblical tests. But he only thought these things in his own study or lying in his own bed or on a Sunday afternoon of searching scripture and meditating further on them.

Come Monday, as he sat in the Salem Village Meeting House with the rhythm and rituals which were soon established -- with the afflicted, his fellow magistrate and the latest hapless accused playing out their prescribed parts -- he no longer knew the right of it. There was too much to be said on either side. Details and definitions remained unclear. The principles seemed to waver and bend and divide into contraries with different sorts of practical applications. He fell back on the assured tone of Mr. Hathorne and the somber visages of the black-clothed ministers — as well as the memory something very like this had been done hundred of times before elsewhere and now a few, now a dozen, now a hundred times right here among us, by the hand of Mr. Hathorne . . . and by his own.

He had wider grounds for sympathy toward both afflicted and accused than any other magistrate presiding over the trials. But that, too, was a double-edged sword affecting his ability to bring justice. His mother-in-law had once been accused of witchcraft, as we have mentioned, and thus his wife drawn near the suffering of the defendants' relatives; but his son was one of the first numbered among the contemporary victims of the witches.   Thus he was pulled by strong emotion in both directions, which only served to maintain the stationery inertia or equilibrium that made him so ineffectual.

In short, he who had the larger stewardship entrusted to him, buried it most deeply in the earth. He who had the most and best understanding with which to resist the false processes of our troubles, was stymied by a reflective nature, source of that understanding, as well as by his peculiar circumstances and an instinctive unwillingness to lead.

Judge Hathorne will be remembered best for his doggedness and for his rhetoric — sharp, but soon predictable. Judge Corwin will be remembered for his silence. The dogged pursuit of the wicked by the one and the silent complicity of the other were both under the spiritual guidance of the Reverend Noyes and the other Salem divines.

The magistrates also had the best of assistants -- in the afflicted girls.

Chapter Nine — Courts of Injustice

It is certain he never works more like the Prince of Darkness than when he looks most like an angel of light. -- Deodat Lawson, **Christ's Fidelity the only Shield against Satan's Malignity,** lecture delivered at Salem Village the day of Rebecca Nurse's examination.

These many years later, outsiders who have the temerity to ask a Villager about the trials are treated either to a detailed discussion of the weather or a withering look and retreating back. Perhaps this will be the case for many generations. It is one thing to learn to forgive — it is another to show one's scars in public. It is only when someone else denies the scars or shows the wrong sort of sympathy toward those who inflicted them that one is inclined to display them more openly.

But to some degree in Boston and more so in London and at other places where our troubles can be discussed without offense, the chiefest question must be, how could these things happen in the law courts of a Christian country? How could there be this degree of injustice within justice's auspices? The answers vary according to philosophy, but there are some answers upon which most agree.

First, there is the idea that in great calamity ordinary niceties of civilized justice may legitimately be set aside. That they are seldom fully recovered is something men are slow to learn. It quickly became the accepted opinion in Salem Village, and in the colony at large that we were involved in some sort of calamity.

Second, every level of our community contributed to it. The learned provided foundations by publishing sensational accounts and arcane scholarship, our leaders built upon them, and every man jack of the community contributed the lumber of fear and suspicion. There was a community propensity toward the ideas of witch and witchery, and a readiness to believe anyone capable of extraordinary secret evil. Ministers, magistrates, jurors, witnesses and even relatives were prone to believe the accused guilty.

In addition to Reverend Willard's account of Elizabeth Knapp and Cotton Mather's account of the Goodwin children, we had memories of a number of prior outbreaks in the colonies, resulting in several executions. The accusers in our colony drew on the memory and records of the East Anglian witch hunts. We also shared with the East Anglians (at the time of their witch trials) the effects of ongoing disruptions and vengeful attitudes which go with or follow war (the Protestant Revolution in England, the Pequot and King Philips Wars here).

Third, the officers of the courts had personal ties and associations which made objective judgments more difficult for them. Both as officers and as family men, our leaders felt the cold breath of spectres on their own necks.

Fourth, the rulers, the courts, the laws, and the offices were in the midst of flux — from the Government under the Colonial Charter, the subsequent revocation of the Charter and the Andros Government, the Protestant Revolution and Commonwealth in England, the Restoration in England and new Phips Government in the Colony, and finally the continual political wrestling over the relative power and authority of the courts versus the "freemen," represented in the Assemblies, throughout these changes. This flux in authority did two things: it made the officers of the law feel they were a last, if temporary, bulwark against anarchy; and it obscured their own legal accountability.

Fifth, the legal precedents were varied enough to give the magistrates lee-way for all that they did. There was enough superstitious and unbiblical matter in print to offer support for almost any opinion or procedure. The extensive witchcraft trials of East Anglia and Europe a generation earlier left explicit "principles," both theological and "practical" for finding and proving witches, most of which had been preserved in books. The writings of two chief British witch hunters — Jonathon Stearne and Matthew Hopkins — were much used by our magistrates, both in the early examinations and later trials of 1692.

But the nexus of the legal question always comes back to one issue: how could our ministers have advised the magistrates and carried on themselves at such odds with the process of law laid down in scripture? How could a community claiming a primary allegiance to God's word as the guide for life and doctrine so mistake what God says about how He wants things done — especially when that community believed itself in the midst of a zealous campaign against God's enemies!

Again, the answers vary. The "freethinker" will say, religion being a sham, one cannot look for any consistency among its adherents. The Papist will say, the Protestant being separated and in revolt from the true church cannot help but live in conflict and contradiction. The Episcopal will say without bishops to shepherd and mediate, the people will always be sheep astray. The Anabaptist will say serving two masters always tears apart—and that we do so by living with one foot resting on this world's government and the other in the church. The Quaker will say our living by the sword has brought us upon its tip. And no doubt there is a germ of truth in most of them.

The particulars of how God would have his courts conduct themselves were not foreign to our fathers fifty years ago. *The Massachusetts Body of Liberties* (1641) was a law code conscientiously based upon the scriptures, and the moral and civil code in the Mosaic law in particular. Here we see the rules of "due process" reiterated— two or three witnesses required for a capital crime, equal penalty for false witness (death in a capital case), legal defenses, impartial judges, public execution—with the witnesses casting the first stones. Witchcraft is indeed listed among the capital crimes there as it is in scripture, but no special rules of evidence are allowed for it. (In England at the time of our *Body of Liberties*, there were nearly two hundred crimes for which one could be executed, while by our code there were but a dozen.)

But neither the Massachusetts Body of Liberties nor even the Bible expresses any need for definitions of "seeing" or "witnessing". It is difficult to imagine Moses either doubting the reality of supernatural appearances (the burning bush, the rod become serpent, the ten plagues, the passover, the parting of the sea, the cloud by day and fire by night, the manna, the judgments, the mountain and commandments given, and so on) or believing someone who claimed to see one of these while other godly persons could not! It is true Baalam's Ass could see the angel when Baalam could not. And Elijah saw Israel's enemies surrounded by the hosts of the Lord—divine armies which his companion could not see until Elijah prayed for him. It was given to Elisha alone to see Elijah's ascent in the fiery chariot. Saul of Tarsus saw the Lord on the road to Damascus while his companions only heard His voice. But these were special revelations of God, not intended for use in human justice.

In fact none of these ought to have been admitted as a legal witness in a capital trial, according to God's own stipulations. Certainly no criminal or capital case was ever hung on such testimonies in scripture, not excepting the accusing of Achen and his family by lots. In that case there was indeed a drawing of lots, but there was also a confession by the accused before sentence was pronounced. Finally, there is no biblical record of a sin or crime committed which was visible to some eyes but invisible to others.

The idea of "witness" and "seeing" may in some sense be applied to dreams (as of Mary and Joseph, or Peter and Cornelius) but not for use in criminal trial. How much less the idea of "appearances" or "spectres". With the difficult and, for the Bible interpreter, humbling exception of the Ghost of Samuel (to which two of the defendants pointedly referred) -- and the figures of Moses and Elijah at the Mount of Transfiguration -- there are very few "appearances" of people in the Bible—and no "apparitions" of living people (in the sense of presences in more than one place) anywhere in scripture. (The descriptions of Christ's appearances after the resurrection would seem to put the resurrected or glorified body outside these categories. Yet even glorified, He does not seem to have appeared in two places at once.) Jesus could perceive the essential problem of the demoniacs—could "see" demons, if you will—but he instructed his disciples that these difficult cases could only be "cured" by prayer and fasting.

From whence then came this idea of an "appearance," this "spectre," who became the most significant figure in our witchcraft trials! The idea and the thing itself, so far as it can be said to be a thing at all, came from deluded minds.

But once the pagan mind, then the Roman church, then the Protestants of Europe allowed for such a thing; and once the Puritans of England and Richard Baxter allowed of such a thing; once Increase and Cotton Mather allowed of such a thing, it was very easy for congregational Salem to allow of such a thing. That it was brought into the courtrooms of Salem with an unprecedented level of respect seemed but proper honor to an ancient family friend. That the Spectre should be seated at the head of the magistrates' table seemed only appropriate to its dignity. That every defendant be required to acknowledge the Spectre's authority showed but a minimum of courtesy. That the Spectre should be allowed to put the noose about each condemned neck was but holy respect for ancient prerogatives. Indeed once admitted, the Spectre ruled the colony, haunted the pulpits of many wise, and dispensed life and death, but chiefly the latter, wherever he walked or she flew.

This then was the chief departure from godly jurisprudence in the midst of a general departure from the Bible as rule of faith and conduct. Who or what exactly was this Spectre, the great host at our bloody feast?

We might describe the Spectre as a monster, the union of three other mythical "beasts". First there was the ancient pagan "ghost", which is recorded as far back as the ancient Greek "shades" of the Odyssey, and, despite Christian teaching to the contrary, continues to "haunt" many a house and Walpurgis night to this day. The ghost is supposed to be the spiritual remains of some person dead and, so far as body, gone, but for some reason either held in an earthly captivity, or brought back on some occasions from a mysterious "other world," (a world other than heaven or hell—for from neither of these is there any return to earth. "It is given for man once to die, then comes the judgment," saith the scripture.)

That some form of this superstition was current in Christ's day is evident from the reaction of the others when Peter was unexpectedly released from gaol. When the damsel Rhoda came running in with the news that he was at the door, first they said "thou art mad" and when she persisted, "it is his angel." Since there is a resurrection of the dead, a rising of the eternal soul or spirit to judgment, the idea of a "ghost" of the dead appearing near the time of death is not entirely foreign to the gospel. We say he "gave up the ghost" at death—indeed so the gospels report of Christ. Curiously, however, among the cataclysmic events surrounding the crucifixion, it was not spirit "ghosts" that came out of their graves and appeared to those in Jerusalem, but "many bodies of the saints which slept" — early harbingers of the resurrection.

Nevertheless, the ghost (both in simple and as part of the spectre-monster) came to Salem Village all too frequently during our troubles. Fifty or sixty dead persons appeared to the "afflicted" according to their sworn testimonies. These were said to have reported various important facts—such as who killed them (inevitably a witch), why they were killed (for offending the same in some small matter), and how they were killed (familiar details of witchery). Several of the afflicted girls became quite famous for their ability to see, hear, and speak with these appearances of departed ones. At last, late in our troubles, witnesses swore several "ghosts" of executed "witches" came and told them they had been wrongfully accused and condemned!

The second mythical beast which had a part in our monster spectre was the "familiar". This beast is also ancient, going back to the pagan gods of Greece, Rome and Egypt. Certain beasts were supposed to be associated with certain gods, as the owl with Athena, the cow with Hera, the deer with Artemis, and so on. These beasts served as messengers and spies for the gods, and the gods themselves took the forms of the beasts when it was convenient for them. Particular beasts were therefore thought to have particular powers, somewhat in the same way as various creatures came to have particular emblematic significance in Christian imagery. In pagan lands today and among our Indians, magicians and shamans often appeal to particular animals to help with various ritual activities.

In the Bible, Satan appeared to Eve as a serpent, and God spoke to Balaam through his beast of burden. But these occurrences have little to do with the "familiar" of witch lore, except that in the first we see that the devil prefers some other identity or intermediary in his transactions with men. And in the latter we see God will use any messenger when those in the first rank refuse to see, hear, or respond to his message. (Jesus declared that where human witnesses abdicated their offices the very stones would cry out.)

In the witch trials of the last century in Europe and East Anglia, one of the primary evidences of witchcraft was thought to be a "familiar spirit," which was a demon who worked at the bidding of the witch, and often took on a characteristic visible form—a black dog, a small hairy man or ape, a cat, a bird, a wolf or a half-man-half-beast. The familiar was thought to come and go at the witch's bidding—afflicting the witch's enemies and victims, and bringing news from distant places.

In our own trials the "familiar" (again in simple form, as well as a part of the spectre-monster) was frequently referred to. The "yellow bird" was perhaps one of our great innovations and contributions to the history of witchcraft. From the very first accusations of Sarah Good and Sarah Osborne by Tituba, and on through trials, there were few witches who could not reliably be placed in conjunction with mysterious yellow birds. But black dogs, black men (both small hairy and tall dignified ones), wolves, cats, blue boars, and various other beasts also appeared. A serpent familiar was mentioned only twice in our troubles, and one of those was a result of the examiners misunderstanding the words of the youngest child accused.

Finally, the third mythical beast who contributed to the composition of our monster-spectre was the emanation, projection, or "apparition" of the living witch, herself. This "apparition" was supposed to be an image of her very body (and voice and mind, etcetera) sent to a great distance while her "other" (one can scarcely say "real," for the emanation was just as real, indeed more real so far as our courts were concerned) body remained in its place – at home, at the bar of court, or even in prison. The projected "self" could inflict pain on a victim, external and even internal, it could move heavy objects, kill persons or cattle, break vehicles, produce invisible barriers and hindrances, yet it could pass through walls, or at least very small holes in walls, go up chimneys, and fly at tremendous speed, occasionally with other witches upon a stick, going back and forth to the witch who sent it. The strangest thing about this "apparition" of a living witch was that many of our most learned men confirmed its nature by means of their most advanced science.

The "Spectre" of our trials was composed of all three of these marvelous beasts. It was a ghost, a familiar, and a projection. It could go anywhere it wanted, do anything it wished, appear, disappear, hurt, hinder, further its mistress's cause and both send and bring her communications. In short it enabled the witch hunters who studied it to do what Eve thought the forbidden fruit would enable her to do – to know good and evil, and to be like gods.

These two great departures from Christian faith and practice – the dismissal of the scriptures as the primary book of law, and the admission of the Spectre into our courts – were the things which made them into places of cruel injustice. Both departures were made and sustained by a concert of leading ministers, doctors, and lawyers and supported by the community at large. Once they were made, the process of justice slipped its reins and ran away with its highest officers. The institutions of justice were thus given to Satan's work. Never did he appear more as an angel of light – and as a monster.

The Nurse Place

Chapter Ten—Eyes Further Opened   (March 1-9)

*. . . Though Satan hath his devices to draw souls to sin, yet we
must be careful that we do not lay all our temptations upon
Satan, that we do not wrong the devil, and father that upon
him that is to be fathered upon our own base hearts.*
— Thomas Brooks, First of Six Propositions
Concerning Satan and His Devices, ***Precious Remedies
Against Satan's Devices***.

The magistrates deliberated all the long afternoon
following the first examinations. The three women were all bound
over to prison. Tituba and Sarah Osborne were kept at Salem Village
that night, but Sarah Good was sent to Ipswich gaol.

Joseph Putnam, one of nearly twenty people present at the
examination, stood outside the Meeting House speaking with several
men, most of whom seemed nervously boisterous, and not inclined
to talk about the immediate subject. Captain Jonathon Walcott came
out and spoke to someone. He turned to Giles Corey and observed,
"What brought you, Goodman Corey? I saw you only came in
toward the end."

"Aye," said Corey, with rough good-humor, "My wife took
my saddle off my horse and hid it in the barn. She would not have
me help to prosecute witches!" Like many remarks carelessly
dropped during our troubles, this one came back to haunt its
speaker. Those present at the earliest examinations had heard Tituba
speak of three as yet unidentified witches, one of whom was a man.

Since it was late afternoon when the proceedings came to a
close, Constable Joseph Herrick took Sarah Good to his house in
Royalside, which was part-way to Ipswich. She was to be delivered
to Ipswich gaol the next morning. He employed Samuel Brabrook,
Michael Dunnell and Jonathon Baker, his neighbors, to guard her.
They testified the next day that she had disappeared that night "bare
foot and bare leg," that is to say without shoes or stockings. She was
there in the morning, however.

Elizabeth Hubbard knew a great deal more, however. The
next day she claimed Goody Good had appeared to her that night at
Dr. Grigg's home, not only "bare foot and bare leg," but also "bare

breast," in which state she had afflicted Elizabeth. Samuel Sibley was at the Grigg's home that night. He said Elizabeth told him to strike out with his sword at the apparition standing upon the table. Although he could not see it, he swung his sword and Elizabeth said he had struck the apparition across the back, after which it disappeared. The next morning Joseph Herrick found Sarah's arm to be bloody from the wrist to the elbow. The other men affirmed this.

Others suggested Sarah Good injured her arm by a rough attempt at suicide. Constable Herrick subsequently testified she threw herself from her horse three times the next day as he transported her to Ipswich. He said she was trying to kill herself on those occasions. Nevertheless the authorities did not regard her bloody wrist in that light.

The accounts of Elizabeth Hubbard and Samuel Sibley were taken as evidence Sarah Good had gone witching that night. Although Elizabeth said Sibley struck the apparition across the back, Sarah Good's wounded arm was accounted to Sibley's sword. Thus were the fancies of the girls tailored to cover events.

Tituba was further reexamined the next day (March 2) at the Salem gaol. In response to plodding interrogation she gave more detailed accounts of making a covenant with the devil by signing his book in her blood and pledging to serve him six years. Pressed about the other signatures in the book, she increased the tally of the witches to include nine others, but she said she did not know any of the names, except Good's and Osborne's. She said more about pinching Abigail Williams and Betty Parris, for whom she nonetheless protested her great love. She repeated that she did this only after being "hauled" and forced to do it by other witches. The examiners were chiefly seeking information to help them identify the other witches, but at least in those early days of our troubles, some of them were also looking for variations or contradictions in the testimony to test the veracity of the "confessor". Tituba was consistent, however, having a good memory and a store of fanciful material drawn from the girls' games and those elements of the Knapp account the girls had shared with her. She was also savvy enough to learn from the examiners.

Most of the other questions sought elaborations on what Tituba had already confessed. She said the half-animal, half-woman described the previous day was Sarah Osborne. She spoke again of a hairy imp that "the man" would have given her, but that she would not take.

With Tituba's suggestion of nine names in the devil's book, the ministers and magistrates expanded the scope of their fears and investigation.   Tituba said lived in Boston and the rest of the nine were from "this Towne".   Based on Tituba's description of the band of witches, the elders of both Salem Village and Town began to look for old or contemporary cases of what might be witchery.

Sarah Osborne was also examined in gaol, but although she shook with fright, cold, and hunger, she again denied the allegations and offered no new information.

On March 5th, Tituba and Sarah Osborne were examined once again.   Among the new questions asked Tituba in her third formal examination (recorded by Ezekiel Cheever while Magistrate Hathorne asked the questions) was whether she had "hurt" Mr. Corwin's eight year old son George, who had become feverish and ill.   She replied she had been told to do it, but would not, though persecuted by the other witches.   She said Goody Good and Goody Osborne had hurt Mr. Corwin's child.

Also giving evidence in this March 5th examination were William Allen (whose wife was a Goodell) and John Hughes, both of whom told of hearing strange noises, seeing strange beasts, and being followed into their respective bedchambers by strange lights which were connected somehow with Sarah Good, Sarah Osborne and Tituba.   These events were said to have taken place on the nights of the March 1st and 2nd.   The men were apparently coming from Samuel Sibleys, having dined too well, as the saying goes.   Many imaginations in the Village had been aroused by these first examinations.   These men, like the three deputies guarding Sarah Good the first night, were much quicker to give supernatural explanations for strange things seen after dark than to talk about how much they'd had to drink.

William Good was again examined and when asked if his wife had any unusual marks on her body, he asked what the magistrate meant.   When Judge Hathorne spoke of a place where a devil might suck, Good Will stammered a bit, then said she had a little tit below her right shoulder which he never saw before.   His answer trailed off into smothered chuckles.   He asked Sarah Ingersoll if she didn't see it when she searched Martha, at which he went off in chuckles again.

Samuel Brabrook gave in his testimony of Sarah Good's attempts to kill herself by leaping off her horse on the way to Ipswich.   Anna Putnam was said to have "seen" these suicide attempts at her father's house in the Village and described them to those around her. Brabrook said Sarah Good told him she would not admit she was a witch unless she were proved one, and that she told him there was only one witness and that an Indian (Tituba), for which reason she was not afraid. He claimed she continued to rail against the magistrates between her efforts to injure herself.

In the first three examinations a site had been cleared for all that was to come. We had chosen our mountaintop, burned the brush, and laid the lines for the high altar of our sacrifices. We had gathered fuel for our rituals, stirred up the whirlwinds, and called down lightning. We had appointed priests and acolytes. The liturgy was composed with the responses and antiphonies established.

We had begun a foundation, and finding the great stone of ancient justice in our way, we had set respected men to pry it up — to make level our shrine in the wilderness. As we moved that stone, we started it rolling in a career that would dash through many lives. He who will not build on the corner stone will never find it serviceable for other purposes. He who moves the ancient boundary marker must ever stumble over it.

Though none admitted it then and few now, some in places of leverage who started the stone on its precipitous path were shaken by its first revolutions and immediately regretted having put their weights behind it. It was a big stone, a massive boulder. Its first few movements were ponderous and unsteady. Indeed, most expected it would soon teeter up on a projecting corner, and settle back at full halt. Even when it kept rolling beyond the first and second revolutions and through the third round of examinations, it was ponderous enough that we expected it would soon come to rest.

But the landscape and the weather were propitious for its journey. The storm grew, the wind blew, and the slope of the Village hill upon which it was uprooted seemed to grow steeper. It kept rolling. For the next few weeks, its roll was but slightly steadier than it had been — it still might have halted. All watched and waited, and only a few considered how either to block or clear a path for it.

There were more desultory examinations of those in gaol. There were formal inquiries for the purpose of clarifying the next steps the magistrates might take. But the ministers and magistrates asked few questions about the doctrine or morality of the legal proceedings thus far. Nor was there much doubt expressed about the guilt of those already accused. The agreed object of the further inquiries was to obtain clues toward finding the other witches, yet to be identified.

Any one of the magistrates or ministers might have slowed the stone by expressing uneasiness. Any one of them might have spoken his doubts about where the proceedings would lead, or the kind of evidence that was being encouraged. In the privacy of their own bedrooms, Mr. Corwin and others expressed such concerns to their wives. But no reservation was expressed when these wise men met together. Each was certain that, although he himself might feel insecure, the others were confident and ready to proceed to a sure conclusion. Most who felt reticent assumed it was some foible of their own that gave them pause.

"I don't know," that simple and humble expression comes least readily to men's lips. It is not ignorance that destroys human endeavors, but ignorance of ignorance, or ignorance of the importance of expressing ignorance, or plain unwillingness. Where a man serves God, he does not fear to say "here I lack knowledge, here is my incapacity, here is mystery," but when he lives chiefly in the fear of men, he must say, "I'm sure we can explain that," or "of course, I certainly agree."

Yet among men of lesser standing who saw the injustices and had courage to resist them, there were few with sufficient wisdom to do it effectively. It requires not only courage to resist unjust authority, but wisdom, and the fear of the Lord is the beginning of wisdom. There is a kind of terror in standing, and a further terror at acting, in defiance of those to whom one has always submitted. Even with the strongest of moral and theological convictions, and a commitment to obey God rather than men, it is against a good man's habits to oppose those he has long been taught to obey.

This repose is a natural one for us and there is a natural and opposite reflex, but they are both dangerous — with the danger of holding back from disagreement while evil becomes established — and the danger, often subsequent to that, of breaking out, loud and vehement, like a horse kicking over the traces. The effect of this second reflex may feel like a new freedom of conscience for the one breaking free, but it neither encourages the authorities to respect his perspective, nor encourages other good men to follow suit him.

Those who were quickest to react against our leaders broke forth loud and belligerent and so were quickly swallowed up. John Procter and Giles Corey were two of the most outspoken, and although the stone had not rolled upon them yet, it had run across the borders of their lands, and was to go right through both their houses. Both were ever pugilists, having been to law against one another on several occasions. When they saw which way the stone rolled, first Giles and then John stood up and tried to stop it by main strength. Both were crushed by it—one literally.

But a few less bold among us, so as to be less precipitate, joined a very few of the wise, and began during this time to marshal a resistance to the new leviathan, an opposition which was not angry, loud, or open.

Even as Tom Preston began to repent of his signature on the first complaints, Joseph Hutchinson called Daniel Andrew aside in the second week of March and gently sought his opinion of the witch trials. The ostensible purpose of the visit was a building project Mr. Hutchinson was considering.

"Well, Daniel. You are getting quite a reputation for yourself as carpenter and mason."

"Thank you, sir. Most of my custom seem happy, and with any that aren't, I try to make it up."

"You can't go far wrong that way. There's a good deal fewer of that mind than once there were. I saw you at the examinations. What a deal of noise and accusation that was."

"Yes, sir. I heard your name on some of the complaints, if I'm not mistaken."

"So you did, so you did. I'm not sure I'm happy about that now. To my knowledge another of the complainants is equally unhappy. Things seem a good deal muddled. And I wonder what we can do as we reconsider."

"Well, I suppose a criminal case is better muddled at the beginning than at the end—especially when there might be a noose at the end."

"Only for the guilty, I hope, Daniel. So I suppose the Indian woman will hang, but . . . well come out and I'll show you the barn. I want to put in a long shed on the north side to get more of my hay under cover."

They walked across the springy turf of the farmyard, past several small outbuildings. The barn stood tall and narrow, its door toward the house and its back to the woods.

"I saw little reason to think the other two guilty," Daniel volunteered, in a conversational tone, "It's a good solid barn. How old is it?"

"Thirty-five years this month. Did you hear nothing that made you suspicious?"

Daniel considered for a time, discovering in Mr. Hutchinson's tone that this matter was as importance to him as the barn extension. "No," he said, "In fact I would argue the contrary. Both of them came in so sure of their own innocence that they were quite unprepared to defend themselves. A guilty evil-doer would have done a better job. To be quite honest, I'm not sure Tituba testifies from a free conscience either."

"H-m-m. A deep matter. Didn't you think Goody Good's passing of the blame to Goody Osborne a low trick?"

"Alas, she has become a low creature. But neither of them would have been there but for Tituba accusing them. If Tituba is a witch, why was she believed? If she is, she seems to me disqualified as a witness. But I am not sure Sarah Good was so much accusing Goody Osborne as desperately suggesting Mr. Hathorne did not need to repeatedly ask her who afflicted the girls, since there were others to ask."

"Aye, there was a good deal of confusion in his dogged questioning. I cannot for the life of me see the point in reasoning with the defendant that she ought to admit she is afflicting the girls since they seem at that moment afflicted. Either she is guilty and won't admit it because she is in league with the devil, or she is innocent and will not give a false witness against herself."

"Ah, that's the rub, it seems to me. One thing's sure, somebody is bearing false witness."

"Yes. That's why I so thoroughly regret signing that complaint. That question should have been thrashed out before we went to law, for now that we are at law, the stakes are too high."

"I understand you. If—I suggest it for purposes of discussion—the girls are shamming, their witness is false in a capital case. Technically the penalty for such is death."

"Some of these at least are below the age of discretion and thus, I think, immune to that severest penalty. Yet, should I discover tomorrow that my child had lied in such a matter, I should feel like Jepthah—or worse, for there would be no semblance of a noble cause associated, and her a much less innocent sacrifice. I don't know if I would say so or not."

"You are more honest than most to admit the difficulty. Most men would boast they would certainly do it—as most certainly would not."

"Well this much is certain—I will never sign another of those complaints—not unless a witch comes down my chimney and personally belabors me with a burning faggot."

"I suppose we must needs pray for justice and consider what we may do now to seek it," mused Daniel, and he gazed absently toward the woods as he said it.

"You've been a representative at court — dost thou recall a man withdrawing his name from a complaint?"

"No, I don't. And I think it would do no good, since all his signature means is that he found the complaint credible at the time he signed it. So you did. However, a man may testify against his own complaint, if reason shows itself."

"I have not yet anything of matter to testify. Sad to say, however, I agree with you in finding nothing about those two homely ladies to support the charges.

"Now, as for this barn. I'm happy enough to have the shed open on the three sides, with but one new door cut through the barn in the middle. The door should be wagon wide. Make it fully the barn's length, and give a price in the next few weeks."

"I will do that, sir. It has been an education talking with you, as always."

"Aye — the young may learn something from the old — not to be such fools! Learn that, and the old may feel less useless, Daniel."

Daniel laughed. "No, quite the opposite. Those who teach the young humility are indispensable. The Lord knows how slowly we learn it in any case. The hoary head is usually well-earned."

"One other thought, Daniel. I have had a talk with Joseph Putnam . . . you and he might find profit in comparing opinions."

"We have often been of similar minds. Most of us felt he showed gumption in opposing his brothers with our new church council."

They parted, and Daniel walked back up the road.

All three prisoners were then in Salem gaol. As in English gaols, they were dependent on their families and friends for clothing, bedding, food, and medicine. Sarah Good and Sarah Osborne had poor families, and few friends, especially under the circumstance of their charges.

While Tituba was kept in Salem, the other two prisoners were soon transported to Boston, where under the gaoler, John Arnold, they were treated with even less compassion than the Dountons showed them in Salem. The Arnolds had to deal with a wide range of offenders, but they, like most of us, were especially wary of witches. For this reason, Goodman Arnold wasted no time when on

March 9ᵗʰ he received directions to place the prisoners in chains. Thus poorly clothed, under-fed, and far from their few family and friends, Sarah Good and Sarah Osborne were further punished by being shackled in cold iron.

The first three "witches" sat in prison through a dismal and very cold March, while the ministers and magistrates of Salem trained their perceptive eyes about them in search of six more suspects. They looked particularly for a short one, a tall one, and a tall, strong "man dressed in black" — a description often applied to ministers.

Ingersoll's Ordinary

Chapter Eleven — Hiatus — Vengeance Naps
(12 - 19 March)

Lying: Whereas truth in words as well as in actions is required of all men, especially of Chistians who are the professed Servants of the God to Truth; and wheras all lying is contrary to truth, and some sorts of lyes are not only sinfull (as all lyes are) but also pernicious to the Public-weal, and injurious to particular persons; it is therfore ordered by this Court and Authoritie therof,

That everie person of the age of discretion [which is accounted fourteen years] who shall wittingly and willingly make, or publish any Lye which may be pernicious to the publick weal, or tending to the damage or injurie of any particular person, or with intent to deceive and abuse the people with false news or reports: and the same duly proved in any Court or before any one Magistrate (who hath heerby power graunted to hear, and determin all offences against this Law) such person shall be fined for the first offence ten shillings, or if the partie be unable to pay the same then to be set in the stocks so long as the said Court or Magistrate shall appoint, in some open place, not exceeding two hours. . .

And for all such as being under age if discretion that shall offend in lying contrary to this Order their Parents or Masters shall give them due correction, and that in the presence of some Officer if any Magistrate shall so appoint. Provided also that no person shall be barred of his just Action of Slaunder, or otherwise by any proceeding upon this Order.
    -- Laws and Liberties of Massachusetts, 1648.

Although little Betty Parris had been present on March 1st, her parents became alarmed at her state during the examinations. Afterward they decided to send her away from the village to a safe haven where she might remain secluded. Mistress Parris preferred her Eldridge relatives in Boston, but the magistrates asked that she stay closer, since her testimony might be required in further examinations. Mr. Stephen Sewall of Salem Town offered his home. (He was to become secretary to the high court and his brother Samuel, one of the justices.) His wife had some acquaintance with Mistress Parris. Thus Betty was removed to Town, and was carefully kept from contact with her playmates and fellow "afflicted" during the rest of our troubles. The Parrises and Sewalls succeeded in convincing the magistrates that she was too young and deeply disturbed to be of use in the examinations and trials.

The seclusion of this original "afflicted" girl so early in our troubles would seem to indicate her guardians suspected other causes than the purported ones. Both the Parrises and the Stephen Sewalls must have believed the girls were at least partly responsible for each other's fits, although this was never admitted publicly. But Betty's removal obscured the origins of our troubles and facilitated their forward motion.

The other girls continued their game. Abigail Williams (remaining with the Parrises), and Anna Putnam, were intoxicated with their preeminence. Abigail at eleven years was the youngest remaining "afflicted evidence." Together with Betty Parris, she had established the early rules of the game, and now she was the foremost, though youngest.

Anna, next youngest, at twelve, had entered into it wholeheartedly. She was old enough to suspect the punishment her martial father would bring to bear should their "game" be exposed. Yet Sergeant Putnam and his wife Anne seemed quite as much in the game as their daughter. Their involvement drove her to greater dedication rather than slacken in her part. At first she could not afford to bring shame on herself and her parents by admitting her visions were fantasy. Then, as her parents became increasingly involved, she could much less afford to tell the truth and contradict them.

It is a curious fact that the best liars in the world are often those who have grown up under the greatest penalties for lying. Simply speaking, it appears greater penalties for failure give the best motives for success! But on a spiritual level, it is an example of how the law causes sin to abound.

A harsh parent is often gullible. (The more gullible leader is the one who thinks he has the greatest control. If he believes in his own competence, he will believe anything!) Once such a parent assents to the tale of Goody So-and-so's malevolent deeds, a further milestone is passed along the road of no return. For the harsh parent is also the most jealous of public opinion and the most susceptible to its blackmail. Once the matter became public, such parents sided with and reinforced their child's accusation. The only other choice was to admit their child was a serious sinner, and by implication, they terrible parents!

At each of these steps the risk was raised. The child risked a beating on persisting in her tale. The parent risked public humiliation in supporting the child's story. The next step was the community's involvement. What does the community put up in their gamble—what did the community risk when the people of Salem Village decided either to reject or to accept the accusations?

Elizabeth Hubbard (who lived with Dr. William Griggs, her uncle by marriage) was seventeen, a lonely girl, whose parents and other family had been killed by Indians near Andover. Nor was her loneliness much assuaged at Dr. Grigg's, two miles east of the Village, off the Ipswich Road near the Royalside Schoolhouse. She and her Aunt Rachel labored there at the tasks which kept many hands busy even in larger families. She counted few close friends her own age—Mary Warren, Mercy Lewis, and Mary Walcott were among them. As the great stone rolled down on us, Elizabeth Hubbard may have understood the enormity of events better than the younger girls, but she was no less of an enthusiast. Her uncle, called in for his medical opinion, was one of the first who diagnosed the fits of the Parris girls'as the results of "haggery." He, too, was thus committed and could hardly withhold his support when his wife's niece began to claim affliction by witchcraft.

At the beginning of the third week of March, Mercy Lewis, seventeen year old maid at Sergeant Thomas Putnam's and principle companion for Anna, joined in the drama, although only in small part, at first. Also in March, Anna's seventeen year old cousin, Mary Walcott, daughter of Jonathon Walcott, the Village militia captain and deacon in the church, joined the circle of the "afflicted".

Meanwhile other confabulations were taking place among the adult movers of the witch trials.

Sergeant Thomas Putnam spoke with his wife, Anne, whose sister, four years dead, had been the wife of Reverend James Bayley.

"You have no doubt about these three, then, Anne."

"Nay, Thomas. I felt the very evil in the air as the girls were being tormented in the meeting. Indeed I have felt it since. I dreamed last night of my sister Carr, who cried out that she had been bewitched to death. Think how the ministers of our church have been so much afflicted—every one of the first three to lose his wife and children, too. Reverend Burroughs lost two wives! My own sister mysteriously dead. The devil is loose among us, and these three are but his catspaws."

"And they are not the whole company. Tituba spoke at first of at least three more—two more women and a man. She said he was the master over the others -- tall and darkly clothed. She made him sound like some dignitary."

"Oh, Thomas! Who might it be?"

"I don't know, but these things begin to come to light. If it is a Village man, it would have to be either some gentleman or elder. Her description was too respectable-sounding for any other. It could hardly be Reverend Parris, for he has been the most eager to reveal the witches. Maybe one of the former men."

"But how that we are yet afflicted if it be a former man?"

"These witches and wizards can do much evil even at great distance. So the magistrates have read in books the ministers have provided them. They know a great deal about this business, and have said as much. They swear themselves ready to do a full job of it, though it take them five years to find all the miscreants."

"Since it could not be brother Bayley, that leaves Reverends Lawson and Burroughs among our former ministers. Can it be either of them?

"If I was put to it between them, I'd wager on Burroughs, for he was a thorn in uncle's flesh and no great friend to the Putnams. But neither was Lawson in the end. Yet I know nothing out of the way about either of them."

"Nor did we of these! Not until the girls were afflicted and Tituba spoke. Did you hear how the girls called out against Good and Osborne! Perhaps they will call out upon the others soon, if they are taken in fits again."

"Ah, but it is not just for two or three we look. When they examined her last in gaol, Tituba spoke of nine signatures in the devils book! Truly we have a tribe attacking us, and these far more subtle than Indians. They are in our midst and who knows how long they've been planning their evil!

"But now they seem to be working that plan against many of us. I was talking to cousin John – the weaver – on Monday, and he said he fears he and his child may have been bewitched."

"Oh, Thomas, does he know who does it?"

"He did not say, except that he thinks it may be someone connected with the Townes of Topsfield. You remember the bad blood stirred up between them and Uncle John over that land this side of the river. Well it seems John heard then that old Mother Joanna Towne was rumored to be a witch in England. Her family were called Blessing – but it seems she did the opposite.

"John mentioned it to some Village men a few weeks back,

and the very next day he came down very sick – and although he recovered, his baby has come down with an illness like his. They fear it may not live long."

"Why, which Towne kin does he suspect?"

"He wouldn't say, but only that there are some daughters hereabouts now become grandmothers. I intend to find out more. Perhaps Uncle John will know. If they are among those who afflict Anna or the Parris girls, no doubt they will be able to tell us."

"It is well we listen to the girls then, and inquire who it may be that hurts and threatens them. We must search them out. We cannot abide these witches among us."

Meanwhile Sergeant Thomas's half-brother Joseph Putnam and his wife, Elizabeth, had a different conversation, although on the same subject. Joseph, youngest son of the patriarch, Lieutenant Putnam, who died six years before, had married Israel Porter's daughter only two years before our troubles. Neither he nor his wife, were comfortable with what was going forward.

"It was incredible to hear! I'm glad you weren't there, dear."

"But so many have said it made them feel so sorry for the girls and angry with the witches."

"Do not call them witches, Elizabeth. Only one of the accused has confessed so, and she more anxious to please than uncle Nathaniel's Mary. (In fact the slave Mary was accused as a witch later, on evidence more insubstantial than most.) It is a good thing to feel compassion, but the compassion must conform to the facts, not vice versa. I heard all their answers to the questions and proofs offered, and wrote down most of what was said. I have reflected on it and I tell you the whole crowd did not bring forward one fact to be relied on."

"We both know our nieces Anna and Mary (Walcott) can be fantastic little creatures, but is the same true of the Parris girls, and the Doctor's maid?"

"Aye, all of them and who knows how many more. Are all girls not foolish things, my dear?"

"Oh, aye, they must be, else why would they ever marry men? But yes, I suppose a gaggle of girls is always as prone to alarums and fantasies as a gaggle of geese. Given the opportunity, children will often break out in headlong foolishness, particularly when their fathers are as intolerant of nonsense as Thomas, Jonathon and the minister. Is that all they do—these supposed afflicted ones—act foolish?"

"One cannot tell. It is the strangest business. At the examinations it is as if there had been an agreement among them all—the magistrates, ministers and girls—to act out this strange drama. First the magistrates ask some question, then the accused answer so and so, then the "afflicted" cry out such and such, then the magistrate refers to what the afflicted have just cried out, and so on. If it were not for the men of office giving constant affirmation I would call it but foolishness, but in the court of law, it becomes deadly serious and cannot be given so light a name."

"What then?"

"Why, it becomes false witness, at least if it is false, as I begin to think. It would otherwise be like any time a few children play fantastic games. One of them says, 'I am a bear,' and another says, 'and I am a wolf, oh you bit my arm off!'. Or it would be like other times when children are caught out in something they should not be doing—some one of them makes a flimsy excuse and the others chime in agreeing.

"But here they have been made the chief accusers of adults under criminal law, and the most respected adults believe and support their fantasies, so that the whole thing becomes more terribly serious than the children themselves can realize.

"The great horror is that the magistrates and ministers seem unable to realize the children are being childish—or perhaps I should say the girls and maids are being girlish."

"Do none of them see it? Not ministers Parris, Noyes, Hale or Higginson?"

"No, my brother and Reverend Parris are the strongest plaintiffs. Both the magistrates belong to Reverend Nicholas Noyes' church, but though he was there, I heard nothing cautionary from him. Reverend Higginson, too, seems convinced the girls are indeed bewitched. Reverend Hale mentioned like things he has seen in the past. I heard no voice express doubt about it except Goodwives Good and Osborne, but none gave their objections a moment's thought."

"What can you do?"

"I don't know, but it's certain I must do what I can."

In Salem other colloquies took place, among the principle men of that place. They gathered at Mr. Hathorne's or Reverend Nicholas Noyes' houses, usually with the latter convening. The magistrates Jonathon Corwin and John Hathorne were commonly in attendance, as was John Higginson, assistant pastor at Salem, son of the patriarchal teacher of the same name. In addition ministers, Samuel Cheever of Marblehead and John Hale from Beverly, frequently joined them. Through the first weeks of the examinations, Deodat Lawson, a former minister in the Village was also among us.

They met to discuss the "witch business" as the innkeepers came to list it in their ledgers. Reverend Noyes philosophical insights dominated the meetings with advisory contributions from Reverend Higginson and anecdotes from Reverend Hale. Many issues were discussed, but the main headings were spectre evidence, and other traditional proofs of witchcraft.

In March the weather produces two apparently opposite phenomena upon our landscape. The last fitful snows blow down upon us and accumulate in little drifts in the lea of trees, rocks and buildings. As soon as the snowfalls cease, the thinner snows begin to melt during the day and freeze at night, humping up the ground and disturbing rocks and roads in great heaves where the ground has soaked in the melt. During the day, as the first insubstantial warmth of weak sunlight touches the ground, the warmth of the earth rises to meet it and mists arise, sometimes obscuring the fields and farms so thoroughly that the world seems packed in wool.

During the early weeks of March in 1692, there were similar obscure gatherings and dispersings of persons and ideas. Elizabeth Hubbard went to see her friend Mary Warren in company with Mercy Lewis and Mary Walcott. They found the household March-moody, not only under the weather, but in that uneasiness common to innkeepers in early spring when travelers are few and woodpiles shrunk to nothing. Mistress Procter asked Elizabeth about the Parris girls and her Uncle Grigg's diagnosis. The conversation lagged after a few exchanges and John Procter came in surly about lack of business and the presence of the young visitors who kept Mary from more productive tasks.

On the way home, Elizabeth and her companions saw a strange shadow like a wolf that seemed to crouch beneath a tree and then disappear, then follow them in the foggy and shadowy woods. The damp and frozen darkness echoed their whispers and magnified their forebodings. Many others traveling or working in the echo-less snow or mists saw and heard strange things and felt thrills of the uncanny. Clouded minds were confused with shadowy events and unexplained things accumulated in drifts in the lea of obscure memories.

When Tituba was examined in gaol a few days later,

Reverend Noyes asked her, "Who was it that appeared like a wolf to Elizabeth Hubbard as she was going from Procter's?"

Tituba answered, "It was Sarah Good. I see she set the wolf on her."

Mary Walcott visited several times with her younger cousin Anna, and the two of them discussed the recent examinations. They retailed the game back and forth between them so that what formerly were more momentary and imaginary ideas moved further into the realm of memory for both. They shuddered and thrilled together and repeated the new rumors that there were many witches in their small community. They could not help but speculate about who they might be.

After Lecture, the girls talked with other friends in an effervescent huddle. Some of the others recollected strange deaths and accusations which the "afflicted" had not heard. The mysterious "wizard" who was said to be the head of the coven was mentioned and Tituba's description enlarged upon and adorned by small touches of speculation and deduction. A mist of ideas and fears grew into a common density like the woolly fog.

Not just the girls, but many in the Village speculated on these questions, and remembered old mysteries, painful and unexplained events, sicknesses, deaths and disasters, some minor, some made ominous by the possibility they were the result of witchcraft. Few gatherings were without mention of the subject. There was much to discuss and late winter leisure to discuss it. More than a few persons took to wearing a red thread about the neck – an old charm against witchcraft, and men began to prefer "rowan" or mountain ash walking staves -- another such.

Arising like the mists, without clear source or destination, two more names began to be mooted about. The first persons known to voice them were members of the Sergeant Putnam's household. These names were Martha Corey and Rebecca Nurse.

Martha Corey first came to Sergeant Putnam's attention when he heard mention of her husband's joke about her unwillingness for him to help prosecute witches.

Rebecca Nurse came to the Putnam's notice a little later, when Goody Holten, who lived in the Village, paid Anne, Sr., a visit, purportedly to bring her some eggs.

"Lord knows, the hens don't like this weather any more than the rest of us. They are laying as poorly as I remember. But we have less need of eggs now than we once did. Benjamin used to love his eggs."

"I'm sure you miss much more than his appetite, Sarah. And they look like good eggs."

"Oh, yes. And how are your girls? I have been much in prayer for them since I heard of their fits."

"As well as can be expected, I suppose. We are all of us much upset with the news of witches."

"Yes. It is a terrible thing to think of. And yet, I have wondered . . ."

"You mean you have thought it might be so before this?"

"No, only that I've wondered. Tell me, is it true that Indian woman of the minister's said one of the witches was thin and pale?"

"Yes, that's what Thomas told me. And they say there is a man, too — a respectable looking man who dresses all in black."

"Have any other names been spoken? I mean of Village folks?"

"Well, yes, there have been names brought up, but no one charged. You know they are saying now there may be six more beside the three in gaol."

"And has anyone said anything about. . . about Goody Nurse?"

"One of the daughters, you mean?"

"No, the mother. I mean she is thin and pale and. . ."

"Have you had reason to wonder?"

"Yes, you see, when Benjamin died so sudden and awful like, it was just after she had come over and spoken very hot to us about our hog that got into her garden. It seemed to me she was almost beside herself. And she said she would have her son shoot the hog. Poor Benjamin rushed out and brought it back. But he took sick right after and failed very fast. It wasn't natural. And I wondered.

"But I would not like to say it to the judges or anyone. I was only asking to see if anyone else had said so. Some are saying all these illnesses and awful deaths might be the work of witches and naturally I thought of Benjamin."

"Do you know what family Goody Nurse came from, Sarah?"

"Why, yes, she is sister to Goodman Towne up in Topsfield."

Thus was Anne Putnam able to descry another name through the mist. Here was someone to ask the girls about when the opportunity arose.

Nor did these names remain mere mist for long. Just as the girls lent substance to each others fantasies, so the various ministers and community leaders bustled about and lent substance to any rumor that entered their ears.

On March 12th, at the advice of Reverend Parris, Ezekiel Cheever, zealous brother of the Marblehead minister, together with Deacon Edward Putnam, both of our Village, decided it was their duty to take one of the rumors seriously. Anna Putnam had mentioned Martha Corey. Deacon Edward and Mr. Ezekiel Cheever wasted little time before setting out to question that woman. They claimed they pursued this ministry in order to defend her, since she was in covenant with them as a member of the Village church, but their testimony in court seems to belie that intention.

Back in 1656, Mistress Ann Hibbins was one of the first "witches" hanged in Massachusetts. One of the main "proofs" of her witchcraft was that she knew too much. She had confronted two of her neighbors who had been whispering about her, and the fact that she knew of their words and intentions was taken to prove she was a witch. A similar pattern emerged with Martha Corey.

Deacon Putnam and Mr. Cheever first went to inquire of Anna Putnam about the spectre's clothes, after which they immediately went down to the Corey's. The two investigators were practically speechless when Mistress Corey all but confronted them at the door with words to the effect of "I know why you are here." When she went on to ask if the girl mentioned what she had been wearing, they were very much taken aback. To coin the old phrase, she had been too clever by half, and to coin a new, they became too clever by the other half. She was soon to find herself in the same situation as Mistress Hibbins.

But at least these churchmen had followed through on the letter of the scriptures — the Matthew 18 passage which tells how we should proceed when we think our brother has sinned.

Mistress Corey also knew the scriptures, as a "Bible woman," and being told that Anna Putnam had somewhat against her, she determined to pursue a reconciliation in keeping with a related passage from the Sermon on the Mount (Matthew 5:23-24):

> Therefore if thou bring thy gift to the altar, and there rememberest that thy brother hath aught against thee; Leave there thy gift before the altar, and go thy way; first be reconciled to thy brother, and then come and offer thy gift.

The next day after church, Mistress Corey went to pay a visit to the Sergeant Putnam house where she stood accused. There she spoke with Anna and Mercy Lewis, under the oversight of Deacon Putnam. But Anna not only fell into violent fits, claiming Mistress Corey was tormenting her then and there, but she described various other strange witcheries—a man being turned on a spit over the fire, various familiar creatures, and so on. Further, Mercy Lewis, who hitherto had tended Anna in her fits, began to be "afflicted" as well, and in the latter half of the evening, had fits and cried out in tandem with Anna.

Edward Putnam asked Mistress Corey to leave when the fits became severe, which she did with little demurrer. But this effort to seek biblical resolution and reconciliation resulted in more damage to her reputation and the accumulation of more ammunition for her examination and trial.

That week, Sam Nurse and John Tarbell, much indignant at reports their mother had been mentioned, yet completely unaware how great the indignities to come, rode two miles northwest of town to Sergeant Putnam's, where they confronted Anne, Sr., and young Mercy Lewis. Mistress Putnam was not happy to see them, especially since her husband and daughter were at Walcott's in town. This disappointed John and Sam at first for they wanted to talk to Anna, but it turned out to suit their purposes.

They were not invited in, but talked at some length at the hitching post before the door.

John discussed the relative health of the Nurse and Putnam families, the weather and farming before coming around to the matter they came to discuss.

"We're sorry to miss Anna," John said, "for it is said she mentioned our mother in her fits."

"Indeed, I think she did so once. Although she has spoken much of others," answered Mistress Putnam. She seemed nervous and spoke warily about it. This made John bolder.

"And when did she first speak of Mother Nurse?"

"'Twas in her fits."

"And did she speak of Mother Nurse before others mentioned her?"

"Why, yes," Mistress Putnam said, but she looked nervously at Mercy Lewis, who had come out with her, and stood stiffly on the doorstep.

"She told us she saw the apparition of a pale, fast woman that sat in her grandmother's seat but did not know her name."

"But who was it that told her it was our mother?" There was a pause as Mistress Putnam again turned to look at Mercy, in response to which Mercy spoke first.

"It was you, Mistress Putnam!" Mercy answered.

"Why, no, Mercy, it was you!" replied Mistress Putnam, "Don't you remember?"

"No, ma'am, it was you." Mercy came back.

"No, dear, it most certainly was you!" said Mistress Putnam. There was iron in her voice this time and Mercy made no more reply, but it was clear to the men how the matter stood, and they could hardly help smiling.

"Has anybody else been afflicted here?" John asked, for they had been trying to make a list of the afflicted.

"No, just Anna," answered Mistress Putnam, grateful for a different subject, and not at that moment willing to give Mercy the status of being "afflicted," "but the two girls at Parris's have had awful fits, and Doctor Grigg's maid, Elizabeth Hubbard, is said to have been threatened."

"Well," John concluded, "We would be much obliged if you would make no more suggestions about Mother Nurse. If we hear any more of it, we will report this conversation to the magistrates. One of you put mother's name in Anna's mouth, and there is trouble enough without giving people ideas."

Sam and John rode away chuckling at how the two women had put each other on the griddle. They felt a great relief, for how could any testimony from such witnesses be taken seriously. Hadn't they both seen and shown that the mention of their mother was but a guess at a supposed phantom suggested to a silly girl? They were confident this would be the last they heard of it. Their sense of relief was to be but brief.

Chapter Twelve – Warning

*Blessed are ye, when men shall revile you, and persecute you,
and shall say all manner of evil against you falsely, for my
sake. Rejoice and be exceedingly glad: for great is your
reward in heaven: for so persecuted they the prophets which
were before you.*   -- **Matthew 5:11-12**

Oِne morning a week later Francis Nurse awoke to the
sound of his wife closing their front door.

"My old dear, have you been out in the cold!" he said.

"So say my bones, Francis, but if we are to keep this cruel
winter out of the house, I must fetch fuel."

"Oh, my old saint. Didn't Benjamin fill the woodbox?"

"No, Francis, he is gone to John's to help with a calf, and I
think to get breakfast there, too."

"We are too old for winter, Rebekah. Winter grows stronger
the older it gets, while we grow weaker and prone to freezing. And
you have been ill."

"I thought as I came along the path from the shed that winter
wind it is so unrelenting. It is like God's pursuit of one unrepentant
or perhaps like the torment of hell—without relief."

"Aye, I guess there are nearly one and the same—for the
unrepentant."

"And yet, the wind is more like God's judgment of the two,
for though it slay me, yet behind it is his presence — whereas in hell .
. ."

"Yet here we huddle before the fire, which is a chief symbol
of that eternal place."

"Yes, so often the hidden things put the seen things at
seeming contraries. The porridge boils. Would you have it now? I
have new butter from Mary and John. "

"New butter! How came it?"

"Two of their cows are milking strong. Benjamin brought it
home last night. He also brought further news of those afflicted girls.
Oh, Francis, it is worse than winter wind, these young ones plagued
by evil like this. And that heaped upon the sufferings of sickness
and death for so many this winter."

"It is a plaguey time. Aye, little has gone right for the colony or for Salem Village since we went on Phip's Quebec campaign."

"But Tom says it is more than illness. He says the girls are naming some among us as the authors of their afflictions — as witches to put a plain and ugly name upon it."

"Witches -- among us? Who have they named?"

"Mary says Sarah Ingersoll told her they have accused the Indian woman of Parris's, and Sarah Good and Sarah Osborne."

"Tituba, they call her. The minister is harsh upon her, so they say. Yet it might be she still holds secretly to heathen ways. The scriptures do say the gods of the heathen are demons."

"But not Sarah Osborne, or even Sarah Good, though she has a tongue in her head that could start more than a small fire, as James saith."

"From what they say, William is a hard come-down from the way of life she once knew. I have grown to like him, but he is a poor excuse for man, though it sound uncharitable to say it. Whether she be partly the cause of his spinelessness or whether it causes her outbursts, I cannot tell. "

"But anger and outbursts are not in themselves deviltry, Francis!"

"I should say not, woman. Thou and I have been known for such.

"Oh, be no second witness to what my own heart testifies! When I think Benjamin Holten died not two months after my winter words blew on his bald head, I am deeply ashamed."

"Now, now! It's gone and past. Your anger is most always the biblical kind — quick, godly, and over before sundown. "

"Yet Sarah would not forgive me when I asked it after the burial. It is my sin that pains me more than winter winds. I long the more to be home, these days. Do you, Francis?"

"No, no more than always, but I have not your infirmity to better remind me where home is."

"Nor have you my quickness to anger."

"Come now, we both can remember a outburst or two I regret. But my father more often said I had the contrary fault — in fact a few times he chastised me in the same terms I used of William — spineless and unmanly. I do not see it of myself. I have flared up more often than I like, especially after we first got this place. And even when I am meeker, it seems to me I am being but careful. Yet I would not make as bold a general as Governor Phips, and my boys have maybe wished for a more forthright father."

"**Y**et you have been a good one. They know what a Father's love is, while many among us know only a Father's discipline."

"Hark, now, are there not voices outside beside the wind? And there, someone's at the latch? Come in! Come in!"

"Why it's Israel and Elizabeth Porter! And brother Peter with Daniel Andrews. What, are you out in this cold!"

The visitors laughed and stamping their feet greeted Rebecca and Francis with that joviality peculiar to the middle-aged in speech with the elderly.

"This winter we have no choice. We must be out in the cold, or else sit as starved skeletons around a cold hearth at home."

"**N**ay, Israel," said his wife," do not speak of skeletons and death in these times. But he is right, Rebecca, as to this winter, it has no mercy on any of us."

"Those were almost the very words I spoke to Francis just now. It has been a cruel winter and unforgiving."

"**A**nd how are you, Rebecca. It is chiefly to ask your health we come."

"**I** rejoice in Christ, Elizabeth. But I continue in some bodily affliction. It is now almost a week that I have had a colicky stomach and have not gone out, but for wood and water."

"**A**nd how the health of thy soul?"

"**I** bless God, Israel, for I have felt more of his presence in this sickness than I have sometimes had in health, yet I desire more. I seem to understand better these days what the Apostle says—caught between the desire to be with Christ and to continue in this world. There is much that draws me heavenward, but many for whom I would remain here.

"**M**y Benjamin told us those poor girls continue in their affliction. Have you heard they are saying some among us are the source of their plagues? How hard it must be for Minister Parris, that his own daughter be under attack."

"**I**t is so. Some say his servant Tituba did cause it by spells and other acts of witchcraft. I heard she had confessed as much."

"**D**espite illness and age I would have visited the Parrises, except that among my infirmities, as you know, I have betimes been subject to fits myself. And as they say it is quite awful to behold, I feared that I might bring no comfort but become another such spectacle myself."

"**N**o one expects it. You are better to stay at home and gain back your own health."

"I have been praying much for them—for Betty, for the Parisses, for the Putnam girl, and for this Tituba, also, that all would be revealed. But Benjamin says they accuse others also—that some whom I would say to be as innocent as I myself are called witches. It is hard to hear."

"So it is. But the devil was always a deceiver. Scripture says he often comes disguised as an angel of light."

"It is so. And that were it possible, he would deceive even the elect. Yet of those we have heard named, one certainly is no less godly than most among us, and the other but one of the poor whom we have with us always. That she is angry and speaks often in outbursts may indeed be sin, but it is hard to imagine her in league with the devil."

"However, her uncle who raised her did make off with himself. And her first husband died early—and the second—well, he is as lackadaisical as one can imagine."

"Elizabeth, Sarah Good was but a child when her uncle murdered himself—as young as these that are now afflicted. And if we are to suspect those whose husbands died young, we must suspect a thousand widows left from King Philips's War and the Quebec Expedition! Surely the works of a witch would be more plain than that."

"Yet they say Baxter's and Mather's books describe wonders none would have guessed."

"And also things we should continue to doubt," added Francis, who had been devoting himself to finishing his buttery porridge.

"In truth, some are named who cannot be under his power," said Elizabeth, and then, both hesitant and deeply attentive, "Martha Corey's name has been mentioned - and, though none believes it, even yours, Rebecca."

Francis sat up abruptly and his pewter spoon clattered on the maple table. Rebecca raised her eyes and looked at Elizabeth's face.

"If it be so, then the Lord's will be done," she said slowly. She sat awhile as in a fugue. None spoke, until Rebecca, summoning her strength, "As to these things, I am as innocent as a child unborn." After which she returned to an bewildered study.

Then, again, as though alone in her meditations she asked, "What sin is there which God hath found in me unrepented of that he should lay such further affliction upon me in my old age?"

Francis answered with a hint of the anger he had just mentioned, "There is no such sin, my old saint. The accusations are but those of the evil one come to stir up and confuse us! The devil's chief work is as accuser of the brethren—a work we should oppose!"

The Porters shifted the conversation to easier ground. They exchanged a few commonplaces and then made as if to depart.

Rebecca stirred herself and spoke to Peter Cloyce, "How does sister Sarah, my brother?"

"Well enough, Rebecca. She is feisty as always and sent me down a purpose to make sure you heard of this foolishness. She sends her love and this jar of preserves."

"Thank you, Peter. Ah, wild cherries! She spoils me.

"And you, too, Mr. Andrews. Thank you for coming out in the frost to us."

Daniel bowed and replied, "It is always a privilege to call upon the godliest woman in the Village, Mistress Nurse."

"Nay, I am no mistress, but only an old 'goodwife' by courtesy. My greetings to your wife, who is indeed a good one."

Mistress Porter spoke at the door, "It will come to little, Rebecca. You are too well known and too well-loved for any to listen to this gossip."

As their feet crunched back along the beaten footpath she spoke again, "Surely you are right, Daniel. If ever there was a saintly woman among us, it is she."

"She is indeed, "answered Daniel, "but elsewhere not even the saintly have been immune from such accusations."

"Yet the accusation of one so godly would never be received in a court of law!" protested Goodman Cloyce.

And as the faintest kiss of sun's warmth touched their chapped cheeks, Mr. Porter replied, "If ever one was surprised to hear such untoward news, it was she. I much regret being bearer of it."

As Thomasin, Benjamin Nurse's wife descended the narrow stairs carrying the newly fed and cheerful Thomasina to the warmth of the fire, she found her old mother-in-law speaking what sounded riddles.

"Francis, I'm all at sea! Surely this is God's discipline of me on account of Goodman Holten."

"No, dear. God's discipline does not come against particular deeds, but out of his directing love. Job was the most righteous, but his hardships remained a mystery until his dying day. Yet he was in the end more righteous. Indeed he saw and heard God. Perhaps you are meant to pray for the whole benighted Village, as he for his misguided advisers.

"But as for this witch talk—it is very evil, and such evil can only come from the evil one himself. Good morning, Thomasin. We have had disturbing news about these afflicted girls in the Village."

"But where do they get it?" Rebecca mused, as she reached out for the baby, "Does the devil have the liberty to whisper such things in children's ears? Not even Job had to contend with that kind of accusation, although many false ones were made to his face."

"They have all read Mather's book and he Baxter's, and he, who knows what popish monk's book before that. It is but another form of rumor, borne down the ages. Baxter and Mather are godly men, at least Mather's father is, but some fleshly flea has bitten them with this old wives tale. No—I should not blame old wives, for I would not trade my old wife for anything. And I would sooner believe a tale from her than from a thousand afflicted girls."

Chapter Thirteen - Respect No Object
(19-21 Mar)

Whence cometh it that pride, and luxury,
Debate, deceit, contention, and strife,
False-dealing, covetousness, hypocrisy,
(With such like crimes) amongst them are so rife,
That one of them doth over-reach another?
And that an honest man can hardly trust his brother.
-- Michael Wigglesworth, ***God's***
Controversy with New England (1662).

The aspiring wrestler or marksman at first competes with lowly opponents. But if he do well over the course of time, he seeks stronger competitors against whom to try his strength and skill. In the same way the "afflicted" accused the least influential and powerful early in our troubles, but afterwards more respected persons. After the first three accusations, the next "witch" named was of more stature.

Mistress Martha (Penoyer) Corey was the third wife of Giles Corey. Although we knew little about her before she married Giles, it was generally recognized that her partner in this last marriage was beneath her own class and education. She was the widow of Henry Rich, though it was said she had a child out of wedlock in her youth before she married him. Perhaps partly due to this smudge on her record and partly due to her gentility, she was not quickly accepted by her neighbors, yet she was gracious in her carriage toward them. Furthermore, when she transferred to the Village church, we learned she was a "Bible woman," who visited the sick and shut-in to read scripture and bring food and alms. Never did a woman have a more hard-headed husband, but she opposed his forcible personality by careful wisdom and small charities. She became the next victim of our troubles, perhaps due to resentments toward her or grudges against her husband.

There seemed an increase of caution on the part of the authorities, and there was therefore a last pause before this further plunge into accelerating perfidy. We have spoken of the three weeks during which no new accusations were taken to law, as many deliberated about what should be done next, while some took the cautious but progressive steps by which Mistress Corey was first named and "tested".

On March 19th, a complaint was issued against Martha Corey, wife of Giles, in the names of Deacon Edward Putnam and Henry Kenney, whose farms were in the same neighborhood as those of Sergeant Putnam and Ezekiel Cheever. (Kenney subsequently gave testimony against Rebecca Nurse and her sister.) The arrest warrant stipulated Mistress Corey was to be brought to Lieutenant Ingersoll's on Monday the twenty-first about noon.

On Lord's Day, Mistress Corey shocked the congregation by coming to worship in the Village very much as usual. That evening she made the visit to Anna Putnam that made matters worse for her.

On Monday, March 21st, Constable Joseph Herrick arrested and delivered her as required. The examination was held at the Meeting House much in the same manner as the previous three. However, due variuosly to the rapidly spreading reports of the first three examinations, the higher standing of Mistress Corey, and the two day interim between complaint and examination, a much larger crowd gathered, filling the Meeting House.

Reverend Nicholas Noyes of Salem prayed at the opening of the court. But when Martha Corey was brought in, she asked if she herself might pray before she was examined. The magistrates and ministers were indignant that a woman should want to engage in public prayer with church leaders present, much less in these circumstances and before so large a crowd. She was told she could not pray — since neither they nor she were there for that purpose.

"You are now in the hands of authority," said Mr. Hathorne, and he began the examination, " Tell me now why you hurt these persons?"

Drawing her dignity about her, she answered, "I do not."

"Who doth?" he asked.

"I must needs pray if I am to answer such questions. Pray give me leave." she asked again.

"We did not send for you to go to prayer," replied Mr. Hathorne with considerable asperity, " But tell me why you hurt these?"

"I am an innocent person. I never had to do with witchcraft since the day I was born. I am a gospel woman."

(Anne Hutchinson was fresh in the memory of the Massachusett's leaders. Her independence had been thoroughly despised by them, and because she too was a "gospel woman," that term had come to carry a certain ambivalence in their minds.)

The "afflicted" had been uneasy and moaned when first she was brought in, but the large crowd seemed to subdue the girls. However when Martha Corey said she was a gospel woman, Mistress Putnam raised the volume as she cried out, "She is a gospel witch!" and the girls followed with various outcries.

Of the four "afflicted" girls in the earlier examinations, only Betty Parris was missing. But the new voices of two older girls joined the official clamor: Mercy Lewis of the Thomas Putnam household, and Mary Walcott, daughter of the captain of the Village militia. In addition four married women cried out against Mistress Corey: Anne Putnam (Anna's mother); Mistress Pope; Goodwife Bibber from Wenham; and Mistress Goodell, the old mother of the distracted Jacob, who had died under the harsh treatment of Martha Corey's husband, Giles.

"Do you not see these complain of you?" asked Mr. Hathorne.

"The Lord open the eyes of the magistrates and ministers. The Lord show his power to discover the guilty."

"Tell us who hurts these children."

"I do not know," she answered with dignity, "how should I know?"

"If you be guilty of this fact, do you think you can hide it?"

"The Lord knows . . ." she began, but Mr. Hathorne interrupted her

"Well, tell us what you know of this matter."

"Why? I am a gospel woman. Do you think I can be a gospel woman and have to do with witchcraft, too?"

At that point, Mr. Hathorne leaped to another subject—the visit which Mr. Ezekiel Cheever and Deacon Edward Putnam had paid Mistress Corey a week earlier (on March 12th) with a view to seeking evidence regarding the accusations by Anna Putnam.

"How could you tell, then, that the child was bid to observe what clothes you wore when some came to speak with you?" he asked.

Before she could answer a word, Mr. Cheever interrupted her and said, "Do not begin with a lie!"

Nor could she answer before the magistrates conferred a moment and decided the report of the visit ought to be given before the questions were pursued. Deacon Putnam read part of an account of the visit he and Mr. Cheever paid Mistress Corey on March 12th:

We found the abovesaid Corey all alone in her house and as soone as we came in, in a smiling manner she sayeth, "I know what you are come for. You are come to talk with me about being a witch, but I am none. I cannot help peoples talking of me."

Edward Putnam answered her that it was the afflicted person that did complain of her that was the occasion of our coming to her.

She presently replied, "but does she tell you what clothes I have on?" We made her no answer to this at her first asking, whereupon she asked us again with very great eagerness, "but does she tell you what clothes I have on?" Which questions with that eagerness of mind with which she did ask made us think of what Anna Putnam had told us before we went to her.

To which we told her no she did not for she told us that you came and blinded her and told her that she should see you no more before it was night that so she might not tell us what clothes you had on. She made but little answer to this, but seemed to smile at it as if she had showed us a pretty trick.

Mr. Hathorne addressed Martha Corey again. "Who told you that?"

She seemed confused by what the two men had said, and her answer was hesitant. "He said the child said. . ."

"You speak falsely!" interrupted Mr. Cheever, again.

Deacon Putnam began to read more of the deposition.

We had a great deal of talk with her about the complaint that was of her and how greatly the name of God and religion and the church was dishonored by this means, but she seemed to be no way concerned for anything about it but only to stop the mouths of people that they might not say thus of her.

She told us that she did not think that Sarah Good and Sarah Osborne were rightly accused. But she said if they were, we could not blame the devil for making witches of them for they were idle slothful persons and minded nothing that was good, but we had no reason to think so of her for she had made a profession of Christ and rejoiced to go and hear the word of God and the like. But we told her that it was not her making an outward profession that would clear her from being a witch for it had often been so in the world that witches had crept into the churches.

Much more discourse we had with her but she made her profession a cloak to cover all. She further told us that the devill was come down amongst us in a great rage and that God had forsaken the earth and after much discourse with her, being too much here to be related we returned to the house of the abovesaid Thomas Putnam and we found that she had done as she said she would for she came not to hurt the abovesaid Anna Putnam. They told us all this at the time but after we were gone we understand that she came again as she did used to do before, greatly afflicting her.

"Why did you ask if the child told what clothes you wore? asked Mr. Hathorne.

"My husband told me the others told him," she said, but did not seem at all confident about it.

"Who told you about the clothes!" demanded Hathorne, "Why did you ask that question!"

"Because I heard the children told what clothes the other wore," she answered, but Magistrate Hathorne seemed to have scented blood. He turned to Goodman Giles Corey, who sat in the third row behind the girls.

"Goodman Corey, did you tell her?" he asked.

Eighty year old Corey, sat up and became alert at the question directed to him. He answered, "No!" his voice gruff as always. But his answer was more belligerent than responsive. Some of us were doubtful he had fully understood the question put to him. In fact his wife was referring to his accounts of earlier examinations, in which descriptions of the clothing worn by apparitions were often asked for and given.

"Did you not say your husband told you so?" Mr. Hathorne went on, confronting the defendant. At that juncture she seemed to lose her poise and her face grew paler, while she struggled with what to answer. She said nothing.

"Who hurts these children now?" asked Mr. Hathorne after the pregnant silence, during which their moans were quite distinct. "Look upon them!"

The girls had been whimpering, but they responded to the question by growing louder and writhing about on the bench.

"I cannot help it," Mistress Corey answered, and there was a new note of frailty in her voice.

"Did you not say you would tell the truth why you asked that question. How came you to the knowledge. . .?"

Mistress Corey interrupted Mr. Hathorne, "I did but ask."

Magistrate Hathorne responded with high indignation, "You dare thus lie before all this assembly. You are now before authority. I expect the truth. You promised it. Speak now and tell what clothes . . . who told you what clothes?"

"Nobody," she answered.

With a sharp edge of anger in his voice Magistrate Hathorne reiterated, "How came you to know that the children would be examined what clothes you wore?"

His words came out forcefully, though little less awkwardly than they had in the previous questions, but she too, was upset, and her answer was also awkward and impulsive, "Because I thought the child was wiser than anybody if she knew."

"Give an answer! You said your husband told you."

"He told me the children said I afflicted them."

"How do you know what they came for! Answer me truly."

She was bewildered by the anger and the constant return to this minor point which somehow told against her. Again she answered nothing.

But Hathorne was relentless, perhaps in part due to the large audience. "Will you say how you came to know what they came for?"

She was weary, but she made another effort, "I had heard speech that the children said I appeared and troubled them and I thought that they might come to examine . . ."

"But how did you know it!"

"I thought they did."

"Did you not say you would tell the truth? Who told you what they came for?"

"Nobody."

"How did you know?"

"I did think so."

"But you said you knew so!" Mr. Hathorne declared in exasperation, and turned from where he stood, wiping his brow with his handkerchief, to confer in a low rumble with Mr. Corwin and the ministers.

He then turned back and asked Anna Putnam to testify. She said Goodwife Corey had afflicted her.

"When did Goodwife Corey hurt you?"

"One day when Lieutenant Fuller was at prayer at our house, I saw the shape of Goodwife Corey and another praying to the devil."

"Who was the other?"

"I thought it was Goodwife Nurse."

"Are you sure it was Goodwife Nurse you saw?"

"I am not sure, but I am very sure I saw the shape of Goodwife Corey."

Suddenly Anna Putnam called out, "There is a black man whispering in her ear!" The other girls began to shout out similar things and to perform in their "afflictions".

"What did he say to you!" Mr. Hathorne demanded of Mistress Corey.

"We must not believe all that these poor, distracted children say," she answered.

"Cannot you tell what that man whispered?" Mr. Hathorne went on.

"I saw nobody."

"But did you not hear?"

"No."

Suddenly all the girls and Mistress Putnam screeched and the girls rolled about, some on the benches, some on the floor. Those present said it was the most intense pandemonium seen or heard previous to Mother Nurse's trial. They cried out of the black man and of yellow birds, and of being hurt by Mistress Corey. Several other women in the large audience broke into tears and some into moanings. A few seemed to undergo afflictions of their own.

"If you expect to find mercy of God, you must look for it in God's way by confession," proclaimed Mr. Cheever, from his seat next to Reverend Parris.

"Do you think to find mercy by aggravating your sins?" agreed Reverend Noyes.

"A true thing," added Mr. Hathorne, "Look for it then in God's way."

"So I do," she answered.

"Give glory to God and confess, then," he said.

"But I cannot confess," she replied.

"Do not you see how these afflicted do charge you?" asked Mr. Hathorne—he was more calm and reasonable now.

"We must not believe distracted persons," she replied.

Mr. Noyes addressed her then. "It is the judgment of all that are present that these are bewitched and only you, the accused, say they are distracted."

"Who do you improve to hurt them?" Mr. Hathorne asked.

"I improved none," she replied.

"Did not you say our eyes were blinded. That you would open them?"

"Yes—to see they accuse the innocent."

Continuing his effort to justify the greater outrage with the jots and tittles loved by the barrister, Mr. Hathorne picked up a written deposition of Henry Crosly, the nearest neighbor to Corey's. He read an account of a conversation in which Martha Corey told Goodman Crosly that the magistrates were blind guides leading the blind, and said that, if she were arrested, she would do all she could to open their eyes. She also told Goodman Crosly that the girls could not stand before her (meaning that their false accusation could not stand up, but the court put a different interpretation on it.) One lesson many of us learned during our troubles was that language susceptible to more than one interpretation is dangerous in a court of law.

Henry Crosly was called to affirm that this was his testimony.

Mr. Hathorne addressed Mistress Corey. He did not look directly at her, but rather regarded a ray of light where it came through a small gap in the wood shakes above the beams.

"Why cannot the girls stand before you?"

"I do not know," she answered with some chagrin.

"What did you mean by that?"

Not realizing the question had to do with her conversation with Crosley she answered, "I saw them fall down."

"It seems to be an insulting speech, as if they could not stand before you."

"They cannot stand before others."

"But you said they cannot stand before you."

Before she could sort out this confusion of the literal and the metaphorical, Mr. Hathorne jumped to another line of attack. He asked questions based on Anna and Mercy's accounts of bewitchment at the time of her visit to the Putnam house the previous evening. She had heard the girls' accusations and descriptions of what they "saw" at the time. She could not therefore claim complete ignorance.

"Tell me what was that turning upon the spit by you."

"You believe the children that are distracted. I saw no spit. The scriptures say you cannot accuse but by the testimony of two or three witnesses."

The girls then began to cry out again. Anna Putnam and Mercy Lewis particularly, began to reiterate various of their previous accusations, claiming to see strange things appearing near her.

"Here are more than two that accuse you for witchcraft," concluded Mr. Hathorne as the volume died down, "What do you say?"

"I am innocent," she replied, but now she leaned heavily upon the bar.

Mr. Hathorne read further from the Crosly deposition.

"What did you mean by that—that the devil could not stand before you?"

"I did not say it."

"Henry Crosley!" called out Mr. Hathorne, and that gentleman stood up again.

"Did you hear Mistress Corey say as we have read?"

"Yes." said Henry Crosly, putting much nervous energy into the one syllable.

"Deliverance Crosly!" Mr. Hathorne called again. An extremely agitated woman stood and also affirmed the account.

Mr. Hathorne turned to Mistress Corey, whose shoulders slumped as she leaned heavily on the bar. Before he could ask again, however, she spoke.

"What can I do if many rise up against me?"

"Why, confess!" he answered.

"So I would if I were guilty," she replied.

"Here are sober persons. What do you say to them?" he countered, "You are a gospel woman! Will you lie?"

Suddenly Abigail Williams cried out, "Next Sabbath is sacrament day, but she shall not come there." (She voiced the general disapproval over the fact Mistress Corey had come to service the previous day, despite the complaint made against her.)

"I do not care what she says," mumbled Mistress Corey.

But Mr. Hathorne was relentless. "You charge these children with distraction. It is a note of distraction when persons vary in a minute, but these fix upon you. This is not the manner of distraction.

Mistress Corey who seemed to be mulling over some recent development, interrupted with a new desperation in her voice, "When all are against me what can I help it!"

"Now tell me the truth will you," Hathorne continued with hardly a pause, "Why did you say that the magistrates and ministers eyes are blinded and you would open them?"

Martha Corey laughed suddenly, and although it began as a polite and politic laugh, it ended with a ragged note almost of hysteria, for suddenly she realized what interpretation the court was putting on that casual statement, and the wheels within wheels of irony. "I did not," she choked out.

"Now tell us how we shall know who doth hurt these if you do not."

"Can an innocent person be guilty?" she retorted.

"Do you deny these words?" he countered.

"Yes," she said.

"Tell us who hurts these. We came together to be a terror to evil-doers. You say you would open our eyes — that we are blind."

"If you say I am a witch you are blind," she answered.

"You said you would show us."

"I did not."

"Why do you not now show us?"

"I cannot tell. I do not know."

Magistrate Hathorne leaped to another line of attack.

"What did you strike the maid at Mr. Thomas Putnam's with?"

"I never struck her in my life."

"Here are two that saw you strike her with an iron rod."

"I had no hand in it."

"Who had?"

"I know not."

"Do you believe these children are bewitched?"

"They may be for ought I know. I have no hand in it."

"You say you are no witch. Maybe you mean you never covenanted with the devil. Did you never deal with any familiar?"

"No, never."

"What bird was that the children spoke of?"

Anna Putnam cried, "There it sits upon her shoulder!"

"What bird was it?"

"I know no bird."

"It may be that you have engaged you will not confess, but

God knows."

"So He doth."

"Do you believe you shall go unpunished."

"I have nothing to do with witchcraft."

"Why were you not willing your husband should come to the former session here?"

"But he came for all that."

"Did you take the saddle off?"

"I did not know what it was for."

"Did you not know what it was for?"

"I did not know that it would be to any benefit in finding witches."

Henry Crosly cried out from the crowd, "She would not have us help in finding out witches!"

"Did you not say you would open our eyes? Why don't you do it?" Mr. Hathorne repeated.

"I never thought of a witch."

"Is it a laughing matter to see these afflicted persons?"

"No, it isn't."

"Goodman Crosly!" That neighbor stood again, and Mr. Hathorne asked him if Mistress Corey had not said these witch accusations made her laugh.

"She did, " said Henry Crosly.

Goodwife Crosly was called upon and answered the same.

Mistress Parker, another neighbor, was called and answered the same.

"Did you not say it was a laughing matter?" asked Mr. Hathorne again.

"Ye are all against me and I cannot help it." And for a moment her voice indeed broke.

"Do not you believe there are witches in the country?"

"I do not know that there is any," she replied through tears.

"Do not you know that Tituba confessed it?"

"I did not hear her speak."

"I find you will own nothing without several witnesses," retorted Mr. Hathorne, with some asperity, "and yet you will deny for all."

Mistress Pope broke out in moans and angry shrieks. "She afflicts my bowels even now, " she said, and to punctuate her accusation threw her muff at Mistress Corey. It fell harmless upon the floor, but Mistress Pope, not to be defeated, took off her shoe and rushing up, hit Mistress Corey on the head. The constable in attendance took her arm and gently led her back to her seat.

Weary and now literally brow-beaten, thus subjected to open public indignity, Mistress Corey bowed her head upon the back of the bench where she stood.

In a lull, Abigail Williams cried out, "She bites us as she bites her lips."

Mr. Hathorne immediately addressed Mistress Corey, "You bite your lip, do you not?"

"What harm is it?" she answered with some spirit, lifting her head and somewhat restored by her anger.

She shifted her feet, and the afflicted girls began to stamp noisily on the floor. They began to imitate her slightest gesture or expression as they continued to cry accusations of her hurting them. Abigail Williams cried out "Why do you not go to the company of witches which muster before the meeting? Did you not hear the drum beat?"

Mr. Noyes, who had said little, beside the notes he had occasionally passed along to Mr. Hathorne, now spoke up, addressing not so much the defendant as the other ministers and magistrates, "I believe it is apparent she practiseth witchcraft in the congregation. There is no need of images for her to practiseth upon. She useth her own members."

Mr. Hathorne turned to Mistress Corey again, "What do you say to all these things that are apparent to the wise?"

"If you will all go hang me, how can I help it," she answered — and this was the first time that chilly thought was put into official words during our troubles.

Mr. Noyes addressed her.

"Were you to serve the devil ten years?"

"No."

"Tell how many."

She laughed in a half-hysterical manner, at which the girls cried out again, "There! There, the yellow bird is with her, again."

Mr. Hathorne spoke up, even while the girls were still crying and wailing, "What is this yellow bird?"

"There it sucks betwixt her fingers!" cried Anna.

The Marshall and Mr. Hathorne went to her and spread her fingers to look for a sign, but Anna cried again, "It is too late, she removed a pin and put it on her head."

The Marshall looked and pulled a long pin from Mistress

Corey's hair.

The crowd sucked in its breath and a clamour of wonder broke out.

Mistress Corey laughed again. She seemed near to be losing control.

The girls cried out and said she pinched and hurt them.

"Why do not you tell how the devil comes in your shape and hurts these?" Mr. Hathorne entreated her, "You said you would!"

"How can I know how?" she answered in a voice grown weary.

"Why did you say you would show us?" he asked, in response to which she began to laugh again, holding her hand to her mouth and spluttering as she tried to control herself.

"What book is that which you would have these children write in?"

"What book? What should I have a book? I showed them none, nor have none nor brought none."

"The black man whispers in her ear!" cried Abigail Williams. And Mary Walcott repeating it added, "He carries the book to me now."

Mr. Hathorne, too, seemed to be growing tired, but he kept on, "What book did you carry to Mary Walcott?"

"I carried none."

Then driven into the corner, Mistress Corey made the statement, which by the dim lights of the ministers and magistrates, was fundamentally an admission of guilt.

"If the devil appears in my shape I cannot help it, " she said.

Another neighbor was ready to accuse her. Goodman Needham was called to testify and said that (John) Parker some time ago thought this woman was a witch. He said that at the time of the death of his son, George Needham, Goodman Parker had seen her making mysterious gestures at the head of his lane, not long after which Parker lost two children himself.

Mr. Noyes then asked her some questions about her faith. "Who is your God?"

"The God that made me," she answered.

"What is His name?"

"Jehovah," she replied.

"Do you know any other name?"

"God Almighty," she said.

"Doth he whom you pray to tell you that he is God

Almighty?"

"Who do I worship but the God that made me?"

"How many Gods are there?"

"One."

How many persons?"

"Three."

"Cannot you say, 'so there is one God in three blessed persons?' "

Mistress Corey was confused by this leap from courtroom questioning to catechizing — as if a particular form would be the "right" answer where her conduct was under examination. She came almost to tears again, and was silent.

But the afflicted, notably Mistress Pope and Mistress Putnam, took the occasion for further outbursts.

Mr. Hathorne changed subjects.

"Do you not see these children and women are as rational and sober as their neighbors. Yet when your hands are clenched, immediately they are seized with fits as the standers-by can see."

"I am but squeezing my fingers," she said, her voice dull and weary. However, Constable Herrick and Marshall Herrick came forward and opened her hands. They held them firmly, further humiliating Mistress Corey. The marshall began to watch her closely. After a minute he said "She bit her lip!" at which the girls and women cried out.

Mr. Hathorne repeated the old litany, "Do you hurt these?"

"No."

"Then who doth hurt them?"

"I know it not. I have no hand in it."

Mr. Cheever had passed a note down the judges table, and Mr. Hathorne read the question — the last question of that examination.

"Why did you say if you were a witch you should have no pardon?"

"Because I am a gospel woman," she answered, "and you cannot prove me a witch."

The examination was brought to a close. Marshall Herrick and Constable Herrick led her from the meeting house. She walked stiffly, but they kept hold of her two hands that she might not further bewitch.

As soon as she left, the last fits of the afflicted came to an end. After some consultation during which the audience was dismissed, the magistrates issued a mittimus to have Martha Corey committed to the Salem Gaol. Given into evidence were the depositions from Parker and Needham, the two Croslys, and Giles Corey, her husband.

Goodman Corey's "evidence," extracted from an earlier interview, shows him describing a number of slightly unusual events almost as if he himself was accusing his wife of witchcraft. In fact, his questioning by Deacon Edward Putnam and Mr. Cheever was not at all accurately reported in the "evidence". They had gone to this interview several days before confronting Mistress Corey. They were armed with Corey's mention of his wife putting away his saddle when he was on his way to the examinations at the beginning of the month. Giles had thought they were investigating the three women already accused, while in fact the two men were searching for clues to his wife's witchery. Thus, all unsuspecting, he gave them occasion for many inferences which they took as ammunition against Martha. The several "unusual" events had been carefully picked out of an hour's questions.

The magistrates approached Mr. Corey before he left the Meeting House. Mr. Hathorne asked him to sign the account Mr. Cheever had written of their interview. Reading the much-abbreviated "deposition" over, Mr. Corey's face grew red and he threw it down on the table unsigned with but one word, "Lies!" He turned and strode angrily out the doorway.

Another sad aspect of this particular examination was the willing participation of the Croslys and (via Mr. Needham) the Parkers. Henry Crosly, and John Parker were not two of the Corey's closest neighbors by accident. In fact, they were married to Giles Corey's step-daughters, the daughters of his first wife, Margaret.

Their participation—in a way that ultimately might be said to have led to patricide—was the beginning of another ugly feature that cropped up frequently as our troubles progressed. Lust for power and land had already pitted brother against brother and mother against daughter, but now that a few well-placed rumors and a vivid recollection or two could cast one's adversaries into prison, feuding family members and neighbors began to testify against each other. Perhaps few such testimonies were consciously fabricated. The enmity already existed, and genuine memories of suspicious wrongs. But when Martha said "Ye are all against me," she was referring to her husband's step-children who had just testified, more than to the magistrates and ministers.

Four months later, himself accused, Giles Corey was to write his will in gaol — a will that conspicuously included two sons in law, William Cleaves of Beverly, and John Moulton of Salem. (John's father Robert was another Corey neighbor.) Conspicuously missing from the will were Henry Crosly, John Parker and their wives.

Only two days later, Mistress Anne Putnam joined the full-fledged "afflicted" and accused Rebecca Nurse. Reverend Deodat Lawson was then summoned to Sergeant Thomas Putnam's and there he found Anne, Sr., lying in bed recovering from "a sore fit," with Deacon Putnam and Mercy Lewis in attendance. Thomas and Anne both asked Reverend Lawson to pray with her, although she told him "the apparition said I should not go to prayer". He began to pray, but soon she went off in a fit, yet kept silent while the minister prayed, so that he thought she was asleep.

When he finished, Thomas went to her and found her in a fit, so he lifted her from the bed and set her on his knees, although she was so stiff at first that she could hardly be bended. After some maneuvering he got her into a sitting position, but she then began to thrash about with arms and legs and complain as though she were talking directly to someone. It soon became clear to whom she spoke.

"Goodwife Nurse, be gone! Be gone, are you not ashamed, a woman of your profession, to afflict a poor creature so? What hurt did I ever do you in my life! You have but two years to live, and then the Devil will torment your soul, for this your name is blotted out of God's book."

(Had the minister but known, he was not only hearing false witness, but false prophecy, for Rebecca Nurse was not to live another six months!)

Anne went on, "And it shall never be put in God's book again. Be gone for shame, are you not afraid of what is coming upon you? I know, I know what will make you afraid: the wrath of an angry God. I am sure that will make you afraid. Be gone, do not torment me. I know what you would have, but it is out of your reach. It is clothed with the white robes of Christ's righteousness."

(In the minister's account he noted that they judged "what you would have" referred to Anne's soul)

Reverend Lawson recorded that Mistress Putnam then seemed to have some sort of debate with the apparition over some text of scripture, the apparition denying it, but Mistress Putnam holding firm to it.

Then the Sergeant's wife said she would recite it and the specter would have to depart being unable to stand before the scripture. At that, in the minister's words, "she was sorely afflicted; her mouth drawn on one side, and her body strained for about a minute."

And then she said, "I will tell, I will tell; it is, it is. . ." repeating the same words over several times, but seemed to be hindered from going ahead.

At last, she broke forth and said, "It is the third chapter of the Revelations."

Mr. Lawson, another scientist of the spirit, said that, despite his unwillingness to cooperate with the devil in anything, he warily went ahead and read the passage because, he "judged I might do it this once for an experiment."

He began to read and before he had finished the first verse, she opened her eyes and said she was well. Her "fit" had lasted about half an hour.

Sergeant Thomas and the others told the minister that reading scriptures she named had often given her relief during fits.

Thus were a number of witnesses and accusers led into suspicion of Rebecca Nurse before any accused her to her face.

Perhaps Anne Putnam attributed these severe fits to the nominal influence of Goodwife Nurse's spectre because of the suggestion of Widow Holten. Perhaps she needed ammunition against John's threat to reveal the conversation in which she and Mercy Lewis attributed the mention of Goodwife Nurse to each other. Perhaps she convinced herself there was something to her "affliction" beside pure performance. Certainly many who performed similarly over the ensuing months seemed to have done so. But she was not a child or even an adolescent playing a game. Perhaps she was partly driven by jealousy of the attention afforded her daughter and Mercy, or perhaps she entered into it to please her husband. Long after our troubles when we think of deliberate evil-doing, it is difficult to avoid thinking of Sergeant Thomas and Anne Putnam.

Samuel Parris

Chapter Fourteen – Fifth Examination
(23-24 March)

The old heresy of the Sadducees, denying the being of angels either good or evil, died not with them . . . How much this fond opinion has gotten ground in this debauched age is awfully observable; and what a dangerous stroke it gives to settle men in atheism is not hard to discern. . . It has also been made a doubt by some whether there are such things as witches -- Cotton Mather, **Memorable Providences, Relating to Witchcrafts and Possessions,** 1689.

A few weeks later Goodwife Nurse was arrested.

We don't know to this day just how Rebecca Nurse's arrest took place. Sam or John could have asked Francis—there were occasions in the years after when the question was on the tips of their tongues—but they could never pronounce it. There is a privacy to grief, a right to be lonely with dark memories, that is honored by silence.

Now these many years later, the Village still seems walled in with caution against intruding upon mourning continued or completed—or in some cases, not yet begun. So we never ask many of the questions we would ask if we were listening to a mere tale told by a hearty sailor or Indian trader.

It was long after dark on the twenty-third of March. No one but the senior Nurses was there when Marshall George Herrick and Constable Joseph Herrick, his nephew, came to take Rebecca Nurse into custody. Goodman Nurse may have spoken hard words, he may even have raged, but more likely the sudden event simply overwhelmed him. There is no evidence the officers needed to restrain him by force. Benjamin, who was always a sound sleeper, heard nothing until Thomasin awakened him. She had heard the sounds of Marshall Herrick below, searching the house somewhat perfunctorily. (At the first three arrests they had searched for the paraphernalia of witchcraft. Later, witnesses in Bridget Bishop's trial claimed they found "poppets" or magic dolls with which she was supposed to torment her victims.)

By the time Benjamin was dressed and down stairs, they were already far across the meadow with his mother in custody. His father looked deathly. He stared out the door after them until they were lost in the gloom, then sat upon the bed, saying nothing. Benjamin wanted to rush out and gather the rest of the family to take back his mother by force, but out of respect for his father's silent suffering, he choked down his rage . After a time, he went over and told the others.

Goodwife Nurse was taken to Ingersoll's Ordinary, in the middle of the Village. There Mary (Preston) Ingersoll received her with confusion and embarrassment—for she had lived at the Nurse place with her brother after their mother died. It was Rebecca who introduced her to young "Nat". (While Deacon Ingersoll was the owner and proprietor of the Inn, the young couple, Nat and Mary, were the working innkeepers.) That morning, Mary was made to act, for all intents and purposes, as prison wardress for her matchmaker, the woman practically her foster mother. It was still the wee hours, so Mary urged her to go to bed, but Rebecca demurred, and said she must pray, for that was all her old heart was inclined to. Mary sat with her for an hour and prayed, too, until Deacon Ingersoll came. He politely, but officiously, told her to come away and let Goodwife Nurse take the occasion for private reflection. He had many important guests and could not spare Mary. Deacon Ingersoll's guests that night included magistrates, marshals, constables, witnesses, interested ministers, and all of their horses. And every time a coin dropped in the till, another demon flew down to hell.

George Herrick, our gentleman Marshal, had ambitions like those of young Nat Ingersoll—not that either would have expressed them. Theirs were hopes of increased wealth, respect, reputation, influence, and security. They hoped to obtain these during at the same time as they helped purge the community of evil. But Nat, although nephew of a deacon in the church, was merely a merchant, while George Herrick considered himself a "gentleman born" and a high officer of the law. (In fact, while Nathaniel did marginally well out of our troubles, Herrick was nearly ruined. And while Nathaniel came to regret his part, Herrick seemed to end up oblivious of his. In his plea for personal compensation afterward, the Marshal cited his gentleman's heritage and said he was not used to hard work. Rather his work made him so hard, that his gentleman's heritage was to all appearances lost in the slough, not of despond but of despite.)

Regarded as timber, Herrick may have ended up hollow. But on the night he arrested Goodwife Nurse, he had not lost his high foliage. He treated her with condescension, brooking no delay, but showing no excess of harshness. At Ingersoll's she was left relatively undisturbed. Joseph Herrick was placed on guard at her door with orders to look in from time to time to see if she was doing anything peculiar.

Mary brought her some breakfast, and Rebecca drank some tea, but would eat nothing. The ordinary rapidly filled with the sounds of doors opening and closing, boots tramping, voices conversing and men going out, as they trooped across the Rowley Road to the Meeting House.

When all the rest were gone, Marshall and Constable Herrick escorted Rebecca across. Mary Ingersoll followed them from the ordinary. She stood with one hand on the rail and one on the door latch watching them depart: Marshall Herrick, broad in shoulders and girth; Rebecca thin, and tall, though a little stooped; Joseph Herrick, smaller than his uncle, but strongly built. The officers, one at each elbow, were anxious to turn over their charge to higher officers. Unintentionally, they hurried her and tugged at her arms, which made her feel for the first time a prisoner — one caught up in something moving more swiftly than she.

When they entered the meeting house, it was filled with a gathering greater than on most Lord's Days as it was again at Lecture that afternoon. It was not a quiet crowd — and there was only the slightest pause in the crowing of its voices when Goodwife Nurse was escorted in. Most there were her friends, however, and the bustle and drone were nervous, but not hostile. Constable Herrick stayed beside the door as Marshall Herrick escorted her to the defendant's bar, which was nothing more than the back of a pew-bench. There she stood leaning on the "bar" and facing, for the first time, the row of magistrates and ministers, across from the afflicted girls.

The men were more than she expected, and by the time Reverend John Hale, of Beverly, had stood and quieted the crowd sufficiently to open with prayer, her old eyes had accounted for Magistrates John Hathorne, Jonathon Corwin, Reverend Hale, Reverend Lawson, Reverend Parris, and Sergeant Putnam, as well as Deacons Ingersoll and Edward Putnam. Captain Walcott was there, too, and Ezekiel Cheever. Rebecca's own ministers, Reverend Noyes and Higginson of Salem were absent.

Reverend Hale's prayer was lofty and somber, but called upon God more for the revealing of evil than for the doing of justice. Many of us noticed he referred to Rebecca, not as "our sister," but as "this one we have called our sister," a hint of the quarter in which the wind lay.

Then the girls began to manifest their "afflictions". Though this phenomenon became familiar to all who attended the trials, none of us desire to witness it again. To describe it is to describe something out of hell.

Perhaps it is because the female voice is capable of such beautiful sounds—sounds of pure song, sounds of gentle praise, sounds of amusement and joy. These sounds were quite the opposite—for song, substitute cacophony; for praise, substitute accusation; for amusement, substitute horror; and for joy, agony.

Yet that does not begin to describe what developed among those girls and women. Although by most accounts they had not yet reached the peak of their performances when Goodwife Nurse was examined, most of them were well on their way.

Yes, cacophony, accusation, horror and agony, but just as strong as these and uniting them, a diabolical accord of mind, heart, and will, which lent great credence to the idea that they were all under the same powerful influence of evil. Indeed they were, but it was not the purported covenant made in hell between witches and fallen angel, but one being made on earth among fallen sinners.

The fits came upon them in waves, but carried from one to another with words and accusations cried out and repeated, elaborated upon and affirmed. One of the girls would fall into beast-like antics, and another would call out a narrative describing the unseen influences, calling the steps of that particular demonic dance.

Many of us have heard a wild cat scream, a wolf howl, and a deer moan. We have heard a stag bugle, a bull bellow, and a mad dog gurgle and growl. But if one ever heard all of these together, joined by mating cats, alarmed geese, a cow in labor, and ten colicky babes, he might have heard something like these horrors. The effect on the gathered crowd was like the unexpected onset of a sudden thunderstorm, lifting the back hairs on every neck, and upsetting the weightiest equilibrium.

The beams of the meeting house which so often resounded to God's glory, now vibrated to things more animal and awful than echoed through any barn—yea through any slaughterhouse or battlefield of our Indian wars!

Anna Putnam, Mercy Lewis, Abigail Williams, Mary Walcott and Elizabeth Hubbard all were present. The first frenzy of these "afflicted" lasted only a short time after the prayer. While this initial outburst went on the judges and clergy alternated between watching the afflicted and Goodwife Nurse. Most of the afflicted were gathered together on a bench to the judges' right and near the fore. Ann Putnam, Sr., with a number of other women, stood behind the girls. The judges faced Goodwife Nurse at a more direct angle, and watched her with alert eyes, looking for clues of witchery.

The afflicted ran out of breath and a lull came, whereupon Judge Hathorne addressed Rebecca and began the examination. Sergeant Putnam also participated in the questioning, with Reverends Hale and Lawson occasionally passing notes along. Reverend Parris sat with pen and transcribed something of the proceedings.

Goodwife Nurse appeared less taken aback than many of us crowded into the meeting house. Those seeing the display for the first time found it beyond anything the descriptions had prepared them for. One could scarcely imagine having to face such accusers as these girls.

Judge Hathorne turned to Mercy Lewis and asked "What have you been saying? Have you seen this woman hurt you?"

"Yes," Mercy replied, boldly, like a saucy child, "She beat me this morning."

Francis Nurse, Sam, and John with many others drew in their breaths at this first open accusation. There had been a low murmuring and a tension in the place, but now there were whispers and not a few voices saying "shame!"

"But she was in custody at Ingersoll's!" croaked the voice of Father Nurse at his ear, and as Sam turned to look at his eyes, he was disturbed to see the most helpless expression he'd ever beheld there. The clamor rising in our Village had seemed distant to Francis. He did not comprehend that our Village vulcans had been forging a chain to which he was now linked and welded by fire -- to be dragged where ever it was drawn.

Mr. Hathorne looked out over the crowd from under lofty brows and the voices quieted. He then turned to Abigail Williams and asked, "Abigail, have you been hurt by this woman?"

"Yes," Abigail replied, in the innocent tones of a child who makes believe.

Again there were voices in the crowd saying "shame!" Now all the judges and ministers looked out sternly over the crowd, but before they could put words to their rebuke, Anna Putman in a high-pitched screech cried out, "She hurts me now!" The other afflicted cried out again as though all had sighted some great terror. One or two new voices joined in, notably Mistress Anne Putnam.

After this new chorus, Judge Hathorne went on, and addressed Rebecca, "Goody Nurse, here are two, Anna Putman, the child, and Abigail Williams who complain of your hurting them. What do you say to this?"

Sam could not but feel a thrill of pride and encouragement as he heard Rebecca's voice respond to the first question without quailing.

"I can say before my eternal Father I am innocent, and God will clear my innocency."

Judge Hathorne, a little surprised by her calm directness, went on. "Here is never a one in the whole assembly but desires that, too, but if you be guilty, we all pray God will discover you."

The judges and ministers then conferred for a moment. Reverend Lawson rose and went out. He was to preach the Thursday Lecture there that afternoon and left in search of more solitude in which to prepare. Henry Kenny was called upon to speak. He stood to give his testimony before the judges, but seemed much disconcerted in facing Goodwife Nurse and the crowd. Judge Hathorne urged him on.

"Goodman Kenny what do you say?"

Henry Kenny participated as a witness on this occasion alone—when he entered his complaint against Goodwife Nurse and gave evidence that was also to lead to the arrest of her sisters. He was, however, one of those who signed the complaint against Martha Corey. He was a stalwart yeoman of the Village. But like Tom Preston and so many other pillars and posts of the community, he had been caught up in the contagion. (Further, his wife was a distant cousin of the Putnams, many of whom were leaders among the accusers and witnesses. One of them had told him what he testified.) In the same subtle ways as the rest of us, he had been primed to see and remember mysterious mishaps as evidences of witchcraft.

Goodman Kenny began by saying he had heard reliable accounts that there had been questions in the past about Goodwife Joanna Towne (mother of Rebecca Nurse, Sarah Cloyce, and Mary Easty. Joanna's maiden name was Blessing.) Kenny went on to tell how two of his milk cows had dried up because there had been an argument over the borrowing of a butter churn, and the return of it improperly scoured. Sarah Cloyce had spoken angrily to him about her churn, and said something about the future of his dairy and farm.

A few days later, his cows began to dry up, although they had been good cows for several years. He said with what they had heard about Goodwife Towne this led him to think they had been bewitched.

After pausing, he haltingly added more. It seemed he only went on out of embarrassment at the pitiful paltriness of his testimony thus far.

"And Goody Cloyce is Goody Nurse's sister, they both being daughters of Goody Towne. And two different times Goody Nurse when she came to my house to visit, I was made most dazed in my mind, so that after she left, I had to sit for a time and pray to recollect my wits."

As Henry Kenny turned, and to his small credit hung his head as he shuffled back to a bench, Anne Putnam, the mother, screeched and began a confused and broken narrative. Standing with her hands upon her daughter's shoulders, she cried out that Goodwife Nurse had come to her home and tempted her to sign her name in a little red book to make covenant with the devil. The girls became a chorus around her, crying out, "She did the same to me," and "Even now she threatens," adding cries and descriptions of torments which they said Goodwife Nurse inflicted upon them at that very moment.

Waiting until Mistress Putnam had finished her diatribe, Hathorne turned to Rebecca Nurse and addressed her.

"Here are not only these girls accusing you but also the wife of Mr. Thomas Putman, who accuseth you by credible information, both of tempting her to iniquity, and of greatly hurting her."

Again Goodwife Nurse spoke directly as little shaken as possible, "I am innocent and clear and have not been able to get out of doors these eight or nine days past. "

Hathorne turned to Deacon Putnam and asked him to give his testimony.

Where Henry Kenny, benighted as his words were, had at least given account of some things which he himself experienced, Edward Putnam could not even do that. His whole testimony was an account of two occasions when, as near neighbor of his brother, Sergeant Thomas, he had seen and heard Anna Putnam and Mercy Lewis at their fits, during which they claimed to see a ghost or apparition of Goodwives Nurse and Corey tempting and threatening them. He said the girls claimed the two women tormented them with bites, pinching, sticking pins in them, and other wracks and pains when they would not sign the devil's book. He also spoke about being present during recent fits of Mistress Putnam, in which she said she was plagued by appearances of Goodwives Nurse and Corey. Never a thing did he say about seeing or hearing anything out of the way himself. In fact, when ever such a witness was asked, he always said he did not see the "apparitions" or "appearances" or "spectres," although he was present when the afflicted parties said they did.

Other than the tales of the girls themselves, this was the chief kind of testimony during those examinations and trials. From the very outset, the incontrovertible principle of scriptures that for any capital crime there must be two or three firsthand witnesses, was thus set aside in favor of "hear-say" or "second-sight-say". The wonder of it was not only that Deacon Putnam thought he had contributed something of moment against Goodwife Nurse, but that none of the judges or ministers showed any reticence in allowing such testimony. It was unquestioned hearsay built upon childish fancies, and the failure to question it is the most remarkable thing of all. Not only did these testimonies fail as eye-witness accounts, but they included explicit testimony to not seeing what others claimed to see! We were ready to believe lies on the basis of lying testimony supplemented by the testimony of witnesses who said that although they had seen the contrary they had heard the liars tell the same lies before.

Judge Hathorne proceeded.

"Is this true, Goody Nurse?" he asked.

She answered clearly, "I never afflicted no child. No, never in my life."

But Hathorne answered, and there was contradiction in his voice, "You see these accuse you. Is it true!"

"No." she replied.

Then Sergeant Putnam rose from the front row of benches and joined in, although he had no office there. He spoke angrily, as one who has been putting up with nonsense long enough.

"Are you an innocent person relating to this witchcraft?"

But before she could answer, Mistress Putnam screeched again and cried out in these words:

"Did you not bring the Black man with you? Did you not bid me tempt God and die? How often have you eat and drunk your own damnation? What do you say to these questions!"

Rebecca Nurse had gazed upon Mistress Putnam as these

queries were thrown at her like barbed spears. Her face, held patient and impassive until then, began to cloud and wrinkle in folds of sorrow about eyes and mouth. As Mistress Putnam's onslaught reached its peak of volume and intensity, Goodwife Nurse's head bowed and she lifted her hands from the bar and spread them out toward heaven, sobbing, "Oh, Lord, help me"

At which the girls began to fall about and shriek in furious pandemonium.

Francis Nurse had grown tense between Sam and John. John found himself resting both hands on his arm. Awkwardly he patted his father-in-law's shoulder with one hand while he held his arm with the other—willing him to stay still, to keep his iron control, to keep silent.

Mr. Hathorne seemed to muse until the noise died back enough for him to speak. Then sharply he fired the third sort of barrage by which the generals of the witch trials waged war:

"Do you not see what fearful condition these are in? We see that when your hands are loose these persons are afflicted."

Father Nurse stumbled against Sam, and the Nurses were momentarily distracted in finding someone to give him space on a bench. When they put him there, he bowed over, his face in his hands, overwhelmed unto a blank study.

Goodwife Nurse's hand clenched the bar as she shook her head slowly side to side like one who had received a blow.

This was another "evidence" our leaders and lawyers accepted as constituting firm proof. Here we not only heard of some past torments carried out by an apparition of the accused; here we not only listened to some other party's account of observing supposed afflictions while hearing them attributed to the accused; but here, in the very midst of the trial we were treated to seeing the accused person, by gestures so slight as blinking or looking at the girls, grievously afflict them and so prove herself a witch.

Mary Walcott cried out then, and said Goodwife Nurse was hurting her by the motion of her head. Elizabeth Hubbard cried out of the same affliction.

Mr. Hathorne continued to apply the fresh "proofs" in questions to the accused:

"Here are these two grown persons who now accuse you. What say you? Do not you see these afflicted persons, and hear them accuse you!" (He spoke in a tone that implied surely none but a shameless liar would controvert such testimony!)

Goodwife Nurse replied, but her voice was now much troubled,

"The Lord knows I have not hurt them. I am an innocent person."

"It is very awful to all to see these agonies," continued Hathorne, "And you an old professor of Christ thus charged with contracting with the Devil, too, by the effects of them. And yet to see you stand with dry eyes when there are so many others wet. . ."

(One of the published authorities which the ministers and magistrates consulted asserted an absence of sorrow was one of the signs of a witch – thus it became one thing our officers looked for.)

But Goodwife Nurse interrupted him, with the silent support of many in the meeting house.

"You do not know my heart," she said, with a return of her resolve and a new firmness in it.

"You would do well if you are guilty to confess and give glory to God."

"I am as clear as the child unborn."

As if her renewed stand were a signal, the "afflicted" broke out with a fresh set of accusations, focused on other favorite themes which came up in many a trial. Elizabeth Hubbard cried out – "see it is the black man, who is her familiar come. Look, he whispers in her ear!" The chorus of furies rose again. Anna and Abigail fell down and clambered under the chairs.

Mary Walcott took up the theme "See, the yellow birds fly about her head, and now do rest upon her shoulders. Oh, she turns and speaks to them. And now they come and fly at us!" Whereupon the older girls, too, fell down. Mistress Putnam ducked and held her arms about her head, her shriek failing only so long as it took her to get another breath.

Immediately after the wave of clamour abated, Hathorne was ready.

"What uncertainty there may be in apparitions I know not, yet this with me strikes hard upon you that you are at this very present charged with familiar spirits. This is no apparition but your bodily person they speak to. These poor afflicted say now they see these familiar spirits come to your bodily person.

Anne Putnam, Sr. echoed with a shriek "The spirits come to your bodily person."

"Now what do you say to that!"

"I have none Sir."

"If you have, confess and give glory to God. I pray God clear you if you be innocent and if you are guilty, discover you. And therefore give me an upright answer. Have you any familiarity with these spirits?"

"No, I have no familiarity but with God alone."

Then, catlike, Mr. Hathorne pounced to another subject.

"How came you sick? For there is an odd discourse of that in the mouths of many."

"I am sick at my stomach."

"Have you no wounds?"

Mr. Hathorne had mounted another favorite hobby — asking about "wounds" or "teats" which were supposed to be on a witch's body and from which the devil himself or demons or familiar spirits were supposed to suckle blood! It is the most ludicrous of ideas and superstitions, but that it should be brought into a courtroom before Christian magistrates, ministers, and deacons as though it were an article of the creed shows how pagan we were.

"I have none but old age," answered Goodwife Nurse, which was slightly less than the full truth. Yet it was as much as any should be expected to answer in public court about intimate matters. However, this point was used against her in her trial later, when physical examinations were to make much of the smallest scars or deformities.

Then the cat bounced back, turning full circle in air.

"You do know whether you are guilty and have familiarity with the Devil, and now when you are here present to see such a thing as these testify a black man whispering in your ear, and birds about you, what do you say to it?"

Few questions to be found in the transcripts of those courts are more puzzling than this of John Hathorne's, although he asked many like it. It is a confounding of such ideas, evidences, and reasons together as drive one distracted in attempting to make order of them. He implied first that she knew she was guilty and that she had familiarity with the devil, which is mere lawyerly talk; but then he continued to say 1/you are here present, 2/to see such a thing, 3/ as these testify, 4/a black man whispering in your ear, and birds about you, 5/what do you say to it? What is the question! It was essentially a demand that Rebecca deny what she knew to be true according to her own heart, mind, conscience and senses. In the place of these, she is adjured to accept what she "sees" in the courtroom, that which is not only contrary to her own seeing and her own spirit, but affirmed through no seeing, but only through *hearing* a group of deeply disturbed women claim to see it! Yet Goodwife Nurse, unlike many of the younger and more susceptible persons who were accused and confused by such demands, saw and spoke clean through it:

"It is all false. I am clear."

The cat changed from stalking to purring.

"Possibly you may apprehend you are no witch, but have you not been led aside by temptations that way."

"I have not."

Sergeant Putnam struck in again:

"What a sad thing it is that a church member here and now another of Salem, should be thus accused and charged."

Elderly Mistress Pope, from whom we heard nothing before this, cried out suddenly, "A sad thing sure enough!" and she seemed to fall into a grievous fit, crying out as though stabbed or struck.

Then the chorus began to shriek, howl and fall about, again. Reverend Lawson who was strolling along the road rehearsing his afternoon lecture said afterward that the noise coming from the Meeting House was such as he'd never heard the like of before.

The cries at last subsided and Mr. Hathorne continued. In the interim Mr. Hale had passed him a paper, from which the next questions seemed to come.

"Tell us have not you had visible appearances more than what is common in nature?"

"I have none nor never had in my life."

"Do you think these suffer voluntary or involuntary?"

"I cannot tell."

"That is strange. Every one can judge." Hathorne commented.

"I must be silent," she replied.

"They accuse you of hurting them, and if you think it is not unwillingly but by design, you must look upon them as murderers!"

Again, this question came from Reverend Hale. He had in mind the scriptures which address false witness — requiring that one who testifies falsely against another is to receive the penalty which that other would have received. At least one at that table of magistrates and ministers was applying the scriptures to the situation — why was that logic never followed? Like the scribes and Pharisees, our teachers knew the law of God, but for reasons of their own, failed to apply it's weightier matters.

Goodwife Nurse was in good company then, when she replied, "I cannot tell what to think of it."

"What do you mean, you cannot tell what to think? Are you of two minds?"

"No."

"Well, then what do you think about it?"

"I do not hear as well as I once did, and so I did not understand aright what was said." This about her hearing was well known among her friends and family, and would prove her bane.

"Well then give an answer now. Do you think these suffer against their wills or not."

"I do not think these suffer against their wills."

Of the many assessments of the afflicted by those standing at the bar, this was one of the most charitable in its restraint.

Sergeant Putnam spoke again, blunt and hostile:

"Why did you never visit these afflicted persons."

"Because I was afraid I should have fits, too."

She swayed slightly at the bar, and this, together with the mention of fits seems to renew the license of the chorus. They shrieked, shuddered, and flopped about, although this time none fell on the floor. (No doubt that exercise was quite uncomfortable. It is no wonder bruises were found on some of them.) In the transcript of this examination which Reverend Parris made, he made note at this point of a correlation between Goodwife Nurse's motions and the girls' fits.

Judge Hathorne also picked up this cue, once more.

"Is it not an unaccountable case that when you are examined these persons are afflicted?"

And Goodwife Nurse, wilting in body, but not in spirit, lifted up her hands again but for a moment and spoke, almost as if praying, "I have got nobody to look to but God."

Anne Putnam, Sr. shrieked one of her best head-splitters, and Abigail and Anna took to the floor. The others thrashed about, writhed and wailed. It really was amazing to behold—it struck many of us as indecent to watch—almost as if one had come upon them bathing. Perhaps that's why so many came to the trials.

During the most recent chorus, another center of sound and motion had erupted half-way back along the right side of the meeting. Mistress Procter, whose husband ran the ordinary to our south down the Boston Road had brought Mary Warren with her, and she was having sympathetic fits. Reverend Parris and the magistrates made note of this. Parris referred to "another sufferer" in his transcript.

Hathorne had struck what he thought was a fruitful line of questioning.

"Do you believe these afflicted persons are bewitcht?"

Rebecca considered for a moment and spoke slowly,

"I do think they are."

"When this witchcraft came upon the stage," said Mr. Hathorne, "There was no suspicion of Tituba, Mr. Parris's Indian woman. She professed much love to that child Betty Parris, but it was her apparition did the mischief. Why should not you also be guilty, for your apparition doth hurt also."

(This was the last official reference to Betty Parris, that "afflicted" who struck the first spark of our great inferno.)

Goodwife Nurse cut to the heart of Hathorne's question, "Would you have me belie myself?"

She rolled her head to one side as she often did in relief of her rheumatism. At this four girls upon the bench tossed side to side and cried out, holding their necks in exaggerated postures — to which Mistress Putnam added the affirmation of a fine shriek.

Abigail Williams cried out, "Set up Goody Nurse's head."

Sheriff Herrick who stood beside the judges and behind Goodwife Nurse, stepped forward obediently and straightened her head with his two hands, at which most of the afflicted fell silent again. Afterward Sam said he found that one gesture the most repulsive of all that went on that day — the treatment of his mother as though she were a doll to be manipulated by a dotard like Herrick. He had a first taste of the overwhelming anger that was to well up on other occasions.

Then Mr. Corwin consulted with Mr. Hathorne, whereupon Reverend Parris was asked to read an account Reverend Lawson had made of Mistress Putnam's fits some days earlier. It was much the same thing as she herself cried out earlier, including the apparitions of Goodwife Nurse, the devil's book, etcetera. He read it with some feeling and a few flourishes, no doubt fruits of his Harvard education.

The afflicted murmured and groaned, but mostly in undertones as the reading went on. The moment it was completed, however, Mistress Putnam, its chief subject let loose with such a string of shrieks and caterwauling, that we put our hands over our ears. She was joined by the others, but she kept it up, her face growing red and the chords standing out on her temples more and more, until we feared she would suffer an apoplexy. Sergeant Putnam approached the judges. After a moment's conference, he walked over and picked up his wife in his arms to carry her from the meeting house. The moment they were out the door, her cries ceased, and a general sigh of relief blew through the crowd.

Mr. Hathorne addressed the accused again.

"What do you think of this?" he said.

Raising a central issue upon which the colonial teachers so weightily misled us — that teaching which was only corrected with the most indistinct sound of the trumpet and only toward the end of our troubles, Goodwife Nurse answered,

"I cannot help it," then, in a murmured afterthought, "The Devil may appear in my shape."

There was another surge of fits and fantastic flailings with attendant cries and shrieks, as the wise men conferred together a few minutes before declaring the examination at a close.

Unbeknownst to her, like two of those accused earlier, she had as good as confessed to witchcraft, according to the "doctrine" current then — that the devil only appears in the shape of one who has made a covenant with him. And for this they had the authority of many respected divines — derived from who knows what doctrine of their high science and philosophy — certainly not from their Bibles.

It was a mercy not given to many of the accused that the examination only lasted two hours. Others, even those considerably younger, were driven to physical and emotional exhaustion by much longer examinations later — indeed, this seemed to become one of the deliberate aims of the examiners.

But Rebecca Nurse was led out by the Marshall and back to Ingersoll's, while the judges and ministers conferred, as the rest of us were dismissed.

As we filed out, Aaron Way bustled up to the ministers, where he stood holding his hat and bobbing until he was able to speak with Reverend Parris. The transcripts reveal he had been seized by that strange and universal urge to be important, to contribute something that might have eluded the officials. He had seen a correlation between the position of Rebecca Nurse's neck and that of the afflicted Elizabeth Hubbard, as if the afflicted and the judges had not already made this rather ponderous point often and emphatically. Nevertheless, Reverend Parris noted his corroboration, and both Sergeant and Deacon Putnam were to put in affidavits of similar observations.

The judges needed little time to come to their conclusions. In writing they said, "Upon heareing the aforesaid and seeing what wee then did see together with the Charge of the persons then present — wee Committed Rebekah Nurse the wife of Francis Nurce of Salem village unto theire Majesty's Goale in Salem as per a Mittimus then given out, in order to farther Examination. John Hathorne, Assis'ts. Jonathan Corwin, Assistants."

Over at the ordinary, Mary Ingersoll gave the Sheriff and the Constable food and drink, and at last prevailed on Rebecca Nurse to eat some cheese and bread. They took her to Salem from there, where she was put in the keeping of William Dounton and his wife at the gaol.

When most of the crowd had left, the three ministers went over and spoke with Mistress Procter and Mary Warren. Later we learned they invited them to attend that evening, when the "afflicted" were gathered together again, and further "observations" were made. Thus Mary Warren was brought into the fantastic fold.

Father Nurse was in a strange state. When Sam and John told him they should go home, he rose from the bench, but did not seem to heed what they said. He panted hard like a man excited and ready to act or speak, yet he stared in a fixed way, and said and did nothing. All the power of his will seemed to be busy at restraint, and their hearts felt toward him as they would toward a sorrowing child.

Elizabeth, John Nurse's wife, had come up after the hearing began. She came forward, and hugged Father, who still almost absent-minded, patted her on the back. The four of them went out, Elizabeth and Sam more or less leading Father Nurse.

The day had unfolded in the first delicate warmth of spring. It seemed a mockery of what they had been through — it seemed a mockery of man, his moods, and his madness. Father Nurse, his son, and the spouses of two other children walked side by side down the road past Hutchinsons, Haynes and Holtons. There was a stillness in the woods, a waiting, leaf upon leaf, a pregnancy in bud and bulb; a smell, even, of waiting rising ever so softly from the leaf mold and the small ponds and from among the stones of fences. But all their springs seemed in the past. Not even the cheerfulness of birds gathering and twittering and flitting...

"Birds! Why had they spoken of birds flying around Rebecca Nurse?" Sam felt the faint but persistent tug of an obscure memory and connection.

They took the footpath off the road between Sarah Holton's and Sam Rea's.

As they slogged through a little runnel, Father Nurse spoke for the first time since we left the Meeting. "Will she be all right in Salem?" he asked, in a pathetic voice, but a voice trying to sound brave.

"Yes, I think she'll be fine tonight. The Dounton's know her from church, don't they?" said Sam.

"Yes, they do." He was silent as the house came into view ahead of them. "But so do all these others." At which, without warning, Sam began to weep. Dropping behind and furiously rubbing the tears from his eyes, he waited until he could speak again. Elizabeth was in the same state, wet-eyed, though holding to Father's arm. John was not far behind.

"Tomorrow Mary and I will take her what she needs."

But they had come to the homestead, and his eye sweeping once across the house and yard, Francis looked across at the woodpile and the chopping block, then turned and walked at a determined pace across the worn ground.

He picked up the ax, set up a sawn piece and swung a mighty blow. The two halves leaped from the block. He set one half up and split again. And then the other. He picked up another sawn piece. Rather than speak, they left him, and walked on down and over the fence where they were met by Mary Tarbell. When she saw the marks on Sam's and Elizabeth's cheeks she too burst out crying. It was all the explanation she needed. Her husband then began to weep. In sympathy, little Jonathon began to wail in her arms. After they hugged around the child, Elizabeth went on her way, and Mary and John went on toward home.

"How is Father?" Mary asked John.

"All right, for now, I think." John said, "As long as we hear his ax." Steady and strong the sound of splitting rang down from the hill and through the copse. And after they had eaten, and as John, Jr. read *Pilgrim's Progress* to young Mary and Cornelius, their father went outside again, where the ax still knocked at his heart. Very late, when the light was gone, Mary took over a basket of food, and a few minutes later John heard the ax go silent.

Chapter Fifteen - The Fellowship of Suffering
(25 -26 March)

And as all facts and grosser acts,
So every word and thought,
Erroneous notions and lustful motion,
Are unto judgment brought.
No sin so small and trivial
but hither it must come,
Nor so long past, but now at last
It must receive a doom . . . .
-- Michael Wigglesworth, ***Day of Doom***, 1662.

One enters Salem Town on the Common Highway which becomes Essex Street, the main thoroughfare. The Gaol, William and Mary Dounton's house, is on the North River side of Salem Town, near the end of a lane turning off Essex Street. The lane is just beyond Gedney's Ship Tavern. As one goes or is taken in that direction, one first passes Samuel Beadle's house. Goodman Beadle served as assistant gaoler and kept prisoners when the Dounton's had no more room.

On the next lane off Essex Street, not an eighth of a mile east of the gaol is the house of Reverend Higginson, son of the patriarch of Salem ministers, while on the lane west of Dounton's stands the home of Nicholas Noyes, the pastor and philosopher of the Salem church. Across the way from Reverend Noyes is the town home belonging to Bridget Bishop, the first of the accused who would be tried by the higher court. At the intersection of Essex Street and that same lane, the two south corners are occupied, on the west, by Judge Hathorne's home and on the east, by the Town Meeting House. Thus are justice and mercy, faith and works, the keys and the sword juxtaposed in less than two furlongs square.

On that same day, Rebecca Nurse woke in the chilly attic room of Dounton's house and recollected that she was a prisoner bound over for trial. She said her prayers, and found new meat for meditation in "forgive us our debts as we forgive our debtors." Benjamin Holten was no longer her chief regret. She felt like Jonah cast overboard and swallowed by the great fish. She might still be fleeing God — There might still be some distance between them, but He had sent a monstrous and alien power to engulf her, to turn and carry her toward His will.

Yet at the same time she knew this beast was wild and even iniquitous. She knew she was here under man's judgment and the furthest thing from righteous judgment. Nevertheless, she was not full of anxiety or fear or anger or stratagems, but preserved in a strange new kind of waiting, a stillness, almost a suspension. She felt as the newborn child must when some great pair of hands takes it from its cradle and lifts it in alien motion into the strange and insubstantial air. She did not know anything of the mode of her motion or where she would be set down, or what would happen then, but she felt no need to try to know. She prayed and meditated leisurely, back and forth between tallies of her loved ones and randomly remembered promises of the prophets or observed with interest a knothole in a shake above her head.

It was not early, but even the lifelong urgency and rote of rising were stilled. She heard the regular breathing of her fellow prisoner lying on the same mattress with her. She heard below the hollow sounds of the Dounton household coming and going, cooking and bringing in firewood, talking and tramping. Next to her Martha Corey stirred. "I will trust and not be afraid," Rebecca recited to herself, then she rose to sitting, and rolled carefully from beneath the quilt and rug.

The gentle movement woke Martha. She sat up sharply, her eyes instantly bright and alert. Almost as quickly, she sank back within herself and yawned.

"Good morning, Mistress Corey!" Rebecca tilted in a rheumatic curtsey.

"Good morning and well-met to you, Mistress Nurse!" Martha replied from the mattress, "Though not the best of meeting places."

Mother Nurse laughed — and found herself marveling she could laugh, that she was laughing naturally.

"Not the place either of us would have chosen. Like the disciple Peter, we have been bound and led by other hands where we would not go. But I must say, I am honored to be in your company if this is where I must be."

"And I likewise, though should there occur an early occasion to part from you, of which I am not hopeful, I would not spare your feelings by abiding."

Again Mother Nurse laughed, and the dusty rafters seemed to listen, to pick up the vibrations and to repeat the unfamiliar sound to one another, a fantastic rumor.

"Nor do I think I would remain a moment longer with you should a similar occasion arise for me. So I think the better of you for it, though I thought no ill before."

"Nevertheless, I hope Giles will come today, although I do not think so."

"My, I had not thought about visitors. I suppose our families must feed us here."

"Yes, food, fuel, clothing and bedding — and physic if it comes to it — all are to be supplied by us and fees to the gaoler for transportation and wood. It is not a rat-infested London dungeon, nor on the other hand, any kind of inn. Mr. Dounton is neither our host or our innkeeper, nor his wife a cheerful hostess. Apart from leading us out daily to empty the necessary article, they are merely our keepers. We are in a new world — the model of things to come."

"Martha, you wax eloquent. I will excuse myself because of recent infirmities, but I think more of food than philosophy."

"Of course. Your examination was yesterday was it not? I have never been so weary and worn in my life. Not even childbirth comes close to the ordeal. Did you ever see such a thing in all your days as those girls — and indeed those women! I do believe the Village has been given over entirely to lunacy. We're well out of it now, though it was not a pleasant passage.

"But I have food here. Let's call down for a coal to start a fire on this little hearth. We'll make some tea. We'll toast some bread and have a bite of cheese with it."

"I believe I could stomach that. Although I have been ill, I feel a strange difference, as though yesterday's ordeal was a spring cleaning and I a carpet well-beaten. "

"Let's not talk of it until after breakfast. There's a great deal there still spoils my digestion."

"Then, Mistress Corey, please direct me how I may help with our chores."

The two fell into a harmony of hand and habit around the small brick hearth.

The next morning Francis Nurse, John Tarbell, his wife Mary, Rebecca (Nurse) Preston and John's wife, Elizabeth Nurse went down to Salem. It was past mid-afternoon when the Nurses got back home. They had just started when they came upon John Procter who strode purposefully north toward the Village, having just finished a wayside conversation with Samuel Sibley in which he had angrily expressed his attitude toward our troubles.

Procter greeted Francis Nurse more civilly than he had Goodman Sibley, out of a deeper respect for Francis, and perhaps already with some regret over having been so abrupt with the other man.

It was cold but still, and thin wisps steamed up from the fields coming out of frost. Tom and John carried wicker hampers on their backs with bedding and food. The women carried smaller handbaskets. It was pleasant to walk together, to stretch out the tensions of the night, during which none had slept well and some not at all. The cold served to freshen them, but by the time they reached Salem, the sun-suffused air and exercise combined to make them warm.

The two prisoners had just finished their toast and tea, when Martha heard klocking at the wooden stairs—feet and voices. Rebecca could not hear as clearly, being mildly deaf, but her joy was instant when Francis entered, followed by the others. Tom Preston came last.

All embraced Rebecca—Francis holding her old face between his hands for a time and gazing into her young eyes. Mistress Corey, too, was greeted by all, after which she retired to the far end of the attic to sit at a small table her husband had brought up after her examination.

Tom kissed Rebecca without words, and tears started in his eyes. He kept on the fringe of the little circle thereafter, and remained silent the whole time.

They awkwardly looked about, and grouped themselves uneasily about Rebecca, unsure what to say. Sensing this Rebecca helped by asking about the children, and what John, Sam and Mary, Benjamin and Thomasin were up to. This recital took no more than ten minutes, during which John strolled about the attic looking at the rafters and the floors and the two small windows, one at each end. By the time he returned to the knot of Nurses around the small hearth, Mother Nurse was speaking and the others were attentive.

"We must forgive them," she was saying, "whichever it be. If one or two of them have set out to hurt us deliberately, it is a great evil, and one to be brought into the light if it may be, but we must forgive them.

"This is my second chance with Holten's hogs, Francis. They

had no business in our crops. Some were unyoked. Fences were broken through. We are in the right and they the wrong — but we must forgive them. More than anything else I want all of you to pray for me that I will forgive them and not become angry."

None of the family replied. What she said was so far from what they felt or wanted to feel, they were each embarrassed — and all embarrassed together — not for themselves, but for her. To talk of forgiveness then and there seemed a greater lunacy than the raving of a distracted girl. They kept silent and let it pass, as if she had babbled something incoherent.

"We brought you food, mother, although you seem not to have wanted for breakfast."

"No, Mistress Corey kindly shared her bread and cheese and tea. But thank you. She says we must supply all our own things — food, clothing, bedding, and so on. We must pay the gaoler for our keep, our transportation and any extras it seems."

Francis broke out at this. "A fee for the gaoler! I wouldn't pay ha'pence for the whole town! "

"Father, father!" his wife laughed, and her laugh softened him like no rebuke or blow could have. "No one's asking you to buy the town — nor take it for free. I don't want it, either, for we've more than enough to care for at home. Only — we must forgive them, even if we must rebuke them, dear."

"Well, what can we bring you else?" Francis gruffly but affectionately changed the subject.

She looked at him and knew what she might say, and knew he could not hear it, and loved him and answered him according to his query.

"I would like my sewing basket and the little dress I began for Thomasina. And a chair. My woolen cap and my heavy shawl. A change of clothes — Rebecca would you pick them out? My hair brush. A basin, pitcher, and soap. What food you think best. Somehow I feel better able to eat than I have for some time. Spoon, forks, a ladle. We have but this fire to cook with, but I see it has a hook — so a covered pot as well."

"Mother," John said, as the others knitted their brows wondering what else she might need. "We are not idle. You have many friends and even now some are studying how we may end this madness quickly and get you home where you belong. We are sending round a petition."

"Thank you, John. And thank you all for your love. It warms

me more than this little fire to see you gathered around me. Seldom have we gathered lately. It is my one regret that Christmas is not our fashion—to see all your faces in one circle is sweet."

Mary and Rebecca went over to Mistress Corey and asked her what other things she thought needing. They came back with a longer list. Soon after that, Mr. Dounton came up the narrow stairs.

"It's time for you to go. An hour a day is the rule. Daylight visiting hours. No weapons, no knives or rope. No tools, saws, chisels, awls. The court pays fees, but you pay extras. Any questions?"

They were all silent. The William Dounton they knew—he who knew Rebecca well from the Salem church—had become a cold and distant official. There was not a drop of kindness, nor warmth of friendship, nor familiarity in his rote tone or words. Again they all felt tremendously awkward—embarrassed this time, not by fanatic forgiveness, but by deathly disinterest.

As they walked back up Essex Street and past the meeting house, Tom spoke for the first time, "She seems all right," he said. "I would go crazy shut inside like that."

"It's a mercy she's a woman," said his wife, "We care not so much about the shutting up part. It is the separation that is hardest for her—from Father."

"I shall come down every day!" Francis vowed.

"It would be well if you did, Father, " Mary said, "And some of us with you. I suppose they will permit us to bring the children. They would cheer her."

"It seems not she but we who need cheering!" Tom replied. "Forgive them, indeed! I am mad between anger at myself and anger at . . ."

"Nay, Tom, wait at least until we are out of town to speak your mind, " John said.

"I'm sorry," Tom's tone changed immediately and he put on the shame-face he'd worn so often over the previous weeks.

"No, you do no great wrong—nor have. But neither can we speak our whole minds openly here."

Outside the town, south of the bend in the road toward Salem Village just after we crossed the Town Bridge, they passed a solitary hill, all silent and unknowing. That height was to become their own Golgotha not many months later.

At about the same time, over a rise in the road ahead came Marshall Herrick on his big roan horse. As he drew near, they moved to the side and the men refused him even their visages. The women, however, saw that upon his saddle crupper bounced a small person wrapped in a dark green and spotty cloak. It was Dorcas Good. After Mother Nurse's examination but prior to the lecture the previous day, she had been brought to the Ingersoll's where the ministers and magistrates had briefly questioned her and decided she too was a witch. Even this five year old child had been committed to gaol. Not knowing this, the Nurse women assumed she was being taken to see her mother, whom they supposed was being kept somewhere in Salem.

Tom did not take up his theme again, even after they were well out of town. Francis was silent, too, and the foggy sorrow to which he had awakened seemed to return in full after the brief sunshine of the visit. Back at the farm they dispersed. Soon there came the sound of Francis's ax at the chopping block again and for the rest of the day.

As Francis and the children departed from her, Rebecca's initial peace of mind seemed to depart with them. Sitting still in the chair borrowed from Martha Corey, she found herself flung from the high plain of patient perspective to the recollection of the shriek-contorted faces of the girls at her examination. Suddenly she was tossed from the calm of waiting into the mist and oceanic swell of bewilderment.

"Why am I here?" she asked herself in a low voice. "What is it for?"

But she was not alone. Mistress Corey watched her from her chair by the small table under the gable window. Now she came over, carrying the chair.

"The first few days were hardest for me, " Martha said, "It would do us good to pray together."

"Yes," said Rebecca, the word drawn out as she herself drew out of the mist, "yes, it would be good to pray." They arranged themselves close to the fireplace and bowed their heads.

That afternoon, largely restored to equanimity and her earlier poise, Rebecca condescended to the luxury of an afternoon nap, something which at home she would have considered an iniquity if she had considered it at all. Mistress Corey was writing a letter, as Rebecca lowered herself stiffly, but stately, onto the mattress and blankets. She moved her shoulders and hips about until she was quite comfortable, and tucked the comforter up about her neck. She breathed deeply, and looked up again at the knothole in the shake above her.

It seemed queer to her this new world, empty of myriad objects and tasks which had been her landmarks and touchstones. It was an alien and, yes, an exciting thing to be cast on the deserted island of this bare attic. It would take some getting used to. She fell asleep.

When she awoke from her brief nap, Rebecca and Martha spoke of their respective trials. They both remarked the salient features — the unchecked and unquestioned authority given the girls by both magistrate and minister, and the stifling or drowning feeling this produced in their own minds and hearts. Martha remarked that they were not alone in the gaol.

"You mean the others are here?"

"Some, I think. There is another in the basement — most probably that Indian woman of Parris's."

Martha went on, "These tiny windows don't give much light nor much of a view, but if you look out the one by the table, you can see a little of this street, and I believe I have seen Mr. Noyes, Mr. Higginson, and Mr. Cheever come and go."

Rebecca got up and walked to the window. She could indeed see part of the small street below and just a corner of Beadle's house back toward Essex Street. At that moment there was a horseman coming up the street.

"Why, it's George Herrick. Who is that he has with him?" Mistress Corey scrambled to her feet and pressed her face below Rebecca's.

"It's a child!"

"It's the little Good girl. They sometimes call her Dorothy, but she was christened Dorcas. Why do you suppose he has brought her here? Her mother has been in Boston gaol with Sarah Osborne about two weeks now, according to the Dountons."

"Perhaps they have made another accuser of her," Rebecca commented, her voice sorrowful almost unto a rebuke.

"You think he brings her to confront us with more wild tales? But if that were the case, the magistrates and ministers would be here to solemnize and record the business. Somehow I doubt it."

"They have accusers and afflicted girls enough without this poor child," said Rebecca, "but what else can it be?"

The mystery was solved for them as the door of the attic stairs opened below, and Mistress Dounton came up guiding Dorcas Good before her.

Anna Putnam had told her parents of the conversation at Reverend Parris's in which Dorcas had spoken about witchcraft. Sergeant Putnam informed the magistrates. Dorcas was brought to the Village Meeting for examination. The four girls began to be "afflicted" the moment she was brought in, each of them reaching the greatest pitch when Dorcas looked at her. The marshall held her head to keep her eyes from them, but the child could not help turning her eyes about, and at every slightest glance, the girls cried out.

The girls were asked if she afflicted them and they complained of being variously afflicted and particularly of being bitten by her. Mary Walcott showed the marks of teeth upon her wrists — and the magistrates and ministers judged them to have come from a set of small teeth.

Dorcas Good was accordingly bound over to prison.

"Here is another prisoner, if you please. It seems even your Village children must be witches," said Mistress Dounton, but frightened by her own temerity, she opened wide her eyes, turned quickly, and clumped down the stairs, leaving little Dorcas standing solitary at the top.

Suddenly both women were overcome with a rush of motherly compassion, and both rose and went to Dorcas, where they bent and reached out a comforting hand to her.

"Are you hungry, dear?" asked Rebecca.

Dorcas silently nodded, her dark eyes staring at the two old women.

"Are you witches?" she asked in a small dry voice. " I am to be a witch, too."

Later in the day, Magistrates Hathorne and Corwin came to the Prison-Keeper's House in order to further examine the child. They questioned her further about her mother's "yellow birds" and asked if she also had something that came to her.

Of cocurse she did not understand, but Mr. Higginson explained, "Do you have something that came to you like your mother's yellow birds — a dog or a cat or some other thing?"

Dorcas pondered for a moment then said, "I had a little snake."

"And did it come to eat from you like your mother's birds?" asked Mr. Hathorne, his boldness softened in horror over this small child being a witch.

"No, I had nothing to give it." she answered, "it would not

eat seeds."

"But did it not suck blood from you?" Mr. Higginson asked.

Again she pondered before answering. "It tried to bite me," she said at length.

"And where did it bite you?" Mr. Higginson continued.

She did not answer, so Mr. Higginson took her little hand and pointed to her palm, asking, "Was it here?"

"No," she answered.

He suggested several other places until at last she herself pointed to the lowest joint of her forefinger.

The men looked closely and thought they could make out a red spot. They glanced knowingly at one another.

"Who gave you the snake?" asked Mr. Hathorne, "Was it the black man?"

"No," Dorcas answered, "It was my mother."

The next morning, as Dorcas still stirred in her sleep between them, Rebecca and Martha read the scripture together before they prayed. They then arose and made a fire, tea and toast. After breakfast Martha entertained Dorcas with a bit of sewing, while Rebecca borrowed Martha's Bible and set herself to memorize a psalm.

Francis, John Nurse and Elizabeth appeared again, carrying up all the things they had brought in a cart. There was a great deal of bustling about while they brought furniture, clothing and food up the stairs. The prisoners were not allowed to leave the attic unescorted, so the visitors did the work. Rebecca was afraid Francis might overdo it, but John was careful to carry the heavier items.

The Dounton's gave them a half-hour beyond the unloading and carrying. Mistress Corey had fixed some tea for them, to which the visitors sat down before the all too brief time came to an end and they departed. That afternoon, Rebecca and Martha planned and arranged the furniture, including Dorcas in their decision-making. They left Martha's table and chairs under the window where they could sit to write or read. They set a heavier table of Francis' making to the left of the fireplace—for preparing and taking their meals. Rebecca's chest was set next to Martha's, in the eaves. They piled her bedding on top of Martha's, intending to sleep all in one bed as long as the cold weather continued. They placed a circular braided rug next to their mattresses.

In place of the makeshift screen of garments with which Martha had veiled the corner containing the chamber pot, they fastened a curtain. Francis had smuggled in a few nails, which they were able to fix by blows of an iron ladle. Thus they strung a rope for their curtain, and hung up clothing and utensils.

The gaol attic, like its inhabitants, was thus suspended between two states, caught up and made part of two worlds and of neither, their tabernacle for a year — or an hour. Over the following week, the two women developed a flexible schedule of waking, praying, Bible reading, sewing and talking or playing with Dorcas, visits, resting, memorization, meal preparation, eating, gossiping, looking out the windows, taking out the pot, singing, and sleeping. They were prepared to remain for another decade or to leave immediately.

Procter's Inn

Chapter Sixteen — Turnings
(28 March)

*FORASMUCH as the free fruition of such Liberties, Immunities,
priviledges as humanitie, civilitie & christianity call for as due to everie
man in his place, & proportion, without impeachment & infringement
hath ever been, & ever will be the tranquility & stability of Churches &
Comon-wealths; & the deniall or deprivall therof the disturbance, if not
ruine of both: It is therefore ordered by this Court, & Authority therof,
That no mans life shall be taken away; no mans honour or good name
shall be stayned; no mans person shal be arrested, restrained, bannished,
dismembred nor any wayes punished; no man shall be deprived of his
wife or children; no mans goods or estate shal be taken away from him;
nor any wayes indamaged under colour of Law or countenance of
Authoritie unles it be by the vertue or equity of some espresse law of the
Country warranting the same established by a General Court &
sufficiently published; or in case of the defect of a law in any particular
case by the word of God.*

    -- Preamble to the Book Of The General Lauues And
Libertyes, in the ***Laws and Liberties of Massachusetts*** (1648)

Mary and John were worried that Father Nurse would go
back to splitting wood as he had for the last three days, laboring as
though he were a younger man, wearing himself down to nothing.
But "Good Will" Good was sitting on the chopping block when they
returned, and seemed to inspire Francis. At least he diverted him,
for they went into the turning shed instead.

    Over the years Good Will had often stolen in to sit in the
corner of the turning shed, where he watched Father Nurse at his
woodworking, sometimes for hours. Will was famous as an observer
of steady and repetitive labors. Once Joseph Hutchinson had come
looking for him and Father Nurse advised him. "Go back up to the
Village and tap on something for a while," he said. "Good Will will
just naturally come around." Will was no good at repetitive tasks,
but he liked to watch repetitive motion. Curiously, he was quite
good at complicated jobs that involved a number of steps: like
putting together a chair or repairing a saddle — but he wasn't much
use for turning.

A few times Francis Nurse had tried to occupy him with running the spring pedal which pulled the strap that spun the flywheel, but Will couldn't keep it up. He would focus on the turning, and before you knew it, he had forgotten he was supposed to keep it going. The flywheel would wind down, and Will would sit there watching the turned piece until it came to a dead stop and only then look up sheepishly.

Good Will went into the shop and sat on a stool in the corner beside the door, waiting for Father Nurse to start up the lathe. The lathe stood before the big window, in the light of which Will often watched the shavings spurt steadily off the spinning wood like streamers over a waterfall.

Mary encouraged her husband to stay a while and make sure Father was all right, while she went on home. She told John to bring him down for supper, if he could be persuaded.

John sat on the chopping block. He could hear Father Nurse picking through his collection of turning lumber, and pretty soon, the sound of the spring pedal being jogged, and the flywheel beginning to rumble faster and faster. There was a brief slow down, as he made some adjustment, then the speed picked up again, and soon John heard the tap of the tool against the toolrest and the rasp of the gouge against the wood as he roughed it out.

John watched a high line of geese returning — nearly silent — and heard the turning tool grow quieter and quieter as it ran more and more smoothly on the nearly rounded wood. When he glanced in through the doorway, Good Will sat enthralled, hugging his knees and watching Father Nurse spinning a length of aromatic cedar, the rust-red paring flying sinuously to his right and piling a fragrant heap on the floor. John withdrew and went back to his own work.

As a last line of geese came up out of the ruddy southwest, he returned to see how the turners were doing. The geese were calling — for as it grows dark, they stay together so. Francis and Good Will were in the same positions. Only the pile of shavings had changed. The shed reeked like a great clothes chest, and Francis held a thin smoothing stone edgewise against the grooves and ogees of an elaborately worked spindle. Three identical ones lay upon a worktable.

He looked up.

"This is the tenth set of these I've made," he said, "most of them oak. They were job-work for James Symonds, who used them on valuables cabinets. Marshall Herrick's brother owns one. So does Joseph Pope, whose wife cried out against Mother at the meeting."

And then he began to sob. Good Will looked on silent and unmoving. Awkward as a duck, John put his arms around his father-in-law, and could not stop his own tears. They were good, those tears, like the shavings and the smell of cedar — the necessary sawdust.

When he glanced back at the corner, Good Will was gone. After sweeping up, the other two men walked on down to Tarbell's place, where the lamp in the window made glad the night.

"She is the best of all saints," Father said, and John knew it was not Mary of whom he spoke.

That night, when Father Nurse had gone back up to the lonely house, John read the Bible with the children, and kissed Mary good night, before he went to keep his rendezvous with Daniel and Sam.

Sam and he had talked themselves confused while building fence on Saturday, at the very time our magistrates were questioning Good Will's child just prior to locking her up. They knew not how to proceed, or who else they ought to enlist, but they were determined to find confederates and do what they could to stop the evil that had come upon them.

Tom Preston was not of much use to them, for he was all awash with guilt and nearly beside himself for putting his name to the complaints against the first accused. He condemned himself for feeding the injustice which grew and pursued Martha Corey and then his own mother. Young Benjamin, on the other hand, with his delicate wife and baby, seemed too volatile. He was quickly angry and far too ready for some form of belligerence. They feared to encourage him. John Nurse, as oldest son, was better left to the management of the farm until his father was himself again. But they had chanced to speak with Daniel Andrews, sometime school-teacher, and carpenter who had also served in the colonial courts. Daniel had showed a surprising degree of open opposition to those who accused their mother, and he had suggested the three of them get together and talk.

As John drew near to Sam's, he saw Daniel coming across from the road abreast of a companion. It was William Rayment, Jr. and John felt a moment of doubt, for William's father was a respected stalwart of Beverly and the Village. But Sam met and welcomed them, before leading them into his cow shed.

"I brought Rayment because he has the latest news, and some that may be valuable to us," Daniel said, after grasping hands around.

"But first," said Sam, somewhat diffident, "perhaps we ought to commend our ways to the Lord." And in response to murmurs of agreement, he asked the God of all justice to guide them.

As he finished, John raised his head and addressed Daniel. "Have you spoken to Mr. Rayment about the dangers of associating with us?"

"I have, and further, I have sounded him and found he is of like mind—that if we do not oppose these things immediately and as well as we may, much greater dangers loom ahead."

"I am committed to submission to those God has placed over us," Rayment went on, "but during the Andros business, I heard someone read Calvin's thoughts on the scriptural limits of submission. It does not extend to obeying those who command what God forbids or forbid what he commands. "

"That's good to hear," spoke Sam, from the pile of hay where he had made himself comfortable. "I'm glad we can be advised by such as you and Daniel, for many of the learned men seem to have caught this strange fever."

"Yet, we must not oppose them too abruptly, neither learnedly nor in the manner of yeomanry," said Daniel. "We must be active but careful, for what we are opposing is a fever, but a fever masquerading as sense. Such a fever is transmitted quickly to all kinds of people. We certainly should seek wisdom before we act, so that our actions be not dangerous to others beside ourselves.

"How is your Mother?" he added.

"She is remarkably well," John answered, "considering her trials. She slept well the first night at Dounton's. She has freedom to converse with Mistress Corey, and is so much taken up with bearing burdens of others that she often seems to forget her own. Another blow came to her, however, for they brought in the Good's child, and locked her there with them. That and Goodman Kenny's mention of her mother and sister weigh upon her. Mother had thought they could do no worse injustice until then, but now she wonders what they may not do next."

"The godliest woman and the most neglected child among us—no it is hard to believe they can find someone less appropriate to accuse. But it seems likely they will find others. Tell them of today's developments, Thomas."

"First, I will tell you of what I just heard, for it shows the root of these accusations. Had I not been there I would scarce believe it, yet not an hour ago I heard two of our "afflicted" speak in such a way as to make my blood run cold.

"Dan Elliott and I had gone into Salem, and coming back, we stopped for supper at Ingersoll's. We spoke a while with Mary Ingersoll about those in gaol. As we finished our supper, Abigail Williams and Anna Putnam came over from the Meeting House where Reverend Parris and Sergeant Putnam had brought them to consult with the magistrates. The men had more to discuss, but first they sent the girls to Ingersoll's, and after Mary Ingersoll had given them to eat, they two fell to gossiping before the fire. Daniel and I sat musing about their afflictions, and Mary Ingersoll knitted. The three of us talked of tomorrow's examinations.

"I mentioned I had heard Mistress Procter was to be examined. 'Surely, not,' said Mary, 'for I have heard nothing about it.' Suddenly Abigail cried out, 'There's Goody Proctor. Goody Proctor there!' and she pointed to the chimney corner. Anna Putnam looked at the same point and joined in, 'Old witch, I'll have her hanged!' she cried, and the very hair stood up on the back of my neck.

"I was horrified to hear them talk that way, and I said, ' You are telling a great lie.' They stopped, as though surprised.

"Then Mary spoke up, too. 'There is nobody there,' she said, ' you ought to be ashamed saying such terrible things.'

"And then, the sugar on the pudding, Abigail answered in such a way I wanted to thrash her then and there. 'We are only doing it for sport,' she said, 'we must have some sport.' And Anna nodded her head saucily.

"It was but a jest to them! Five women and a child in prison for their jests!"

"Did you speak to their fathers of it?" Sam asked, and there was eagerness, and hope in his voice. "If these girls say openly it was but a jest, all might be brought to a rapid close and the horror end no worse than with a few girls well-spanked!"

"Nay," answered Rayment, and he spoke slow and troubled, "The girls went out then, back to the Meeting, and I did not know if I should go across and speak then or not."

Daniel concluded for him, "I came along and found him on the stoop, and hearing his tale in brief, I brought him here."

"But surely," John said, rising from his seat, "this is all we need to end this thing! We have all suspected they were shamming, but that they would openly say so shows what a light thing it is to them. How far they are from understanding the seriousness of their behavior!"

"Go slow, John, go slow," said Daniel, "for there is more that has happened in the last few days than just this incident, enlightening as it is — and as strengthening to our resolve as it may be.

"Did you go to meeting on Lord's Day?"

"No," John said, "With so many there a part of Mother's arrest, we could not bring ourselves to it."

"Have you talked to any of the church members since?"

"No."

"Well it seems the Reverend Parris had Mary Sibley up before the whole covenant and practically blamed the present afflictions on her. It seems he found out it was she gave Indian John the recipe for a witch-cake to catch witches, if you can believe it. And the pastor says that was going to the devil to find out a devil, and that it is what has made this plague of apparitions and afflictions much worse among us. After he dismissed the householders, he read a paper to the covenant members about how sinful she had been, but also saying he was convinced she did it out of ignorance.

"He posted the paper afterward and I made a copy:

'It is altogether undenyable that our Great and Blessed God, for wise ends hath suffered many persons, in several families, of this little Village, to be grievously vexed, and tortured in body and to be deeply tempted, to the endangering of the destruction of their souls; and these amazing feats (well known to many of us) to be done by witchcraft and diabolical operations. It is also well known that when these calamities first begun, which was in my own family, the affliction never broke forth to any considerable light untill diabolical means was used by the making of a cake by my Indian man, who had his direction from this our sister Mary Sibly : since which apparitions have been plenty and exceeding much mischief hath followed. But by this means (it seems) the devil hath been raised among us and his rage is vehement and terrible and when he shall be silenced the Lord alone knows. But now that this our sister should be instrumental to such distress, is a great grief to myself, and our godly honoured and reverend neighbours, who have had the knowledge of it.

'Nevertheless, I do truly hope and believe that this our sister doth truly fear the Lord and am well satisfied from her that what she did, she did it ignorantly, from what she had heard of this nature from other ignorant, or worse persons. Yet we are in duty bound to protest against such actions as being indeed a going to the devil for help against the devil. We have no such directions from nature or Gods word. It must be and is accounted by godly Protestants who write or speak of such matters as diabolical and therefore calls this our sister to deep humiliation for what she has done and all of us to be watchful against Satan's wiles and devices.

'Therefore in duty as a church of Christ are deeply bound to protest against it as most directly contrary to the Gospel, yet in as much as this our sister did it in ignorance as she professeth and we believe, we can continue her in our holy fellowship upon her serious promise of future better advisedness and caution and acknowledging that she is indeed sorrowfull for her rashness herein.'

"The pastor had charged her with it earlier in the week and gotten Mary to agree with all. After reading it he asked the congregation if they thought it was sinful behavior, which they all agreed. He then had her up personally to express her sorrow and repentance. They had a vote whether they were satisfied and all signified they were.

"After that they celebrated the Lord's Supper together. It seems she's not to be accused as a witch, despite all that."

"That ought to encourage us," said John, "It seems there is some room for repentance in this thing, and at least a little Bible sense. That business about going to the devil to cast out devils is reminiscent of Saul. And did not the Pharisees accuse Christ of it?"

"Yes, but don't think 'forgive and forget' is to be the new rule. Some near Sergeant Putnam hint of new rumors of accusations."

Sam groaned, and John, who had been standing, leaned back against a stanchion.

"No," they both said, and John, "tell us the worst."

"First let me ask you, Rayment, where you had heard Goody Proctor's name mentioned."

"It was in Salem. It was but a shopkeeper's servant who said it. I supposed it must be noised about."

"That is how such rumors fly — for all you know, the one you heard it from heard or remembered it wrong. Perhaps that servant heard part of a conversation. Suppose someone barely within his hearing said, 'Reverend Lawson coming up to the witch trials stayed at the inn of John and Elizabeth Proctor' — out of which the servant heard only 'Reverend Lawson coming up to the witch trial . . . of . . . Elizabeth Proctor.' But no, I too heard a reference to Mistress Proctor, and I think it is connected to Mary Warren. She was brought to speak with the ministers and girls after Rev. Lawson's Lecture on the night of Goodwife Nurse's trial.

"But there is at least one more who stands in danger now — your Aunt Cloyce."

"**Aunt** Cloyce," Sam sputtered, and he jumped to his feet, beginning to pace back and forth, "what is there about us that they must accuse us of being witches! Why Dan Elliott is her son-in-law! He at least will want to speak up about what he and William heard. We must go to Sergeant Putnam and Reverend Parris and tell them their girls admit to doing it for sport! "

"**Who** says what of Aunt Sarah?" John asked, and then he remembered Henry Kenny's silly testimony at his mother's trial.

"Oh, no. You mean Henry Kenny!"

"**Yes**," said Daniel. "Did you hear his testimony."

"**I** was there the whole examination. However, it was so overwhelming I have not much weighed the pieces. Kenny's testimony was early, and so lame as to pull no weight, I thought. Not even the magistrates thought it worth asking him questions."

"**But** this is the sort of thing we've to deal with — even a whisper of the most unreasonable suggestion, whether in the court, or in the corner of a barn, may quickly become a capital charge."

"**It** is too much," said Sam, groping in his shirt, "I must smoke a pipe if I am to hear anymore. Come down to the edge of the woods with me, that I do not burn my cowshed around our ears."

They followed him out and while he went into the house for a coal, the others ambled across the corner of the meadow. A horn of the moon showed above the woods. Daniel spoke to John.

"**When** I tell you about Procter, you will see why I'm unsure about sending Rayment to talk to Parris and Putnam."

Sam came down, already puffing on his pipe, and only William Rayment accepted his offer of the coal. The two of them sent up fragrant trails of smoke as Daniel commenced.

"**It's** true, isn't it, that Mary Warren was also taken with fits during your mother's examination."

"So she was. Mistress Procter was with her, and seemed mortified. It was toward the end that Mary cried out and fell, it seemed, into a swoon."

"We all know she has a history of it. At any rate, the ministers and magistrates noted it and asked Mistress Proctor to bring her after Lecture that they might speak with her. They kept her late, and although Mistress Proctor went home, Mary stayed at Ingersoll's the night. The next morning Sam Sibley was on his way down to Phillips when he met John Proctor in high dudgeon coming up to bring Mary away. "

"Yes, we saw Goodman Procter coming up when we first went to Salem to see Mother!" John said.

"Sibley took offense at Proctor's shortness when he greeted him and asked him what he meant by it. Proctor said he was going up to 'fetch his jade,' because if he left her to jabber to the magistrates, they would end up accusing everyone. He spoke strongly about the girls, according to Sibley, saying, 'if they were let alone so, we should all be devils and witches quickly. They should rather be had to the whipping post.' He also said 'he would take his jade home and thresh the devil out of her and stop this crying out of "hang them, hang them." ' "

"Here, here," said Rayment, and for the first time in several days, Sam and John laughed.

"Apparently Mr. Procter gave Sibley quite an earful. He said when Mary was first taken with fits he kept her close to the wheel and threatened to thrash her, to the result that she had no more fits as long as he was in the house. He said the same treatment ought to be used on all the girls. Sibley said he was angry."

"No wonder he was so red in the face when we met him. He had just parted from Sibley," commented John.

Daniel went on.

"I am afraid of your Aunt Cloyce's name being mentioned, no matter how weightless the fashion of it. John Procter's resistance to Mary Warren's involvement may well end in his being accused, too. The arrests of Sarah Good and Sarah Osbourne seem to have arisen in Tituba's testimony. My guess is she mentioned them only to shift the blame. If your Aunt Cloyce and John Procter are arrested we may conclude that everyone accused, or anyone who openly opposes this madness is certain to be brought in. If, on the other hand, I am wrong and these things come to nothing, we may take it as a sign that sense again prevails and there may be some openness to reason among our judges and ministers.

"Until then, I think we should hold our fire."

"But," John objected, "Would you have us wait and do nothing!"

"Far from it," Daniel replied, and his calm was much comfort to the others, "we should act wisely, but indirectly, until we see what befalls your Aunt Cloyce and Procter."

"But we should warn them!" Sam added.

"Yes, we should," Daniel agreed, "But what can they do with our warning? If they flee short of being accused, they will certainly be accused thereafter. If it were someone without family, I would advise them to at least make preparations to flee, but in their cases, I wonder how they could. Where would they go?"

"Aunt Cloyce could go to Wells — they have family there — and Reverend Burroughs, formerly of the Village, too." (How foolish he would feel when he remembered this last suggestion, although the first part of it bore fruit late in our troubles.)

"In any case, warn her, but if she is inclined to speak and act her mind as you say, she sounds more likely to stay and do that. I will try to speak a word to Proctor, but I am no more sanguine about him."

"But we must do more than that," contributed Rayment, "am I to keep silent about these girls and their 'sport'? "

"No, no. You are as well-placed to resist this tide as any of us, Rayment, and I would not have you be silent, but I think we need to use your information where it will be of the most use, and that means in some official capacity. You say Elliott was with you. Sam has said he will be sure to want to help, so we can ask him to write an account. What do you Nurse men think the chances are that Mary Ingersoll would also sign an affidavit attesting to what those girls said?"

William Rayment struck in, "I think they both would. Certainly they were as flabbergasted as I by the episode. Mary cannot help but be upset at Mother Nurse's arrest. Everyone knows how warmly she regards her."

"Mary as good as begged my forgiveness two days ago when I stopped by," John added, "as if she was the sinner, and I the sinned against. I will ask her."

"That's good," Daniel said, "Tell her to put it in her own words. William, will you ask Elliott? Meanwhile, sit you down tonight and write out a deposition yourself. You can show it to the others. It will make them feel less out on a limb and more likely to follow."

Daniel's experience with the courts stood them in good stead, but Sam and John had been thinking of a plan themselves. John put it forward.

"Sam and I want to act right away, as you say, indirectly, on behalf of Mother Nurse. What would you think of circulating a petition on her behalf among her more respected friends in the Village?"

"It's a good idea. What sort of petition did you have in mind?"

"Why, a petition for her release!" said Sam, emphasizing it by knocking out his pipe on his heel.

"That is what we all desire, but such a petition is not likely to do as much good as one attesting to blameless character and conduct," Daniel advised. Both Sam and John felt this was too little.

"What good a petition about her character and conduct!" John said. "Everyone knows she is blameless."

"The magistrates do not seem to know it," Daniel said, "and if these matters are brought to the higher courts, as they must be, such a document may be very valuable. It would be much the same as bringing in everyone who signs it as a witness, which practically speaking, would be more difficult."

"Will you write it?" Sam sighed.

"I will compose it, but it would be better if one of those respected neighbors wrote it. How about Israel Porter?"

"Of course! He would, I'm almost certain." John said, enthusiastic again with the prospect of doing something. "Weren't he and his wife with you when you came to warn mother?"

"Yes, in fact, it was their idea, I think."

"Who will ask him?" Sam said.

"Israel is my wife's uncle," Daniel said, "Nevertheless it would be best if you could get your father to make the request."

"And it would serve the purpose of encouraging Father to be doing it!" John felt much better. His thoughts suddenly ran high. They would act! They would prevail, and Mother Nurse would be restored to her family and her rightful respect.

"It is late. I must be going." Rayment said. "I will try to feel out my neighborhood and Royalside. Perhaps you can find some signers for your petition there, although the Herricks are not likely, nor Dr. Griggs, who considerably colors official opinion."

"We will begin tomorrow," John said. "When shall we meet again?"

"Let's come here again in a week." Daniel proposed, "Meanwhile we can speak to one another after lecture Thursday — but we must use caution."

"Done!" said Sam. "Will you close?"

The stars were clear and cold when they raised their heads and went their separate ways.

Chapter Seventeen — Petitioners
(29-30 March)

. . .Witches make witches by persuading one the other to subscribe to a book or articles . . .
. . .If he [the devil] can prevail upon those that make a visible profession, it may be the better covert unto his diabolical enterprise.
    -- Deodat Lawson, **Christ's Fidelity the only Shield against Satan's Malignity,** lecture in Salem Village the day of Rebecca Nurse's examination.

John Tarbell put the plow on the cart and took it down to John Nurse at the west end of Governor's plain where he and Tom were preparing to plant. With the colter re-forged and a new tip on the share, the implement was ready to be put to work again. But it was another plow to which John intended to put his hand that day. After conversation kept short by a common desire to get on with their different tasks, John rode back to the Nurse Place.

There he met Sam in front of the main house, where they heard Father Nurse quietly going about his solitary business inside. After a time he emerged and was surprised to see them.

"Oh ho! So these are the sort of lazy bones I have raised up! Why, when I was your age. . ." then his bluff tone of camaraderie slipped away ". . . I'm not sure I remember ever being your age. But what are we about today, my yeomen?"

"John and Tom were early at the plow in the corner above Governor's. Benjamin says we have another week of clearing near Holten's. Those maple stumps are all rooted in boulders by his account. Sam and I are planning to traipse across the country, with your approval."

"Traipse?"

"We are going to take a petition around to the neighbors for Mother, and once we have their signatures, take it to court on her behalf."

"Bless you, boys. That's a fine idea. . . a fine idea." He turned half away to brush something out of his eye.

"But, Father, we need your help," John added. "We have

been advised it would be better received from the pen of one of our leading men. If we come up with the proper wording, do you think Israel Porter would write it for us?"

"I'm sure of it, John. Why, he and Elizabeth came over to warn us at the first. I know he would."

"Would you be willing to ask him?" Sam said.

"Well, I suppose I could . . . I was going to . . . of course I will!" he concluded, like them, suddenly excited with the prospect of doing something for Rebecca.

John was halfway up Topsfield Road on the way to Daniel's place, north of Porter's Hill, when he met him coming the other way. Daniel had a draft petition already written. John sat down on the edge of the wooden bridge to read it, while the stream flowed beneath him. There were ducks already along the brook. A glimmer of warmth was in the air, and the water chuckled hopefully.

"We whose names are hereunto subscribed being desired by Goodman Nurse to declare what we knew concerning his wife's conversation for time past; we can testify to all whom it may concern that we have known her for many years and according to our observation her life and conversation was according to her profession and we never had any cause or grounds to suspect her of any such thing as she is now accused of."

"Have you talked to your father?" Daniel asked, as John finished it and complimented him on the lawyer-like language.

"He's on his way to Porter's, now."

"Then you can take this directly, but make sure Porter writes it out himself and signs it first—on such things as those barristers love to wrangle.

"I spoke to your cousin Peter this morning, and warned him about your aunt. He says they had cause to be sensible of it already, but that he would warn his father and mother, again. I did not like to be too open, but I asked him if his mother might consider going away. He said there was not a chance of it. It seems your Uncle Peter has already urged her, but she won't budge. She says it would be abandoning her sister."

"These hard-headed old settlers!" John burst out, "Our generation is all tallow next to them."

"Tallow, talk and tobacco-smoke", added Daniel, "But be of good courage, I suspect you'll need a large sheet for all the signatures. In fact, I brought you paper!"

"Daniel, I will not overpraise you, for I dislike it myself, but you have become that friend closer than a brother to us."

"The closest friends give blows not praises! So here's a friend for you." And he pummeled John on the shoulder. It delighted John. Daniel seemed all of a sudden less superior and professorial—indeed more like a brother—and John warmed all the more to him.

"I go now to test the sea air of Salem Town," Daniel said, "I suspect our events are being shaped by the philosophers there as much as by our own temperaments and humors."

By then they were come to the Ipswich Road. Daniel continued south upon it, while John turned east toward Wenham, then took a field path to Porter's. But he had new food for thought.

Francis Nurse and Mr. Porter sat in the sun on a settle. The logs of the garrison lay log on log, gray above their silver heads. Israel Porter rose and gave John his hand.

"Your father has honored me with a request to begin a petition. He tells me you boys have given it some thought."

"Yes, sir. We have made up a draft, which I brought over. I will read it for your approval." And he did.

"I think it's fine—above board and respectful, but a clear statement of support for your mother. It opposes these accusations, without saying exactly so."

"I have brought you some paper on which to write it," John added, at which both older men laughed.

"If I'm not careful, Francis, this son in law of yours will be guiding my writing hand. Have you brought me pen and ink, too, John Tarbell!"

"No sir, " he answered, somewhat embarrassed, "I apologize for appearing disrespectful and hasty. But Sam and I intend to take it around as soon as you find time to write it out."

"Not disrespect at all, not a bit of it. I find no disrespect in young men who are active on behalf of their mothers. None such will find any opposition or hindrance in me. If you'll have that table down off the porch, there, I'll write it out now." And with that he went in the house to find pen and ink.

"That's well writ." Francis said, as he helped John place the table. "Sounds like somebody with a lawyerly knack."

"Yes," John answered, reluctant to reveal his co-conspirator, even to Father Nurse, "somebody else who looks up to you and Mother."

Mr. Porter wrote out the petition in a clear hand. He not only signed it, but brought out his wife to sign, as well. Elizabeth Porter was sister to magistrate John Hathorne. Thus it seemed worth four or five other signatures to have hers upon it. Israel, himself, was one of the more respected men in the village. He has frequently stood up against men who wished to run the Village like lords, yet he and two brothers were members of the Salem Town council, which by rights made them big fish in a little pond. His son Joseph was on the newest board of the Village Church (with Daniel, and Francis Nurse, Jr.) elected the previous October. His nephew by marriage, Joseph Putnam, was also elected to that board.

But Mr. Porter was not content to write the petition and sign it with his wife, he insisted he would go up the Ipswich Road with John and canvass some prominent Royalside neighbors.

"In fact," he said, "we might even try a long-shot or two."

The road wound through the fields as they crossed Frost Fish Brook. There were wood-thrushes calling from the vaults of the forest near Leach's Hill.

John thought they would turn in at Benjamin Porter's, but Israel didn't turn. He walked right by their road, steady with long strides like an old woodsman. He didn't turn in at Rea's or Watt's or Bishop's either, so John supposed he was going to Rayment's, but he went on further and John began to wonder if they were going to start in Ipswich. The thought went through his head that he should have brought more paper.

But Israel had decided to take his most difficult long-shot first. They turned in at the farmstead of Joseph Herrick, Sr. — older brother of Marshall George, and father of Constable Joseph. John felt his stomach muscles tighten as they walked up the hill and through the wood-lot toward the house. Just as Reverend Parris and Thomas Putnam wished to draw a line to exclude evil, he wanted to draw a line that left out Herricks altogether. The problem was in the drawing. He told himself Joseph Herrick was in no way responsible for what had happened to Mother Nurse. Not even his brother and son were responsible. They were only doing their duty, as many an officer before and since — to good or evil ends depending on the drawers of the lines. It flashed upon him that this desire to draw lines, to define and exclude was a deep and desperate thing. Yet despite all his philosophy, he still found it hard to ask a Herrick to sign the petition.

Of course, Israel was wise in trying — precisely because having Mr. Herrick on their petition would make it hard for others to draw lines that would exclude supporters of the accused. As Daniel had prophesied, a time was rapidly coming in which speaking on behalf of the accused would be dangerous. It may well be that Mr. Porter, too, had that possibility in mind.

The view from Mr. Herrick's place on Alford Hill led one's eye down the valley almost to Bass river and Beverly-side. The faint blush of new green in the woods beyond Horse Bridge seemed an illusion—it made John blink his eyes and look twice. But no, the woods were changing from gray and brown, charcoal and tan. There was a Redbreast on the wide lawn as well as a Hermit Thrush in the bushes.

Joseph Herrick was glad to see Israel. He was one of lordly stock, the grandson of Sir Somebody, but he had an easy manner toward them. An ancient respectability grows lonely in these hills unless it deigns to befriend the leading yeomen.

When he heard Israel's errand, however, Mr. Herrick grew more distant.

"I have not heard much concerning the substance of these things," he mused, as the fired flickered in the brass of his firedogs, "but it's plain my brother and son and a nephew or two are involved in it, as public officers, and I don't like to do anything that would appear to oppose them."

"No, sir," Mr. Porter said, and it sounded so strange to John to hear him call someone sir, "there is nothing of opposition to public office or law in this petition, otherwise I would not sign it either. My own brother-in-law is a magistrate and has been officiating at these examinations. But John's mother-in-law is one of the godliest women we know and that she has been accused of this great evil is far from just or right. Our petition is an opportunity for the many who know her to testify to her good character and conduct."

"How many signatures do you expect to get?"

"I should think we could find a hundred if we wanted them. Rather we intend to get forty of the most respected citizens of the Village and surrounds. That is why we have come to you at the outset."

"Ah—flattery—how I enjoy it. Nevertheless, I fear if I sign next to such a radical as you, Israel—and you fail to get any other signatures—you and I will be next for witches! And then what will poor George and Joseph do!"

"No doubt their duty, sir! But no, I would not have your name stand out overmuch, although we covet it. How of this—you sign near the bottom, so that as we gather the others, we will fill in and obscure your part just enough that neither your brother nor any other feel uncomfortable. At the same time, your name upon the document will ease the fears of others whom George might be more comfortable clapping in irons!"

"Well thought, Israel! I can play that part with good conscience. For between you and me, John here, and the gatepost — I do not like this business overmuch myself."

With that he did sign, near the bottom, leaving a goodly stretch between the Porters and his own name, and adding "Senior".

John shook his hand as they parted, and it was a sincere handshake.

Mr. Porter then led down the road. No Rayments were in evidence, but they got the signatures of many in Royalside, including Edward Bishop and his sister Hannah. Edward, Sr., the sawyer, was out at work, and Israel did not think it much use to ask his wife Bridget, who ran the ordinary there. Her reputation was none too good, though neither of them suspected she soon would be accused.

They stopped at Joshua Rea's next, where he and his wife Sarah cheerfully signed. She invited the two men to have tea with them, but they did not stay. Between walking and making conversation with their few but important petitioners, the day had gone very quickly. John returned with Mr. Porter to his door where he thanked him for his kindness.

On this, the fourth day since Rebecca's arrest, Francis did not come to Salem at his normal mid-morning hour, and she plunged into despair. She prayed and recited her psalms, but found she was only doing these things as one would whistle in the dark — and about as effectively.

At the same time as she chatted with Martha and Dorcas, she was distracted and down-hearted. "What is wrong with me," she wondered. "Are my joys built so much on his coming that I lose them entirely when he cannot? Is not this the opposite of faith?"

But when Francis did come in the early afternoon, explaining about visiting the Porters and the petition being circulated, she was a bit short with him.

"But I was expecting you! And I did not know what had become of you!" she complained.

He apologized and said he would send some one if ever again he could not come on time.

Afterward she was in the midst of righteous self-pity and the beginnings of anger at herself, when she happened to glance over at

Martha and Dorcas sitting at her little table, with the weak light falling on the old head and the young up-turned face. Suddenly she realized that after four days she had yet to see Giles Corey or William Good. She was ashamed.

Now her solitary prayers took on a new and more serious cast and her afternoon nap became even more luxurious. She had begun to realize the requirements of holiness and the privileges of enjoyment were higher for her as a prisoner than they would have been at home.

During the two weeks Rebecca was kept at Salem gaol, old Francis visited her nearly every day, twice with a cart when it was necessary to carry goods, often on foot with daughters and sons, but several times on horseback by himself. He invariably started out early. Thus his mid-morning visit, regulated officially to an hour, became the central point of every day for the prisoners.

Just a little further west on Essex Street and on the north side again, is the home of the Sewalls, where Stephen and his wife maintained the retreat for young Betty Parris. There they wrestled in prayer for Betty's soul and body. They had found her a difficult charge. The 25th of March, she had "sore fits" and claimed a black man came to her, promising her if she would be ruled by him she should have whatever she desired and be taken to a Golden City. The Sewalls were just beginning to understand her more basic needs — for discipline, for faith rather than outward shows, and for a self-respect based not on her father's office, but on her Savior's merits. But these further attacks of demonic affliction left them feeling much in the dark. They had read Willard's account of the Knapp case, however, and more carefully followed his conduct and attitude than most in Salem. Therefore, instead of asking her who afflicted her, they commended her to God in prayer. Mistress Sewall told Betty the "black man" was a liar from the beginning, and that if he came again to her, she should tell him so. When the fits came upon her again that evening, the girl did so. "Satan, you are a liar," she said, "The Lord is Way and the Truth and the Life. In his name depart."

At the same time, the Sewalls began to demand more consistent obedience and self-discipline from Betty than she had hitherto known. Where her parents had alternately spoiled her and demanded rigid conformity, often for the sake of public appearance, the Sewalls were more steady in their oversight. They gave her regular responsibilities and chores, and called her to examine her soul in terms of particular scriptures they required her to memorize. She fought energetically against this unfamiliar, and at first stifling, discipline, having many more fits the first few weeks. Several times when Mistress Parris came to visit she complained so brokenheartedly that her mother nearly took her home. But she wisely did not, and over the difficult months to come, Betty was eventually "cured".

Daniel came up from Salem Town that night and stopped in at the Tarbell's. After John gave him the petition, the two men walked up toward the Nurse place to talk. Daniel was much heartened by Mistress Porter's and Joseph Herrick's signatures.

"This makes the thing so much safer for the rest of us who sign," he said. "It shouldn't be difficult to fill the page now. Let me take it with me and try my neighbors tomorrow."

"What goes on in Salem?" John asked.

"I heard little. Although I stopped by the gaol, I did not see your mother. Did you know I laid those bricks? Too good a job, I'm afraid. We'll have to break your mother-in-law out by book rather than crowbar. I was too generous in my mortar.

"I did see your sister Rebecca and brother Ben leaving there. The bad news is talk of irons. Imagine, irons on small children and seventy year old ladies! The accused claim they are still bewitched by those in gaol, despite the great distance. The wise men think by binding hands and feet they can stop the devilish gesturing by which the witchery is done! I'd rather be a pagan than a Christian who believes such nonsense. What am I saying. Those words in the wrong hearing and I'd be in irons myself. At any rate they haven't done it yet, but there have been few things suggested in these matters that have not come about—in fact that seems to be the creed—not 'I think therefore I am' but 'If you can think of it, it is'."

"I'm too tired for philosophy tonight, Dan," John replied, "Even on a good night I cannot keep up with you. Do you think we can fill up that sheet tomorrow?"

"I will do what I can up my way in the morning and bring it back after noon. If one of you can take it around here, that ought to fill it. Of course, we must constantly remind ourselves that we don't want even one questionable signature and we most want those of influence and reputation. Does Sam understand that?"

"Yes, we talked about it when I came home tonight. He stands ready to take it around tomorrow — I will tell him it will be afternoon. If there is still space left, we can get a few more signatures at lecture tomorrow. It is set aside as a solemn fast day, you know."

"So it is! I had forgotten. The whole community is supposed to be praying about these matters. May God swiftly answer and bring them to a clear end."

"That brings up a question I would like to ask you," John said, " but not tonight!" he exhorted himself, "Remind me the next time we have space for philosophy – for among the things that puzzle me in our troubles, there is one that persistently comes back. But not tonight!"

The next day, Daniel went around his neighbors. Using the same principle as Mr. Porter, he went to the most prestigious with the most connection to the "other side" as they were coming to call those who promoted the witch trials. He got the very valuable signatures of Captain John Putnam and his wife Rebecka. Captain John was brother both to Nathaniel, a Nurse neighbor, and to Lieutenant Thomas, who had been the wealthiest man in Salem Village when he died four years earlier. Thomas's sons, Sergeant Thomas and Deacon Edward, along with their brother-in-law Jonathon Walcott were the most active men on "the other side" (along with Reverend Parris and various Salem divines.) So now they had among their petitioners both Putnam and Herrick patriarchs. Further, Mistress Putnam, the Captain's wife, was of the Hutchinsons, another leading family.

Another signator was Sarah, wife of John Leach (Junior) of a respected Village family, and Daniel's nearest neighbors.

Daniel then stopped in at Jonathon Putnam's, on the strength of his father's (Captain John's) signature, and Jonathon and Lydia both signed, despite his being a constable and brother of John the weaver, who signed the complaint against Rebecca Nurse! (These Putnams are Cloyce's nearest neighbors and Lydia is Israel Porter's niece.) They put there names just under the signatures of Daniel and his wife, Sarah. Daniel's own was the boldest on the sheet.

As Daniel brought the petition down to the Nurse's again, he went aside to Joseph Hutchinson, Senior, another patriarch of a leading family, whom he knew to be sympathetic on the basis of earlier conversation. Mr. Hutchinson and his wife, Lydia, signed.

Finally, with his characteristic willingness to take a risk, Daniel went to Joseph Holten, Senior, as well. The Holtens were often allies with the Putnams – particularly in the land controversies among us. More important, one of the most bitter accusers of Mother Nurse was the widow of Benjamin, Sarah Holten, who lived right across the road from Joseph, senior, her father-in-law. But the older Holtens had been good neighbors to the Nurses. Furthermore, according to Daniel, they were considerably impressed with the other signatures on the petition. Both Joseph Holten, senior and his wife Sarah (Deacon Ingersoll's sister, not to be confused with Sarah Holten, widow of Benjamin) signed.

Daniel delivered the petition to Sam. He said he was off to do some calculations for a new house Francis Peabody was building above his grist mill in Topsfield.

John was at work sawing furniture wood with Father Nurse. Sam set off immediately to seek more signatures among the neighbors to the south. Seeing Daniel's success with the Joseph Holten's, he came up with a bold idea of his own—but it did not turn out as well.

However, he began by stopping in at the first neighbors' on the road south, and Walter Phillips, senior, signed cheerfully. His wife and daughter-in-law were gone to Salem that morning, but he said that if Sam stopped back by, they should be home by mid-afternoon.

Sam went on along to Mr. Felton's, of an old family, for whom the big hill is named, and found old Nathaniel quite willing to sign. All this success went to his head, however, and spurred him ahead with his plan. He stopped in at James Holten's back on the Ipswich Road. James was building a hog pen, and perhaps that helped bring the old association fresh to his mind. In any case it quickly became clear he had not the forgiving spirit of the older generation, and not only still blamed Mother Nurse for her angry rebuke of his brother Benjamin, three years earlier, but was in full agreement with his widowed sister-in-law, Sarah, that Mother Nurse had bewitched him. He said so in no uncertain words and added that he thought she deserved whatever she got.

Sam was so unprepared for this rejection, that he could not speak a word in reply, but turned shaken and bewildered, and so stumbled out of the yard and back to the road.

That he found Margaret and Talitha Phillips home and ready to sign was not sufficient encouragement to restore his dashed hopes or perspective. They saw his weariness and discouragement, and tried to speak cheerful words.

"Few who know Rebecca can countenance these charges," said Margaret. "We and many others, both of Salem and the Village are praying for a quick end to her imprisonment, and a restoration of such as she to their homes. If some of the others are indeed witches, she is so far different that the court must see it and justice be done."

Sam came back to find Francis and John at the saw-pit. He showed them the petition and told them of his encounter with James Holten.

"The Lord's ways are past finding out," said Francis, when Sam's recital was finished. "That very incident with Benjamin Holten so weighs on your mother's conscience that she still prays daily for forgiveness and that she might be reconciled to Sarah. It got to where I rebuked her for bringing it up again and again. And yet, here it is, not forgotten nor forgiven on earth — and one wonders how it stands in heaven."

"Surely done and covered in Christ's blood!" John insisted. "The sin is now theirs, for they have let a thousand suns go down on it and ever resisted Mother when she tried to make what recompense she could."

"Truly, the Lord's ways are past finding out," answered Father Nurse and John could say no more.

To Sam, however, John gave as encouraging a talk as he could, pointing out James Holten was but a very small fish in our pond, and that the four other signatures were each worth ten of such as his. But underneath it Sam felt, and so did John, that there was more to all this than their small minds could fathom, and indeed, some shadow of a larger thing that lay over us all.

As these things settled uneasily and oppressively on John's mind like storm swell on the ocean, he suddenly determined on a bold course of his own.

"Sam," he said, "Would you help Father finish the saw-work. I'm going to have this out with these Holtens, for it seems to me if we cannot reason with our neighbors, we have little hope with high officials who know us not."

Sam looked at John, first taken aback, but then enthusiastic again. "Go on, John! I'm glad to trade labors with you, for it seems to me I am not cut out for fighting with words. Are you going back to talk to James?"

"No," John said, "I think I will go to Joseph, junior, instead, for he bears more weight with the family, and I am determined to show him the reluctance to be reconciled is all on their side."

John made off then, up past Sarah Holten's, the site of the infamous encounter between Mother Nurse and Benjamin Holten, marshaling his arguments and scriptures to give Joseph Holten, junior, a talking-to.

But when he got there, and found Joseph sharpening a harrow, his reception was as mild as butter. Stealing away John's thunder, Joseph consented to sign the petition with no resistance at all. While he signed it with a fine steel nib, John hardly knew what to say. Greatly reduced in fervor, he asked Joseph why his sister-in-law and brother were so dead set against Mother Nurse. Joseph said he didn't know, but supposed it was that grief had hit them differently, the one his wife, the other ten years younger and looking up to his brother.

"I was closer to Ben than anybody else in the family," Joseph Holten said, "but for me the grief was not helped by poisoning it with blame. There have been so many strange deaths over the last few years, that demanding to understand and explain them by blaming them on someone else seems to me like demanding to be God." And then he echoed what Father Nurse had said that same afternoon, "The ways of the Lord are past finding out."

Greatly heartened, though somewhat subdued, John decided to continue on his mission until dark. He went back and down across to Samuel Endicott's, another ancient name among us, with whom the Nurses had fought over borders. He did not quite have the heart to go to Zerubabel, the brother whose loggers Tom and John had roughly opposed some years earlier. But Samuel signed readily, and shook his hand, saying, "We have had our differences, the Endicotts and the Nurses, but in this thing, we must agree." Which saying subdued John yet more, and made him begin to wonder if in fact the Lord's unsearchable ways in this thing might not have to do with humbling such as himself who were not easily humbled otherwise.

Joseph Buxton's place lay more than a mile to the south toward Salem, but he reckoned he had just time to get there before supper. He struck off down the road, and finding only Mistress Buxton at home, obtained her signature and encouragement.

Goodman Samuel Aborn came up the Salem road as John came out. John acquainted him with his purpose, after which nothing would do, but they must go in again to Buxton's, where Goodman Aborn borrowed the pen and ink, and affixed his signature as well. Daniel was to point out later that Aborn had been one of the accusers in a witch case at Marblehead 25 years earlier!

It was with a much pacified heart John arrived back home, and acquainted Father Nurse, and Mary with their successes. Sam had already gone home to Mary and supper.

"We have twenty-five signatures, and are sure to fill up the rest of the page if we take it to Lecture tomorrow at the Village. How can the court fail to consider such an affirmation of Mother's character!"

"And mayhap I will have another surprise for you at Lecture tomorrow." Father said, and there was the old twinkle in his eye. But more he would not say.

"Mother seems in good spirits," said Mary. " I went over to Rebecca's. She and Benjamin took a load of firewood down to Town. She said Benjamin did an intolerable amount of fuming on the way, but that Mother calmed him and made him promise to take his burdens to the Lord instead of letting the flesh batten on them. Speaking of battening, Mother passes around everything we take her to eat. She is a-mothering of everyone in the place, Mistress Corey, Dorcas Good, and even Mistress Dounton, by their account! What a woman she is. She seems to think the gaol as good as a meeting house for charity."

"It's a good deal better!" said Father, but he choked on his bread, so that they had to pound him on the back.

After he had gone home, Mary told her husband the news from Ipswich — that Rachel Clinton was arrested and gaoled there that day. The fervor of witch accusation was spreading outside the Village.

John went over to Sam's and he had some more news. He said he had been surprised to see John Houghton come walking down, when he was finishing up the split-rails Tom and John had started the day of the first complaints.

"How's your mother?" John Houghton asked.

"As well as can be expected," Sam answered, which has become their standard answer.

"Well, I couldn't help but come over and tell you something," John said. "Sam Barton and I were over at Sergeant Putnam's today, helping to keep an eye on their two girls. You know they've got a regular watch going on 'em to keep 'em from throwing themselves into the fire when they have those fits.

"Things were pretty quiet most of the day, except that just after noon, Mercy Lewis had a tumbling fit in the parlor, and pretty much jerked about, and then lay on the settle all stiff and deathly for maybe half an hour. But just at the beginning of it she cried out "There she is!" and began shaking. None of the rest of us saw anything. Anyway Mistress Putnam was with her, and talked quiet to her and read some scripture, and then she was all right, and got up and had a drink of water, so Sam and I got to visiting and we was in the kitchen shed when the Sergeant come in from a trip to Town.

"We heard the Mistress telling him what happened, and then the two of them started talking to Mercy and pretty soon we heard them telling her she had cried out 'Goody Procter—there she is.' Mercy said she didn't remember that. Then the Sergeant said, 'but you did cry out Goody Procter, Mercy,' and Mistress Putnam repeated it again and asked her, 'Didn't you cry out Goody Procter, Mercy?'

"Well, Mercy seemed to get het up over that, and she said, 'No, I did not cry out Goody Procter nor nobody. I only said "there she is," but did not tell who it was, because I could not tell.'

"Barton and I come in then and the Sergeant saw us and no more was said.

"But afterward when we left, we talked and decided it was something that ought to be known—them saying things about who Mercy saw when she didn't even know herself."

"I told him I was grateful he told me," Sam Nurse said, " I said it fit with some things others had heard and seen. I asked him if he and Barton would write the whole thing down as they heard it and give it in to the courts if anything more came of it.

"He looked nervous at that suggestion, but said he would talk to Barton. I told him that they should write it down now while it was fresh in their mind, but that they need not give it in until later, and only then if they thought it might help. He seemed more comfortable with that.

"We parted company then, but it's like what Rayment and Elliott saw at Ingersoll's and the conversation you and I had with Mistress Putnam and Mercy over who first named Mother. It looks like things have got to where the Sergeant and his wife are putting ideas into those girls heads a-purpose."

John and Sam were both staggered by this. They had seen and heard much they did not like about the Putnams, but this was the first they'd heard that sounded like deliberate malice.

"What do you think the Putnams have against us all?" John asked.

"I can't think," answered Sam, " I have been wracking my brains over it all the while since. Mr. Procter is known to be hardheaded at times. So is the Sergeant. I suppose there have been a few times they banged those hard heads together."

"Well, we will ask Daniel and Joseph what they think. At least it's good to know there is more reliable evidence to the unreliability of these witnesses. Tomorrow being Lecture, we'll get a few more signatures on our petition there."

Sam Barton was quite willing to testify to the events he witnessed -- against the Putnams and on behalf of the Nurses et al -- because he was married to Hannah Bridges, daughter of Sarah Cloyce (Rebecca's sister) by her first marriage. His parents were among those driven out of Maine during the Indian wars, and back to Salem and Boston.

However, in the next few days Sam Barton's own mother-in-law was to be accused, whereupon he became more chary of testifying. The words and actions, even of the relatives of those accused was coming under official scrutiny.

Cotton Mather

Chapter Eighteen — Solemn Humiliation and Fasting
(31 Mar)

God's judge Himself, and Christ attorney is,
The Holy Ghost registerer is found;
Angels the sergeants are, all creatures kiss
The book, and do as evidence abound.
All cases pass according to pure law,
And in the sentence is no fret nor flaw.
-- Edward Taylor, **Sacramental Meditation** #38

Many in the Village prayed long and hard the next
Lecture Day, which had been set aside throughout Massachusetts
Bay Colony as a Day of Solemn Humiliation and Fasting. But prayer
is a mystery. It is conversation with God in which he says nothing
clearly. His clearest speech is in the scriptures and there He
encourages us to pray for all that we have on our minds and hearts.
We are told to ask for the desire of our hearts, with the promise that
what we ask "according to his will" we shall receive. But we are also
told we do not receive because we ask amiss. Prayer is a vehicle of
thanksgiving and of praise as well as of complaint and supplication.
It is the most important place for the church to agree — more
important even than synods and assemblies. But it is not a substitute
for other kinds of faithfulness.

He who robs the widow will not gain God's ear by any prayer
but that of thorough repentance, and that only in conjunction with
restitution. He who remains unreconciled to his brother goes to the
altar in vain. He who serves mammon may spend every morning,
every evening, and all day on the Sabbath in forms of solemn
humiliation, fasting, and prayer — yet God will not hear him. Even
when the righteous pray, God answers according both to his
revealed will — and his secret will.

So God did not answer all our prayers of that day on that day
or for many another day. He did not answer because we asked for
things that were contrary to his revealed will, much less his secret
will. He may have answered some who were humble or were being
humiliated, that is driven to the very humus. Many of us were just
beginning to learn humility. Perhaps he answered all those who

were eventually humiliated. For humus is ever fertile. It was from that dust we came, in that dust we raised our sustenance, and to that dust we would return. What strange creatures, dust and glory, earth and spirit, futility and hope! The scriptures say God draws near the dusty humble, but opposes the proud.

We went to meeting in the Village and in our midst were the afflicted girls, except of course, for Betty Parris. The Reverend Parris lectured on the great passage "Greater is he that is in you, than he that is in the world," which would have been better had he not added so many jots and tittles. Several of the "afflicted" cried out strange and ridiculous things during the service, although those near them restrained and quieted them when they could. Reverend Parris looked drawn and harried. As the service ended, Mary Tarbell heard Abigail Williams exclaiming she had seen a great number of persons in the Village in a mock sacrament with red bread and red drink.

Nevertheless the word was a comfort, and it was almost cheerfully that Sam, Daniel and John scurried about with their petition afterward. They asked a number of the respected members to sign. One or two refused, but a great number were quite willing. Daniel had brought a pen, and had people signing on the front stoop, but the ink got spilled, and made a rather ugly stain on the boards beneath the railing. They rounded up a few more who were willing and betook themselves to Ingersoll's, where Mary found them more ink. There they filled up the paper.

The additional signatures included: Isaac and Elizabeth Cooke, neighbors and relatives of the Goodells and Coreys; Benjamin and Sarah Putnam, Daniel's neighbor from up above Davenport Hill and cousins of Thomas and Joseph; Job and Esther Swinnerton, who lived between the Nurses and the Goodells; Samuel Sibley, whose wife gave Tituba and Indian John the recipe for the witchcake; Daniel and Hephzibah Rea, from east of the road beyond Porter's Hill toward Daniel's; William and Hannah Osborne, who live down toward Salem and one more.

Before the last signature was placed, however, Sergeant Thomas Putnam and one of the constables came in looking around suspiciously.

"What have you got people a-signing, Tarbell?" the Sergeant asked.

"No secret thing, Sergeant. Read it yourself and sign if you like," John replied.

He did read it, and although he looked hard and long could

find little to censure. Nevertheless he said, "That's a fine way to be spending a day set aside for prayer and fasting."

That angered John so he replied, "Jesus said one might pull an ox from a ditch on the Sabbath. I don't suppose he minds a Christian trying to pull his mother from prison."

As the Sergeant glared at him, his half brother Joseph, more slender but no less manly, shouldered his way in front of Thomas, and with considerable show of it, dipped the pen, raised it in the air and added his signature which filled the last space on the petition.

Joseph then turned to his brother, looked him brazenly in the eye, and said, "Now that's too bad, Thomas. Uncle John and several of our cousins have signed, too. It's a shame there's no room left for you!" Daniel was to berate them later for "unnecessarily stirring up antagonism" as he put it, but at that moment John looked as though he could have kissed Joseph.

Francis Nurse had left after the service, but as they came out of Ingersoll's, Nathaniel Putnam, Sr., Joseph's other uncle—he with whom the Nurses had long contended over the land at the creek forks above Crane River -- walked up to Sam Nurse, and handed him an envelope saying, "I missed your father. Please give this to him with my compliments."

John and Sam, suspecting the envelope contained some further lawsuit about the borders, were nonplused as they walked home. When they gave the envelope to their father, however, he broke into a broad grin, and said, "This is the surprise I was promising you boys. Here you open it, Sam."

Sam opened it and read:

> Nathaniel Putnam, Senior, being desired by Francis Nurse, Senior, to give information to the court of what I could say concerning his wife's life and conversation: I the above said Putnam have known this above said woman fourteen years and what I have observed of her, human frailty excepted: her life and conversation hath been according to her profession: and she hath brought up a great family of children and educated them well so that there is in some of them apparent signs of godliness: I have known her to differ with her neighbors, but I never knew or heard of any that did accuse her of what she is now charged with.
>   Signed, Nathaniel Putnam

"**I** went over and asked him myself," Father said proudly. "That night you went out to talk with young Joseph Holten, I knew the Lord was trying to humble me, too, so I went to Mr. Putnam and asked a favor—the first I ever asked in all the years I've known him. It felt like the first time I took the Lord's Supper! And it seemed to do him good, too!"

"**Well** done, Father! Wait until Daniel sees this, " exclaimed Sam.

"**Daniel?**" asked Father.

They stood dumb and, Sam grew red.

At last John answered, "Well, since you've heard the name, Daniel Andrew has been helping us—but not a word to anyone else. We promised."

"**Why** all the secrecy?" Father asked, puzzled.

"**We** are waiting to see whether this thing is coming to a quick end—or if there is more madness ahead. If this is only the beginning, then anyone may become fair game for the magistrates."

"**You** mean you think there will be more arrests?"

"**Yes**, Father. We're afraid there will be."

Francis paused and raised his bristly brows toward the tops of the trees.

"**I** think I should rather die than stand before such an examination as Mother faced," he said.

"**Nay**, Father, no one has mentioned your name. And if they do, we will be ready this time."

John's own words frightened him. Sam, and Francis, too, looked at him with surprise.

That evening Daniel came over and brought Joseph Putnam with him.

"**Welcome**, Joseph. You must feel torn by this thing!" Sam said, unsure how to address him.

"**Nay**, Sam. My half-brothers and I have long been opposite sides of many things. You know my father gave me the home place by his will six years ago—which puts me solidly in the place of the biblical Joseph so far as his brothers' feelings about me. But more than that, I think they are educated above and beyond their wits, and inclined to be wrong in many things.

"**I** am here because I was at the first three examinations, and I heard and saw the first battles of this campaign. Those girls and the accused women weigh upon me. I must do what I can to stop this."

"**You** know how high our own stakes are," John said, "but

you should also know that any one or all of us could fall suspect easily—especially after today when your brother the Sergeant witnessed us circulating our petition."

"He cannot charge his uncle and cousins with witchcraft—at least I don't think he will. If he thought he could get away with it, he might charge me."

"We have your other uncle's petition as well!" Sam exclaimed, and he proudly offered that paper to Joseph. While Joseph read it, with Daniel looking over his shoulder, Sam asked, "Where is Rayment?"

"He won't be here tonight," Daniel replied. "We have talked and he thinks we would be better without him just now. Apparently his father has got the wind up over this affair. It seems he had kinfolk amidst the witch hunts in England during the Commonwealth, and wants his family to keep far from it. William says he will help if he can from time to time, and get any new information to us. He has written an account of his evidence about those girls and their 'sport' at Ingersoll's. He has asked Mary Ingersoll and Elliott to do likewise, although Mary is torn between her husband's allegiances and us. I think Rayment's well out of it right now. We each have our callings."

They spent a good part of the evening telling Joseph all they knew and questioning him about the first three examinations. He was particularly interested in Rayment's evidence about the girls' at Ingersolls and their naming of Mistress Procter in "sport" and Sam's reiteration of the things John Houghton and Samuel Barton had heard at Sergeant Thomas's—the Sergeant and his wife trying to convince Mercy Lewis she called out of Goody Procter in her fit.

"Whew!" said Joseph, when he had finished. "I think I'll change my name to Jones. I am ashamed to be related to such people. What drives them?"

"I don't know," answered Daniel after some reflection. "Perhaps they heard the earlier rumors elsewhere and are so caught in the madness that they suspect every rumor to be true. I'd prefer that to thinking they are cold-bloodedly trying to get even with the Procters for some past injury. Do you know nothing that would explain it, Joseph?"

"Thomas and I do not have the best fraternal relationship, and I am therefore inclined to doubt my own interpretations of his actions. Lord knows Thomas has been in plenty of brawls over one thing or another—land and the Village church, especially, but I can't connect Procter with those. I do know that Elizabeth Hubbard and Mercy Lewis are friends with Mary Warren, the Procter's maid, and that John Procter is not always kind to Mary. Then, too, Mistress Procter has some reputation as a midwife and Elizabeth's uncle Griggs, being a doctor, no doubt dislikes the competition. But that doesn't bring it back to Thomas and Anne. Except that the girls are friends."

"They say Griggs was one of the first to suggest witchery when the Parris girls first had fits. Is he a close friend of your brother?"

"My half-brother, if you please. Yes, but not so close to him as Jon Walcott and Edward. I think Daniel's first guess is the better. Something Tituba said in the days after her examination convinced the ministers and magistrates that there were nine more witches besides her. Considering they have arrested only four others—five if you count the Good child, that leaves four unaccounted for. If they are fully convinced there are still four active witches among us, I can imagine them doing anything to pick them out and have them charged."

"Then any of us might be next, or more likely our wives," groaned Sam.

Joseph filled the others in on what had occurred at the first three trials. He had transcribed what was said and remembered quite a bit more.

Most interesting were his comments on the examination of Tituba.

She was at first stubborn and answered much as the other two—saying she did not hurt the children and did not know how the devil worked. But seeing Reverend Parris's mounting anger, she changed horses and began to describe how the devil had come to her.

Thereafter she was so completely under the domination of Reverend Parris, that she looked constantly to him as she testified, and added or modified what she said in response to his expressions.

Joseph commented, "You remember when I made the great mistake of going to Mr. Parris over Ezekiel Cheever's unlicensed borrowing of my horse? Well two things I concluded from the minister's mishandling of that affair. First, he does not understand people and how to deal with them. Second, he is obsessed with his own authority, and exercises it highhandedly in order to maintain it.

"Under that high hand, Tituba openly charged Sarah Good and Sarah Osborne and spoke of other witches from Boston, whose names she did not know. She said the other witches threatened and afflicted her, even then, so that she was afraid to answer. The four girls cried out during the first part of her examination, saying they, too, were afflicted, by knives, pinches, and so forth. Tituba repeatedly said the others would cut off her head if she told. "

Daniel wondered aloud if this detail might derive from the gory death of Christian Trask, which some had attributed to witchcraft, though the coroner's jury on which he and Rayment had served, concluded it was suicide.

Tituba went on to confess she had given in to the witches and a mysterious man, who seemed to be their leader. Joseph had heard they questioned her again in gaol, where she said she signed a book with nine other signatures. She said she was ordered to hurt the Parris girls and did hurt them once, but afterwards refused, even though the others told her she must continue. They supposedly alternated between offering her rewards, such as a yellow bird of her own, and threats, of death, etcetera. She confessed only to minor involvement and spent most of her time describing how she had held out against the other witches. But she did say she flew on a pole to Dr. Griggs with Goodwives Good and Osborne, where they afflicted Elizabeth Hubbard. She said she had never gone with them again, but they might have sent something like her on other occasions.

Daniel said the spectre doctrine must have been taught her by her interrogators or the girls. He also attributed many of the features of Tituba's testimony directly to the Elizabeth Knapp report—such things as the appearances of a black dog and a wolf, and the hairy creature which walked upright and had the head of a woman, but turned into a woman. Joseph said she later told the magistrates that woman was Sarah Osborne.

At the end of Tituba's examination she herself went into a fit. When she was asked who afflicted her she said they blinded her and would not let her see who they were.

Joseph was adamant that neither Sarah Good nor Sarah Osborne gave any evidence upon which a sensible juror or magistrate could build a case. It was true, he said, that Good rather desperately seemed to suggest Sarah Osborne must be the one who afflicted the girls; at least she told the magistrates to ask her about it, but that could have no weight.

He reiterated that the central evil of this thing was the seriousness with which the ministers and magistrates listened to and believed the girls.

Joseph then said he had read over his own account and talked with others about it until finally he felt he needed to talk to the girls themselves. He found, however, that his half-brother Thomas would not allow him to talk to Anna privately, and he was only able by surreptitious means to speak for a few minutes with Mercy Lewis, who had not then been involved in the accusations, or "afflictions".

She told him the same things that the others had inferred from the conversations at the Sergeant's house — that Mistress Anne Putnam first mentioned the names of Mistress Corey and Mother Nurse to Anna, thinking they fitted the vague description Tituba had given of the two unnamed witches. Mother Nurse was thought to be the tall one and Corey the short one. When next Anna had a fit, Mercy said Mistress Putnam asked if it was Goody Nurse or Goody Corey who afflicted her and Anna answered it was Goody Corey. Within a week, however, Anna claimed she thought she "saw" Rebecca Nurse, too, as she testified at Mistress Corey's examination. Within a few days of that, several of the girls were naming both of them.

Daniel vetoed John's suggestion that Joseph write a deposition about his conversation with Mercy. "What we are coming to learn is that our petitions and depositions are only likely to tell with a reasonable set of judges, which means they must be more than solitary accounts or hearsay. At this point, we have a much bigger problem, which is the degree of credibility afforded these girls. They always corroborate each other. That is our greatest obstacle."

"Daniel," John said, "I mentioned to you some time ago a thing that has troubled me. Joseph's tale has helped me with it some, but I would like to have it clear. Is it possible Tituba is a real witch and the source of these afflictions?"

"I'm sure we have all given the question of real witches serious thought. If there are any among us, however, we have yet to hear evidence that proves it." Daniel replied. "No reasonable court gives weight to testimony that has been compromised so thoroughly as that of these girls. We know for a fact that two of the chiefest — indeed at this point the two most chief — have confessed openly before three reliable persons that they were having "sport" in accusing Mistress Procter. We know in addition that they have been supplied at least two names by their mother — that your mother's name and apparently Mistress Procter's was give Anna by Mistress Putnam. Furthermore, we can find the sources for nearly all of their witchcraft descriptions in several written accounts easily available to them and those who instruct them.

"As for Tituba's confession, it has been simply and plainly made under duress. The man who has complete authority over her life has as much as required her to say she is a witch. She is no more responsible for it than a small child."

"But are there no mysteries in this thing for you!" John protested.

"Aye, I'll admit to one great mystery. I have been searching the Baxter, Mather and Willard accounts, but I can find no mention of yellow birds. These yellow birds have been the one original feature our witnesses have introduced."

Sam laughed aloud. "Then I have something to tell you!" he said.

The others looked at him in surprise as he began his tale.

"Last October I went down one day to talk to one of the Goodell's about buying a cow. Although it was a cool morning, when the sun was well-risen I began to grow hot, so I stopped and sat down near Sam Abbey's where a clearing reaches back from the road. I sat but a few minutes before I heard voices coming through the still air. I looked back up toward the head of the clearing and saw Sarah Good and Dorcas come out of the woods.

"They went up and down gathering something from the dried plants along the edge of a garden plot. After doing this for a while, they sat down on some rocks. I was behind a bush from them and I did not like to watch them secretly, but neither did I want to disturb them, so I stayed still. Sarah put aside her pipe and seemed to scatter something from her hand. After a bit I could see some birds flying about at the edge of the woods near them. It struck me that they must have been gathering seeds and were feeding them to the birds.

"The child sat very still as the birds flitted from the brush at the edge of the woods. I could hear her mother talking to herself like she does, while she, too, sat, and extended her arm on her knee. Her fingers were very still.

"By then I could make out the birds were goldfinches, and seemed quite friendly. A bird with black wings, a cock, settled on the ground where Sarah had scattered a few seeds on a bare patch. Then three females joined him and they twittered as they ate. The cock rose and alighted on Sarah's fingers. I guess she had kept a pile of seeds there. She seemed to have stopped her murmuring, but the bird flew away after a moment and sat on a low branch. Cocking his head and twittering, he flew out over the patch of garden, then dashed back and landed again on Sarah's finger. I shook my head in amazement over it. Sarah and Dorcas were both very still as the bird pecked up a seed and raised his head to swallow it, then snatched another. A yellow female joined him and she, too ate from Sarah's outstretched palm.

"After swallowing four or five more seeds, they flew back to the twig, but before they could return, the other two skipped from the bare patch to Sarah's hand, and ate there, too—facing Sarah and scrutinizing her face like they were puzzled at what manner of tree she might be. The pair on the twig flew back, and frightened the others away. They pecked up a seed each, but Sarah suddenly flapped her hand and all four scattered back into the woods.

"Then Sarah spoke loud enough that I could hear her, 'There was plenty for all, ye ungrateful creatures! Why must ye drive away the poor ones! Have you been a-studying at the rich people's houses?'

"Dorcas clapped her hands. 'Let me feed them! Let me feed them!'

"'They won't be back this morning, Dorothy-bird,' she said, 'P'raps tomorrow you may feed them. We have few friends enough, and it is well to care for what friends we have. We shan't be like some of them.'

"Muttering again, she put her pipe back in her mouth and began some haphazard gardening, pulling up the dried plants drooping and lying across last year's rows. Dorcas followed her, imitating her movements and piping to herself, with sounds that were cheerful imitations of the birds. I slipped away on down the road after that, but ever since I first heard the girls talk about 'yellow birds' I guessed someone must have told them about Sarah and her goldfinches."

"Wonderful!" exclaimed Joseph. "Perhaps one of the girls saw the same thing on another occasion—or Sarah or Dorcas spoke of it to someone. That is all there is to that! But making our potentates believe it is another matter! No matter what interpretation we put on it, they would have quite another. I think it would be best not to tell it to anyone else just yet, otherwise they will have you up as another witness against Sarah and her child."

"I marvel at you, Sam," said Daniel who had been mulling over his story, "you are deeper than I thought to keep this secret so long from us."

"**Nay**, I did not keep it from you so much as never think to tell you. I am not deep, but slow! I think I had forgotten it myself, until the girls started talking about yellow birds, and the memory began to stir."

"**Still** waters run deep, so saith the ancients. Well," continued Daniel, "as Joseph says, it may put our reasonable minds to rest, but it gets us no farther in putting quit to the madness. At least we must agree that apart from compelling and independent evidence, there is no reason to believe there is so much as a whiff of witchcraft among us, despite the great efforts being exerted to extirpate it. Does that make things any clearer for you, John?"

"**Yes**," he answered. "It puts my heart at peace in one way and makes it much simpler in my mind. But it also puts us at complete odds with our magistrates and ministers. It means we quite disbelieve what they completely believe."

"**That** is so. And it means our great day of prayer and fasting cannot end tonight. If the ministers and magistrates believe there are four more witches and perhaps a wizard still loose among us, they are only beginning their witch-hunt."

Standing to take his leave, Joseph responded, "I have given that some thought, and I have resolved that whoever comes to arrest me or my wife will be met with powder and ball. I am keeping my best horse ready to saddle, and two brace of pistols loaded. As long as the fantasies of silly girls are taken as gospel among us, I will not go tamely before the law."

This was the strongest statement any of them had made yet, and the other three were at a loss for words.

"**Furthermore**," said Joseph, I am going to make my preparations known!"

"**You** may well be the safer for it, Joseph." Daniel said, slapping his thigh. "However, it is not a plan that would work for many others in the Village. We still need to do what we can to get this mockery of justice exposed and end it."

After Joseph left them, Sam asked Daniel, "Weren't you with Israel Porter and his wife when they came to warn Mother?"

"**Why**, yes, I think the Porter's had heard her name mentioned and they told your Uncle Cloyce and me. We all thought she and your father should know."

"**Couldn't** you or they write up an account of it that would do Mother good in court?"

"**I** hadn't thought of it. But now that I do, I agree it would be wise. Her remarks and surprised reactions spoke strongly of her innocence. Come to think of it, the Porters remarked upon that as we departed. That would certainly bear some weight if we can get reasonable judges. I will try my hand at a version of it and talk with the Porters and your Uncle Peter. A fine idea, Sam.

"And furthermore," Daniel went on, "it is time I began to do what I can to get these matters before a reasonable court. A court of assistants would inevitably have better men on it—there would be five to seven, and there are not five such blind men in all the colonies as the two we now have—though I doubt not they are all right as farmer and merchant.

"I will go to Boston tomorrow and see if I can find a few sympathetic ears to help in bringing about such a change. Why don't you two talk to the Porters and your Uncle Cloyce. Then all three of us will be able to keep our minds occupied with something more useful than bloodthirsty thoughts."

When they had left, John spoke to Sam, "What Joseph said reminded me of my own words today with Father Nurse."

"Me, too," said Sam, "Only Joseph has a unique position as Daniel said, and he has already made his plans. I almost want to make the same for us, only Mother Nurse is in Salem gaol, and it wouldn't do her any good to open a rebellion in the Village."

"Especially when we have so many of the best people on her side—I guess it could only do her harm. Daniel seems to be right—it is the court and especially the girls and their families whom we must fight—and that not with powder or ball."

Chapter Nineteen — Sarah Cloyce and the Procters
(4, 8, 11 April)

*If the party suspected be the son or daughter, the man-servant
or maid-servant, the familiar friend, near neighbor, or old
companion of a known and convicted witch, this may likewise be
a presumption; for witchcraft is an art that may be learned, and
conveyed from man to man.*
-- William Perkins, Point Six in "**A Discourse of the
Damned Art of Witchcraft**," 1608.

For the first two days of April a cold and driving rain
dampened the enthusiasm of the witch finders. Daniel was in Boston
speaking with some influential people there. Sam and John went to
Mr. Porter again, and asked him if he and his wife would consider
writing an account of their visit to Mother on the occasion they first
told her of the rumors. The Porters had the same reaction as
Daniel — surprise they had not thought of it themselves.

"Nay," John said, "We each find it hard to see the things
directly before us!"

Recollecting the conversation on that occasion, the Porters
said they would ask Peter Cloyce and Daniel Andrew to witness the
account as well.

Mercy Lewis, now officially one of the "afflicted," reported a
vision on April 1st. Mercy was a young woman who had served as a
maid in three households of the Village: first in Reverend
Burrough's; then for nine months at William Bradford's (whose wife
was cousin to William Rayment); and now in Sergeant Putnam's.
She had, therefore, been companion and overseer to Anna Putnam
during her "afflictions," which began in the second week of March.

Mercy first dabbled in "the game" upon the visit of Martha
Corey to the Putnam home in mid-March. She then joined the
general tangle and confusion during the trials of Martha Corey and
Mother Nurse. But she had accused no one directly, despite the
insistence of Sergeant Thomas and Anne that she had accused
Mistress Procter in her fits. On the first of April, according to
ministers who visited her that day, she had a vision of a glorious
man in white who came to her in a place full of light and sang her

songs and psalms from the scriptures to comfort her in her fits. She was very reluctant to leave this place, she said. The ministers were much impressed. Thus the "afflicted" were further anointed as recipients of heavenly visions as well as of hellish ones. (The account was much the same as Cotton Mather's published record of comforting visions the Goodwins had in the midst of their afflictions a few years earlier.)

Mercy Lewis, although involved in many of the trials, was nearly always an "indirect" accuser—having fits and being "afflicted" but seldom saying who was responsible. Others, notably Abigail Williams and Anna Putnam, frequently told the court which witch was afflicting Mercy on a particular occasion.

As Mercy Lewis was often an indirect accuser, Sarah Cloyce was one indirectly accused. Her sisters were Rebecca Nurse, and Mary Easty (soon to be complained of). All three were daughters of Joanna (Blessing) Towne, whom someone somewhere sometime mentioned to John Putnam, the weaver, in connection with witchcraft, and he in turn mentioned it to Henry Kenney, who attested to it at Rebecca Nurse's examination. (Many of those arrested hereafter had chiefly this against them—that they were kin to another accused.)

On April 3rd, the Lord's Day, Goody Cloyce, made a mistake. Failure to attend meeting was one of the things which had been brought against Sarah Good and Sarah Osborne. Sarah Cloyce did not like Reverend Parris and had not attended much since he came. But that Lord's Day she came at the insistence of her family, who due to Goodman Kenny's testimony, feared she might be suspected. There were small disturbances from the "afflicted" during the service but no great outbreaks. Goody Cloyce reacted vigorously, however, after Reverend Parris rose and named his text, John 6:70. When he began to read it, "Have I not chosen you twelve and one of you is a devil," she became very angry at the thinly veiled reference to her sister (and others) recently arrested. Sarah got up abruptly and stalked out of the meeting. The wind was blowing strongly, and the door slammed to with a bang, but many thought she had slammed it a purpose. Later two of the afflicted girls claimed to have seen her go out to a black sabbath meeting with other witches.

On Monday a complaint was filed against Sarah Cloyce, wife of Peter Cloyce, for witchcraft. Captain Jonathon Walcott and Lieutenant Nathaniel Ingersoll signed the complaint. Cited as "afflicted" were Abigail Williams, Mary Walcott, Ann Putnam,

Mercy Lewis, and John Indian.

Peter Cloyce, Sr. came to Francis Nurse that afternoon. Peter was Sarah's second husband (her first had been Edmund Bridges) and she his second wife. They had fifteen children between them, but only six at home, and two of them in their twenties. The magistrates had wasted no time after Sarah's exit from the Meeting House.

"They're coming for Sarah," he told Father Nurse when he found him in the turning shed.

Francis took him by hand. "Nay, Peter. Of all things a man could never imagine, this has got to be about the worst."

After commiserating a while, they went off on in Peter's wagon, and Francis didn't return again until the next morning, when Rebecca's other brother-in-law, Isaac Easty, Sr., brought him home.

Mary Tarbell sat them down for a midday meal, and Francis told her they had tried to get Aunt Cloyce to go down to Peter's family in Maine, but she wouldn't budge. Not her husband or her two brothers-in-law, nor various other Towne connections — not her own children and sisters — could prevail to persuade her to flee.

Nor would Mary Easty, another sister, make any provision against being arrested, when she was charged two weeks later. It was not until more than a dozen people had been put to death, including two of her own kindred, that a Towne sister-in-law did not forthrightly submit to the authorities.

The Townes were loyal to one another and stubborn — and no one had yet been hanged in April — while Aunt Cloyce sat at her spinning wheel for four days, expecting to be arrested at any moment.

Our officials seem to have been proceeding more cautiously, however, since no action was taken on the complaint until that Friday, when a warrant was issued for her arrest. In fact all the "afflicted" were interviewed before the warrant was issued, and other inquiries were made. But the "afflicted" said much the same things they had said about the others, so even a more circumspect magistry would have been hard-put to treat Sarah Cloyce differently.

On Friday, George Herrick came to the farm and seemed surprised to find her there. He did a lackadaisical search, picking up a few hanks of cloth and wool, but discarding them as not fancy enough to be a witch's "poppets".

Elizabeth Procter, wife of the strong-minded John, was complained against at the same time as Goody Cloyce, and both women were included in the same arrest warrant. Further, their examinations were combined. In addition to the afflicted mentioned in the complaint, Mary Warren, the Procter's maid, was required to come as a witness.

On Monday, April 11th, Goody Cloyce and Mistress Procter were examined in Salem Town at the Meeting House before a more substantial set of judges. Daniel Andrew's consultations in Boston seemed to have done some good.

While all prior examinations had taken place before only two magistrates, this one included Thomas Danforth, deputy governor (still under the Bradford government, which was not replaced until May); Isaac Addington, secretary of the colony; Mr. Hathorne; Major Samuel Appleton; James Russell; and Captain Samuel Sewall; as well as Mr. Corwin. This then, was a "council" the highest court of the colony under the judicial laws then in force. It was also the first examination to be held in Salem Town rather than the Village. Most of us wondered about the reasons for the expanded court and the change of venue. The consultations leading up to these examinations perhaps accounted for the longer duration since the warrant.

The examinations of Sarah Cloyce and Mistress Procter had a few new features. Reverend Parris was appointed by Deputy Governor Danforth to be secretary, and make a transcript of the examination. We were most curious about the silence of Mr. Hathorne, since this was one of the few times he was not in the fore. He passed a few notes to Deputy Danforth, however, and once or twice spoke in his ear during the examination.

Reverend Noyes opened the session in prayer.

Deputy Governor Danforth conducted the questioning. At first it seemed he was a more circumspect interrogator than Mr. Hathorne. He began with Indian John, perhaps as the weakest witness.

"John, who hurt you?"

"Goody Procter, first, and then Goody Cloyce."

"What did she do to you?"

"She brought the book to me."

Mr. Danforth seemed to exhibit more skepticism than had been Mr. Hathorne's wont. "John! tell the truth. Who hurts you? Have you been hurt?"

"The first was a gentlewoman I saw."

"Who next?"

"Goody Cloyce."

"But who hurt you next?"

"Goody Procter."

"How oft did she come to torment you?"

"A good many times, she and Goody Cloyce."

"Do they come to you in the night as well as the day?"

"They come most in the day."

"Who?"

"Goody Cloyce and Goody Procter."

"Where did she take hold of you?"

"Upon my throat, to stop my breath."

"Do you know Goody Cloyce and Goody Procter?"

"Yes, here is Goody Cloyce."

Attention being directed to her, Sarah Cloyce asked John, "When did I hurt thee?"

He answered, "A great many times."

"Oh! You are a grievous liar!" she replied.

"What did this Goody Cloyce do to you?" Mr. Danforth continued, after looking sternly at Sarah Cloyce for a moment.

"She pinched and bit me till the blood came."

"How long since this woman came and hurt you?"

"Yesterday at meeting." (The lecture in the Village.)

"At any time before?"

"Yes a great many times."

Mr. Danforth then began to question the other witnesses.

"Mary Walcott! Who hurts you?

"Goody Cloyce."

"What did she do to you?"

"She hurt me."

"Did she bring the book?"

"Yes."

"What were you to do with it?"

"To touch it, and be well. . ."

Mary Walcott then started into a rigid and trembling fit which lasted but a minute, but stirred up the other girls to further "afflictions". Mr. Danforth, however, looked at them as sternly as he had Goody Cloyce. They became subdued and he went on.

"Doth she come alone?"

"Sometimes alone, and sometimes in company with Goody Nurse and Goody Corey, and a great many I do not know . . ."

Mary started into a fit once more.

Mr. Danforth again regarded her sternly, then addressed

Abigail.

"Abigail Williams! Did you see a company at Mr. Parris's house eat and drink?"

"Yes, sir, that was their sacrament."

"How many were there?"

"About forty. And Goody Cloyce and Goody Good were their deacons."

"What was it?"

"They said it was our blood, and they had it twice that day."

Mr. Danforth turned back to Mary.

"Mary Walcott! Have you seen a white man?"

"Yes, sir, a great many times."

"What sort of man was he?"

"A fine grave man, and when he came, he made all the witches to tremble."

"Yes," Abigail blithely contributed, "the witches all were afraid of him and they had such a sight at Deacon Ingersoll's."

"Who was at Deacon Ingersoll's then?"

"Goody Cloyce, Goody Nurse, Goody Corey, and Goody Good."

Sarah Cloyce, bold as she was, found the strain too much at this moment, and she sat down abruptly, asking for water as she bent forward in a faint.

The girls fell into vigorous fits at this. Anna and Abigail cried out, "She is afraid!" and "Her spirit has gone to her sister Nurse in prison!"

The magistrates conferred and a constable brought a dipper of water to Goody Cloyce. The court called up Ephraim Sheldon, young son of the Widow Sheldon, Sam's closest neighbor to the south. (His eighteen year old sister, Susannah, was to join the "afflicted" in testimony against Giles Corey and Reverend Burroughs). Ephraim testified he had been at Ingersoll's on the Lord's Day and seen Mercy Lewis in one of her fits.

"I heard her cry out Goody Cloyce and when she came to herself she was asked who she saw. She answered she saw nobody."

"Who asked her this?"

"Mistress Putnam and Sergeant Putnam."

"What did they ask her?"

"They demanded of her whether or no she did not see Goody Nurse or Goody Cloyce or Goody Cory. She answered she saw nobody."

Once again the testimony of a witness presented the issue of "seeing" and "witnessing" to the court, but this interrogator did not take it up any more than had Mr. Hathorne.

Among the reasons that Deputy Governor Danforth did not behave more objectively than the two Salem magistrates was a connection of which most of us were ignorant at the time. His sister was married to Reverend Parris' brother. His sterner demeanor toward the "afflicted" was somewhat subverted by his sympathy for his wife's nieces.

The judges had heard all they needed to bind Goody Cloyce over to gaol, charged as a witch. They conferred and the Marshall was told to take the defendant, somewhat recovered, across to Ingersoll's. Elizabeth Procter was then called forward to the bar.

"Elizabeth Procter!" began Mr. Danforth, "Do you understand whereof you are charged: That you are charged to be guilty of sundry acts of witchcraft? What do you say to it? Speak the truth."

He turned to the girls, "And so you that are afflicted. You must speak the truth as you will answer it before God another day."

Those of us familiar with the previous examinations found this an unusual warning — unique in even mentioning the possibility of deceit among the afflicted.

"I am guiltless in this and know nothing of it," said Mistress Procter.

"Do you worship God?"

"Yes."

"How do you pray? Can you say the Lord's Prayer?"

"Our Father which art in heaven hallowed. . . (here the ministers, who were listening intently, thought she said "hollowed" and objected, thinking it a blasphemy. They asked Mr. Danforth to have her start again.)

When she was nearly through the second time, she said, "Deliver us from all evil. . ." rather than "Deliver us from evil," which the ministers fine-tuned ears somehow took as a possible prayer to Satan! They had her start again at "Give us this day. . ." but they seemed to find more suspicion in those two small matters than in the recitation of the rest of the prayer.

Mr. Danforth turned again to the witnesses.

"Mary Walcott! Doth this woman hurt you?"

"I never saw her so as to be hurt by her."

"Mercy Lewis! Does she hurt you?"

Mercy Lewis did not answer, as though in a fit of dumbness, which was her characteristic behavior through many of the examinations.

"Anna Putnam, does she hurt you?"

Anna, did not speak, either, and appeared not to have heard.

"Abigail Williams! Does she hurt you?"

Abigail thrust her hand into her mouth.

"John! Does she hurt you?"

"This is the woman that came in her shift and choked me," John said.

"Did she ever bring the book?"

"Yes, sir."

"What to do?"

"To write."

"What, this woman?"

"Yes, sir."

"Are you sure of it?"

"Yes, sir."

"Abigail Williams, does this woman hurt you?"

Still Abigail made no answer.

"Anna Putnam, does this woman hurt you?"

But Anna, too, remained silent.

"What do you say, Goodwife Procter, to these things?"

"I take God in heaven to be my witness, that I know nothing of it, no more than the child unborn."

"Anna Putnam! Doth this woman hurt you?"

"Yes, sir, often."

"Does she bring the book to you?"

"Yes."

"What would she have you do with it?"

"To write in it and I shall be well."

Abigail Williams spoke up, addressing Mistress Procter. "Did not you tell me that your maid had written in it?" (She meant Mary Warren.)

"Dear child, it is not so," replied Mistress Procter, "There is another judgment, dear child."

Abigail stood up, angrily it seemed, and went toward Mistress Procter with her fist curled in front of her. Immediately Anna joined them, and the two of them drew near, menacing her, but when they came so near as to touch her, Abigail's hand opened and she but brushed Mistress Procter's hood and then cried out,

"My fingers, my fingers burn!"

Both Abigail and Anna broke into fits again, shaking and contorting their limbs, and Anna would have collapsed had not her mother and another woman held her up by her arms.

Deputy Danforth had looked upon these events with disapproval and seemed about to rebuke the girls, but he was forestalled by another observer.

John Procter, who had thus far been sitting near the front of the court, could no longer countenance what went on. He cried out angrily at the girls who nearly struck his wife, then stood and demanded the court be kept in order.

Deputy Danforth who was accustomed to maintaining a great deal more dignity in his courtroom than this, was quite obviously growing incensed, but did not seem to know what to do about it. He turned his stern countenance upon the bold man who seemed the latest author of disorder.

Abigail, "recovering" from her fit, turned and pointed up crying out, "Look you! There is Goodman Procter upon the beam."

This was one of the regular features of the girls "second sight," – seeing the accused "on the beam". Strangely the magistrates never asked for a more exact description of this phenomenon. At first those of us who heard it thought it was the same as the childhood game of seeing figures in the exposed grain of the beams – something most of us had indulged our youthful fancies in. But the judges and ministers seemed to take it as meaning the "spectre" of the accused were suddenly taken up and sat upon the beam – straddling it as one would a broomstick.

Then Anna joined in and they both cried that Goodman Procter was a wizard.

All the rest of the "afflicted" began to have fits.

Mr. Danforth, now himself bewildered, addressed Anna with considerable solicity.

"Anna Putnam, who hurt you?"

"Goodman Procter and his wife, too."

Abigail cried, "There is Procter going to take up Mistress Pope's feet!"

Whereupon, Bathsheba Pope raised her feet straight out before her.

Mr. Danforth turned to Mr. Procter, who had been sitting in front, and trying to control himself and at the same time encourage his wife. Long before his burst of outrage, his face had grown dark with anger at the accusations of the girls.

"What do you say, Goodman Procter, to these things?"

Procter had been so concerned for his wife that he scarcely was able to assimilate the turn things had taken.

"I know not. I am innocent," he managed to answer, but his voice was still choked with passion.

Abigail shouted out again, "There is Goodman Procter going to Mistress Pope."

Mistress Pope fell into a fit.

Still addressing Mr. Procter, and once more on a familiar course, Mr. Danforth went on, "You see the devil will deceive you. The children could see what you was going to do before the woman was hurt. I would advise you to repentance, for the devil is bringing you out."

Again Abigail cried, "There is Goodman Procter going to hurt Goody Bibber."

Goodwife Bibber fell into a fit.

Abigail continued down the line, "prophesying" Mr. Procter's afflictions upon Mary Walcott, Anna Putnam, and Mercy Lewis. Each responded by going into fits.

When the noise of the girls had subsided, Benjamin Gould was called up.

"Benjamin Gould! What do you know of these things?"

"I saw them witches a-gathering last Lecture Day."

"Where saw you them?"

"They come into my chamber."

"Did they hurt you?"

"No, I did but see them."

"Who were they?"

"There was Goodman Corey and his wife and Goodman Procter and his wife and Goody Cloyce and Goody Nurse and Goody Griggs." (How quickly he rolled Mr. Procter into his story. Not only the girls, but also many of our witnesses were adept at assimilating accusations!)

"Were they the only ones?"

"Yes, sir."

A few other witnesses were called, who gave in the same kinds of remote circumstantial evidence we heard in other trials, and which would hear much more of. Arthur Abbott claimed to have seen some strange sights at the Procter home. Although the magistrates listened carefully (so carefully, in fact, that Major

Appleton later charged Abbott with false testimony because of an impossible date to which he testified) the magistrates quickly tired of this.

The magistrates ended the testimony, consulted together and not only committed Sarah Cloyce and Elizabeth Procter to Salem gaol, but they also committed John Procter! He went along without a struggle, bewildered, but relieved for the moment to be able to stay with his wife.

There were a number of new "facts" to be derived from the examinations of Goody Cloyce and Mr. and Mistress Procter. Abigail Williams mentioned forty witches, which quadrupled the size of the supposed coven, and went a long ways toward promoting wholesale suspicion throughout the Village and Salem. Abigail also mentioned Mary Warren as having "signed the book," the sure sign of a true witch. This became the basis for Mary's imminent arrest. Her witchery, however, was attributed to the influence of the Procters about whom she was to be questioned on several occasions.

John Indian testified to being afflicted first by "a gentlewoman I saw." Mr. Parris seems to have been unwilling to record any more specific identification for this "gentlewoman," but subsequently we found she was a relative of Mr. Corwin's! Further, Benjamin Gould testified not only that the Procters, but Goody Griggs had been among the witches! Mistress Rachel Griggs was the wife of Doctor William Griggs, he who early suggested witchcraft as the cause of the Parris girls' behavior. These were two of several cases where the magistrates deliberately and inconsistently ignored plain accusations as if they had never been made and did not further investigate someone who was accused (or at least not officially or publicly)!

There had been other omissions. Anna Putnam earlier, during the lecture by Reverend Deodat Lawson, spoke of a little yellow bird sitting upon his hat where it hung on a pin at the pulpit. Those around her hushed her and no more came of it, although everyone else remotely associated with the apparition of a "yellow bird" was accused as a witch.

On another occasion during later trials one of the afflicted cried out of seeing the appearance of the Reverend Samuel Willard of Boston. There the magistrates told the "afflicted" one that she had mistaken the identity of the spectre and sent her out of the courtroom for a while. In plain, the magistrates were not objective and had their own standards as to who was likely a witch and who not.

This higher court, which sat for only this examination, had begun with a more objective attitude toward the accusations and the testimony of the afflicted. But these men, too, were heavily influenced by their familiarity with "precedents" of witch prosecution which had come down to us. Thus Deputy Danforth's reference to the devil "bringing you out" when he addressed Goodman Procter. Despite an initial intention to maintain the dignity of the court and the standards of due process, the additional magistrates were quickly brought under the spell of the afflicted. Thus the ministers and magistrates were spontaneously willing to receive the accusation against John Procter.

The next day the court formally charged Goodman Procter. Reverend Parris submitted a summary of the accusations against him, beginning with Abigail William's saying that he, Mistress Procter, and Goody Cloyce had afflicted her on April 4th, and again the night of April 6th, and that the Thomas Putnam household had also been afflicted by these three on the 6th.

The magistrates sent Marshall Herrick up from Salem to the Village in order that he might get from Reverend Parris's a clear copy of the record of the previous examination. The marshall came to the Meeting House where Mr. Hathorne and the Village deacons sat with the minister as he finished the copywork. He found them at their task amidst continuing fits by John Indian, Abigail, and Mary Walcott. These continued to cry out of John Procter afflicting them. Abigail said "There is Goodman Procter in the magistrate's lap!" Mary Walcott affirmed seeing this. John cried out there was a dog under the table, and said "Come away," to the dog, and "Come away Goodman Procter," for he claimed Goodman Procter was upon the dog's back. Then John cried out "Goody Cloyce, oh you old witch," and fell into another fit, so that the marshall, Captain Walcott, Deacon Ingersoll and Reverend Parris together could barely restrain him.

During these agitations, Mary Walcott sat quietly knitting, but commented as John had this great fit, "There was Goodman Procter, and his wife and Goody Cloyce helping him."

John and Abigail were both taken away so that Reverend Parris might finish his written summary. Mary Walcott continued knitting beside him, but while he was writing she said, still calmly, "There Goody Cloyce has pinched me now."

Mary Walcott said she had never seen spectres of Mr. Procter or his wife until she was coming back from their examination the previous night. She said she saw Goody Procter riding behind her brother Jonathon all the way from Widow Gedney's to Phillip's farm, where Jonathon stopped to visit a while. Mary claimed, however, to see John Procter three times during the time Reverend Parris wrote his summary. As Reverend Parris was finishing, Mary cried out, "Oh yonder is Goodman Procter and his wife and Goody Nurse and Goody Corey and Goody Cloyce and Good's child." She then said, "Oh, Goodman Procter is going to choke me," and immediately acted in fulfillment of her prophecy with audible effects..

 Deacon Ingersoll gave a deposition of "evidence" he heard from Joseph Pope (the afflicted Bathsheba's husband). Mr. Pope said John Procter had told him and several others that if Reverend Parris would give John Indian into his custody he would soon drive the devil out of him.

 Mary Warren , the Procter's servant, was one of the three "afflicted" cited in the indictments against John Procter, but, although she was present at the Salem examination, she did not testify against them then. Those who soon began to question her cited the 26th of March as the first day Procter had afflicted her – the day Samuel Sibley had seen John striding angrily up toward the Village to bring Mary home in order, as he told Sibley, to "thrash the devil out of her".

 Back at Salem, having in hand Reverend Parris's record of the previous day as well as his notes of the morning's afflictions at the Village, the magistrates quickly concluded their formal charges against John Procter.

 Reverend Higginson closed that proceeding in prayer.

 Late the previous afternoon, two and a half weeks after Rebecca's arrest, her sister, Sarah Cloyce, was brought to the prison along with John and Elizabeth Procter. While they had been examined that morning, John Nurse had come to visit his mother in place of his father, explaining that Francis was at the examination to console and support the Cloyces.

 Rebecca's equipoise failed her and she reeled at the news of Sarah's arrest. She and Martha had recently speculated about the apparent slowing and perhaps an end of the accusations. They had wondered aloud if the girls might have been caught out in their lies at last or if the magistrates had been corrected in their foolishness by some of the ministers. At first, Martha and Rebecca did not like to talk too much of such things before the child, but Dorcas was a difficult little book to read. Doubting she understood what they discussed, they had come to talk more freely before her. Always their speculations carried a gleam of hope, and an expectation of justice restored.

But the warrant for Sarah and Elizabeth Procter, written almost a week earlier, sharply checked their optimism. Martha and Rebecca faintly hoped those examinations would end better than their own.

The two older women welcomed the newcomers and made them as comfortable as they could, vacillating among worrying over their own and these three further cases of gross injustice, and the practical complications connected with having a man bound over to their boudoir. Mr. Dounton solved that problem for them toward evening by moving the Procters to the cellar.

The three "old prisoners" and three new ones did not get time to reorganize themselves, however, nor did the two sisters get much time to embrace or mull over their common distress, for after Mr. Procter's examination the next evening, Mr. Dounton came up and told them they were all to be transported to Boston the following morning.

Thus plans and fixities were thrown about in fluctuations of the wind. That night, lying wakeful and somewhat less warmly blanketed (for she had given her mattress and half of the bedding to the Procters for the night) Rebecca found herself anxious and angry. She said a number of unkind or at least ungrateful things to her God. The three women and the girl lay snuggly on their mattress as doubt and anxiety quickly turned themselves into morning.

After Sarah's examination, Francis Nurse had welcomed Peter Cloyce and his son of the same name to stay with him in the Village. Daniel came over and Sam and John asked if they might include cousin Peter in their "conspiracy." Daniel knew Peter as a neighbor and readily agreed, so the four of them planned to gather the next night at Joseph Putnam's.

Their meeting, however, was put off . The Nurses and Cloyces were told at the last moment of a prisoner transport. They made an unexpected trip to Boston to re-settle their mothers there.

Chapter Twenty—Cold Comfort
(Apr 12 - 13)

*. . .Be thy calling never so mean and homely and never so hardly
accepted, yet, if thou hast lived by faith in thy calling, it was a
lively work in the sight of God; and so it will be rewarded when
thy change shall come. Many a Christian is apt to be
discouraged and dismayed if crosses befall him in his calling. Be
not afraid; let this cheer up thy spirit — that whatever thy calling
was, yet thou camest into it honestly and hast lived in it
faithfully; your course was lively and spiritual, and therefore
you may with courage look up for recompense from Christ.*
-- John Cotton (1585-1652) , ***Christian Calling***

On Friday, the 12th of April, Rebecca Nurse, Martha Corey,
Sarah Cloyce and the Procters with several others from Salem were
transported to Boston gaol. The Nurse tribe was weighed down with
the further hardship of a five hour ride rather than an hour's ride or
two hours walk. There was only the mildest sort of comfort for
Rebecca — and it seemed perverse to find any satisfaction in it — in the
fact that her sister Sarah was now with her. Nor did any of them
know the gaoler at Boston. For the first few months John and Mary
Arnold were to prove less sympathetic than the Dountons had
become.

The Arnold's were accustomed to unusual prisoners. Their
gaol had held "fanatical" Baptists and "heretical" Quakers, Indians,
and pirates, as well as more ordinary felons. But now they were
being commanded in the name of their sovereign majesties William
and Mary to keep witches in the gaol, which building was also their
home. Sarah Good, who was with them from the second week of
March did little to ease their minds. She and Sarah Osborne were
brought down in chains and were soon put back in chains. The court
so ordered not long after the first arrests, and, although the prison-
keeper could have modified the order (and indeed ignored a similar
one months later), he enforced it another month and a half after
Rebecca and company were transported to Boston.

After the exhausting trip, the cart lumbered to a stop a few
yards from the door. Rebecca saw it was neither a new building nor

an elaborate one. The dark lumber was not yet the silver-gray of the older homes, but in the back half of the building nearly a quarter of the boards had been replaced with newer lumber. Though tired from the jolting, Rebecca was alert enough to notice this.

Mr. Procter kindly helped his wife and Dorcas down, and then Rebecca. Mistress Corey and Sarah Cloyce followed. The see-saw motion of the single-axle cart had so pervaded Rebecca's mind that the ground felt unsteady. As her head cleared, she thought how nice it was to feel the motion stopped as well as the creaking of the wheels.

Ivy grew at one corner of the prison, and a gnarled and stunted rose next to the door. The prisoners swung their heads about taking in the neighborhood. Marshall Herrick had dismounted and tied his horse to a post. He, too, was tired of traveling and impatient to turn over his charges to their next keeper. He knocked loudly on the gaoler's door.

Mistress Arnold answered and finding it was he, shut the door again in order to summon her husband from within. A few minutes later he appeared, adjusting his dress and hastily swallowing some savory.

"**P**risoners from Salem," said Marshall Herrick.

"**M**ore witches?" asked Mr. Arnold.

"**A**ye."

"**T**hey aren't as crazy as that Good woman are they?"

"**N**o, this is a respectable lot, here. There is a child, though."

"**A** child? Well bring 'em in. You got a mittimus for me? Can't take nobody without paper."

"**P**aper I have, if you have ink. I need your mark on a receipt."

"**R**eceipt is it now! Every time some judge gets five minutes free for scheming, he figures out one more piece of paper to be carried back and forth. First you sign, then I sign, then he counter-signs, then we all make copies and send them out to each other, and pile up a few, and lose a few, and amend a few. Seems to me it would be easier if we just kept the gaols full of paper and let the prisoners go."

"**Y**ou would be wise not to let anyone hear you talk of letting these ones go. You never saw such a nervous country as Salem Village right now, with Salem Town close on its heels. No, I advise you not to be talking of letting these prisoners go!

"**A**s for me, I'm glad to be rid of them. I'm that tired I could sleep in the gaol myself, " continued the Essex County Marshall, "Where is a reasonable inn hereabouts?"

"No reasonable ones hereabouts. You got to go back out of town to find reasonable ones. Cost you twice as much to stay in this great city, just for the honor of it."

"Ps-shaw! I'll sleep on my horse before I pay that much, though they tell me I will be repaid when this is over.

"The sad thing is two of these prisoners kept the inn where I would have stayed! I'm that tired, I might stay there anyway, though their sons murder me in my sleep."

While the sleepy Marshall made small talk with the Boston Gaoler, a constable, who had driven the cart, and the gaoler's wife carried forward the more practical business of escorting the prisoners through the door and into the dwelling where four out of the six would spend most of the rest of their lives.

As Mistress Arnold led them through the door (which was not at the front, but at the front of the side of the building) and down a narrow hallway to the left and toward the back of the building, Rebecca smelled cooking, coming, she supposed, from the Arnold's own quarters off that corridor to the right.

Mistress Corey who followed Rebecca, said something about supper.

They came to a heavy locked door, which, once opened, admitted them to a single large room which took up the back and a little more than half of the building. The first thing Rebecca noticed was that it was much darker than the attic room some of them occupied in Salem. Two gunslits high on the back wall allowed what little daylight entered the room. Some of the others, who had been kept in the Dounton's cellar, however, expressed appreciation at being above ground. In the middle of the end wall a small fireplace contained some glowing coals, and before it on a three-legged stool, sat the squat figure of Goody Osborne. Her chains were draped over her knees, where she held her hands close wrapped in a musty wool shawl.

"Goodwife Osborne, is it you?" spoke John Procter, his hearty voice abrupt in the brown, quiet place.

Sarah Osborne turned her shoulders slowly toward the new prisoners, as the door behind them closed. Her cheeks which they had known as round and cheerful, hung much shrunken in pale folds. The rest of her complexion was still reddened, which they might have taken for a good sign, were it not for the heavy moisture shining on her brow. But her small eyes stared out feebly as from some depth, and they realized she was trembling. Her whole body vibrated minutely in a steady tremor, so that Rebecca stooped instinctively and put her own manacled hands upon the woolen bundle of her lap.

"My poor dear," she said, "You are ill."

Before Goody Osborne could answer, a high-pitched voice shrieked from the corner behind them to the left.

"It's my Dorothy-bird!" cried Sarah Good, "Here you are with the gentry come to call on us all wrapped in our chains!"

There was affection in the first sentence, but in the latter more of mad exultation and latent rebuke.

"May you all be ill as she, aye sick unto God's good death!" continued the voice, lower with a single note of anger, then quieter in triumph, "how art the mighty fallen."

Then another voice sounded, a thin high near-whisper from Sarah Osborne, "Pray, pay her no mind, she has been like this since the beginning." She broke off in a wheezing cough, which stirred her shivering into waves of shaking.

Elizabeth Procter and Sarah Cloyce both spoke then, "you poor dear," and "we must see if we cannot make you warmer."

Among the four women they sorted out more wrappings to put around the feverish woman. Mr. Procter knocked upon the door and asked for firewood, which Mr. Arnold brought just inside the door, repeating as his servant dropped each armload that the prisoners would be charged for it. John built up the fire and began to survey the dark room as his eyes became adjusted to the half-light. When the fire was crackling, he began to inspect the structure to find the sources of the frigid drafts that moved in sharp streams through it.

As he walked around the circumference of the room, he overheard the conversation back in Sarah Good's corner. The small figure with her pale oval face sat beside her mother. He shook his head, still wondering at this particular injustice. Going to the other women he spoke in a low voice.

"The child. She must be hungry. Do you think she is safe with her mother, after all."

Mistress Corey rose and pulling a part of a loaf from her ample pocket, went to the corner where she presented it to Goody Good.

"Thank you, marm," Sarah said, without a trace of irony, or

apparently any sense of the inconsistency with her earlier tone and words.

She broke it in half and gave half to Dorcas. "Say thank you, Dorothy bird."

"Thank you, Granmer Corey."

"What!" squawked her mother, "Why are you calling of her granmer?"

"We spent a few days together at Salem," explained Mistress Corey, "She and I and Mistress Nurse. We became friends, didn't we, Dorcas?"

"Yes, marm," said Dorcas, muffled by bread.

"And are you well?" asked Mistress Corey.

"I haven't got her ague, if that's what you mean," answered Goody Good, glancing toward the others gathered around Goody Osborne, " but that flibberty-gibbet William starves us down here. We've seen him but thrice, and if the Arnold's don't pity Dorothy-girl, we'll have nary a thing to eat." She slipped into her old long-suffering tone, " I'm eating for two now, you know."

Mistress Corey realized then, that the bundle on Goody Good's lap was not her hands or a bundle of chains, but her middle. They had last seen her almost six weeks earlier, and had not known of her pregnancy. Sarah stood and stretched as she finished her bread, and it was plain now.

"Then you must take double care of yourself," she said, "Perhaps it is the Lord's provision he has sent you some midwives."

"Nay!" shrieked Mistress Good, "Do not be dragging him in to what goes on in this place! His ministers and holy magistrates have called me witch and I will not hear his name no more — not until we are well out and they brought here in our places, the filthy liars, they and their bits of baggage, those mad girls. Nay do not name him!"

This outburst straightened the backs and turned the heads of all the others, saving Goody Osborne who repeated in a hoarse whisper, "She's been like that since the beginning."

"Then I will pray to him instead," answered Mistress Corey, swallowing a sterner answer. "When do you expect this child?"

"The signs would be some six weeks more," answered Goody Good, suddenly civil again. "I hope I may speak of signs. I hope I may. Do you think there would be any objection?" She asked it with a simple and solicitous tone.

"No, " faltered Mistress Corey, "no, of course not." And then,

to escape this bewildering conversation, "Come, Dorcas, come and
help Granmer Nurse toast some bread."

Dorcas looked up at her mother, who cocked and twisted her
head in gesture. "Go on," Sarah said.

Later as they arranged the blankets, the only furniture they
had been allowed to bring with them, Martha Corey spoke quietly
with Rebecca and Sarah Cloyce.

"Do you think it's good for Dorcas to be with her mother?"

"Yes," answered Rebecca, after a moments reflection, "I think
it is the best to be made of an ill situation. God seems to give
children special protection—even against their parent's
shortcomings. It's hard to imagine living with a mother like that, but
she is all Dorcas has known, and they love each other in their own
ways."

"Perhaps you're right, but I tremble when I put myself in the
child's place. Sarah is so unpredictable—one moment raging, the
next as polite as pie."

"The girl makes me think of my own Hepzibah," said Sarah
Cloyce, and Rebecca saw the tears in her eyes."

"Oh, you poor dear. We have been so taken up with all this
change that we have forgotten you. Martha comforted me so much
the first few days. She spoke the truth when she said they are the
hardest." And Rebecca hugged her sister.

After a decent silence, Martha went on, "There, there. We
have indeed neglected you. For all her suffering, Goody Good has
had more time to get used to these things than the rest of us. And no
doubt all her rages are seen as proof of the charges against her.
There is that in all of us would like to rage, Lord knows. Let us
encourage each other. For most of us, under the circumstances, are
even more inclined to despair."

There was another prisoner already incarcerated in Boston
gaol, a young woman. Rebecca did not recognize her, although
Martha soon did. Martha introduced herself but the woman was
very reticent to speak. Finally Martha asked, "Are you not Elizabeth
Emerson?"

At which Elizabeth nodded her head, then turned away.

A year ago in May, Elizabeth, the 28 year old daughter of
Michael Emerson of Haverhill, reached the end of a secret pregnancy.
She was not married and thus far had successfully concealed her
condition from her family. She gave birth to twins in her father's
house, most amazingly without her family knowing. The children

were both dead soon after birth. She concealed their bodies and then buried them. Although variations in her confession left some of us in doubt, the court found her guilty of deliberately killing the babies. She was tried in September 1691 and found guilty. She was sent to prison in Boston where she was to remain for almost two years.

Meanwhile her tale spread quickly through the environs of Ipswich and Essex County, where, together with other strange events, it heightened the sense of secret sins and evil deeds ready to break out among us.

Martha quietly told Rebecca who she was.

They finished laying out their bedding. After consultation with the Procters, they made their makeshift beds on either side of the earlier prisoners', which were laid close before the fire. The gaoler had sometime painted a yellow line three feet before the hearth. At dusk he came in to repeat a stern warning against any bedding or clothing left closer to the hearth and the danger of fire to such as they, locked up in gaol.

Mr. Procter built up the fire with a large backlog before they went to bed and twice during the night he rose to put on more wood. The wind still sifted through the large room, but John had stuffed clothes in some of the larger cracks, and the fire and their blankets made it tolerable.

Nevertheless, Sarah Osborne coughed and murmured all through the night, and Rebecca did not sleep as well as she had at Salem. She was thankful that her sister Cloyce slept more soundly. But deep in the night Rebecca found herself staring at the dim beams and shakes above her head. She began to pray through the long list of her other loved ones, who now were farther away and seemed obscure.

The Nurses and Cloyces brought a wagon down the next day, bringing the small furnishings from Dountons with additional food and clothing. Due to the distance and weather only Francis, Peter Cloyce, Sr., and John made that first trip. On the way down the wagon got stuck in the mud innumerable times. The three of them were thoroughly wet and worn and that much more discouraged when they reached Boston prison.

The sight of Mother Nurse in this distant dismal place was far worse than the weather. Francis held her bony wrists in his hands and looked into her face. He was more heart-broken at the smile than the tears. But the thing that brought hot tears to John's eyes and cold rage boiling to the rim of his heart was the sight of little Dorcas

Good there. The picture of her tender figure in the bleak prison came back to him often over the next weeks. It was that which led him to consciously entertain his first blood-thirsty thoughts.

Mother Nurse was full of compassion for the others, particularly Dorcas whom she and Mistress Corey had been mothering. Now that Dorcas was reunited with her half-crazed mother, Rebecca was even more solicitous of her welfare. Goodwife Osborne was very sick, largely because of inadequate clothing, the cold chains, and poor food and sanitation. Rebecca, Sarah, Mistress Corey and Mistress Procter were doing what they could for her, but it was to prove too little too late. They also reached out to Elizabeth Emerson, who remained aloof and silent most of the time.

The Arnolds were very strict. (For the first weeks they would not allow the prisoners to pray together — no doubt for fear they were praying satanic prayers. There was even some debate about allowing them Bibles, though ultimately they could scarcely deny them those.) They spared the visitors but one hour to visit, strictly by the glass, and then they were peremptorily dismissed. Peter Cloyce protested, but to no avail. When they hastily kissed Rebecca and Sarah and told them they did not think they would get someone down but two or three times a week, the two women comforted them and said they had their work there, while the others had theirs in the Village. Sarah was still emotional over the new hardships, but Rebecca was calm. Her superior peace made John angry again, although he would not admit it.

The night after their visit, the three men stayed with John's brother in Charlestown. He and his wife tried to comfort them, but being some distance from our troubles, they could not fathom the depth of the men's discouragement.

During the trip back they said little, although the weather was better, and the wagon less prone to stick in mudholes. When they got back, Peter went on home, but the Nurses held a family council of sorts at Sam's and Mary's.

The children played in the woodlot under the care of the older ones. They pretended to be wild Indians. The adults gathered about the fireplace while Sam added wood. Tom was still in a distant mourning, crippled by his fatal signature on those first complaints, and the rankling conviction he was the doorway through which this affliction had come to the Nurses. He said nothing. His Rebecca, sensitive to his guilt and confusion, said little more than he, although she made some good practical suggestions about gaol visits.

  Sanguine Ben, the youngest, talked a lot and both amused and alarmed the rest. Nevertheless he contributed little of moment, except to make a vague suggestion they needed to take some stronger measures. This fanned up the tinder smouldering in John's heart. John heard little else, at least not to meditate upon. He watched the children playing joyfully and thought of Dorcas Good shut up in the dark gaol. His thoughts were beginning to boil around the idea of more active resistance.

  The rest of them set up a plan for visiting their mother twice a week by teams, four going down at a time. Mary volunteered John's brother's for overnight lodging, looking worried when she realized he had not heard her. But John caught the tail of the conversation and quickly agreed, so that she only knew he had been chasing other thoughts over distant ground.

  John took Ben aside afterward, and Sam naturally drew aside with them. Down by Sam's well, John asked Ben how far he was willing to go to rescue Mother.

  "How far? I—I guess I'm not sure what you mean, John. I'd go to London or Quebec if I thought it would do any good."

  "No, Ben, I'm talking about what you said tonight, about needing to take some stronger measures for Mother. What did you mean?"

  "I don't know particularly, but I feel strongly about the principle! We have got to do more. The rest of you haven't even seemed willing to talk about it."

  Sam and John looked at one another before John went on.

  "Well, Sam and I and one or two others have been doing a few things. You saw that petition we circulated. There have been more things of that sort. But when I saw Mother and the Good child in gaol and Goody Good and Osborne in chains, I was fit to bust. I think there could come a time and place where we would be right to take up arms. If that happened, would you be with me?"

  Ben looked frightened. "Of course, John! I'm for fighting right now if only you'll work out who we should fight," he said, eager, but with a note of caution in his voice, "But you're going to have to work it out, first, because if I'm going to leave Thomasin and Thomasina widow and orphan, I want to do it to good purpose."

  "Agreed!" John said. "I promise you I'm not more eager to leave a widow and orphans than you, nor any more willing to go off half-cocked. But neither am I willing to be merely sweet and patient, either. We'll talk more."

Mary had rounded up the children and stood looking quizzically across the farmyard. "What are you up to?" she asked when John joined them.

"In better times I would have said 'the devil's business', but there's no more light talk in that direction."

"No, but just you make sure you are not about that business in earnest!" she said. He silently marveled at her uncanny ability to read his mind.

As Sam and John walked with Peter up to Joseph Putnam's the next night, Sam said to him, "I don't think you should talk to Ben like you did. He's already too much of a hot head without you putting in fuel." John was surprised, for this was the bluntest correction Sam had ever given him. Between them John was used to being the director and corrector.

"Well, Sam, I aim to talk more about that subject tonight, but right now I feel like hotter heads is what we need.

Chapter Twenty-One — Revolution or Repentance
(14 Apr)

Are these the men, that now Mine eyes behold,
  Concerning whom I thought, and whilom speake,
First heaven shall pass away together scrolled,
  Ere they My laws and righteous ways forsake,
Or that they slack to run their heavenly race?
  Are these the same? or are some others come in place?
-- Michael Wigglesworth, **God's Controversy with   New England**, 1662.

Joseph welcomed Peter coolly but with courtesy. For a moment John saw them as the aristocrat and the country bumpkin — for Peter's clothes were homely and his sandy hair stood up in an unruly roostertail in contrast to Joseph's wellkempt hair and dress. Then he reflected they all were equal as conspirators — in a democracy of resistance, which bound them, and in an aristocracy of justice, which equally anointed them. Between the two, the threat of death certainly leveled all, if only by the ducking of their heads. His musings took a further democratic turn, that Joseph was only a little better educated than they, and indeed the things he wrote were often worse spelt than his own.

Daniel began with a summary of things that had happened over the twelve days since they last met.

"We have completed an honorable petition for Goodwife Nurse and found many friends along the way. We have been given another valuable deposition by Joseph's Uncle Nathaniel. We have also, in this process, discovered a few who are not our friends, and perhaps made a few more enemies.

"We have the deposition from the Porter's and Peter's father with my humble subscription concerning Mother Nurse's evident surprise at the news we brought her before her arrest.

"We have ready to our hand depositions by Rayment and Elliott and Mary Ingersoll as to the girls admitting they named Mistress Procter 'for sport'. We have John Houghton's and Sam Barton's testimony of the Thomas Putnams putting Mistress Procter's name in Mercy Lewis's mouth.

"We have found that those who oppose the accusations and speak or act publicly against the accusations are very likely to be themselves accused. The arrests of John Procter, and Goodwife Cloyce reinforce this conclusion.

"I might add a related discovery, that mild and well-considered statements in legal form are more likely to be effective than other kinds of opposition. This is due to a number of things: more people will sign a mildly worded statement; many signatures as with the Nurse petition makes any one of the signers feel safer and; by bringing such things into the legal forum before counter-accusations are made, we may pre-empt the higher ground as it were, and require the officials themselves to operate in our defense, at least to the degree we succeed in appearing law-abiding friends of the court. Because we have only had examinations thus far and no trials, the degree to which our petitions may affect the magistry and the final outcomes is unknown.

"Furthermore, after inquiries which may have gotten me on the wrong side of the magistrates, we find that there is not much use trying to impeach the witnesses at the examination stage.

"I was planning to present Rayment and Elliott's testimony about the two girls 'having their sport' at Ingersoll's. I also considered the possibility of having John Houghton and Samuel Barton repeat their account of Thomas and Anne Putnam coaching Mercy Lewis. All four men were ready to speak, although Mary Ingersoll was not so sanguine, due to her husband's allegiances. Nevertheless, I know she would. But Mr. Hathorne with Mr. Corwin assenting silently, made it clear to me they will not hear evidence against the witnesses.

"After I described the evidence in general, indicating the five witnesses were all of high character, the magistrates said they saw no use to it. In fact Mr. Hathorne fixed me with his magisterial countenance and said that since most witnesses had proved themselves reliable, this matter would not be brought to a more just conclusion by any attack on their testimony. As I say, all I succeeded in doing was putting myself in their black books. Perhaps a trial court with judges from other places will prove more reasonable. Although I admit Deputy Danforth and the additional assistants at the examinations of Peter's mother and the Procters did not inspire great optimism.

"Things went better in Boston. I was able to talk with two eminent pastors and other men of influence. There is already considerable discontent with what goes on in Salem. Thus far, most of the reports they receive are coming from men like Mr. Lawson and Mr. Hale, who show the witch prosecutions in a favorable light. A few men, like Mr. Allen, who is still your landlord if I'm not mistaken, Sam, have heard a different perspective from people of the community. He was quite stout in defending your mother, and ready to do what he could. Withal, I gave extensive information to counter the stories of justice being done. I do not think you will be surprised when I say that Reverend Willard is also much opposed to this business. Indeed, he openly regretted having written his report on Elizabeth Knapp, especially when I told him that we had seen it re-enacted almost to the letter at various points.

"These men are speaking with others and trying to bring about several things. They are looking for one of reputation and ability to publish in opposition. But that is delicate, even in Boston. They are working among them to bring about some serious review of the spectre evidence question. The two men I have mentioned both recognize serious problems with it, especially as it is being played out here.

"Of course they have many other claims on their time and their good intentions may be slow in becoming fruitful. However, they have said they will exert what influence they can to get these matters out of the hands of our Salem magistrates. I hope a higher court will be convened to deal with these matters, perhaps even at the examination stage. The appearance of a number of assistants in this last examination was not altogether a coincidence. "

John had been girding his loins, and he spoke up then.

"Daniel, you have done all that could be done and more, so far as the judicial and political side of this thing goes, but I am not satisfied. When I saw little Dorcas Good locked up, something snapped in me, and I felt we had gotten past the point of politely objecting. I have come to be more of Joseph's mind. We must ready our saddles and load our pistols, and take a more active part in stopping this madness.

"You heard what happened to Mr. Procter at his wife's examination. At his first outcry against the open injustice of the girls being allowed to walk up to his wife in order to strike her -- a thing of which I never heard tell of in any court of law in my life — they began to name him as afflicting them and as a witch. The court hardly batted an eye before they packed him off to gaol with no more ceremony than that.

"We are up against madness," John continued. "These girls and the few mad women who have joined them, are become rulers over us. They are despots every bit as tyrannical as James or Mary or Charles at their worst. Their whim is the magistrates' command. Their folly is the doctrine of the ministers. They have been granted complete absolution from original sin or even any question of error. Your interview with the two magistrates only makes official what we've all seen!"

Daniel had listened patiently, where he sat across the table, his hand around a cup of ale. Joseph Putnam, too, had given John his full attention. Peter looked on wide-eyed, while Sam, knowing him better and being more intimately involved with him, fidgeted the whole time John spoke.

"Dash it all, John!" was Sam's comment when he finished. He seemed to want to say more, but was at a loss for words.

Joseph asked, "But what would you have us do, Goodman Tarbell?"

Daniel picked up this dangling end of the conversation, as John joined Sam in exasperation over concrete formulation.

"Let me take your thought to some of its logical conclusions, John, hoping dearly that there is no spectre hovering about to report it to any but the most loyal ears." He glanced at Joseph as he said this and Joseph nodded to assure him.

"We could all of us load our pistols and saddle our horses and go tonight or tomorrow and murder the six or seven members of the tender sex who rule us as you so aptly say, like despots. We would doubtless be caught soon enough, and doubtless executed. But perhaps our five lives would be a good trade for those nine persons we know to be bound over for trial as witches. And also for others of the "forty witches" who now are sought among us.

"For the moment, let us pass over the morality of that action and ask: What would be the result? Would those nine accused be released? Would their trials come to nothing for lack of the principle despots? Or would more despots arise to fill their thrones? And would not our action be taken as the veriest proof that all were indeed witches and we loyal members of the great coven so bound in diabolical ties that we would resort to an extreme effort to save them? In short, even if we could for a moment justify murder in any circumstance, would not the result be quite contrary to what we intend?"

"I'm not talking about murder!" John objected. "I only mean

we have got to resist what is happening."

"But in what then does this resistance consist?" asked Daniel, so much the school-teacher that John felt briefly like throwing his mug at him. "You spoke of ready saddles and loaded pistols. What do you intend to do with our cavalry once we have mustered it?"

"Well, after seeing what I saw in Boston, I thought about a plan to break those innocent prisoners out of their dungeon." He had nearly boiled off his heat and was beginning to feel a little foolish, but the frustration had not gone, nor the profound sense that they must do something.

"And after your cross-country expedition to storm the Boston Gaol, assuming it is successful where would you take your hearty band of buccaneers and escaped defendants?"

"I don't know, I tell you. Perhaps to Maine — perhaps to Canada, where we might join the French. Can their tyranny be more evil than ours right here!"

John felt he had scored a good point, there.

"No." Daniel answered after another draught of ale. "No, Frontenac cannot be a worse ruler than these small despots here in the Village. If the French decided to execute you, it would be because you were English, a thing you truly are, whereas here we are all threatened with the fantastic accusations of being what we aren't. We have no idea which of us will be accused next or of what deeds in particular."

"But I do not think you really want to storm the gaol or go to Quebec. I think you want to effectively end the reign of our maiden empresses as soon as possible so that our friends, loved ones and community can return to some semblance of a safe and normal life."

"Of course that's what I want! It's just that nothing we have done so far seems to be getting us anywhere nearer it. In fact, all that has happened is the horror grows and the power and malice of the girls."

"Ah, there you hit on a key question which is not at all clear to any of us — no not to you, either, John. How much malice is there in what these girls say and do?"

"Joseph, you are kin to two of them. Do Anna Putnam and Mary Walcott say these things and reinforce each other and the other girls out of malice would you say?"

Joseph stood and walked to the window of the parlor where we sat. He turned and answered, "I think there are malicious forces and even evil persons involved in this business. I believe, in fact, that the devil is really and truly attacking us through particular ones. However, I find the great fallacy in the official view of this thing to be the idea that the devil chiefly uses those who consciously and voluntarily agree to be used by him. In fact, this is not the reformed faith as I have learned it. The devil is indeed wholly intent on evil, but the will of every man, infected by original sin, is what provides our enemy his redoubt in the world.

"Perhaps a pagan priest or a wizard or witch are of especial use to him. But the prevalent evils are done by people acting out of sinful motives, as often hidden from themselves as not. Our actions performed without reflection and even our actions performed with shallow reflection are as likely to oppose God and aid the devil as things done with diabolical intent.

"I would say these girls have not given a moment's reflection to what they are doing and saying. I would go so far as to say not many of them are capable of such reflection. It is for this reason that God gives us parents and churches and civil leaders. Part of the purpose of each of these is to insure one does not act without some measure of reflection and oversight."

"There you are, John!" Daniel responded, emphasizing himself with a hearty swat upon the table, "If you are going marauding, it must be the parents, ministers and magistrates you shoot!"

This was a terrible thought, and all quailed at Daniel saying it, as far from earnest as he was.

"Well, why not!" he continued. "Joseph is certainly right. Even to the degree these girls may be consciously pursuing their petty jealousies and revenges, they are so far from mature and sober in their reflections that they might be said to have no idea what they are doing. It is those who ought to, can, and in many instances certainly do reflect on what goes forward who should be held responsible. What is there to restrain us from carrying out justice against these?"

For a moment John's imagination quailed at the image of huddling in the dark along a lonely stretch of the Ipswich road, pistol in hand waiting for Mr. Hathorne, Sergeant Putnam, or Sheriff Herrick, ready to put a ball through one or all of their hearts.

"We could not!" he gasped.

"It would be open rebellion pure and simple!" added Peter, almost as alarmed.

Sam gave a guttural agreement.

258.

"No," said Daniel, "Just plain murder. Rebellion or revolution is too complex an idea to apply to it. Our Scots divines, Rutherford et al, clarified a theology of revolution, and if it be lawful, it must be the ultimate result of a great many lesser efforts and a great many more injustices, under the leadership of some better magistrates after all that. It can only follow the same sorts of warnings, clarifications, and preliminaries required for any godly war. No, murder this would be, and as contrary to God's law as to all our best desires.

"Listen, John, and I will tell you who you must shoot if you would apply powder and ball to this matter. You must shoot us and yourself and the whole community. For what we deal with here is the product of all our sin. These little despots who rule us and the foolish guardians who give them absolute power have been raised up by the Village and Salem and all of New England. We will take a great deal of shooting."

For the moment John felt like a target himself. He was confounded by what seemed to him an artillery of philosophical bombast, too thick and rapid to stand against. He saw, however that Joseph had followed Daniel's argument, for he had bemused eyes and a wry grin as he sat toying with his empty mug. Sam, too, seemed quiet, as though he understood the bones if not the flesh of Daniel's logic. Peter but watched. John had little more to say.

"Then what are we to do. This cannot go on!" he threw out, his tone plaintive and hopeless.

"It will go on a while," answered Daniel, but he was being tender of John, "Yet we must do what will bring it to the quickest end. It is unlikely that will involve any use of firearms – although it may involve saddle leather.

"I have given Joseph's well-known preparations some thought, myself, and while I do not think I will keep my pistols loaded, I will indeed flee if necessary – if I can do it without endangering others, and particularly my family. So far no one has tried it, but I am certain many others now give it careful thought. The scriptures are full of flight. Think how many of the great men of the Bible fled when injustice turned its jaws upon them.

"Paul, the upholder of the God-given authority of 'Caesar' in Romans 13 and Titus 2, gives us the capstone of his apostolic credentials in II Corinthians 11. There he says he evaded commissioned constables of the Governor of Damascus, whom he knew to be seeking him for arrest. Yea, he enlisted co-conspirators to lower him over the city wall in a basket. He makes no apologies nor sees any contradiction in his innocent flight to escape unjust arrest.

"All Protestant authorities are agreed, and not a few papists as well, that flight from injustice, where it has reasonable chance of success, may be preferable to active resistance to unjust rulers.

"Is that not the primary motive under which our Puritans and nonconformists, and even Baptists and Quakers, have come here? Massachusetts was at first a retreat for those who fled. Why not flee again?

"The great danger in flight is not our own, but that of those we leave behind. Therefore I suggest we consider it seriously, and make what preparations we think reasonable against our own arrests or the arrest of other loved ones. But meanwhile our community sins are best dealt with by our repentance, if you will allow me to call it that. We must, in the words of John the Baptist, bring forth works in keeping with our repentance. We must turn back, and retrace the wide path that has led to our idolatry and the ascendancy of sin.

"If our despots are children, we can only topple them from their thrones by bringing them back under the rule that God intends for them—that of parents and rulers of church and government.

"But John is very much right, too," Joseph spoke, setting aside the pipe he had kindled, "We must take greater risks, even as the risk increases to us. We must speak to more people and say the things you have so excellently summarized. These girls are sinners, yet they are being treated as though they were both sinless and infinitely wise. Most of our leaders seem to have a blind spot regarding the girls, but some of those who oversee their lives, private and public, are all too cognizant of the effects of their sin. In other words, some of their guardians are more guilty than the girls, who cannot as fully appreciate the evil they do.

"We must confront ourselves by confronting these others. We must say what I have been all too hesitant to say to my half-brother, that this a great evil, and to be repented of, not encouraged. There are many forms of resistance. If we can but encourage some to keep silent where they would have agreed and others to speak where they would have been silent—if we can but help some not to smile or frown in concord with words they might otherwise have consented to—we will stop the madness. We can but hasten our own flight, or even our own arrests, it may hap. But to take no risks or fewer is to give our own consent.

"Which of the prophets is it who is warned as a watchman?"

"Ezekiel," answered Sam. "If the prophet does not warn those going to destruction, their blood is on his hands. But if he warns them, and they continue in sin then the blood is on their own heads."

"Yea, but what of the innocent blood!" John answered, in a weary but deeply discontented humor.

"The Proverbs say, 'hold back those being dragged to slaughter'. The same passage says there is no excuse for those who say 'we did not know,' " Daniel answered, "For me the greatest horror is imagining my sons growing up in a community where such godless injustice prevails. I suppose I would like to see the world 'safer' for them and their families.

"But let us turn to practice," he went on, "It has done me some good to have you raise these things, John, for believe me, we have all felt bloody-minded on many occasions over the last weeks."

"Aye," said Joseph, "Did you hear Ephraim Sheldon's testimony? It was very like the tale of Houghton and Barton, except that he claimed to witness Mercy actually naming Mistress Cloyce in her fit. Yet he said after her fit she denied seeing or naming anybody. No doubt the magistrates and ministers took it to strengthen the case against your mother, Peter, but a judge who took seriously the law concerning witnesses, would draw other conclusions.

"By speaking to as many as we can, we will find other such accounts that show the lies in what the girls say or at least that these afflictions are either deliberate games or some disease that causes mad dreams and false visions. I have read over Reverend Willard's account of the Knapp case, lately. It was his careful listening as she accused one who supposedly bewitched her that allowed him to catch her in the lies which put paid to the idea of bewitchment."

Peter struck in, speaking up for the first time. "And what would a fair judge make of accusations based on blood relations? It is said both Aunt Nurse and my mother were named because our grandmother was once suspected."

"Yes," Daniel agreed, "Guilt by association is no guilt. The sins of the fathers are not to be visited on the children in the Christian court. Have you heard who are next to be named?"

"Thus always you become the prophet of doom, Daniel," John groaned.

"Nay, that is Wigglesworth, friend. I am only the bearer of evil tidings, nowhere loved, but nonetheless useful.

"Do you hear Mary Warren spoken of as signing the book?"

"Yes, and Indian John is said to have spoken of Mistress Thacher of Boston, although he would not name her in court. Also Benjamin Gould named Mistress Griggs. Will they not be next?"

"Indeed! I missed that. Were those two truly named?"

"Yes. The Indian told the court "a gentlewoman" first afflicted him, but elsewhere he put the name on her. And Benjamin said Mistress Griggs attended a gathering of witches during a prayer meeting at Joseph's half-brother's. The other witches mentioned are all in gaol."

"Did they ask any further questions about either Mistress Thacher or Mistress Griggs?"

"No, not a one. They went on as though they had not mentioned them and as though none heard their names."

"There we learn another thing," said Daniel, and he mused for a few moments. " I do not think either of them will be arrested, because Mistress Thacher is Mr. Corwin's mother-in-law and Doctor Griggs is too closely allied with and too deeply respected by our great ones. Why, Mistress Griggs' niece Elizabeth is one of our despots! There are probably a great many who the girls will not name, or if they should, who would nonetheless be considered inviolate.

"See then, John, the little despots' rule is not absolute, and although the ministers and magistrates maintain the principle of the girls' infallibility, they refuse to submit to it in practice. That ought to give us some hope."

But why don't they rebuke the girls and discount their other accusations, if they are going to ignore some of them!" John said.

"That is the extent of our leaders' blindness. They are so committed to the idea of a coven among us, that they see such things as only minor distractions, and not as the grounds for impeaching the witnesses which they ought to be. We can only pray for the restoration of their sight, or for the advent of wiser judges.

"But meanwhile our practice must be to do as Joseph has suggested, to speak clearly and persuasively where we may, albeit at risk to ourselves. Our objects must be to encourage those who recognize the injustice of the thing and to find further instances in which the girls have been caught out in lies or in making a party to pursue their accusations. Obviously this is most dangerous for us where it implicates adults in deceits. Beyond that, we must look for positive steps that will contribute to the defense of the accused, as we have done with our petitions. Surely we can raise similar petitions for your mother, Peter and for the Procters. I will speak to Benjamin Procter tomorrow. Are any of you on more cordial terms with Giles Corey than I? I find it difficult to speak with him."

Sam and John laughed, as both Peter and Joseph joined in a chuckle.

"No," John said, "I fear he is not on very cordial terms with anyone — not even with his own children as their testimony against his wife doth prove."

"Well, perhaps, in keeping with our new bravery, we can agree that the first of us who has an opportunity should advise him about circulating a petition on his wife's behalf.

"But I mentioned Mary Warren — is it true she now stays with Elizabeth at Doctor Grigg's?

"Aye, she and Elizabeth Hubbard have been friends a long while."

"I don't like that. But anyway, I suspect she will be accused, since both her master and mistress have been named and her name said to be in the devil's book. I wish we could warn her, but she is not able to escape by herself and too unstable to be trusted with the fate of confederates. I know no more direct thing to do than to pray for her.

"And now . . . I am worn to a frazzle as I'm sure we all are!"

"Nevertheless, I would impose upon your weary mind for a few more minutes," said Joseph. "At the same time as we are accumulating what support we can for those accused, I fear others are accumulating more 'evidence' as they call it, of guilt. My poor cousin John Putnam — John the weaver, you know, son of Captain John — lost a child two days ago, and he and Hannah are inclined to believe it was the malignant work of the Towne sisters. It seems he is the "reliable source" from whom Henry Kenney heard the rumor of your Grandmother Joanna being a witch, and he dates the decline of the child from a few weeks after he told Kenney of it.

"I tell you this not because you need any more excuse for anger, but because I saw in his broken-hearted father's face a great deal of suffering. We need to keep sharply before us the fact that the 'laymen' of our community are drawn into this through a legitimate desire to reduce the pain and suffering of their own loved ones. They are being told there is a "cure" and "preventative" for the kind of suffering they and their families have gone through. Like a very sick man or the husband of a very sick wife, they are willing to try desperate remedies. When my Mary was born, a year ago February, and my wife seemed near death's door, there was such a desperation in my heart that I might have done nearly anything to prevent it. The wise ones tell these sufferers that the elimination of the infectious "disease" of witchcraft is the cure for their sorrows.

"I mean to say John Putnam's is one more case where the teachers among us have the greater responsibility. The patient seldom refuses the physic the doctor gives him. The sheep feed where the shepherd leads them. As long as they are driven up paths supposed to lead to greener pastures, they will walk those paths, precipitous as they may be.

"We are all as worn out as Daniel, but since you gentlemen still have some walking ahead of you, as a proper host, I will adjourn," concluded Joseph.

He bowed and prayed, "Oh Lord Christ, there hast not yet come so great an injustice as thou didst take upon thyself. Therefore we acknowledge thou knowest far better the injustice bound up in man. Have mercy upon us and speedily end these evil days among us. We pray in thine holy name. Amen."

They walked nearly silent down through the Village, conspirators indeed. They gave their partings in muffled words as Sam and John turned south and left Peter and Daniel to go up the Ipswich Road.

Before they too parted company, Sam said to John, "I guess you'd better straighten out things with Ben."

John gulped guiltily. "Yes," he said, "I will."

Chapter Twenty-Two -- Wider Nets
(14 -19 Apr)

*. . . They bore sundry years with much patience, till they
were occasioned by the continuance and increase of these
troubles, and other means which the Lord raised up in those
days, to see further into things by the light of the word of
God. How that not only these base and beggarly ceremonies
were unlawful, but also that the lordly and tyrannous power
of the prelates ought not to be submitted unto; which thus,
contrary to the freedom of the Gospel, would load and burden
men's consciences and by their compulsive power make a
profane mixture of persons and things in the worship of God.*
-- William Bradford, *Of Plymouth Plantation* (1669)

Our "prelates" had heard there were forty witches among
us. They now knew their task as defenders of the flock to be
immense and all the more urgent. With the woods full of wolves and
the bay full of sharks, caution must be abandoned and desperate
measures taken. Every hunter must keep his musket primed. The
widest nets must be deployed. The constables began to bring in
suspects at a greater rate.

The day Mary Warren's master and mistress were examined
and gaoled, Mary was invited to stay with her friend Elizabeth
Hubbard at the Griggs. The next day Anna Putnam accused Giles
Corey, husband of Martha.

Mary Warren's own warrant was issued three days later (18th
April) in combination with warrants for Giles Corey, Abigail Hobbs
and Bridget Bishop. The plaintiffs were John Putnam, Jr., and
Ezekiel Cheever. (This John Putnam, thirty-five year old father of
eight, and his wife had signed the petition on behalf of Rebecca
Nurse.) The "afflicted" victims named in the warrant were Anna,
Mercy, Abigail, Mary and Elizabeth Hubbard.

The four accused were examined the next day. Before Mary
Warren's examination, Abigail Hobbs was brought in. She became
the second to "confess" to being a witch and soon she (and her
mother) did as much damage as Tituba in naming and affirming
other "witches".

Mr. Hathorne conducted her examination, with Mr. Parris and Ezekiel Cheever taking down minutes.

"Abigail Hobbs, you are brought before authority to answer to charges of sundry acts of witchcraft committed by you and upon the bodies of many, of which several persons now accuse you. What say you, are you guilty or not? Speak the truth.'"

"I will speak the truth. I have seen sights and been scared, " answered Abigail, "I have been very wicked. I hope I shall be better if God will help me."

"What sights did you see?"

"I have seen dogs and many creatures."

"What dogs do you mean? Ordinary dogs?"

"I mean the devil."

"How often? Many times?"

"But once."

"Tell the truth."

"I do tell no lie."

"What appearance was he in then?"

"Like a man."

"Where was it?"

"It was at the Eastward at Casco Bay."

"Where? In the house or in the woods?"

"In the woods."

"In night or in the day?"

"In the day."

"How long ago?"

"About three or four years ago."

"What did he say to you?"

"He said he would give me fine things, if I did what he would have me."

"What would he have you do?"

"Why, he would have me be a witch."

"Would he have you make a covenant with him?"

"Yes."

"And did you make a covenant with him?"

"Yes, I did, but I hope God will forgive me."

"The Lord give you repentance. You say you saw dogs and many sorts of creatures."

"I saw them at that time."

"But have you not seen them at other times too?"

"Yes."

"Where?"

"At our house."

"What were they like?"

"Like a cat."

"What would the cat have you do?"

"She had a book and would have me put my hand to it."

"And did you?"

"No, I did not."

"Well, tell the truth, did you at any other time?"

"Yes, I did, that time at the Eastward."

"What other creatures did you see?"

"I saw things like men."

"What did they say to you?"

"Why they said I had better put my hand to the book."

"You did put your hand to the book, you say?"

"Yes, one time."

"What, would these others have you put your hand to their book, too?"

"Yes."

"And what would they have you do then? Would they have you worship them?"

"They would have me make a bargain for so long and do what they would have me do."

"For how long?"

"Not for above two or three years."

"How long did they agree with you for?"

"But for two years."

"And what would they then do for you?"

"They would give me fine clothes."

"And did they?"

"No."

"When you set your hand the last time to book, how long was that for?"

"It was for four years."

"How long is that ago?"

"It is almost four years. The book was brought me to get my hand to it for four years, but I never put my hand but that once at Eastward."

"Are you not bid to hurt folks?"

"Yes."

"Who are you bid to hurt?"

"Mercy Lewis and Anna Putnam."

"What did you do to them when you hurt them?"

"I pinched them."

"How did you pinch them? Do you go in your own person to them?"

"No."

"Doth the devil go for you?"

"Yes."

"And what doth he take? Doth he take your spirit with him?"

"No. I am as well as at other times, but the Devil has my consent and goes and hurts them."

"Who hurt your mother last Lord's day? Was it not you?"

"No."

"Who was it?"

"I heard her say it was Goody Wildes at Topsfield."

"Have you been in company with Goody Wildes at any time?"

"No, I never saw her."

"Well, who are your companions?"

"Why, I have seen Sarah Good once."

"How many did you see?"

"I saw but two."

"Did you know Sarah Good was a witch when you saw her?"

"Yes."

"How did you know it?"

"The Devil told me."

"Who was the other you saw?"

"I do not remember her name?"

"Did you go and do hurt with Sarah Good?"

"No, she would have me set my hand to her book also."

"What mark did you make in the Devil's book when you set your hand to it?"

"I made a mark."

"What mark?"

Abigail Hobbs seemed confused as though she did not know how to answer this. Mr. Hathorne went on in a patient and almost a fatherly mood.

"Have you not been at other great meetings?"

"No."

"Did you not hear of great hurt done here in the village?"

"Yes."

"And were you never with them?"

"No, I was never with them."

"But you know your shape appeared and hurt the people here."

"Yes."

"How did you know?"

"The Devil told me if I gave consent he would do it in my shape."

"How long ago?"

"About a fortnight ago."

"What shape did the Devil appear in then?"

"Like a black man with a hat."

"Do not some creatures suck your body?"

"No."

"Where do they come? To what parts when they come to your body?"

Abigail was a good deal disconcerted by these questions, and blushed exceedingly. "They do not come to my body. They come only in sight."

"Do they speak to you?"

"Yes," said Abigail, and she seemed to be growing more uneasy.

"How do they speak to you?"

"As other folks," she said, and her tone was petulant.

"What? Do they speak to you as other folks?"

"Yes, almost." She seemed to choke on her words and to become dumb.

"What say they?" asked Mr. Hathorne, but Abigail Hobbs seemed not to hear him.

The other girls began to cry out now, as if in a wave of affliction.

"See Goody Good and Goody Osborne come to her!" cried Mary Walcott.

"Oh Goody Good, you should be ashamed!" cried Mercy.

"See, they put their fingers in her ears!" cried Elizabeth, and Anna affirmed this.

Abigail now stared before her in a daze. The magistrates stared at her, and the Marshall stepped forward to look around her and to feel about her head. After a while she seemed to recover and spoke again.

"Sarah Good," she said, "Shall I not speak!"

She said no more for several minutes. The magistrates ordered that she be taken away then.

It was noted by the magistrates and ministers that the afflicted had suffered no attacks during the whole time Abigail Hobbs had made her confession, indicating to them that the malignant spirits were kept away and her confession thus a true one.

The officers and ministers were also grimly satisfied to hear their theology and science reinforced in this "confessor's" testimony. She was a sharp student or had been taught well, for she twice said the reason people had seen her appearance was because she had given the devil permission, "The devil told me if I gave consent he would do it in my shape". They were increasingly certain that none could "appear" and afflict, but those who had done likewise.

The court further questioned the afflicted girls about her, and all testified they were very sorry for her, and believed her to be telling the truth. She was committed to Salem Gaol on the strength of her own confession.

The next day, Abigail Hobbs was further examined at the gaol. She told the examiners that while she was on the way to her previous examination, an apparition of one Judah White, who used to live with Joseph Ingersoll at Casco Bay, came to her together with Sarah Good and told her to flee rather than be examined. Abigail said she would not flee, but would go to the examination. The apparition then told her if she did go, she should not confess anything. She replied that she would confess all she knew. The apparition then told her that Goody Osborne was a witch.

When asked what this Judah White looked like, she said she was dressed in fine clothes, including a sad-colored (dark) silk mantle with topknot and hood. Abigail also said the Devil came to her in the shape of a man and told her to afflict Anna and Mercy and Abigail Williams. She said the Devil brought her wooden images of them and gave her thorns, telling her to push them into the images. She said that she did this to each of them and then the Devil told her they were afflicted. She said they were indeed afflicted then and cried out that they were hurt by Abigail Hobbs. She also said she was at a great meeting in Mr. Parris' pasture where the witches administered their sacraments and she ate red bread and drank red wine there.

After Abigail Hobbs had been taken back to the lock-up, Mary Warren was examined. When her fits made further questioning fruitless, the next suspect, Bridget Bishop was brought in.

Perhaps more witnesses came forward against Bridget Bishop than against any other during our troubles. She ran an unlicensed ordinary on the Ipswich Road in Royalside, where drinking and games went on late into the night. That ordinary had fairly good success with the younger men and old soldiers, few of whom had reputations or influence they could or would bring to bear in her defense. She had been three times married, and twice widowed. Some thought the death of her second husband, Thomas Oliver, was mysterious. She had been charged with witchcraft the year after he died in another connection, but was found innocent. Her marriage seven years later to Edward Bishop had led to notorious public conflicts between them, at least one of which had brought them before a magistrate. On that occasion they were punished by being gagged and bound back to back in the Town Square of Salem for a day.

Among us worldliness is a virtue only so long as one is no more worldly than one's neighbors. Although Bridget Bishop was a member in good standing of Reverend Hale's church in Beverly (and indeed he had testified on her behalf when she had been charged with witchcraft twelve years before), her appearance, business, reputation, and demeanor were not such as was expected of a churchwoman. Yet her presence commanded personal respect, even in her church.

The event which brought her under the greatest suspicion was the death of her neighbor, Christian Trask. Some six years before our troubles, Christian was found dead, and the coroner's jury concluded she ended her own life with a pair of sewing scissors. Some talk went forward of charging Goody Bishop with witchcraft at that time, but Reverend Hale's account of Goody Trask's melancholy and her good relationship with Goody Bishop sufficed to prevent further efforts at prosecution then. Nevertheless, as soon as our troubles broke out in 1692, Reverend Hale began to reconsider. He began to wonder if the "fits" suffered by our afflicted were not very like the "melancholy fits" suffered by Christian Trask. He began to consider whether he had not done wrong in diverting the charge of witchcraft from Bridget Bishop. When it was mooted about that there were forty witches in our neighborhood, he decided Bridget Bishop must be one of them.

Samuel Braybrook, John Hutchinson, and John Lewis brought Bridget into the Village Meeting House before the two magistrates and several ministers, including Reverend Hale. Once more Reverend Parris and Ezekiel Cheever sat prepared to take minutes of the examination.

The afflicted girls immediately fell into fits, as they had toward the end of Abigail Hobb's examination and early in the course of Mary Warren's.

Mr. Hathorne began the questioning.

"Bridget Bishop, you are now brought before authority to give account. You stand here charged with sundry acts of witchcraft by you done or committed upon the bodies of Mercy Lewis, Anna Putnam and others. What do you say?"

"I take all this people to witness that I am clear," she said, sweeping the whole crowd with her eyes.

He addressed the afflicted. "Hath this woman hurt you?"

Abigail and the three older girls each said she had hurt them. A number of women offered timid assent as well.

"You are accused by four or five for hurting them. What do you say?"

"I never saw these persons before nor never was in this place before. I am innocent."

Mary Walcott spoke up then. "She came to me this morning, and Jonathon struck at her with his sword. See her coat is cut by it!"

"Is not your coat cut?" asked Mr. Hathorne?

"No." she said, but the Marshall and Mr. Hathorne examined it and found a three-cornered tear.

Mary spoke up again and said she had seen and heard the coat tear when her brother had struck at her.

Jonathon Walcott was asked if he had struck at an appearance, and he replied that he had struck as his sister instructed him, not with a naked sword, but one still in its scabbard. The ministers and magistrates considered the tear might well have been made thereby.

The afflicted then broke out in their usual manner, but more intensely than before.

Anna cried out, "You bewitched your first husband to death!"

"What say you to this?" asked Mr. Hathorne.

"If it please your worship, I know nothing of it," Bridget replied.

"You would have us sign the devil's book!" cried Abigail.

Goody Bishop shook her head vigorously in denial of Abigail's accusation, saying, "It is false." At the shaking of her head, however, they fell into a greater clamour.

The next few times she moved her head, the girls cried out in concert.

Samuel Braybrook was called and testified of a conversation he had with her that morning as he brought her down to court. She had told him some had accounted her a witch for ten years, but that she was not a witch. She also told him "the devil cannot hurt me."

"Are you not a witch", Mr. Hathorne asked her.

"I am no witch," she replied.

"What contract or covenant have you made with the devil?"

"I have made none."

"Why, if you have not written in his book, yet tell me how far you have gone? Have you not to do with familiar spirits?"

"I have no familiarity with the devil. I never saw him in my life."

Anna cried out, "She calls the devil her god!"

Mercy Lewis cried out, "Oh, Goody Bishop, did you not come to our house the last night and did you not tell me that your master made you tell more than you were willing to tell?"

"What say you to all this that you are charged with. Can you not find in your heart to tell the truth?"

"I do tell the truth. I am innocent. I never hurt these persons in my life."

Mr. Hathorne went on, "Tell us the truth in this matter. How come these persons to be thus tormented and to charge you with doing it?"

"I am not here to say I am a witch to take away my life!"

"Who is it that doeth it if you do not. They say it is your likeness that comes and torments them and tempts them to write in the book. What book is that you tempt them with?"

"I know nothing of it. I am innocent."

Here another wave of affliction boiled up among the girls.

"Do you not see how they are tormented. Why, you seem to act witchcraft here before us, by the motion of your body which seems to have influence upon the afflicted!"

"I am innocent. I know nothing of it. I am no witch. I do not know what a witch is."

"How do you know then that you are not a witch?"

"I do not know what you say."

"How can you know you are no witch and yet not know what a witch is?"

"I am clear. If I were any such person, you should know it."

Mr. Hathorne was well enough convinced of her guilt, that he heard a threat in this answer. He answered back, "You may threaten, but you can do no more than you are permitted."

"I am innocent of a witch," she reiterated.

"Have you not given consent that some evil spirit should do this in your likeness?"

"No, I am innocent of being a witch. I know no man, woman, or child here."

Marshall Herrick addressed a question to Goody Bishop.

"How came you into my bed chamber one morning, then, and asked whether I had any curtains to sell?" (This question was based on an idea put about that she might have been the mysterious murderer of a stranger whose body was found wrapped in cloth some years earlier. The inference was that she had sought the material of the curtains to wrap the body in — another of those speculations made by piecing together fantastic fragments of old incidents.)

Mr. Hathorne continued. "What do you say of those murders you are charged with?"

"I hope I am not guilty of murder. I know nothing of it."

In saying this she raised her eyes in exasperation and immediately all the afflicted aped her action, raising their eyes, too.

"What do you say to these things among us, these horrible acts of witchcraft?"

"I know nothing of it. I do not know whether there be any witches or no."

"It may be you do not know. Have you not heard that any have confessed today who were examined before you that they are witches?"

"No. I know nothing of it."

John Hutchinson and John Lewis were called by Mr. Hathorne and asked if they had told her of Mary Warren's and Abigail Hobbs' confession to witchcraft. They both replied they had so told her.

Mr. Hathorne rounded on her, "Why look, you are taken now in a flat lie!"

"I did not hear them," she said and again raised her eyes in exasperation.

The girls broke out in new paroxysms of affliction, as all five charged her with afflicting them.

She was taken out then and across to Ingersoll's under the supervision of two assistant constables. At the ordinary, Samuel Gould, who was there for refreshment with his brother Will and John Buxton, Jr., talked with her and asked her if she was not troubled to see the afflicted tormented. She answered flatly.

"No, I am not troubled for them."

"But don't you think they are bewitched?" he asked.

"I can not tell what to think of them," she answered.

After a brief consultation, meanwhile, the magistrates and ministers bound Bridget Bishop over to Salem gaol.

Giles Corey was arrested on April 19th, but much to the magistrates chagrin, he refused to answer any questions whatever, and therefore his examination was very short!

It is said Goodman Corey, now in his eighties, had come to the colonies as a young apprentice, and got into trouble a number of times for stealing from his master, as well as from Mr. George Corwin, Salem's greatest merchant (father to our magistrate, Jonathon, and grandfather of our Sheriff, George). In the 1660s Goodman Corey obtained a small farm west of Felton's Hill and married the first of three wives, by whom he had several children who married and settled near him. We have already spoken of his conflicts with John Procter, and the suspicion concerning his part in Jacob Goodale's death as well as the arrest of his third wife Martha.

Giles had been fiercely angry at the court ever since he saw how his wife was treated. He was enraged that his unwitting comments, as well as his children's witting ones, were used against her, and further that the court would have him sign a damaging and misleading deposition. As soon as he was arrested, he resolved to give the court nothing more by which to injure his wife or himself. He was just such a man as was able to keep such a resolve even at great extremity, as we shall soon describe.

But the magistrates were greatly frustrated by his refusal to be examined, because this effectively halted their official proceedings against him. Evidence could not be taken in court except before the accused, and the accused could not even be prosecuted if he would not "put himself upon the court," acknowledging the court's authority and entering a plea in response to the charges.

The "confessors" could still give depositions, however, and Goodman Corey was thereafter named among the witches.

Daniel had attended that day's examinations and was seething with frustration at what he had seen transpire. John, however, had worked from sun-up to sun-down in the field, where Daniel found him before supper. He dragged John off to Joseph Putnam's, where Mistress Putnam, Sr., and Joseph's wife kindly fed them both. Afterward, the three men retired to Joseph's barn, where Daniel undammed the emotion he had stored up that day.

The courtroom has become another nursery for them, a place to play in fanciful worlds.

"And the magistrates are also their playmates! Mr. Hathorne puts the capstone on each fantasy, by turning to the poor one at the bar and asking 'What do you say to that!' Most fall back on plain denial, but today we had another such as Tituba. Abigail Hobbs for all her embarrassment over being asked how she suckles demonic creatures, was the veriest friend of the court, confessed witch, and fellow victim of the afflicted. They made hardly a peep during her whole examination, except at the end where she fell into a trance herself.

"The silence was so refreshing it was almost enough to make one wish all the accused would confess right off, so that our nerves might be spared!

"Oh, I am beside myself. I do believe I shall go and confess to being sore afflicted myself. I cannot stand to see our organs of justice used so. It makes a mockery of all government!"

Both Joseph and John listened to Daniel without comment. He was plainly too overwrought for argument or even discussion. All they could give him was a pat on the back.

They heard a few more details of the day and prayed with him. He seemed to find solace, and thanked them. Sheepishly he said, "It is a good thing you reached your own thoughts of violence another night than this one, John, else I would never have talked you out of them."

"Nay, you need no talking out," John answered, "In attending these examinations you have borne much more of this than the rest of us, excepting those in prison. . . . and those who love them," he added, thinking especially of Father Nurse. "But you must rest your mind and soul, too. If we allow this madness to become all our meditation, we will be of no use in resisting it."

"It is so. I think I will go fishing tomorrow!"

"A wise resolve," said Joseph, "and I shall go with you to be sure you concentrate on the business before you."

"Not I," John laughed. "I have the privilege of forgetting my troubles again behind a plow and a horse!"

"One last curious information before we begin our forgetting," said Joseph. "Today I was in Salem and stopped at Gedney's Tavern, where I heard a generous sentiment from one of our constables, young Willard from Topsfield. He was with two other constables and after they had talked a while of the witch examinations, he tossed it all aside saying, ' The whole of Salem Village is possessed. We ought to hang them all.' "

On that note of comfort the conspirators parted.

Israel Porter's House

Chapter Twenty-Three -- The Price of Contrition
(19-20 Apr)

*2. If any man or woman be a WITCH, that is, hath or consulteth
with a familiar spirit, they shall be put to death. Exod. 22. 18. Levit.
20. 27. Deut. 18. 10. 11.*

*11. If any man rise up by FALSE-WITNES wittingly, and
of purpose to take away any mans life: he shal be put to
death. Deut. 19. 16. 18. 16.*

-- Capital Lawes in **Laws and Liberties of
Massachusetts**, 1648.

In any war, the forces of attack, defense, counter-attack,
espionage and counter-espionage roll back and forth like waves
between a ship and a shore. In agriculture, a particular disease,
weed, or insect makes headway until the farmer learns to overcome a
that pest. After only a brief respite, there is soon an insurgence of
others. The thorns and thistles spring ever up, so that it's always in
the sweat of one's brow one brings forth bread. The forces of false
purgation worked night and day in our Village and the just labored
against them. The tactics of each was modified by those of the other.

Although she might be called an unwitting initiator of our
troubles, Mary Warren did not become actively involved until her
master and mistress Procter were arrested and imprisoned. Both
Anna Putnam and Abigail Williams testified that Mary signed the
devil's book, wherefore she was under suspicion. Since the Procter's
arrest, she was staying with Elizabeth Hubbard and the Griggs
family. Thus she was thrown more closely together with the older
afflicted girls, including Mary Walcott and Mercy Lewis.

Mary's arrest indicated how far the cabal of girls would go in
defense of their "sport". Her examination was held the same day as
Abigail Hobbs' and Bridget Bishop's.

At twenty years old, she was the youngest of those thus far
accused, except for little Dorcas Good. The "afflicted" were her peers
and sometime friends. Thus there was a new atmosphere to the
proceedings.

The defendant was led into the Meeting House and
immediately Elizabeth Hubbard, Abigail Williams, and Anna

Putnam fell into fits, but without much outcry. Most of the girls sat rigid, staring balefully at Mary.

Mr. Hathorne began the examination.

"Mary Warren, you stand here charged with sundry acts of witchcraft. What do you say for your self? Are you guilty or not?"

"I am innocent"

He turned to the other girls. "Hath she hurt you?" he asked.

Most of them continued to stare silently at the defendant, which the magistrates and ministers interpreted per usual -- that they were kept dumb by diabolical means.

Elizabeth Hubbard spoke up. "She has lately hurt us." Then Elizabeth fell down in demonstration.

"You were a little while ago an afflicted person," said Mr. Hathorne, "yet now you are an afflicter. How comes this to pass?"

"I look up to God," said Mary, "and take it to be a great mercy of God."

"What!" replied the magistrate, "Do you take it to be a great mercy of God to afflict others?"

"No," said Mary, "But it is a great mercy not to have fits nor to pretend it."

Mr. Hathorne again addressed Elizabeth Hubbard.

"What have you to say about this."

"It is the same as she did say three days ago at Ingersoll's. She said that all of us who were afflicted did but dissemble."

At this, all the afflicted girls and Mistress Pope, as well, threw themselves about and cried out loudly that Mary afflicted them right there, that she bit them and pinched them and stabbed them with pins. There was a great deal of writhing and moaning. Only Indian John seemed unaffected at first, but when he saw the others at it, he joined in.

Elizabeth cried out, "Here she is a-tormenting of us now and we see her doing it and hear her saying she has made a league with the devil."

Then Mary, herself, began to tremble and fell over backward, so that the Marshall, standing behind her, barely caught her and set her down at his feet.

Elizabeth cried out, "She is going to confess."

But after a little time Abigail Williams cried out, "No, see, Goody Corey, Mr. Procter and his wife. They have struck her down. They say she must be silent!"

Mary continued for perhaps ten minutes, lying back against

the Marshall's legs, and apparently unconscious, while the others went through squalls of fits, as those around them tried to restrain and calm them.

After a time Mary seemed to recover, and she stood up and said. "I will speak." Then she cried out, "I am sorry for it" and began to wring her hands, then fell again into a fit, but this time the Marshall was ready. Catching her beneath the arms, he lowered her onto a bench. In a short while, she again recovered and in a weak voice, said she would speak, but she became rigid again, her jaws set, and her body began to jerk. In the midst of it, she cried out, "Oh Lord help me. Oh Good Lord save me!"

Strangely, the rest of the afflicted grew quiet. All in the Meeting House watched and waited as Mary's latest fit subsided, only to be repeated as she again sat up and said "I will tell, I will tell," before falling into a fit again, remaining still for another five minutes.

This time she recovered enough to sit up and say, "I will tell, they did, they did, they did!" and then fell into a shaking fit again.

After a few minutes she recovered again and cried in an exhausted voice, "I will tell, I will tell. They brought me to it!", and back into a fit she went, which continued so that the magistrates ordered she be taken out, at which time they brought in Bridget Bishop for her examination as we have described.

After Bridget Bishop's examination, Mary was brought in again. She immediately had another fit and was set upon the bench. The magistrates indicated she could stay sitting rather than stand at the bar, and thus, when she recovered sufficiently she got through two questions.

"Have you signed the devil's book?"

"No."

"Have you not touched it?"

"No."

She fell back along the length of the bench, hitting her head. At the suggestion of one of the ministers, she was led outdoors for some air, after which she was brought back, but could give no more answers.

After the court adjourned that afternoon, the magistrates and ministers brought Mary Warren back once more for a private interview.

"Mary can you tell us anything more?" Mr. Hathorne asked, with unusual tenderness.

"I shall not speak a word. But I will speak, Satan! She saith she will kill me. Oh! She saith she owes me a spite, and will claw me off."

"Who saith it?"

"It is not. . . No. I must not tell. Avoid Satan, for the name of God avoid! " She then fell again in a fit, crying out once more, "Will ye, I will prevent ye in the Name of God!"

And when she was calm again, Mr. Hathorne went on, "Tell us, how far have you yielded?"

But she had another fit. When she sat up again, one more question was asked her.

"What did they say you should do and you should be well?"

But her body became rigid and she so bit her own lips that they bled, so that they sent her back to Ingersoll's and entered into consultation together.

The chief resolve of their consultation regarding Mary Warren was to bind her over to Salem gaol, where they would continue to question her in hopes of getting to the bottom of her testimony.

In Salem gaol, which became crowded during this time, Mary Warren had a chance to speak with other accused persons. Over the next few days, even as the ministers were questioning her at length, she was able to tell other prisoners the gist of the truth.

She said "the magistrates might as well examine Keyser's daughter who had been distracted many years and take notice of what she said as any of the afflicted persons."

That Thursday, our Lecture Day, the two magistrates and several ministers came to the gaol and examined Mary exhaustively. These included Reverends Higginson, Noyes, and Hale. They saw her as an object for hope, caught between the desire to confess and fear of further affliction. Because this was their convinced perspective on her, everything they said and heard was tailored to the ideas that Mary was: 1/a witch who had afflicted the other girls; 2/herself afflicted by other witches for recalcitrance in cooperating with them, and therefore; 3/torn between confessing and protecting herself by keeping quiet. What the ministers could not fathom was that she desired to speak the truth, but was indeed truly afflicted both with her life-long propensity to distempers and fear of the other girls' threats, which brought on and intensified her fits.

Another interpretation of Mary Warren's "confession" and her description of the "dissembling" of the afflicted is suggested by some: that since the things that she "saw" during her own fits were, afterward, obviously false; she assumed the same pattern applied to the other girls. If this was so, then she did not see their "dissembling" as deliberate falsehood, but merely as false perception resulting from some disability like her own, which led to their fits. She was not to be allowed this interpretation, however, any more than she was allowed to blame the afflicted girls for deliberate malice. The ministers and magistrates were determined to come to conclusions that fit the categories they had forged.

In the accounts of English and colonial witchcraft up to the time of our troubles, a high place was given to that well-established institution, the devil's book, in which witches were supposed to sign away their souls. Thus Abigail Hobbs confessed to having set her mark in the devil's book. Reverend Lawson, an early assessor of our troubles, was told by Edward Putnam that Mercy informed the magistrates Mary Warren signed this diabolical document in order to gain relief from her afflictions. The magistrates repeatedly asked the young woman about it at her examination. When the ministers and magistrates received no answer that satisfied them, they continued to browbeat her until they did.

When Mary was brought up from the basement cells, the ministers found her far more composed than when she was first examined. They questioned her in the Dounton's parlor. Reverend Noyes began:

"Did you not tell Mercy Lewis that you signed a book?"

"No," Mary answered, and although rational, her attitude and response were cold and defensive.

"Did not your mistress bring you a book to sign?"

"No, she brought me none. My master once brought me a book."

"Did you sign it?"

"No."

"Did you not touch it?"

"I touched it."

"Did you not see a mark where you touched it?"

"There was a spot upon it like a letter."

"What color was the spot?"

"It was black."

Mr. Hathorne then showed her a Bible. "Was this the book that was brought to you and that you saw the flourish in?"

"No."

"Did your master not threaten to run hot tongs down your throat if you did not sign it?"

"He told me once he would burn me out of my fit."

"Did you not make a mark in the book?"

"I made no mark, but perhaps with the tip of my finger."

"But was it wet?"

"It may have been wet with sweat or cider."

"Were you drinking cider?"

"I do not remember if I was or not."

"But you did say there was a mark where you touched it?"

"Yes, it had a black mark."

"Was any but your master and mistress with you when they threatened you with the hot tongs?"

"No."

"Do you know that if you signed the devil's book by your own voluntary act that you agreed to belong to the devil and do his will?" She began to grow uneasy as her own fancy responded to the minister's suggestions.

"But my master gave the book to me, and that was what made me touch it."

"The devil could have done nothing if you had not yielded for the ease of your own body, "continued Reverend Noyes. " It was not for the good of your soul!"

For the first time, Mary seriously considered this suggestion that the Procters might have deliberately misled her, so that she unwittingly endangered her soul. As the thought came home to her, she cried out in fear, "Then I am undone body and soul!"

The ministers elaborated until she openly wept. She began to remember and tell the ministers of times her master and mistress had threatened her, now made so much more horrible. She said they had threatened to drown her and to make her run through the hedges.

"Have you not seen your master and mistress since you came to prison?"

"I thought I saw my master when I took the chamber pot out."

"What said he to you?"

"Nothing," she said trembling, then she fell into a fit.

At this point the ministers resorted to a kind of spiritual warfare they used with many other defendants. Reverend Noyes began to make a rapid clipping motion around her head with his hands. He did not at first touch her, but only moved his hands close

284.

to her eyes and ears as though he were shooing away the spirits that attacked her – and indeed, this is what he thought he was doing.

Mary did recover after a little while. She cried out, "I will tell. I will tell. Thou wicked creature, it is you stopped my mouth. But I will confess the little that I have to confess."

"Who is she you would tell of? Is it Goodwife Procter or no?"

"O Elizabeth! Procter? It is she. . . It is she I lived with last!"

Again she fell into a fit, and the minister administered his "treatment". Recovering, she cried again, "It shall be known, thou wretch. Hast thou undone me body and soul? She wishes to have me make a thorough league."

"What was it your finger was blacked with when you touched the book?"

"I know not that my finger was blacked until I saw the mark."

"Was that where you put your finger?"

"Yes, I touched the book."

"What did you then?"

"I was eating bread and butter."

"Did your finger black the bread and butter?"

"Yes, for aught I know."

Perhaps suspecting malignant spirits were behind what sounded like insolence, Reverend Noyes again moved his hands rapidly up and down before her face and around her ears.

"What does thy mistress now say to thee when you have complained of her?" He went on.

"She bid me not to tell she was a witch."

Again she had a brief fit, and again the minister labored to drive away the spirits with his hands.

"I will tell!" she cried out, "My master bid me not tell. He has sometimes been beside himself because of his wife's quarreling with him."

"Did you know your mistress was a witch before you touched the book?"

Again she fell into a fit, and this time the minister not only moved his hands near her head, but softly pummeled her ears and brushed his hands rapidly back and forth across her brows

Afterward the question was repeated and she answered, "She said I had set my hand to the devil's book that night I was thrown out of bed."

"What night was that?"

"It was the same Sabbath night that I put up a note of thanksgiving in the Meeting House for going so long without a fit."

"Did your master and mistress know of this?"

"Yes."

"Did they approve of it?"

"Yes, my mistress said I should. My master told her he did not like the putting up of bills for public prayer."

"How did your mistress come to you that night? Was it merely her shape or in body?"

"It was her body for aught I can tell."

"Is your mistress a witch."

"It may be so."

"Have you seen any of the witches since you came to prison?"

She had another fit, and it was severe. Her lips were bleeding again and she was growing exhausted. More light blows were rained about her head. The question was repeated.

"I saw Goodman Corey and the daughter of Sarah Good."

"What did they? Did they bring a book to sign?"

"When first I came, some brought a book to sign." (This was the log book which the Dounton's required the prisoners to sign)

"But do you not admit that you knew your master a witch or wizard?"

"No, I knew it not."

"Did you not know your finger would make a mark in the book he brought you?"

"No, but Mr. Procter and his wife asked me to read."

"What did you read there?"

"The first word was Moses."

"And what after?"

"The next word I could not tell."

"What did your master and mistress say then?"

"They bid me if I could not pronounce the word that I should hold the book."

"Why will you not tell the whole truth?"

"I do, I do. . ." and she began weeping again.

"Nay, do not weep, but answer. Why do you not tell the whole truth?"

"I did not tell the whole truth before because they threatened they would tear me in pieces if I did. But I could not go on thus. And now I tell the whole truth."

"Did you not suspect it was the devil's book you touched?"

"I did not suspect it before you told me my finger blacked it."

"Why did you do it?"

"My master saith I must."

"What did he say might happen to you?"

"He saith when I am in my fits I might run into the fire or water and destroy myself."

"Have you not been used to afflict the afflicted persons?"

"No."

"But they say they are afflicted by your shape."

"I fear it is the devil that afflicts them."

"Have you images in which you stick pins or thorns to hurt people by?"

"No."

"Did the devil ever ask your consent to hurt in your shape?"

"No."

"Have you heard your master or mistress speak of hurting persons with images and sticking thorns in them?"

"Yes, I heard them speak of it."

"Had they such images in the house?"

"No."

"Do you know of any ointment they had in the house?"

"My mistress put ointment on me once upon a hurt."

"Where came it from?"

"It came from Mistress Bassett's of Lynn." (Elizabeth Procter was the daughter of William Bassett of Lynn. Her sister Sarah Bassett was later accused.)

"What was it like?"

"It was green."

"How smelt it?"

"It smelt very ugly to me."

"When you touched the book, was it your finger made the mark?"

"No. The mark was there already."

"When you touched the book, did your finger go to the mark?"

"Yes."

"Then," said Reverend Noyes, "You touched the book twice. Did you not suspect it was the devil's book before you touched it the second time?"

"I fear it was not a good book."

"What mean you it was not a good book?"

"I fear it was a book to deceive."

Mary was finally allowed to go back up to the Dounton's cellar, where the other women comforted and fed her after this second ordeal. The magistrates and ministers departed sadly shaking their heads over the terrible deceptions of the devil and especially his malignant book.

The *New England Primer* which Benjamin Harris had begun printing in 1690, based on the English primers, had an alphabet section, wherein most parents and teachers were wont to begin their students on their letters. Under the letter "M" we find "Moses was he who Israel's host led through the sea." This was the horrible book full of black marks which the Procters had given to Mary Warren.

If the misidentification of Mary Warren's book was a principal error of the ministers and magistrates, an even greater one was the misidentification of her tormenters. "They did it," a statement she repeated both in her examination and in this interview in gaol, referred not to the Procters and witchcraft, but to the other girls' dissembling and threats. She had resolved to testify they were only pretending to see witches and to be tortured by the accused. The magistrate's mistake of believing she spoke of the Procters was made plausible, once it was made, by Mary's expressions of fear of the girls' threats. The magistry assumed the witches threatened her, when in fact it was Elizabeth Hubbard and the other older girls who threatened to hurt her, should she try to expose their deception.

If at this juncture in our troubles it had been published that the afflicted were playing or pretending or even deluded, it would have spread shame and ill repute over many — afflicted, parents, ministers and magistrates. It was nevertheless nearly the last juncture at which parents and local leaders could have exercised their responsibility to halt the forward march. Within a few weeks, the advent of the new court of Oyer and Terminer under the single-minded leadership of Deputy Governor Stoughton would work an alchemy transmuting the local potentates from whales into small fry.

Ever scientists, Reverend Noyes and the other men "proved" by experiment that the action of their hands could thwart the diverting influences of the malign spirits. They were confident in this conclusion, not only because they saw it to be consonant with Cartesian principles of physics, but because it so obviously worked with Mary Warren. She had been terribly afflicted in her examination and unable to answer much at all, yet after they began to "help" her by "driving away" the bewitching spirits with motions and light blows, she was able to answer at length and to openly "confess". They did not reflect that her master, John Procter, had already spoken of the success of such methods with her – saying that when he threatened here with beating she always came out of her fits.

The ministers and magistrates had tormented Mary Warren within the just meaning of that word and they would torment her further. Perhaps she had not been injured or even caused physical pain by the rapid motions and light blows of the ministers' hands, but she had been harshly driven. This kind of violence was to grow into a pattern of torment which always was justified in the minds of these tender shepherds. They who spoke with horror of the Spanish Inquisition or the Marian tortures were true imitators of their worst spirit. But any suggesting such a thing at the time would have seemed to them much deranged — or probably bewitched.

William Phips

Chapter Twenty-Four — The Number of the Elect
(April 21-22)

*A ship that bears much sail, and little or no ballast, is easily overset;
and the man whose head hath great abilities, and his heart little or
no grace, is in danger of foundering.*
-- Anne Bradstreet, **Meditation #4** , 1664.

The last week of April saw a great effort toward filling up
the number of the elect witches — for it was now almost a doctrine of
predestination that the magistrates and ministers pursued. The
number "forty" had been given out and the gaol door swung wide to
bring in those chosen. Nine new candidates were named in a
warrant dated April 21st, with an additional half dozen inscribed in
the book of death on the 30th .

As in our churches so with the witches it was a weighty
matter to be admitted to the visible body. Thus the magistrates and
ministers, the guardians of this insubstantial "church," were very
particular about the ritual of admission. They developed an
elaborate test only barely less stringent than those of the nominating
girls. This ceremony of initiation involved a catechism, which was
fixed according to the two orders of membership.

Some of the candidates were immediately received into the
first order, of "deacons," as it were, who by their open "confessing,"
became members not only of the nominating committee, but fellow
participants with the ministers and magistrates. Others were
admitted unconfessed. These gave the second set of answers, in their
humility, denying they were worthy of admittance. Thus they
proved the highest witches, worthy of the supreme sacrament of
execution, and not to be wasted in lesser offices.

The prophesied number was not yet made up, and it was
only to be expected it would grow larger, since it had gone from one
to three to five to nine to forty in so short a time. Each new member
was expected to add new understanding to the scope and variety of
their number. Old relationships and old rumors of secret evils could
be sure to open up new avenues for study and meditation. The
ministers and magistrates saw themselves called to an ever
expanding task of bringing in the harvest. Theirs was a new Great

Commission. They sent out to the Village, to the larger Salem country, and even to the ends of the colonies, making disciples and drawing them into the irresistible circle of the damned.

The circle was being opened to a wide range of candidates from every walk of life, discovered through a variety of factors. The latest admissions included one chosen for blood ties; one selected for his "support" of witches (his criticism of a member of the nominating committee); the wife of the same, no doubt one in fleshliness with him; three nominated by a new "confessor"; one an African slave; one a leading wife of Salem; and, rarest to behold, one case of mistaken identity. Indeed this set of examinations, for the first and only time found one nominee unworthy to be received.

Sergeant Putnam had a new partner signing the complaint, John Buxton of the Village. The girls afflicted according to the complaint were Anna, Mercy and Mary Walcott.

Benjamin Hutchinson testified how two of the principle girls made new accusations. Benjamin, twenty-seven year old son of Joseph Hutchinson, Sr., lives about a mile east of Nurse's toward Fairmaid's Hill, a quarter mile south of the Andover Road. His wife, Jane, daughter of Reverend Phillips of Rowley, consented to keep Abigail Williams at their place for a time, in hopes the change of place would give both the afflicted girl and the Parrises some relief. The Parrises pursued the plan of farming her out because it seemed to be working so well for their Betty.

Unlike Betty, however, Abigail still went to church in the Village with the Hutchinsons. Ben carried her up to Lecture in his cart late in the morning of the 21st. But just as they were passing William Buckley's place (whose wife Sarah was accused a few weeks later by the girls and this same Ben), Abigail cried out, "There he is!"

"Who is it?" asked Goodman Hutchinson in some alarm.

"It's the little black minister," she replied.

"What is his name?" Ben asked.

"He says he lived at Casco Bay," she went on, "and that he killed three wives. Two were his own and one of Mr. Lawson.

"He says he made nine witches in this place. He says he can hold out the heaviest gun that is in Casco Bay with one hand, though no other man can hold it out with both."

"Where is this little man?" Benjamin asked.

"Just beside the cartwheel he goes," she answered.

Goodman Hutchinson had a three-groined pitchfork in his hand and he threw it where she said the spectre stood. Abigail immediately fell into a short fit, and when it was over she said, "You have torn his coat for I heard it tear."

"Where did it strike him?" Benjamin asked.

"On one side." Abigail answered.

When they came to Ingersoll's, about noon, Mr. Hutchinson went in with Abigail behind him, but as soon as they came into the main room of the inn, Abigail said, "There he stands."

"Where?" asked Benjamin, as he drew his rapier.

"He has gone!" she answered, then "There is a gray cat."

"Where abouts does it stand?" he asked.

"There!" she said and pointed with her finger, whereupon Benjamin struck out with his rapier. Abigail again fell immediately into a fit, but afterward said, "You killed her and immediately Sarah Good came and carried her body away."

In the late afternoon after lecture Mary Walcott joined Abigail in more "spectre visions" back at Ingersoll's. According to Benjamin Hutchinson, they said Goody (Deliverance) Hobbs of Topsfield bit Mary in the foot. Both girls fell into fits and said William Hobbs and his wife were coming toward them along the table. Goodman Hutchinson again drew his rapier and stabbed about. According to both girls, he hit Goody Hobbs in the side.

The two girls said the room was full of witches. Therefore Goodman Hutchinson and Eleazer Putnam (26 year old son of Captain John), who had just come in, both stabbed out randomly all around them. Mary and Abigail told them they had killed a great Black woman from Stonington and an Indian who came with her. The girls said the floor was covered with blood. The girls went and looked out the door, claiming there was a crowd of witches gathered on a hill with the three dead ones laid out there, that is the Black woman, the Indian, and one more whom they did not know.

The magistrates named the two older Hobbs in warrants issued that day, but they did not name "the little minister" yet, for this was more exalted quarry. In fact this accusation caused a wave of doubt to pass swiftly, though imperceptibly through the staunch band of magistrates and ministers. Like the proverbial wonder it was, it kept them from acting upon it for nine days. Meanwhile they seemed to proceed with new caution during the examinations of the next day, April 22nd.

Those examinations, which so incensed Daniel Andrews, convened at midmorning in the Village. The two magistrates thought to verify the identifications by bringing in the accused unannounced. This approach, although commendable in principle, did not work out to much effect. The girls were supported by the immediate presence of fathers, mothers and elder brothers with whom they freely talked. Usually these stood just behind them as they sat upon their bench, and regularly gave the girls advice or direction during the examinations. On this occasion, they helped them identify the accused.

Deliverance Hobbs was the first of the accused to be brought into the meeting house. She was mother of Abigail, who had been accused by all of the girls at the instigation of a seventeen year old neighbor, Lydia Nichols, supported by things Deliverance had told her friends. Abigail, as we have seen readily "confessed". Goodwife Hobbs was charged after Abigail Williams and Mary Walcott cried out of her apparition at Ingersoll's the previous day.

Goodwife Hobbs started out in staunch denial, but she made one of those errors which precipitated a number of defendants on the path to "confession," that is, she spoke of seeing supernatural things.

Mr. Hathorne had asked her if it were true that she herself had been afflicted. Grateful for some relief in her interrogation amidst the usual caterwauling, she answered, "I have seen sundry sights." This somewhat coy reply was almost the same as the one her daughter used earlier.

"What sights?" Mr. Hathorne asked.

"Last Lord's Day in this meeting house and out of the door, I saw a great many birds, cats and dogs and heard a voice say come away."

Once she had begun to recount fantasy, she had no foothold against slipping into what followed. She went on to say she had seen apparitions of persons, that these had tempted her, and that one of them had been Goodwife Wildes.

When Mr. Hathorne accused her of going from being tormented to tormenting, she tried to stop her downhill slide, but the girls cried out that she was "on the beam," and Mary Walcott said they could "see her not" where she was supposed to be.

The girls began to cry out as the magistrate questioned her about signing the devil's book. Goodwife Hobbs, bewildered, looked from face to face of the afflicted, but as her glance fell on each, they fell into fits. She desperately answered that she was unable to speak, but he questioner kept on. Mr. Hathorne asked again "Have you signed the book?" She replied, "It is very lately then." Thus she became a confessed witch. She said she had only done it "the night before last."

Goodwife Wildes was given credit for tempting her, for providing the book and the pen and ink. Mr. Hathorne asked if she was tormented and thus made to sign. He was not surprised when she affirmed it. She confessed to being forced to stick pins in images, and to hurting John Nichol's child, in particular. She mentioned other witches including Goodwife Wildes, Goodwife Osborne, and a tall man in black in a high-crowned hat.

In recounting her affliction by Sarah Wildes, she also mentioned an appearance of Mercy Lewis! Mr. Hathorne was taken aback by this, yet no more questions were asked about it. The apples of the court's eye could not be touched.

As soon as Goodwife Hobbs began to "confess," the afflicted grew quiet, in the pattern that began with Tituba and continued with all the "confessors". This was duly noted by the court.

The magistrates and Mr. Parris formally ended the examination, but after conferring a few minutes they spoke privately with her before she was taken out. They asked her if she had received any hurt the day before. She said she had felt a prick when she was in a trance. Their questioning led her to settle on the place of the pain as being her right side.

Further questioning of Mary Walcott, and Abigail Williams with Benjamin Hutchinson brought the ministers and magistrates to the certain conclusion that her apparition had indeed been struck by Benjamin's rapier the previous day at Ingersoll's.

William Hobbs was brought in next. He kept obstinately to short answers in denial of any guilt or knowledge of witchcraft in himself or his wife or daughter. He was nonetheless bound over to gaol.

Sarah Wildes was brought in. Also from Topsfield, Mistress Wildes was the wife of a magistrate, John Wildes, of that town. Any respect due his office, however, proved no barrier to witch fever, in fact some of his judgments provided motives for those of Topsfield and Ipswich who accused his wife. She was also the mother of Ephraim, one of the constables who was active during our troubles. Both men later testified to the grudges behind old witch accusations dragged up against her.

The afflicted gave their customary enthusiastic greeting to Sarah Wildes as she was brought to the bar, most of them falling into fits.

"Hath this woman hurt you," asked Mr. Hathorne.

"Oh, she is upon the beam," cried out Abigail.

Goodwife Vibber agreed. Her status had grown from an emotionally sympathetic observer to being one of the chorus of afflicted.

"Goodwife Vibber, do you know this woman?"

"Nay, I never seen her before, but now I see her upon the beam," she answered, after which she feel into a blubbering fit.

"What say you to this?" Mr. Hathorne asked Mistress Wildes. "Are you guilty or not?"

"I am not guilty, sir," she replied.

"Is this the woman?" he asked the afflicted.

"Yes," cried Abigail and Anna together, followed by Mary, "yes," and Mercy, "It is she."

"What do you say? Are you guilty?" he asked Mistress Wildes again.

"I thank God I am free," she replied.

"Here is clear evidence that being not only a tormenter, you have caused one to sign the book the night before last. (The "clear evidence" was Goodwife Hobb's "confession") What do you say to this?"

"I never saw the book in my life nor these persons before."

Anna cried out, and several of the girls thrashed about on the bench.

"Do you deny this thing that is going on before you?"

All the girls and two women cried out and chorused back and forth in accusation that she hurt them then and there. As they had begun to do in past examinations, they reacted to motions of her body, hands, head or feet, by contorting their own in grotesque imitation.

"Did you never consent that these be hurt?"

"Never in my life."

"Anna cried out, "It is she who hurt John Herrick's mother." (John Herrick was the Marshall's brother. Reverend Hale was to testify later, just before Mistress Wildes was sentenced to be hanged, that John Herrick's mother-in-law, Mary Gould Reddington, came to him fifteen or sixteen years earlier complaining Mistress Wildes, her Topsfield neighbor, had bewitched and afflicted her. Other witnesses repeated this story later at Sarah Wildes' trial.)

"Is that so?" asked Mr. Hathorne.

"No, it is not true," Mistress Wildes replied.

Captain Abraham Howe was called to give evidence. He was

husband of Sarah Peabody Howe, sister to the wives of Daniel Rea and Thomas Perley, several of whom testified against Sarah Wildes, Bridget Bishop, Elizabeth Howe, and others. He testified in confirmation of Mary Reddington's complaint that Mistress Wildes previously bewitched her.

Mistress Wilde was bound over to gaol. There was general relief among the crowd since another of the elect number was now accounted for.

The next candidate brought in was Nehemiah Abbott, Jr., a sixty-year-old weaver from Topsfield.

Mr. Hathorne began questioning Goodman Abbott without identifying him.

"What say you, are you guilty of witchcraft of which you are suspected, or not?

"No, sir, I say before God, before whom I stand, that I know nothing of witchcraft."

"Who is this man?" Mr. Hathorne asked the girls.

"He is Goodman Abbott," answered Anna.

"I knew not his name, but have seen his shape," said Mary.

"What do you say to this?" Mr. Hathorne addressed the accused.

"I never did hurt them."

"Who hurt you Anna Putnam?" asked Mr. Hathorne.

"That man."

"I never hurt her."

"Look, he is on the beam," said Anna, with less than her characteristic enthusiasm.

"There was just such a discovery made of the person who was just carried out," (meaning not Goodwife Wildes, but Goodwife Hobbs) said Mr. Hathorne, "and she confessed. And if you would find mercy of God, you must confess."

"If I should confess this, I must confess what is false," replied Goodman Abbott, in a plain honest tone, yet without the rancour shown by the men previously accused.

"Tell how far you have gone. Who hurts you?"

"I do not know. I am absolutely free," he replied.

"Why then do these say you hurt them?"

"God knows."

"As you say, God knows if you will confess the truth. We desire nothing else, that you may not hide your guilt if you are guilty, and therefore confess it so."

"I speak before God that I am clear from this accusation."

"What! In all respects!"

"Yes, in all respects."

"Doth this man hurt you?" Mr. Hathorne again addressed Mercy, but there seemed to be more than the usual note of query in his question.

Mercy was silent, which some took as her usual dumb fit brought on by witchery.

"You hear several accuse you, though one cannot open her mouth."

"I am altogether free."

Again Mr. Hathorne addressed the girls with an uncharacteristic neutrality, "Charge him not unless it be he."

"This is the man," said Anna.

"He is the one," said Mary.

"It is very like him," said Abigail.

"How did you know his name," he asked Abigail.

"He did not tell me himself, but other witches told me."

"It is the same man!" cried Anna, and she went into a fit.

"Mary Walcott, is this the man?" asked Mr. Hathorne, paying no attention to Anna, and with a rising impatience in his voice.

"He is like him. I cannot say it is he."

"Mercy Lewis, is this the man?"

"It is not the man," she replied calmly.

Then several of the girls murmured in agreement.

"The man had a bunch on his eyes," Mercy continued.

Anna, still performing as in a fit, cried out a question, "Be you the man? Aye, do you say you be the man? Did you put a mist before my eyes?"

The ministers and magistrates conferred among them for a time, after which they had Goodman Abbott taken out. His case puzzled them and they planned to bring him back later in the day.

Edward Bishop, Jr. was brought in. He had three factors which told against him. First, he was the step-son of Bridget (Oliver) Bishop who was examined and gaoled three days earlier. Second, his wife was the daughter of Sarah Wildes (and sister of Constable Ephraim). But the principal reason he was accused was the sharp way he had dealt with John Indian after the examinations conducted at Salem eleven days earlier.

Following those examinations, John Indian had continued to have "fits" even when the party escorting most of "the afflicted" stopped at Gedney's Tavern for supper. Bishop had also stopped there, and did not like having his meal interrupted with John's antics. He dealt with John firmly by threats which effectively halted the fits. John Indian remained quiet and sober until they were riding back toward the Village. He rode double behind a young man, but suddenly he went off into another fit, clamping his teeth on the young man's shoulder so that his companion cried out in pain and surprise. Edward wasted no time about it, but broke off a stout switch and began to beat John severely across the back. John soon left off biting the young man, and apologized to Edward.

"I'm sorry, Mr. Bishop, sir. I won't do it no more."

"I am sure you will not," replied Edward," as I am equally sure I could cure all you afflicted people in the same way."

Three of the girls, Abigail, Anna, and Mercy were also of the party. As soon as Edward and the others of Topsfield parted with them at the forks above Phillips, they began to discuss what he said. Even as they were riding along they began crying out of Goodman Bishop afflicting them.

There was, therefore, considerable clamour raised among them when Edward Bishop was brought in. Nor were there many dumb fits or periods of silence during his examination. Goodman Bishop had come prepared to speak directly and strongly, but such was the level of noise made not only by the girls, but by the older women and Indian John, that his eloquence was largely wasted.

The result was that although Goodman Bishop declared his own innocence, he had no real chance to confront the afflicted as shamming and dissembling. At one point he became frustrated and bellowed like a bull, "They need but a good thrashing for the cure of their afflictions." Many others silently agreed, but the ministers and magistrates were not sympathetic.

He was bound over to gaol.

His wife Sarah was greeted with comparatively little enthusiasm when she was brought before the court. She gave no ground to Mr. Hathorne's questions. She stated that she did not think either her husband or her mother was a witch. She said she herself was completely innocent and trusted in the Lord Jesus Christ. She offered no explanation for the behavior of the afflicted.

Sarah too was bound over to gaol. But neither she nor her husband were to stay there very long.

Goodman Abbott was brought back. The Meeting House was so full of people that many sat or stood in the windows. It was hard to see, wherefore the magistrates had the accused go outside and the girls, too, so they might see him in the daylight. There the magistrates and ministers talked with him and asked the girls if he was the witch or wizard whose spectre they had seen. There they all agreed he was not, because he had not "the wen" on his face, although he was "very like" the man. They said they had been mistaken because of his much-lined face and the hair hanging over his forehead.

Mr. Abbott was released by the court and walked away from the Meeting House feeling far freer than he had thitherto. Many of us, particularly the families of others accused were much heartened by this apparent diminution of the power of the accusers.

However, with the forgetfulness of the Unforgiving Servant, Mr. Abbott soon became a witness in the June trial of Elizabeth Howe, where he attributed several maladies among his cattle to her agency. Perhaps he meant to fully establish his innocence by coming in on the other side.

Chapter Twenty-Five — The Third Sister
(22 April)

But after these things they could not long continue [in England]
in any peaceable condition, but were hunted and persecuted on
every side, so as their former afflictions were but as flea-bitings
in comparison of these which now came upon them. For some
were taken and clapped up in prison, others had their houses
beset and watched night and day, and hardly escaped their
hands; and the most were fain to flee and leave their houses and
habitations, and the means of their livelihood.
-- William Bradford , *Of Plymouth Plantation* (1669)

After Goodman Abbott was taken out, Mary Easty was
brought before the magistrates. Mary Easty was a few years older
than Sarah Cloyce, but still fourteen years younger than, Rebecca
Nurse, oldest of the Towne sisters. The Easty place was well up into
Topsfield, about a mile north of Smith's Hill and Joseph Porter's
place. Isaac Easty was a solid and respected farmer, with close ties to
other Towne kindred in Topsfield.

Francis Nurse, Rebecca (Jr.), Mary and John were there in the
Meeting house. They had come to support their uncle Isaac and
cousins Isaac and Sarah during the examination. It was heroic of
Francis, especially, who appeared to be reliving a nightmare
throughout the questioning.

Isaac and Mary were so respected the magistrates were hard
put to find any beside the girls to say a word against her.
Nevertheless Goodwife Easty was brought in to a vigorous chorus.
Perhaps to renew themselves in the favor of the court after showing
fallibility over Goodman Abbott, Abigail and Anna immediately fell
into fits.

"Does this woman hurt you?" asked Mr. Hathorne.

The girls acted as though struck dumb, then Mary Walcott
and Mercy Lewis went into shaking fits.

Abigail cried out, "It's Goody Easty! She hurts me!"

"Oh, she hurts us now!" cried Mary Walcott. Anna Putnam
and Mercy Lewis joined in.

"I see Goody Easty and Goody Hobbs upon them," said John

Indian, who had been brought in during Goodman Bishop's examination.

Mr. Hathorne turned to Mary Easty and asked "What do you say? Are you guilty?"

"I can say before Christ Jesus, I am free." Again the Nurses felt, as they had with their mother, a depth of pride in this hardy saint who could speak calmly and openly in the face of these chaotic accusations.

"You see these accuse you."

"There is a God."

"Hath she brought the book to you?" he asked the girls.

They were silent, although several appeared to be playing at their dumb fit.

"What have you done to these children?"

"I know nothing."

"How can you say you know nothing when you see these tormented and accuse you? Can you say that you know nothing?"

"Would you have me accuse myself?"

"Yes, if you be guilty. How far have you complied with Satan whereby he takes this advantage against you?"

"Sir, I never complied but prayed against him all my days. I have no compliance with Satan in this. What would you have me do?"

"Confess if you be guilty."

"I will say it, if it was my last time, I am clear of this sin."

"Of what sin?"

"Of witchcraft."

He turned to the girls again, with the same note of genuine query he had used over Goodman Abbott.

"Are you certain this is the woman?"

All the girls were silent, and it seemed for a moment as if there might be another case dismissed! A great hope surged up in many hearts. But after a time Anna spoke, "This is the woman. It was like her and she told me her name."

"You hear them say it was you bewitched them."

"I am free of it."

"How then do you think it is they are thus afflicted?"

"I do not know if they be bewitched or perhaps not."

"It is marvelous to me that you should sometimes think they are bewitched and sometimes not, when several confess that they have been guilty of bewitching them."

"Well, sir, would you have me confess that I never knew?"

Goodwife Easty had joined her hands together and Mercy Lewis imitated her in an ostentatious manner. Seeing this, Mary opened her hands and let them fall before her.

"Look now your hands are open, her hands are open," observed Mr. Hathorne.

"Is this the woman?" he again asked the girls.

The girls made signs with their hands, pretending they could not speak, but after a minute or two of this, Anna cried out, "Oh Goody Easty! Oh Goody Easty," while Mercy cried out, " You are the woman! You are the woman!"

Mary Easty bowed her head, and immediately the girls imitated her and cried that she hurt them. All hopes were dashed. They had made up their minds, our little despots, and this victim would not be spared.

Mr. Hathorne directed the Marshall, "Put up her head, for while her head is bowed the necks of these are broken." Her husband Isaac began to rumble at this. John was deeply fearful he would speak out. He turned to his cousin Isaac and whispered, "It would be the worst thing for him to say anything. If you think he may, you should take him out."

"What do you say to this!" Mr. Hathorne demanded of Mary.

"Why, God will know."

"Nay, God knows now!"

"I know he does."

With the encouragement of his son, Isaac Easty seemed to have gotten hold of himself again.

"What did you think of the actions of the others before your sisters came out? Did you think it was witchcraft?"

"I cannot tell."

"Why do you not think it is witchcraft?"

"It is an evil spirit, but whether it be witchcraft I do not know."

Elizabeth cried, "She brought us the book!"

"She bid us sign!" joined in Mary Walcott. Then all the girls and several women fell into their fits.

With little consultation, the magistrates bound Mary Easty over to Salem gaol.

Goodman Easty's countenance was churning, but not at all as Francis Nurse's had been. He was not so much dazed as very alert and looked around him sharply as though he had been lowered into a pit of serpents. His children Isaac and Sarah rose and urged him before them as they went toward the doors. John knew the weight upon their hearts that dimmed their eyes and made their shoulders stoop. Francis and he went with them, and outside, hugged them and wept. At last Father Nurse urged them to stay the night, but they would not, and only asked a few things about what they should take to the gaol, before they hastened away home.

After Mary Easty, the magistrates brought in another defendant with little testimony against her. Mary Black, Nathaniel Putnam's slave, was there apparently due to the suspicions of her master's son, the constable Benjamin Putnam. He had become very sensitive to hints of witches among us. He thought his father might be harboring one of the forty recently numbered.

Mary Black had more integrity than Tituba, or more dignity, perhaps, for she made no concession to the demands of the court or her master's son.

"Mary, you are accused of sundry acts of witchcraft," said Mr. Hathorne, "Tell me be you a witch?"

Mary shook her head silently.

"How long have you been a witch?" he urged.

"I cannot tell," she replied.

"Why do you hurt these folks?"

"I hurt nobody."

At this point, Benjamin Putnam struck in, "Who doth!" he asked, with a certain amount of mastery in his voice.

"I do not know," Mary replied, with courtesy but no show of subordination.

Nathaniel Putnam (who had written a petition for Mother Nurse) testified that Mary had said a man appeared to her and sat down in her room about a year ago.

"What did the man say to you?" asked Mr. Hathorne.

"He said nothing," she replied.

Turning to the girls who had been fairly quiet, perhaps due to their day-long exertions, Mr. Hathorne asked, "Doth this Negro hurt you?"

"Yes," said Abigail, "she does."

"Yes," echoed Anna and Mary Walcott.

"Why do you hurt them?" asked Mr. Hathorne.

"I did not hurt them," she answered.

"Do you prick them with sticks?" he asked, for several of them had just cried out to that effect.

"No. I pin my neckcloth, though."

"Well, take out a pin and pin it again," instructed Mr. Hathorne, with the predictable result that the girls cried out of further injuries. Mary Walcott even demonstrated a bleeding mark on her arm. Abigail claimed to be stabbed in the stomach, while Mercy said her foot was injured.

Mary Black was bound over to gaol.

Thus the magistrates became wizards themselves! Like alchemists of old, they combined science and magic in the laboratory of their courtroom. To prove Mary Black a witch they ordered her to perform "a spell" in order to see the affect of that "magic" upon the afflicted. Mr. Hathorne was thus as much the agent of the girls being stabbed as Mary who was commanded to use her pin. In the earlier words of Reverend Parris, he used the devil to bring out the devil. This sort of wizardry was carried out increasingly, the magistrates instructing the accused to perform or themselves performing bits of "magic" during examinations.

The last of the elect to be catechized on April 22nd was Mistress Mary English, but she was by no means the least. She was wife of one of the most successful merchants in Salem, Philip English, who owned a number of ships. He did not come from an old Salem family, but had immigrated to the colony from the island of Jersey in the 1660s. His wife was daughter of William Hollingsworth, a wealthy merchant, even more respected than her husband.

The girls greeted her with an unusual intensity of fits, especially considering how long they had been at it that day! As with Mistress Corey and Mistress Wilde, one had the feeling they particularly enjoyed bringing down one of high standing.

Mr. Hathorne treated her with moderate respect, but asked all the usual questions, and although she gave clear answers denying any knowledge or involvement in witchcraft, he pointed out to her she must be guilty when all of the afflicted cried out of her. He suggested that therefore she ought to confess.

She said, "They do not know what they are saying."

He replied, "They have spoken the truth about several who have today confessed to be witches. You would do well to confess your guilt as they."

Mistress English was bound over to gaol with the rest, including all named in the complaints except for Nehemiah Abbott.

While these two days passed with a great filling-up of the numbers, Joseph and Daniel went blithely fishing in the nether

regions of Andover, more likely to be taken by an Indian for their
scalps than a witchhunter for their necks. But instead they claimed
to have been taking fish of colossal size and in incredible numbers —
so many that they could not bring them back but had to let most go.
When the others went over to Joseph's the night of the 23rd, Peter and
Sam and John were able to see two large salmon and eight trout of
about one foot in length, being kept in a barrel in the springhouse.
The fishers assured them , however, that this was but a miniscule
remnant of the great quantity caught. They said they had to eat all
the larger ones on the spot, due to their great weight and the
difficulty of carrying them. Not only had their fishermen's
imaginations been revived, but they seemed genuinely refreshed.
Smelling the campfire smoke heavy upon their clothes, the others
were envious, but nevertheless glad for them.

Mistress Mary (Veren) Putnam, Joseph's widowed mother,
another who was opposed to the proceedings, visited with the
conspirators while Joseph's wife Elizabeth fried up six fish for the
benefit of the late-comers (although most had eaten somewhat
already). It seemed necessary to the fishermen's complete happiness
that these also partake and extol the fruit of their labors before any
other topic could be raised. So all did their duty, and found the fish
excellent.

The two ladies retired upstairs and the five men sat about the
table again, where they reluctantly turned their conversation to the
matters that brought them together.

"Have you heard the latest tally?" John asked.

The two fishermen nodded silently.

"And did you hear that one of them was let go!" Sam asked.
"You are not the only fishermen who throw back the small fry!"
They had not heard any details of it, so Sam gave them a somewhat
exaggerated account of Goodman Abbott, emphasizing the
bewilderment of Anna at being out-of-step and out-voted, and then
the fanciful means by which the girls were able to harmonize their
momentarily divided forces."

"Old Abbott is a good enough soul," commented Peter, "He
was fair scared to death, so he told me, for I walked part way home
with him after. He said he would be praying for Mother and for
Aunt Rebecca and Mary, now, for he knew a little of what they had
been through. But he is too frightened by the whole thing to be any
use to us, I'd say."

"And Mary English!" Daniel said, blowing out pipe smoke.

"They can find but twenty people within fifty miles who are as respected and established as she. Your despots grow in power, John."

"**P**lease, Daniel, don't call them my despots," John begged, "I feel about that as Joseph feels about calling Sergeant Putnam his brother."

"**M**y half-brother, if you please," commented Joseph, "and if we wish to follow the pattern established by the ancient Greeks, we ought to call these girls 'the benevolent ladies,' for that is what they called the Furies, in order to avoid becoming objects of their wrath."

"**M**y point is made," John said.

"**I**t is always important at the beginning of any serious discussion to make sure of definitions and nomenclature," said Daniel dryly, " Having done so, let us move on. Has anyone anything more to report?"

"**Y**ou know Mary Warren has said more?" John asked. When their expressions indicated they had not heard, he went on. "Aunt Mary Easty spoke long with her at Dounton's. She said Mary nearly bites through her lips during the examinations, so hard they go at it with her. It seems three days ago they got her to say she had indeed signed a book, and that her master and mistress told her not to tell anyone they were witches. Two days ago, she was so beside herself she admitted to a great many things they asked her — seeing other witches, gathering to afflict, and so on. So now she is regarded as a 'confessed witch' and her words are being used to accuse others.

"**B**ut here is the main thing. Aunt Mary says Mary Warren is open with the other prisoners in denying the truth of any of this — or the truth of what any of the afflicted say — when she is given the chance. She told Aunt Mary, Mistress English and others that the magistrates might as well question that distracted Keyser girl and believe what she said as any of the afflicted. She says her fits are pure distraction. She said her head is so distempered, she can't remember anything she says during them outside of her fits, nor believes any of it to be true. She says what we have all along supposed, that most of the "afflicted" girls are dissembling.

"**B**ut Aunt Mary says she is deathly afraid of the other girls, who seem to have threatened her, and is also afraid of the magistrates and ministers who belabor her with words. Apparently they even slap her face if she does not go along with them. Several witnesses among the prisoners at Dounton's have heard these things from Mary Warren, and Aunt Mary says they are all ready to swear so in court."

"That is good!" said Daniel, "It will not have as much weight with the court as it does with us, but that is good, John. Almost as good as the big salmon I hooked, wouldn't you say, Joseph?"

"I'd trade the greatest of your poor minnows for a good method of getting around these girls and magistrates. It seems strong irony that Mary Warren may be the model for the Parris girls' original games, and now is dragged in herself against her will! What better irony it would be, if her testimony became the means of exposing the whole deception!"

"But you see, that is why I spoke somewhat reservedly about the court's reception of such testimony," Daniel went on. "As soon as authority admits to supernatural evidence inaccessible to any but an elect group of seers, it makes itself dependent on those seers for all its actions in the purview. The magistrates will only admit the girls are shamming and deceiving is if they are willing to abandon the whole enterprise. If they are not willing, then they will hold out indefinitely against truth, be it ever so well attested to.

"Furthermore they have the means by which to justify themselves to themselves, for the essence of this business is that ultimately everyone involved is being afflicted. The ultimate author of that affliction is the devil. Those who give in to the affliction become witches. Those who repent become confessed witches, but are again subject to affliction. Those innocent whom the devil wants to drive to himself or the confessors he wishes to bring back, he afflicts through the apparitions of his witches.

"What is likely to be their explanation when Mary either says or is quoted by three or four others as saying, she and the others were only dissembling?

"They will conclude she has given in once again to the devil in order to avoid further affliction. In fact ultimately everyone who speaks the truth about these girls will be supposed to serve the devil. The truth has never been so unpopular."

"If I recall," said Peter, "The prophets and church fathers treated the same way. The more truth they told, the more they were hated. In such times, it is hard to keep track of earthly reasons for speaking the truth."

"Certainly the earthly reasons are not very evident, nor show up very quickly in earthly results. It is a bare and brave thing to speak merely because it is the truth and because God is Truth, and he requires it."

"To speak the truth in love," added Sam. "That's what I find impossible. To love my enemies, to love a village full of spoiled, proud, small-minded and evil-doing people. I would as soon love King Philip or Frontenac, whose weapons and reasons I can somewhat understand."

"That is something we can only pray for, for none of us can find it in ourselves," said Joseph. "Think how it feels to me to see my grandfather's and father's names dragged into such a pigsty by these incomprehensible half-brothers, brothers-in-law, and other relatives of mine. How do you suppose the Lord was able to love Judas?"

"Perhaps that struggle had a part in the bloody sweat at Gethsemane," said Daniel. "But we must disperse. John, will you pray for us?"

So he did, and a whippoorwill called from the dark woods as the four walked home.

They passed Sam Sibley as they came to the Meeting House. He grunted a greeting after peering suspiciously at the four of them. They stopped and spoke lightly until he had gone on a little. Then Peter spoke in a low voice, "Perhaps we ought to make a point of not being seen together like this. It might be enough to get us named one of these days."

"You're right," said Daniel, "We must agree and plan against that next time we gather. Meanwhile be careful."

Sam and John turned toward home as the other two continued down the road.

Woodcut from Wonders of the Invisible World, 1693.

Chapter Twenty-Six -- Conspiracy Fails
(1 - 9 May)

With bold resolvedness, these stout soldiers of Christ reply: "As death, the king of terror with all his dreadful attendance, inhumane and barbarous tortures doubled and trebled by all the infernal furies, have appeared but light and momentary to the soldiers of Christ Jesus, so also the pleasure, profits and honors of this world set forth in their most glorious splendor and magnitude by the alluring lady of delight, proffering pleasant embraces, cannot entice with her siren songs such soldiers of Christ, whose aims are elevated by him many millions above that brave warrior Ulysses."
    -- Edward Johnson, **Wonder-Working Providence of Sion's Savior** (1654)

The Arrest and Examination of Reverend George Burroughs dominated the attention of Salem and the Village during the first half of May. Nevertheless, other arrests and examinations went forward rapidly. Such was the pace and scale of events, that the little band of conspirators could do little. They continued at a few small tasks and hoped for the best from the trials to come. So many were the arrests, however, that all hopes of a quick end appeared but illusions. The conspirators were coming to feel their enterprise must hopelessly fail.

On May 1st, Deliverance Hobbs was further examined in prison. She repeated all she had "confessed" and added she was invited to a witches' meeting the previous morning. Many of the arrested were there, she said, but there was also a wizard, who preached and administered the "sacrament" of red bread and red wine like blood. She said these were distributed by Goodwife Nurse and Mistress Wildes. She said the meeting was in the pasture by Mr. Parris's house and that she saw Abigail Williams run out to speak with them, but that when she had come a little way, she was struck blind and did not know to whom she spoke.

Deliverance's daughter, Abigail Hobbs, was brought down to speak with the magistrates and ministers. As she entered the room, she had a great fit and blamed it on Giles Corey. Deliverance said it was indeed him, and that she could see both him and the gentlewoman from Boston trying to break her daughter's neck. (The gentlewoman from Boston was identified by several as Mrs. Thacher, Judge Corwin's mother-in-law.)

The next day five more examinations were held in the Village. Those examined by our two magistrates were Sarah Morey and Dorcas Hoar of Beverly, Lydia Dastin of Reading, Susannah (North) Martin, a widow, of distant Amesbury, and Philip English of Salem. These were complained of in the same warrant that named Reverend Burroughs.

Sarah Morey, a young woman, was arrested by the Beverly constables.

Lydia Dastin, an aged widow, was brought in by Constable John Parker of Reading. Both of these were put through the usual ritual—fits of the afflicted, berating by Mr. Hathorne, and a denial of everything on their part—before they were both bound over to prison.

When Dorcas Hoar was brought into the Meeting House, the two magistrates and three ministers (Mr. Parris recording) waited quietly, but the afflicted girls immediately went into fits.

Dorcas Hoar was a near neighbor of Reverend John Hale of Beverly, who was one of her primary accusers. A number of years earlier, after his beloved daughter died he recalled a suspicious event. He once confronted that daughter for the theft of some articles from his house. It seems the theft was carried out by the Hoar children, but Reverend Hale's daughter had not told him this, because the children threatened her. More specifically, they had told his daughter that Widow Hoar had a magic book which would tell if Miss Hale revealed the secret to her father. They said if she did tell, their mother would bewitch her.

Reverend Hale said he had heard of this book many years before. It was said to be a fortune-telling book. Years earlier he had exhorted Widow Hoar it was not lawful to have or use such a thing. She indicated she had taken his exhortation to heart and gotten rid of the book. She told him she had once had such a book from John Samson, but gave it back twenty years ago and told no fortunes since. Samson, however, told Reverend Hale he had sold his book about thirty years earlier in Casco Bay and not seen it since. When Reverend Hale spoke with Thomas Tuck about this, more than a decade before our troubles, he confirmed Widow Hoar still had such a book. Further, she spoke to Reverend Hale of seeing the ghost of Thomas Tuck nearly ten years after he died. After his daughter's death, other friends told Reverend Hale that the poor girl had lived in constant fear of Widow Hoar and her book.

Mr. Hathorne began the examination by addressing each of the afflicted in turn, asking if this woman hurt them. Elizabeth and Anna both said she had hurt them a week ago last Sabbath. Elizabeth and Mary said Widow Hoar told them she choked her own husband. Abigail made the remarkable claim that she was the first "witch" whose apparition she had seen, prior even to Tituba's.

Eighteen year old Susanna Sheldon of the Village, accused Widow Hoar of hurting her last Monday night. Both Abigail and Anna said she had choked a woman in Boston recently.

Elizabeth cried out, "Why do you pinch me?" Those standing by looked and saw the mark of the pinch. Marshall Herrick said he saw Widow Hoar pinching her fingers together at that time.

Mr. Hathorne addressed her, "Dorcas Hoar, why do you hurt these?"

"I never hurt any child in my life," she responded with indignation.

"It is you or your appearance," he said.

"How can I help it?" she answered.

"What is it from you that hurts these?"

"I never saw worse than myself," she said, which unusual answer at first seemed to Mr. Hathorne a confession, but he thought for a moment and realized it was a disclaimer, so he responded cleverly,

"You need not see worse. They charge you with killing your husband."

"I never did," she said, and addressing the girls, "I never saw you before."

"You sent for Goody Gale to have her head off!" said Susannah Sheldon, "What do you say to that?" (This was one of the many obscure bits of testimony that remains a mystery. Perhaps Susannah referred to Reverend Hale's first wife, who had died nearly nine years earlier. Susannah Sheldon became noted among the "afflicted" for connecting old deaths with witchcraft.)

"I never sent for her upon that account."

"What do you say about killing your husband?" Susannah challenged, and went on, "You came in with two cats and brought me the book and I fell into a fit and you told me your name was Goody Buckley"

"No, I never did. I never saw thee before."

"What black cats were those you had?" Susannah continued, so that it seemed the afflicted were now to conduct the examination rather than the magistrates.

"I had none," Widow Hoar replied, looking to Mr. Hathorne in surprise that the girls were allowed to question her like this.

Mary Walcott, Susannah and Abigail cried out, "Oh!"

"See!" said Mary, "A black man whispers in her ears!" The others cried out in agreement.

"Oh! you are liars!" cried Widow Hoar, "And God will stop the mouth of liars!"

"You are not to speak after this manner in the court," warned Mr. Hathorne, demonstrating his selective concern for propriety.

"I will speak the truth as long as I live," she answered. She maintained a degree of courage which many of those listening admired.

Again Mary, Susannah and Elizabeth cried out, saying a black man whispered in her ear.

"He says she should confess!" said Elizabeth.

"Oh, see, the black man with her!" cried Goody Vibber, who had been in blubbering fits up to this time, and she lapsed as quickly back into her fits.

"What do you say to those cats that sucked your breast? What are they?" asked Susannah.

"I had no cats," she answered.

"You do not call them cats," said Mr. Hathorne, "what are they that suck you?"

"I never sucked none but my child," she answered

"What do you say, you never saw Goody Buckley?" Susannah called out.

"I never knew her," answered Widow Hoar.

"Goodman Buckley," Mr. Hathorne addressed that man, "Did this woman know your wife?"

"She was often at my house," Goodman Buckley replied.

"I know you, but not the woman," replied Widow Hoar.

"You said you did not know the name," observed Mr. Hathorne, ever willing to catch someone in words, though not so careful of the words themselves, as in this case.

"I did not know the name so as to go to the woman," she replied, still with strength of voice and character.

"Look!" said Susannah, "there is a blue bird!"

"It has gone down her back!" cried Abigail.

The Marshall struck her upon the back, and afterward some in the meeting said they saw something fly up like a moth.

Goody Vibber cried, "Oh!"

"What did you see, Goody Vibber?" asked Mr. Hathorne.

Goody Vibber lay half-supine on the bench wide-eyed, but apparently unable to speak further.

Turning to Widow Hoar, Mr. Hathorne demanded, "What! Can you have no heart to confess!"

"I have nothing to do with witchcraft," Widow Hoar replied.

"They say the devil is whispering in your ear!" he went on.

"I cannot help it if they do see it," she answered.

"Cannot you confess what you think of these things?"

"Why should I confess that I do not know?" she replied.

"Oh, Goody Hoar, do not kill me!" cried Susannah, and she fell into a fit. When she recovered she said, "There was a black man whispering in her ear and she brought me the book."

"I have no book but the Lord's Book," replied Widow Hoar.

"What Lord's book?" asked Mr. Hathorne.

"The Lord's Book," she answered.

"Oh!" Mary cried, and the others joined in, "There one whispers in her ears."

"There is somebody will scrub your ears shortly," said Widow Hoar.

Immediately all the afflicted cried out and thrashed about.

Mercy Lewis cried out, "Why do you threaten they should be rubbed?"

"I did not speak a word of rubbing," she answered.

"Yes, she did!" cried Susannah. Several others loudly agreed.

"My meaning was God would bring things to light."

"Your meaning for God to bring the thing to light would be to deliver these poor afflicted ones, not to rub them!" declared Mr. Hathorne, "This is unusual impudence to threaten before authority. Who hurts them now!"

"I know not," she answered.

"They were rubbed after you had threatened them!" he declared.

At this point the magistrates had several of the afflicted brought toward her for the "healing" that was supposed to occur when the afflicted touched the afflicter, but the girls held back and acted like they could not approach her.

"What is the reason these cannot come near you?"

"I can not help it. I do them no wrong. They may come if they will."

"Why! You see that they cannot come near you!"

"I do them no wrong."

After that, the magistrates wasted little time in having Dorcas Hoar bound over to prison.

(Despite her tremendous courage under fire and her apparently unshakable resolve not to retreat, Dorcas Hoar was to become a "confessor" by September.)

Next to be examined was Susanna Martin of Amesbury. Orlando Bagley, the constable of that town brought her in. We do not know who first named her, but six accusers were named in her warrant and Abigail, Elizabeth, Mercy and Anna, as well as John Indian, accused her at her examination. Although long the subject of witch rumors in the country about Salisbury, she was a hardy, cheerful woman. Coming fresh onto the scene of our troubles, she seemed better prepared than most. She proved the best theologian examined thus far.

Mr. Hathorne began by addressing the girls, who had already presented the requisite fits in greeting.

"Do you know this woman? Hath she hurt you?" he asked.

Abigail answered, "It is Goody Martin. She hath hurt me often."

The others were silent.

Elizabeth Hubbard said, "I have not been hurt by her." (Which was particularly interesting in that she was listed as one afflicted in the warrant.)

John said he had not seen her, but Mercy pointed and fell into a dumb fit.

Anna had a fit and in the process threw her glove at her.

Goody Martin laughed at this.

"What!" said Mr. Hathorne, "Do you laugh at it?"

"Well, I may at such folly," answered Goody Martin.

"Is this folly, the hurt of these persons?" challenged Mr. Hathorne.

"I never hurt man or woman or child," replied Goody Martin.

"She hath hurt me a great many times and plucks me down!" cried Mercy.

Goody Martin laughed again.

"This woman hath also hurt me a great many times!" cried Mary Walcott.

"What do you say to this?" asked Mr. Hathorne.

"I have no hand in witchcraft," the woman replied.

"What did you do? Did not you give your consent?" asked the magistrate.

"No, never in my life," she answered.

"Pray, what ails these people?" demanded Mr. Hathorne.

"I do not know," she replied.

"But what do you think?" he persisted.

"I do not desire to spend my judgment upon it," answered Goody Martin.

"Do not you think they are bewitched?" he asked.

"No, I do not think they are," she replied.

"Tell me your thoughts about them."

"Why, my thoughts are my own when they are in, but when they are out, another's their master," she answered.

"You said their master," Mr. Hathorne responded, then half-turning toward the girls he asked, "Who do you think is their master?"

"If they be dealing in the black art, you may know as well as I."

"Well, what have you done towards this?"

"Nothing."

"Why! It is you or your appearance!"

"I cannot help it."

"That may be your master."

"I desire to lead myself according to the Word of God."

"Is this according to God's Word?"

"If I were such a person I would tell you the truth."

"How comes your appearance just now to hurt these?"

"How do I know?"

"Are not you willing to tell the truth?"

"I cannot tell. He that appeared in the shape of Samuel's shape, a glorified saint, can appear in anyone's shape."

"Do you believe these do not say true?"

"They may lie for ought I know."

"May you not tell a lie?"

"I dare not tell a lie if it would save my life."

"Then you will speak the truth."

"I have spake nothing else. I would do them any good."

"I do not think you have such affections for them whom just now you insinuated had the devil for their master."

Elizabeth Hubbard, afflicted for the first time by Goodwife Martin, if her earlier testimony were to be believed, cried out and fell into a fit. Marshall Herrick standing by said Goody Martin pinched her fingers. Several of the afflicted cried out.

"She is on the beam," said Abigail, and Anna and Mercy echoed her.

"Pray God discover you if you be guilty," said Mr. Hathorne.

"Amen. Amen. A false tongue will never make a guilty person," Goody Martin replied.

Mercy Lewis called out to her, "You have been a long time coming to the court today, but you can come fast enough in the night!"

"No, sweetheart," Goody Martin replied, with gentleness, at which Mercy fell into uncharacteristically vigorous fits, and all the others joined her.

John Indian then fell into one of the violent fits for which he was noted, thrashing about on the floor and gnashing his teeth. "She bites, she bites" he called, as Goody Martin bit her lips.

"Have you not compassion for these afflicted?" asked Mr. Hathorne with great pathos of his own.

"No, I have none," answered Goody Martin.

"There is a black man with her," cried Abigail, and others joined in agreeing.

Goody Vibber, for the first time in this examination, cried out in agreement.

The magistrates tried the experiment of bringing the afflicted near, but as in the last examination, they held back and claimed they could come no nearer. Abigail, Mary Walcott, Goody Vibber and John Indian all thus acted and spoke.

"I will kill her if I come near her!" shouted John Indian, which no one but he made any sense of. He threw himself down as he came near her.

"What is the reason these cannot come near you?" asked Mr. Hathorne.

"I cannot tell," she replied, "It may be the devil bears me more malice than another."

"Do not you see how God evidently discovers you?" asked the magistrate.

"No, not a bit for that," said Goody Martin.

"All the congregation think so," replied Mr. Hathorne.

"Let them think what they will."

"What is the reason these cannot come near you?"

"I do not know but they can if they will. Or else if you please I will come to them."

"What is the black man whispering to you?"

"There was none whispered to me."

The magistrates then bound Sarah Martin over to prison.

Mr. Phillip English was the last of the accused scheduled for examination on May 2nd, but the constables, marshal and sheriff reported he could not be found. The conspirators rejoiced at this news, for at last someone had fled rather than be arrested. In particular they were glad Mr. English had evaded arrest. The Nurses knew of him through William Russell, husband of Elizabeth Nurse, another of Rebecca and Francis's daughters. Mr. English built and bought fishing boats to send out from Salem for twenty years past. He owned a wharf and warehouse and more than a dozen stores and sheds in Town. William, a fisherman, said he was a good man to work for, although a careful businessman.

Mr. English spent about a month in hiding with friends in Boston, but at the end of May, he was caught and given into custody at Boston, where he joined his wife. They were among a number of wealthier "witches" who were able to put up bail money, and be released on recognizance of others who were willing to provide surety. Later, they were able to escape and go far enough away to have no more trouble until the trials drew to a close. Meanwhile Sheriff Corwin confiscated the English property, which was of considerable value

On May 3rd the magistrates again examined Deliverance Hobbs at the gaol. Some of the girls had told the officers she further afflicted them. She acted nervous when brought down to Dounton's parlor.

"What have you done since last we saw you, whereby there is further trouble in your appearance?"

"Nothing at all."

"But have you not since been tempted?"

"Yes, sir, but I have not done it, nor will not do it."

"Here is a great change since we last spake to you, for now you afflict and torment again. Now tell us the truth who tempted you to sign again?"

"It was Goody Oliver (Bridget Bishop — Oliver was her name from her previous marriage), she would have me to set my hand to the book, but I would not neither have I. Neither did I consent to hurt them again."

"Was that true that Goody Wildes appeared to you and tempted you?"

"Yes, that was true."

"Have you been tempted since?"

"Yes, about Friday or Saturday night last. "

"Did they bid you that you should not tell?"

"Yes, they told me so."

"But how far did they draw you or tempt you , and how far did you yield to the temptation?

"I did not do it."

"But do not you acknowledge that was true that you told us formerly?"

"Yes."

"And you did sign then at the first, did you not?"

"Yes, I did, it is true."

"Did you promise then to deny at last what you said before?"

The ministers and magistrates were always one step ahead of the devil. In this case they had worked out a theology for denial. If a "confessed" witch recanted her testimony it was clearly a result of renewed temptations and afflictions by her fellow witches. The great magi could see this before it was told them. So gifted was their intuition they could discern it in the features and demeanor of the one who was turning back.

"Yes, I did and it was Goody Oliver (alias Bishop) that tempted me to deny all that I had confessed before."

"Do you not know the man with the wen?" (Mr. Hathorne referred here to the man who was like Nehemiah Abbey, according to the girls, but with a "bunch" or "wen" on one of his eyes. The magistrates would not be content until they had hunted down every last witch or wizard.)

"No, I do not know who it is. All that I confessed before is true."

"Who were they you named formerly?"

"Osborne, Good, Burroughs, Oliver, Wildes, Corey and his wife, Nurse, Procter and his wife."

"Who were with you in the chamber?" (Apparently some of the "afflicted" had "seen" others talking with her privily in her bedchamber.)

"Wildes and Bishop or Oliver, Good and Osborne. And they had a feast of roast and boiled meat and did eat and drink and would have had me to have eat and drunk with them, but I would not. And they would have had me signed, but I would not then nor when Goody Oliver came to me."

"Nor did not you come to the children in your likeness?"

"I do not know that I did."

"What is that you have to tell which you cannot tell yet, you say?

But she was at a loss for words. The magistrates concluded she was struck dumb.

That same evening, Mary Walcott claimed to see the apparition of Rebecca Nurse telling her she had bewitched a number of persons to death: Benjamin Holten, John Harrod, Rebekah Shepherd and several others.

On May 6th the Massachusetts Assembly passed an act calling for a general fast to be celebrated on May 26th throughout the colony, specifically that prayer might be offered for the godly prosecution of our troubles.

Two days later, on the Lord's Day, a complaint was issued for four more women: Bethia Carter of Woburn, her daughter of the same name, Ann Sears, and Sarah Dastin, the unmarried daughter of Lydia.

On the 9th, Ephraim Bock, Constable of Woburn, brought Widow Bethiah Carter, Sr., and Mistress Ann Sears to the examination. Sergeant Putnam and Constable John Putnam, Jr. had made the complaints on behalf of Anna, Mercy, and Mary Walcott. Neither woman had much to say, except to deny the charges. Both were bound over to gaol and remained there until early December, when two men from Lynn put up bond money for their recognizance.

Bethia Carter, Jr., however, followed the example of Mr. English and fled, so that we heard no more about her. In Mr. English's case a general warrant was issued and sent throughout the colonies. In the case of young Mistress Carter, the magistrates seem to have made no further efforts.

Sarah Dastin was brought in by Constable John Parker of Reading, who earlier arrested her mother. Her examination was according to pattern and was as dreary as oft repeated performances, no matter how dramatic, must inevitably become.

Sarah and Lydia Dastin were sent from Salem prison to Cambridge Prison.

Reverend Burroughs was examined on May 9th. By the middle of May, Joseph Putnam, Daniel Andrews, John Tarbell, Sam Nurse, and Peter Cloyce, Jr. felt the failure of their conspiracy was written large. The magistrates, however, with the arrest and examination of Reverend George Burroughs became convinced their own efforts had gloriously succeeded.

Jonathon Corwin's House

Chapter Twenty-Seven — Forged Links
(13 Apr - May 7)

Ninth Device : By presenting to the soul the crosses, losses, reproaches, sorrows, and sufferings that do daily attend those that walk in the ways of holiness.
    Thomas Brooks, "Satan's Devices to Draw the Soul to Sin" in *Precious Remedies Against Satan's Devices*

The Arnolds of Boston Gaol were in much the same position as the poor centurion detailed to accompany Paul on his journey to Rome. No doubt our accused ones differed from that apostle in many ways. They had not appealed to Caesar or otherwise initiated the link with their gaolers. John and Mary Arnold, nonetheless, were joined to the "witches" willy-nilly so that their lives were dominated by them over the next ten months. The centurion was actually chained together with the apostle, at least during Paul's last months in Rome, while the Arnolds had a stout door separating them from the Salem defendants most of the time. But they lived in the same building and their waking hours were largely spent in administrating for and administering to the prisoners.

Neither the centurion nor the Arnolds could escape a deepening involvement — not only through dealing with their charges' basic needs, and in meeting their visitors, but through being forced to watch their manner of life and listening to their conversations. Both the apostle and the Salem prisoners appealed to their guardians' better natures in both deliberate and unconscious ways. The Arnolds, like the centurion, began with substantial resignation, and went no further than a degree of resentment toward their prisoners in the first months of this new duty.

Somewhat hardened, like the Dountons of Salem and the Fosses of Ipswich, all of whom spent a lot of time and energy as wardens of accused witches, the Arnolds were initially as nervous about witchcraft as the rest of us in Massachusetts. They endeavored in those first months to keep their children completely insulated from the prisoners, trying to obscure the identities of their two sorts of charges from each other. When the children asked about the shrieks and mutterings of Sarah Good during the second week of March, they told them not to concern themselves — that she was a mad woman who had been incarcerated for acts of great wickedness.

The children nevertheless learned about the prisoners from remarks made by playmates in the neighborhood, and soon came to refer to them as "witches" rather than "prisoners". Once when one of the children came down with a fever, and another time when one of them tripped and cut her head while playing tag, Mary Arnold was nearly beside herself for fear the family was being injured by diabolical means.

The number of prisoners kept increasing, and although this was desirable and even a bit of a windfall from the standpoint of remuneration, it made the administrative task an increasingly difficult one, taking more and more time and energy. This contributed to the Arnold's increased harshness and impersonal treatment of their wards during the first months.

It was without any desire to cause the prisoners suffering, but equally with no great concern to protect them from it that John Arnold, upon order of the court, hired a smith to put chains on the new prisoners a few days after they arrived at Boston. One by one, he brought the prisoners out and along the street to the smithy, where the smith measured each prisoner for ready-made wrist and ankle bands. Efficiently the smith then placed the bands in the forge, heated them red-hot, removed them to the anvil where he bent the flanges, and punched a hole in each. He then dropped the hot bands in a bucket of water and placed them, still warm, around the prisoners wrists, after which he inserted an open chain link through the hole, and hammered it shut upon either end of a length of chain. He repeated the operation on the ankles, seating the prisoners on a high box next to the anvil. Then John led each prisoner in awkward shuffling gait back to the gaol, while each wondered dazedly over this newest indignity and hardship. None of the adults lost their long-suffering composures, except John Procter, who angrily asked the gaoler what kind of madness possessed him to do this, to which John Arnold only answered,

"Go careful now." And, once he judged Procter was properly subdued, "Ask your magistrates, sir, for they command it."

Sarah Good, who was in a benevolent mood the first part of the morning, was very helpful in showing the others various stratagems she had learned by which the chains and bands could be made less uncomfortable and inconvenient.

But when both John and Mary Arnold came to take little Dorcas out, her manner changed. Sarah's eyes grew hard, her shoulders hunched and stiffened and she began to mutter, then growl, then suddenly began to shriek in rage.

"**Y**ou it is! You are the fiends! You, the witches to think of such a thing! Leave her be! She is but a child! Nay! Put the pretty bracelets on your own children then! Do not go, Dorothy-bird! "

But Mary Arnold already led Dorcas out the door, as John stood between, ready to restrain Sarah, should she offer any violence.

After they left, all of the women began to weep, and John Procter dragged his new chains up and down one side of the room, trying to stifle his deep anger and sense of unbottomed frustration.

When they brought Dorcas back, she shuffled in with her little hands hanging before her weighed down by the chains. Every eye was on her as she shuffled silently the first four steps into the room. But as the door shut behind her, she held up her arms suddenly and lifted her feet awkwardly, first one, then the other.

"**S**ee, Momma, now I'm just like you!" she said. The women remained wet-eyed and silent, but John Procter spun and sat down in a heap, where he began to choke out unpracticed sobs.

If Mary Arnold lay that night some time awake and red-eyed, so that her husband was bad-tempered with her and told her abruptly to go to sleep, none of the prisoners ever knew of it.

Within three days, they had grown accustomed to the shackles. In wonder at this, Sarah Cloyce asked Rebecca what there was a person could not grow used to? To which Rebecca answered the question certainly gave one pause.

Elizabeth Emerson, as a mere murderer and not a witch, was not in chains, and she was deeply chagrined at her privileged status, but the other prisoners came to appreciate her help at the few things which the chains made difficult, and she jumped at every opportunity to be of service.

Dorcas quickly grew used to her chains. Both the smith and the gaoler had insured they were significantly lighter, being in fact little more than bridle chains. She and the ladies concocted several games with them. Mistress Corey showed Dorcas how a tune could be played on the links if they were held suspended while another played on them. The handle of a heavy spoon worked well on Dorcas' chain, while its bowl was better for ringing those of the adults. Dorcas also found she could perform a complicated maneuver like that of the children's game called "skinning the cat" while lying on her back—using her chains instead of the usual bar.

The women cooperated in caring for Sarah Osborne. Mistress Procter took the lead, since she had the most medical experience. All three of the other ladies were amateur nurses and midwives, and Elizabeth had worked with her uncle, a physician. They kept Sarah Osborne well-covered, and fed her as much hot liquid as they could get down her throat. They coaxed her to take naps several times a day, but after another week, she needed no coaxing, and spent all of her time beneath blankets and rugs.

Her coughing was terrible to listen to. It sounded as though parts of her were breaking up and in imminent danger of tumbling out. Warm mixtures of honey, spirits and lime juice quieted it, but only temporarily, and each day less.

The visitors came faithfully—the older Procter children, the Nurses and Cloyces and twice, in the week before his arrest, Giles Corey. Peter Cloyce, Jr. and Mary Preston, in contrast to the rest enjoyed the long journeys to Boston as extended periods for courting, variously chaperoned by their families.

Francis Nurse brought Alexander Osborne and Will Good down with him on two occasions. It quite made Dorcas's day to see her father, though Will and Sarah hardly talked. Alexander Osborne was nearly beside himself with nervousness, and seemed nigh to bursting with desire to get away, but his wife found considerable comfort in his presence.

On the two occasions he came, Giles Corey was hardly more affectionate toward his wife, stalking about morosely as she talked quietly to him. His obvious anger was partly due to outrage over his wife's arrest, and partly due to being in the same room with John Procter, with whom he had often feuded. Within a week of his wife's arrival in Boston, however, he, too, was arrested, and he was never to see Martha again on this earth.

Tituba, since she was a "confessor," was kept elsewhere in Boston. The others never saw her except briefly when they were transported back to Salem for hearings and trials.

Gradually the life of the eight prisoners in Boston Gaol took on its own order. The women arranged the chores of cooking, cleaning and laundry among them. Mr. Procter led them in daily worship meetings. At first the Arnold's forbid and fought this. Mr. Procter refused to submit in the matter, however, and after John Arnold had come bursting in a number of times demanding that they stop singing or praying or listening to Mr. Procter's readings, he gave up. So it appeared to the prisoners.

In fact, John Arnold sat a number of times just outside the door with a pen and ink. There he listened carefully and filled up a sheet of paper with quotations and comments from their meetings. After two or three such efforts, he realized there was nothing but Christian piety expressed among them, and he tossed the papers in his stove. He decided whatever their crimes or purposes, they were not celebrating any black masses in his gaol.

They ate together. The women worked together on sewing and knitting. Elizabeth Emerson had come to be the laundry-woman, since both washing and hanging clothes wearing chains was difficult. Each of the prisoners did what she or he could to entertain Dorcas. A kind of equilibrium seemed to settle into their much constricted life together.

The arrest of Martha's husband brought fresh grounds for communal suffering and commiseration. She hoped Giles would soon be among them, but more in line with John's secret hopes, Giles was sent from Salem to Ipswich gaol, where he was to spend most of the rest of his life.

Mary Warren and Abigail Hobbs, "confessors" arrested and examined at the same time as Giles Corey, were kept at Salem. No new witchcraft prisoners were brought to Boston until the first week of May.

On May 2, after their examinations in Salem, four more prisoners were sent directly to Boston gaol, threatening John Arnold with an administrative crisis. He was barely able to fit Lydia Dastin, Dorcas Hoar, Susannah Martin and Sarah Morey into his establishment. At night, when their bedding and a few chairs and tables were all in place, there was barely so much as a path to the chamber pot. The older ladies, in particular, found it difficult to make the journey without stepping on the sleepers. Like prisoners everywhere, they adjusted their schedules and arrangements to suit the circumstances. By day, they folded their blankets and piled their mattresses in a corner, except for those of Sarah Osborne, who now remained abed.

John Arnold began to plan and explore alternative arrangements. He appealed to the Boston magistracy and had some of the prisoners sent to Cambridge gaol, but since he lost the income these prisoners brought him, he began to canvas the neighborhood in an effort to find subcontractors. He could still profit if he placed his safer prisoners with neighbors who had sturdy facilities. It seemed a certainty yet more prisoners would come out of the Salem investigations.

Meanwhile the prisoners rearranged their furniture and their lives to accommodate the four new women. The experience of those longer established made them wise in comforting the newcomers during their initiation. The stages of suffering were familiar to them.

First the new prisoners reeled under the shocks in rapid succession, of charge, arrest, examination, and being bound over to gaol. In conjunction with these came the physical shocks of sleeplessness, transport (through various inclemencies of that year's wet weather), and the unfamiliar discomforts of the dark and crowded place. Hard upon the heels of these came the shackles. Then to each came several days of remembering and reflecting on the bitter scenes which had led to this degradation. After the tears, reliefs, and depressions of the first week of initiation, each arrival was well-launched upon the career of prisoner. Hard wars make veterans quickly.

Each new personality made a difference, especially as the place became crowded. The Widow Dastin was a sturdy ancient of few words, who seemed "to possess her own soul." However, she was only kept a week at Boston and then sent on to Cambridge, with several newer arrivals.

Dorcas Hoar, a younger widow, was another of those who respond to hardship by becoming tempered -- harder and more brittle in her relations to the rest of mankind. During her examination she had been accused of killing her own husband, which seemed particularly malicious of the girls. Her hard words in reply had been taken as demonstrations of a hard heart. She was barely known to the other prisoners, but now Martha and Rebecca took her under their wings. Nevertheless, she remained independent and sometimes resorted to Sarah Good as a companion of similar temper, if not identical mind.

Susannah Martin and Sarah Morey forged one of those peculiar partnerships of unlikes in their first weeks in gaol. Susannah had a highly developed instinct for precipitating offense, which may partly account for the fact that she had more accusers and witnesses against her than any other. Yet she was open and free-spoken, without any apparent edge of bitterness, as though every negative that occurred to her was given immediate vent, so that while all those around her might grow bitter, she herself did not. Sarah Morey, a younger woman, found Goodwife Martin a tower of strength. While not herself overly meek, the younger found relief in the older woman's instinctual expression of opinion. It was as if she felt Goodwife Martin would inevitably say what needed to be said, so that she needed only silently agree.

Susannah Martin, for instance, railed nearly two hours with barely a pause when taken out and brought back wearing the common jewelry. When she was done commenting upon the gaoler, the blacksmith, the magistrates, and the sorry state of all the inhabitants of their majesties dominions, however, she was indeed quite finished. Sarah Morey found relief for her own tears in this diatribe, and was as cheerful as Goodwife Martin when it was over.

John Procter found the addition of the new female contingent nearly too much for him. He became much more reticent to take initiative and manifested much more discomfort over the increased problems of privacy and decency created by the crowded room full of women. (Nevertheless, somehow, either in Salem or Boston gaols, he fathered the child upon his wife which was to prove the instrument of her deliverance.)

Gaoler Arnold instituted a new policy for the visitors, allowing only four at a time, so that those who arrived early got in right away, but those arriving later might have to wait much of the day. Since there was no room in which to wait, the late comers were assigned a time for their visit, and often went away in the interim, sometimes to an inn.

But again, after two or three days, the new prisoners, too, settled into a pattern of daily life, labor and mutual ministry. Sarah Osborne's night-long coughing sounded a continual memorial that linked their shared suffering even in slumber.

George Burroughs

Chapter Twenty-Eight—The Archangel Falls
(May 5-9)

You are to ordain elders in every church: make you use of such as Christ hath endowed with the best gifts for that end; their call to office shall be mediate from you, but their authority and commission shall be immediate from Christ revealed in his word – which, if you shall slight, despise or condemn, he will soon frustrate your call by taking the most able among you to honor with an everlasting crown, whom you neglected to honor on earth double their due, or he will carry them remote from you to more infant churches. You are not to put them upon anxious cares for their daily bread, for assuredly (although it may now seem strange) you shall be fed in this wilderness whither you are to go with the flower of the wheat, and wine shall be plentiful among you (but be sure you abuse it not). These doctrines, delivered from the word of God, embrace. And let not Satan delude you by persuading their learned skill is unnecessary: soon then will the word of God be slighted as translated by such, and you shall be left bewildered with strange revelations of every fantastic brain.
   --Edward Johnson, **Wonder-Working Providence of Sion's Savior** (1654)

T hat our witch trials should reach to our furthest settlements "to eastward" may be said to highlight one more conflict among us. The original settlers of that region now called York County came not under Massachusetts Bay but under the Gorges Administration – as "The Colony of New England" in "the province of Maine" in 1639. Nantucket, too, was assigned by royal patent to Sir Fernando Gorges, and our settlers there, most of them from Salisbury or the coast "to eastward," were Quakers, escaping both Indians and the governing officers of Massachusetts Bay.

The ultimate failure of the Gorges Administration and the separate colony was due to two factors: 1/ that they never established a sufficient permanent government of respected men to hold the colony and resist the inroads of Massachusetts Bay, and 2/ the great aggressiveness of Massachusetts' officials, who repeatedly sent commissions up the coast demanding that the colonists there take oaths of allegiance to the Massachusetts government.

Massachusetts timed these take-overs to coincide with the

absence of the higher officials of the Gorges Administration – first in 1653, then again in 1668. Eventually those loyal to the Gorges gave up resisting the tide, but there persisted the feeling that Massachusetts was less interested in extending its help "down east" than extending its power of oversight and taxation.

Many of those "to eastward" were either inclined toward a dissenting religion or had little interest in religion at all. Reverend George Burroughs, formerly of the Village, had gone there because he found fruitful ministry among people more grateful and less fractious than those in Salem Village.

The events leading to the arrest of Reverend Burroughs, of Wells, Maine began when Tituba, our first named and first confessed witch, mentioned a mysterious man who was the head of all the witches. In her early examinations she described him as tall, dignified in appearance and dressed in black. Thereafter, in nearly all of the girls' descriptions of witch gatherings, this "wizard" figured largely. Therefore while the ministers and magistrates peered about them through the lenses of the afflicted girls' vision, they were particularly searching for clues to the name of this evil captain over the devil's forces. It was assumed he was a masterful man, thus John Procter and Giles Corey and lately Edward Bishop had been eagerly gathered in. But he was also a "black man" and "a man dressed in black," descriptions which were most often applied to ministers. This clue was much discussed—and to such a degree in the Parris and Sergeant Putnam households that names of possible candidates were discussed with details of their histories.

Anna Putnam is credited with the first "afflictions" attributed directly to Reverend Burroughs. These she claimed to experience the evening of April 20th. She testified later she saw an apparition of a minister and cried out, "Oh dreadful, dreadful! Here is a minister come! What are ministers witches too? Whence come you and what is you name, for I will complain of you, though you be a minister, if you be a wizard!" She said she was immediately tortured and choked by him and tempted with a book, et cetera.

She said that after she refused the book the second time he told her his name was George Burroughs. He told her he had three wives and that he had bewitched the first two to death, as well as killing Mistress Lawson (the wife of Reverend Lawson) because she was unwilling to leave the Village. She said he killed Mr. Lawson's child because Mr. Lawson went to the Eastward with Sir Edmund Andros and preached to the soldiers there. She further said Mr.

Burroughs bewitched many of the soldiers and made Abigail Hobbs a witch as well as several others. And finally she said, he told her he was even greater than a witch, for he was a conjurer.

The first public mention of these things came to us through Benjamin Hutchinson, who told how he and Abigail Williams encountered the spectre several days later on the Andover Road. This description was very specific and so perfectly parallel to Anna's, it was certainly communicated from Anna to Abigail. The wizard was no longer the tall man of earlier descriptions, but "little". He was not just a man in black but a "minister," who lived at Casco Bay, where he performed specific feats of great strength. These particulars not only narrowed the field of inquiry, but pointed to one man only, George Burroughs, former minister of the Village church, and for some ten years, minister near Casco Bay in Falmouth and Wells, Maine.

The next day after Abigail's public confirmation, Anna's father sent a letter to the magistrates. Sergeant Putnam wrote:

> After most humble and hearty thanks presented to your Honors for the great care and pains you have already taken for us, for which we are never able to make you recompense (and we believe you do not expect it of us; therefore the full reward will be given you of the Lord God of Israel, whose cause and interest you have espoused, and we trust this shall add to your crown of glory in the day of the Lord Jesus); and we, beholding continually the tremendous works of divine providence—not only every day but every hour—thought it our duty to inform your Honors of what we conceive you have not heard, which are high and dreadful: of a wheel within a wheel, at which our ears do tingle.
>
> Humbly craving continually your prayers and help in this distressed case, so praying almighty God continually to prepare you, that you may be a terror to evil-doers and a praise to them that do well, we remain yours to serve in what we are able.

Despite his avowed piety, Sergeant Putnam's use of the scripture image of "making their ears tingle," was blasphemous. God speaks of making his people's ears tingle in fear at the judgments he brings upon persistent iniquity, whereas Sergeant Putnam and his family, to the best of our knowledge, were bringing judgment upon others out of their own persistent iniquity. The sensation he calls "tingling" was manmade like false doctrine (in that other scripture) tailored to those with "itching ears".

The nine days between this revelation and the warrant for Reverend Burrough's arrest were given to great consultations among the ministers and magistrates, the gathering of evidence and cross-examinations of the afflicted to make sure of their accounts. For it was a momentous step to arrest a Harvard-trained minister, even one who was not ordained and therefore just short of the highest rank.

Once the threshold was reached, however, the ministers and magistrates were never so zealous as they became in the prosecution of this man. Cotton Mather opened his account of Mr. Burrough's trial written after our troubles with these words: "Glad should I have been, if I had never known the name of this man; or never had this occasion to mention so much as the first letters of his name."

In a letter written during that late summer trial, Mather rejoiced in the discovery of more confessed witches in Andover who had not only affirmed the guilt of the five recently hanged but were "all agreeing in Burroughs being their ringleader".

Beginning from about the first of May, not only all the confessed witches, but all the afflicted, and many new witnesses affirmed Mr. Burroughs as the central figure in their witchcraft accounts.

> . . . *He was accused by eight of the confessing witches, as being head actor at some of their hellish rendevouzes, and one who had the promise of being a king in Satan's kingdom, now going to be erected: he was accused by nine persons for extraordinary lifting, and such feats of strength, as could not be done without a diabolical assistance. And for other such things he was accused, until about thirty testimonies were brought against him; nor were these judg'd the half of what might have been considered for his conviction: however they were enough to fix the character of a witch upon him according to the rules of reasoning, by which the judicious Gaule, in that case required.* (Cotton Mather)

Mr. Mather's " Judicious Gaule" was the English Rector, John Gaule, who opposed the more zealous extremes of the "Witch-finder General," Matthew Hopkins, some fifty years earlier. He wrote *Select Cases of Conscience Touching Witches and Witchcraft*, published in 1646.

It was politic of Mr. Mather to cite Reverend Gaule, who proposed more moderate methods for prosecution, unbiblical as many of them remained. Despite this and like rhetoric, it was not sanity of prosecution, but a new intensity of madness that we continued to witness in Salem.

The complaint against Mr. Burroughs was dated April 30th and the plaintiffs were the two stalwarts Sergeant Putnam and Captain Walcott. Six afflicted persons were listed: Mary, Mercy, Abigail, Anna, Elizabeth, and Susannah Sheldon.

A special arrest warrant from the Governor and Council was conveyed to the magistrates in Portsmouth, New Hampshire. Elisha Hutchinson of that settlement commissioned Marshall John Partridge to make the arrest, which was effected on May 4th. Marshall Partridge took several men with him, not knowing what diabolical resistance he might meet. They found Reverend Burroughs at table with his family, and took him away without delay.

After riding night and day, Marshall Partridge delivered Mr. Burroughs to Salem on May 5th. There he was kept at Thomas Beadle's house next to the Dounton's, since the regular gaol was full. Eleazer Keyser, he of the distracted daughter, dropped by Beadle's for a glimpse of this great wizard. Captain Daniel King of Lynn, who commanded one of Governor Phip's ships on the ill-fated Quebec expedition, was there also. Seeing Goodman Keyser lurking about, Captain King invited him to come upstairs and talk with Reverend Burroughs, but Mr. Keyser showed great unwillingness to do this, whereupon the Captain asked him why not?

"Nay, sir, 'tis not for such as I to discourse a learned man like he.' "

"But he is a child of God like you," answered Captain King.

"I have heard the other way, sir," Keyser replied.

"But he is a child of God, a choice child of God! And God shall clear up his innocence!" said King, with some vehemence.

"I am of the fear, sir, that he be the chief of all them as is accused for witchcraft and the very ringleader of them."

"Well, man, if you are of such an opinion, why not speak with him and see if he seem such a one!"

"Nay, sir, for I believe if he is such an one, then his master will have told him what I said of him before now." Keyser had become as good a student of the science of witchery as many others among us.

Captain King, who was in Salem on business and not very

familiar with the tenor of our troubles, grew angry with Goodman Keyser and called him a superstitious fool. Keyser retired from the fray, but that afternoon he came back for a look at Burroughs, and was greatly frightened by the fact that Mr. Burroughs stared at him for a moment. Later that night Keyser's digestion or imagination produced a spectre or two in his own bedroom, which would be dutifully attributed to Burroughs at his trial.

On May 7th Mercy Lewis was afflicted at length by the spectre of Reverend Burroughs, whom she had known as an inmate of his household. She testified he tempted her to sign the book by telling her it was one she had often seen in his library, but she refused, saying she had seen many books in his library, but never that one. He went on to say he had many books she did not know about — for conjuring with, and raising the devil. He threatened she would see his two wives (that is she would join them in death) unless she signed. She still refused. She claimed that when his threats were not effective, he imitated his master in taking her up upon an exceeding high mountain and showed her all the kingdoms of the world, saying he would give them to her if she signed. She replied that they were not his to give and that she would rather be thrown down on a hundred pitchforks than to give in. Both Thomas and Edward Putnam said they witnessed her extreme afflictions at this time, and heard her attribute them to Mr. Burroughs.

Mr. Burrough's examination took place on May 9th. It was distinguished by the presence of two more magistrates, William Stoughton and Samuel Sewall, in addition to Mr. Corwin and Mr. Hathorne. William Stoughton, our new deputy governor, was to become the head of the Court of Oyer and Terminer which carried out the capital trials to come. He proved to be as intently bent on the elimination of our witches as Mr. Hathorne.

Before his public examination, the four magistrates examined Mr. Burroughs privately at some length, without the afflicted being present. They asked him about his own faith and ministry. They fastened particularly on his acknowledgment that he had not taken the Lord's Supper for several years, although he was still officially in full communion at Roxbury. Since he had been a solitary unordained minister in a remote outpost for many years, there was little remarkable in this. They also made a point of his testimony that his oldest was the only one of his children who had been baptized.

They pursued particularly the question of whether he had any unusual experiences, or been in any way peculiarly tempted.

They asked if his house in Maine was haunted. He laughed at this, and said that they had been troubled considerably by Indians (Wells had been fiercely attacked over the previous months) but not haunted in any way he could suggest. On the basis of some informant or other, they asked him if there were not toads in his house, to which he answered there had been numerous toads in the neighborhood in some years and seasons.

Attention was also focused on his relationships with his wives. Quite a bit of testimony was offered in both his examination and trial about his harshness toward them. There seemed to be some basis for this, but little of substance was brought forward. He was asked if he had made his third wife swear not to write her father (John Ruck of Salem) without his approval of each letter and its contents. He denied this. (That their relationship was not a perfect one was evident in her subsequent conduct. After his arrest she packed up her belongings, sold much of his property and moved out with her own children, leaving his by former marriages to fend for themselves.)

When the public examination was begun, he received the usual enthusiastic greeting from the afflicted girls.

Among those testifying against him during the examination was Captain John Putnam, who had heard the remarkable tale that Burroughs was able to lift the heaviest musket to a horizontal position by one finger inserted in the muzzle, admirably illustrating how a story grows with the repeated telling of it. Captain Putnam did not claim to have seen it, but had only heard Reverend Burroughs boast of it. However, as one of the patriarchs of our Village (both he and his wife signed the petition for Mother Nurse) the Captain was highly respected. His hearsay evidence was given as much weight as the evidence of another man's eyes.

The next witness, Captain Wormwood testified he had seen the feat of the gun performed, and that in fact Reverend Burroughs held it just before the lock and rested it upon his breast. The same witness denied another tale that was told many times over before and after, about Reverend Burroughs lifting a full barrel of molasses by means of two fingers placed in the bung.

However, the following witness, John Brown (related by marriage to the Corwins) testified to hearing Reverend Burroughs had indeed performed this feat with a barrel of cider.

Reverend Burroughs denied a story put about by a young woman who had lived with his family in Wells which featured a mysterious white calf haunting them there. It seems she was also responsible for the report of the plague of toads.

Captain Putnam testified concerning Mr. Burroughs and his second wife, which two had lived with the Putnams when first they came to the Village. The Captain said Reverend Burroughs had required his wife to take a vow to reveal none of his secrets. The Putnams advised the Burroughs their marriage vows covered keeping one another's lawful secrets, so that nothing further in the ways of vows was necessary.

Abigail Hobbs testified Reverend Burroughs had appeared to her and urged her to sign "the book," after which she did sign it, under his compulsion. This dove-tailed nicely with her signing the devil's book "at Eastward".

Benjamin Hutchinson testified Abigail Williams had indeed claimed to see the apparition of the "little minister" from Casco on the 21st.

Mr. Burroughs was bound over to prison, with all the others accused in the warrant with him. The power of the girls' accusations was brought to another successful proof. Thereafter no office or honor could be trusted to keep one safe from them.

But the magistrates were much relieved. They believed they had finally found the Ringleader, as Mather and Keyser called him. Now all that was left was to round up the ten or so witches left undiscovered among us — if our young despots would be satisfied with that.

Chapter Twenty-Nine — I Bear in my Body the Marks

A man knows not what afflictions shall come upon him whilst on the earth. This is true concerning particular persons: they may know in general that afflictions shall attend them in an evil sinful world, but what those afflictions in particular shall be they know not. Thus the Apostle speaks: (Acts 20. 22,23) "I go bound in spirit to Jerusalem, not knowing what things shall befall me there, save that the Holy Spirit witnesseth in every city, saying, that bonds and afflictions abide me : so that he knew in general that he should meet affliction, but not in special what the affliction would be.
-- Increase Mather, *Man Knows Not His Time*.

T he apostle Paul wrote to the Galatian church that, as a result of his afflictions, he bore in his body the marks of the Lord Jesus. The rational faculty is inclined to object to that bare statement, for all Christendom stands on the idea that the Lord's atoning sufferings were unique. But in Corinthians, the second letter, Paul recounts a summary of some of his more severe sufferings, making it easier to understand what he meant. For although Jesus never suffered for his own sins nor ever sinned against another, and although he entered into the suffering of the cross freely for the salvation of mankind, he was not at all unique in the physical particulars of his sufferings — not even in being crucified. Two others received very similar marks in their bodies on the day he died, and thousands more before and after. It is said the hills of Jerusalem were covered with Roman crosses bearing other Jews in agony during the great persecution of Vespasian, sixty or seventy years later. Those marks too were like Christ's.

Our troubles branded innumerable men, women, and children with the marks of suffering, which to the extent that they were innocent, were like the wounds of the Lamb, and to the extent that they were his faithful people, were indeed the marks of Christ.

Early on, in the middle of March, when Reverend Deodat Lawson made some first records of our troubles, he was greeted by one of the girls who demonstrated to him marks on her own body of purported supernatural affliction:

. . . presently after I came into my lodging, Captain Walcott's daughter, Mary, came to Lieutenant Ingersoll's and spake to me; but suddenly after as she stood by the door, was bitten, so that she cried out of her wrist, and looking on it with a candle, we saw apparently the marks of teeth both upper and lower set, on each side of her wrist.

In that same report, Reverend Lawson wrote of Martha Corey's examination:

It was observed several times that if she did but bite her under lip in time of examination the persons afflicted were bitten in their armes and wrists and produced the marks before the magistrates, ministers and others.

Three days later Rebecca Nurse was examined and again:

... Some of the other [afflicted] said that they had seen her, but knew not that ever she had hurt them; amongst which was Mary Walcott, who was presently, after she had so declared, bitten, and cried out of her in the meeting-house; producing the marks of teeth on her wrist.

Dorcas Good was also examined:

being between 4 and 5 years of age, and as to matter of fact, they did unanimously affirm, that when this child did but cast its eye upon the afflicted persons, they were tormented, and they held her head, and yet so many as her eye could fix upon were afflicted. Which they did several times make careful observation of: the afflicted complained they had often been bitten by this child, and produced the marks of a small set of teeth, accordingly, [she] was committed to Salem prison, ...

These early marks of affliction were taken particularly seriously by the magistrates, demonstrating to their eyes visible proof of bewitchment and affliction. Reverend Lawson himself, expressed no doubt about this proof.

On the 25th of March, Edward Putnam deposed that, at about 2 o'clock that afternoon, he had witnessed Anna Putnam's afflictions which she attributed to Rebecca Nurse. Deacon Putnam described the marks:

> . . .she was struck with her chain, the mark being in a kind of
> a round ring and 3 strokes across the ring. She had 6 blows
> with a chain in the space of half an hour and she had one
> remarkable one with six strokes across her arm. I saw the
> mark both of bite and chain.

These particular visible "proofs" of biting and chains was
only found in that first month of the examinations, and chiefly
during that one week in March. Some minister or magistrate seems
to have questioned the strange resemblance of the "chain" marks to
teeth, and the difficulty of distinguishing the marks of one set of
teeth from another, and suddenly they became less common.
Throughout the trials, however, "marks" of supernatural affliction
continued to be demonstrated. Sarah Nurse, Rebecca's daughter-in-
law, testified in June that she watched Goody Vibber surreptitiously
place pins between her fingers and inflicted wounds upon herself
during Rebecca's trial.

But the chains that the prisoner's wore made real marks on
their own wrists. No one disputed the sources or validity of those.
So deep went the marks of the freezing chains about her wrists, that
Sarah Osborne was to die in Boston gaol two and a half months after
she was sent there. Death, the ultimate bodily mark of affliction, was
visited upon others in prison as well: Sarah Good's second child,
born in prison, was to die during Sarah's transport at the beginning
of June; Doctor Roger Toothaker, in Boston gaol on the 16th of June;
Rebecca Chamberlain of Billerica, in Cambridge gaol on the 26th of
September; Ann Foster, the 3rd of December; and ancient Lydia
Dastin, the 10th of March in Cambridge, just two weeks before the last
of the prisoners were released to an earthly parole. (Of the nineteen
prisoners killed by order of the court we will speak in due course.)

Many marks of affliction, not of teeth or chains or visibly
manifested in the cold flesh of death, remained throughout various
sufferers' lives. Several young men were treated particularly cruelly.
John Procter described these tortures in a letter to five Boston
ministers toward the end of July.

> . . . Two of the 5 (Carrier's sons) are young men, who would
> not confess any thing till they tied them neck and heels till the
> blood was ready to come out of their noses, and 'tis credibly

believed and reported this was the occasion of making them confess that [which] they never did ... My son, William Procter, when he was examined, because he would not confess that he was guilty when he was innocent, they tied him neck and heels till the blood gushed out at his nose, and would have kept him so 24 hours, if one more merciful than the rest had not taken pity on him and caused him to be unbound.

The most notorious torture of the prisoners was that used upon Giles Corey, the obstinate husband of Martha Corey, of which we shall also say more. Suffice it here to say Goodman Corey was tortured to death.

Less extreme tortures were used extensively, although perhaps our ministers and magistrates did not regard them as such. Many of the accused were treated to rapid motions and blows about the face, eyes and ears during examinations, particularly in prison, as we have described in the case of Mary Warren. This was thought to be in accordance with the Cartesian philosophy that the malignant spirits operated through fine particles of matter upon the vision, hearing, and minds of witches and afflicted. The theory was that the malignant operations of these streams of particles were disrupted by such physical means. These methods were used particularly upon the "confessors" like Mary Warren at those times when they were either reluctant or appeared to be "recanting" their confessions. In October, Thomas Brattle of Boston, a much respected man, was to write a letter to a gentleman in England concerning the evils of the trials. He mentions the "rude and barbarous methods that were afterwards used at Salem" and in a side note writes:

> You may possibly think that my terms are too severe; but should I tell you what kind of blade was employed in bringing these women to their confession, what methods from damnation taken; with what violence urged; how unseasonably they were kept up; what buzzings and chuckings of the hand were used, and the like, I am sure that you would call them (as I do) rude and barbarous methods.

Although he uses the term "blade" as a metaphor, the rest is but understatement.

(The use of rapid motions and slaps of the hand about the

face and head to drive off demons seems to be very ancient, perhaps of Mannichean origin, for Augustine in his *Confessions* makes reference to something very like it practiced in his time.)

The marks of affliction upon the minds and memories of the "confessors," particularly those whose confessions led to the deaths of their own loved ones, can scarce be calculated. Tituba, Mary Warren, Deliverance and Abigail Hobbs, Margaret Jacobs, and Sarah Churchill were made consenting participants in deathly deceit. This was through their own weakness and sin, certainly, but no less culpably through the proud and fleshly force of their spiritual overseers. Later Dorcas Hoar and the many Andover "confessors" submitted to what was by then common knowledge — that to confess was to survive. It became the examiners' habit to propose this very equation — thus these confessors, intent on the preservation of their innocent lives, received fewer external marks of agony upon their bodies. Even their loved ones in many cases pleaded with them that they confess and so preserve their lives.

However in the course of their "confessions," these not only falsely accused themselves and gave false testimony of their own deeds, but implicated or reinforced charges against friends, loved ones or even strangers. The serious consequences of this could not help but cause affliction of soul and leave lasting marks upon them.

William Good under the kind oversight of Benjamin Putnam applied for compensation after our troubles, as we have said. The document stated that little Dorcas, whom Reverend Lawson described as looking "hail and as well as other children" at the time of her arrest, had afterward such marks upon her as to scar her for the rest of her life:

> . . . a child of 4 or 5 years old was in prison 7 or 8 months and being chained in the dungeon was so hardly used and terrified that she hath ever since been very chargeable [burdensome] having little or no reason to govern herself. (Brattle)

No one now, that is none but the staunchest and most self-serving defenders of those atrocities, believes Mary Walcott bore any marks of affliction but those she deliberately placed on her own body. But the genuine and enduring marks of affliction which the accused wore, were real, horrible, and none of their doing. The great wonder is not that Dorcas Good grew up with scars on mind and heart, or that her mother was beside herself with rage and fear on the scaffold, but rather that any among the accused or their families lived or died without severe scars.

The judges, accusers and witnesses disfigured their own souls to such an extent that in some cases, not even years or generations would seem sufficient to eliminate the scars.

One is driven to ask what could possibly prevent, relieve or remove such marks? Yet one further wonders how it is that in some cases they seemed to heal within a few short years? If the horrors of our troubles are nigh impossible to imagine, how imponderable the means whereby so many were able to bear up and continue to show charity toward their persecutors. Truly those bore in their bodies the marks of the Lord Jesus Christ. For his most enduring marks remain in his hands, feet and side -- and in those other innocent sufferers who repeat, "Father, forgive them for they know not what they do. "

Chapter Thirty — Conspiracy Succeeds
(May 10 - 14)

[The Assistants] delivered their several reasons, which all sorted to this conclusion, that strict discipline, both in criminal offenses, and in martial affairs, was more needful in plantations than in a settled state, as tending to the honor and safety of the Gospel. Whereupon Mr. Winthrop acknowledged that he was convinced, that he had failed in over much lenity and remissness, and would endeavor (by God's assistance) to take a more strict course hereafter . . .
      -- John Winthrop, *Journal,* January 18,1636.

On May 10, warrants were issued for Margaret Jacobs, Daniel Andrew's niece, and for Goodman George Jacobs, Sr., her grandfather. Constable Joseph Neale zealously executed the warrants, and the magistrates as zealously began their examination late the same afternoon. These charges originated with Abigail Williams, youngest of the girls still active, and unwearyingly zealous. She originally accused George Jacobs, Sr., claiming he had caused many other members of his family and household to sign "the book". From among these, Margaret Jacobs and Sarah Churchill, his maid, gave in early to the examiners and became themselves "confessors".

Sarah Churchill had been interviewed informally the previous afternoon by Reverend Noyes and Ezekiel Cheever. Informal as it was, Reverend Noyes was dogged, increasingly assailing Sarah with his words and fastening on her small confessions on the basis of which he demanded larger ones. Sarah was not yet bound over, and she was immediately beside herself with remorse over what she had been made to say. She went and poured out her heart to Sarah Ingersoll, the Deacon's daughter, who was skeptical about Sarah Churchill's sincerity at first. The older woman testified to this when the worst of our troubles was over.

Sarah Churchill was crying and wringing her hands when she found Sarah Ingersoll taking in washing. At first the girl received short shrift.

"What ails you!"

"Oh, Goody Ingersoll, I have undone myself!"

"In what?"

"I belied myself and others in saying I set my hand to the

devil's book, when I never did at all."

"I believe you have set your hand to the book."

"No, no, no. I never! I never did!"

"Well, what made you say you did!"

"Oh, Goody Ingersoll! They said I would be put in the dungeon with that terrible wizard Burroughs and the other witches, Good and Corey. They said I must confess and then it would be better for me, and the devil would have no more claim upon me. When I said I knew nothing or did nothing, they became angry, and Mr. Noyes told me hell was a place of terrible torment and I was going there.

"Oh, I have undone myself, for now I have lied indeed, and against others, and I have writ it down and signed it sure enough."

"Why did you write it if it was a lie?"

"Because I stood out against it so long, that I dare not any longer."

"You should go to the ministers and confess the truth of it."

"No, no. It was Mr. Noyes was the worst of all. When I told him but once that I set my hand to the book he fully believed me, but if I told him the truth and said I set not my hand to the book a hundred times, he would never believe that."

On the 10th, Sarah Churchill and Margaret Jacobs were examined formally. Mr. Hathorne allowed the accusers, particularly Abigail Williams in this case, to question the accused directly. The afflicted quieted themselves as soon as weak-willed Sarah Churchill gave in and spoke of signing the book. After some coaching, she said George, Sr., made Margaret Jacobs and George, Jr., sign it, too.

The magistrates were continuing a new approach to examination in which the girls provided not only a background chorus of fits and accusations, but became themselves the examiners.

Mr. Hathorne flourished his hand toward the afflicted and spoke to Goodman Jacobs, "Here are them that accuse you of acts of witchcraft."

"Well, let us hear who are they, and what are they," said the defendant, with a short bark of laughter.

"Jacobs laughed!" said Abigail accusingly.

"Because I'm falsely accused," he answered. He then turned his head and appealed to the five men sitting at the bench. "Your worships, all of you, do you think this is true?"

"Nay, what do you think?" countered Mr. Hathorne.

"I never did," said Goodman Jacobs.

"Who did it?"

"Don't ask me."

"Why should we not ask you? Sarah Churchill accuseth you. There she is."

"I am as innocent as a child born tonight. I have lived thirty-three years here in Salem."

"What then?" asked Mr. Hathorne.

"If you can prove that I am guilty, I will lie under it, Sarah."

To Sarah's credit, she was in great distress at first, and seemed ready to cry, but she soon got over it. "Last night I was afflicted at Deacon Ingersoll's," she began.

"It was a man with two staves!" Mary Walcott encouraged her. (George Jacobs, Sr. was partially crippled and traveled by means of two walking sticks.)

"It was my master!" said Sarah, in a wail.

"Pray do not accuse me. I am as clear as your worships. You must do right judgments."

"What book did he bring you, Sarah?"

"The same that the other woman brought."

"The devil can go in any shape," answered Goodman Jacobs. (These things were being talked of all around the community, and Susannah Martin's observation about Samuel's ghost was soon well-known. Nonetheless it was in flat contradiction of the doctrine current with the magistrates and ministers.)

"Did not he appear on the other side of the river and hurt you? Did not you see him?" Mr. Hathorne asked Sarah.

"Yes he did!" she replied.

"Look there, she accuseth you to your face!" Mr. Hathorne challenged the defendant. "She chargeth you that you hurt her twice. Is it not true?"

"What would you have me say? I never wronged no man in word nor deed."

"Here are three evidences!" replied Mr. Hathorne

"You tax me for a wizard. You may as well tax me for a buzzard. I have done no harm."

"Is it no harm to afflict these?"

"I never did it."

"But how comes it to be in your appearance?"

"The devil can take on any's likeness."

"Not without their consent."

"Please your worship, it is untrue. I never showed the book.

I am as silly about these things as the child born last night."

(This saying "I am as innocent . . . ," or "I am as silly. . . ," or "I am as ignorant . . . as a child unborn" has been so common among us, that beginning with the earliest, a great many of the accused used it. The ever vigilant magi began to hear it, therefore, as one more evidence of guilt! One section of Wigglesworth's popular poem, *Day of Doom*, made a point of the wickedness of the newborn and even the unborn child.)

"That is your saying. Yet you argue that you have lived so long, but what then! Cain might live long before he killed Abel, and you might live long before the devil had so prevailed on you."

"Christ has suffered three times for me."

"What three times?"

"He suffered the cross and gall and . . ."

Sarah Churchill interrupted him, perhaps hoping he would save himself as she had, "You had as good confess if you are guilty!"

"Have you heard that I have any witchcraft?"

She paused for a moment, and then said, haltingly, "I know you lived a wicked life."

"Let her make it out."

"Doth he ever pray in his family?" asked Mr. Hathorne.

"Not unless by himself," Sarah answered.

"Why do you not pray in your family?"

"I cannot read," said Goodman Jacobs.

"Well but you may pray for all that. Can you say the Lord's prayer?"

"Yes."

"Let us hear you."

He made a false start, then went through it, but as we saw with Mistress Procter, the smallest mistakes were grounds for dark suspicion in the minds of the ministers and magistrates.

"Sarah Churchill, when you wrote in the book, you was showed your master's name, you said."

"Yes sir."

"If she says so, yet you do not know it, what will you say?" responded Goodman Jacobs.

"But she saw you or your likeness tempt her to write!" answered Mr. Hathorne.

"One in my likeness? The devil may present my likeness."

"Were not you frighted, Sarah Churchill, when the representation of your master came to you?"

"Yes."

"Well burn me or hang me, I will stand in the truth of Christ. I know nothing of it."

"Do you know nothing of getting your son George and his daughter Margaret to sign?"

"Nothing at all."

The magistrates brought the examination to a close since it was late in the afternoon, but determined to recommence the next morning. Goodman Jacobs was locked up at the Watch House overnight.

It was intimated to the magistrates the next morning that the chief witness had expressed doubts, so that Sarah Churchill was not in the Meeting House during the second examination of George Jacobs, Sr. Nevertheless, in his August trial, she was induced to swear out testimony against him, albeit in much reduced form.

When Marshall Herrick brought him in the next morning, the girls were in fine fettle and screeched and tumbled about like chickens with a fox among them. Mr. Hathorne began the ritual again.

"Is this the man that hurts you?"

"This is the man!" cried Abigail, and fell on the floor writhing.

"This is the man!" cried Anna, "He hurts me and brings the book to me and would have me write in it. He says if I do I shall be as well as his granddaughter."

"Mercy Lewis, is this the man?"

Mercy was immediately taken with fits, but at last said, "This is the man. He almost kills me!"

Elizabeth Hubbard said, "This man never hurt me until today, when he was on the table." (That some of the girls were occasionally reluctant to fabricate tales of afflictions made us wonder whether they had less imagination or more conscience than their companions.)

"Mary Walcott, is this the man?"

Mary, too, had immediate fits, but managed to say, "This is the man. He used to come with two staves and beat me with one of them."

Mr. Hathorne having gathered this insurmountable weight of testimony turned to Goodman Jacobs and asked "What do you say? Are you not a witch?"

"No, I know it not. Though I were to die presently."

Mercy Lewis then acted as if she wanted to come near him, but could not and fell into fits instead.

A written account of some evidence Mercy had against him was read.

"What do you say to this?" asked Mr. Hathorne.

"Why, it is false. I know not of it, anymore than the child that was born tonight."

"Yes," said Anna, "You told me so—that you had been so this forty years."

Anna and Abigail both cried out that their hands had been stuck with pins, "Oh it is he that pricks us!" they said.

A written account of Abigail's evidence was read.

"Are you not the man that made disturbance at a Lecture in Salem?"

"No great disturbance. Do you think I use witchcrafts?"

"Yes, indeed."

"No, I use none of them."

But Goodman Jacobs, Sr., was bound over for prison, where he was to remain until the middle of August.

Margaret Jacobs, his granddaughter, was examined next. She had given in to the threats and persuasions, after being accused by her companion, Sarah Churchill. Margaret "confessed," testifying that both her grandfather and George Burroughs were witches. She was later to write:

> They told me, if I would not confess, I should be put down
> into the dungeon and would be hanged, but if I would
> confess I should have my life; the which did so affright me,
> with my own vile wicked heart, to save my life; made me
> make the like confession I did, which confession, may it
> please the honoured court, is altogether false and untrue. The
> very first night after I had made confession, I was in such
> horror of conscience that I could not sleep for fear the devil
> should carry me away for telling such horrid lies . . .

Yet her recantation was not to be written for several more months. The threats by which confessions were forced were to become all the more persuasive a month later when the alternative began to be illustrated.

The day when the first two members of the Jacobs family were arrested (10 May,) Sarah Osborne died in Boston prison. That same day James Kettle, the twenty-seven year old potter who lived near the mouth of Frost Fish Creek witnessed Elizabeth Hubbard in several fits at his neighbor's, Doctor Griggs'. During these, she said, Kettle's two dead children came to her and cried out for vengeance against Sarah Bishop, Edward Jr.'s wife. She said Sarah Bishop told her Kettle was going to burn a kiln of pots and that she would break them if she could. Kettle indeed planned to fire a batch of pots, but that prediction needed no witchcraft, nor did the bursting of a few during firing.

On Thursday (12 May) Mary Warren was examined again. She was by then given over wholly to the role imposed upon her. Where before she resisted and labored to tell the truth, now she told the same stories as the other afflicted and confessors. However, even among these tall tales, there were places where reality was part of the fabric. Mary said her master (Mr. Procter) told her he wished she were more afflicted because she brought out innocent persons. However, she then described a "poppet" her mistress used to afflict others – and her own participation in pushing pins into it. She also confirmed the guilt of Goodwives Parker and Pudeator, and Reverend Burroughs. She spoke of further appearances of Mother Nurse, Sarah Cloyce, the "Good's Child" and Goody Oliver (Bishop). By this time, between Mary's affliction, which was real, the threats of the other girls, and her constant harrying at the hands of the ministers, her conscience had been trodden down by main force.

Ann Pudeator and Alice Parker, both of Salem Town were first named by the newest "confessor," Sarah Churchill. Whether she originated the accusations we don't know, but other girls joined in at once. Mary Warren was best acquainted with Goody Parker. The two women were examined on the 12th. Nothing but the girls' standard accusations was brought against Ann Pudeator. She did not have a proper examination for two months, by which time various witnesses had been gathered to make a more substantial case against her.

Alice Parker, wife of the fisherman, John Parker, already had a reputation for hard words and dark predictions of disaster. Mary Warren was made her principle accuser, but many others in Salem already believed her a witch. Next to Sarah Good, she was one of the more sullen defendants to be examined.

She was asked if she had not been responsible for a number of drownings and shipwrecks – the kind of superstitions that flourish among seamen. The officers who arrested her testified they had mentioned there might be two score of witches among us and she replied there might be three score of witches. Thus, on the basis of a railing reply, the number of candidates was once more raised.

Goodwife Parker was vehement in all her answers. At one point she said, "I wish God would open the earth and swallow me up presently, if one word of this is true, so that he might make me an example to others."

It seems that she was neighbor to Mary Warren's parents when Mary was a child. There had been some lingering conflicts, and Mary blamed the deaths in her family on Goodwife Parker's malevolence.

Mr. Noyes had been involved with witchcraft charges against her before. During the examination he spoke to Goodwife Parker. "Do you remember in your time of sickness this winter how I spoke with you of charges of these same sort, how some accused you of witchcrafts and I asked you then if you were guilty of such?"

She replied "If I was as free from other sins as from witchcrafts, I would not need to ask the Lord mercy".

Mary Warren had meanwhile gone into another rigid fit, her arms stiff at her sides and her tongue clamped between her teeth, so that it hung out until it turned quite dark.

"Why will you not have compassion on these? Do you not see how her tongue turns black!" Mr. Hathorne demanded.

"Her tongue will be blacker before she dies," replied Goodwife Parker.

"Why do you thus afflict and torment her!"

"If I do, the Lord forgive me," she answered.

Both Goodwives Parker and Pudeator were bound over to Salem prison.

On Friday, the 13th, the following prisoners were sent to Boston from Salem gaol: George Jacobs, Sr., William Hobbs, Edward Bishop (step-son of Bridget), Sarah Bishop his wife (the daughter of John Wilde), Bridget Bishop (formerly Oliver), Sarah Wilde, Mary Black, Mary English, Alice Parker, and Ann Pudeater. Giles Corey, still maintaining his silence before the magistrates, was kept at Ipswich.

A great caravan of families with carts and horses went down to Boston afterward to take these prisoners furniture and supplies. John and Ephraim Wilde went humbly among them, although Ephraim had arrested several of those in gaol. They two were as faithful as any to their loved ones.

Those remaining in Salem Gaol included: Mary Easty, Deliverance Hobbs, Abigail Hobbs, Mary Warren, Sarah Churchill, and Margaret Jacobs.

Also on May 13th, Sarah Procter (daughter of John Procter) and Abigail Soames, were added to the number. Mary Warren was the principle afflicted again, with Margaret Jacobs the second in that office. Sarah Procter was of course suspected on the basis of kinship. Before our troubles were over, nearly half the accused were derived from the families of those earlier arrested.

Abigail Soames, an invalid, lived with Goodwife Gaskins of Salem. (Her father was one of those killed in the Narragansett Campaign of 1676.) Various afflictions were attributed to a crochet needle which was found in Abigail's apron. According to the astute observations of Reverend Noyes, after the needle was removed, Mary was no longer afflicted as she had been. However, Abigail's laughter and even her glance were found to be malignant. After a point was made of this, she was commanded to look at Mary, and refused, but closed her eyes instead. Mary was then brought to her and when she touched her she was "cured," but when Abigail opened her eyes at the touch and looked upon her, Mary was again afflicted. At one point Abigail Soames was asked who hurt Mary.

"It is the Enemy who hurts her," she said, "I have been myself distracted many a time and my senses have gone from me, and I thought I saw many a body hurt me. I might have accused many as well as she doth."

"Whom did you see?" asked Mr. Hathorne.

"I really thought I had seen many persons at my mother's camp at Gloucester, and they greatly afflicted me as I thought. But it was all distraction."

The court experimented with the "healing" by the touch of the witch several times during Abigail's Soames examination – proving to their satisfaction that she was a source of the malignant afflictions.

Both young women, Sarah Procter and Abigail Soames, were bound over to Salem Gaol.

The scope of the accusations, arrests, examinations, confessions, incarcerations, and transportations with the great crowd of witnesses that was gathered in—a new company for every new accused witch—accumulated to a scale that was overwhelming and beyond comprehension. Not even the magistrates could keep track or think straight about what was to be done. Those opposing the witch business felt like pebbles trying to dam a river or grass stems holding back the wind. Many whose loved ones were in prison felt a strange relief that their examinations were behind rather than ahead of them—but they also felt ashamed and repentant at such thoughts. They were strange and perverse times, and almost any joy or delight felt illicit, out of place, foreign, and doomed.

But on May 14, just when the small band of conspirators were convinced their various efforts had been entirely for nothing, they were given the encouragement of their enemies. A warrant was issued for Daniel Andrews.

One who would defend a victim from an assailant enters into a morally complex situation. To do nothing or to do too much, to do what one ought to do, but in the wrong way, to do it with the wrong spirit—any and all of these can be morally reprehensible and counter to justice. Presumably love of God and love of one's neighbor are the original motive for any such act. But it is very easy for hatred of one's enemy to take over from these. When Christ enjoins love of enemy, he is not arguing against love of neighbor—thus most Christians (excepting our stalwart Quakers) have approved of war carried on according to strict moral parameters. To restore justice, one may sometimes use force against injustice, as long as one does not depart from justice in doing so. The Bible defines justice and lays out the narrow path which must be followed.

But on a more basic level, one who would defend a victim, must identify with the victim—so that the assailant realizes he cannot further harm the victim without reckoning with the defender. This in an allegory, is one way we follow Christ. He so identified with us to the degree that God the Father poured out his (righteous) wrath, which had been stored up for us, upon God the Son, who had voluntarily interceded between us.

Thus there was a profound sense in which the conspirators felt a kind of elation, a sense that they had won a battle when Daniel was accused along with the other "witches." They felt this even as they also felt more commonplace regrets and fears.

Susannah Sheldon, recent addition to the growing chorus of "afflicted," was among Daniel's more vocal accusers. A former, and rather dull, student of his, she was able to carry out the sort of revenge against her teacher of which many another scholar has dreamed. In her early depositions she still called him "Mr. Andrews," respectfully accusing him as a witch.

Chapter Thirty-One -- Into Hiding
(May 14 - 16)

*And whom the Lord will honor by suffering for His cause, by
imprisonment, etc., He gives them spirits suitable thereto; whom the Lord
will reserve for other service or employ in other places, he inclines their
hearts rather to fly, giving them an heart suitable to such a condition. It is
a case of conscience frequently put and oft resolved by holy Bradford, Peter
Martyr, Philpot, and others, in Queen Mary's bloody days, viz. Whether it
was lawful to flee out of the land: to which their answer was that if God
gave a spirit of courage and willingness to glorify Him by sufferings, they
should stay; but if they found not such a spirit they might lawfully fly: yea,
they advised them thereunto. Those servants of Christ, though full of the
spirit of glory and of Christ to outface the greatest persecutors in profession
of the truth unto death, yet did not complain of the cowardice of such as fled
because they deserted them and the cause, but rather advised diverse so to
do, and rejoiced when God gave liberty to their brethren to escape with their
lives to the places of liberty, to serve the Lord according to His word.*
    -- Thomas Shepherd, ***A Defense of the Answer made unto the
Nine Questions or Positions sent from New-England against the
reply thereto by Mr. John Ball*** , 1648.

On May 14th, Sir William Phips, the new governor of our
re-chartered colony arrived in Boston from England, and with him
Reverend Increase Mather. They brought with them not only the
new charter, but its list of new officers, largely put forward by Mr.
Mather, himself. The new charter ended the 1684 prohibition on self-
government which had come to us with Governor Andros' absolute
commission. At the time of the Glorious Revolution of William and
Mary most of us hoped to revert to the ancient charter, but many of
those in office and places of influence opposed this. We had formed
"committees of safety" which operated meanwhile coordinating the
general defense and upper courts, while for the most part the local
courts and militia ran themselves.

    A few days later Governor Phips ordered the removal of the
chains from the witch-trial prisoners. This order encouraged their
relatives to hope that the new governor would pursue better justice.
But Governor Phips became immediately occupied with the

depredations of the French and Indians, particularly in Maine, and he delegated oversight of the witch trials to William Stoughton, his new lieutenant governor. The governor paid little attention to the trials during the first five months of his administration.

On the day Governor Phips arrived in Boston, Deacon Ingersoll and Sergeant Putnam complained against Daniel Andrews at Salem Village. Our chief conspirator, although highly accomplished and reputed, was described as a "bricklayer" in the complaint. Others charged included his brother-in-law, George Jacobs, Jr. and Daniel's sister, Rebecca (Andrews) Jacobs, as well as Sarah Buckley (wife of William, the cobbler), and Mary Witheridge (Sarah Buckley's daughter). Four more from Lynn were complained of as well: Thomas Farrar, Sr., Elizabeth Hart (wife of Isaac Hart), Elizabeth Colson, and Bethia Carter, Jr. (daughter of Bethia Carter already arrested). The three Village women were arrested, but the two local men, Daniel and George, Jr., could not be found.

After Sarah Churchill and Margaret Jacobs had "confessed" and added to the testimony against George Jacobs, Sr. and Reverend Burroughs, these two young women went on to implicate other Jacob family members and acquaintances. Daniel Andrew was both the brother-in-law of George's son and, equally suspicious, a known opponent of the witch-finders.

Perhaps it was inherited weakness of mind like that of Mary Warren that made Margaret Jacobs so susceptible to the demands and harangues of the magistrates and ministers. She had submitted to affirming all sorts of falsehood. As we have mentioned, a similar weakness of mind had long plagued her mother, Rebecca, who as we have mentioned, had experienced fits of melancholy for ten years.

Daniel and George evaded arrest, but they were not the first, as we have seen. Earlier on, Philip English and two accused women fled before they could be arrested.

Just three days previous a warrant was issued for the former constable's assistant, John Willard, he who had commented the whole village ought to be hanged. That hard-sounding comment apparently came out of a soft-heart, for he was said to have broken down in tears during one arrest and finally resigned his office, refusing to bring in any more suspects. The warrant for former constable Willard was issued on complaint of Thomas Fuller, brother of Joseph Fuller who had been murdered by persons unknown. Willard could not be found. He had made his way to relatives on the Nashawag River, where Constable John Putnam, Jr., apparently acting on information received, found him working in a field with a hoe.

Willard was brought back the 17th of May, as a second warrant was issued for George Jacobs, Jr. and Daniel. This was a general warrant "To the Marshall General or Lawful Deputy of Constables in Boston or Elsewhere," reading:

> You are in their Majesties names hereby required to apprehend forthwith; or as soon as may be, Daniel Andrew and George Jacobs both of Salem Village, who stand charged with high suspicion of sundry acts of witchcraft by them done or committed on the bodies of Mary Walcott, Abigail Williams, Mercy Lewis and others of Salem Village lately: where by great hurt and damage hath been done them contrary to the laws of their Majesties, who being found you are to convey unto Salem and deliver them unto authority in order to their examination relating to the premises and hereof are not to faile.
> Dated, Salem, May 17th, 1692
> John Hathorne, by order of the Governor.
> Jonathon Corwin, by order of the Governor.

Daniel's wife was Sarah, the daughter of John Porter, brother of Israel. Sarah's mother was Mary Endicott. Thus two of the oldest and strongest families in the Village were connected closely to him. But Israel Porter was married to Judge Hathorne's sister, too, and there were many other marriages among Herrick, Corwins, Ingersolls, Hutchinsons, and Putnams, so that what went forward was not a sharpening but a confusion of the lines of battle. Loyalties were mixed as further accusations were made, resulting in increased tensions within families and communities. The forces of witch-finding and family bonds were contrary, like those of water freezing inside a jar of the sort Goodman Kettle burns in his kiln. If such a vessel is filled and left out in the winter, there comes a point where the freezing liquid pushes so hard against the baked clay that it must break. The tensions in the Village among and between families and family members were as certain to result in destruction. Both the stronger and the weaker vessels among us were already much cracked.

That day (the 17th) Marshall George Herrick had brought five more suspects to be kept in the Watch House in the Village, when Constable John Putnam arrived with John Willard. It chanced some other traveler brought news of his imminent arrival and many of the afflicted were gathered at Ingersoll's where they broke into extensive fits as Willard was brought down the road. Seeing the terrible effect he had on the poor girls, Marshall Herrick not only locked him in the Watch House, but pinioned his arms and legs, so he might not work any more of his supposed witchery.

Meanwhile less than a mile away, Daniel and George Jacobs, Jr., sat snuggly before a fire awaiting the first of the conspirators' rendezvous since they had been declared outlaws.

Among the craggy rocks at the back or north side of Thorndike Hill, sometimes called Whipple Hill (after the first land-holder), Joseph Putnam had found a cave when he was eleven years old. Out on a solitary expedition, he had followed a falcon's flight, hoping to find the nest. He had failed at this, and frightened himself climbing steep cliffs. Half way up he entered an unexpected crevice in the rock. There boulders and smaller stones had filled up a great crack until it accumulated a sloping tongue of soil, which was covered by grass. The little lawn extended back perhaps twenty feet, curving to the right, and then ended abruptly in several cracks, mostly thin ones that ran up the vertical rock, which rose on all sides about forty feet to the top. But at the very back of this grassy strip, and on the right (or west) wall was a triangular opening where two large cracks converged. Peering in Joseph had discovered a roomy cave. It was about the size of a wigwam.

Joseph made it his hideaway. He repaired there whenever he could, bringing homely furnishings, and building a small fire ring near the door. The cave tended to fill with smoke above the level of the door, but if he was careful that his fuel was well-seasoned and the fire kept small, he could keep his cave warm into the late fall without asphyxiating himself. After exploring all the surrounding terrain, he found the cave was well below the peak of the hill, and completely inaccessible from the town-ward or southerly direction. Each year he furnished it a little better. One summer he took a saw to the hilltop and cut sections from some fallen timber, which he dropped down into the crevice from the cliff top. These he used for chairs and table.

When Joseph heard rumors of Daniel's warrant on the 13th, he had traveled up Topsfield Road and put a plan before Daniel. He offered the cave to him and George. He promised the other conspirators would supply them if they decided to use it. He argued that distance was not necessarily of more use in flight -- since every mile they traveled would risk them to exposure or discovery by more people. He argued that although no one had ever found the cave but himself, it was close enough for easy communication and supply.

Daniel was greatly torn. He felt to leave his own wife or for George to leave Rebecca would be irresponsible abandonment. Joseph did not know if the women were named in the warrants. He admitted the flight of the two men could lead to the arrest of their wives. However, Daniel's wife was a Porter and probably as safe as any in the community, while Rebecca's chances could hardly be made worse by her husband fleeing, since both her daughter and her husband's father were already in prison. Both agreed it would be impossible to sustain the women in hiding with them, particularly because of Rebecca's infirmities of mind. Neither could the children be abandoned or taken along. Joseph promised he and Elizabeth would take Daniel's six children, should Sarah be arrested, and that likewise, they would make sure the Jacobs children were cared for in the case of Rebecca's arrest.

Joseph pledged support of them whatever they decided and told them the conspirators would come to the cave in three days. If they had chosen some other plan, their absence would tell the story. The men prayed fervently together. After repeating his directions to the cave, Joseph departed, leaving further deliberations to Daniel and George. His parting words were a hearty encouragement of their resolve. "However you choose to do it, the time has come for flight."

The morning of the 16th, Constable John Parker of Reading went to arrest Elizabeth Colson of that town, for whom a warrant had been issued two days before. He found her gone. The constable obtained information leading him to believe she was in Boston seeking passage out of the country.

That same afternoon, Joseph and John met along the Rowley Road near the fork toward Osborne's. They walked another quarter mile along that branch, to a place where three old pines crowded next the road. After looking backward and forward, Joseph led suddenly off to the southeast. John followed him into the woods, and they made their way by game paths toward Thorndike Hill.

"If they are here, we will bring a cart down from my place with supplies. We can hide them near the road, then come back to pack them in. We cannot afford to carry anything openly on the roads, for the constables will have their eyes skinned for those who have fled or any sign of collaborators. But I don't know that we shall find them here. Daniel was not much inclined toward the cave when we talked."

"But we know he and George have at least fled," John pointed out, "and your argument was good for them staying nearby. I hope they are here, although it makes it more dangerous for us."

"Yes, maybe that's why I hope they are here, too. One feels uncommonly feeble when he is doing so little against the evil striking all around him. Those of us upon whom no danger has alighted must do what we can to create a middle position in which we share the danger of the others or at least its threat.

"We draw near, now. See that slight parting in the rock-face about two thirds up? It hardly looks as though it would admit a man from here, yet it is four feet wide at the front. If they are here they will have found the rope. I did not tell them, because it would not help them get up the first time, but I keep a stout rope there, which is just long enough to reach the ground. It makes the climbing easier and faster, but of course one cannot leave it out except for brief trips down and back. I will try a crow's call. We'll see what we may."

With that Joseph gave a passable imitation of an alarmed crow, then repeated it twice more. The harsh sounds echoed against the cliffs and across the thick woods that extended a half mile in all directions. They both stood against the trees, easily visible from the cleft above. Suddenly a low whistle sounded above, like the peeping of swallows.

"How can I signal them about the rope?" asked Joseph, excited, "We can't shout."

"No need," John replied, "They have figured it out themselves."

A brown strand came slapping down the rocks almost to the bottom.

A few minutes and considerable exertion later they were shaking chafed hands with the two fugitives from the law.

"What of our wives?" Daniel asked, as they retrieved the rope and clambered back up to the cave. They were still puffing, but Joseph turned to George and said, "Rebecca has been taken, and she is at Salem with your daughter."

Tears welled in George's eyes. "Have I done wrong?" he sobbed.

"Nay, brother," Daniel said, as he put his arms around him in a great hug. "You would not serve her better to be there, too. So I am convinced myself, or I would not be here either."

"Where is the justice for those who trust us?" George said.

John was taken aback by what seemed to him flippant rhyme in such circumstances.   He was soon to learn that rhyming came naturally to George, as it did to his father.

Joseph continued, "Sarah has brought the little ones home with her, and my Elizabeth and her father have gone with stores to help her. No one will question Israel Porter doing charity."

"But how long before they come for her?" mused Daniel, plainly not entirely convinced of his own wisdom yet.

"There is no perfect plan in these times. Yet I am the more convinced you two have done best," answered Joseph.

"He's right," John put forth, desperately concerned to encourage them. "There have been several who have taken flight. Philip English is in hiding. Two of the women named with you, one of Woburn and another of Reading are gone. Even John Willard, our former Topsfield constable fled. Unfortunately Joseph's cousin captured him, out on the Nashawag. Some traveler must have seen and reported him."

"And that is why I am glad you came here," continued Joseph. "There is too much chance of being recognized on the roads. This cave has been a private place for me, which I have always been jealous of sharing, but it is a blessing to offer some small sacrifice to hardy comrades. From this hidden place we can continue to conspire for justice and perhaps a return to reason."

"May God send us a return to reason before the start of the freezing season!" said George, bluffly.

"It would indeed be a blessing if it came soon!" said Daniel, also trying to be cheerful, largely for George's sake. "I hope you two criminal accomplices have brought more than dreary news, for we have considered eating the grass that grows about here, but hoped for better fare!"

Back in the cave, they broke out the food wrapped beneath their shirts, and never was Easter Feast received more gratefully than those bits of bread, cheese and meat. While they were eating, and washing it down with a bottle of Joseph's ale, John and Joseph gave accounts of the many most recently arrested. They told a little about the examinations, but in consideration of the fugitives' feelings, made small mention of Sarah Churchill and avoided reference to George's daughter, Margaret. The two men had cause enough for melancholy.

"We cannot stay much longer," said Joseph. "And we must take great care not to be seen in groups or in any suspicious actions. Our signal shall no more be the crow, but three small swallow peeps such as you answered us with. Tomorrow we intend to bring a cart along Osborne's Road and hide such goods as you need in the woods. We will come back later and bear those things here, so that we may leave you well supplied for a few days. It would be best for the time being if you stayed hidden here. By no means show yourselves on the ridges or peaks during the day, for they can be seen from several roads and farms. However, if you are cautious, you might explore the ground around your bivouac. Take care not to form trails or leave footprints in muddy places. I suppose you can dig a latrine at the far side of the grass back along the crevice. You must regularly put ashes in it so nothing gives you away."

"It would be an ignoble way to be discovered!" commented Daniel, then, "Get what news you can of Rebecca."

"Thank you both," George said, still emotional as he shook our hands, "We're glad to know what friends are true – even when we find them few."

The two conspirators made their way back through the woods by a different route, coming out across from John Hutchinson's.

Joseph turned to John unexpectedly and said, "I think we shall win after all, John," as they parted along the road.

Chapter Thirty-Two -- The Mystery of Christian Trask

*I wish New England have not a great deal of innocent blood to
answer for both in former and in later times.*
    -- Gershom Bulkeley, **Letter to Benjamin Davis**,   15
    March 1700.

No accusation brought against Bridget Bishop was more
serious than the murder of Christian Trask. There were other people
Bridget Bishop was said to have bewitched, and other deaths laid at
the feet of other defendants. But among these charges the hardest to
refute were the ones having to do with unsolved murders, and no
murder in our midst was quite as mysterious as the death of
Christian Trask.

Christian was the daughter of Humphrey and Elizabeth. She
grew up on the Beverly side of Bass River, only a few miles from the
farm of her husband, John Trask, son of Osmond Trask. John, who
was eight years older than Christian, was a widower. John and
Christian were married in April 1679, when she was eighteen. They
had five children, the oldest dying at the age of seven, and the
youngest born only five months before Christian's death. They were
members in full communion of the Beverly Church to which
Reverend John Hale ministered. Christian's death came in 1689. At
that time John Hale's testimony was given a great deal of weight by
the coroner's jury — and thus, likewise, his revised (or we might say,
reversed) opinion was taken very seriously by the Court of Oyer and
Terminer during out troubles.

Reverend Hale remembered that Christian had come to him
some five or six years earlier with complaints about Bridget Bishop.
The Trasks were one of the nearest neighbors to the Bishop's
Ordinary on the Ipswich Road. Christian came to ask Reverend Hale
to withhold the Lord's Supper from Goody Bishop until she had
given Christian "satisfaction for some offenses that were against
her". These consisted chiefly of the late night drinking and gambling
at the ordinary which were causing discord in the neighborhood and
were in danger of corrupting young persons.

Reverend Hale related that Christian said she had "once gone
into the house and finding some at shovelboard, had taken the pieces

they played with and thrown them into the fire, and reproved the said Bishop for promoting such disorders, but received no satisfaction from her about it." Reverend Hale advised her how to proceed further, himself concerned that Bishop's Ordinary would become nothing but a house of profaneness and iniquity if such things were not checked.

Later Reverend Hale heard that Christian was "distracted," and inquired of her husband when this began, to which he replied she was distracted the night she came home from Hale's after complaining to him about Goody Bishop. When he said "distracted," he explained, he meant she had "lost her reason". She continued to be distracted for some time, and many in the Beverly church fasted and prayed for her recovery, until "The Lord was pleased to restore the said Trask to the use of her reason again." Reverend Hale was often with Christian during this time and his later testimony was that he "took it then to be only distraction, yet fearing sometimes somewhat worse."

Subsequently, in May 1692, having seen the fits of the "afflicted evidences" in Salem Village, Reverend Hale revised his analysis for he called "to mind some of hers to be much like some of theirs."

When Christian Trask recovered from that first period of fits, she expressed the possibility that she had been bewitched by Bridget Bishop and was much adverse to any conversation with Goody Bishop. Reverend Hale said this bothered him a great deal, because he hoped for better things from Goody Bishop, and thought the two of them should be reconciled toward that end.

Some time later, Christian had another fit of distraction on the Lord's Day in the public meeting, and had frequent fits thereafter for about a month — "continued sometimes better, sometimes worse." During this time she showed, by her actions and words, that she was under a temptation to kill herself or possibly somebody else.

Reverend Hale said he spoke to Margaret Ring who was close to the Trasks during the time of Christian's last difficulties, and asked her what she knew of Christian's last days. Margaret Ring told him Christian was given much to reading and searching the prophecies of scripture. Margaret further said that a day prior to Christian's fits in meeting she had met with Bridget Bishop and told Margaret that they were now reconciled as friends.

Reverend Hale assured the Court that he had often prayed and counseled with Christian in the days before her death. He said she seemed most rational just a day or two before, and wanted Edward Bishop to come by so she could be reconciled to him. Reverend Hale asked if she had wronged Goodman Bishop, to which she replied not unless it might have been by burning his shovelboard pieces. She said if she did evil she was sorry for it and desired that Bishop would be friends with her and forgive her.

On the sabbath before Christian died, her husband brought a note from her to Reverend Hale. The note, which the pastor judged was in her own handwriting, asked for prayer.

Christian was found dead on June 3rd 1689, her throat apparently cut with sewing scissors. Reverend Hale described the wounds as "three deadly ones": "a piece of her windpipe cut out, and another wound above that through the wind pipe and gullet to the vein they call the jugular." Reverend Hale testified later that he felt it "impossible for her with so short a pair of scissors to mangle herself so without some extraordinary work of the devil or witchcraft".

A Jury of Inquiry or Coroner's Jury was convened from among the Trask's neighbors. It included Joshua Rea, Sr., James Putnam, Joshua Rea, Jr., Edward Bishop, Sr., Joseph Herrick, Daniel Andrew, Nathaniel Hayward, Thomas Rayment, Benjamin Balch, James Kettle, William Rayment, Jr., and Edward Bishop, Jr.

The jury reached its conclusions on the 24th of June (Friday if 1689, Sat if 1690), finding:

> Christian, wife of John Trask of Salem, being violently assaulted by the temptations of Satan, cut her own throat with a pair of scissors to the astonishment and grief of all, especially her most near relations.

Daniel Andrews, a neighbor as well as a member of the Coroner's jury, was much disturbed by the case. Several witnesses described Christian's fits and history of distraction. Four or five witnesses were called who testified to the nature of the wounds by which Christian had died, but Daniel, who together with the rest of the jury, saw them firsthand, was not satisfied that the death wound, that is the cut vein, could have been inflicted with the scissors. However, the emphasis upon Christian's melancholy and distracted "fits," and particularly those of the month before her death, made most of the jury feel suicide was the proper verdict.

Generally speaking one is wise to let official conclusions

stand, unless there is good cause to question them. However, in this case since the conclusions of the coroner's jury were considerably altered to death by witchcraft during our troubles, the way was opened for further speculations. As the two fugitives whiled away the days in or near their cave, Daniel talked with George at some length about the mystery of Christian Trask's death. Having their own stock of experience with melancholy women, they agreed this singular form of death did not seem consonant with the kind of such a woman might carry out.

Being themselves fugitives from law, they felt more free to speculate about things they otherwise wouldn't have spoken of, as they talked at length one afternoon.

"Let's be bold, George. Christian's death has long weighed upon my mind. Let's make a list of the persons who might conceivably have killed her, if in fact, as I think, it was not suicide. I'll stick my neck out first. I nominate her husband John Trask."

"Oh, that's cruel, Daniel. But I suppose you could make an argument for why he might want to do it. Lord knows, a distracted wife can weigh on a man at times. And particularly if he was dallying or sallying with some other — it could happen, I suppose."

"Let's add a few more to the list before we debate the likelihood of any one. My second nomination is a marauding Indian, name unknown."

"No, that's too far a stretch. If an Indian had come sneaking up and done away with her, he would have done it quicker and neater — and taken a few trophies."

"It's true. John said there was no evidence of robbery. Still, I leave my Indian on the list. Have you any nominees?"

"Well, how about a would-be lover? Some footloose bachelor trying his hand at a little adultery, but plumb rejected by a wife that was too Christian?"

"Good! It's a possibility with a man of the right temperament or who had just the wrong amount to drink over at Bishop's. He would take that rejection as a deadly insult to his manhood and flare up in anger. The scissors as the instrument could be taken to argue for a sudden resolve, rather than a premeditated deed."

"We've got husband, marauder, and rejected plotter. What other possibilities are there?"

"Well, one doesn't like to speak ill of the dead, but I suppose we could speculate of the other sort of lover — one that was accepted. Then we have two other possibilities -- her husband again, but jealous, or the wife or sweetheart of the lover, also jealous."

"**Y**es, scissors do seem a more female weapon.

"**O**f course, the Bishops, either husband or wife are possible suspects for plain murder, even if it wasn't witchcraft."

"**Y**es, but one or both of them would more likely have had a plan, and they wouldn't have used scissors would they?"

"**A**h, I've been meditating on that," answered Daniel, " What do you think of this. When the murderer inflicted the fatal wound, whether cold-bloodedly or suddenly in a passion, it spurted blood all over. We had testimony to that at the hearing, by the way. Probably the murderer ended up a bit bloody, too, and even a hot-blooded person would then begin thinking about evidence and suspects. He (or she) knew of Christian's recent distraction (that lets out the Indian doesn't it!) and decided to make it look like suicide. The murderer then took up Christian's own sewing scissors and made those strange cuts in her windpipe, and left the scissors in her own hand. When she was found, as the murderer predicted, all of us thought the source of both wounds was the same instrument—and the scissors were the one in evidence."

"**O**h, that's a bit frightening, Dan. It sounds too likely to be light-hearted about."

"**I**t does, doesn't it. Does it eliminate any of our suspects, I mean beside the Indian?"

"**N**o, I suppose not. All the others would likely know of her distraction, except perhaps the rejected suitor, if he were a stranger. But if it were a sudden or angry attack, I suppose a plan would be less likely. Cold calculation usually goes with cold blood."

"**T**hat's true, except that my experience leads me to think that intense action causes one's mind to race and formulate plans more quickly than usual. I can imagine a hot-blooded murderer taking a few minutes to elaborate on his hasty action in order to direct any investigators away from his trail. But still cold-blooded does seem to go better with that theory."

"**W**as Christian completely alone in the house when it happened? Did no one hear anything?"

"**J**ohn was supposed to have been in Salem. I seem to remember talking to someone who saw him there that morning. It was he who discovered her body when he returned toward evening.

"**M**argaret Ring, who was often there helping Christian, had taken the four children including the baby, over to a neighbor's. Trask's friends were making efforts to give Christian such peace and quiet as they could. So, no, I heard nothing to suggest anyone was near their place all day."

"But wasn't she nursing the baby?"

"At five months, one would certainly think so. Now that you mention it, I don't think Margaret left with the children until mid-afternoon, presumably after the baby had been fed."

"That makes it all the more incredible to me," said George. "A nursing mother doing away with herself with a pair of sewing scissors an hour or two after feeding her baby and sending her children to a neighbors with a friend."

"I agree. I have always been uneasy about the conclusions we reached on that jury. Let's examine our suspects. You know John—can you imagine him doing such a thing?"

"It's hard to imagine. He was seven or eight years older than Christian. They had been married about ten years, and although she had a couple periods of distraction, they seemed to be well-paired."

"If you knew he was involved with another woman, could you imagine him doing murder?"

"Ah, that's a hard one. He's a bold enough man, all right, and I don't suppose there's anyone I couldn't imagine doing murder. Not with the what we've seen lately. But would he? Only if he was downright crazy over his stolen fruits, I suppose. Then maybe."

"Which would lead us to. . ."

"Now Dan, I feel like a true criminal talking this way. Of course the logic of all that, if it was logic, could lead us to his new wife, Mary."

"Mary Dodge—she can't be more than nineteen or twenty can she, George?"

"No, I don't suppose so, though she's quite a ripe young woman for all that. But if that was the case, they were pretty careful about it. I never heard a peep. And it must have been a year and a half after her death that they got married."

"Well, let's leave them for a while. You've driven my Indian away, so how about frustrated suitors who might have been rejected by Christian?"

"There's not much use speculating along those lines—too many possibilities, but nothing to go on."

"Well, to my mind, the one big factor that supports that possibility is the proximity of Bishop's Ordinary. You know the crew that gathers to it. I think half the sailors coming through Salem end up there. And footloose plowboys, all the way from Ipswich or

Boxford, looking for a lively evening, wandered along the road to drink Goody Bishop's cider."

"But though it's only a quarter of a mile to Trask's, it's a pretty big leap for any of them to have met Christian in circumstances where they might have gotten ideas about her."

"Not necessarily. The wrong sort of fellow, particularly a hard-bitten sailor, soldier, or woodsman doesn't need more than a glimpse to get ideas. And there must have been plenty of them that got a glimpse of her coming and going. After all, the Trask's lane comes out almost across the road from the ordinary."

"You're more of Calvinist than I am, Dan. I guess I lose track of how ugly the human heart can be."

"That's a charitable thing for a man in our situation to say, George!"

"I suppose it is, yet somehow this organized madness is easier for me to grasp than a wild act of lust and murder on the part of some wandering ne-er-do-well."

"They're much the same thing, it seems to me. It's just that the organized madness is an accumulation of sin, reinforced by the mob, while the individual act takes a little more initiative, maybe."

"But," said George, struck with a new idea, "If we're going to be downright cold-blooded about the human heart, why should it be a stranger—why not a local man, even a respected one?"

"Perhaps that is even more likely. Especially if it was a local man heated up with Goody Bishop's cider and deathly afraid of his reputation being ruined. That way he could fit in either category—the rejected lover or the accepted one, suddenly fearful of being exposed."

"You mean, in the second case, if Christian had come under conviction and threatened to confess their adultery?"

"Yes! That might be argued to fit pretty well. Reverend Hale said at the hearing that she had been 'distracted' for a while before. Although you and I know a woman can be distracted without reasonable cause, certainly it might make a Christian wife 'distracted' to have something like that eating at her conscience."

"I'd hate to make a list of men who might fit into that picture. Don't you think we've gone too far?"

Daniel hesitated only for a brief space. "No, I don't. We certainly aren't swearing out a complaint against anyone, nor attempting to hurt any reputation. Our purpose is not to get anyone in trouble. We aren't likely to come to a conclusion sitting here. It may feel a bit like gossip, but talking about the possibilities is only evil if we're being selfish or destructive. The fact that her death is being blamed on witches is what makes me wonder about it again."

"I don't see how we can go much further. We could list every man for ten miles around."

"But, perhaps we can come up with a much smaller list by approaching it from a different angle. For instance, we might ask who tried to pin the blame elsewhere?"

"You mean on Goody Bishop? Do you remember who first accused her?"

"No, that wouldn't have been easy to figure out—not even then. Much less now. You see, there were already old rumors about her—from around the time Tom Oliver died—her first husband, you know. And there were plenty of other rumors in between. So it was easy to start new ones when Christian was killed."

"Well who testified against her?"

"I don't remember anyone testifying directly about her killing Christian. It was a little like our present troubles in that a few people testified to the bad blood between her and the Bishops, then others told about cases where Bridget was suspected of witchery. But Reverend Hale pretty much scotched that by testifying he had met often with Christian, that she felt she had sinned against the Bishops and said she wanted to make it right. Both Margaret Ring and Reverend Hale said Christian had made up with Bridget, and wanted to make up with her husband, too, if I rightly recollect."

"Speaking of her husband, could he have had those same two motives? Might he have been trying to kill two birds with one stone by getting rid of Christian and Bridget, too?"

"It could be, although it doesn't fit with what we know of Edward. I think you might be on to something else there, though. Maybe somebody planned to gain more from it than just silencing Christian. The old lawyers often ask "cui bono?" that is, who got the good out of it? If we could argue somebody not only got the good of silencing Christian but another good as well, that would give us a shorter list of likely suspects."

"Well, none of the Bishop's neighbors seem to have been very happy with the ordinary. I suppose anyone of them would have been happy to have it shut down—which would likely have happened if Bridget had been hanged for Christian's murder."

"Hm-m-m—let's see, the immediate neighbors are: John and James Rea, Jeremiah Watts, the two Tom Rayments, Captain and son.

Ben Porter and Dr. Griggs are a bit further away. After them you get into a circle of ten or twelve families, including ours."

"We have nothing to make any one seem more likely, do we?"

"No, but, for purposes of speculation, we could go beyond immediate neighbors to local men who sometimes visited the ordinary. Obviously they wouldn't have the motive of wanting to get rid of the ordinary, but they might have developed another kind of grudge against the Bishops. Or there might be old grudges about land or something."

"Well, you and I know that there are local men that go there occasionally."

"Like Sergeant Putnam and Captain Walcott, you mean?"

"Yes, those two certainly. But also Will and Zach Perkins come to mind."

"You know, it's amazing how many of those men are involved in our present troubles. "

"It is, isn't it. Zach Perkins has done things in the past that might put him on the short list, as the brand on his face attests. And Sergeant Putnam and Captain Walcott are among the chief complainers against witches. We're suspicious they're pushing their daughters in this. Wouldn't it be something if one of them was Christian Trask's murderer!"

"I suppose any of them would be likely if we add in the motives of a rejected lover or a lover afraid of exposure. Despite their patronage of the ordinary, I don't suppose any of them would balk at naming Goody Bishop in those circumstances."

"The way sin works, it would be all the more likely such a man would harden his heart and accuse various other people, like Putnam and Walcott now do. "

"Well, I don't suppose we'll solve the mystery sitting in this cave—or likely would outside it, either."

"No, I don't know anything to back up our other theories, either, so I guess I am inclined to agree with you. Short of conviction and repentance—maybe on somebody's deathbed—I don't suppose we'll ever know.

"But one thing I'm pretty sure of—even if Bridget Bishop did it by plain human violence—Christian Trask did not die by witchery, nor by her own hand either."

The two man sat silently for a time, then Daniel spoke again.

"You know, there isn't a whole lot that I'm thankful for about being stuck here, but this is the first time I've ever been able raise all the questions that death raised in my mind. One good thing about the present circumstance, we have time and freedom to talk."

"Dire deeds and desperate times do make room for discussion"

"Generally, in less horrible times we keep up a courteous face and don't talk about the ugly side of the human heart.

"There is one other way to look at the Trask mystery," said Daniel, now in a meditative mood. "You remember John Bunyan has a character of that name in his book."

"But his Christian was a man," said George.

"Yes, a man and everyman. But he also has an 'everywoman' named Christiana in the second part. I can think of a greater conundrum than the death of Christian Trask, though much like it in a way. I mean the mysterious death of Christian New England?

"Did we kill ourselves with the instruments of our huswifery? Was it marauding Indians, adulterous neighbors, or a passing suitor, rejected or repented?

"Or are our severe wounds the result of the righteous anger of our husband and master, who so long tolerated our fits of distraction, but would not abide our unfaithfulness?"

After a time during which neither said anything, George answered, "You turn the story like a poet, change the names and greater grow it."

"No!" laughed Daniel, "It is you who can always turn things to poetry!"

Chapter Thirty-Three -- Isolation and Community
(8 - 16 May)

*Oh! Long to be in the bosom of Christ! Long to be at home! For this world,
this wilderness, is full of snares, and all employments are full of snares, and
all enjoyments are full of snares. In civil things, Satan hath his snares to
entrap us; and in all spiritual things, Satan hath his snares to catch us. All
places are full of snares, city and country, shop and closet, sea and land:
and all our mercies are surrounded with snares. There are snares about our
tables and snares about our beds; yea, Satan is so powerful and subtle that
he will oftentimes make our greatest, nearest, and dearest mercies to become
our greatest snares. Sometimes he will make the wife that lies in the bosom
to be a snare to a man, as Samson's was, and as Job's was. Sometimes he
will make the child to be a snare, as Absalom was and Eli's sons were; and
sometimes he will make the servant to be a snare, as Joseph was to his
mistress. Ah! Souls, Satan is so cunning and artificial that he can turn
your cups into snares, and your clothes into snares, and your houses into
snares, and your gardens into snares, and all your recreations into snares.
And oh! How should the consideration of these things work all your souls
to say with the church, "Make haste, my beloved, and be like a roe, or a
young hart upon the mountain of spices,' and to love, and look, and long
for the coming of Christ (Cant. 8.14)   -- Thomas Brooks, **Precious
Remedies Against Satan's Devices**

F*our more prisoners were bound over to Boston gaol on the
8th of May, arriving there the next afternoon. These included the
great "wizard" George Burroughs, Ann Sears, Sarah Dastin, and
Bethia Carter, Sr.

Poor Sarah Dastin had barely alighted and stumbled into the
crowded gaol, when she and her mother, Lydia, were loaded up
again and taken on to Cambridge. Thus, at points where no
harshness was deliberately intended, yet in the cause of efficiency,
prisoners were often treated worse than cattle. This was the second
of the Dastin's several transports, of which the penultimate led to the
release of both, but in different ways.

While Lydia Dastin was reunited with her daughter in the
transport and imprisonment at Cambridge, Bethia Carter, Sr.,
another widow, had been separated from hers.   Bethia, Jr., was

named in the same warrant as her mother and Ann Sears, but when
Woburn Constable Ephraim Bock went to arrest them, the daughter
was not to be found. She had joined the growing number of hardy
escapes.

Generally speaking, it is not good for man to be alone, and
this applies to more than his marital condition. Certainly Jesus went
directly from his baptism into the wilderness alone, but that and his
isolation in the garden and on the cross were deliberate challenges to
the devil in his own domain — a willing entry into his best-laid
ambushes. But Jesus made himself part of a race, a people, a family,
a community, and a church. He brings people out of isolated
conditions and unites them. The devil's best strategies may fail
before the onslaught of God's will — but isolation is still one of his
favorite tactics.

There was much isolation during our troubles. Perhaps this
is sometimes as necessary to those who are called his workmanship
as it was to Jesus in the labors by which he created that work. But it
was exacerbated by many things. Being chosen out and falsely
accused of heinous crime enforces a strong sense of isolation. He
who becomes a martyr for his faith is similarly innocent, but he is
isolated from men over cause or creed in which he knows he has
union with righteous men and with heaven. He holds to a sure hope
of eventual vindication on earth and abiding glory in heaven. Nor
are his accusers usually of his own family, church, or pastors. In
other words the same formal lines which separate most martyrs from
their persecutors, unite them with their fellows.

Not so in our troubles. The principle union reinforced
through the arrests was with others accused, while only the strongest
family bonds were maintained. Nor did the nature of the charges
render union among the accused a thing happily to be embraced.
Our "witches" were peculiarly isolated from the outset.

Differences of station, haphazard variation in treatment, and
peculiarities of individual suffering increased that isolation. Since
the deprivations of imprisonment turned small commonplaces into
valued luxuries, there were many opportunities for bitter
competition for these: such things as standing for a few minutes in
the sunlight coming through a window, or taking out a slops jar for
three or four minutes under God's own sky. Being allowed to read
one's Bible in relative quiet became a royal privilege. The more
prisoners there were, the more rare peace and privacy became.

Strange outbursts — not just the kind all came to expect from

Sarah Good—but sudden breaks of violent anger from such quiet souls as Martha Corey and young Sarah Morey shocked the more sensitive and amused the more cynical. One afternoon these two and several other women were working on a quilt which they held on their laps in a circle, when Sarah Morey suddenly stood and began screaming. "If you do that again, I'll scratch your eyes out!" The rest of them were at a loss to know what had sparked this explosion, but it was Martha Corey toward whom it was directed. As suddenly in complementary sympathy of emotion, she stood, too, the sagging quilt the only barrier between their naked souls, and said, not as loudly, but with an intensity as violent, "I have dealt with naughty kittens before my dear, and shall know how to deal with you." Afterward Rebecca and Sarah Cloyce spoke quietly with each of the two women and achieved a reconciliation of a sort.

Such outbursts did further damage where they were communicated to the magistrates. More than a few such exchanges were repeated in official ears, but the greatest damage was in the further sense of isolation and futility which grew out of such incidents and contributed in turn toward more of them.

The callous treatment of the prisoners increased the sense of isolation, particularly in the constant breaking and reshuffling of relationships. While little is fixed or reliable in life, it is the constant habit of man to build schedule, procedure, and ritual into life. Prison life offers just enough grounds for this habit to expose it regularly to disappointment.

George Burroughs was a great relief to John Procter, and indeed those two, like Martha and Rebecca, were to become boon companions in prison. Outside of it they had both been distant, and too masterful to draw close to other men. But now they had been forced to stoop, and were thus able to go together through the humbler door of fellowship. George Burroughs fulfilled the expectations of the magistrates and he did become spiritual ringleader among the "witches" at Boston, as chief chaplain to his fellow accused.

But first there was another of the great rearrangements of life which each new influx brought. Since it was no longer possible to house all the prisoners there, John Arnold had found lodgings for some nearby in a sturdy barn, and in a cellar. He calculated he must keep his most dangerous prisoners in his own gaol, but he sent four of the women to these dark and dirty quarters: the two newcomers with Sarah Cloyce and Sarah Morey.

The weather was sufficiently milder that the damper basement and the draftier barn did not put those prisoners into any great danger. They spent the first few days in the respective new establishments cleaning and arranging. All four had visitors as it happened, and were made more comfortable than they would have been at Arnold's. They indeed did not have to suffer the most difficult night and day that the other prisoners had gone through.

That night, the 9th, and into the next afternoon, Sarah Osborne coughed up the last of her life in hoarse chokes and heartbreaking wheezes. Martha Corey and Rebecca sat up all night with her, bathing her burning brow, offering fresh warm cloths into which she coughed. They were continually praying for her. In the early hours of the next morning, the others, groggy in fitful sleep, heard the two old voices blending in a rustic rendition of a psalm. Not long after noon that day, Sarah Osborne became the first among many to die in our troubles. Her last intelligible words were, "It seems so long."

William her husband had not seen her for a week, but he dutifully arrived the next day with an official claim for her body from the Salem magistrates. He had to wait a day while a coroner's jury convened to determine she died naturally. The older women felt very mortal for the next few days, but Reverend Burroughs, newly transported from Salem, preached on the resurrection of the dead, taking as his theme "Well done, thou good and faithful servant." He intimated his own recent conviction that good and faithful servanthood in this world may not appear such to others or, at times, to ourselves. He said that as there is no forgiveness, except of sin, so there is no resurrection, except from death, no sanctification, except through mortification, nor glory, except for that which is sown in dishonor.

But without Sarah Osborne to minister to, and with her sister incarcerated elsewhere, Rebecca suddenly felt very old and empty again—much as she had after her examination.

Meanwhile other examinations went continually forward in Salem Village. George Jacobs, Sr., was sent to Boston on the 13th, along with William Hobbs, Edward and Sarah Bishop, Bridget Bishop, Sarah Wilde, Mary Black, Mary English, Alice Parker, and Ann Pudeator.

Marshall Herrick was busy during this time, and with the many arrests and examinations—short-handed. Because of this, the custom became that a single officer went as driver and guard in these transports of prisoners. A large hay cart was employed, with Deputy

Harris driving it on this occasion. The prisoners were in shackles, but unbeknownst to the officials, Edward and Sarah Bishop had been at work with a file over the last two weeks. Their shackles were held together by only a thread of steel, the gaps left by the file being filled with a putty of wax and filings.

After the wagon with its ten prisoners had been on the road to Boston for about three hours, Deputy Harris happened to stop to clean the mud from his wheels, and out of the corner of his eye saw something not quite right about the prisoners. Still holding a muddy stick, he raised his head and scanned his charges. There were only eight of them! Two of them had disappeared, and he had no idea how or when. He did not even know for certain what their names were. None of the other prisoners would give him a straight answer to his questions, though he tried both railing and cajoling approaches. Indeed, they acted like they had no idea what he was talking about when he spoke of the two missing prisoners.

Angry and confused, Deputy Harris calculated how best to fulfill his commission without getting deeper into trouble and decided he would continue on to Boston, hail the first rider whom he met and require him to take the news back to Salem. He realized he would have to give names to the messenger, however, and so he stopped the wagon again and demanded that the prisoners identify themselves. He was unfortunate in addressing himself first to Bridget Bishop, who had known of the younger couple's plans and given them advice, electing not to join them for fear of hindering their flight. She laughed scornfully and said she had not found it did her any good to speak with officials of the law. He then tried reading down the list and demanding that those present indicate when their names were spoken—but no one did. At last he gave himself to trying to recollect all their names, but could only succeed with five.

About forty-five minutes later a young man from Salem rode up the road, and when Deputy Harris hailed him and told him what had happened the young man laughed long and loud. The Deputy got angry again and said it was no laughing matter, at which the young man tried to stifle his humor. He agreed to look for the Marshall in Salem or failing there, in Salem Village, and to take a message to him which consisted of the news of the escapes and the five names the Deputy could remember. Deputy Harris then went on to Boston, punishing the recalcitrant remnant by waiting nearly an hour after they complained of a need to stop, refusing to let the women go out of his sight (although he did allow them to go a distance away) and verbally abusing them for being so slow about it.

The newcomers were bursting to share the news with the other prisoners at Boston, while the Deputy reluctantly told John Arnold what had happened. The new prisoners, except for Bridget Bishop, answered submissively to their new gaoler's demand for names. Since Deputy Harris by then recalled who Bridget was, he now knew who the two escapes were. The deputy set out again for Salem immediately, despite the condition of his horses.

That night all the new prisoners made shift in the crowded gaol, but the next day Alice Parker, Ann Pudeator, Mary English and Mary Black were distributed between the neighboring barn and cellar where the four others were lodged.

Before the latest arrivals were moved, the others questioned them eagerly and learned of the new developments in Salem and the Village. George Jacobs, Sr., Bridget Bishop, and William Hobbs, particularly, did not take kindly to the shackles. Mary English broke down and cried despairingly most of the afternoon. They did not wear them long, however.

On May 16th, an order arrived from the Governor, who was newly apprised of conditions among the prisoners, partly through friends of Phillip English, still in hiding in Boston. The friends had visited Mary the previous day and gone directly to Governor Phips, complaining particularly of the shackles — emphasizing those of little Dorcas Good. The governor issued an order on the 15th that the shackles were to be removed and upon the 16th much of the day involved a procession the reverse of the earlier one, in which each was taken to the smith, where the bolt was riven through on his anvil, the bands and chains removed. More than one prisoner got a scrape or bruise in the process, but none preferred their former condition.

Although greatly relieved, the prisoners continued to experience daily disruptions. Constantly increasing in number and continually being rearranged, they had many occasions to feel isolated. Nonetheless, in many ways they indeed formed a community. Reverend Burroughs remarked to John Procter that in all his years of ministry he had never had a more agreeable congregation nor one that paid him much better. Like much else in that community, the remark spread quickly and was shared among them all.

Chapter Thirty-Four — Hope Deferred Makes the Heart Sick
(May 17- 26)

. . . I will also plead by Polybius in my excuse: "It is not the work of an historian to commemorate the vices and villainies of men so much as their just, their fair, their honest actions; and the readers of history get more good by the objects of their emulation than of their indignation." Nor do I deny that, though I cannot approve the conduct of Josephus (whom Jerome not unjustly nor ineptly calls "The Greek Livy") when he left out of his Antiquities the story of the golden calf, and I don't wonder to find Chamier, and Rivet, and others taxing him for his partiality towards his countrymen; yet I have left unmentioned some censurable occurrences in the story of our colonies, as things no less unuseful than improper to be raised out of the grave, wherein oblivion hath now buried them . . .
-- Cotton Mather, *Magnalia Christi Americana* (1702)

John Tarbell and Joseph Putnam drove the cartload from Joseph's farm. They came to a stop at the three pines which they had marked out earlier. There they took turns sitting ready to whip up the horse at any moment, while the other man took armloads of supplies back into the woods. These they concealed in a hollow beneath a haw-thorn bush. John was at the reins when someone came down the road from the direction of Osborne's, so he whipped up the horse and made as if he had stopped but for a moment. He glanced back and saw Joseph peep from between the pines. The interloper proved only a hired man from James Putnam's place and soon passed by. When he was out of sight, John turned back, and they unloaded the rest of their contraband.

That night Peter Cloyce, Jr. and Joseph carried the goods to the rocks and sent them up the rope to Daniel and George. Afterward Joseph told John and Peter to stay home and lie low for a few days.

During the day John Willard had been examined by the magistrates, and finding he could not get the Lord's Prayer right, he laughed nervously and said the girls must have bewitched him. He and two women from Lynn were committed to gaol.

The next day was so exciting neither John nor Sam could stay home. In fact, half of the Cloyces together with as many of the Nurse tribe went into Salem and came back all the way to nether Topsfield in joyous celebration over the first great news they had heard in six weeks. Their Aunt Mary Easty was released from gaol, found by the magistrates to be wrongly charged.

We never knew exactly how this came about, due to the breaking of subsequent storms. From things Mercy Lewis said a few days later we understand almost all the "afflicted" agreed to Mary Easty's innocence during individual interviews with the ministers. Perhaps the magistrates had weeded out her case as one of the weakest, or maybe the dire deeds attributed to her had been subsequently attributed to another person. In any case it was decided by the officials that Mary Easty, like Nehemiah Abbott, was not a witch after all. She was released without charges or further restraint on May 18th.

The Eastys stopped to tell the news to friends and kin as they hurried on their way to Salem to get her. The Nurse party followed within half an hour and met them just leaving town at the bridge overlooked by the ominous hill. Mary was practically suffocated with all the hugging, as they bubbled with hilarity over her, the first fruits, as it were, promising further deliverances from gaol. The Cloyces and Nurses saw this joyful event as an assurance their own mothers and grandmothers would soon be released to them.

The celebration at the Easty's was the occasion for much exuberance. During the feasting, prayers and conviviality, two young people seemed to enter into the joy of it with a particular vigor. These were Mary Preston, daughter of the still melancholy Tom, and Peter Cloyce, Jr. Despite the dominant atmosphere of fear and mourning which would continue many months, these two found occasions to form an attachment that was to grow with peculiar immunity to the unsuitable climate, sustaining something of the joy shared briefly by all that night.

That same Wednesday, Dr. Roger Toothaker of Billerica was examined. He was then sent from Salem to Boston Gaol along with Thomas Farrar, Elizabeth Hart of Lynn, and John Willard.

Elizabeth Booth had joined the afflicted girls. She testified against Daniel and strangely, against one of her fellows. Mary Warren, after another clear day in which she tried to tell the truth about the girls' dissembling, was again accused. Elizabeth Booth claimed both of these "witches" tried to get her to sign the devil's book.

We soon discovered the great Leviathan who pursued us

would not give up its prey easily. Unlike Jonah's great fish, this one did not willingly disgorge whom it swallowed — nor left as free. Through secondary causes like those operating on Jonah's monster, it's contrary actions in regard to Mary Easty seem to have been connected with internal disagreements.

Two days later, all hopes founded on Mary Easty's release were crushed to the ground. A further complaint was issued against her for acts of witchcraft against Anna, Mercy, Mary Walcott and Abigail. The plaintiffs included John Putnam, Jr., Benjamin Hutchinson, Sam Brabrook, and James Darling, who was Mercy Lewis's uncle.

Marshall George Herrick testified he saw the "afflicted" in extremity on the 20th, crying out of Goody Easty tormenting them. He himself re-arrested her about midnight, after which their suffering was supposedly relieved. Mary Walcott and Elizabeth Hubbard had been at Putnams on the 20th where they, Mercy, and Anna had fits alternately, and variously. Abigail and Anna testified that they, Sam Abbey and their friend, Sarah Trask, had been on their way to comfort the suffering Mercy at the home of Constable John Putnam where she was temporarily staying, when an apparition of Mary Easty with other "witches" appeared, spoke, and afflicted them.

Mary Easty's second arrest was a reassertion of power. Up until Nehemiah Abbott's release, the group of "afflicted" had been growing in numbers and sway. But on that day (April 22) the additional magistrates had suddenly checked the girls, and questioned their inerrancy. The girls has disagreed among themselves and finally been forced to agree on an explanation which explained Abbott's innocency — that he resembled "the man with the wen," a witch they agreed they'd seen. The release of Mary Easty, who was examined just after Goodman Abbott, was an even more direct challenge to them, for all had agreed in accusing her of bewitching them. The magistrates seem to have combined doubts over lack of testimony to previous bewitchments, and the possibility the girls were mistaking her for one of her sisters, Cloyce or Nurse. When the ministers spoke with the girls individually, they brought them to agree to her innocency. But once Mary Easty was released, the girls came together and were indignant over being found wrong. Thus the renewed and intense "afflictions," which Mercy Lewis began, and the others joined.

The day Mary Easty was rearrested, the magistrates took

further depositions on Bridget Bishop's case. Reverend Hale gave evidence against her in the old mystery of the death of Christian Trask. Also testifying were Major Gedney, Reverend Parris, Joseph Herrick, Jr., his wife, Thomas Rayment, his wife, John Trask, Margaret Ring, Hannah Baker, Captain William Rayment, Sr., William, Jr. and, James Kettle. Daniel Andrew, when told of William Rayment, Jr.'s involvement, made excuse for him, saying he was no doubt dragged into it. The conspirators were nevertheless glad Rayment was no longer meeting with them and ignorant about the hidden escapes.

On May 23rd, Mary Easty was examined on new charges and primary attention paid to the great afflictions of the 20th which all the girls blamed on her, John Willard, and Mary Witheridge. Mercy Lewis, afflicted at Constable Putnam's where the other girls were gathered around her, said Goody Easty appeared to her and said she would kill her "because she did not clear her so as the rest did." Sam Sibley, John Putnam, Jr., and Edward Putnam joined George Herrick. These solemnly affirmed that they had seen the girls afflicted and heard them say Easty caused it.

The Eastys, Nurses, Cloyces, and Townes came closer to despair through this series of events than at any point thus far in our troubles. They were made so vulnerable again through their joy in Mary Easty's release that when the new accusations and sudden rearrest came, they were deeply wounded.

Also arrested and examined were Mary Derrich, and Benjamin Procter (son of John and Elizabeth). Benjamin's parents and sister were already in gaol. His brother William was soon to be arrested as well. Mary (Bassett) Derrich was the second sister of Elizabeth Procter to be accused, and mother of sixteen year old John Derrich. Young John would testify in September about a spectral assault committed against him by the repentant accuser, Margaret Jacobs. Attack and counterattack through accusations became increasingly common after the June trials.

Also on May 23rd, another transport of Salem prisoners took place. Like our surgeons, who bleed our bodies for our own good, and like magistrates who would exorcise evil for the good of the common weal, the gaolers regularly purged the gaols of their excess humors by means of transports — from Salem to Boston and Ipswich, from Boston to its "annexes" or to Cambridge or back to Salem, and so on, in a sort of Cartesian vortex. Most transported prisoners, in reflux, so to speak, would be brought back to Salem for their trials —

the first of which were swiftly approaching.

The following day the magistrates examined Mistress Elizabeth Cary of Charlestown, who was committed to gaol. The callousness of the magistrates and ministers had reached the point where they ordered her to be held pinioned by the Marshall and his deputy throughout her long examination, despite her tears and protestations of great distress. So grueling was her examination that her husband, Nathaniel, protested loudly but vainly during it. Such were his protests we were much surprised he was not accused and charged after the pattern of John Procter. Although he was ineffective in the Salem Court, Mr. Cary soon wrote an account of his wife's examination which did some good toward opening the eyes of Boston officials and ministers.

On May 25th, Sarah Pease was examined and gaoled. From Salem to Boston went Mary Easty, Abigail Soames, Susannah Roots, Sarah Bassett, Mary Derrich, Benjamin Procter, and Mistress Cary. (Sarah Bassett was another sister of Elizabeth Procter, while Susannah Roots was a widow from Beverly.)

Upon their arrival in Boston, there were various emotional reunions among the prisoners. The following day the standard re-arrangements took place, with only Mary Easty and Benjamin Procter of the new prisoners being kept at the Arnold's, while the others were transferred to one of the annexes.

Nathaniel Cary applied for and was granted a writ of habeus corpus by which his wife was transferred to Cambridge. There she was put in shackles, and nothing her husband could do would induce gaoler or magistrates to remove them.

Shackles had been ordered anew by the magistrates, due to an intensified period of complaining and "affliction" of the girls. They claimed the prisoners in Boston and Cambridge were still afflicting them in "apparitions". The gaoler at Boston had grown more confident, however, and was in no hurry to put his prisoners (and himself) through that ordeal again. Mr. Arnold decided to put off further shackling until after the trials, which were scheduled to begin in a few days.

The 26th of May (a Lecture Day) had been set aside as the General Fast by act of the General Assembly on May 6. Even Salem Town closed most of its shops, and the citizens remarked it was long since the waterfront was as quiet. The Village was more unified in its prayers than for many a year, though never so divided in its doctrine.

William Stoughton

Chapter Thirty-Five -- Toil and Trouble
(19 - 20 May)

It is therefore most wholesome for magistrates and officers of the church and commonwealth never to affect more liberty and authority than will do them good, and the people good: for whatever transcendent power is given will certainly overrun those that give it and those that receive it. There is a strain in a man's heart that will sometime or other run out to excess, unless the Lord restrain it; but it is not good to venture it. -- John Cotton, "Limitation of Government" in ***An Exposition of the Thirteenth Chapter of Revelation***, London, Chapman,1655.

On the 19th of May, Thomas Farrar, Elizabeth Hart, John Willard and Roger Toothaker were sent to Boston gaol.

John Willard was accused chiefly by his own in-laws, the Wilkins clan of Boxford. The Wilkins laid the mysterious death of young Daniel Wilkins, in particular, at Willard's presumably cloven feet. They had called "The French Doctor," Anthony Randall of Salem to make a diagnosis, but Dr. Randall had merely sent word back that it was not a natural disease and certainly witchcraft in his judgment. Perhaps Dr. Randall had figured out it was better to keep as far away as possible from witchcraft cases. (Dr. Toothaker, now in chains with John Willard, was accused chiefly by Elizabeth Hubbard, partly because he claimed to know too much about hunting down witches.)

Anna Putnam had accused Thomas Farrar of Lynn (whom her father called "Old Pharoah") for alleged afflictions on the 8th of May. Thomas Putnam, and Robert Morrell signed the complaint. Anna also accused Elizabeth Hart of Lynn, after that woman visited her personally on the 13th. Anna said Goody Hart did her no hurt until that time, but hurt her "most grievously" several times thereafter. Many took note that both Martha Corey and Goodwife Hart were accused after visiting Anna. Visitors to that household suddenly became scarce.

The four new prisoners had their chains removed when they arrived at Boston. The two men were kept at the gaol, while the two women were "farmed out" to quarters in the neighboring barn. Rebecca had been grieving and growing a bit melancholy over the ten days since she was separated from her sister, Sarah. But a new development captured her attention. Not many days after Sarah Osborne died, Sarah Good began to have labor pains. The remaining women rallied around, arranging for the advent of a baby in their midst. Dr. Toothaker was ill with an infection of the head and lungs, but he declared himself well enough to preside over the event, which took place early in the morning.

Reverend Burroughs and John Procter with John Willard and the supernumery women retired to one corner where they played with Dorcas, prayed, and caught snatches of sleep. Rebecca, Martha Corey, and Elizabeth Procter aided Dr. Toothaker in the delivery.

Dorcas Good was taken aside by Elizabeth Emerson and another of the younger women, who tried to entertain her. Nevertheless, she regularly turned from the games toward the mysterious ceremony taking place around her mother.

Sarah Good became much quieter than was her habit, although she still muttered and glanced nervously about as the pains grew and the event rapidly approached.

At the moment of birth she cried out in great shrieks full of irrational references to William, the magistrates, her little Dorothy-bird, and her own extremity. The women spoke soothingly, but applied themselves vigorously toward a speedy delivery, Elizabeth Procter helped push downward on the baby in her womb at the crucial moment (for which Sarah never quite forgave her judging from remarks over the next weeks).

A baby girl came forth — well, though small. Every face in the dark chamber broke into a broad smile at the first tiny wail. Dr. Toothaker took a great deal of the credit for this marvelous advent, as men and doctors are often wont to do. After the women had rubbed her vigorously, he held the child up and gave her a kiss. None of the women approved of it — for he was clearly feverish and breathing hoarsely, but it was done before they could object.

Sarah seemed to improve amazingly, becoming wholly quiet over the next days, except for coos and whispers to the baby, whom she shared cozily with Dorcas. This event seemed to restore her beyond what anyone could have predicted, and the ladies commented over the next days upon the providences of God.

Even the Arnolds were moved by the event, and brought soft warm blankets and knitted caps and boots for the child. Mistress Arnold brought fresh milk for Sarah twice a day during the next weeks. The whole body of prisoners became attentive to the needs of the mother and baby. Visitors were cautioned to be quiet and not to admit drafts. The news went quickly back to the Village, and William came down with Father Nurse to see the new member of his family.

Francis seemed to join in the celebration of the new baby with some restraint. When he and Rebecca were able to talk alone, he told her that Mary Easty had been arrested again with all of the afflicted girls saying she had lately bewitched them. It struck Rebecca very hard. It was as if her heart was more vulnerable for the happiness they had felt over the baby — like a settler's home where the door is thrown open to welcome a loved one, only to find there are attacking Indians on his heels.

Roger Toothaker grew steadily worse over the ensuing days, with an abiding fever. Soon his spells of coughing reminded the older inmates of Sarah Osborne.

Some days after the child's birth, early in the morning, Martha Corey visited with mother and child in their privileged spot among the blankets before the fire. Afterward Martha came anxiously to confer with Rebecca.

"I am fearful for the baby," she whispered.

"What is it, dear? I've never seen Sarah more quiet or more in her right mind."

"No, it's not Sarah. Her milk is come along fine and the child sucks well. I want you to come over and feel her head."

Rebecca knew what that meant, and hastened to rise and dispose her clothing in a presentable manner. Going directly, but without appearance of haste, she bent her old knees beside Sarah and the child and asked, "How is baby today? And how is Momma?"

"Both well, God be praised. But I had forgotten how little they sleep between meals, so I had. Dorothy bird was no better, but it takes getting used to again."

Rebecca saw a red flush on the child's brow, but it was not until she casually held her wrist upon the tiny forehead, that her concern increased. Continuing to make cheerful conversation, she asked Sarah if there was anything she needed, to which Sarah said a cup of tea would be nice. As Rebecca rose and went to the fireplace to heat the kettle, she glanced back across the room to Martha. The glance between the two friends was enough to signal and signify their agreement.

After Sarah had her tea, and Dorcas, a cup, too, Rebecca and Martha busied themselves making some toast and boiling water for the others. They could not very well whisper together so close to the Goods, but after others were up and about, they retired to the door end to sit down and talk.

"If only it's not that infection of Toothaker's!" said Martha.

"Oh, do not say it!" answered Rebecca, "it doesn't bear thinking about. There are so many milder sicknesses it might be. I am coming to fear he will not survive it, much less would this darling mite."

"We must pray for unseasonably warm weather and think what remedies there may be."

"Let us ask Elizabeth. She has more experience with physic than I, although my children had every minor disease known to man. I lost two, but two survived even the pox. Oh, this is too bad. Let's pray now."

The two gray heads bowed and whispered their supplications and complaints. When they were finished, they looked more gaunt than even their years or trials accounted for. They gazed wordlessly at one another for a time, until Martha spoke, "Why must there be so much suffering?" Her voice was as dreary as a dream.

"Why do the heathen rage?" answered a cheerful male voice.

"Indeed, Mr. Burroughs," said Martha looking up, "and the nations imagine a vain thing. I think that is a question we all have been asking fairly often."

"The kings of the earth . . . but that will not tell you anything you have not learned yourselves. . . and you asked a more basic question Mistress Corey."

George Burroughs was a small man, and his voice, like his movements, was nimble and lively, with little of the ponderous self-consciousness which was common to most of the Salem ministers. On the other hand as Rebecca remembered from his days in the Village, he had a strong sense of personal dignity. In his own household, at least, he was quite intolerant of any appearance of resistance. Yet here, with all his formal offices stripped away, there were no such challenges. This was one more factor which helped two strong personalities such as he and John Procter get along as alien captives.

"Scripture offers at least three reasons for suffering. First because of sin. Second because of God's love. And third, because of his secret will, which works all things together for his glory and the good of those called according to his purpose."

"Those whom the Lord loveth he chasteneth, and scourgeth

every son whom he receiveth," quoted Rebecca.

"Yes," said the minister, "and the first part of that passage indicates the two responses to God's discipline which are most natural to fallen man. 'My son, despise not thou the chastening of the Lord, nor faint when thou art rebuked of him.' Despising and fainting — rebellion and unbelief. When the mysterious hardship comes, our hearts incline either toward anger or despair or sometimes both."

"Please don't say anything to Sarah or the others yet, but we are afraid the baby may have Toothaker's fever."

"Oh, Lord Jesus, let it not be!" He lowered his eyes for a moment. "Yes, I see. These are the hardest things — when the innocent and helpless suffer. Was it this you prayed about?"

Seeing the affirmation in their faces and nods, he went on, "Then let us pray again, for my own weak heart's sake. We do not need philosophy, but the Spirit's groans -- too deep for words."

Afterward, as the minister left them and went over to look at the baby, Rebecca spoke in a high thin voice of her reflections, "The child has seemed like a second chance and a symbol of hope to us. There have been so many hopes deferred."

"And hope deferred makes the heart sick," answered Martha, then deliberately raising herself up, "but perhaps we imagine and prophesy evil. Let us continue to hope."

When Mr. Burroughs came back his eyes were dull with pain. "Can the little one be taken? She is such an encouragement to us and to her mother, like the children of Perpetua and Felicitas."

"Who were they?" Rebecca asked.

"Perpetua was a young widow and Felicitas a servant , both martyred for their faith in the third century. They lived in Carthage, that great city in North Africa so long at war with Rome. Perpetua was from a wealthy noble family, but when she heard the gospel, she believed and was baptized. The Christians were much persecuted at that time. Her father and even the governor of the province begged her to deny her newfound faith, but she would not, and was condemned to be thrown to the beasts with a number of others. She had a young son whom she was nursing. At first he was taken from her and she almost despaired. But while she was in prison awaiting her sentence, she was allowed to have the child with her — and her prison which had first seemed so dark to her -- became so comfortable she said she had no wish to be anywhere else.

"Felicitas was eight months pregnant when she was put in

prison. Just as with us here, the law did not allow a pregnant woman to be put to death. She was upset by this both because she wished to die with her friends, but also because she did not want to be put to death later with common criminals. She and her friends prayed and soon after she went into labor. When she was in the travail of birth she cried out in pain, whereupon some guards in the prison mocked her and said 'if you suffer so much now, what will you do when you are eaten by the beasts!'

"She answered, 'Now it is I who suffer what I suffer; but then another will be in me, who will suffer for me, because I am to suffer for him.'

"Immediately when Felicitas' child was born, she too rejoiced.

"When at last they were marched into the amphitheater where the beasts were to be released, it is said they looked as though they were going to heaven, so peaceful were their faces. And if they trembled at all, it seemed as though it was with joy rather than fear."

Both Martha and Rebecca were moved by the story. The three of them were silent some time after Reverend Burroughs finished.

"Yes, I can see Perpetua's and Felicitas' joy in Sarah," said Rebecca, "The joy of motherhood. But joy while being fed to the beasts! I've never seen it and can scarcely imagine it!

Chapter Thirty-Six — Cave-Dwellers
(May 21)

Satan has raised, maintained and continued against the Saints, from time to time, in one sort or other; sometimes by bloody death and cruel torments; other while imprisonments, banishments and other hard usages; as being loath his kingdom should go down, the truth prevail and the churches of God revert to their ancient purity and recover their primitive order, liberty and beauty. . .
    -- Governor William Bradford, *Of Plymouth Plantation.* (circa 1650)

Although the two men hiding in the cave at the back of Thorndike's Hill had stone around them rather than wooden walls, they were but a little freer than the prisoners in Boston. They could indeed see the sky from the vantage point of their little lawn. They could sometimes go for short walks in the woods below in the evening. But they lived in constant awareness of farmsteads within a mile of their hideaway, and in constant apprehension of hunters or wanderers coming near their cave. Daniel found solace in scholarly and literary pursuits. He spent some time each day writing about our troubles and reading what books the others brought him. George read his Bible daily, but other times showed the yeoman's ability to rest quietly with little to occupy his mind. Yet during their first days, between the burdens of their loved ones in various states of difficulty and their own inactivity, they too felt oppressed, isolated and at times nearly surly with each other.

Plato speaks of a cave in terms of philosophy. He presents the choice between seeing reflections in the firelit shadows or reality itself in the broad light of day. The sunlit world of Salem Village certainly contained no smaller measure of illusion than the dim world of their cave. It was true, however, that the cave's chief features at those times when its inhabitants were most disgruntled seemed to be damp, darkness, and smoke. They looked forward to the visits of their friends with lively anticipation.

The conspirators planned a full meeting for Saturday the 21st. At dusk the other four came by several routes to the cliff face, where they ascended the rope. After the rope was retrieved, they crowded together in the stone cell where Daniel and George had lived for a week .

Joseph opened the meeting, and more than one conspirator thought of ancient precedents while the words of his prayer sprang distinct and reverberant from the walls of their catacomb. He finished and went on to welcome the motley members of the band.

"David may have had more robbers in his cave," he said, "But I doubt he had a hardier band." The others chuckled at this pure rhetoric.

"We gathered last a month ago, and, although we have met by twos and threes since and continued our efforts, we all know things have come to a much worse pass."

"There have been more than sixty persons charged, of whom perhaps seven, including our stalwarts here, have evaded arrest. All the rest, with one exception, have been bound over to gaol, and will be brought before a jury of inquiry, then tried. One, Sarah Osborne, has died in gaol.

"Mary Easty, Sam and Peter's aunt, was arrested on the day we last met. Three days ago she was released, in what seemed a belated version of Goodman Abbott's case, that is being declared free and innocent with the apparent approval of our dear afflicted despots. Yesterday she was rearrested for supernatural attacks on four of them. (Peter Cloyce choked on his emotions as Joseph spoke.) Our despots, the benevolent ladies, apparently felt their powers were diminished by this release. They do not kindly brook rebuffs to their authority.

"Mercy Lewis claimed she was afflicted because she alone refused to clear Goodwife Easty, who had blinded the eyes of the others. They rounded up Elizabeth Hubbard, Mary Walcott, Abigail, and Anna, under the supervision of such citizens as Sam Abbey, Sam Braybrook and my half-brother's wife. The girls all affirmed the apparition of Goodwife Easty afflicting Mercy. My cousin John, the constable, and Benjamin Hutchinson signed another complaint."

As Joseph's tone took on an unusually sharp note of bitterness, Daniel, John, Sam, Peter, and George regarded him silently in the flickering red light of the fire.

Daniel broke the silence. "I am almost made to think Satan has an imagination after all. Certainly there is a kind of variety to these things. But better things are more predictable — and your presence here with George and me seems more momentous than the torment the Eastys and the rest of the Towne clan are being treated to."

"Nay, " John rejoined, "the Jacob's clan has been treated more shabbily and endured as much pain as we." Even as he said this, George leaned forward and he bowed his head where he sat, to hide the tears that welled along the furrows of his cheeks.

"It has been very hard," he said, addressing the floor of the cave. He collected himself for a while and then went on.

"But let's stay on guard. I want to hear as much as you know — though it involves Sarah Churchill telling lies, and even . . . my own Margaret."

"Be not burdened under, brother!" Daniel chided him, "I need you to bear up for me. It's not only this den we share together."

"No," Sam Nurse joined in, " Sarah Churchill and your own Margaret have been coerced to say things that are being used for evil, it is true, but they are not in any wise unique, and we have some news to encourage you."

"Were you at the meeting house for those examinations?" asked Joseph, for there had been a multitude of things about which the conspirator's had not conferred.

"I got in on most of the examinations of the 10th and 11th,"said Sam, "But I also heard through Mary Ingersoll of another crack in the witch-hunters' armor. Abigail Williams started the Jacob's accusations as near as I can make out. I don't know if she is getting her ideas from the Parris's, from your half-brother and his wife, or cooking them up on her own. In any case, she seems to have named your father, George, then your daughter and Sarah Churchill.

"The wiley magistrates brought Sarah Churchill in first for an informal interview with Reverend Noyes and Ezekiel Cheever. They frightened the poor girl with actual threats about being thrown into the dungeon with the terrible wizard Burroughs and so on. Eventually she broke down and said what they wanted, which was that George, Sr. was a witch and had made her sign the book, and done the same to other members of the family.

"Like everyone else in the Village, old George had a pretty good idea how these things were done, and how fatal it was to admit to any supernatural event whatever, so he warned your daughter not to say anything at all that could be used by the magistrates. However, they brought her up before the little despots, and the girls terrorized her so far that she, too, gave in and said she had signed the book and her grandfather had made her do it.

"Nay, do not let your heart break over it, brother, they have done the same mean set of tricks to about ten young women so far, and it reflects no evil on you that she hadn't the strength to hold out against them."

Daniel spoke. "I suppose he fears, I suppose we fear, that she has been driven to the same kind of confusion my sister, her mother has fallen heir to," he explained with his arm about George's shoulders.

"It did not appear like that, but only the kind of distraction that great fear and their babble might cause in any tender heart.

"In any case, I will give you the better news. They issued warrants then, as you know, for you two and Rebecca. Sarah Churchill, after her first interview with Reverend Noyes, ran to Sarah Ingersoll, and poured out a confession in which she said it was all lies and that she feared she had undone her soul. Sarah Ingersoll listened to her and finally told her she ought to go back to the minister and tell the truth, but Sarah Churchill said he would not believe her. Sarah Ingersoll told Mary and she told John, who asked her to get Sarah Ingersoll to write a deposition. She is willing to do it."

John struck in, "Some at Salem gaol say Margaret has told them what really happened, too. We think there is a good chance that when the actual trials come about, these witnesses may be encouraged to speak the truth—especially when some of the depositions we have are brought forward."

"Ah, I see you are becoming barristers in my absence!" said Daniel.

"You have given us a good apprenticeship!" laughed Peter.

"A great many of the prisoners are now at Boston," continued Joseph. "But Edward and Sarah Bishop have recently escaped—and we guess they have gone up to Maine. The Indian attacks have been frequent up there lately, by all reports. Peter's Cloyce and Littlefield relatives are constantly sending petitions for more help. I don't suppose our officials are particularly interested in traveling through that territory if they can help it. The magistrates don't perceive the Bishops to be as important a catch as Reverend Burroughs was."

"But time runs on. Get out the refreshments, John, though let's not pause in our business. What matter's would you discuss, gentlemen?"

"The list of the arrests and related events grows too long to discuss. Roger Toothaker of Billerica, the doctor, is in gaol, accused by Elizabeth Hubbard, niece of his rival."

"Rather than recite the list, I have brought a copy with dates and a few notes," Joseph said, offering some folded sheets to Daniel. "Look it over and ask any questions you wish, but I would rather keep to the question of what we can and should be doing, than use this time to exchange information.

"Peter, you have said little enough. What suggestions have you to make?"

Peter shook his head of reddish straw in an awkward gesture. "I don't know. . . I guess one thing I think is that we should keep looking for others who are of like mind with us."

"Good suggestion, and one to be emphasized. Does anyone have anything to add on that heading?"

"Well, I have a name to add," said John, as he cut up a pie and distributed it, "I heard Ben Balch was saying some strong things against the magistrates, so I sounded him out, and found it was true. He said he had a lantern and a horse to lend to anybody that was accused by those girls. I told him that was good to know and that his lantern might be of use yet, but that he should be a lot more careful who he said it to. He was pretty gruff with me and demanded to know what I meant. I reminded him that John Procter, Giles Corey and Edward Bishop all ended up in gaol through speaking too loud and clear. 'Never you fear!' he said, 'if I have to use my own lantern and horse, I'll know how.' "

"But wasn't it young Ben's wife — Elizabeth — who testified against Sarah Bishop?" objected Daniel.

"Without a doubt," John replied, "I remember being struck then how she sounded like a proxy for Sarah's husband, Edward, Jr. Mostly she repeated things he once said, no doubt in heat, about his wife entertaining the devil in their house and so forth. It could be Ben Balch's stand is partly to make up for his wife's involvement. He told me he has charged her to hold her tongue."

"May the Lord grant us a great repentance!" sighed Sam. "If our sins have not thus been dealt with by the day of judgment, it will take the whole heaven of angels to sort them out."

"Yes," mused Daniel, "the blood of Christ is indeed the most efficient justice, with so much injustice concentrated in its shedding."

"But back to business!" said Joseph, in the manner of an unrelenting taskmaster. "What important matters would you raise, John?"

John said, "After watching these girls performing their afflicted antics over the last months, I'm ready to propose that we recognize different categories among them. This may not get us much further in any immediate way, but it may give us some landmarks as we arrange our tactics.

"A few seem to be originators. I believe from all we've heard that Betty Parris and Abigail derived this whole "game" from observing the girls with real afflictions and distractions of mind. Since Betty is young, the youngest of the bunch, and since she has been taken to Salem and kept at Stephen Sewall's, we have seen no more of her in the examinations. It appears she is not allowed near the other girls. In the unlikely event that someone might get her to admit to starting the whole game for fun and in pure imitation, she could be of great value to our efforts.

"But a second category is those who continue to elaborate along the lines that have been established. Abigail Williams seems to be the foremost of these, with Anna Putnam, Mary Walcott and Susannah Sheldon three more. They seem to have almost a ritual by which they require each new girl who is added to name a few more witches as well as further accusing those already in custody.

"A third category is those who merely follow the lead of the others. These are the most changeable—being ready to accuse or exonerate depending on what their friends do and say. Elizabeth Hubbard and Elizabeth Booth seem to fit this description. Mercy Lewis also seems in this category some of the time, although it is said she initiated the new accusations against Mary Easty.

"A related category is those who follow the lead of their parents and guardians. These may be our greatest problem, for they cannot be swayed, except by those same parents or guardians. Anna Putnam is the foremost of these. In the Nehemiah Abbott examination, she was the least willing to allow the possibility that he was innocent, although she finally did. And in the re-accusation of Mary Easty, Mercy Lewis took a very active lead. Behind both of them are Thomas and Anne Putnam.

"Although I place her in the second category, Abigail Williams is still a mystery to me. She seems to me an originator herself, now that Betty Parris is out of the picture. It might even be that she was the leader from the first. There is no discernible influence of the Parris adults on her, and this mightily puzzles me. Do they encourage her or do they attempt to restrain her? If neither, why not?

"Sam thinks Reverend Parris doesn't want to inquire more closely into what Abigail and the others are doing, because he takes a lofty view of his role as a spiritual leader, who must withhold his judgment and remain objective. He does not seem willing to admit he was the first to turn the girls' games into a public spectacle. But it could be he also regularly questions Abigail and thus gives her more ideas."

Sam spoke up, "I think he suspects how flimsy the girls' evidence really is, and is afraid to know more. Is it possible the Parrises fear Abigail, themselves? Quite a number of such maids have accused their masters and mistresses."

When John had finished, George spoke up, "Aye, the magistrates used Sarah Churchill against father that way, it seems — and Mary Warren against the Procters."

"Yes, George, but you would have been proud of your father. He gave not an inch. He said they might as well accuse him for a buzzard as a wizard. And he called the girls 'witch bitches,' according to your family style of rhyme."

"An excellent summary, John," Daniel said, with a dip of his head. "The girls have certainly been the key, but is it a key we can accurately understand or expose in court?

"The lock, however, into which that key has fitted so well, is the mind of the ministers and magistrates. And the door which they open and close is the general fear and ancient superstition of the whole colony.

"That door is well nigh fully open, and those who are about to become the door-keepers on the Court of Oyer and Terminer are likely to be higher men yet. Pray that they are godly men led 'sola scriptura,' rather than these half-Christian, half-magicians who have so far directed us."

"Mr. Andrews, what deep meditations have you formulated here in your 'den' as you call it."

"No offense was intended to the kind landlord, Joseph. We are deeply grateful. Nor have we been at all troubled by bears, although I have once or twice mistaken George's snoring for the same."

After a smile from Joseph and a grin from George, Daniel went on.

"This habit of analysis, which John demonstrates, may be one of the more important things we can cultivate. All disorder must at last be some kind of departure from or parody of an order. Further, the processes which lead to it must have beginnings and patterns, agencies and motives. This is not some colossal accident that has befallen Salem Village, nor simply a mysterious act of God, though he intend to use it for our humiliation.

"Analysis, of course has its limitations. As Augustine concluded, evil is the absence of good and it does not ultimately make sense, nor can rational explanations get to its roots. It does follow certain patterns, however, otherwise we could not define particular sins, nor apply particular remedies to them.

"We need imagination, that great gift of God, to counter the destruction wrought by fancy, the finest plaything of the devil. "

"I hope you are aware," Joseph interrupted him, "That the elegance and profundity of your insights are lost on most of the rest of us. Perhaps if you could bring them down to words of two syllables and sentences of but ten words."

"As you wish, sir, I will save the philosophy for the cave bears which roar when George is asleep.

"I propose that we continue to look for the odd events, odd statements, and persons who seem out of place in these matters. An apparent anomaly in a mysterious matter is often the first opening into its secrets."

"Thank you. That is fairly clear. Let's all take it seriously. And now, Sam—although you contributed something earlier, is there anything you would add?"

"Just one odd event, as Daniel calls them. Mary Ingersoll, who unbeknownst to herself, is practically a member of this group, told me the girls mentioned Mistress Thacher of Boston last week. It seems she has been spoken of formerly during examinations, possibly by Tituba, by one of the Sheldons and by John Indian. The name did not mean anything to me, but Mary mentioned it to the Deacon, and he rather abruptly said those were old and evil rumors, which made Mary more curious. She then asked her husband, who said Mistress Thacher of Boston was Judge Corwin's mother-in-law. If these girls go looking for more witches in such lofty places, that seems to me one sure-fire way these mockeries will come to an end."

"Oh, that takes the prize, Sam! All those in favor say 'aye'!"

A chorus of hearty "ayes" filled the cave and as quickly sank into the stone.

"Tom Preston helped me with that one," said Sam, nearly blushing.

"Oh, yes. Tom," said John, remembering something on his mind.

"I would like the permission of the company to open up what

we are doing to Tom Preston. He is so heartily sorry for his signature on the first complaints and has stewed so long in his misery, that I am certain he has as strong a desire as we to throw his weight against this evil. He has said as much to me, and I nearly bit my tongue off not to do more than commiserate with him."

"An important practical consideration — on a broader scale as well as in regard to the particular person you suggest," said Joseph after finishing a puff upon his pipe.

"We still have Will Rayment on our books, although we have been careful of him since his testimony against Bridget Bishop. Dare we widen this circle any more?"

"My counsel," said Daniel," is that we not widen this circle in the sense of inviting others to conclaves such as this. On the other hand, each should widen his own circle as carefully as he can, so that we involve others in the kinds of stratagems we find to be most effective. I think, for instance that John, or John and Sam, might well tell Tom what they have been doing, without mentioning the rest of us. There is no purpose in letting all those who think like us know all our names. In the unlikely event one proves a weak link, the damage to our enterprise might thus be limited, and the rest of the conspiracy continue to operate."

"Do you fear Tom might expose us!" asked John, with some heat.

"No, I intend no such implication," answered Daniel, "but I see no purpose to giving anyone else a list of our names. Beyond that, there is already an inefficiency to our meeting — a good month it has been — which could be overcome if each of us were free to operate in his own circle, involving those he deems reliable so far as he thinks it necessary."

"He's right," said Joseph, "we can operate as teams, pulling the same load, without all being harnessed shoulder to shoulder. Do you see the point, John?"

"I suppose I do," said John, still mulling this over, "each of us in our daily rounds can do what he can without consulting all the rest on every decision. I confess I find great comfort in the greater wisdom of the rest, though."

"We need not dispense with that, so far as policy and general direction," answered Daniel. "We should still meet, perhaps every week or two, when we can, but meanwhile we need to keep about our father's business."

"And we can take every opportunity for informal

consultation between times, where any feels unsure about a particular course of action," Joseph added.

Two bats, dropping from the back of the cave, punctuated the discussion by flying over the low fire and out the cave door.

"At least you two needn't grow lonely!" Sam remarked after a startled moment.

"Some witches have familiar cats --see, we two have only bats," George said.

"Well, the rest of us had better flit on our ways, too," Joseph concluded, "Peter, would you do us the honor of a benediction?"

After the descent of the rope, the four visitors went through the dark woods by pairs as far as their respective roads. There they divided again and made their solitary ways toward home.

The next day the magistrates sent four more prisoners, those examined that morning, to Boston gaol.

Chapter Thirty-Seven — Trial Preparations
(27 - 30 May)

Even so, brethren, it will be between you and your magistrates. If you stand for your natural, corrupt liberties and will do what is good in your own eyes, you will not endure the least weight of authority, but will murmur, and oppose, and be always striving to shake off that yoke. But if you will be satisfied to enjoy such civil and lawful liberties, such as Christ allows you, then will you quietly and cheerfully submit unto that authority which is set over you, in all the administrations of it, for your good. Wherein, if we fail at any time, we hope we shall be willing, by God's assistance, to hearken to good advice from any of you or in any other way of God. So shall your liberties be preserved in upholding the honor and power of authority amongst you.
  -- John Winthrop, ***Speech to the General Court*** (1645).

On May 27th, the day after the General Fast, and perhaps in answer to its prayers, Governor Phips, hitherto preoccupied with war on the eastern borders, was sufficiently informed about our troubles to intervene. He decided the situation was too serious to wait until October when the legislature was expected to reorganize and convene the courts. Governor Phips therefore issued a commission for a Court of Oyer and Terminer (Hearing and Determination) and appointed judges.

The members of the court were Lieutenant Governor William Stoughton of Dorchester; Bartholomew Gedney and John Hathorne (members of Mr. Noyes' Salem Church); John Richards of Boston (of the Mathers' Old North Church); Samuel Sewall, Peter Sargent, and Waitstill Winthrop (all of Boston and Reverend Willard's Old South Church); Thomas Danforth of Framingham; and Nathaniel Saltonstall of Haverhill. A quorum of five was necessary for this high court to sit.

The high court was scheduled to convene on the 2nd day of June. William Stoughton, as Lieutenant Governor, was appointed President of the court. Thomas Newton was appointed King's Attorney General to prosecute the cases. Stephen Sewall, brother of Samuel and temporary guardian of Betty Parris, was appointed Clerk.

On May 28th, in what seemed further evidence of the alliance of Indians and witches, Captain John Littlefield (brother of Peter Cloyce's first wife) wrote a petition to the General Assembly from Wells, Maine. The petition asked that a chaplain be sent them "due to ye distressed condition of ye inhabitants of Wells who are not only objects of pity with reference to ye enemy and ye length of ye war but also with reference to their spiritual concerns". The settlers "to eastward" had been frequently subject to Indian attack during the previous two years, and had several times petitioned for troops and aid. At the top of the list of signatures on the previous two petitions had been the name of George Burrough's. This plea for new chaplain was due to Reverend Burrough's arrest and transport to Salem. The "wizard" had been the only minister in the vicinity of Wells.

On that same Saturday, magistrates Corwin and Hathorne issued a warrant for Elizabeth Howe of Topsfield/Ipswich. The next day, Constable Ephraim Wildes of Topsfield brought Elizabeth Howe to Ingersoll's. Reverend Parris once more recorded the examination. Mercy Lewis, Mary Walcott, Mary Warren, Susannah Sheldon, John Indian, and Anna Putnam acted out their afflictions throughout the questioning.

On May 29th the daughter of Ann Douglas died in the Village. Reverend Parris wrote in the church records that she died "by witchcraft I doubt not."

The next day a complaint was issued by our two magistrates against Elizabeth, wife of John Fosdick of Malden, and Elizabeth, wife of Stephen Paine of Charlestown. The complaint was signed by Nathaniel Putnam and another representative of an old Village family, Joseph Whipple, on behalf of the "afflicted," Mercy Lewis and Mary Warren. The girls were casting their accusations far beyond the borders of the Village, and Lieutenant Putnam, who earlier supported the Nurses, had been enlisted in their cause.

Tuesday, magistrates Hathorne, Corwin and Gedney examined Martha Carrier, John Alden, Wilmott Redd, Elizabeth Howe and Philip English. Mr. English had been apprehended in Boston after evading arrest for several weeks.

The arrest of Wilmot "Mammy" Redd (of Marblehead) originated in old accusations arising from a grudge between Mistress Simms who once threatened to charge Mammy Redd's maid for stealing. After that Mistress Simms was afflicted with severe constipation and an inability to pass urine supposedly for a considerable period of time! Mistress Simms left the area and recovered. But for this and other witchery, Mammy Redd's reputation was established.

Rumors had been circulating that the famous Captain John Alden, seventy-year old son of the Mayflower stalwart, was also accused. His name stood so high that it might have been ignored, like that of Reverend Samuel Willard, but early descriptions of a dignified looking white-haired man from Boston had kept the magistrates' eyes sharp for some high wizard in addition to Reverend Burroughs and John Procter.

Captain John Alden, son of the highly respected Plymouth patriarch, was as famous a Christian gentleman and ship's captain as lived in all the colonies. His was the highest rung of the colonial ladder to which the accusations had yet climbed. Captain Alden was formally charged on Monday, July 28th. Although he was well known to all the leading men of Boston as a member in good standing of Old South Church, Deputy Governor Stoughton did not hesitate to send him to Salem to be examined by Mr. Hathorne, Mr. Corwin, and Mr. Gedney.

Sarah Rice of Reading was also listed in the mittimis with John Alden.

Two days later Mistress Cary escaped from Cambridge prison.

The next day Mr. Alden was examined.

By arrangement a number of Captain Alden's friends came into the meeting house at the same time he was brought in, and the magistrates did nothing to indicate which was he.

The afflicted girls put on their customary display of torments and "juggling tricks," to use the captain's own words.

Mr. Gedney addressed the girls and asked them several times who hurt them? Anna Putnam pointed several times at one of the other men, Captain Hill, but said nothing until someone who stood behind her stooped down and whispered to her. Thereupon she cried out, "Alden, Alden is the one who hurts me!"

Mr. Hathorne asked if she had ever seen Captain Alden. "No," she said.

"Then how do you know it is he who hurts you?"

"The man told me," she replied.

The magistrates were not satisfied with that answer. Attempting once more the roughhewn test for identity they used with Nehemiah Abbott, the magistrates sent everyone in the Meeting out in the street. There a ring was formed of all the men from

Boston. The afflicted were then brought out and asked to identify the guilty one.

"There stands Alden," cried Susannah Sheldon, "a bold fellow with his hat on before the judges! He sells powder and shot to the French and Indians, and lies with the Indian squaws, and has Indian papooses." These vicious rumors seem to have come to the girls' ears in conversations at home and among themselves.

"Take away his sword," cried Abigail, "for he afflicts us with it."

The marshal took his sword away and took him across and up the street to Dounton's. He was kept there for short time. Then he, the witnesses and the officials formed a strange cavalcade, going to the Salem Village meeting-house, where the three magistrates conducted his examination.

Captain Alden is not a tall man and so many of us were crowded into the Village meeting house, many standing, that most of the spectators could not see the defendant. The magistrates consulted and required Captain Alden to stand upon a chair.

When the girls cried out that he pinched them, Mr. Hathorne told the marshal to hold Captain Alden's hands.

They brought Anna forward in a fit and held her hand out to touch him, at which she recovered at once.

Captain Alden asked the magistrates why they thought he came to the Village to afflict the girls, whom he did not know and had never seen before?

Mr. Gedney suggested the devil was "bringing him out" and advised him to confess, and give glory to God.

Captain Alden said, "I hope I shall give glory to God, and never gratify the devil. But I ask all you that know me, if you ever suspected me to be such as I am now accused of. Can you offer any evidence from your own knowledge, that might give you suspicion of me being a witch?

Mr. Gedney said, "I have known you many years, and have been at sea with you. In the past, I always looked upon you as an honest man, but I now have seen cause to alter my judgment."

"I am sorry for that," said Captain Alden, "but I hope in God to make clear my innocence, so that you recall that judgment again. I hope with Job to maintain my integrity till I die."

"Look again upon your accusers," said Mr. Gedney.

When he did, nearly all the girls tumbled down upon the floor.

"Why do they fall when you look at them?" asked Mr. Gedney.

"Why is it you do not fall down when I look at you?" answered Captain Alden.

The girls were again brought "to be healed by his touch."

Captain Alden, for all his boldness was beginning to be shaken by all this. He said, "what strange providence of God is this, to suffer these creatures to accuse innocent persons!"

"Why do you speak of the providence of God?" asked Mr. Noyes. "God by his providence governs the world, and keeps it in peace. He does not disrupt it or send to afflict innocent persons. Otherwise the world would be given over to chaos!"

"What say you why these are afflicted so?" asked Mr. Gedney.

"There must be a lying spirit in them," answered Mr. Alden, " for I can assure you that there is not a word of truth in all these say of me."

However, by the time the examination was over his former friends among the magistrates were quite satisfied he was as guilty as the rest. Captain Alden was bound over to Boston gaol. John Arnold received him respectfully and thereafter was even more lenient with the other prisoners.

He remained in prison nearly 15 weeks, keeping informed of the progress of the trials in Salem. Finally, in early September, when all hope of justice before the court had been dashed, Captain Alden allowed his pastor, Mr. Willard, to prevail upon him to escape, and did not come back until early the next spring.

Unfortunately that opportunity was not available to most of the accused. They had no hope other than in the court — and that hope remained tenuous.

The 31st of May was a day of gatherings and formulating, of planning and expandings, of preparations for the next weeks and months which were to jolt and toss us into the sorest depths of our troubles.

Thomas Newton, the King's Attorney-General, sent an official letter to Isaac Addington, Suffolk County Sheriff, requiring that a number of the earliest accused be brought from Boston gaol back to Salem for trial before the Court of Oyer & Terminer to be held at Salem on Thursday the second day of June:

. . . Sarah Good the wife of William Good of Salem farmes

*husbandman, Rebeca Nurse the wife of Francis Nurse of Salem
Village husbandman, John Willard of the same place husbandman,
John Procter of Salem farmes husbandman, Elizabeth his wife,
Susanna Martin of Amesbury widdow, Bridgett Bishop alias
Olliver the wife of Edw'd Bishop of Salem Sawyer, Alice Parker the
wife of John Parker of Salem seaman, & Tittuba Indian in our
prison und'r yo'r custody as it is said detained together with the day
& cause of the taking & detaining of the s'd Sarah &c . . .*

Testimony in the trials indicates the "afflicted girls" were
making a fuss about these prisoners in particular. That Tituba was
included seems to indicate that the early plan of the high court was
to try the "confessors" like the rest.

Warrants for "grand jurors" for the "Jury of Inquiry" were
sent out. They were called to attend the opening day of the high
court, that is June 2nd.

Warrants were also sent out for the jurors of the Jury of Trials
of life and death which was to bring in the final verdicts:

> *To the Sheriff of the County of Essex*
> *You are required in their Majesties Name to impanel and return
> forty good and lawful men of the freeholders and other freemen of
> your bailiwick duly qualified to serve on the Jury of Trials of life and
> death at the next session of their Majesties Special Court of Oyer
> and Terminer, in Salem . . ., whom you are by your self, under
> sheriff, or deputy, to summon to attend the said court at the time
> above specified.*

Anne Putnam, Sr. from whom we had heard little for weeks,
swore out a deposition before magistrates Hathorne and Corwin that
day which spoke of being afflicted by a number of those already
accused. The next day she claimed to be particularly plagued by
Rebecca Nurse.

Also on 31 May, Cotton Mather sent a scholarly and pastoral
directive, "An Essay concerning Witchcraft," to John Richards, the
judge who was a member of his congregation. In it Mather makes a
distinction between "lesser criminals" (by which he seems to mean
confessed witches) and the others.

> What if some of the lesser criminalls be onely scourged with
> lesser punishments, and also put upon some solemn, open,
> publicke and explicit renunciation of the Divil? . . . Or what if

the death of some of the offenders were either diverted or inflicted, according to the success of such their renunciation?

Apparently Cotton Mather and his parishioner Mr. Richards, were beginning to recognize the potential results of what went forward, and to wonder about alternative sentencing.

In his letter to Secretary Addington, Attorney General Newton requested the records of Bridget Bishop's 1679 charges and trial for witchcraft. In addition he indicated his desire that Tituba, and "Mistress Thacher's Maid" be "transferred as Evidences, but [we] desire they may not come amongst the prisoners but rather by themselves."

Others besides the witch-hunters were making preparations for the trials. In keeping with the conspirator's resolution to set up peripheral circles, the Nurse men went around among their kinsmen and asked them to keep their ears cocked for any reference that might show up the "afflicted" as shams and games-players. Within a few days, their effort bore some fruit.

The potter, James Kettle, who had testified against Bridget Bishop and eagerly affirmed Elizabeth Hubbard's accusations against Sarah Bishop two weeks earlier initiated a conversation with Peter Cloyce. Goodman Kettle had suddenly grown more skeptical about Elizabeth Hubbard, wherefore Peter persuaded him to commit his reservations to paper. It seems Goodman Kettle had "some discourse" with Elizabeth on May 29th, and in the course of it found her to speak several untruths. He said she "denied the sabbath day" saying there was no need for her to keep it. Furthermore she said she herself had not gone to meeting but rather had gone up to James Holten's. Goodman Kettle not only lost his enthusiasm for the afflicted girl's veracity, but began to wonder if, rather than an instrument of good, she herself might have signed the devil's book.

Peter's brother-in-law, Joseph Trumball, reported something he had heard from Robert Moulton (father of one of Giles Corey's sons-in-law) concerning some things Susannah Sheldon had said. Sam and Goodman Trumball spoke with Goodman Moulton and were able to persuade him to write out his account of those things. It read:

The testimony of Robert Moulton senor who testifieth and saith that I, waching with Susannah Sheldon since she was afflicted, I heard her say that the witches halled her upone her

bely through the yeard like a snacke and halled her over the
stone walle & presontly I heard her contradict her former
discource and said that she came over the stone wall her selfe
and I heard her say that she rid upone a poole to Boston and
she said the divel caryed the poole.

The opponents of the witch prosecution were hopeful that the
higher court would take such testimony seriously and begin to
regard the "afflicted" more critically. We were poised on the brink of
a new, if cautious, optimism.

Chapter Thirty-Eight — Whither Thou Wouldest Not
(John 21:18)

*And this seems to be the meaning of Solomon in the text: "An adverse or
evil time" (Eccles. 9.12) Some times the times favor the enterprises of men,
sometimes they frown upon them. At one time, wise and good men stand
up for the defense of their country and liberties thereof, and prosper in it;
the times favor them, there is a concurrence of all manner of the
furtherances and advantages. At another time, they may endeavor it and
the times frown upon them, the spirit and humor of the people is
degenerated, and they swim against the stream and are lost in the attempt.
And we say, such a man was worthy of better times, had been a brave man
if he had lived in better times, his worth had been more known and prized,
and he would have had better success. So when the time of judgment upon
a people is come, then wrath ariseth against them without remedy; and then
the strong man may fight for the defense of such a country, and the wise
man endeavor to deliver the city, but all in vain: they shall miscarry in the
undertaking. -- Urian Oakes, **The Sovereign Efficacy of Divine
Providence** (1677)*

T he first prisoners to be tried by the high court were
transported back from Boston to Salem. The accused were not tried
in the order of their arrests or examinations. Whether these were
thought most wicked or selected for other elusive reasons, the
transport included: Sarah Good, Rebecca Nurse, John Willard, John
Procter, Elizabeth Procter, Susanna Martin, Bridget Bishop, Alice
Parker, and Tituba Indian. Tituba was the only confessed witch
among them, and she was brought as a witness. Also brought as a
witness, but never giving public testimony was "Mistress Thacher's
maid".

Sarah Good had become almost cheerful caring for her new
baby. Although the child was by now very sick, Sarah did not
recognize or else would not acknowledge the fact. Dorcas had
responded to her sister's advent and her mother's joy by becoming
much livelier. All the members of the little family group brought
comfort to the other prisoners. But Dorcas was not named in the
transport order. Nor could Reverend Burroughs, John Procter or
any of the older woman persuade the gaoler or the deputies to send

Dorcas with her mother. Sarah grumbled when first told, but looking down at her baby, she reconciled herself. She gave her older child a kiss and allowed Dorcas to kiss the baby before she turned and went out the door after the deputy.

As her mother withdrew, two women knelt beside Dorcas. Martha Corey put her arm around the child's shoulders, as Elizabeth Emerson spoke haltingly to her. Dorcas watched her mother disappear in faded brown down the dark hall. Martha looked into the windows of that small soul and saw shutters drawn across them. But even after Martha was eventually transported to Salem, Elizabeth remained in gaol with Dorcas. For the rest of Dorcas' imprisonment, the young woman tried to be for the girl what she had not been for her own babies.

The prisoners emerged from Boston gaol into a fine spring day. As their wagon set out across the countryside, they found it rich with smells of flower and field, sounds of birdsong and running water, and white clouds floating across blue skies. Rebecca and Elizabeth Procter took occasion aboard the rocking wagon to enjoy these things — things foreign and delightful after their dismal confinement. But most of their time was given to watching Sarah Good and her tiny daughter who was by then in the deep throes of congestion. Her whistling breath and tiny coughs seemed to drown out the cheerful birds and dominated the thoughts and prayers of her fellow voyagers.

Sarah herself still seemed quiet and gentle, a "new creature," the Perpetua of Reverend Burrough's account, whose joy was centered in the baby in her arms. Her companions were deeply concerned over the seriousness of the child's illness, particularly since Sarah acted as though the child were well. They thought perhaps she felt it her duty to be cheerful for the infant's sake.

About half an hour after the deputies stopped the transport in Lynn to give the prisoners food and offer opportunity for relief, Rebecca heard what she had dreaded now for many days. After a series of small, but profound wheezes, the child inhaled for what seemed an impossibly long time, then gave a tiny sigh as of greatest contentment — and became silent.

Sarah looked down at the child with no more concern apparent in her countenance and manner than she had manifested since its birth. She gently arranged the blanket which haloed the little face, and gazed with affection on the baby as though she had at last fallen asleep. Rebecca and Elizabeth looked at one another wide-eyed, almost in horror at the realization that Sarah did not know or would not acknowledge the child had gone. Both looked back at her in wonder, then gazed around the wagon as every other face looked to them in interrogation.

Tears rose and ran down both women's cheeks and they bowed their heads as they struggled to remain silent themselves. The child had been a blessing. As quickly as the knowledge of its death spread to all, each reeled as under God's sentence. All sank into despair. Most saw in the innocent child's death a sign their lives were required and would be taken.

Alice Parker was the first to break the silence. She began to sob through clenched teeth, and shake at each sob with her face dropping into her hands again and again as her whole body shook free of her fierce restraint. At this the men, too, began to cry freely, though more silently. John Willard could be heard in soft staccato sobs emitted through his nose as he kept his mouth firmly shut.

After the first fit of sorrow, Elizabeth and Rebecca again focused upon Sarah, who held the child to her as the wagon continued to jolt over the rocky road. If she seemed to listen for some missing sound, it was only as though some obscure thing were slowly occurring to her.

Thus they continued for another two hours, until, as the wagon came into the eastern road which approached Gallows Hill, Sarah opened her blouse to give the child her breast.

Rebecca and Elizabeth sensed what was coming. They moved close to her on either side of the wagon floor. Sarah carefully placed the blanket over her shoulder and raised the child. She placed the tiny cold lips against her and held the child thus for a minute. She reached in and gave the child the smallest shake, and only a moment later threw off the blanket and lifted the tiny body to gaze intently into the little face. She shook it again then, sharply and when the small head rolled limp and lifeless she screamed. The remaining half hour was the closest any of them had come to seeing one of their number truly possessed.

The wagon had halted upon her first scream.   The two deputies on horseback came crowding against the wagon and began to shout at Sarah to be quiet. She replied with malediction and curse, her face transformed into a malignant mask of suffering and hatred. She spoke explicitly of hell and of the devil, and called them every evil name she knew. When her fellow prisoners tried to restrain her or speak to her she turned on them with like language and violent gestures.

Now Rebecca began to cry uncontrollably herself. After a few minutes wrestling, the deputies tied Sarah's arms to her sides and put a gag around her mouth. Their greatest effort had been expended trying to take the child away from her after they realized it had died. They set the small bundle on the tailgate as they put Sarah under forcible restraint. Elizabeth recovered the fragile form and held it in her arms close to Sarah. For her efforts she received only the muffled curses of the mother.

The horses had become restive and were skittish for the rest of the journey. The driver cursed them in restrained echoes of his gagged prisoner.

At Dounton's Gaol, the child's body was taken away. The prisoners were taken down a narrow stair to the basement where, in contrast to the open attic, small rooms had been partitioned off, each with but a small opening through the brick foundation to give the only light, excepting one lantern in the central area. The cells had no doors, and the hard earthen floors were cold. But they spread what bedding they had and ate sparely of the few cold victuals they had brought.

Sarah Good was shackled head and foot, although her gag was removed. Her shackles were further tied to a staple set in the wall. There she banged her head for nearly an hour, until she lapsed into hoarse cries which toward the middle of the night became grumbles and whispers. At midnight those near her began to hear her calling for Dorcas and this did not cease until the wee hours of the morning. Few of the others slept, or found much rest for their souls that night.

Some kinder official had spread the news of the transport, so the families did not have to go to Boston to learn of it. The next morning Francis, John, Francis, Jr. and wife Sarah (come up from Reading) and Rebecca, Jr., came to see Mother Nurse. William Good came to claim the child's body, which was given him only after the learned doctors determined it had not died of something diabolical. The other families brought food and a few clothes, assuming correctly that the authorities with characteristic insensibility had not shipped their paraphernalia from Boston. There were many visitors, and all were crowded into the basement cells at the same time.

When Rebecca told her family about the end of Sarah Good's child, she wept again and turning to Francis sobbed, "It's so hard!"

"Aye, Mother," he answered with that gruffness with which

she knew he always covered his emotion, "It's hard as nails and we can but pray it will be softer presently."

"At every turn it seems harder to forgive them," she sobbed.

Thus far, during the ten weeks in which she had so often repeated this theme, Francis had repressed his anger, or turned it and the conversation in other directions, but the cumulative frustration was too much for him now. There was anger in his voice as he answered.

"Forgive them! No, we should not even try. They are the evildoers, theirs is the sin, the injustice. To forgive them is to let them go on, to pursue this madness to the horrible end it will surely go to—unless instead of forgiving them we oppose them with all our hearts and with all the means God gives us..."

He paused then, hearing his own tone and seeing her dear and tearful face before him.

". . .few though they seem," he abruptly ended, but with little vehemence left.

John interposed in that awkward way children do when they think their parents are beyond their depth.

"All Father means, Mother, is that it seems ill timing to speak of forgiveness now, when so much is at stake. The time to forgive will be when this madness is ended, and the judges and deputies gone back to punishing evildoers. Offering forgiveness at this time seems like giving them further license to pursue what these lunatic girls have brought upon us."

Rebecca Nurse listened carefully to her son, and saw his father nodding his head. The others, too, gave affirmation in their countenances. The older woman turned her head to the side and down and seemed to ponder what he said.

"Yes," she replied after a time, "I think I see what you are saying. And I have grown less sure of many things over these weeks. I think it may be a difference of callings. For surely all of us here pray that those on the outside will do whatever can be done to right this wrong.

"But you see, that is all we can do in here—comfort each other and forgive. The gospel is much simpler in gaol. The good works are few and clear and right before one. The chief thing we can do for one another is help bear the spiritual burdens that come with despair and bitterness. We have no choice but to encourage one another to forgive.

"So long as what you are doing is for the good, perhaps it is not the main thing for you. But for us there are continual opportunities either to hate and curse as poor Sarah Good does now again — or . . ."

Rebecca interrupted her mother then, fearful to hear the word one more time. It sounded so foreign there, huge and meaningless and not fit to be spoken in the cell or even in the building. She did not feel the same anger the men seemed to feel, but rather an impatience to speak of things that would make a difference — that would bring relief to her beloved namesake, and the many other godly people who shared this dishonorable dwelling with her. She did not want that comfort crowded out by something so alien and unsympathetic as forgiveness.

"They say the trials of inquest will begin Monday," she said. "Have you heard the governor has appointed a high court headed by Mr. Stoughton, who was minister at Dorchester and with other respected men who will certainly see the errors in all this."

"Oh, how much I hope so!" said her mother, "It would be so lovely to go back to my own home and have the little ones about me again. How are they all?"

Francis, Jr. and Sarah brought Rebecca up to date on their children, the youngest, Jonathan, born only three weeks before her arrest. She made much of having three grandsons named Jonathan, born within a few weeks of one another.

They spoke further of the family. Francis and John mentioned the crops and cattle. Finally Francis brought from behind his back a bouquet of wildflowers they had picked on the way.

"Oh, they are beautiful" she said, and her lined face was transformed in her smile. "Consider the lilies of the field, my dear ones — we also must take no thought for the morrow."

As the Nurses rode back along the road, Francis, Jr. said, "Take no thought for the morrow! With all this madness there's little else I think about!"

Chapter Thirty-Nine -- Fair Days of June

S(alem). We are willing to hearken to reason.
B(oston). That's well: Do you really believe that all the persons accused
are witches?
S. God forbid that I should be so uncharitable.
B.This is plain contradiction: for if you believe the former conclusion,
you must either suspect the accusers of falsehood, which you will not hear,
or of delusion, which you deny, or that all so accused are guilty.
--Some Miscellany Observations On our Present Debates
Respecting Witchcrafts, in a Dialogue Between S. & B. By P.E. and J.A,
Printed by William Bradford for Hezekiah Usher, Philadelphia,
1692.

The beautiful days of June, with intermittent rain, seemed
to mock the events of those first days of trials before the Court of
Oyer and Terminer. There was still an element of uncertainty
beneath blue skies curtained every few days by low, smoky clouds.
More people were coming and going in the streets of Salem, but
words were often cut short, and emotion restrained. We did not yet
know much about the higher court and the judicial officers who were
to continue in pursuit of our "witches".

Soon we were to get the first sight of the goal toward which
our magistrates were leading us. The pace of events continued to
accelerate. Most of us had our minds occupied in keeping up with
them.

Public interest was much aroused when complaints were
rumored against Margaret Thacher of Boston, widow of Reverend
Thomas Thacher and mother-in-law of Judge Corwin. She had been
subject of witchcraft rumors for a number of years. Several among
our "afflicted" named her.

Reverend Thacher had been minister first at Weymouth, and
afterwards at Boston's Third (Old South) Church, where he was
joined by Reverend Willard in 1678. Her first husband was Jacob
Sheaffe, the wealthiest man in Boston when he died in 1659. Her
daughter, Elizabeth, was first married before she was sixteen to
Robert Gibbs. After he died, Elizabeth married Jonathon Corwin.

The case—or non-case—of Margaret Thacher provided a

stark example of the divide between God's law and that by which our trials were conducted. "My brethren, have not the faith of our Lord Jesus Christ, the Lord of glory, with respect of persons," says the book of James, and goes on:

> *For if there come unto your assembly a man with a gold ring, in goodly apparel, and there come in also a poor man in vile raiment; and ye have respect to him that weareth the gay clothing, and say unto him, Sit thou here in a good place; and say to the poor, Stand thou there, or sit here under my footstool: Are ye not then partial in yourselves, and are become judges of evil thoughts?*
> *(James 2:1-4)*

So far as any of us knew, whether or not she wore a gold ring, Mistress Thacher was never even summoned before the magistrates—while many of those poorer and less well-connected, were made to sit for months on the cold floors of gaols.

The dangers of favoritism in law is both warned against in scripture, and guarded against in our written codes, as in this oath taken by Thomas Newton, King's Attorney-General for our trials:

> *You Thomas Newton, Gentleman, being appointed to perform the Office of their Majesties' Attorney-General in the prosecution of the several persons to be indicted and tried before their Majesties' Justices of Oyer and Terminer now sitting, and from time to time to sit, by vertue of the commission now published, and in all other matters that may be requisite in the execution of the same do swear, that according to your best skill, you will act truly and faithfully on their Majesties' behalf, as to the law and justice doth appertain, without any favour or affection. So help you God.*

While only a few were active agents of the "favour or affection" shown some, many of those in office knew of their machinations. No public announcement was made that Mistress Thacher would not be tried, nor that her maid's bewitchment was being attributed to some other "witch" rather than to the mistress she accused, nor that the "afflicted" accusers of the Village were told they were in error every time Mistress Thacher's name had been raised.

Thomas Brattle, one of the first to question the trials in print, eventually wrote:

416.

I do much admire that some particular persons, and particularly Mistress Thacher of Boston, should be much complained of by the afflicted persons, and yet that the Justices should never issue out their warrants to apprehend them, when as upon the same account they issue out their warrants for the apprehending and imprisoning many others. This occasions much discourse and many hot words, and is a very great scandal and stumbling block to many good people; certainly distributive Justice should have its course, without respect to persons; and although the said Mistress Thacher be mother in law to Mr. Corwin, who is one of the Justices and Judges, yet if Justice and conscience do oblige them to apprehend others on the account of the afflicted their complaints, I cannot see how, without injustice and violence to conscience, Mistress Thacher can escape, when it is well known how much she is, and has been, complained of.

Mistress Thacher's stature and wealth were well-known. Her husband been respected as a broad-minded minister and physician. In 1677 a year before his own death, Reverend Thacher published *A Brief Rule to Guide the Common People of New England how to order Themselves and Theirs in the Small Pocks or Measels,* recommendations for dealing with the epidemics that continued to sweep among the settlers and the Indians. Although it was said he had Anabaptist relatives in England with whom he maintained cordial relations, his reputation in Boston was very high. Reverend Thacher wrote a letter defending Welthean Richards, a member of his own congregation accused of witchcraft in 1654, which was one of the reasons that woman was not tried.

The early references by Tituba and others to a witch or witches "from Boston" had kept the magistrates and minister's ears cocked in that direction. By May, several of the afflicted had spoken of Mistress Thacher by description and name. Furthermore, investigations in Boston uncovered the fact that one of Margaret Thacher's own maids, Mercy Short, had recently accused her.

Mercy Short's family had lived "to eastward" at Salmon Falls, not far from the Reverend Burrough's parish of Wells, Maine. During a fierce Indian raid in March of 1690, Mercy had been captured by Indians. Her parents and most of the rest of the white settlers at Salmon Falls were killed, but she, three brothers, and two sisters were taken to Quebec by their captors. Six months later, through the mediation of a trader, they were brought back to Boston where they were indentured. Mercy became a servant in the household of the widow, Margaret Thacher, a year and a half before our troubles.

In mid- May 1692, Mistress Thacher heard that Dr. Roger Toothaker, an acquaintance of her first husband was ill in Boston gaol. She sent Mercy Short to the prison with some food and goods for the doctor. While at the prison Mercy encountered Sarah Good (a few days after Sarah's baby was born). Cotton Mather recorded a version of that meeting in his manuscript work, *A Brand Pluck'd From the Burning*, privately published the next year.

Mercy Short was allowed to enter the gaol in order to deliver her mistress's gifts to Dr. Toothaker. As she was leaving after her act of charity, Sarah Good approached her in her habitual way and asked,

"Hast thou any tobacco to loan a poor woman?"

On this occasion Mercy showed none of that virtue for which she was named.

"No!" was her sharp reply — then, after a moment's hesitation, she bent and scooped up a handful of straw which she threw at Sarah Good, saying, "that's tobacco good enough for you."

"May God treat you the worse!" snarled Sarah, and went off into more curses, less audible, while shaking her fists at Mercy.

Cotton Mather claims Mercy Short was immediately taken with fits like those of the other afflicted girls — then and frequently thereafter. However, the story seems to have been tailored to cover the awkward fact of the accusation of Mistress Thacher by the Village girls and Mercy Short, herself.

One wonders if being sent to take gifts to accused witches in gaol may not have clinched Mercy's suspicion of her mistress. Rumors and accusations had come to her ears before.

Attorney General Danforth did subpoena "Mistress Thacher's maid" along with Tituba as witnesses for the June trials before the Court of Oyer and Terminer. Nevertheless, no hearing or trial involving accusations against Mistress Thacher took place.

Nor did Mercy Short testify. Instead, Cotton Mather took Mercy Short into his own household in order to cure her of the bewitchment which he attributed to Sarah Good. He had done the same with the oldest Goodwin girl in 1688, inspired partly by the example of Reverend Willard and Sarah Knapp. And he was to "adopt" Margaret Rule six months after ministering to Mercy Short —

for similar reasons of scientific observation and Christian charity.
(He later claimed to have done the same with two or three others.
Some said that , for a time, Tituba was in his custody.) There were
very many "afflicted" at the time, however. Many wondered what
inspired him to choose Mercy Short out of all their number. This
solution to the awkward situation involving Mistress Thacher and,
through her, Mr. Corwin, is said to have been arranged through the
magistrates.

There is no reason to believe Margaret Thacher was any more
a witch than the others, but neither was she more innocent than they.
(Probably the accusations contributed to that lady's failure and death
the next year.)   Few felt any particular animosity toward her, but as
Mr. Thomas Brattle wrote, there was considerable heat generated
over the fact that such as she were not treated in the same manner as
the others accused. The "reign" of the afflicted girls was finally
brought to an end largely because they accused more and more
highly respected persons. Therefore it stands to reason that their
"reign" would have ended sooner had their earlier accusations been
treated equitably, that is, with equal seriousness.

Nor was Mistress Thacher alone in being treated in a
privileged manner. Mr. Hezekiah Usher, a sixty-five year old Boston
merchant was also accused, as Mr. Brattle mentioned:

> I cannot but admire that Mr. H.U. (whom we all think
> innocent,) should yet be apprehended on this account, and
> ordered to prison, by a mittimus under Mr. Lynd's [Jos.
> Lynde, 1637-1727, of Charlestown, member of council under
> the new charter] his hand, and yet that he should be suffered,
> for above a fortnight, to be in a private house; and after that,
> to quitt the house, the town, and the province, and yet that
> authority should not take effectual notice of it. Me thinks the
> same justice, that actually imprisoned others, and refused bail
> for them on any terms, should not be satisfyed without
> actually imprisoning Mr. U. and refusing bail for him, when
> his case is known to be the very same with the case or those
> others."

(Hezekiah Usher was also purported the agent of a
publication opposing the Salem trials. This dialogue between two
men -- of Boston and Salem, -- was published by William Bradford
in Philadelphia. Most now believe it was written by Reverend

Willard.)

   Other prominent citizens accused during the ensuing months included Reverend Willard himself, Mistress Moody (wife of his assistant minister), members of the Bradstreet family of Andover, and even Mr. Saltonstall after his resignation from the court. None of these were taken up by the courts, however, so they did not influence the course of the trials. So far the most prominent people accused and arrested were Reverend Burroughs, Mr. and Mistress English, Mistress Cary and Captain Alden. Most agree the first was fastened upon because of the early rumors of a "great wizard" who was a minister, but the other four were all to escape from prison through the help of influential friends.

   Mr. English, who had at first eluded the authorities, but was apprehended in Boston on May 31st, joined his wife in prison, where they posted bond and found two sureties, so that they were allowed to go out during the day, as long as they were back "by candlelight."

   Mary English wrote a deposition from gaol concerning the statements of Mary Warren in Salem a month earlier. She said Mary said the afflicted girls were all distracted and their testimony no more reliable than the well known distracted ramblings of Eleazer Keyser's daughter.

   As the Jury of Inquiry began to hear cases in preparation for the trials, Mary and Deliverance Hobbs, always useful sources of information, were again examined at Salem gaol. Now that several of the "unconfessed" witches were incarcerated in proximity to the "confessed" ones, the authorities hoped to find further proofs and confirmations. It seems the ministers and magistrates were unsure about three accusations in particular, and sought more insight from the "confessed witches". Both the Hobbs women were quick to oblige. They spoke of Rebecca Nurse and the two Proctors afflicting them then and there. Mary Warren testified further against Bridget Bishop the same day.

   Sarah, wife of Nicholas Rice of Reading, who had been named in the complaint with Captain Alden, was taken into custody and sent to Boston where she was to be kept for a long time without trial.

   We had come to the eve of the trials of the Court of Oyer and Terminer. The hope of justice had been continually deferred by the local magistrates. However we looked forward to a greater measure of justice from this higher court.

Chapter Forty — First Convicted
(June 1-7)

S(alem). But if the afflicted persons testifie that they see such an one afflicting them personally, must not this be convictive? . . .

B(oston). . . . supposeing the afflicted capable of giving a testimony, we will say; that if two witnesses aver such a thing, concerning a person, and he cannot prove himself to be in another place at the same time, he is legally convicted, and (if innocent yet) he must adore God's sovereign providence, and acquit the judges and juries: but what do you say, when they do it whilst the accused is in presence, and many witnesses must say it is not he? For he cannot be in two places at once.

S. That is the witchcraft in the case, which is hereby discovered; for it is the devil who doth all the mischief, only it is by their consent; otherwise they could not be supposed to be witches.

B. But when it is so, it still remains to prove their consent, which they deny; and your argument is not valid to evince it; it being a conclusion which you draw at leaff from uncertain premises, how then should it be certain? Where the Word of God requires that the thing be certain.

S. Witches then must not be known but by their personal confession: and this is to prevent the finding out of such abominations.

B. Otherwise innocent persons may be condemned for witches: and what a fearful thing is that? And know it, that God never intended to bring to light all hidden works or workers of darkness in this world; nor will it be imputed as a sin, that men did not punish secret sins without clear discoveries: but if in a precipitant zeal, they should cut off for crimes not proved, it will be imputed.

--***Some Miscellany Observations On our Present Debates Respecting Witchcrafts***, in a Dialogue Between S. & B, 1692.

T he suppression of charges and refusal to hear the case of Margaret Thacher as the Court of Oyer and Terminer opened in early June was an exception to the tenor of the hour. In fact the hurly-burly of judicial activity reached out from the court into nearly every corner of Essex County — magistrates and constables in every settlement trotted along roads and paths to serve complaints, and summons upon more and more defendants. Clerks burned their candles late into the night scribbling out documents: warrants, complaints and depositions. When they found time, they made clear copies of the notes from examinations and inquests. Servants came and went with refreshment for human, and fodder for animal, couriers. Witnesses, relatives of the accused, and curious neighbors were drawn to Salem as flies to the orb of a web. There in the center sat our justices at their bench.

A Jury of Inquest or Grand Jury began to hear and rule on all cases which had been brought thus far. This body of men was to decide whether each case was "Bill Avera," that is a "true bill," to be passed along to trial by jury before the Court of Oyer and Terminer. The Grand Jury was hearing depositions of old accusations "owned," that is, attested to, by the witnesses who had given them in earlier examinations, but they were also hearing new testimony — as various other people manifested that fever which turned nightmares or old mysteries into certainties of witchcraft.

The Jury of Inquest could have ruled that none of the cases were "true bills" and ended the trials then — but they were made up entirely of ordinary citizens like ourselves, who did not understand too much of what was going on, except that the magistrates had concluded we had many witches among us, and that most if not all those accused were witches indeed. The freemen on this jury expected that innocent persons, if any, among the accused would be exonerated in the trials, themselves, before the anointed men who were the appointed justices.

Within the circle of the afflicted girls, several of the late-comers such as Goodwife Vibber tried to improve their stock by making more accusations at this time. Susannah Sheldon began to see more ghosts, particularly of young children formerly thought to have died of disease, who cried out and told this "witness" which witches had killed them. For instance, Susannah claimed the ghosts of Thomas Green's twin babies appeared to her and told her Bridget Bishop had killed them by driving them into fits. A new witness, Joanna Childrin deposed that the apparition of Rebecca Nurse and the ghost of Goodman Harwood appeared to her, the latter claiming the former had killed him by pushing him off a cart, and driving the breath from his body.

The cases which the Jury of Inquest sent forward were by then recorded on paper, which is to say they were made up largely of old depositions newly attested to, or new depositions recorded by Secretary Stephen Sewall or the Attorney General, Mr. Newton, in support of indictments brought against the accused. But the depositions were not valid substitutes for the witnesses, who must be called and once again affirm their testimonies before the inquiring Jury.

The first Jury of Inquest had John Ruck as its foreman, of the family of Reverend Burrough's third wife, Sarah Ruck, she who is said to have abandoned the minister's children by earlier marriages not long after his arrest. There were originally nine trials scheduled for the first week of June: those of Rebecca, Sarah Good, John Willard, John and Elizabeth Procter, Susannah Martin, Bridget Bishop, Alice Parker and Tituba. The hustle and bustle was such, however, that the trials were carried forward more slowly than planned over the next months. The Jury of Inquest began it's job with dispatch, however, handling two or three cases per day for several days, and found "true bills" against all the cases brought before it. These then were passed on to trial before the high court and the Trial Jury, where things went a bit slower.

During the first two days, depositions were owned and testimony given against Bridget Bishop, Elizabeth Howe and Sarah Good. The cruelty of the girls' words reached such a pitch that Susannah Sheldon testified Sarah Good had killed her own "second child" by witchcraft. The look on Sarah's face when she heard it was enough to send even a calm person into fits. The afflicted girls were more obliging yet.

On the second day, two more preliminary examinations took place. The accused were Elizabeth Fosdick and Elizabeth Paine, who were complained of by Peter Tufts of Charlestown for afflicting his Negro woman. Peter Tufts was the second husband of Prudence Putnam, sister to Sergeant Thomas, Deacon Edward and Deliverance (Putnam) Walcott.

Also on the second, a Lecture Day, Sheriff George Corwin ordered physical examinations for six women, Bridget Bishop alias Oliver, Rebecca Nurse, Elizabeth Procter, Alice Parker, Susannah Martin and Sarah Good. Those subpoenaed to help in these examinations included nine women, but their chief was Dr. John Barton, "chyrurgeon" from Marblehead. They examined the women first at ten in the morning, then at four in the afternoon. Someone apparently had figured out the devil's feeding schedule — and part of the examiners' job was to perceive the differences in the women's bodies between the two examinations. Their official findings from the morning were:

We whose names are under written being commanded by Capt George Corwine Esq'r Sheriff of the County of Essex this 2'd day of June 1692 for to view the bodies of Bridgett Bishop alias Oliver, Rebecca Nurse, Elizabeth Procter Alice Parker, Susanna Martin, Sarah Good. The first three, namely: Bishop; Nurse; Procter, by diligent search have discovered a preternatural excrescence of flesh between the pudendum and anus much like to teats & not usual in women & much unlike to the other three that hath been searched by us & that they were in all the three women near the same place.

As expected, the afternoon physical examination revealed a change — the "witches" obviously had failed to heed the old warning, about those who sup with the devil using a long-handled spoon.

We whose names are subscribed to the within mentioned, upon a second search about 3 or 4 hours distance, did find said Bridgett Bishop alias Oliver in a clear & free state from any preternatural excrescence as formerly seen by us. Also Rebecca Nurse in stead of that excrescence within mentioned it appears only as a dry skin without sense & as for Elizabeth Procter which excrescence like a teat red & fresh, not anything appears, but only a proper procedeulia ani & as for Susanna Martin whose breast in the Morning search appeared to us very full; the nibbs fresh & starting, now at this searching all lank & pendant which is all at present from the within mentioned subscribers. And that that piece of flesh of Goodwife Nurses formerly seen is gone & only a dry skin nearer to the anus in another place.

Thus were the women treated to further invasive humiliation. Thus was Rebecca's secret ailment revealed — namely piles. The fact that she had any "excrescence" at all was enough to constitute "medical" or "scientific" evidence of a relationship with the devil. The fact that the "excrescence" changed — appeared deflated later in the day was further proof it was a "devil's teat". And further, Mr. Hathorne, at least, remembered the direct questioning during her examination in March, when Rebecca had denied having any "wounds" or physical maladies -- "I have none but old age". Nor was one mention of Rebecca's condition enough for the examiners — someone insisted more minutiae about her private parts be appended to the end of the afternoon report. Like her Lord, she was in effect, displayed naked before her persecutors.

All this was preliminary to the actual trials in the Court of Oyer and Terminer. The first full trial before this august body was that of Bridget Bishop on June 2. She was arraigned upon five separate indictments corresponding to each of the victims she was supposed to have "afflicted".

Had the first "confessed" witch, Tituba, been tried first, as would have been just, things would have gone differently. Not only was Tituba never tried, but neither were any of the others who confessed. On the contrary, the "confessors" became primary witnesses against the others in the high court trials – in partnership with the afflicted girls.

Apparently Goody Bishop was put at the head of the list because of earlier charges. There was an abundance of witnesses against her. She had originally been accused of witchcraft more than twenty years earlier, and tried in the Court of Assizes in 1679. Her original accuser then was Samuel Gray, who renounced his accusation on his deathbed. The accusation lingered, however, and at the death of her second husband, Thomas Oliver, rumor-mongering enemies said she had bewitched him to death. She was again accused openly in 1689 at the death of Christian Trask, but on that occasion she was staunchly defended by Reverend Hale. Now he had reversed his position, and was a witness against her. There were many witnesses against her: enemies from her neighborhood, rivals in business, as well as "good" people fearful and ready to go to extremes to end what they thought was a dark night of witchery among us.

The trial went on the next day, and the "evidence" summarized carefully before the jury by Mr. Stoughton at the end. The jury was sent out, and the Meeting House was not only full, but had a crowd around it such as never had been seen before in the history of Salem Town.

All those gathered knew witchcraft was a capital crime. All had discussed the possibility that some of the accused would be hanged. Many believed the sooner we began hanging them the better and Bridget Bishop was a popular first candidate. Nevertheless we were all shocked when the jury came back with a guilty verdict, and the justices issued a sentence of sorts.

They called for the "full penalty of the law," but did not specify what that was. At that juncture not even the judges seemed certain. Cotton Mather had written to Judge John Richards suggesting various alternative sentences. Our laws were betwixt and between under the new charter and administration. It wasn't until four months later that our legislature passed an explicit witchcraft law in an effort to make it clear again.

So even with Bridget Bishop's conviction, the outcome was still dubious and those interested in stopping the witch hunt were ready to let out a small sigh of relief. The Court had not rushed to hang the first one found guilty. Surely the Court of Oyer and Terminer would now step back and deliberate toward a more moderate conclusion. And indeed, the court did not go on immediately to try any other defendants, and did seem to withdraw into consultations.

All in all the progress of the high court during the first week of June was much what had been prophesied by Attorney-General Newton's letter to Secretary Addington on the 31 of May:

> I fear we shall not this weeke try all that we have sent for, by reason the tryals will be tedious, & the afflicted persons cannot readily give their testimonyes, being struck dumb & senceless for a season at the name of the accused.

Chapter Forty-One — The Walls Raised Higher

S(alem).But what then do you mean by the testimony of human witnesses?
B(oston). I mean, that the testimony it self be humane, as well as the witnesses; or, to speak more plain, that the thing testified be that which he came to the knowledge of, after the manner of men.
S. What do you mean by that?
B. I intend, that which one man can know concerning another by his senses, and that according to the true nature, and use of them; whatsoever comes in any other way, is either by extraordinary revelation from God, or by the insinuation of the devil; and what credit is legally to be given to a thing, which an humane person swears, meerly upon the devils information?
--Some Miscellany Observations On our Present Debates Respecting Witchcrafts, in a Dialogue Between S. & B. , 1692.

O n the 8th of June the news spread as fast as horses' hooves could carry it—that a death warrant had been issued for Bridget Bishop. That warrant was born out of a long labor and many midwives. The physician who delivered it was William Stoughton, but its parentage evades our metaphor. Perhaps we could say the birth pangs came suddenly upon the members of the high Court of Oyer and Terminer a few days after the jury brought back a verdict of guilty on June 3rd. Somehow none of the judges, except perhaps Stoughton, seem to have given much consideration to the end toward which the trials were leading.

It is a queer characteristic of committees in all places and times that no one member ever feels as responsible as he would alone. They share responsibility, but none feels responsible. It might be argued that the sense of responsibility felt by a committee in sum never quite equals that felt by a sole bearer of the same commodity. Committee members seem to remember Christ's parable of the workers in the vineyard—and always count themselves, if not those who came in the eleventh, at least those who came in the sixth hour—never those who are called to labor all day. After all, the wages are to be the same for all. There are two complementary tempers in most committees—those who say, "he seems to know what he is talking about" and those who say, "they aren't disagreeing with me, so I must be right." Each sort is able to justify a share in decisions that turn out well — and to distribute the blame to the others in those that don't.

Nevertheless, when the jury found Bridget guilty, all of the judges suddenly felt some of the weight upon their shoulders. Each and all became more zealous in seeking guidance toward making further judgments.

Mr. Gedney and Mr. Hathorne went to seek direction from Nicholas Noyes; Mr. Richards inquired further of his pastors, Increase and Cotton Mather, while Mr. Winthrop sought advice of the younger Mather as a friend. Mr. Winthrop, Mr. Sewall, and Mr. Sargent spoke briefly with Mr. Willard and Mr. Moody, their pastors, but unfortunately these two ministers were quite busy and at that point insuffiently aware of the court's inclination. Mr. Saltonstall applied to Mr. Phillips of Boxford for clearer theological and biblical perspective, and came away from that interview much troubled. Ministers Higginson, Samuel Cheever, and Hale were sought out by several magistrates. Lieutenant Governor Stoughton had supreme confidence in his own theological acumen, and sought direction from none. Nevertheless he and the other justices more assiduously reviewed various books of law. The chiefest of these were:

King James the First's *Demonologie* (1597); William Perkins' *Discourse of the Damned Art of Witchcraft* (1608); John Cotta's *The Tryal of Witchcraft, Shewing the true and right method of the Discovery with a Confutation of Erroneous Ways* (1625); Richard Bernard's *Guide to Grand-Jury Men* (1627); *Lawes Against Witches and Conivration* (1645); John Gaule's *Selected Cases of Conscience* (1646); Matthew Hopkins' *The Discovery of Witches* (1647); John Stearne's *Confirmation and Discovery of Witchcraft* (1648); John Wagstaffe's *Question of Witchcraft* (1671); as well as such venerable Catholic sources as *Malleus Maleficarum*, "The Hammer of Witches," originally published in 1484, for those magistrates who could read Latin.

They also perused more anecdotal accounts of witchcraft, including: Thomas Bromhall's *Treatise of Spectres* (1658); Thomas Cooper's *Pleasant Treatise of Witches* (1673); Joseph Glanvil's *Sadducismus Triumphatus* (1681); and Richard Baxter's *Certainty of the World of Spirits* (1691). Witchcraft pamphlets had become almost a written entertainment in England from about 1645 to the time of our troubles. Thus is more abbreviated forms there were many more tracts and treatises in print concerning particular cases of purported witchcraft, including those recent ones of our own shores by Governor Winthrop, Samuel Willard, Increase and Cotton Mather.

The magistrates with least experience talked with others who had more, including particularly Mr. Hathorne and Mr. Corwin. Judges Stoughton, Sewall, Gedney, and Danforth of the court were also consulted as well as magistrates Samuel Appleton and James Russell, Secretary Addington, and King's Attorney Newton, a trained lawyer. Of course many a farmer or tavern keeper contributed his sage advice, if only to his companions where opportunity offered.

After four days of assiduous consultation and study following the conviction of Bridget Bishop, the high magistrates met at the home of Mr. Corwin in Salem. There Lieutenant Governor and Chief Justice Stoughton convened the meeting toward a determination on the Bishop sentence, and establishing the parameters within which to conduct the rest of the trials.

All the justices were there: Stoughton, Gedney, Hathorne, Richards, Danforth, Sargent, Saltonstall, Sewall and Waitstill Winthrop, with attorney Thomas Newton and their host, Jonathan Corwin.

Perhaps it was calculated or perhaps poor judgment, but Chief Justice Stoughton had Reverend Noyes open the meeting and give another description of the "physics" behind the various arcane "proofs" used thus far in the trials. Several of the more scientific men followed much of it—but the others would have understood it no worse in Ugaritic. These were happy to conclude their colleagues assented to its gist. Refreshments were served, Mr. Noyes departed, and Mr. Stoughton put on his mantle of leadership.

William Stoughton was a careful man, and we might even say a deliberate man, but he was not a man of caution. He knew he was not all-knowing, but he also believed there was none more competent than he. Therefore, for everyone's good, as he saw it, he led confidently and with authority. He had a sense of divine right, and divine calling as he took up his role as chief justice of the court. He was dedicated to the elimination of witches from our New Jerusalem, our New England, but he would have been as dedicated to any task equal to his sense of personal authority.

Although born in England in 1631, his parents came to the colony and sent their son to Harvard, from which he graduated in 1650. He returned to England and received a further degree from Oxford two years later. He was given a fellowship there. Apparently enjoying the life of a scholar, as well as a growing reputation as a preacher, he remained at Oxford for eight more years, but at the Restoration he was ejected. He returned to New England and was called by the church in Dorchester, but did not settle there, preferring to preach in various settings as he became increasingly involved in government courts. His ability was widely respected. His sermons were carefully ordered and imperatively presented. His doctrine was carefully arrived at, and determinedly maintained. But his ambitions were chiefly political.

With the revocation of the colonial charter and the imposition of the Royal Commission under Governor Andros, he had been appointed Deputy President of the temporary government from 1674 to 1676. He was back in England as an agent for the colony at the royal court from 1677 to 1679. And he was Deputy President again from 1680 to 1686.

William Stoughton's appointment as Deputy Governor under the new charter was officially made by the king. Unofficially, however, Increase Mather picked nearly all the colonial officers. While the other New England commissioners opposed Mr. Mather's fight for the new charter, William Phips had supported his effort to get it approved by the royal court. (The other commissioners had been holding out for the reissuance of the old charter, with its election of officers and the franchise limited to the Congregational men. Mr. Mather knew this would never be approved by King William, thus his advocacy of a charter which compromised on those points.) Increase Mather also knew Governor Phips was an experienced leader of men. But he recommended Mr. Stoughton as Deputy Governor because of his high standing as a colonial-born Oxford theologian. Stoughton had gained some influence in court circles during his years at Oxford and thus had backing in his own right.

Chief Justice Stoughton was a theologian with experience in office. He had found over the years that wielding authority suited his gifts and his humors. He was quite ready to act directly to hold the colony together. He was ready to begin by completing the messy but necessary task of ridding New England of witches. His goals included his own elevation to higher office — not out of selfish ambition, but because he felt the colony could do no better.

William Stoughton had little respect for the man who was placed over him as governor. As a party to the debates over the new charter, he was alert to the dangers of the wider "franchise," by which less educated and less orthodox men could vote. Apparently he came to see Governor Phips as a prime example of that danger. We learned through his public behavior at the end of that year and throughout the next that he despised Governor Phips, as a scholar may sometimes despise a successful man of humble origins. (Some say there was an old romantic rivalry between them, as well.) In the year following our troubles, hostility became open between them.

It is not always true that the proud man is haughty. There is a kind of pride which is founded in unbelief, fearfulness and desperate self-trust. Studying, planning, and acting energetically can all be the products of faith. They can also arise from severe doubts about God's love and sovereignty over human affairs. Diligence sometimes is a refusal to leave the secret things to God. William Stoughton was driven by the conviction he must hold back the forces of evil if God's kingdom were not to collapse. His was that almost royal combination of diffidence and determination, caution and resolve, but he was more fitted for a usurper than a king.

Justice Thomas Danforth of Boston, the former Deputy Governor, was also on the high court. He had been acting governor during most of the administration of aged Governor Bradstreet. While Increase Mather and the other commissioners wrangled with the court in London over the charter, Indian depredations again become a serious danger. Deputy Danforth and Governor Bradstreet had also to cope with the ruinous effects of the failed Phips expedition against Quebec. Justice Danforth, therefore, had extensive experience of directing and defending the colony during times of attack and hardship. He was prepared once more to set his face like flint against an enemy.

Although we had little opportunity to find where he may have led us, there are many now who remember Deputy Danforth's oversight of the examinations at Salem in May, during which the afflicted girls were more restrained and one defendant, at least, found not guilty. As we have said, his objective temperament was sadly offset by his wife's relationship to the Parris family.

Justice Nathaniel Saltonstall of Haverhill, son of the founding stalwart, Richard Saltonstall was then on the verge of being the first judge to resign. He is chiefly regarded now as one whose acuteness of conscience was greater than his ability to persevere.

Justice John Richards of Boston belonged to Cotton Mather's North Church and from the beginning sought the advice of the younger Mather regarding the trials. Like most of the others, Mr. Richards was a militia commander, having served during King

Philip's War. (He was then made a captain in 1675, and a major of the Suffolk Regiment from 1683 to 1689.) Curiously, Major Richard's own mother had been accused as a witch back in 1653. Welthean Richards seems to have had a sharp tongue when wronged or angered, and various afflictions of those with whom she was angry were attributed to her. Her pastor was Mr. Thacher, however! And his letter in her defense contributed to the result that she was not brought to court. The Richards thus owed a debt to the Thachers — perhaps one more reason Mistress Thacher was never tried.

Mr. Richard's first wife had died the previous November. He was sympathetic to the bereaved relatives of those supposed bewitched to death. Furthermore he was then courting Anne Winthrop, whom he married later that fall. Thus his allegiances were many and tangled.

Justice Samuel Sewall was born in England in 1652. He graduated from Harvard at the age of nineteen. He was early interested in biblical prophecy, and the peculiar place of the American colonies in God's plan. With most other leading men he was thus susceptible to an interpretation of events that located the front lines of the war between heaven and hell in Massachusetts Bay Colony. He married Hannah Hull, daughter of a successful merchant, and beginning in 1681, he ran the colonial press for a number of years. His present office on the Court of Oyer and Terminer was an extension of his appointment as judge in May, 1691, under old Governor Bradstreet's administration. He said at the time of his original appointment, "Let us serve our generation according to the will of God, and afterwards fall asleep," drawing on the description of David's temporary role as ruler over God's people in Paul's sermon at Antioch of Pisidia. He belonged to Boston's South (Third) Church under the care of Samuel Willard.

Justice Peter Sargent of Boston was husband of Elizabeth Corwin, and thus Jonathon Corwin's brother-in-law, although his wife died a number of years before our troubles. He was to marry Mary Spencer (Rogers), widow of Governor Phips, nine years later. Judge Sargent had been part of the cabal against Governor Andros, signing the petition asking Andros to surrender and abandon his royal commission. He, too, was a member of Willard's South Church.

Justice Waitstill Winthrop was son of former Governor Winthrop. His sister Margaret married John Corwin, brother of Jonathan Corwin, and thus he was also an uncle to Sheriff George

Corwin. Although belonging to Reverend Willard's church, he was closer to his friend Cotton Mather — who dedicated his earlier book *Memorable Providences Relating to Witchcrafts and Possessions* (1689) to him: "I reckon among the best of my friends and the ablest of my readers. Your knowledge has qualified you to make those reflections on the following relations." During our troubles, Mr. Winthrop remained under the penumbra of his powerful friend, whose opinions he valued as highly as those of his own pastor.

Justice Bartholomew Gedney was the second justice from Salem beside Mr. Hathorne. (That is to say, these were the only two Salem men on the original Court of Oyer and Terminer. Soon Jonathon Corwin was also added.) His father was a Quaker. Partly because of conflicts with the Town's leaders, his father first opened "The Ship" Tavern in Salem outside the jurisdiction of the town, on a wharf projecting over the water. Major Gedney's brother Eleazur, operated a shipyard nearby. Major Gedney joined the Salem congregation and thus became a freeman in 1669. He joined his brother in shipbuilding, and flourished as a shipowner as well. From 1680 to 1683 he served on the Court of Assistants and was Commander-in-Chief of the colony's militias for a number of years. His daughter Lydia was married to Sheriff George Corwin.

Justice John Hathorne was of course well known to us. To the rest of the high court he was an invaluable resource, since he knew the defendants, one might say "intimately" by then, and had made mental and literal notes of the strongest points of the cases against them. For Judge Hathorne, the advent of the Court of Oyer and Terminer was a tremendous respite. He had led the attack for four months, and had expended himself more than he showed in public. Mr. Hathorne found it a singular relief to be taken into the large and capable fellowship of the larger court. He felt like a man who comes in from cold.

The Court of Oyer and Terminer had to determine the question of the code to which they stood responsible. It is a common rule of mankind that a society operates on the last official laws laid down until some authoritative act changes them, thus the laws of the colony had never ceased to operate. Nevertheless, the new charter which Increase Mather and Governor Phips had brought back did represent a change — a change after many changes — and left some ambivalence, which was not to be entirely eliminated, even on the 15th of June when the General Court convened and passed its first temporary bill under the new charter. That bill stated that all the laws of the colony "being not repugnant to the laws of England nor inconsistent with the present constitution" shall remain in force until November 10th. The General Court expected to overhaul the laws more carefully by then.

Furthermore the commission which created the Court of Oyer and Terminer on May 27th instructed the justices to "enquire of, hear, and determine for this time, according to the law and custom of England and of this their Majesties' province, all and all manner of crimes." The expression "according to the law and custom of England" in one sense meant 'do as we've always done.' But the very reason New England existed was the strong sense that there had been significant errors in what we'd always done. The phrase was therefore a far cry from the original polity of New England which required all jurisprudence to be founded in the scriptures – made explicit in the Body of Liberties of 1641. What the court was to make of these ambiguities was a central question addressed by the ten men who gathered in Judge Corwin's home.

All of the justices had experience in various sorts of courts and public offices, as well as in military commands. Any one of them might have led the court in his own right, but since Mr. Stoughton was Deputy Governor and since he stepped naturally into a superior role, the rest stepped as naturally into subordinate ones.

When they had been served refreshment by Judge Corwin's servants and settled themselves, Mr. Stoughton rose and presented the situation in simple terms.

"We have been appointed to a momentous task, gentlemen, and I know you will not flag or fail at it. Due to the persevering efforts of Mr. Hathorne, Mr. Corwin, and many lesser officers, there is no doubt about the horrible scope of the witchcraft among us. We have seen that men and women from the highest to the lowest have given themselves to diabolism and blasphemy. We have seen that they are not content with their evil worship, or even with the minor spells for which many of their brothers and sisters have been executed in England and Europe. But as we have learned during the trial of Bridget Bishop, these are the very vilest of witches. Due to the devil's particular hatred of our settlements and government, they have been given over to every form of evil, including, it would seem, the wholesale murder of innocent men, women and infants.

"Some of these who are in covenant with the devil first made that covenant more than twenty years ago. Several, including she who now stands guilty by verdict of jury and sentence of this court, were accused and in some measure prosecuted long before this. But at that time, with what we now see as too nice a care for adequate evidence, their cases were set aside. We now know there were five or six such cases, and that while none alone seemed at the time to warrant guilty verdicts, together they should have been recognized for what they were. By our lenience and too great care lest some innocent be convicted, we allowed a terrible invasion of Satan's kingdom in our very midst. We are like the Israelites when they met the Gibeonites disguised as wanderers, and failed to recognize their true character. Thus they failed of the Lord's command to eradicate the enemy in their midst, which sin continued to draw them into severe trials for many generations.

"This is not just a matter of dealing with heretics or criminals, gentlemen, it is a war. It is a war between the kingdom of light and the kingdom of darkness, between heaven and hell — and as we have the Lord's promise that the gates of hell will not prevail against his church, we have the special office of leading the charge that will storm those gates and bring down the one who sits within upon his black throne.

"I can do no more than repeat the exhortation of Reverend Lawson a few months ago in Salem Village. We must 'Arm! Arm! Arm!' against our foes.

"There are times in the history of the world where things are done that change history's course. Those who act in faith at such times may feel a measure of trepidation. Nonetheless, their actions are of great moment. I may say of you what Mordecai said of Esther, "Who knoweth whether thou art come to the kingdom for such a time as this?"

"Some parts of our task daunt us. During this first trial we heard many things that troubled us and a few that raised doubts. Like Abraham, we have been called to an unknown destination, and we have feared our steps might lead us astray into byways far from God's will. Is it not always thus when one lives by faith? Does not every one to whom God gives authority over great things in this world feel so? Is that not the very essence of faith — to go forward to a city whose builder and maker is God, without being able to see it until the day we arrive?

"I suggest that our task is of a piece with all acts of faith — to do what is set before us. To go forward step by step without hesitating, and to believe that God will lead us through each step to the next, until we find our task is finished.

"Many questions have been raised — and many more will be raised. But those who question our conduct have not been called to the task we are called to. Theirs is not the grace to do it. Has not the Lord promised those who go through particular trials that they — they and not some other — shall have grace sufficient for it? Does not God tell us that he is faithful and will provide a way of escape — not a running away, but a way through, as Israel passed through the Red Sea and through the hoards of Baal-worshippers in Canaan. We will pass over dry shod and we will not turn back no matter how giant our foes. Soon the walls of Jericho will come crashing down.

"I propose to you, then, that we ought not to let the questions and the doubts much occupy us. Some of them are merely another stratagem of the enemy. Others, while sincerely meant and expressed by godly men, are but the musings of those who are not given to see as we are, because they are not called to the task to which we are called.

"The questions should be turned upon their heads. The issues are not why we should proceed as we do — and as godly men have proceeded in like circumstances for hundreds of years according to many authorities — but rather why we should not! It is our commission and calling to proceed. If there be some who have serious reservations about some means by which we proceed, let them study the authorities and correct us where we err. But meanwhile it is not our task to debate and study, but to judge the cases presented to us.

"I have, for instance, heard some say we ought not to allow the testimony of the victims about the apparitions of these witches which they have seen about their demonic tasks. We have heard from Mr. Noyes that this method of the devil accords well with both science and scripture. Further I look to the Bible and I find several cases where apparitions are attested to. If not the substance, then the method of scripture tells me it is permissible to take apparitions seriously. But I am not left to my own assessment — for we all know that private interpretation is not to be respected. Rather I look to the works of many good Christians and many good Puritans among them. These I find attest to apparitions without apology and list their appearing as a valid indications and even proofs in the trying of a witch.

"What, I ask, would be the fate of our war if we disallowed this testimony! Would this rank witch Bishop have been convicted were it not for this sort of testimony from so many. True, there was much testimony to the ills she worked and to her malevolence toward those who suffered them, but these are poor evidence next to the firsthand evidence of her appearing and working the ills. Seeing these things go on in the very court has convinced the jury and ourselves.

"But more serious yet is the objection some make that the devil might appear in the form of an innocent person. What a mockery we make of God if we allow that the devil has been able to use the form and powers of a man or woman without such a one submitting to him. Is God not sovereign and does he not love his people with a saving love? Has he not delivered his people from the domain of darkness and into the kingdom of his beloved son? How then is it possible that the devil take the images and voices and powers of God's own children with which to injure others? It cannot be, indeed it seems to me blasphemy to suggest it. If it were allowed, it would make chaos of our understanding, our world, and human justice. For if the devil can take the form of an innocent person for purposes of witchcraft, could he not also do it for purposes of murder or theft or adultery? Thus all our criminal law would be cast aside, and no testimony of any eye witness could be given any weight.

"If we disallow the testimony concerning apparitions and other such proofs as are complained against, we will fail to convince a jury and to convict the wicked malefactor. That is not my sense of calling nor how I would prosecute a war.

"A tender heart toward an enemy in battle is as good as a sword at one's throat. We cannot allow our fleshly compassion and the tears or protestations of the accused to sway us. Neither can we allow the qualms of the questioners to infect our souls.

"Others have asked how we can allow men or high reputation like Captain Alden and the Englishes to be accused. They point to this as evidence that the accusations are not sound – but these are ignorant of the Enemy's stratagems, which others of better discernment have understood since this wave of witchery began in early spring. Reverend Lawson, preaching at Salem Village, spoke directly to this point – that the devil most of all seeks to subvert the greatest among us, since only to draw the lesser into his covenant would make his purpose of much less effect. That there have indeed been some errors in accusation, we know, and we have tried to correct such at an early date. But the apostle Paul says that even if he or an angel from heaven should preach another gospel such a one ought to be accursed — therefore we can say if even ourselves or the most respected person among us make covenant with the devil, he ought to be prosecuted — aye and punished to the full extent of the law. Though there is room for discernment, there is no room for favoritism.

"We are charged with the equitable application of the law. We have been called to lead in this battle between dark and light and we can allow of no shadow of doubt if we are to keep the light clear and eradicate the darkness.

"Enough from me, gentlemen, only let us pray before we continue.

"Lord Christ, we ask that thou receivest our humble prayers through thine own shed blood. We desire to lead thy people through this sea of troubles and into thy glorious presence. Bless our ministers, oh Lord, some of whom have been singled out for special attack by the great enemy of our souls. Keep your servants the civil princes. Lead them always in your light. Reveal thine enemies, the minions of the devil, oh Lord, and give us zeal to strike them mortal blows. Make our faces as brass and our hearts as adamant, that we may be zealous always for the good, and merciless toward them that hate you. We pray in Christ's name. Amen."

The others joined in the "amen," but the silence which had grown deeper during Justice Stoughton's homily continued for a while. At last, Judge Hathorne spoke.

"Judge Corwin and I have had to deal with these questions and qualms, of course. I could well say we have been persecuted for righteousness sake at some points. Some who were our friends avoid us and will barely give a civil word. Yet any who had seen and heard the devastation these fiends work among us cannot help but steel himself and grow ever more determined to stop them. To allow this to go unchecked would be the same as trusting one's wife and children to the tender mercies of the savages who ravish our borders.

"It has not been as hard as some of you might fear. God gives grace at need as Mr. Stoughton reminds us. We found once we got through the first few examinations that we began to see our way more clearly. The devil has not so much imagination as many credit him. After a while one anticipates his next trick and learns how to scotch it. What seemed all smoke and fog at first gradually becomes a marked path."

"That encourages me," answered Mr. Richards. "For I confess, I was completely at sea through this Bishop trial. It seemed to me so much of what we dealt with by way of testimony and deposition was the sort of thing that would not be admitted in any other trial — rumor, allegation, things seen by one but not by another in the same room, and so on. I do not feel competent to sort through such things to the bones or marrow."

"And that is why I speak of war," answered Mr. Stoughton. "For it is sure that a court martial or an admiralty court has few of the niceties of a London court of chancery, yet all are convened to bring justice. The circumstances warrant a rough and ready justice in the former and a more careful and exhaustive course in the other. Which would you say we have here?"

"I'm not — I'm not sure if either is entirely analogous. For certainly the defendants here, if they be guilty are indeed foot-soldiers of an enemy — indeed The Enemy. But if there be some innocent among them, then they are citizens and soldiers of the Lord's own, and it would be a great sin to mistake them for the others."

"Yet in a pitched battle such as General Gedney here has led, it can hardly be helped that there are sometimes men who fall from the accidental shots of their fellows."

"Oh, aye!" said Mr. Gedney, glad to find something he felt competent to speak to, "At the Narragansett Fort after the smoke cleared we found five or six of our dead with holes in the wrong side of 'em."

"Thus it may be that one mistake out of a hundred might befall us — but what soldier would stay home from the battle for fear of such a thing? Every Christian in the colony is of our colors. I believe most are ready to give their lives for their King. There is a worse judgment awaiting the nation that does not deal with it's criminals. Especially witches — 'You shall not suffer a witch to live' is not a command that admits of long interpretation."

"Perhaps so," struck in Mr. Saltonstall, "but the scriptures are also clear that God hates the shedding of innocent blood — and indeed will require it of the land that allows or causes it to be shed."

"The context," answered Mr. Sewall, "is indeed that of justice, but it has more to do with allowing criminals to go unpunished than any mistakes of justice. No justice under human administration has ever been perfect, and since capital crimes must be prosecuted there cannot help but be rare cases where an innocent man is put to death. I do not think this need be a question that holds us back more than in any other capital case. However there are many issues of procedure and evidence which are unclear — at least to me — and I would like to hear them gone over.

"What for instance are bases and guidelines for this proof by touch?"

"That, and it's connection to torment by means of the witches own bodily movements were explained to us by Reverend Noyes when Mr. Corwin and I first began the examinations in March," answered Mr. Hathorne. "He said there was a unity of scripture and science behind it. As he said again today, this physics of Descartes ties to and is supported by the Bible. It was clear he understood what he was talking about, and it seemed to me Jonathan understood, but I could not lay it out for you — not for love nor money."

Mr. Corwin responded, "I understood his argument and the correspondence he drew well enough. To the degree we are sure of Descartes', and Mr. Noyes' interpretation of the relevant scripture, we may certainly agree to his conclusions."

"But even those of us who understand less well may rest from trying. For we have no obligation to do it," said Mr. Stoughton.

"Although some of us are theologians, some physicians and some otherwise learned, we have not been appointed to the office of scholar, but of magistrate.

"The things which we need to know need neither be discovered nor explained by us — the crime of witchcraft is as old as scripture. So is its prosecution and the proofs to be used in doing so.

"Those of you who have not had a chance to peruse them, may borrow from among these texts which we have gathered on the sideboard there. They include many books dealing with the law and legal proofs. There are also a number describing observations of witchcraft victims, including those of four unimpeachable witnesses, the venerable Mr. Baxter, Mr. Willard, Mr. Increase Mather, and his son.

Another two hours of discussion followed with tentative questions and objections by a few, but the inertia carried forward by the Chief Justice.

Mr. Stoughton ended the gathering with the following statement.

"Well, gentlemen, I am much encouraged at your resolve and unity. If anyone fears we are not adequate to the task before us, the rest of us are ready to disabuse him of his misapprehension.

"The jury delivered a verdict of guilt against Bridget Bishop and after conferring we upheld that verdict and prescribed the sentence required by law. I can tell you that there is no ambivalence in any authority from the Bible onward as to what that sentence is to be. Assuming there is therefore no objection, I will execute the responsibility under which we stand. The verdict was handed down last Friday, so I will issue the death warrant for this Friday, the tenth of June.

"But," asked Mr. Richards, remembering his own mother's struggles with witch accusations nearly forty years earlier, "are not lesser penalties available to us? Mr. Cotton Mather has suggested to me that we might resort to banishment, at least for some of the confessors and more doubtful cases."

"Perhaps so, but I do not think any of us believe Bridget Bishop's to be such a case," answered Mr. Stoughton. "Let us take up that question when and if it arises."

"No further question? Then I thank you for your labors together. I count it a high privilege to be part of such a gifted court. May God prosper our further deliberations."

To which, with various emphases, the others said, "Amen."

Samuel Willard

Chapter Forty-Two — The Few Grow Faint
(June 8)

. . . Instead of all apish flouts and jeers at histories, which have such undoubted confirmation, as that no man that has breeding enough to regard the common laws of humane society, will offer to doubt of 'em, it becomes us rather to adore the goodness of God, who does not permit such things every day to befall us all, as he sometime did permit to befall some few of our miserable neighbours.
  -- Cotton Mather, ***Another Brand Pluckt Out of the Burning****: An Account of the Sufferings of Margaret Rule. (1700)*

That night the conspirators gathered at the cave of their two confederates. They had just ascended and none had as yet told the latest episode in their grim tale. John and Sam offered Peter Cloyce's apologies, but Joseph was also missing as they sat about outside the cave entrance catching their breaths in the new spring perfume rising from the ground.

"Quiet!" said Daniel suddenly, as above them they all heard scraping sounds. They had no time to crowd into the cave before suddenly another rope came coiling down. Directly above their heads they heard warbling like an Indian and Joseph slid down the rope among them. Daniel was instantly angry at Joseph, who stood puffing beside them on the narrow tongue of lawn. George and Sam were wide-eyed as they recovered from the first assumption to which they all had leapt.

"What in the world! . . ." Daniel began, but John interrupted him soberly, "What is your purpose, Joseph? For we know after today you can hardly be skylarking."

At this Daniel turned toward John and his scowl faded.

"What do you mean, John? What else has happened?"

All the others dropped their eyes, except George who sat quite bewildered by these swift turns of events.

"The high court has issued a death warrant for Bridget Bishop," Joseph said, answering Daniel's question. Then after a solemn pause, "and my purpose was only to test our security by seeing if the route of my original coming here was a point of vulnerability. Care is needed more than ever."

Peter had made a brief and solitary visit three days earlier, so the two escapees knew of Bridget's conviction. But none knew what conclusion the court would bring to the case until that day.

"So it has come to this," Daniel said, as though speaking to himself. He turned away then and walked down to the edge of the cliff where he stared out over the woods below, his back still and silent and bowed.

George began to weep, and Sam put his arm around the sitting man's shoulders.

"Nay, then, man. They seemed to pick her out special, because of the old accusations and the special animosity of so many in Salem and Royalside. Did Peter tell you Reverend Hale had joined in accusing her? It seems he was doing penance over an obscure guilt in regard to Christian Trask's death. Remember he defended Bridget then."

The others brought out comestibles for the two hermits. But no one seemed much inclined to eat or speak, and for a while, they did little but sigh and struggle to comprehend.

"We must go forward," Joseph said at last. "We must continue to think and pray as well and wisely as we can. Are we to give in and let them hang us all?"

The others still regarded him passively.

"I cannot discuss today's event without losing perspective myself. Perhaps one of the others can give a summary — but let's leave that to the last. I would like to pursue more fruitful conversation."

Daniel turned and came back to the circle again as Joseph went on

"Let us take the most charitable interpretation possible of the high court's actions thus far. Let us suppose for the moment that Bridget Bishop is indeed a damned witch. Let us suppose the judges and even the jury were convinced of it beyond the shadow of a doubt.

"Even if these things were so, we nonetheless have no choice but to resist and attempt to overthrow their course. For unless there is some amazing intervention, Goody Bishop will be hanged for no reasons, more or less, than that a number of people attributed to her events they neither saw nor otherwise witnessed in any reasonable construction of those terms.

"Though indeed she were a witch, and all the things attributed to her indeed of her doing, yet the process of law by which she was convicted was such that any one of us, indeed any innocent person in the colony could be likewise convicted and sentenced to hang.

"We and many others in this colony know these witnesses should not be allowed to testify except to things which they have seen with their own eyes or heard with their own ears. Further no one should be convicted, in a capital case, unless at least one other witness has likewise seen or heard the same things. The idea that a person can be said to be two places at a time, and be convicted of a crime at great remove from where others swear to seeing her is anathema. This evidence based on "apparitions" seen by some but unseen by others must be shown for what it is — deceit, illusion, false witness, and itself the work of the devil. Until that happens, there is no hope for a glimmer of justice."

"Until our little despots are overthrown, we will be ground to dust," Daniel agreed, his voice still bemused or bewildered with the enormity of the news.

"And now we know this will not happen even among these judges!" John added.

"But I have something of hope to offer there!" Joseph answered quickly.

"As I was hastening home, and perhaps riding my horse too hard, I caught up to Justice Saltonstall, who lives, as you know, in Haverhill. We rode together almost an hour, and no other with us, so I was able to sound his mind.

"At first he would speak nothing of it, even rebuking me when I asked too direct a question about the court's treatment of the evidence. But after we discussed weather and crops and horses and families a while, he began to veer back to the witch business, himself.

"I mostly listened and made only the mildest replies, but as he talked it became clear he is nearly as chagrined as we. He wanted to know if in my experience I had ever seen this spectre evidence allowed in other courts. I replied I had not, and could not see how it was consonant with the biblical requirements for eye witnesses. After the Ipswich fork he asked me to elaborate.

"So I told him my argument that given the nature of spectre evidence, it could not accurately be called witness at all. I pointed out that the whole basis for the Levitical requirement of two witnesses, as well as the penalties for false witness, was the idea that the heart of man was wicked and capable of deceit. It therefore made no sense to allow any testimony that could not be corroborated by another observer. I said it made even less sense to allow as sufficient evidence that which was actually contradicted by another observer who placed the defendant at a great distance from the crime. I suggested it was likewise at odds with the concept of biblical witness to uphold the testimony of one witness, while denying that of another present in the same place at the same time yet explicitly testifying he could NOT see what the other saw.

"Even if spectre evidence were given equal weight with eye witness," I said, "one reliable eye witness to the contrary should at least be considered as discrediting one spectre witness." I further suggested that only one equally competent eye witness, who, though trying, cannot see the supposed spectre from any angle, nor otherwise confirm its existence, should discredit the spectre testimony of a number of others. For he is truly an eye witness while the others are something else. The court seems to hold to the opposite interpretation, as though the "seeing" witness were blind.

I said the logic of the court's present practice allowed nearly any claim to be made by with no possibility of discounting it.

"'But the jury has the right to discount the credibility of a witness or that witness's testimony,' he answered, 'if they see good reason to doubt either.'

"'Yet no jury is likely to deny what our high magistrates so obviously support,' I replied. 'The court has made it plain it sees no contradiction between the eye witnesses and the seers of "apparitions," although by all reason, they are incompatible. No civil court should be expected to judge matters that are unseen. But the jury looks to the justices for its principles. The constructions of those who hold high office will always been given a greater measure of respect and precedence. It is the essence of the very idea of office.'

"We rode a while longer, and passed through the Village, where we would normally have taken different ways. But at the juncture of Rowley Road, he asked the condition of the path below Hathorne's Hill which meets again with the Andover Road at the log bridge. When I told him it was not nearly so good as the main road, but passable, he turned with me north and began to open his mind on two more points.

"'I cannot understand what impels our Deputy Governor, ' he said, and his bewildered tone surprised me. 'Mr. Hathorne is clearly full of zeal for clearing your village of witches, but though it is a matter of trouble in his own backyard, he has not the fierceness of Mr. Stoughton.'

"'**N**or can I understand him, sir,' was all I could think to reply.

"'Especially when persons of high reputation are being accused, there is no reason for the unquestioned support of these girls and their accusations,' he added. He was silent a long while after that.

"'**D**id you hear Mr. Lawson's lecture in the Village after Rebecca Nurse's examination?' he asked at last.

"'**N**o, sir, I did not,' I replied, 'But I have heard the gist of it from others. That the devil is particularly intent upon attacking the church and suborning its members for his purposes and so on.'

"'**A**h, but it seems, according to my fellow judges, that Mr. Lawson went further than that — predicting and explaining the accusation of persons of high reputation,' he said. His tone became ironical.

"'**H**e seems to have said the devil cannot achieve his ends unless he brings some high and respected persons, even those of high standing in the churches, into his covenant. Perhaps that had something to do with all this accusing of reputable persons.'

"**H**e stopped talking suddenly, and seemed to me he felt he'd said too much. I kept silent for a time after that.

"**T**hen I said, 'Is there nothing you and the rest of the magistrates can do to halt the march of this madness?'

"'**N**o!' he said, and he gave a bitter snort. 'For a march it is. It is precisely as a march that Deputy Stoughton describes it — a march in time of war, and therefore to be made hastily and despite all objections, obstructions, and incidental losses. As the magistrates' opinions are given precedence by the jury, so the chief justice is given precedence by the other judges.'

"**H**e said no more for the next ten minutes, and I durst not say anything either.

"'**I** am not fit for this business,' was the last thing he murmured before he turned at Hathorne's Hill Road. He seemed very much dejected.

Joseph went on, "I wonder how many of the other justices feel the same? I suspect the saner justices are caught in a kind of quandary from which only two or three are free — and those two or three are actively bent on error. The active but erroneous ones lead the rest. Therefore it may be only some mighty ones outside their circle again — either Governor or ministers that change this course. The Salem ministers are too deeply involved to be of good use. A few outlying pastors, like Phillips of Boxford may help, but only the combined voices of a number of respected divines can carry sufficient weight. We have more hope from the Boston ministers than our own. Yet although there is hope there—there are also among them several with something to lose by a change of course—including Cotton Mather, who has perpetuated the "science" of spectres. Nor is his father, who loves him, likely to speak unequivocally in opposition.

"Although the governor belongs to Mather's church along with three justices, I think he is our best hope. What are our best means of approaching Governor Phips, Daniel?.

Daniel considered this for a moment. "I don't know too much about him, but since he is governor by royal appointment, he may be easier to approach than you think. Does he not continue the old custom of court days when citizens may bring their cases to him?"

"Yes, I think so, although King William's War and particularly the depredations to eastward—which is, you remember, the region of his birth—have taken most of his attention since he arrived."

"Well, the appeals to a royal governor which are traditionally best received are direct ones from the suffering. Ought we present the several petitions by the hands of the families of the accused? We meant to use them in court, but now that sounds less hopeful."

"By all means!"

"Wait," said Sam, "Do you mean you want representatives of all the families to go to the governor? I don't think most of us would be much good at that."

"No Jacobs, anyway, " said George, "I don't suppose there are many over the age of twelve that have not been arrested." The wonder of this statement was not that he said it, but that no self-pity sounded in it—he was but a stating the fact.

"No, we must do the reverse of what the court did in trying Goody Bishop first—as they tried their worst case, we should take our best one to the governor. I think your mother is that case, Sam. She is older than her sisters, and widely known and respected. None of the testimony against her has been worth a straw nor been much reinforced. If we can succeed with her case, it may turn the whole course of things around."

"I hope you are right, Joseph," Daniel said, "I seem to have lost my ability to get enthusiastic with tonight's news. It is much different to anticipate the worst and to know it has actually begun. It feels exactly as if the Christians were being thrown to the lions."

"Except that Christians are doing the throwing," John commented.

"It has been so often before," Daniel answered. "But at least it was Catholic against Protestant or Anglican against Dissenter in most of those cases. Among us it has been Congregational against Episcopal, Quaker, Baptist, or Presbyterian — until now. Many of these accused are the best members of our own congregations! They are our saints, if we have any at all."

"Well, I call that immodest of you," Joseph answered. "It's all very well for John and Sam and I to call you and George saints, but you really should be more reticent about it yourself!"

Daniel winced and pretended to look sheepish. "I didn't mean us — at least not me. I meant. . ."

"We know what you meant — and we agree with you," said John, "and we do include you and George among our saints. A distant day may come when to have been a friend or relative of a witch will be a source of pride and boasting."

"Say not witch. . . if you have the itch — but one accused as a witch. . . who refused as a witch!" George said, his tone more cheerful.

"So do the other trials go forward?" Daniel asked, his nervous energy beginning to revive.

"Perhaps Peter has told you some of this," Sam said, "But a week ago Friday, the Jury of Inquest heard the testimony of Reverend Philips on behalf of Elizabeth Howe — the same he gave at her examination. He recalled that Hannah Perley's family had told her to blame Goodwife Howe for her fits. They also heard depositions owned and new testimony sworn against Mother Nurse, John Procter and John Willard.

"Captain Putnam and his wife testified that although their son-in-law John Fuller and their daughter Rebecca Shepard both died a violent death and acted strangely at the time of their deaths, yet they judged at the time both died of a malignant fever. They said they have no suspicion of witchcraft of any, nor could they accuse the prisoner at the bar, that is Mother Nurse, of any such thing. This was both courageous and difficult testimony for them, because it primarily rebutted the testimony of their son.

"That son, John Putnam, the weaver, was of a different opinion. Joseph has already told us how he and Hannah lost a baby about the middle of April, and how deeply it affected him. He said that when the child was about eight weeks old he told Henry Kenny what he heard concerning our Grandmother Towne and witchery, after which John, himself, was taken with strange fits. He was the source of Kenny's testimony at Mother Nurse's examination. Although John was delivered from these fits, his daughter came down with similar fits in the middle of the night. They sent for 'Mother Putnam' in the night, and after seeing the child, she said she feared 'an evil hand'. The doctor was sent for, but he could do little, and the child died after two days. John said the child suffered 'grievous fits which were horrible enough to pierce a stony heart'. There was no doubt he thinks the Towne sisters behagged his child in revenge for saying their mother was a witch.

"**On** Saturday Job Tookey from Beverly was arrested and examined. The girls claim he told them 'he had learning and could raise the devil'. They also said they saw ghosts of his murder victims, including John Trask's child, crying 'vengeance, vengeance'. As many as eight people were named bewitched to death by Tookey. One witness testified he heard Tookey say he would take Mr. Burrough's part. We all know how dangerous that kind of statement is. John Putnam further swore to hearing the afflicted blaming Tookey during their afflictions. A number of men testified they had heard him say he could 'as freely discourse the devil' as speak to one of them. When Tookey was further examined on Tuesday, he was confronted by Mr. Hathorne about being able to raise the devil, he replied 'I knew not then what I said.' Judging from the circle of companions brought to affirm his foolish statement, it's likely they'd been drinking heavily when he said it—and probably he truly didn't know what he was saying.

"**Also** on Saturday, Mary Ireson of Lynn was complained of by Deacon Edward Putnam and Tom Rayment, Sr.

"**On** Monday, June 6th, Anne Dolliver of Gloucester was arrested and examined at Salem. There were only two who claimed she afflicted them, Mary Warren and Susannah Sheldon.

"**Elizabeth** Booth has risen to the occasion and become one of the loudest, with new evidence against the Procters and Martha Corey, according to the fashion. Her testimony consists of ghostly appearances by many who have died in the community, which ghosts told her these bewitched them to death.

"**Then** today Justice Stoughton issued the death warrant for Goody Bishop. She is to be hanged Friday morning on the hill south of the road between the Quaker Burial Grounds and the bridge."

All were silent for a time, then Joseph spoke.

"It was much too little and much too late, but I went to my half-brother and his wife. I told them that what they did was a great evil, and that it could not be defended by the word of God or by human reason. They sputtered and threatened and at least once said that I sounded as though I was in league with the witches. I persevered, however, for I had been long preparing to speak my mind, as you know. They said that the ministers and magistrates knew more than I did, and that they were well satisfied that it was all of God. I said I would speak no evil of dignities, but did not think there was one among the ministers of Salem who could support the matter from scripture.

"Thomas said that I was always high and mighty, in which he may be right, but I grew weary with argument and angry at their mindless dedication to these things, until I felt I had to leave them. But not before I told them in no uncertain terms that if they dared to touch any of mine with their foul lies, that they would answer for it."

Another silence ensued, but it was fraught with admiration for Joseph.

"You have often led us in courage, Joseph," Daniel said finally. "If only every one of the accusers had a kinsman who would speak to him or her in such terms, a sea-change might be effected."

"But most have not such a one," said John. "And we greatly fear that our own loved ones will soon follow Goody Bishop to the rope."

"God be merciful to us!" said George, "where else can we turn?"

"Little else can we do," agreed Daniel, "but we must both pray and do what we can, though it seems next to nothing. You and Sam will take your petitions to the governor won't you, John?"

"We will. And our circle all continue in prayer. Our women especially are fervent. God grant that we have better news with which to encourage one another next time we meet."

They asked Joseph to close their meeting. But as they made their ways through the woods, they were as those who dreamed.

Captain John Alden

Chapter Forty-Three — First Hanged
(10 June)

*O foolish Galatians, who hath <u>bewitched</u> you, that ye should not
obey the truth, before whose eyes Jesus Christ hath been evidently
set forth, crucified among you? This only would I learn of you,
Received ye the Spirit by the works of the law, or by the hearing of
faith?* -- **Galatians 3:1**

The Salem Gaol at Dountons had been too full even before
the prisoners were transported back from Boston for trial.

In anticipation of the beginning of the trials and the arrival of
the Boston prisoners, William Dounton had cleared out his basement
cells and moved the "confessed" witches to the attic where Rebecca,
Martha Corey, and Dorcas Good had first stayed. Tituba was placed
there among Mary Warren, Abigail and Deliverance Hobbs,
Margaret and Rebecca Jacobs, and Sarah Churchill. There was more
suspicion among them than in a pack of armed robbers.

The Beadle home next door to the gaol was being used for the
keeping and occasional examinations of prisoners more recently
accused, including Elizabeth Paine and Elizabeth Fosdick from
Malden. Other prisoners were kept at Ipswich, including Rachel
Clinton of that town, and Dorcas Hoar, as well as Rebecca's two
sisters, Mary Easty and Sarah Cloyce, who had been moved from
Boston.

Many recently examined were shipped to Boston during the
previous week. These included the Procter's two sons, Benjamin and
William.

Those suspected as leading witches were kept in the
Dounton's basement. They were: Bridget Bishop, Sarah Good,
Susanna Martin, Alice Parker, John Willard, George Jacobs, Sr.,
Elizabeth Howe, Martha Corey, Rebecca Nurse, and John and
Elizabeth Procter.

The Jury of Inquiry was hearing other cases and the
examinations of newly accused prisoners were going forward at the
same time as Bridget Bishop was being tried at the Meeting House.
Therefore the significance of what their fellow inmate was going
through was not brought home to the rest of the prisoners until June

3rd, when the news came of her conviction. The scuttlebutt was quickly shared by all. Bridget and Sarah Good, alone, seemed to make little of the jury's verdict. The other prisoners were as shocked and full of speculation as the rest of the colony.

The insubstantiality of events over against the undefined condition of the law and government militated against the wholesale sorrow subsequent convictions were to bring. The justices had not made a clear statement of sentence. No one had been along this path before, so no one knew where we were going. To the other prisoners' commiseration Bridget made little response except to sigh and shake her head as was customary among them when speaking of the courts. The others had little more to say, except to speculate privately what the results of this conviction would be for her—and what it meant for the rest of them.

Meanwhile many in Essex County took the opportunity of the trials to accuse more women formerly reputed witches—but always through the medium of the "afflicted girls". The day after Bridget's conviction, Job Tookey of Beverly was arrested. Two days later, Mary Ireson of Beverly and Ann Dolliver of Gloucester were arrested and examined

In between, on the Lord's Day, the prisoners had relative quiet, and held a worship service as had been their wont in Boston. However their worship, which went over into early afternoon, was cut short by Mr. Noyes bursting in behind William Dounton, and demanding that they cease. His eyes were alive with indignation that these worshippers of Satan should make a mockery of the true worship of God. It mattered not that all he heard while listening first at the door was a psalm truly sung and a scripture truly read. He did not need to hear blasphemy to know worship by such as these was blasphemous. Most of the basement prisoners sat where they had gathered, in the larger cell near the steps. He stood in the cell door and delivered his prophet's blast.

"You will not pretend to public worship! Have you no shame at all! Is it not enough that you subvert and tempt so many from God's true worship, but that you must go on to make a mockery of it!"

And to Mr. Dounton, "See to it that this does not happen again. God is not mocked! And you are accountable for them!"

As soon as they left, Rebecca turned to the Procters with tears in her eyes, but before she could say anything Martha Corey began to sing the Te Deum, and several voices hesitantly joined her, then all the rest. When Mr. Dounton burst in again as they finished, all increased their volume "... Praise Father, Son, and Holy Ghost!" He blinked at the zeal of a thousand martyrs shining in every eye.

Thus began a minor battle that continued for the next four months, for the Salem ministers and gaolers led several campaigns during that time to stop all "mockeries" of Christian worship. It reached its peak when Reverend Burroughs was brought up later for trial. In Boston, however, the prisoners' services continued unhindered.

Job Tookey was examined on Tuesday (7th) by the three assistants from Salem. On Wednesday, Elizabeth Booth, the eighteen year old daughter of Alice Shaflin, who lived south of the Village joined the "afflicted". She blamed her neighbors, the Procters, for many of the recent deaths in the community, after they "appeared" to her. She claimed various murdered persons also appeared, some blaming Martha Corey for their deaths.

But this was also the day Chief Justice Stoughton issued the death warrant for Bridget Bishop, and by noon, the news had reached the gaol. The date of execution was set two days hence, Friday the 10th, in the morning. Bridget was one of the last to hear it. Visitors brought the news to the others, but none could bear to break it to her. Finally Martha and Rebecca sat with her and told her and prayed. She was silent, with both tears and appreciation in her face. In the early afternoon, Reverend Noyes and Judge Hathorne came to the gaol. The latter read it out to her in fine official voice. The others were appalled, but Martha Corey stole to her side as he finished and reached out her hand to cover Bridget's which lay clasped in her lap.

"Thy sins have found thee out, Bridget." Said Reverend Noyes, "that these many years lay hidden. Now comes the time to account for them. Repent and even now receive the Lord's forgiveness."

Summoning all her strength Bridget answered him, "My sins are indeed many, but this is not one of them. As for accounting, I thank my Lord, that I have found in him what forgiveness I need."

With a look almost of astonishment, Mr. Noyes turned on his heel, and Mr. Hathorne followed him, adding his own awkward rebuke, "Take care, for you will not be able to hide anything before the judgment that still awaits you."

As soon as they left, the other women crowded to her, but the steel with which she had armed herself, was not quickly set aside, and although she accepted their words and embraces, she did not much soften in response to them.

The next day her fellow prisoners showed her many kindnesses, leaving her seldom alone or in want of anything. But she continued sober and slow to respond. It was unclear to the others if she was but numb, or if she was perhaps reflecting over her sins and her readiness for death.

"I am not sure she grasps it," Martha said to Rebecca as the afternoon drew on. They sat together in Sarah Good's cell, which Sarah had only just left, after they had been trying to comfort her with talk about Dorcas and other subjects.

"Bridget, you mean?" said Rebecca. "Yes, I think she does — so far as any of us do. Martha, do you know what this means? She will be the first, but we. . ." She could not finish.

"It seems so," Martha answered, "Yet we do not know. Surely those old charges told much against her. And now that saner folk see where it is all leading, is it not more likely that it will be put to an end?"

"I do not know. Do you think there is a chance they will not do it?"

Martha did not answer right away. Then the two of them gazed into each other's faces. "No. . . no," she said, "I think there is little chance. They do not act as if there were the slightest hesitancy about it. It would take some strong counter-action, and I cannot hope such is likely. Not the governor, nor any of the ministers, I should think. No, they will do it."

"Then how soon shall we follow?"

Martha made no answer, for there was none to give. After a time, Rebecca fell into tearful prayer. Nevertheless, the two of them were at Bridget's side not long after, cheering her and praying fervently with her.

That night only the more hardened slept. Amidst the snores of Sarah Good, there were many creakings and rustlings to be heard as others tossed on their beds. Several went to Bridget who lay on her cot, staring up at the ceiling, turning briefly grateful eyes to each visitor, but returning soon to her own meditations.

In the morning, the others gave her what breakfast she would take, and Mr. Procter led them in prayer for her special comfort, but Bridget had put on her steel again, and said no good-byes when Sheriff Corwin came for her.

"In the resurrection!" called Martha, as they led the prisoner up the stairs.

Outside, a haycart waited as they put chains upon Bridget's arms and legs. They lifted her in and drove her up the lane where most of Salem lined the way, and crowded thickly along Essex street. The deputy drove the cart, while the Sheriff rode his horse behind. Crowds coming in from Ipswich, Topsfield, the Village, Lynn and Boston waited for them beyond the bridge, and continued to wind up the roads as far as the eye could see.

The Sheriff turned onto the carttrack that led up the hill. There at the top grew an ancient oak, its limbs contorted with age and weather. Under the oak several magistrates and ministers stood before a band of accusers and witnesses. (The levitical requirement that the witnesses cast the first stone was applied in requiring their presence.) The cart was brought to a halt then jerked forward a little, so that Goodwife Bishop sat directly beneath a great limb.

Reverend Noyes climbed upon the wagon and looked out over the great crowd — greater than most he had spoken to, greater than any ever gathered in Salem meeting to hear his sermon. He led in a prayer with much the same burden as his exhortation in the prison — that God would grant this wicked sinner repentance. The deputy raised Bridget to her feet before he began, but she did not close her eyes or bow her head, rather she looked about her with wide eyes — at the blue of the sky and the gray and brown texture of the tree bark. The faces and eyes, the somber earth-tones and white linen. The hands, the heads, the brown backs of the horses. She began to breath deeply.

When Reverend Noyes finished, he turned to her and called her once more to repentance. She looked briefly into his face, but now it was less with steel, than with preoccupation — she hadn't time to pay him attention. There was no time to be wasted. There were last bits of color to see, last memories, a few more precious breaths of sweet air. She did not respond to him at all.

Reverend Noyes stepped down and Sheriff Corwin stepped up. At the moment he threw the rope over the limb, Bridget began to cry and she began to pray desperately, seeming indeed to have great sins unrepented. She prayed and looked wildly about through her tears, until her head stopped turning suddenly. Her eyes met those of her husband Edward, who stood back a ways through the trees. "Oh, Edward," she said, in a murmur as though there were only the two of them. He said nothing back, but held her eyes with his. He spoke no word, but words mean little in parting, and if eyes cannot indeed afflict at a distance, perhaps they can express love and give comfort.

Thus stayed, she did not know the rope had been set about her neck and tightened. She did not know the cart had begun to move. It was not until she toppled and could no longer see him, that she came back briefly to this world. His eyes closed at that instant. Her hands went up to the rope that choked her. They pulled fiercely at it for almost two minutes, then relaxed and slid down to hang at her sides, as with a last sliding whistle of choking, she drooped where she swung.

Some near her wanted to cut her down right away, but others wiser and more merciful held them back until four or five minutes had passed. They knew that should she recover, the Sheriff would put her through the whole ordeal again.

At last her body was lowered to the ground, and several of them carried it to the shallow grave two deputies had dug earlier. They dropped her in and filled it in again. Edward had faded away in the crowd. He knew he walked a knife-edge—his son and daughter-in-law escaped, and his beloved wife now hanged as a witch.

When the news came back to the gaol, those who had been laboring in prayer all morning, rose and fixed themselves some food, with a clearer sense of the path before them now that one of their number had gone its whole length.

Chapter Forty-Four -- The Violent Take it by Force

Verily I say unto you, Among them that are born of women there hath not risen a greater than John the Baptist: notwithstanding he that is least in the kingdom of heaven is greater than he. And from the days of John the Baptist until now the kingdom of heaven suffereth violence, and the violent take it by force. . . . For John came neither eating nor drinking, and they say, He hath a devil. -- **Matthew 11: 11-12, 18.**

It is remarkable the degree to which our founders avowed intentions have become but words to us, and our principal desires the things they most eschewed. The royal charter of 1629 appointed the officers of Massachusetts:

> *. . . for the directing, ruling, and disposeing of all other Matters and Thinges, whereby our said People, Inhabitants there, may be soe religiously, peaceablie, and civilly governed, as their good Life and orderlie Conversation, maie wynn and incite the Natives of the Country, to the Knowledg and Obedience of the onlie true God and Savior of Mankinde, and the Christian Fayth, which in our Royall Intention, and the Adventurers free Profession, is the principall Ende of this Plantation.*

And thirty years later, John Norton, writing principally against the Quakers, said "It concerneth New England alwayes to remember, that Originally they are a Plantation Religious, not a Plantation of Trade," which was repeated and expanded by our own Reverend John Higginson, in 1663:

> It concerneth New England always to remember that they are originally a plantation religious, not a plantation of trade. The profession of the purity of doctrine, worship, and discipline is written upon her forehead. Let merchants, and such as are increasing . . . remember this: that worldly gain was not the end and design of the people of New England, but religion.

These exhortations were addressed to the fact that there was a "new religion" coming to prevail. Reverend Nathaniel Ward, principal author of the *Body of Liberties,* our first law code, wrote a satire against the changed faith of the colony, *The Simple Cobbler of Agawam* (1647), in which he summarized, "Interest is their Faith, Mony their God, and Large Possessions the only Heaven they covet."

Ten years before our troubles, Reverend William Hubbard preached a Fast-Day sermon in which he reminded his congregation:

> [The founders] came not hither for the world, or for land, or for traffic; but for religion, and for liberty of conscience in the worship of God, which was their only design.

The change was not only in the objects of our worship, but in the violence with which we were willing to obtain and defend them. Salem was named by old Reverend Higginson for its primary meaning "peace," which he found the salient feature of the Naumkeags in their relations with the first white settlers there. They fed and sheltered the Salem colonists, and taught them how to raise good crops. Where are the Naumkeags now? We are a long way from what was not so long ago the "principall ende" of the colony.

It is perverse, but perhaps predictable, that Governor Endicott and Reverend Skelton, leaders among people who had been persecuted by bishops, should ship some who wanted Episcopal churches back to England. But they did the same with the first Quakers who arrived. When the "Friends" proved more persistent than the Episcopalians, the governor hanged Mary Dyer and three others in Boston. Then Endicott gave Elder Clark thirty lashes for an unauthorized prayer meeting, making for the colonial Baptists a martyr as holy to them as Latimer and Ridley.

The Quakers were hanged or driven out, in part, because of their loud opposition to violence. They are crotchety and, I think, wrong about much, but they are not wrong about us and the human heart, and the tendency for man's government to run always in the strength and heat of the flesh. The Pennsylvanians have dealt with the Indians far more equitably than we. The Quakers may be wrong in completely discounting war, when God often initiated and approved in the scriptures, but they are not wrong in calling us to consider the motives of our wars. As often as not these are Christian fighting Christian over secular power. Even when the matters of contention are doctrinal—the doctrines are often linked to human power in secular or ecclesiastical office. Would there be wars over the nature of the Lord's Supper were its administration not treated as an instrument of power and authority? Likewise images, preaching, baptism, marriage, offices and so on.

Yet for the violence of tyrannical high-handedness, there is an opposite violence which denies all authority but one's own. Ann Hutchinson was at last driven out after she insisted on her own prerogative to receive binding revelations from God. Not even her staunch defenders like Reverend Cotton could defend her in that. Where every man's a king, every conflict is a war. (After she was banished, she and her family went to Rhode Island and New York, where Indian violence ended her life.)

Among the stated intentions of the Puritan Revolution in England was throwing off the horrors of ecclesiastical violence, yet it used a great deal of violence and determined on the execution of the king, a solution most difficult to justify from scripture. (Our Nathaniel Ward, returned and become a vicar in England, is said to have opposed it in writing.) In turn, at the Restoration, the "regicides" were put to terrible deaths, and as late as the 1680's, their families were still considered "attainted," a thing contrary to the explicit teachings of Christ.

Violence inevitably seems to breed violence, so that the "Witch Panic" in the midst of the English Commonwealth was fed by the blood of English battles just as our troubles here. Matthew Hopkins, "The Witch-finder General," had two hundred English witches put to death upon the heels of the great victories of the Puritan Revolution. The zealotry of war greatly facilitated it. Cromwell turned into a great pacifier once his army had defeated the royalists and achieved an equilibrium against parliament. We, on the other hand, are so familiar with violence of one kind or another that we seem to thrive on it.

We have learned to justify violence over against those who disagree with us and those who are not like us. The Indians were driven back until we no longer pretended to make treaties with them — The Christian Indians as well as the rest. Governor Endicott (who lived on and first owned the farm next which the Nurses ran their plows) led the early expedition to punish the Pequots because they had killed surveyors sent to the Connecticut.

There is a kind of violence perpetrated under color of peace and law. Such was that of the surveyors. There is a self-defense that the scriptures make distinct from violence — such in some measure, was the Pequot's. There is a vengeance against the defender which is merely violence compounded — such perhaps was Governor Endicott's. The next year, of course, the Indians retaliated once more in the Pequot War, the vibrations of which grew to oscillations and rumbled up again into King Philips War forty years later, and still go on in King Williams War, reverberating even now.

By the 1670s, in King Philip's War, we came to offer violence most readily. At that time we murdered the sons of the Indian who welcomed and made treaty with the Mayflower Pilgrims. It is true as a bare excuse that by then the Indians had become angry enough to begin murdering us.

But the red fist of violence thinly gloved in fabrics of faith has clenched the sword so long it is no longer cramped or painful, indeed it can scarcely open to drop it. The clenching and the striking have become second nature to us. Not only have we never beaten our swords into plowshares, but our hands appear more comfortable on the handle of the former — it is from the sword that we think we ought not to turn back, lest we be found unfit for the kingdom. The plow is merely an instrument to maintain our grip. Like the Romans, we seem not so much fighting farmers as farming soldiers.

Papists, Prelates, Quakers, Baptists, pagans, pirates, Indians, neighbors, and finally witches — we believe we were made for our enemies rather than for our God. If in times past, we fought to live, now we seem to live to fight. We had come, before our troubles, to a point where we scarcely knew any other way to live.

From the neighborhood of Salem Village some forty of us had fought in King Philips War — quite a few in the Narragansett Swamp Fort Fight. Fourteen local men died of wounds or exposure in that war, the worst yet fought in the colonies. It is said one out of twenty colonists were killed and one out of twenty homesteads burnt by the Indians. In the Fort Fight our men are commonly said to have been the first inside the Indian stockade and to have carried themselves like ancient heroes. But nearly a thousand Indians were killed in that battle — most of them women and children.

Thomas Shepard wrote about the treatment of the Indians during the Pequot War forty years earlier:

> At last, by the direction of one Captain Mason, their
> wigwams were set on fire, which being dry and contiguous to
> one another, was most dreadful to the Indians: some burning,
> some bleeding to death by the sword, some resisting till they

were cut off, some flying were beat down by the men without, until the Lord had utterly consumed the whole company, except four or five girls they took prisoner and dealt with them at Seabrook as they dealt with ours at Weathersfield. (*Autobiography*)

In the same way, during King Philip's War we killed most of the enemy whom we took prisoner. The rest were sold into slavery in the Barbados.

Like Massasoit, most of the Indians treated the early interlopers with exceeding charity for many years. It was only after the pattern of treaty-made-treaty-broken had been repeated over and over that his sons broke off all appearance of peace, and acknowledged the violence of lies and broken vows with the violence of arrow and bullet. Theirs may have been a less civilized violence than ours up to that point, but effective, too, in reducing the number of white settlements nearly by half. We set aside our other fights long enough to unite in crushing them—succumbing in a kind of further defeat as we took up their weapons of attacking women and children. (Massasoit's son, King Philip was killed only after we captured his wife and family.) When Philip was dead, we returned to fighting with each other.

It was according to this honorable tradition that we responded to inexplicable afflictions, fears, and rivalries with arrests, torture and hanging during our troubles. We are a violent people with generations of violence as the heritage we have brought to the colonies and here nourished.

Land was what we fought the Indians for and land was chief among our local strivings. The land that Francis Nurse rented and bought from Reverend John Allen was first Townsend Bishop's, then Henry Chickering's, then John Endicott's, and then his widow's. They had no children, so it came to the hands of Reverend Allen. There had been much contention about its borders among various neighbors.

There were few conflicts between John Endicott and Townsend Bishop, despite the haphazard fashion in which the earliest grants were made (perhaps with the strange expectation that Christian men could charitably and equitably arrive at agreements regarding their mutual boundaries.) The problems came over choice parts, especially, when ownership changed, and gentlemen's agreements were not detailed in official records. Zerubabel Endicott had gone to court over it—not so much against his brother's widow, as out of frustration over not being certain which was his land. By the time Francis Nurse came, there were long-standing differences with two sets of neighbors, the Endicott heirs, and Nathaniel Putnam.

The piece of ground contested between Mr. Allen on his east and the Endicotts on their west depended for its original north-south survey points on two trees both of which had fallen down, so that the memories of the whitest heads in the village were relied upon for conflicting accounts of where the rotting trunks lay. There were four or five surveys of the same contested lines between Mr. Allen and John Endicott, and between the Nurses and Zerubabel Endicott. The surveys came out variously, depending on which white head was consulted on the position of the trees and the streams. The last several surveys alternated between two sets of lines.

When Francis Nurse first moved onto the land he was ignorant of the conflict. Mr. Allen had his former tenant walk the boundaries with Goodman Nurse. Four months later Francis and his sons were surprised to receive a summons to court in Salem for cutting and carrying away wood from land belonging to Zerubabel Endicott. The Nurses lost the case.

That winter Tom Preston came galloping back to the house with the news that the Endicott men were cutting lumber on the contested stretch of ground. Father Nurse, Sam, Tom, and John hurried down. The Endicotts had indeed cut about fifty trees and loaded the logs in sleds. The Nurses rode up in righteous indignation and threw all the timber out of the sleds, while Francis demanded to know whose men they were. Zerubabel Endicott was with them and said they were his men, for it was his land. Francis hotly contradicted him.

"You may descend from a governor, but I contracted for this land, and its mine alone to cut, clear, or cultivate." His face was red and his fierce eyes those of a self-made man. Endicott ordered his men home, and this time the Nurses went to court for damages, but they lost again. Zerubabel had only one written proof to hold up against John Allen's, but his family was local and deeply respected. It was not long before Endicott was cutting again on the contested land, and Father Nurse went back to court. Cases were fought back and forth for twelve years, with the local courts usually finding for the Endicotts and the General Court finding for the Nurses, but with both sides appealing nearly every decision.

The other conflict over Nurse land involved Lieutenant Nathaniel Putnam. He and Francis Nurse had been on the same side in the boundary war with the Endicotts, but at the north end of the contested area, they had their own conflict. It concerned nineteen acres near the creek which was on or near their common boundary. Lt. Putnam and Reverend Allen had been to court over it in 1678 and again in 1681.

Despite the small size, the piece was good ground, Mr. Putnam felt strongly about it. The Nurses felt hard-pressed. They fought back just as hard on this second front. Several members of the Rea family testified on Lieutenant Putnam's side — various other men on the Nurses' — but both sides had conflicting surveys and official decisions on record, so that final agreements had to come from compromise — which nobody was willing to initiate. There was still contention when the Village troubles began. (Thus it was a considerable act of charity that Lieutenant Putnam wrote a petition on behalf of Rebecca. One small benefit out of our great suffering was that he and Francis laid the old conflict to rest.)

Another such conflict or series of conflicts went on further north between Nathaniel Putnam's brother, Captain John, and Rebecca Nurse's Towne relatives. When Topsfield was founded, in much the same subsidiary relationship to Ipswich as Salem Village has to Salem, the newly incorporated town included land south of the Ipswich River — land which some northerly Salem Villagers considered their own. Various efforts were made to settle the dispute. Much of this disputed land was claimed by Topsfield as "common land," but the town subsequently divided it among the inhabitants, and Thomas Towne (Rebecca Nurse's oldest brother), John and Joseph (Jr.) Towne, and Isaac Easty (husband of Mary) came into direct conflict with Captain Putnam and his sons over the land.

In 1687, only five years before our troubles, Isaac Easty, Sr., Isaac Easty, Jr., Thomas, John and Joseph Towne, Jr., brought suit against Captain John Putnam, his sons and some cousins, for cutting timber "within Topsfield bounds and on Topsfield men's property." When the Topsfield men warned the Putnam timbermen, Captain John responded,

"I have felled the timber here cut down on my orders. I will keep on cutting and carrying away from this land until next March."

"What!" demanded Thomas Towne, to whom the land had been granted, "By violence?"

"Aye," said Captain John, "By violence. You may sue me. You know where I dwell." His crew then returned to their cutting.

Thomas Towne went to court, supported by the testimony of various other Townes and Eastys. They won, and the ownership of the Topsfield men was confirmed. Captain Putnam later sued Isaac Easty at Ipswich for lying in open court, but the case seems to have come to nothing, except as further exacerbation of enmity which was to burn hot in the witch trials.

These "land wars" went on in a very wide circle — for most neighbors had them to some degree — over a few feet of meadow if not a few acres. Family feuds went on — within circles of relatives and between them. Since everybody in Massachusetts is related to somebody else, at least as a 3rd or 4th cousin, every fight is a family fight in some sense or another. And sometimes, as in the Wilkin's family's accusation of John Willard, family fights are the ugliest.

Some fights were about issues of rent. Francis Nurse fought with Reverend Allen, himself, pastor of the First Church of Boston, who sent Captain John Flood of Rumney to Salem to sue for what was owed. (That man, who served as Mr. Allen's attorney, collecting debts and bringing suit around the Village, trampled on many toes, and in May of 1692, the official toes of a constable brought a witchcraft warrant to his door. Captain Flood departed the country in short order.)

Francis Nurse's argument against Reverend Allen, strong on the face of it, was that battles over the borders with Endicott and Putnam ought to have been settled by Allen. He held back part of the rent because, having agreed to rent 300 acres at such and such a rate, the Nurses had ended up with nearly 30 acres less through the land wars. He felt he ought to have his rent adjusted accordingly and perhaps further reduced to cover time and legal fees.

The legal battles were fought mostly with official paper and by the principals themselves, but we also had local "attorneys", men like Captain Flood and Edmund Bridges, Jr. (first husband of Rebecca Nurse's sister, Sarah, now Cloyce) and Edmund Batter of Salem, who prided themselves on their knowledge of the law and their ability to serve as advocates more effectively than those they represented might do. Such men tended not to be peace-makers, but legal duelers — not greatly liked or respected, but increasingly to be reckoned with.

The land wars had many roots, but in addition to greed and the growing willingness to rob the Indians of their ancient grounds, the wars were also intensified by the different perspectives on property we brought with us from different parts of England. The idea of a "commons," including common woodlot and common meadow was strong in some parts of England, and were important to many old settlers in our colony.   But the idea made for a lot of confusion and required continual supervision and regulation. Others of us came from places where a "freehold" was the only alternative to wilderness, and this idea fit better with the desires and inclinations of our second and third generations. Gradually, therefore the commons shrank and were divided and distributed among the settlers, furnishing grounds for new conflicts and resentments.

Some of our battles were even smaller in scope, but loomed large in the battlefields of minds — as well as in the troubles to come. Rebecca Nurse, like many another great-hearted woman among us, was not always as patient as she was at the end. She became angry on a few occasions with neighbors who trespassed on Nurse prerogatives, or allowed their livestock to trespass on Nurse land.

Relative new-comers, only fourteen years in place, the Nurses were working hard to improve and earn their farm. The pressures of law-suits with their landlord and neighbors, as well as conflicts in the church made them as short-tempered as many, and more testy than a few. Rebecca dressed down Benjamin Holten for letting his pig get into their crops. Soon after that, he grew sick and quickly died. Goodwife Holten would not forgive her — which is also a violence. This cloud no bigger than a man's hand became part of the great storm which burst during our troubles.

We used hard words against one another. For over twenty years witch charges had been raised against various people. And even where no person was charged, witch rumors often followed mysterious mishaps and deaths. Reverend Lawson was quick to come to the Village at the beginning of our troubles when witchcraft was mentioned in connection with the death of his wife and daughter. We used violence and we suspected violence.

The violence which had become our reflex, the violence of our habits and hearts swelled up and erupted even in the midst of our meeting, our own church of Christ in Salem Village, our families and our businesses. Our troubles, then, were only a further expression of the same.

At the heart of our many violences were the things we most condemned in our enemies. How often we hate in others those sins which are our own. Anne Hutchinson and the Quakers aroused the rage of the civil and church leaders by claiming some special insight into God's will and an independent assurance that they went the right way. The "inner light" of the Quakers and Anne Hutchinson's revelations were derived apart from scripture. They did not therefore seem susceptible to scriptural correction. But the same sort of independent assurance was the foundation for much we did ourselves—all the sermonizing about our being a uniquely chosen people in a specially chosen place, set apart for God's special purposes in history. Did it derive from scripture? Or at least, was our interpretation of it biblical? And more pointed yet – were the things we did on the basis of that interpretation godly?

As also in our wars against the Indians and our flouting of treaties with them -- as also in our internecine wars over land and local power — the violence against other sects was based on an unsupported sense of absolute right, where in fact only relative right existed, that is, relative to God. In the same way the ministers and magistrates who most zealously prosecuted the witch trials did so on the basis of "inner light" and personal revelation no more biblical than that they violently opposed.

In short, imagining ourselves the vessels of a special dispensation, we hated any who claimed a rival one. To epitomize the accused as witches, as violent subjects of the devil, was to see them as mirrors and therefore rivals of ourselves. How else to deal with them but by violence!

Chapter Forty-Five - High Places
(10-25 June)

*Among others which then sprung up, with but too much advantage,
in the third century, the Maniche did spread his pestiferous sentiments,
and taught the existence of two beings, or causes of all things, viz. a
good and a bad: but these were soon silenced by the more orthodox
doctors, and anathematized by general councils. . . .*

*Might a judgement be made from the books of the modern learned
divines, or from the practice of courts, or from the faith of many who call
themselves Christians it might be modestly, though scarcely, concluded,
that the doctrine of the Maniche, . . . is so far from being forgotten, that
tis almost everywhere professed. . . . The books here printed and
recommended, not only by the respective authors, but by many of their
brethren, do set forth that the devil inflicts plagues, wars, diseases,
tempests, and can render the most solid things invisible and can do
things above and against the course of nature, and all natural causes.*

-- Robert Calef, A Warning to The Ministers in *More
Wonders of the Invisible World*, 1700.

"I will lift up mine eyes to the hills. From whence does my
help come? . . ." says the psalmist. The instinct to look to high places
must be deeply rooted in the human heart. It was upon the high
places the ancient pagans built their altars. It is to the mountain top
the lonely or disturbed soul often directs his feet. And it is to the
high places the helpless and oppressed flee. "And they shall say to
the mountains cover us and to the hills fall on us." Yet though the
psalmist looks to the high places, he does not find his help there,
rather: "My help comes from the Lord, maker of heaven and earth."

The high places of human power, to which men look in times
of trouble, are usually as barren of wisdom as the low ones, but those
inhabiting them are capable of doing more damage. The execution of
Bridget Bishop upon Gallows Hill was the first deliberate act of legal
murder committed by the "witch court". The sheer enormity of it
loomed over us for weeks afterward.

For nearly a month, between the 4th of June and the 2nd of July
no new warrants were issued. Although the court had gone forward
with Bridget Bishop's execution, and the examinations and

investigations continued apace during the first week, there was a
growing conflict in the motive forces of our troubles. If Governor
Phips had been more frequently in Boston and able to pay more
attention to the witch trials and those who began to criticize them,
things would have come to more rapid end. Indeed, the greatest,
though unconscious, allies of the witchhunters may have been the
Indians to eastward whose depredations occupied Governor Phips
for almost three months.

Although there were no new arrests for a month, conference,
criticism and debate continued and intensified in many quarters.

Justice Saltonstall helped precipitate some of it by resigning.
Some say he resigned immediately when the death warrant was
issued, others the day Bridget Bishop was hanged. While the
conduct of the trial and the unease of his conscience at participating
are generally regarded as his reasons, those were not the reasons he
published. He spoke instead of being urgently needed by his family
and community in Haverhill, where the Indians had recently
attacked once more. But Judge Saltonstall did not spend all his time
back in Haverhill defending his family from Indians. In fact not too
much later, Judge Sewall wrote him a stern letter exhorting him to
be careful of drunkenness. (By fall Mr. Saltonstall was awarded the
high distinction of being himself accused.)

If cider was Nathaniel Saltonstall's solution to the witch
troubles, the pastor in nearby Topsfield made better use of the crisis.
On Monday, June 13th, the Reverend Joseph Capen brought three
men together to work out their differences in Christian reconciliation
before the gathered church of Topsfield. The men were Lieutenant
John Gould (his family closely tied to the Putnams), Captain John
Howe, and Ensign Jacob Towne. The feuds between them went back
more than twenty years, and involved not only the three previous
pastors, but three previous governments, ten serious incidents and as
many lawsuits, as well as many other families, including the John
Wildes. The bad blood between Gould and Howe on the one hand
and Gould and Towne on the other had as many kinds of poison and
as strong as sickened hundreds of other relationships before and
during our troubles.

Reverend Capen had realized that Topsfield, like Salem
Village, was riddled with infectious bitterness and hatred which
fueled the witch troubles through which many in Topsfield stood
accused. By the wise pursuit of biblical principles, Reverend Capen
and the other church leaders succeeded in bringing these three men

together to acknowledge at least in principle, the errors in their conflicts one with another. The congregation voted itself satisfied with their repentances, and voted to receive them at the Lord's Table. The three men "in token of the their mutual forgiveness did take each other by the hand, promising better for the future."

Reverend Capen hoped efforts toward Christian forgiveness and reconciliation such as this would go far toward halting our troubles. Unfortunately so much damage had been done already that Elizabeth Howe (sister in law of John) and Sarah Wilde (wife of John Wildes) were already numbered among the accused witches. Nor was John Gould so far repentant as to refrain from repeating twenty-year old hearsay as a witness against Sarah Wildes in her trial at the end of the month. Neither did John Howe find it out of keeping with his repentance to testify two weeks later against his own sister-in-law, Elizabeth.

At the same time as Reverend Capen gathered his Topsfield congregation for the reconciliation of its three members, Governor Phips met with his Council (that is the assistants from throughout the colony) in Boston. The Salem troubles were one of the principle concerns discussed. Despite Deputy Stoughton's insistence that the Court of Oyer and Terminer had things well in hand, the rest of the Council urged the Governor to apply to the leading ministers of Boston for guidance regarding the conduct of the trials. The Governor agreed.

The Boston ministers responded immediately to this request. But there was considerable secrecy about their meeting. To this day we are uncertain who was present, except it is said there were twelve. It is generally accepted that Increase Mather convened the meeting and that Cotton acted as its secretary — writing out the letter to the court that was made public afterward. It is also generally thought that the ministers included Samuel Willard, John Allen, Joshua Moody, and James Bailey. But which ministers made up the balance we do not know. Did they include any of the Salem divines?

Two days later, having met for many hours, the ministers expressed themselves in terms more eloquent than decisive, to the effect that: 1/what the court was doing was very important for the spiritual and temporal welfare of the colony, 2/ that the justices ought to be very careful so as to do no harm in the process; and 3/that everything the justices had done so far showed they were doing a fine job. That was the gist of the document, and that is how it was taken by Chief Justice Stoughton. Nevertheless, the details of the letter included several things on the cautionary side which would have made a great difference had the court heeded them:

> . . . that tenderness be used towards those accused, relating to matters presumptive and convictive, and also to privacy in examinations, and to consult Mr. Perkins and Mr. Bernard, what tests to make use of the scrutiny; that presumptions and convictions ought to have better grounds than the accusers affirming that they see such persons' spectres afflicting them; and that the devil may afflict in the shape of good men; and that falling at the sight, and rising at the touch of the accused, is no infallible proof of guilt; that seeing the devil's strength consists in such accusations, our disbelieving them may be a means to put a period to the dreadful calamities.

The effort of the ministers to be gracious and subtle was wasted on the court. We know the pastors did not all agree. No doubt the verbal vacillation in the document was partly a result of it being the record of compromise. As pointed as the cautionary sections were, they were eclipsed in the mind of the court (or its dominant personality) by the subsequent passages in which the ministers:

> . . .humbly recommend to the government, the speedy and vigorous prosecution of such as have rendered themselves obnoxious, according to the direction given in the laws of God, and the wholesome statutes of the English nation, for the detection of witchcraft.
>
> We cannot but with all thankfulness acknowledge the success which the merciful God has given unto the sedulous and assiduous endeavours of our honourable rulers, to detect the abominable witchcrafts which have been committed in the country; humbly praying that the discovery of those mysterious and mischievous wickednesses, may be perfected.

Since that "success" had consisted in arresting, examining, and beginning to try upwards of sixty persons on the primary bases of spectre evidence and magical proofs, and since their "assiduous endeavours" had resulted in the hanging of Bridget Bishop, the justices must have found it hard to summarize the letter in any other terms than 'keep on with what you are doing, only continue to be as careful as you have been.'

Nevertheless, the gathering of ministers put some steel into some of their fellows. William Hubbard of Ipswich wrote a defense of an accused witch on June 20th. He spoke forthrightly of Sarah Buckley's good character saying he was "strangely surprised" that any person should charge her with that of which she was accused.

At the same time as the ministers were meeting, the General Court (the assistants meeting in their legislative capacity) was passing its first act under the new charter for the continuance of all standing laws, "being not repugnant to the laws of England nor inconsistent with the present constitution."

On Thursday, June 16th, Dr. Roger Toothaker died at Boston gaol. The coroner's jury found that his death was "from natural causes."

On Saturday, Governor Phips met with his Council again. And on that day, Sam Nurse and John Tarbell met him for the first time. He reminded John of Daniel — one of those peculiarly colonial characters who could adapt himself to a wide range of persons and situations, polished or primitive. His secretary received their petitions and the Governor seemed to listen carefully to their brief plea on behalf of Mother Nurse. It was more brief than they wished because both were overawed in the presence of such high office, and said less than they might have.

Their petitions and personal pleas would have received more attention if they had not coincided with other importunities in regard to our troubles. As it was, the governor hoped that the particular problems would fall into place as the general matter went forward, and thus he set the Nurse petitions aside without any immediate action.

The Governor and his Boston advisers had begun to realize the potentials for disaster arising from these matters in Salem. Governor Phips had reached high office by the single-minded pursuit of particular goals. He was only beginning to learn the bewildering lesson that high office requires an ability to fight many heads of Hydra at the same time.

From the Salem trials were emerging not one but several heads dangerous to the governor: 1/the increasing power and rivalry of Lieutenant Governor Stoughton, 2/the many dimensions of the trials of which their Majesties might ultimately disapprove, and 3/the growing potential of rebellion by some of the louder opponents and advocates of the trials. More specifically as to the second, there was good possibility that royal disfavor might be aroused against either extreme – leniency or severity.

Like many another head of household, the governor was disturbed by all the domestic halloo-balloo, and his instinct was to hasten back to the field or business, in this case the field and business of battle with the Indians, as quickly as he possibly could. Governor Phips seems to have preferred lifting up his eyes to the hills of Maine.

The sun was at its traditional high place, the summer solstice, with its midsummer night's eve – or St. John's Eve, on June 23rd. In Europe and England, as a remnant of the old pagan holidays, it was thought to be the one night of the year when supernatural beings had a peculiar freedom to come and go at will, and when human revelry was often raised to a unwonted height. Strangely little was made of it in the colony, and there was no noticeable increase in "afflictions".

The sun was at its highest, the highest of our ministers had been consulted, the highest court continued, but none were adequate to our desperate need. We had lifted up our eyes to the high places and found no help there.

For the high places of the earth are neither God, nor better places to find him.

Chapter Forty-Six — The Silent Souls

*Far, therefore, be it from me, to have any thing to do with those men
your letter mentions, whom you acknowledge to be men of a factious spirit,
and never more in their element than when they are declaiming against men
in public place, and contriving methods that tend to the disturbance of the
common peace.*

*I never accounted it a credit to my cause, to have the good liking of
such men. My son! (says Solomon) fear thou the Lord and the King, and
meddle not with them that are given to change. Prov. xxiv.*

*However, Sir, I never thought Judges infallible; but reckoned that they,
as well as private men, might err; and that when they were guilty of erring,
standers by, who possibly had not half their judgment, might,
notwithstanding, be able to detect and behold their errors. And furthermore,
when errors of that nature are thus detected and observed, I never thought it
an interfering with dutifullness and subjection for one man to communicate
his thoughts to another thereabout; and with modesty and due reverence to
debate the premised failings; at least, when errours are fundamental, and
palpably pervert the great end of authority and government: for as to
circumstantial errours, I must confesse my principle is, that it is the duty of
a good subject to cover with his silence a multitude of them.*

-- *Letter* of **Thomas Brattle**, F.R.S., October 1692.

*But if you altogether hold your peace at such a time as this is, your silence,
at least seemingly, will speak this language; that you are not concerned,
though men ascribe the power and providence of the Almighty to the worst
of his creatures -- that if other ages or countries improve the doctrines and
examples given them, either to the taking away of the life or reputations of
innocents, you are well satisfied.*   --Robert Calef, A Warning To The
Ministers in *More Wonders of the Invisible World* (1700).

T he hanging of Bridget Bishop was like the mason's last tap
on a stone already fractured into three sections. With it the outward
appearance of a united colony disappeared, cloven through along the
fissures which "public safety" and "spiritual warfare" had made
among us.

Upon Gallows Hill there were no longer one, but three sorts
of people gathered: the zealous accusers and prosecutors; the

accused victims; and the standers-by. The top of that hill became the riven peak of our new world. We were no more a single "city set on a hill" and no longer had one mind. The high place of our executions became a Tower of Babel, from which people of different tongues dispersed.

Or if it is too much to say many nations separated and moved apart from the place and time of Bridget Bishop's execution, yet certainly we can say it was evident at that time and place that our "new world" was divided into three. The three parts were the world of the zealots, the world of their victims, and the world of the silent onlookers. Most of the souls inhabiting our colony identified themselves within the borders of one of these worlds. The divisions and boundaries affected all, even where they were obscured.

The world of the zealots was not confined to the witch-hunters. One of the matters most occupying the minds of the governor, his councilors and the ministers of Boston in June was the advent of zealous opposition.

Often the pioneers of opposition are more zealous than the ones they resist. Among worlds where victims have no voice and the silent will not use theirs, this is nearly inevitable. Furthermore, zealous opposition often seems to do its cause more harm than good, at least at first. It is determined, frequently foolhardy, and sometimes borrows the worst of what it opposes. Zealous pioneers seldom are good teachers, though they are prophets. They cannot formulate and communicate the tenets of their opposition so well as they can declare and act upon them.

Thus amongst the subjects occupying the Governor and his councilors, as well as the ministers who gathered in June to advise them, were a few outspoken opponents of the witch trials, whose words, spoken and written were heard during that month.

These opponents, through a strange set of connections, contributed to the ambivalence of the ministers' advice and helped soften it into the ineffectual document it became. At the same time these opponents strengthened the resolve of the justices on the Court of Oyer and Terminer.

Early in June there began to circulate some papers by William Milbourne, a preacher of Baptist proclivity, who like Reverend Burroughs came from the Governor's own province of Maine. Reverend Milbourne had ministered at Saco a decade earlier. He had come up to Boston where he was one of the more vehement voices against the Andros' administration, contributing to the revolution which deposed that governor.

He published papers addressed "to the Grave and Juditious the Generall Assembly of the Province" which attacked the Court of Oyer and Terminer. The papers particularly protested the conviction "upon bare specter testimonie" of "persons of good fame and of unspotted reputation." They included the statement that "the innocent will be condemned and a woeful chain of consequences will follow, inextricable damage will be done to this province. Give no more credence to specter testimony than the Word of God alloweth."

Milbourne found none among those in high office who were willing to publicly identify with him. The Council was unsure of the authorship at first, partly because in circulating them, Milbourne had succeeded in getting a number of additional signatures. The question of their authorship was among the matters the ministers were asked to elucidate. They seem to have taken the papers seriously enough that their own conclusions reflected them. Indeed it is striking the degree to which their own report picked up Milbourne's language in regard to spectre evidence.

Nevertheless, Milbourne was identified and called before the Council on June 25th, his papers characterized as "containing very high reflections upon the administration of public justice within this their Majesty's Province".

Upon examination Reverend Milbourne was bold in saying he wrote the papers. Some suggested he was in fact taking more credit than was actually his.

He was ordered to be committed to prison or give bond of $200.00 with two sureties to answer at the next session of the Superior court. The actual charges against him were "for framing, contriving, writing and publishing the said seditious and scandalous papers or writings."

The high degree to which this retarded the opposition to the trials, rather than strengthening it is due to another connection of Milbourne's.

In New York from May 1689 to March 1691, a Dutchman, Jacob Leysler, held the reigns of government, styling himself Lieutenant Governor of New York. At the outset Leysler overthrew a relatively unpopular government which included several Roman Catholic officers. Many who gave considerable support at first soon found Leysler's administration too high-handed. As his primary partner in this administration, Leysler appointed his son-in-law as secretary. That son-in-law was Jacob Milbourne, brother of this

Reverend William.

In March 1691, newly appointed Royal Governor Slaughter sent his emissary ahead of him from England, which representative arrived with troops and demanded that Leysler turn over his office. Leysler refused to surrender it to any but the new governor, so the troops gave battle. The new governor arrived as the fighting went forward. Soon the governor's troops defeated and arrested Leysler and Milbourne along with six other officers. All were sentenced for treason. The punishment handed down was hanging, disembowelment while still alive, burning of entrails before them, etc. The six others were pardoned, but Leysler and Milbourne were executed in the grisliest fashion possible.

"Leyslers Rebellion" had a mixed reputation among us in Massachusetts. On the one hand it was parallel to our own rebellion against Governor Andros. On the other hand Leysler and Jacob Milbourne were not only reputed violent and profligate in both their rebellion and government, but it was popularly said that when the new Royal Governor arrived, they refused to submit to him. In that point they were universally regarded as treasonous.

Most significant of all, in relation to our troubles, they had been prosecuted by Thomas Newton, now King's Attorney before our own Court of Oyer and Terminer. Newton, of course, would abide no defense of the leaders of "Leysler's Rebellion". When William Milbourne was found to be circulating papers opposed to the actions of the high court, his character and actions was associated with those of his brother Jacob.

Other wiser or more favorably placed opponents of the trials were checked outwardly and inwardly by the Council's edict against Reverend Milbourne. The effect was to stifle others of higher reputation who would have spoken out. Publications in Philadelphia and New York continued to criticize the conduct of the trials, but few such were published or even circulated in Massachusetts until the trials had drawn to a close. And even when the Governor finally dissolved the court, he banned publishing on the subject.

Thomas Brattle's critique, framed as a private letter to a friend, was not written until October and was not widely published, but only circulated among a few, albeit influential men. Thomas Maule of Salem, outspoken Quaker and businessman, did not print his contemporary criticisms until long after the trials came to an end. And Maule's friend and co-belligerent, Joseph Calef, did not publish his extensive critique, *More Wonders of the Invisible World* (the title a parody of Cotton Mather's book) until 1700, and that in London.

An anonymous pamphlet, *Some Miscellany Observations on Our Present Debates Respecting Witchcrafts,* was published (supposedly in Philadelphia by William Bradford, known as a publisher of controversial things) during the trials. This tract written by some Nicodemus, (many said it was the work of Reverend Simon Willard) appeared late in the summer, but even it was too late and too little to save those tried over the next months. (The publisher was imprisoned for "sedition" in Philadelphia during this same year. There he supported the Quaker George Keith who called for a return to the "Friend's" founding doctrines, including non-participation in government.)

Bridget Bishop had been loud and one might say zealous in her early examinations. But in the world of the prosecutors she was powerless, one of the accused made an object of the zeal of others. And at last, upon the hill, after a few tears and prayers, she joined the silent, at the end of a rope. Thus were we divided into three worlds, yet thus were the three worlds brought together in one person, and one community.

It was the silent , however, who predominated. Many continued to speak in muted voices about the errors among us, but to the knowledge of those in Salem Village and surrounds, the best men remained withdrawn from the legal and judicial business that dominated us. Men who had brooked powerful opponents in various causes of conscience, became like wraiths in public, offering no word beyond a pious hope that we all should pray for God's will.

Silence seems simple — an absence of words. But our silence was compounded of many things. Chiefly it was made up of fear and doubt. But it was also motivated by a variety of strong desires which are not immediately attributed to the flesh.

Some there were who kept silence out of the old fear of anarchy, the sense we had following the overthrow of Governor Andros that the slightest further shaking of our foundations could bring them down in chaos. Such people wrestled with the tension between speaking against present abuses of power and the terrors of a society in which the powers were overthrown.

Others stayed silent out of rivalry and an unwillingness to give ammunition to their adversaries. Many leaders among both congregational and nonconformist groups were fearful about raising their voices over anything but their most vital distinctives. The Quakers and Baptists had gained a great deal of ground, and were chary of losing it. The orthodox churchmen were afraid any criticism they might give would weaken their predominancy which, with the growth of the nonconforming groups and the toleration provisions of the new charter, was already much on the wane.

Others, especially those related to or associated with the accused, feared for their necks or for their property and businesses, or for the other members of their families — fears increasingly well-supported by experience.

Several of those few broadsides and isolated expressions of disgust which broke the silence seemed counter-productive, resulting in little but the prosecution or proscription of their authors. Therefore men who genuinely wished to impede or end the injustice were holding their fire in hopes they might be more effective in a short time, when some of the fog had lifted.

A large number of persons kept silent as though their silence was itself a strategy, a weapon that robbed the evil among us of power. But it was quite the opposite.

Many motives for our silence seemed commendable. But our silence was wrong. It was the silence of the prophet's watchman who must share in the consequences of the evil done by those he fails to warn.

The worlds of judgment, victim, and silence were separated by narrow but profound rifts. They could not be joined again except through some power which comprehended all three.

Chapter Forty-Seven — Determined to Go Forward

Authority without wisdom is like a heavy axe
without an edge, fitter to bruise than polish.
-- Anne Bradstreet, **Meditation** #12 (1664)

Thus stands the cause between God and us: we are entered into covenant
with Him for his work; we have taken out a commission, the Lord hath
given us leave to draw our own articles. We have professed to enterprise
these actions upon these and these ends; we have hereupon besought Him
of favor and blessing. Now if the Lord shall please to hear us and bring us
in peace to the place we desire, then hath He ratified this covenant and
sealed our Commission [and] will expect a strict performance of the
articles contained in it. But if we shall neglect the observation of these
articles which are the ends we have propounded, and dissembling with our
God, shall fall to embrace this present world and prosecute our carnal
intentions, seeking great things for ourselves and our posterity, the Lord
will surely break out in wrath against us, be revenged of such a perjured
people, and make us know the price of the breach of such a covenant.
-- John Winthrop, *A Model of Christian Charity* (1630)

In the same way that the hiatus in arrests in March seemed
to renew the examining zeal of Judges Hathorne and Corwin, so the
three weeks pause in the trials in June seemed to give new
inspiration to the Court of Oyer and Terminer. Chief Justice
Stoughton and his several pairs of yoke-fellows lifted their shoulders
again and strained at the tugs which were ultimately linked to ropes
about eighteen more necks.

On June 27th summons were issued for witnesses in the
Grand Jury inquests of Sarah Good and Susannah Martin to begin
the next morning.

Sarah Good's inquest was completed the next day and on the
29th the Jury of Inquest indicted her for witchcraft. Since the deputies
were unable to find several witnesses, Susannah Martin's inquest
was delayed.

On the 28th summons were also issued for the inquests of
John Willard and Martha Carrier, but their trials were put off until
the next round.

The grand jury inquiries against Elizabeth Howe and Sarah Wildes went forward, continuing the preparations for their trials.

On the 29th Sarah Good's capital trial began as the grand juries for Sarah Wildes and Elizabeth Howe indicted both. That day Mistress Mary (North) Bradbury of Salisbury was arrested and brought to Salem.

By the 30th, the witnesses for Susannah Martin were gathered and her inquest ended in her indictment.

Grand jury inquests were completed on the 30th for John and Elizabeth Procter and for Martha Corey. However, with John Willard and Martha Carrier, these three were not tried for many weeks. The channels of the court became choked with much paper and many comings and goings, so that though these inquests handed down indictments, they did not lead immediately to trials. That these witches were still dangerous was sworn to by many, including Sarah Vibber who was afflicted by an apparition of John Procter early in the month.

But the trials began for the five women under indictment. Rebecca Nurse, the first indicted, on March 24, had the highest reputation among them. Sarah Good was a notorious character in the Village, as we have said. Elizabeth Howe's name had been connected to witchcraft rumors in Topsfield and Ipswich for a long time. Sarah Wilde was the subject of old allegations in Beverly and Ipswich. Susannah Martin had an ancient and stained reputation in Salisbury.

During their inquests and trials the "afflicted" Susannah Sheldon made a great noise. She spoke of being afflicted within the last few days by these five women and of hearing from many spectres of those they bewitched to death.

The court proceeded as the examining magistrates had. Although there was a little more restraint in the courtroom, the evidences and testimonies were essentially those of the examinations. And the "afflicted" could still be counted on for immediate and dramatic demonstrations.

Against Sarah Good we have already seen what the evidence was. There was one incident during her trial which once more exposed the unshakable faith of the court in the afflicted. Elizabeth Booth fell into a fit and drummed her heels a while on the floor. As she recovered she called out "Oh, Goody Good, why do you stab me so!" and she pulled a piece of a knife blade from her breast and showed it to the court. It was indeed the broken blade of a knife, but soon after this someone slipped up to the justices and gave them some information that caused them to call a young man to testify. Upon coming up, he brought from his pocket a knife from which the tip had been broken. He further testified that he had broken the knife on the previous day when Elizabeth Booth was present, and that he had thrown away the broken tip. The court then addressed itself to Elizabeth, caught out in her deceit. Mr. Stoughton told her not to tell lies, yet he did not dismiss her from the court even for that day. She was sent back to sit with the other girls and went on with as much zeal, crying out with them in their afflictions.

There is a clarity to surprise, as there is substance to anger and indignation at injustice when it is first witnessed. But even horror and pain fade under long subjection. A few days, a few weeks, a few months dull the clarity, erode the substance, and make horror and pain seem commonplace. When what-ought-not-to-be is perpetuated, what-should-be is obscured. As the shadow of a looming cloud seems more substantial than the house it sweeps over, the effects of injustice obscure the true things they adumbrate.

Thus when we went back into the courts after Bridget Bishop's hanging, fewer of us were looking for justice or truth. Most of us hoped for a few smaller legal obstacles or the coincidence of particulars that might modify the march of the leviathan and somewhat lessen its destruction.

The evidence in the cases against the next five women showed various dreary shades of the darkness at the heart of our troubles.

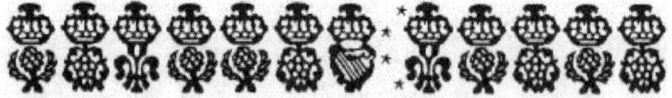

Chapter Forty-Eight -- The Mare and the Pipe

I do believe that the evil angels do often take advantage from natural distempers in the children of men to annoy them with such further mischiefs as we call preternatural. The malignant vapours and humours of our diseased bodies may be used by devils thereinto insinuating as engine of the execution of their malice upon these bodies; and perhaps for this reason one sex may suffer more troubles of some kinds from the invisible world than the other, as well as for that reason for which the old serpent made where he did his first address.
-- Cotton Mather, ***Another Brand Pluckt Out of the Burning:***
*An Account of the Sufferings of Margaret Rule_*(1700)

Although the devastation of the world, the flesh and the devil seem severe in the extreme when they are allowed to reach such a pitch as in our troubles, yet there is a puniness, an insignificance to the effects of sin-serving man, such that the scriptures compare him to chaff and dust, vapor and withering grass. We are told the Lord at times scoffs at the folly of those who oppose him -- "He that sitteth in the heavens shall laugh: the Lord shall have them in derision." (Psalm 2:4)

Even as the court was preparing once again to bring a death sentence to five of our neighbors, it was admitting into evidence things more ludicrous than were ever invented by the fancy of a Chaucer or a court jester.

In the case against Elizabeth Howe, particular emphasis was given to mysterious maladies among livestock, and in particular some mysterious torment which befell a poor mare belonging to Isaac Cummings, Senior, of Topsfield, a deacon in the Ipswich church.

Elizabeth Howe, wife of the blind James Howe, Jr., was formally complained of in late May, and examined on the 31st of that month. But accusations against her had been mooted about among her neighbors for several years. On the basis of witchcraft rumors, the Cummings were among those who opposed Elizabeth Howe's efforts to covenant with the Ipswich congregation some years before.

At that time a small mystery had arisen. Several horses in the neighborhood were ridden to exhaustion by an unknown rider. The

A Gallows Set

particular accusations against Elizabeth Howe were made public just about the time a few neighbors were concluding Isaac Cummings, Jr. had been borrowing their mounts by night to go on jaunts with a young woman. Isaac escaped blame when the horse tales were transferred to the body of rumors that kept Elizabeth Howe out of the Ipswich church.

By the end of June, when the depositions concerning Elizabeth Howe were taken, there emerged the "story of the pipe and mare," as the tale was called long after.

On a particular Thursday, James Howe, Jr. had asked Isaac Cummings, Jr. if his father had a horse he might borrow. Isaac, Jr. replied he had not. James then asked if perhaps Isaac, Sr. had a mare, to which Isaac, Jr. said, yes he had, but he could not loan it, since his father was planning on riding the next day.

The next day, Isaac, Sr. and his wife Mary (nee: Andrews) rode the mare to a neighbor's house and when they returned in the evening, the mare was in fine condition.

During the night, however, something happened to the animal. When Isaac , Sr. came out on Saturday morning, the mare stood before his door, its head drooping, its coat matted and stained, and its mouth severely injured. It looked like it had been very roughly handled over a long ride. In his June deposition against Elizabeth Howe, Isaac Jr., testified "I seeing the same said mare the next morning could judge no other but that she had been rid the other part of that night or other ways horribly abused."

Isaac, Sr. put the ailing mare in the barn, but she would eat nothing he gave her, so a day later he sent for his "brother" (in-law) Thomas Andrews of Boxford, who had some reputation as a horse doctor.

Tom Andrews showed up the next day when Isaac, Sr. was not at home. He looked the mare over and concluded she might have a case of the botts, a digestive disease caused by the larvae of a fly. Andrews gave the horse a concoction to treat that condition. When Isaac, Sr. came home just before dusk, the two men looked the mare over again and Andrews concluded the treatment had done no good. He next suggested the mare might have the "belly-ache," but since he could not tell, he wanted to try an experiment, "which was a pipe and some tobacco which he applied to her thinking it might do her good."

But when "brother" Andrews described the specific method by which he was going to "apply" the pipe and tobacco, Isaac

Cummings said he did not think it was lawful to treat her that way.
His brother-in-law, being the horse doctor, convinced him against his
objections, by saying it was a standard test. Isaac, Sr. recalled:

> My brother Anderos said he wold take a pipe of tobaco and
> lite it and put itt in to the fundement of the maer. I told him
> that I thought it was not lawfull. He said it was lawfull for
> man or beast. Then I toke a clen pipe and filled it with tobaco
> and did lite it and went with the pipe lite to the barn. Then
> the said Anderos used the pipe as he said before he wold.

In his own testimony, Tom Andrews described his reasoning
and the effects of his experiment:

> I could not tell what to doe for her. I perceived she had not
> the botts which I did att first think she had, butt I said she
> might have some great heat in her body & I would applie a
> pipe of tobacco to her. That was concented to and I litt a pipe
> of tobaco and putt itt under her fundiment. There came a
> blew flame out of the bowle & run along the stem of said pipe
> & took hold of the haer of said maer & burnt itt.

Isaac, Jr. was looking on during this operation, and both he
and his father were alarmed at the result:

> When they used the pipe with tobacco in itt abought the said
> maer the pipe being litt itt blazed so much that itt was as
> much as two persons could putt itt ought with both of their
> hands upon which my father said wee will trye no more,
> brother.

Isaac, Sr.'s testimony was:

> The pipe of tobacco did blaze and burn blew. Then I said to
> my brother Anderos you shall try no more. It is not lawful.
> He said I will try again once mor which he did and then thar
> arose a blaze from the pipe of tobacco which seemed to me to
> cover the butocks of the said mear. The blaz went up ward
> towards the roof of the barn and in the roof of the barn thar
> was a grate crackling as if the barn wold have falen or bin
> burnt which semed so to us which ware with in and some

that ware with out. And we hade no other fier in the barn but
only a candil and a pipe of tobaco and then I said I thought
my barn or my mear most goe.

True scientist and medical man that he was, Tom Andrews
was not to be put off so easily:

> We tryed itt 2 or 3 times together & itt did the same. Itt
> semed to burn blew butt run like fyer that is sett on the gras
> to burn itt in the spring tyme & we struck itt outt w'th our
> hands & the said Comings said that he would trye no more
> for said he, I had rather loose my mare than my barn.

Isaac, Jr. affirmed his uncle's pertinacity as well as his father's
conclusion:

> My uncle said he would trye once more which he did. The
> pipe being litt, the fyer blazed out of the same said pipe more
> vehemently then before, upon which my father answerd he
> had rather loose his maer than his barn.

Isaac, Sr.'s faith in his brother-in-law as a veterinary seems to
have been finally shaken the next day. "The next day being Lord's
Day I spoke to my brother Anderos at noone to come to see the said
mear and said Anderos came and what he did I say not." One
hesitates to imagine what further treatment brought Isaac, Sr. to this
shocked silence. Whatever it was, combined with the original abuse
and previous day's medical treatments, it proved extreme in results.
He went on:

> The same Lords day at night my naighbour John Hunkins
> came to my hous and he and I went in to my barn to see this
> mear. Said Hunkins said and if I ware as you, I would cut off
> a pece of this mear and burn it. I said no not to day but if she
> lived til tomorow morning he might cut of a pece off of her
> and burn it if he would. Presently as we hade spoken these
> words we stept out of the barn and emedeiatly this said mear
> fell downe dade and never stured as we coold purseve after
> she fell down, but lay stone dead.

Isaac, Jr. made even the death of the horse sound more ominous:

The very nex night folloing the said maer folloing my father in his barn from one side to the other side fell down emediatly dead against the sell of the barn befor my father had well cleerd him selfe from her.

This story will no doubt be told in inns and barns throughout the bounds of Essex County for years to come. But since it was originally told in the context of a capital trial, and since the witnesses were claiming that Elizabeth Howe was the agent of this mare's affliction rather than they, we find it hard to tell it or to laugh at it as heartily as we otherwise might.

Isaac, Jr., who many believe to be the real agent of the mare's original affliction made a point of testifying that this was "the same maer which said Hough would have borowed which semingly was well when my father & mother came home." And Thomas Andrews reiterated:

> I this deponant doe testify that to the best of my understanding this was the same mare that James Hough Junior belonging to Ipswich farmes, husband to Elizabeth Hough, would have borowed of the said Comings .

During the same period of time both Nehemiah Abbott and Jacob Foster of the same neighborhood discovered similar mysterious disabilities of horses that appeared to have been ridden hard during the night and eventually attributed these to Elizabeth Howe. According to Goodwife Cummings, Elizabeth defended herself by suggesting Isaac Cummings, Jr. had taken his father's mare to see his girl friend some distance away. She or her husband apparently also suggested that Cummings or Tom Andrews fed the mare oil and sulphur which caused the spectacular display brought on by the pipe experiment. Goodwife Cummings rebutted this, however, referring to a more recent incident of yet another horse "bewitched" by Elizabeth Howe:

> A short time after, my son Isaac's maer came in sight not fare from the hous and my son Isaac praid me to go out and look on his maer. When I came to her he asked me what I thought on her and I said if he wold have my thoughts I could not compare it to nothing else but that she was riden with a hot

bridil. I said also to Isaac that I hered what they said. [that is the Howe's counter-explanation] For she hade divirse bruses as if she had bin over rocks and much wronged and where the bridel went was as if it hade bin burnt with a rade hot bridel . Then I bide Isaac take the mare and have her up amongst the nagbours that people might see her for I hered that James How jun'r or his wife or both hade said that we kept up our maer that peopel might not see her. And Isaac did show his maer to saveril and then they said How, as I hered, did report that Isac had riden to Lin Spring and caryed his gairl and so surfited the maer the which was not so.

On the basis of testimony like this given by Goodwife Cummings, Elizabeth Howe was to be hanged for witchcraft three weeks later.

Cotton Mather gave a short account of the tale of the horse and the pipe in his account of several of the trials published the next year. True scientist that he was, he found the incident, including the near firing of the barn as a result of the treatment, to be solid evidence of witchcraft.

Chapter Forty-Nine—The Case Against Susannah Martin

If Baalam became a sorcerer by sacrificing and praying to the true God against his visible people; then he that shall pray that the afflicted (by their spectral sight) may accuse some other person (whereby their reputations and lives may be indangered) such will justly deserve the name of sorcerer.

If any person pretends to know more than can be known by humane means, and professeth at the same time that they have it from the black-man, i.e., the devil, and shall from hence give testimony against the lives of others, they are manifestly such as have a familiar spirit; and if any, knowing them to have their information from the black-man, shall be inquisitive of them for their testimony against others, they therein are dealing with such as have a familiar spirit.

And if these shall pretend to see the dead by their spectral sight, and others shall be inquisitive of them, and receive their answers what it is the dead say, and who it is they accuse, both the one and the other are by scripture guilty of necromancy.

. . .As long as witchcraft, sorcery, familiar spirits, and necromancy, shall be improved to discover who are witches, etc.

So long it may be expected that innocents will suffer as witches.

So long God will be daily dishonoured, and so long his judgments must be expected to be continued.
-- Joseph Calef, ***More Wonders of the Invisible World*** (1700)

Susannah Martin was among the earliest tried for the same reason Bridget Bishop was tried first—that she had an old reputation as witch, and had been charged with it in court. More accurately (for a "reputation" is no more a substantial thing than a spectre) we should say there had been those in Amesbury and Salisbury who called her a witch and blamed their troubles on her from as long as thirty-five years earlier.

Cotton Mather reflected her reputation at its worst in the account he wrote of her trial, published the next year:

> Note, this woman was one of the most impudent, scurrilous, wicked creatures in the world; and she did now throughout her whole trial discover herself to be such an one. Yet when she was asked, what she had to say for her self her chief plea

was that she had led a most virtuous and holy life!

This sort of gossip had resulted in a legal complaint of witchcraft in April 1669, but her husband George countersued for slander and William Sargent was forced to pay token damages. Several years later, after the death of Richard North, her father, she went to court claiming his will had been a forgery—and had some fairly sound arguments for it. However, one of her claims was that magistrate Thomas Bradbury had neither written or witnessed it—that his hand and signature had been forged. He swore that he had written it and that the will was genuine. Thus the matter ended.

It was partly due to Anne Putnam's origins that Widow Martin, though of Salisbury, was known by the Salem Villagers and named among the earliest accused. Anne was the daughter of George Carr, Sr. of Salisbury, and sister of George Carr, Jr., as well as sister-in-law to Elizabeth Pike, daughter of magistrate Robert Pike of Salisbury. All these were connected with the earlier charges against Susannah Martin. (There were many such connections between the Villagers and their Salisbury neighbors to the south.)

We heard Widow Martin was arrested in early May upon complaint of Sergeant Putnam and Captain Walcott. Her chief contemporary "victims" were said to be Anna Putnam, Abigail Williams, Mary Walcott and Mercy Lewis. Others including Goodwife Vibber, Indian John, Susannah Sheldon and Elizabeth Hubbard, joined in accusing her at her examination. During that examination she often replied to Mr. Hathorne's questions with more wit than he returned. Reverend Parris and Deacon Ingersoll joined the complainants in the customary testimony that they had witnessed the girls afflicted while she was examined.

Robert Pike, magistrate of Salisbury (who later opposed the proceedings, and despite his Carr and Putnam connections, particularly opposed the charges against Mary Bradbury) took further testimony from among Widow Martin's old detractors during the weeks following her examination. He was fastidious insofar as he uncovered simple explanations for elements of the testimonies that otherwise sounded ominous, nevertheless the testimonies by their nature seemed to give weight to the presumption that Susannah Martin was a witch.

The old testimony against her might be summed up under three heads: mishaps to livestock, incapacitations of neighbors, and various "apparitions." In addition, and in connection to these, there was a significant degree of hostility, rivalry or revenge in most of the tales.

    More specifically, these old witnesses testified at Widow Martin's inquiry on June 28th and 29th:

    From the previous September, Joseph Ring, twenty-seven, testified he and his brother Jarvis were hewing timber, but that when Jarvis took a load home with his team, Thomas Hardy of the Great Island at Puscataway appeared to him and forced him "by some impulse" to follow him to the deserted house of Benoni Tucker, where Susannah Martin appeared with another female he did not know. There they sat with Hardy, before a fire, talking and drinking cider most of the night. Toward morning, Goodwife Martin who had been "in her natural shape" got up, made a noise and turned into the shape of a black hog, which went away with the others. Joseph Ring was meanwhile strangely carried away, until he came to himself by Samuel Wood's house in Amesbury. (Joseph Ring further testified to various supernatural rough handlings by Thomas Hardy, who appeared at the head of a mysteriously devilish crew — but magistrate Pike decided this testimony was tainted, having ascertained that Joseph Ring owed Hardy money lost at "shuffle board or some like game".)

    From several years earlier, Robert Downer of Salisbury , fifty-two, testified that when Widow Martin was first brought to that town's court, Goodman Downer told her he believed she was indeed a witch. She responded angrily that a she-devil would fetch him away shortly, which did not scare him at the time. The next night, however, as he lay in bed, something in the likeness of a cat came in through his window and took him by the throat. This spectre then lay hard upon him a good while, almost strangling him, until he remembered Susannah's threat, at which time he said, "avoid thou she devil in the name of the Father and the Son and the Holy Ghost." His attacker let him go, slumped to the floor, and jumped out the window. The next morning before he could say anything about it to them, some of the Martin family inquired about it. Mary Andrews, aged forty, affirmed she had heard Widow Martin's threat about the she-devil. She also heard from a family member that Goodwife Martin told them how Downer was served that night. Moses Pike (of the magistrate's family) said he heard Susannah Martin tell how Goodman Downer was handled, the very next day, to the best of his memory.

    From five years previous, John and Susan Atkinson testified

of buying from one of Susannah's sons a cow which behaved "so madd that we could scarce get her along," particularly when it came to crossing water. (It is common lore that witches and the bewitched are much affected by running water.) Goodwife Atkinson also found it remarkable that Widow Martin could travel through "dirty" weather and stay so dry and tidy.

From about six years earlier, Ensign Joseph Knight, about forty years old, testified he and Nathan Clark, Jr. of Newbury, went out in the woods to fetch their horses and there met Susannah Martin with a little dog running at her side. When she saw them she took the little dog into her arms, but when they approached, the dog turned into a small keg or half-firkin under her arm. Knight told her the keg was a little dog, and Clark said it was indeed a dog. When they went on and found their horses, they brought them to the causeway, but every time they brought them up to pass over the causeway the horses ran in circles around a small knoll—and thus throughout most of the day. Finally a young man came driving a yoke of oxen, and after he passed over the causeway, albeit with some difficulty, the other men got the horses over, too.

Elizabeth Clark, wife of Nathan, Jr., testified her husband told her the same story, but specified it was he who told Ensign Knight the keg under Widow Martin's arm was or had been a dog. Goodwife Clark said Goodwife Martin came to their house the same day before Goodman Clark had come home, and mentioned what Ensign Knight had said.

From seven or eight years previous, Jarvis Ring testified he had on many occasions been afflicted in the night by somebody or something which came upon him while he was in bed, and afflicted him so that he could neither move nor speak. He was able to make a slight noise, however, so that others heard him and came to him, whereupon the afflicting force always departed, although he usually did not see who or what it was. However, one night it came upon him and he saw that is was Susannah Martin. She came to him and took him by the hand and bit his fingers and lay upon him and after a while went away. The print of the bite could be seen on his little finger of his right hand for it was hard to heal.

From about ten years previous, Bernard Peach, forty-two, testified he was living with his master William Osgood of Salisbury when George Martin came and asked Osgood for some beef from an injured ox, which Osgood refused. The following day Osgood's best cow went into such a mad fright that two men could hardly get her into the cow house. When she was let out the next day with the other cattle, she seemed fine, but by evening she was very ill, having lumps of matter under her eyes as big as walnuts. She died that same night.

About three years after this, the same Peach testified he was staying at the home of Jacob Morrell in Salisbury when he heard scratching at the window and looking up saw Widow Martin jump through it. She commenced to torment him in various strange ways, including wrapping him up and lying upon him, for about two hours, during which time he could not move or speak. At last he was "loosened or lightened" enough to put out his hand and grasp her hand, which he put to his mouth, biting her in three fingers to the breaking of her bones, after which she fled. Peach then called to the people of the house, and told them what had happened, but when they went outside they did not see her, but only three drops of blood – one in a bucket of water outside the door, and two more in the thin layer of snow beside only two footprints about a foot beyond the threshold. Then three weeks later, when Peach refused to help Susannah Martin husk corn, she and another appeared to him coming into the barn at William Osgood's. He struck at the apparitions, and hit the rafters the first time, but the second time he struck both apparitions. He heard the rumor Widow Martin had a "broken head" at that time.

From more than a decade earlier John Allen, forty-five, said one day after he had hauled timber for George Carr, Sr., at Amesbury, as he was about to depart for home, Widow Martin asked him to cart some staves. He refused her because his oxen were exhausted and needed feeding, but she was unhappy with his response and stated, in the presence of James Freeze, that he should have done it, for now his oxen would never do him any more service. Allen responded by calling her an old witch, and threatened to throw her in the brook, but she fled over the bridge. When he was going home, his oxen grew so tired that he was obliged to unyoke them, and after they got home, he put the oxen with others in the customary pasture at Salisbury Beach.

A few days later, however, as witnessed by their tracks, the cattle were found to have gone to the mouth of the Merrimack River. They were feared drowned, but proved to have gone out to Plum Island. The men who went to recover them approached the cattle gently, but the whole herd ran away as though diabolically pursued and near the mouth of the river ran right into the sea, except for two old ones and one that turned back and ran amuck. The other thirteen were drowned so that they recovered nothing but the hides. James Freeze had thereafter urged the others to prosecute Widow Martin as a witch. No doubt many were reminded of the Gadarene swine.

From about twenty-three years previous, John Kimball (and wife) testified that he bought a piece of land in Amesbury from George Martin, and when he was about to move to it from Newbury, Martin and his wife came for the cattle promised in payment. Kimball gave them the choice of three cows and other cattle, but reserved two cows that were his first and favorites. Susannah Martin wanted one of these, but the Kimball's persisted in refusing, so Susannah said "she will never do you any more good," and by the following April, the cow died for no apparent reason. Kimball also testified that after he moved to Amesbury, he wanted a dog, and went to get one from a litter at Martins. But Susannah would not let him have his choice, so he said he would not take her puppy, but would check some available at Blaisdells, first. Later he told George Martin he had picked out a puppy at Blaisdells. Edmund Eliot heard George tell Susannah that Kimball had chosen one of Blaisdell's, and her abusive reply "I'll give him puppies enough."

Within a few days Kimball was walking from his house to Eliot's when a small squall arose and he was made to tumble over some stumps "by impulse he can give no reason of," such that even when he resolved to avoid them he could not. As he went further, something like a dark puppy shot between his legs, back and forth "like one raking hay." Kimball tried to strike it with the ax he carried, but could not. However, the puppy gave a little jump and seemed to disappear into the ground. A little further on a bigger one appeared which attacked Kimball so fiercely he could not ward it off, but he ran and called out "Jesus Christ" and then it went away. Kimball told no one for fear of fretting his wife. Edmond Eliot claimed he went the next morning by Martin's, and stopped in to light his pipe at which time, Widow Martin asked where Kimball was. When Eliot said he did not know, she said the townsfolk say he was fretted last night with puppies. Kimball claimed that it was only later, through Eliot telling them, that the townsfolk found out about this—since he had worked alone in the woods all that day.

John Pressy testified of twenty-four years before when he was walking at night near the Amesbury Ferry and a field belonging to George Martin, when he became bewildered and wandered three times in a circle. During his wandering in the dark, a light about the size of a bushel basket appeared three times on his left. The third

time he saw it, he struck at it with the stick in his hand and felt
something substantial as he struck. Yet the light grew brighter and
waved from side to side like a turkey cock's tail when he spreads it
out, so that Pressy belabored it further with all his might, giving
perhaps forty blows. He then hurried away, but slipped and began
to slide down, as into a deep pit, where no pit was known to be. He
caught hold of some brush, and rescued himself, but having realized
he had lost his coat, he went back to the strange light where he found
his coat, and took it up and went on home. After going five or six
rods, he saw Susannah Martin standing on his left just as the light
had. She looked at him and turned away, saying nothing, and he
went on.

When Pressy got home he was "seized with fear" such that he
"could not speak til his wife spake to him at the door". His family
was very concerned about him . Telling the tale to others in the town
they heard that Goodwife Martin had been in such bodily pain she
had her body swabbed for the relieving of it. The implication was
that Pressy had delivered the forty blows to Susannah Martin
appearing as the "light". Magistrate Pike made note of the fact that
since Pressy didn't let him know about this until significantly later,
there was no way to confirm the condition of Goodwife Martin in re
her supposed injuries. Pressy testified further that some years after
these events and his testimony against Widow Martin, she
threatened the Pressys and told them they would never have more
than two cows, since when, through disease and mishap, they never
could keep more than two cows alive. His wife agreed to much of
his testimony, however she had no recollection of the cow curse.

From thirty years previous, seventy-year old William Brown
testified his wife Elizabeth had seen the defendant disappear and
reappear a number of times and thereafter was inflicted with internal
complaints. She sought the prayers of her church, which set aside a
day of humiliation and prayer, but the mere appointing of the day
seemed to do the trick, for her complaints ceased forthwith and
instead of a day of humiliation, the church had a day of
thanksgiving. However Goodwife Brown and Goodwife Osgood
were summoned to court to testify before Susannah Martin in that
earlier case , and soon after the defendant appeared and pledged to
torment Goodwife Brown. Within two months, Goodman Brown
came home one day to find his wife out of her mind and claiming
they were divorced — in which demented condition she continues to
the present. Magistrate Robert Pike testified he himself knew

Goodwife Brown to have been a rational woman "before she was so handled" and that he also knew of her present condition and her long continuance in it. "For she remains a miserable creature."

Such were some of the old grievances laid at the feet of Susannah Martin. Carefully considered now with the troubles well behind us, the best of these tales appears no more than a concatenation of actual observations, fearful or drunken fancies, unfortunate events, and unjustified allegations. Most of the witnesses succeeded in frightening themselves a good deal—through bad dreams, misfortunes, or the perverse behavior and diseases of livestock.

John Pressy's tale is particular interesting in that it owed it's most salient detail not to his imagination but to a natural phenomenon which few persons witness, since few travel at night without a lantern. The strange light he came upon three times as he circled the same terrain was a jack-o-lantern fungus. During the day it is a bright orange mushroom that grows on rotten wood, with many large stems and caps emerging in a clump. In the dark it glows with a bright greenish light. It not only grows nearly as large as a bushel basket, but stands up in much the same configuration as feathers in a turkey's tail. Its tough, flexible stems do indeed wave about like so many plumes in the dark, when struck. As for the next episode of his story, to slip in the dark is always frightening and needs no undiscovered pit to give it terror.

Darkness, dread, and drunkenness had more to do with these tales than the tellers will ever admit. But the court did not raise those issues with the jury, and we went forward in lunacy

Certainly to allow a correlation between an object located on one's left and a person later seen on one's left is lunatic. That some evil agency working through some person should be blamed for this great miscellany of mishaps might in other circumstances be attributed merely to a widespread inability to laugh at oneself.

From the sheer number of these stories, it seems Widow Martin, like a number of others accused, had made use of others' superstitions by promoting rather than discouraging their silly associations. She had allowed others to associate her with an ancient house, and thus maintained a false respect, under color of which she felt protected. The broom and caldron proved an unreliable coat of arms.

Chapter Fifty — The Case Against Sarah Wildes

And thou New England, which art exalted in privileges of the Gospel above many people, know thou the time of thy visitation, and consider the great things the Lord hath done for thee. The Gospel hath free passage in all places where thou dwellest: oh, that it might be glorified also by thee. Thou enjoyest many faithful witnesses, which have testified unto thee the Gospel of the grace of God. Thou has many bright stars shining in thy firmament, to give thee the "knowledge of salvation from on high, to guide thy feet in the way of peace" (Luke 1.78,79)

*Be not high-minded because of thy privileges, but fear because of thy danger. The more thou hast committed unto thee, the more thou must account for. No people's account will be heavier than thine if thou do not walk worthy of the means of thy salvation. The Lord looks for more from thee than from other peoples: more zeal for God, more love to His truth, more justice and equity in thy ways . . . -- Peter Bulkeley, **The Lesson of the Covenant For England and New England**, (1651)*

Sarah (Averill) Wildes was the second wife of the widowed Topsfield carpenter, John Wildes. Not long after she married him, she found herself in the middle of old conflicts between her husband and the family of his first wife, Priscilla Gould.

The patriarch, Zaccheus Gould, was the original unordained minister of Topsfield. He died in 1668, leaving 3000 acres of land and a number of children, including Priscilla, Lieutenant John, and Mary (wife of John Reddington). Zaccheus' sister, Priscilla Gould was the wife of another patriarch, John Putnam, and thus grandmother of Sergeant Thomas et al of the Village. The Goulds and Putnams had many adjacent lands and common interests in the area south of Topsfield near the river, including the former common lands they contested with the Townes and Eastys. John Wildes was on the committees that divided and bounded that land between Topsfield and Salem Village. Thus he was said to have made himself disagreeable to his Gould and Putnam relatives, who were not satisfied with the results.

However that may be, by 1682, during the Andros administration, John Wildes was a witness against his brother-in-law Lieutenant John Gould in a case of treason. Gould had made

statements of non-submission to that government because it had
abrogated the old charter. Gould was found guilty, fined and spent
some time in gaol. (It was justly cited as hypocrisy in Wildes that he
once signed a document of similar resolution, that is refusing to
submit to any government that did not uphold the first
Massachusetts charters.)

Soon after this, and many said because of this, Mary (Gould)
Reddington began to spread gossip naming Sarah Wildes as a witch.
When John Wildes caught wind of it, he threatened John Reddington
with a slander suit, but Reddington begged Wildes not to pursue the
suit, since it would "waste his estate" and seeing that "his wife
would have done with it in time". William Averill, Sarah's brother
had gone to Mary Reddington and asked what she had against Sarah,
but Mary told him that she knew no harm Sarah had done her.
Nonetheless, Mary Reddington's gossip not only spread to others,
but she repeated it again during our troubles. Sarah Wilde's bold
and unyielding manner with her neighbors did little to dissipate the
rumors.

John Wildes was actively involved with the Topsfield church
and with ministers Danforth, Capen and Hubbard. Sarah Wildes
testified on behalf of Reverend Hubbard when he charged another
member with slander in 1679. The Goulds, on the other hand, were
active opponents of the first two ordained ministers William Perkins
and Thomas Gilbert. Zaccheus, perhaps resentful at being displaced
by Reverend Perkins, was charged by the minister with "abusive
carriage" toward the congregation, and was also involved in charges
against Gilbert for drunkenness and the like. The Townes and
Bridges defended Reverend Gilbert in the first and in subsequent
cases, including one in which he charged John Gould with assault.

During our troubles, the complaint issued April 21st named a
number of Topsfield defendants including William and Deliverance
Hobbs, Mary Easty, and Nehemiah Abbott. Not only did it include
Sarah Wildes, but also her husband John's daughter, Sarah (Wildes)
Bishop, and her husband Edward, son of the first woman tried.

The morning of April 22nd Marshall Herrick arrested Sarah
Wildes. That same afternoon, Marshall Herrick ordered constable
Ephraim Wildes, twenty-seven year old son of John and Sarah, to
arrest William and Deliverance Hobbs. Ephraim said Deliverance
"showed a very hard spirit" when he arrested her and "looked so
molishly" at him with "revenge in her face," that he thought her
subsequent accusations of Sarah were largely due to his part in

Deliverance's arrest. Their daughter Abigail, who "confessed" before her mother, was also quick to implicate Goodwife Wildes.

Ephraim Wildes testified that his mother "had always instructed him well in the Christian religion and the ways of God ever since he was able to take instructions." He also testified to having courted one of the Symonds girls, until he found that her mother, Elizabeth, believed his mother had done her wrong. He confronted Goodwife Symonds who said she had no grievance except what she had heard from Mary Reddington. After that, however, constable Ephraim broke off the courtship. He claimed Elizabeth Symonds had been angry with him ever since, and joined in accusing Sarah Wildes again for that reason.

Elizabeth (Andrews) Symonds was sister to Mary (Andrews) Cummings and Thomas Andrews (of the horse-and-pipe testimony against Elizabeth Howe). She said that twelve or thirteen years earlier her mother, Elizabeth Andrews, accused Sarah Wildes of threatening her sons, John and Joseph Andrews, and hindering their haying by witchery. Elizabeth said Sarah replied by threatening her mother and herself, and caused her to fall into a fit of trembling. That night she felt something like a cat creep in upon her and lie upon her all night so that she could not move or speak until morning. (Some of these "incidents" were repeated so often that saner judges would have recognized they were merely parroted.)

A while later at lecture, Sarah Wildes walked by Elizabeth, and she immediately felt a pain in her back so great that she fell out of her seat unconscious, until she came to herself in Reverend Hubbard's house where others had carried her. She then pointed out Sarah Wildes as the cause of it. She said she was so afflicted with pains since then she could not come to court to testify in person.

John and Joseph Andrews affirmed the account of hindered haying, only placing the date in 1674, nearly five years earlier than there sister remembered it. They gave the original cause as their "borrowing" a scythe in a high-handed manner. They said "a little lad whose name was Ephraim Wildes" was the messenger who came out to bring them the original threat. The long list of woes that befell them during their haying was quite remarkable, causing some of us to wonder if perhaps twenty years of mishaps had not been summarized in the recollection.

Thomas Dorman testified to afflictions of geese and cattle following a transaction in which he sold some bees to Sarah Wildes. He found it particularly amazing Anna Putnam could tell his wife the details so many years later — as if such tales were ever kept secret.

Both John Wilde's old enemy, Lieutenant John Gould, and Gould's nephew, Zaccheus Perkins, were witnesses to Sarah Wildes witchery — mostly in the genre of mysterious deaths of livestock and difficulties in performing agricultural tasks. Gould gave Mary Reddington's account of John Wildes, Jr. (another son) doing feats of witchcraft, and repeated a number of tales Mary Reddington told against Sarah over the years. Gould said that Mary claimed Sarah was responsible for her final illness. Perhaps his strongest testimony against Sarah was that Mary Reddington's last words to him attributed her approaching death to Sarah.

Reverend Hale of Beverly also testified against Sarah, citing the fifteen year old accusations of Mary Reddington, who came to him with her daughter, Mary (Reddington) Herrick. Reverend Hale admitted he had forgotten the particulars of her stories. He also said that Goodwife Reddington told him John Wildes, Jr. had come to her to say his step-mother, Sarah, was indeed a witch. Reverend Hale remembered John, Jr. had "acted very strangely" twenty years earlier. He and Reverend Cobbett had been invited to advise and pray for young John, whom "some thought to counterfeit, others to be possessed of the devil." Hale said Cobbett was sure it was the latter.

Sarah Wildes, like most of the other women accused, was a bold woman. When younger she had twice been brought before the court for "lewd behavior," which in those days was often connected to the sumptuary laws and dressing too brightly. Her conduct during examination had been straight-forward and respectful, but the resentment among her neighbors coincided too well with the inclinations of afflicted girls and the spirit of our troubles.

The Jury of Inquest accepted all this testimony as valid, and indicted her, passing the case on to the Court of Oyer and Terminer. Neither did Justice Stoughton and his colleagues doubt the evidence of past and present witchcraft, finding it sufficient to convict her. Under their instruction, neither did the jury. She was found guilty, the last of the five tried in mid-summer.

Chapter Fifty-One — Sentence of Death
(29-30 June)

When the righteous God is contending with apostate sinners for their departure from him by his judgments, as plagues, earthquakes, storms and tempests, sicknesses and diseases, wars, loss of cattle, etc. then not only to ascribe this to the devil, but to charge one another with sending or commissionating those devils to these things, is so abominable and wicked, that it requires a better judgment than mine to give it its just denomination.

But that Christians so called should not only charge their fellow Christians therewith but proceed to tryals and executions; crediting that enemy to all goodness and accuser of the brethren, rather than believe their neighbours in their own defence; this is so diabolical a wickedness as cannot proceed, but from a doctrine of devils; how far damnable it is let others discuss.

-- Joseph Calef, ***More Wonders of the Invisible World*** (1700)

O n the 28th of June Rebecca petitioned "the Court of Oyer and Terminer now sitting" concerning her physical malady and the desirability of having other "prudent" women examine her:

> The humble petission of Rebecca Nurse of Salem Village humbley sheweth
> That whareas sum women did sarch your petissioner at Salem, as I did then conceive for sum supernaturall marke, and then one of the said women which is known to be the moaste antient skillfull prudent person of them all as to any such concernd did express hirselfe to be of a contrary opinion from the rest and did then declare, that shee saw nothing in or aboute your honors poare pettissioner but what might arise from a naturall cause. And I then rendered the said persons a suficient knowne reason as to my selfe of the moveing cause thereof, which was by exceeding weaknesses decending partly from an overture of nature and difficult exigences that hath befallen me in the times of my travells. And therefore your pettissioner humbley prayes that you honours would be pleased to admitt of sum other women to enquire into this great concerne, those that are moast grand

wise and skillfull: namely Mrs. Higginson sen'r, Mrs.
Buckstone, Mrs. Woodbery, two of them being midwives,
Mrs. Porter, together with such others, as may be choasen, on
that account before I am brought to my triall. All which I
hoape your honours will take into your prudent
consideration, and find it requisite soe to doe, for my lyfe lyes
now in your hands under God. And being conscious of my
owne innocency — I humbley begg that I may have liberty to
manifest it to the wourld partly by the meanes abovesaid.
And yo'r poare pettissioner shall evermore pray as in duty
bound &c.

In support of this petition, Rebecca (Nurse) Preston and Mary
(Nurse) Tarbell offered an additional deposition to the court:

We whose nams are under written: can testiefie if cald to it
that Goodde Nurs have bene trobled with an infirmity of
body for many years which the juree of women seme to be
afraid it should be something elce.

The more objective women whom Rebecca suggested for a
second physical examination were certainly respected by the court.
But the court did not see fit to give the prisoner another examination.
(Perhaps at some point even Herod's captains grew tired of
humiliating their prisoners.)

Rebecca's inquest before the Grand Jury took place on the 29th
of June within a few days of those of Sarah Good, Susannah Martin
of Amesbury, Elizabeth Howe of Ipswich, and Sarah Wildes of
Topsfield. All five were indicted for trial. Four separate indictments
were handed down for Rebecca Nurse, above the signature of John
Ruck, foreman of the Jury of Inquest. Each indictment cited one of
four "afflicted evidences" as the girls were being called, although all
four of them signed each indictment. They were Anna Putnam,
Mary Walcott, Elizabeth Hubbard, and Abigail Williams. Thus
Abigail's:

Anno Regni Regis et Reginae et Mariae nunc Angliae &c
Quarto: Essex ss
The jurors for our Sovereigne Lord & Lady the King &
Queen presents that Rebeckah Nurse the wife of Francis
Nurse senior of Salem Village in the County of Essex

husband — the four & twentyeth day of March in the fourth
year of the reigne of our Sovereigne Lord & Lady William &
Mary by the Grace of God of England, Scottland, France &
Ireland, King & Queen, Defenders of the faith &c   and divers
other dayes & times as well before as after, certaine
detestable arts called witchcrafts & sorceries wickedly and
feloniously hath used, practised & exercised at and within the
towneship of Salem in the County of Essex aforesaid in upon
and against one Abigail Williams of Salem Village aforesaid
singlewoman — by which said wicked arts, the said Abigail
Williams the said four & twentieth day of March in the fourth
year abovs'd and divers other dayes & times as well before as
after was & is hurt, tortured, afflicted, consumed, pined,
wasted & tormented against the Peace of our Sovereigne Lord
& Lady the King & Queen and against the forme of the statute
in that case made & provided.

   Wittnesses
   Abigail Williams
   Mary Walcott
   Elizabeth Hubbard
   Ann Puttnam Junior

   Bill Avara John Ruck foreman in the nam of the Rest,
No.4

On Thursday, June 30th, the Court of Oyer and Terminer
began a marathon set of trials for the five women, which concluded
on Saturday, the 2nd of July.

   When all were gathered in the Salem Meeting House for
Rebecca's trial and the opening prayer offered, Mr. Stoughton read
the charges and asked Rebecca how she pleaded. "Not guilty, sir,"
she replied.

   Stephen Sewall, clerk of court, then stood and addressed her,
"Culprit, how wilt thou be tried?"

   "By God and my country," She answered, according to the
ancient form.

   "God send thee a good deliverance," the clerk answered. The
trial then went foreword with the readings of depositions and the
swearing of witnesses to them. As with the women tried with her,
the court went but one step closer to caution. One of the few
detectable differences in procedure was that each witness was asked

directly if he or she did truly, in his or her heart, think the defendant to be a witch. No accuser demurred.

Rebecca's trial included few new witnesses. The "afflicted" carried out their cries and contortions with little more restraint than they had used during the examinations. Several of the Nurse family, however, set themselves to watch the afflicted carefully. Sarah Nurse reported in a subsequent deposition that she saw Sarah Vibber faking evidence of injury by sticking pins between her own fingers. But the magistrates paid no more heed to this deposition than to the many testimonies of Rebecca's good character.

The earlier witnesses brought in to reaffirm the testimony of the written depositions included Goodwife Holten, with her original grudge, and (on Rebecca's behalf) Israel and Elizabeth Porter with their early account of their visit to Rebecca before she was charged. Their deposition, originally written after Rebecca's arrest, bore the signatures of Peter Cloyce and Daniel Andrews, stating they would also testify to the truth of the statements, although Peter's own wife was in gaol, and Daniel had been some time in hiding. No doubt that did little to further the court's respect for this document.

Two girls, Sarah Stevens and Margery Pasque were new witnesses, testifying their friend Jemima Rea had been afflicted by an apparition of Rebecca Nurse on June 21, only a week earlier.

Anne Putnam, Sr., the loudest of the afflicted at Goodwife Nurse's examination in March, testified of new afflictions at the beginning of June, connecting them with the gaol transport from Boston to Salem.

Deliverance and Abigail Hobbs were brought in to testify against Rebecca and this surprised her, for she knew they had also been accused and were prisoners at Salem. The prisoners had talked at length about the injustice of "confessed" witches being relied upon as witnesses. Upon seeing them brought to testify against her she said, "What, do you come against me now! Were you not also of our company!" The judges fastened on this and interpreted it to mean she recognized them as fellow witches.

When the jury finally went out, they deliberated but an hour before coming back with a verdict of "not guilty." The members of the Nurse family had so steeled themselves for the opposite verdict, that they could hardly assimilate this wonderful event. The afflicted, however, broke into such a caterwauling as had hardly been heard during the trials before the higher court.

As all those in the courtroom whispered in speculation about this unprecedented event, the justices conferred with one another. A couple of them had risen as if to leave the bench, one of them remarking they would have to bring new indictments, but the chief justice called them back into conference. They seemed to come to a consensus and their chief turned to address the jury, again.

Chief Justice Stoughton with stern civility told the jury members he did not wish to impose upon them. He asked, however, if perhaps they had failed to take account of the words Goodwife Nurse spoke against herself when she asked the confessed Hobbs women if they were not also of her company.

The jury, in turn, conferred among themselves for a moment. Several members thought they ought to deliberate again, so they went out and discussed this statement. But they could not agree about what she had said or meant. The jury, like Pilate, did not want to make the decision alone, and were quite willing to wash their hands of it. Foreman Fisk went back into the court and asked the judges what indeed her words were, to which they repeated them. He then asked the court what construction they placed upon them, which was repeated by several of the judges. Foreman Fisk looked at Rebecca, who sat near him during this discussion, but she made no objection, nor indeed said anything. He then returned and told the jury what the judges had said.

Since Rebecca was sitting still at the bar before which the foreman asked his question, and since she neither corrected or commented on this question and answer, he assumed she had no different interpretation to put upon it, and concluded the court's version of her words must be the right one. When he conveyed this to the rest of the jury, they were left with the choice of opposing the court or abdicating the responsibility of their office by submitting to the judges. Like Pilate, they took the easier way – easier, that is, for them. They changed their minds and voted her guilty. This verdict they brought back the second time after another hour's debate.

So crushed were her family and friends by the reversal that they could neither protest or mourn. They made their way out from the court, stumbling into the fresh air of the street.

On July 2nd the jury brought in the guilty verdict against Sarah Wildes, last of the five then tried under its auspices.

Two days later, at the request of Sam Nurse and John Tarbell, Foreman Fisk was quite willing to explain the jury's decision to the Nurse family, and wrote it out on the following Monday:

July 4, 1692. IThomas Fisk , the subscriber hereof, being one of them that were of the jury the last week at Salem-Court, upon the tryal of Rebecka Nurse, etc., being desired by some of the relations to give a reason why the jury brought her in guilty, after her verdict not guilty; I do hereby give my reasons to be as follows, viz.

When the verdict not guilty was, the honoured court was pleased to object against it, saying to them, that they think they let slip the words, which the prisoner at the bar spake against her self, which were spoken in reply to Goodwife Hobbs and her daughter, who had been faulty in setting their hands to the devils book, as they have confessed formerly; the words were "What, do these persons give in evidence against me now, they used to come among us."

After the honoured court had manifested their dissatisfaction of the verdict, several of the jury declared themselves desirous to go out again, and thereupon the honoured court gave leave; but when we came to consider of the case, I could not tell how to take her words, as an evidence against her, till she had a further opportunity to put her sense upon them, if she would take it; and then going into court, I mentioned the words aforesaid, which by one of the court were affirmed to have been spoken by her, she being then at the bar, but made no reply, nor interpretation of them; whereupon these words were to me a principal evidence against her.

Rebecca, like the Galilean prisoner, had been too lamb-like in her silence. In fact, she had not understood what was going on. Her slight deafness betrayed her along with the fact that she was exhausted by the three days of hearing and trial. She had heard the "not guilty" verdict, and after that fell almost into a fugue. She was ready to rejoice, but she remembered the bitter disappointment of her Sister Easty's release and re-arrest, and was therefore unable to let go the restraints of her heart. Her head had been bowed in wonder and relief. She did not know what Mr. Fisk asked the judges, so she did not catch the dialogue about her statement concerning the Hobbs.

After Rebecca's conviction, in consultation together, the judges addressed the sentencing. Judge Richards once more raised the idea of alternative sentence as suggested by Cotton Mather's letter.

"Do you see any grounds in scripture for such a sentence?" asked Mr. Stoughton.

"I am generally of the opinion that Levitical standards are normative," answered Mr. Richards, "yet as we depart from them in other dubious cases, it seems to me we ought to consider alternatives here. After all the Jury found her not guilty when first they deliberated."

He added hurriedly, and nervously, "Doth not the scripture say that mercy triumphs over judgment?"

"So it does, but is that not about divine justice, rather than human civil justice? " Mr. Stoughton replied, his tone almost brittle.

"Nay, if we begin to depart in this from scripture, even in one case, we open the door to abandoning God's law altogether. Remember it was precisely such a tendency that allowed these servants of Satan to continue their terrible deeds over twenty years or more.

"I am only the president of this court, and have but one vote. If the rest of you are of a different opinion, you ought to prevail, but unless you can make argument from scripture and law, I suggest we throw up our commission in refusing to impose the biblical sentence."

None other spoke, and Deputy Stoughton wrote out the death sentence for the five most recently convicted.

The court gave out its sentence. These five women, at least, would not continue to bewitch their neighbors. The Chief Justice was determined to continue the march of justice against the devil's hoards without looking back.

Sarah Good Wife of William Good of Salem Village, Rebecka Nurse wife of Francis Nurse of Salem Village, Susanna Martin of Amesbury Widow, Elizabeth How wife of James How of Ipswich, Sarah Wild Wife of John Wild of Topsfield, severaly arraigned on several indictments for the horrible crime of witchcraft by them practised & committed on severall persons and pleading not guilty did for their tryall put themselves on God & their countrey whereupon they were each of them found & brought in guilty by the jury that passed on them according to their respective indictments and sentence of death did then pass upon them as the law directs.

As Thomas Fisk wrote out his explanation for the jury's

change of verdict, Secretary Stephen Sewall made copies of all twenty documents bearing on Rebecca's case for the Nurse family, stipulating that some "viva voce" testimony was not included among them (including in particular the fatal words concerning the Hobbs women).

At the urging of her children, Rebecca wrote another deposition in an effort to clarify the testimony misunderstood by the court and jury:

> These presents do humbly shew, to the honoured court and jury, that I being informed, that the jury brought me in guilty, upon my saying that Goodwife Hobbs and her daughter were of our company; but I intended no otherways, then as they were prisoners with us, and therefore did then, and yet do judge them not legal evidence against their fellow prisoners. And I being something hard of hearing, and full of grief, none informing me how the court took up my words, and therefore had not opportunity to declare what I intended, when I said they were of our company.

Their fellow prisoners had already heard the verdicts by the time the five women were brought back to Salem gaol. These did their best to comfort them.

Chapter Fifty-Two—The Two Tables
(3 July)

Wee promise to walk with our brethren and sisters in the congregation with all watchfullness, and tenderniss, avoyding all jelosies, supsitions, backbyteings, conjurings, provokings, secrete riseings of spirit against them, but in all offences to follow the rule of the Lord Jesus, and to beare and forbeare, give and forgive as he hath taught us. -- Third point in **The Full Covenant of the Church at Salem**, 1629

. . . If he neglect to hear the church, let him be unto thee as a heathen man and a publican. Verily I say unto you, Whatsoever ye shall bind on earth shall be bound in heaven: and whatsoever ye shall loose on earth shall be loosed in heaven. Again I say unto you, That if two of you shall agree on earth as touching any thing that they shall ask, it shall be done for them of my Father which is in heaven. For where two or three are gathered together in my name, there am I in the midst of them. -- **Matthew 18: 17b-20**

On Sunday, July 3rd, Rebecca Nurse entered into another form of her Lord's suffering. She was led or rather carried to witness her betrayal by those in spiritual covenant with her—not only the Scribes and Pharisees, but the Judases of her own congregation.

Reverends Noyes and Higginson gathered their flock on the morning of the Lord's Day in the same building where Bridget Bishop, and now five more women had been condemned. The seating was nearly the same as for the court, except there were fewer men at the front, and no defendant. Nevertheless, a sharp reminder of an one condemned and executed, was placed at the fore—for the congregation was to celebrate the Lord's Table.

Reverend Higginson preached to the greater auditory on Matthew 18 -- a double-edged sermon in his estimation, because it not only explained the severe discipline the congregation was about to carry out, but it gave the "almost-persuaded" crowd among them another chance to understand the importance of the covenant.

After the sermon and the singing of a psalm, the "inhabitants" were dismissed, leaving only the church members to celebrate communion.

After the others had departed, but before the elders went

ahead with the communion, Mr. Noyes and Mr. Higginson prepared to crucify Christ once more. Reverend Noyes in somber tones, told the congregation that one of their number had been condemned to death by the civil court for witchcraft, wherefore it was their sober duty to proceed to spiritual discipline against her as a church. He told how Rebecca Nurse had been approached by many over the previous months in accordance with Matthew 18 and that she was completely unwilling to admit or repent her sin.

"Now the church had been told, yet she neglects to hear it. Therefore it is our solemn and sorrowful duty to proceed to cut her off from the communion of the church and the fellowship of the saints."

Reverend Higginson read several related passages, and gave a particular warning albeit a rather extraneous one, that none should keep company or so much as eat with such a one, as per I Corinthians 5:11. He made spiritual application to the Lord's Supper and excommunication.

"For," he concluded, "Christ said he would eat it again with us in paradise — which most sadly will not be true for those such as Goodwife Nurse, who are cut off from it and the church. He will never again sit down to eat it with them."

The congregation voted and was unanimous in consent to the excommunication of Rebecca Nurse. More accurately, those who opposed the measure remained still, rather than raise their hands or voices in opposition. And under the circumstances, even that took great courage.

The Salem Church then celebrated the Lord's Supper.

"This is my body which is given for you. This do in remembrance of me."

"This is my blood of the new testament, which is shed for many for the remission of sins."

Meanwhile Rebecca's husband and daughters had hurried over to town after their own service at the Village. They had spent an hour at the Gaol with her and were on their way home. Her sons were in Boston preparing to present her most recent affidavits and their other petitions in hopes of a reprieve by the governor. But none of her family was present when the gaoler led in two constables and Reverend Noyes.

"Goodwife Nurse, this is a solemn day," he announced, "you are to be brought before the Salem church to be cast out of the covenant, unless it be you will repent of this great evil for which you stand convicted and condemned."

Rebecca had no inkling of this further humiliation until that moment and her first response was almost of terror. Martha Corey sat by her, however, and reached out to touch her shoulder.

"Fear not. They are blind guides, Rebecca. It is but the judgment of men."

Reverend Noyes turned on Martha with great vehemence.

"Be silent, you servant of the devil! Do not interfere! The Lord rebuke you! "

And to Rebecca again. "Fear indeed! For the Lord has given his church the keys by which it binds and looses. But a few days and your eternal soul shall depart into hell unless you repent!"

But just Martha's brief encouragement and the short exchange had served for the girding of her loins.

"Do what you would," she said, "although I do not think I have the strength to walk much."

Whereupon the gaoler was dispatched to find a stout chair, and when Rebecca had prepared herself, she was seated upon it, and her hands shackled together though it. Then the constables carried her thin frame up and out into the bright, rising heat of the day.

Waiting outside were two deacons. The small party made its way down the street, the feet of the men scuffing against the cobbles, and the sounds of the gulls and the smell of the sea blowing gently against the June warmth.

They neared the meeting house as some members made their way back in. When they entered the ministers directed the constables to carry her close to the all-too-familiar place of prominence at the front, where so many of the accused had stood — where, in special dispensation of the court, she had been allowed to sit during her trial. Now they placed her in the center aisle, facing forward. The Lord's Table occupied the place of the defendant.

After a time, she looked back over her shoulders at the congregation and saw the bright hard eyes of many turned strangers. She saw friends, too, but their eyes were cast down. But when she turned to the front again, there came to her the sweet release of grace, a soaring sense of detachment and waiting and an ordered sense of purpose. She bowed her head and began to pray.

Reverend Noyes proceeded once more to read the Matthew 18 passage and to once more exhort Rebecca to repent. He was full of zeal and ardor. He would not let her soul descend into hell without doing his utmost to turn her back.

When she remained silent in response to his direct and candid appeal, he went on to declare to the rest of the congregation that they might profit from her bad example. Indeed, in consultation with Reverend Higginson and the deacons, he had decided to bring her to the meeting for this momentous ritual largely for the public and didactic value of it. Her own repentance was much to be desired, but regardless, it would also serve as a distinct warning—a witch hearing her own formal separation from the people of God pronounced. (Others condemned with her, one a member at Salem Village and one at Salisbury, were excommunicated in absentia.)

"Do not be deceived! God is not mocked!" Reverend Noyes declaimed, "The sentence of the church is as fearful as that of the court. For the court has delivered your body over to destruction— but we deliver such a one as you to Satan for the destruction of the flesh, that perhaps the spirit may be saved in the day of the Lord Jesus.

"Nay, but do not think we hand thee over as thou hast handed over thyself—for the exercise of wanton power and the enjoyment of the things the evil one has promised thee. For thy master is a liar and is under God's thumb. We deliver thee to him only in this, that we cast thee out of the fellowship of his saints, and make a separation between thee and the benefits of Christ's mercy. Therefore we pray that thou may be so tormented in the few days that remain to thee on this earth, that thou shalt gnash thy teeth and tear thine hair—indeed that thou shalt cry out with the very torments of hell here—rather than be subject to them throughout all eternity. For so you certainly must be if you die unrepentant.

"We no longer ask for God's blessing of thee, but his severest cursing. We no longer intercede on thy behalf, but with the Psalmist ask that we may hate thee with a perfect hatred—that as thou art now fully revealed and exposed as an enemy of God, so you may be our enemy, too.

"And it is our prayer, not for you but against you, that you may indeed see your sin, and see the foul blackness of your master, and the desperately putrid corruption of your own sin, and lastly the horrors of eternal punishment toward which you now rush."

He then quoted the poet John Milton:

A dungeon horrible, on all sides round
As one great furnace flam'd, yet from those flames
No light, but rather darkness visible

Serv'd only to discover sights of woe,
Regions of sorrow, doleful shades, where peace
And rest can never dwell, hope never comes
That comes to all; but torture without end
Still urges, and a fiery deluge, fed
With ever-burning sulphur unconsum'd:
Such place eternal justice had prepar'd
For those rebellious, here their prison ordain'd
In utter darkness, and their portion set
As far remov'd from God and light of heav'n
As from the center thrice to th' utmost pole.

"Oh, woman, witch though thou art! Turn even now and call upon the great Christ. For he doth say that if we confess our sins, he is faithful and just to forgive our sins and to cleanse us from all inquity! He is able to provide a way of escape!"

But, as she was tragically unaware of the dialogue between jury foreman Fisk and Justice Stoughton at her trial, Rebecca was now gloriously unaware of the chief purport of Mr. Noyes' sermon.

She heard her Lord's name and the scriptures, but she was occupied in prayer. She turned her head both ways again and her eyes passed slowly over the parts of congregation she could see. For each upon whom they fell, she prayed. To most of them it was the evil glance of a devious and hard-hearted witch, from which they shrunk. Only a few prophets among them saw the saint.

Mr. Higginson stood, the congregation rose, too, and the two men proceeded to pronounce the excommunication. Afterward, the psalm being sung, the two constables came forward and lifted her chair, carrying her down the aisle among the members of the Salem church now formally cut off from the grace and forgiveness of which she had become the foremost repository among them. But she had pronounced no excommunication herself.

As she passed Israel and Elizabeth Porter, she gave them the briefest of silent benedictions. They received it gratefully.

Chapter Fifty-Three -- Last Throes of Justice
(4 -18 July)

So that perhaps there never was an instance of any innocent person condemned in any court of judicature on earth, only through Satans deluding and imposing on the imaginations of men, when nevertheless, the witnesses, juries, and judges were all to be excused from blame. -- Increase Mather, **Cases of Conscience Concerning Evil** *Spirits* (Boston, 1693)

The day the Nurses asked and received Thomas Fisk's account of the jury's about face, another woman was arrested and examined in Salem. There the behavior of the magistrates reached new depths. They examined Candy, a slave from the Barbados belonging to Mrs. Hawkes. When Candy was brought into the meeting house, the afflicted went through their usual antics, including reacting as if tortured when Candy pinned her scarf. The judges observing this, asked her to do it again and again. The afflicted girls cooperated perfectly in repeating their cries and contortions at the appropriate moments.

Candy had brought her lunch to court wrapped in a piece of cloth. The afflicted indicated that this piece of cloth was actually a "poppet," that is a doll-image which could be used for witchery against them. The magistrates decided to test this theory. True wizards, they cut pieces of the cloth and alternately burned them and immersed them in water -- which resulted in the girls experiencing the agonies of fire and water -- as the dullest among us could by then have predicted. Even the similitude of order and justice was in its last throes among us.

(A few months later, Reverend Hale was to belatedly reflect upon this examination and conclude the judges were themselves practicing magic during it. Certainly Mr. Hathorne was as guilty of going to the devil to cast out a devil as Mary Sibley had been with her perilous witchcake.)

Tuesday after Rebecca had written her response to Foreman Fisk's explanation of the guilty verdict, Ben Nurse was dispatched to carry it to Boston and find Sam and John Tarbell, who had gone down Sunday to make another appeal to the governor.

With all their documents in hand, including the various

neighbors' petitions on their mother's behalf, and copies of the court documents from Stephen Sewall, the three men were granted an interview with the governor on Thursday morning. The governor remembered them from their brief meeting in May. They had the sense he was more relaxed with them than with many of the powerful gentlemen who were constantly coming and going on government business.

"**Nurse!** I remember you. We spoke before. Your mother is one of those who has been accused in Salem."

"**Yes**, sir," said John, "And worse than accused. She has now been tried and although the jury found her not guilty, when they brought back their verdict, the Justice Stoughton sent them out again with a confused report of something she had said. The jury could not puzzle out what it meant, but the judges gave their interpretation, which she being deaf did not correct, and so the jury brought back a guilty verdict the second time."

"**Ah**, Mr. Stoughton, my deputy governor has done much the same with me on several occasions -- sent me out with a flea in my ear to deliberate again." He laughed, but quickly became serious again.

"**Well** I'm no lawyer, but there are plenty of them about here. What have you got for documents -- for you know we must have documents!

"**We** have an account of why the jury changed its mind -- written by one of its members. We have our mother's explanation of what she meant by the misinterpreted sentence. We have copies of all the written depositions made up for us by the clerk of court, Mr. Stephen Sewall. In addition we have copies of those several petitions signed by her neighbours as to her good character, the originals of which we already gave you."

"**That** should be enough, I should think. Most important is that juryman's explanation I suppose, but the others will be of use.

"**As** I understand it, my office gives me authority to pardon or reprieve a convicted criminal or to commute a sentence to a much lesser one. But I understand that would not be your first desire?"

"**Oh**, no, sir!" said Sam," For if the guilty sentence stands, regardless if you pardon her, she will bear it all her days worse than if she were branded for any other crime!"

"**Yes**, I can understand that. We have seen how suspicion of these things never seems to die. Well, we will make it our first goal to see if the court can't be persuaded to restore the first verdict of the jury, and throw out the second. If that cannot be done, we will ask for another trial, and if worse comes to worse, we shall have to settle for a pardon or reprieve.

"Are you men staying in town?"

"No sir, I mean we have been, but we planned to return as soon as we might."

"Well, I wish you were staying, for I grow tired of all these merchants, lawyers and ministers -- I would prefer to spend an evening with ordinary yeomen."

"We would stay, sir, if we could serve you so," said John.

"No, no -- you have urgent enough business and so do I, I fear. Not only do I have the devil to deal with in Salem, but also to eastward, and during the next week, here in Boston, in the form of my council! But don't tell anyone I said that, or Mr. Stoughton will be having me up for trial!"

"He seemed to genuinely care," said Sam as they walked along the street.

"Oh, aye, but so he seemed before," John said, "As I think about it, I wish we had stayed to dine with him and pressed mother's case a little more."

"But what more have we to say?" Sam asked.

"I begin to suspect that's not the question for those who make their way with government." answered John, "It is rather who have you said it to and how many times have you said it."

By Friday, when William Phips met with his council, he had developed a much more profound interest in the Rebecca Nurse case than her sons would have guessed. For not only did he see injustice in it, but he found in her exceedingly good reputation and the court's rejection of the original verdict, the proverbial fulcrum for a lever he had been crafting. The one thing he most wished to remove was the growing power of his Deputy Governor.

This desire did not eclipse the governor's sense of justice, nor his particular interest in the Nurses. He thought, however, that their situation had the potential to kill not two, but three birds with one stone : put Stoughton back in his place; slow or halt the troublesome witch business; and do justice in this one case where it was clear injustice was being done.

That he had not similar compassion on the Wildes, Howes, Goods, and Martins was due to a variety of factors, but suffice it to say, none had brought him documentary grounds as extensive as those the Nurses had gathered. Furthermore, in none of their cases had the jury come back with a "not guilty". A diplomat or politician must learn early to make his strongest case where he has one -- and only multiply weak cases where he has none.

So when the council gathered, the governor bided his time for discussions of the agenda, recent Indian attacks, the legislative schedule, and miscellaneous correspondence. But when the subject of the Court of Oyer and Terminer lately convened in Salem arose, he was ready with pointed questions for Deputy Governor Stoughton.

However, the governor had underestimated his deputy. When a self-made swashbuckler meets a highly educated minister, there are many areas where they fail to fairly take each other's measure. The swashbuckler doubts the minister's experience, his courage, and his wisdom. The minister doubts the swashbuckler's information, his sophistication, and his self-restraint. Both are liable to self-doubt, too, and their self-doubt may line up with the doubts of the other -- so that both tend toward a compensating effort -- to be more fully what the other thinks they are not.

Thus, for instance, Deputy Stoughton, exhibited far more raw courage in the face of opposition than one would have expected him to do -- so much so, that it seemed to appear unwavering was of more importance to him than other virtues which better accorded with his calling. On the other hand, Governor Phips so resented the possibility that his deputy might look down upon him for lack of sophistication and education, that he went out of his way, and indeed over his head, in complicated efforts designed to prove the opposite.

Specifically in the matter of the Nurse trial, Governor Phips introduced the whole dossier of documents to the council, and asked the council's advice about how he ought to respond to the Nurse family's requests for reinstatement of the original verdict or a retrying of the case.

This seemed to him a wily maneuver -- one which put his deputy immediately on the defensive and exposed him to the disapproval of the wider council.

But the governor was quickly frustrated in this when not only his deputy, but a number of men whom he expected to be his allies in this, immediately raised the legal questions of jurisdiction and appeal.

The governor had assumed that any appeal to him, such as the Nurses had made, was legitimate, but his councilors told him there was grave doubt about this. Since the appellants seemed to be objecting to the procedure of the court in the one instance and asking for the court to take into account new evidence in the second, the proper jurisdictions for these appeals were, in the first instance, the General Court, and in the second, the court of Oyer and Terminer, itself.

But, objected the governor, am I not bringing the appeal to the General Court now?

No, they replied, though you bring it, you are not the proper bearer or signer thereof. In fact it is an appeal improperly brought to you, and must be sent back in order to be directed to the proper jurisdiction.

"But as governor, have I not authority to pardon or reprieve?"

"That is something else," they told him, "and although a true pardon can only be given by their majesties, yet you have the authority of reprieve while an appeal for such a pardon is made."

"But the family is most desirous that the original sentence might be restored, rather than a reprieve or pardon. So how ought we to advise them?"

At this point, most strategically, Deputy Stoughton interposed what he posited was a more central question.

"Governor Phips, did you not appoint our high court and myself as its president, to try these matters according to justice and to the best of our abilities?"

"I did." Replied the governor.

"Then why do you question our conduct in one of the six cases we have thus far tried? Are you so soon put out of confidence in us?"

"I accepted an appeal, perhaps not entirely in the correct form, but according to ancient practice. The governor's office has always been available to those who are dissatisfied with the conduct of other offices of government."

"But why bring such an appeal to the council -- unless you yourself are greatly dissatisfied with the conduct of the court and its members."

This of course put the governor in the reverse position from which he had intended, for now deputy Stoughton was forcing him either to express a lack of confidence before he knew whether the rest of the council saw good grounds for it -- OR to express a confidence, which would reinforce the court's decisions thus far, and would hinder further limitation or review of its actions.

"I have grounds for question, not only in the appeal before me, but in some other matters which it is not now appropriate to bring before this body."

The governor then fired from the second string of his bow. "But I would like to know from you upon the court if one thing I am told is true. Is it a fact that one of these afflicted girls accused Reverend Willard?"

After a moment, Mr. Richards answered the governor, "It is true that one of the afflicted girls spoke of an apparition which she said identified itself as that of Samuel Willard. The president of the court stopped her testimony, however, and asked her to leave the courtroom for the rest of that session. On one other occasion she was found to have spoken an untruth and was rebuked for it.

"However, on this occasion, many of us think it likely she erred merely in repeating the wrong given name, for the governor may not be aware that one of the defendants is a John Willard of Salem Village. It may well be this was the true identity of the apparition she saw."

"This is the sort of thing we must be careful of," said the governor, "But, of course, the court should proceed. I would however, remind the members of the court that the ministers of Boston issued a letter in response to our request for their wisdom -- and that that letter contained several particular cautions which need to be given the most careful heed. False or erroneous testimony is a terrible thing.

"However, I will return the appeal to its originators, advising them as you gentlemen have recommended. Now let us move on to these other appeals -- for military reinforcement on our northern and eastern borders."

Thus was the governor stymied on his first gambit, and Deputy Stoughton reinforced in his position. In addition, Judge Stoughton was thus apprised of the Nurse's efforts and the governor's second and third plans of attack. For these he was thus able to prepare.

One of the Essex county assistants brought the governor's reply to the Nurses on Monday, and after seeking advice, the Nurses sent two petitions, one to the General Court and one to the Court of Oyer and Terminer, seeking respectively, a reinstatement of the original verdict and a re-trial. It was a case of belt and braces, but they knew there was no time for more deliberate proceeding. In fact neither of these were acted on, partly because they both had been submitted.

Chief Justice Stoughton met with his fellow justices on Monday (11th) and on Tuesday (12th), issued a death warrant for the five condemned women. To what degree this was precipitated by the Nurse petitions, none of us knows.

The Nurses found out that same evening, and Sam, John Tarbell and Benjamin once more set out for Boston. They arrived in the morning (the 13th), after spending much of the night in Lynn at the ferry landing, and went to Reverend Allen their landlord to tell him of their desperate case.

With the help of Reverend Allen, they found one who knew the forms for a petition for reprieve, which was delivered into the governor's hand by Reverend Allen himself. The governor signed it that night, and they returned directly to Salem, where they took it immediately (14th) to Reverend Noyes. This was another mistake.

Had they held the reprieve until the very morning of the executions, and then presented it, there would have been no time for counter-action.

As it was, however, someone or more accurately several someones, took up the matter with the governor on the 15th, at the council meeting in Boston. Down the years we have heard various explanations, but the upshot of that meeting, insofar as the reprieve goes, is that the governor recalled it.

Some say the lawyers there convinced him he had not authority to issue it, after all. Others say he had not followed the correct forms. Some say a gentleman from Salem persuaded him to recall the reprieve not only by pleading that it would undermine the cause of justice and the confidence of the community in the ability of its officers, but also by playing on the governor's fears and emotions by claiming that at the very moment of its issuance, the poor afflicted of Salem and the Village had been subjected to a renewed intense diabolical attack, which most certainly came from the very witch it named. Others say, with some authority, that the nominal reason for recalling the reprieve was that appeal had been made to two lower jurisdictions in the same case, in which circumstance, higher authority is supposed to withhold action until the lower have reached their conclusions. Thus the bureaus of government seem always able to obscure responsibility and avoid the onus of their official decisions.

A further factor which may have influenced the governor was the first reports brought to Boston of a new and extensive attack of

Satan on the nearby town of Andover. After concluding mysterious ailments and afflictions in that town seemed similar to what was rumored in Salem, Joseph Ballard of Andover enlisted the aid of Abigail, Anna, and Mercy from the Village for the exposing of witches there. This action marked the beginning of the Andover witch hunt, which was to carry many of the features of the Salem troubles to new extremes.

When they learned the governor had recalled his reprieve, the Nurse men returned yet once more to Boston, this time with Joseph Putnam as companion. But though they were able to apply to the governor's secretary, they could not get a personal interview again, nor any sympathy from the other assistants who were gathered in that town for yet more meetings of the Council. Like many another farmer dealing with an impasse among officials, the Nurse men ran out of patience at just those points where it was most needed and found their efforts further impeded as a result. They finally left Boston empty-handed and utterly dejected on the afternoon of the 18th, the day before the executions were scheduled.

Chapter Fifty-Four — Colony of Calvary
(July 19)

We resolve uprightly to study what is our duty, & to make it our grief, & reckon it our shame, whereinsoever we find our selves to come short in the discharge of it, & for pardon thereof humbly to betake our selves to the blood of the everlasting covenant.

And that we may keep this covenant, & all the branches of it inviolable for ever, being sensible that we can do nothing of our selves,

We humbly implore the help & grace of our mediator may be sufficient for us: beseeching that whilst we are working out our own salvation, with fear & trembling, He would gratiously work in us both to will, & to do. And that he being the Great Shepherd of our souls would lead us into the paths of righteousness, for his own names sake. And at length receive us all into the inheritance of the saints in light.

-- **Salem Village** *Church Covenant*, 1689.

The condemned slept strangely well, all but Susannah Martin, whose temper until a few days before had seemed so much like Sarah Good's—hardened and ready to return blow for blow or at least word for word. But the last few days she had been brooding, and quiet, and given to slipping in beside other pairs and knots at prayer.

Rebecca rose and found Martha awake already, with a small breakfast set out for her.

"No, Martha, I cannot eat it, although I thank you. Besides— you in church covenant are not supposed to eat with me! "

"You will be feasting in better company ere long, my dear, dear friend."

Martha spoke as well as she could and did not let her own emotions go beyond wet eyes, for she felt it her duty to uphold her companion.

John Procter called down the corridor and hastily summoned the condemned women to gather before his cell. Only Sarah Good stayed behind in her small corner.

"God's grace is sufficient for you, sisters. It is we who remain who need your prayers now. We ask you to continue them before him who was more unjustly condemned even than you.

"We will say a psalm together, but then for the little time we have left, please pray for your families and for us."

He began the psalm, "The Lord is my shepherd," and all joined in:

...I shall not want
He maketh me to lie down in green pastures:
He leadeth me beside the still water.
He restoreth my soul:
He leadeth me in paths of righteousness for his name's sake.
Yea, though I walk through the valley of the shadow of death,
I will fear no evil: for thou art with me;
Thy rod and thy staff they comfort me.
Thou preparest a table before me
in the presence of mine enemies:
Thou anointest my head with oil; my cup runneth over.
Surely goodness and mercy shall follow me
all the days of my life:
And I will dwell in the house of the Lord for ever.

Martha Corey looked around the little circle, about which the other prisoners had also gathered — there was a quality in the four faces closest to Goodman Procter that made her wonder. Was this not how Stephen appeared before the Sanhedrin who "saw his face as it had been the face of an angel." There was something about them that could scarcely be described except in terms of light, yet the gloom of the cellar shadowed them no less than anyone else.

The psalm ended, and the four condemned women entered into prayer. They prayed for their families and for the other prisoners by name. They prayed for a speedy end to the folly and injustice. They prayed for righteous men to rise up from among the ministers and civil leaders. They prayed for each other and the special grace they would need that morning.

Shyly, but clearly, Rebecca prayed for an easy end for each and all of them.

Then she raise her head and realized Sarah Good was not among them.

She slipped away, as Susannah Martin, for the first time among them, haltingly, prayed aloud, asking for the Lord's forgiveness of her many sins.

Rebecca went into Sarah's cell and found Sarah munching on

a crust of toast.

"Sister," she said, "You know we die today."

She looked searchingly into Sarah's eyes as she spoke.

"We have done nothing!" replied Sarah, defensive and drawing back from the soft hand on her shoulder.

"We have indeed done nothing, but nonetheless we die today. And it would be well if you prepared your soul to see the Lord. May I pray with you?"

"I will not! They took my little one. They cannot take me from my Dorothy bird like this. There is a God in heaven and he will hold them accountable for it."

"He will, Sarah, but the world is full of iniquity, and today we shall die under unjust sentence. It is not the first time such a thing has happened. The Lord Jesus himself died thus."

"So his ministers would crucify us, too! Have they not enough in Him that they need some more? No, I will not pray to their God, for they are wrong. "

"But Sarah, in this He is our God, and not theirs. You are right they must account for it, and it will go hard for them in the judgment unless they repent, but that is not for us to work out. Today we must work out our own salvation. We have to prepare our own hearts and see if there is any wicked way we should repent — so we do not appear in judgment with sins uncovered by Christ's blood."

"No, you preach to me as they do. I will not hear it! I will do what praying I must do. Go pray for yourself, Mistress Nurse!"

Thus Rebecca reluctantly emerged from Sarah's cell, and only heard the few last sentences of Susannah Martin's soft and fervent confession before steps were heard clumping down the stairs outside the locked door.

Goodman Procter cast out his last plea to heaven for them.

"Oh, Lord, bless and keep us through these dark hours and may no one of us be missing from the reunion around your throne."

Sarah Good was half-way out the door of her cell when this prayer was prayed, and hesitated, unsure she wanted to be part of it.

The door swung open and banged against a stanchion. Five deputies followed the sheriff, who hid considerable discomfort behind the regimen of office. The door had not stopped vibrating before his voice launched out.

"Step forward at the order of authority. Sarah Good! Rebecca Nurse! Susannah Martin! Sarah Wilde! Elizabeth Howe!"

He continued in a parade voice, while all the other prisoners were caught as bystanders and observers under its rough spell of stillness.

"Line up at the door. Each to go up with a deputy. Climb into the wagon. Offer no resistance. Speak no word.

"Where's the Good woman!"

Sarah had gone back into her cell, where a deputy found her bending over the small pile of her belongings fidgeting and fingering them.

"Come on!" he said, his voice brutal with fear and distaste.

The rest were up the stairs as he came after, beginning to propel her and she beginning to resist. By the time they reached the top they were in physical contest, which was quite all right with him. This he knew how to handle. He practically picked her up and set her in the wagon with the others.

There she began muttering after her old habit, but the sheriff chose not to hear her or to account her muttering as spoken words.

The sheriff and three deputies climbed on their own mounts, while the other three sat at front on the wagon seat. The prisoners sat in the bed of the wagon among the agricultural scraps that bore witness to its more innocent occupations.

Surreptitiously, they encouraged each other, touching a hand, or giving the quick communion of a warm glance, eye-to-eye. Sarah Wildes began to shake, and Rebecca whispered to her, "I will fear no evil, for thou art with me."

As they were placed in the wagon, each and all felt as though that thing time of which they hitherto had seemed to have such a dreary excess was suddenly being snatched away from them. The feeling was almost like suffocating. There was not time enough. Not time to see the last few beauties of this transient earth. Not time to take their partings from the many loved ones. Not time for all the words that ought to be said. Not time. Not time.

Suddenly they were crossing the bridge, and there were crowds around them. From the crowds some loved ones broke forward for an instant. Elizabeth Howe's two daughters urgently led her blind husband. He stood helpless as his daughters leaped forward and kissed her then fell back, as he cried out, "I've never ceased to love you, Elizey." And the wagon went forward into the closing crowd.

The sheriff and deputies on horses were going ahead, trying to make way for the wagon through the crowd. The crowd was cooperative, but since they were mostly moving in the same way, the pedestrians were unconscious of the hindrance they furnished, until the sheriff's voice boomed above their gabble.

"Make way! Make way! In the name of authority, make way!"

As they neared the top, the prisoners saw they were not to depart this world from beneath a tree branch as Goody Bishop had, but from a scaffold that had been recently built.

It was a long platform with two much taller posts canting out from both ends. These in turn supported a long and thick horizontal beam from which the ropes were suspended. Leading to the platform at one end was a ladder. And though the platform was long, it was very narrow, having just width enough for one executioner to stand behind each of the condemned.

As the wagon drew to a stop, many loved ones who had come earlier than the poor Howes, were already gathering. They surged around the wagon despite the sheriff's booming commands and the deputies' hostile grimaces and wild eyes.

The sheriff took his bearings and realized his prisoners had no chance of escape, so he called his deputies off, and allowed the prisoners to be hugged and kissed and many last words spoken among them. The wagon box by tacit agreement became the barrier — the line across which neither the living or the dead would pass, except in the small trespasses of embrace.

As the Nurses overwhelmed Rebecca, the Howe girls dragged their father panting through the last reefs of the crowd and up to the arms of their mother. Widow Martin's sons stepped up and reached out to her shyly trying to say something that bore meaning in the overwhelming mortality of the moment. She shocked them by saying she had been a hard mother and a hard neighbor, she knew. When they tried to deny it, she pressed their two hands — one in each of hers, and said it would be clear in heaven.

Constable Ephraim Wildes came forward, his father, John, half a step behind. He who had been a magistrate trusted now in his son's office to make safe this sally into the precincts of authority. Sarah leaned out over the wagon box and hugged them each in turn. "I needed you to come," she said to John, "now it will be all right."

Many other endearments, tearful embraces and prayers were shared — most of them rapid and brief. Before the sheriff climbed up on the platform to read the death warrant, Ben Putnam from the Village, who had watched what transpired until he was sure it was safe, brought "Good Will" Good up to the wagon, where he leaned over and timidly kissed his wife's cheek.

Sarah had sat the whole time in a corner of the wagon box, sourly muttering, distractedly twisting the corner of her shawl. She looked up sharply at Will and said, "we haven't had enough to eat."

When he mumbled something sympathetic or penitent she asked in a tone not petulant but quizzical, "Should I pray to the God they name? Would it be right?"

Will was decidedly embarrassed about spiritual advice, but Goodman Putnam, seeing this, spoke once, "To ask forgiveness for our sins is always a right prayer."

At this Sarah replied angrily, "But it is not our sins we need pray for, but theirs!"

Rebecca had meanwhile kissed her sons, her daughters, and their spouses, as well as five older grandchildren, and as the sheriff ascended, Francis stepped forward and put his arms a last time about the dear frame he had so often embraced. They looked into one anothers eyes only a moment.

Then Rebecca said, "You are to forgive them, Francis."

Never before in their lives had she spoken to him in the form of a bare command, yet he dimly recognized it was both a gesture of submission and much more than a requirement.

The deputies were arrayed around the condemned and their families, as the Sheriff stepped upon the platform to read the death warrant. He cleared his voice and the rumble of the crowd sank almost to silence.

> *To George Corwin, Gentleman, High Sheriff of the County of Essex; greeting. Whereas Sarah Good, wife of William Good of Salem Village, Rebecca Nurse, wife of Francis Nurse of Salem Village, Susanna Martin of Amesbury, widow, Elizabeth How, wife of James How of Ipswich, Sarah Wild, wife of John Wild of Topsfield, all of the County of Essex, in their Majesties Province of the Massachusetts Bay in New England at A Court of Oyer and Terminer held by adjournment for Our Sovereign Lord and Lady King William and Queen Mary for the said County of Essex at Salem in the said County on the 29th day of June were severally arraigned on several indictments for the horrible crime of witchcraft. . . (here he paused to catch his breath)*
> *. . . by them practiced and committed on several persons and pleading not guilty did for their trial put themselves on God and*

their country whereupon they were each of them found and brought in guilty by the jury that passed on them, according to their respective indictments, and sentence of death did then pass upon them as the law directs, execution whereof yet remains to be done:
        (he paused for another breath)
        These are therefore in their Majesties name, William and Mary, now King and Queen over England and so forth: to will and command you that upon Tuesday next being the 19th day of this instant July between the hours of eight and twelve in the forenoon the same day you bring Sarah Good, Rebecca Nurse, Susannah Martin, Elizabeth How and Sarah Wild from their Majesties Gaol in Salem aforesaid to the place of execution . . . (again he caught his breath)
        . . .and there cause them and every of them to be hanged by the neck until they be dead, and of the doings herein make return to the clerk of the said court and this precept and hereof you are not to fail at your peril, and this shall be your sufficient warrant given under my hand and seal at Boston, the 12th day of July in the fourth year of the reign of our Sovereign Lord and Lady William and Mary King and Queen of England and so forth:
        Signed, William Stoughton

Struggling for last touches and desperate kisses, the families were shoved aside by the deputies, who helped the prisoners from the wagon and led them to the ladder. There each deputy urged his prisoner up and followed close behind to prevent any last act of desperation, such as a self-destructive leap from the top.

Sarah Good allowed herself to be helped down from the wagon, but she immediately began to be recalcitrant once her feet were on the ground. The deputy who had such trouble with her at the gaol had been careful to pick another prisoner, so that Joseph Herrick ended up with her. When he attempted to move her toward the ladder behind the rest, she angrily shrugged against his hands.

"Let go of me, you wretch! If you are law then little law it is!"

Angry and embarrassed, he snarled, "No words from the likes of you. Get on ahead!"

Sarah did move ahead, but very slowly and with much bad grace. When he got her to the bottom of the ladder, he thought about what he would do next. After a moment's reflection, he said, in a low voice to the warder ahead of him, who escorted Susannah Martin, "It might take two of us to get this one up." The deputy glanced at Sarah's contorted face, then moved out of line with his charge and fell in behind Constable Herrick.

When the first three were on the platform, the deputy tried to get Sarah to begin climbing, but she looked up and saw the ropes swinging in the summer breeze, and suddenly seemed to fully comprehend the significance of the time and the place.

The sheriff looked down from above them, anxious to get this business underway and over. Seeing the sheriff, she stiffened and shrieked, "You'll no be a hanging of me, George Corwin. For I have not done anything. You hadn't ought to believe those girls. It was they if anyone was witches!"

"Get her up here!" commanded the sheriff, angry like Herrick over the indignity being heaped upon his severe discomfort.

The deputy tried pushing her, and then he tried lifting her, but she let herself slip back down each time. Finally he mounted the ladder before her, holding the chain of her shackles, by which he began to haul her up bodily. The other deputy briefly abandoned his prisoner and lifted from below.

Sarah shrieked and screamed, partly in pain, during the entire ascent.

At the top, the sheriff and deputy dragged her to the fourth position, and the deputy roughly pinioned her against the back railing by dragging her chain over it , and grasping it beneath the rail.

The last of the condemned climbed the ladder and stood before her rope with her warder, as the sheriff took up his position again at the top of the ladder.

Heroic to the last, the Reverend Noyes stepped forward for one last call to repentance.

The families of the prisoners had taken different paths since their partings. Most of the Nurses had gone away down the hill, perhaps at their mother's request or out of other sensibilities. Tom Preston had stayed—an act of self-torture and penance, such as no Protestant allows in his theology but nearly all in practice.

Blind John Howe stood between his two daughters only twenty feet in front of his wife. The daughters looked down, unable to watch the final suffering by which their mother was to leave this world. John, however, stared directly in Elizabeth's direction—and she found much comfort in gazing upon him.

Ben Putnam and Good Will stood further back in the crowd.

The Martin boys were even further away, warily looking about them, suspicious, as most of relatives of the accused had become, that some suspicion might be directed toward them.

Constable Wilde and his father stood to the side, but near the crowd that had given back a little to let the pastor move before the scaffold and address the five prisoners towering above him.

Reverend Noyes had nothing new to say, and it was as if he knew it, but like the rest of the great ones, he had committed himself to a course from which he found it impossible to depart. He preached and cited scripture. He adjured the prisoners and warned the crowd.

At the end, however, he addressed each prisoner directly and allowed each the opportunity to reply.

"Sarah Wilde, will you not confess your sin?"

There was a pregnant silence before she realized she was expected to speak.

Then she said, "I am no witch nor have been. I have confessed my sins to the Lord, and he is my only hope in heaven and on earth."

"Rebecca Nurse, will you not confess your sin!"

"I am innocent of the sin for which I stand condemned, but my sins have been many. I ask the Lord to forgive what I've neglected."

She added in fuller voice, "Just as we forgive any who have sinned against us, we say to all, you must forgive them, too."

"Elizabeth Howe, will you not confess your sin of witchcraft?"

"I have no such sin, sir, but many others I have. I have often been angry and let the sun go down on my anger. I have not been a good neighbor . . ." here she looked at her little family, "nor so good a wife and mother. Lord Jesus forgive me!"

"He does!" cried out blind James, "and we thank God for you!"

Reverend Noyes turned sternly, but when he saw it was the blind husband, he turned back and went on

"Sarah Good, will you not confess this your sin of witchcraft? For such you know your sin to be."

"Nay!" shrieked Sarah, twisting her body around from the rail where he hands were held, "You are a liar. I am no more a witch than you are a wizard, and if you take away my life, God will give you blood to drink!"

She went on in a litany of names — "Judge Hathorne is a liar! Judge Corwin is a liar! Reverend Parris is a liar! The Indian is a liar!" And so on, but Reverend Noyes ignored her and raised his voice to address the last prisoner.

"Susannah Martin, will you not confess your sin!"

She answered in low voice, surprising in its meekness to those who knew her, "I have confessed them these last days and I believe they are taken from me. But we are innocent of this. Father, forgive them for they know not what they do."

As if to provide the counterpoint, Sarah Good shrieked again. "May God treat you all according as you have done! May your children be as my little Dorothy bird."

Then Rebecca began, "Our Father who art in heaven..."

And the others quickly joined in. "Hallowed be thy name, thy kingdom come, thy will be done, on earth as it is in heaven. Give us this day our daily bread, and forgive us our trespasses as we forgive those who trespass against us. Lead us not into temptation, but deliver us from evil, for thine is the kingdom and the power and the glory for ever. Amen."

Tom Preston had bowed his head as had many in the crowd, and unashamedly with many tears, he prayed aloud with his mother-in-law.

To those who watched closely, even Sarah Good seemed to have joined in, but perhaps her lips were still moving in curses or imprecatory prayers. The news that the last words of the prisoners had been the Lord's Prayer got back to the gaol and those subsequently hung during our troubles did likewise.

The deputies reached out with their swords or staves and pulled the nooses in. They pushed their respective prisoners forward and placed these about their necks, keeping one hand firmly on the shoulder of each. The sheriff helped his nephew with Sarah Good, but she was no longer fighting or angry. Suddenly she called out, "Tell my Dorothy I love her. Tell her, William."

The sheriff raised his sword-arm, glancing once up and

down the line, then dropped it, at which all five prisoners were pushed off the platform.

Rebecca had prayed their deaths would be easy, and indeed, she may have been the last to go, but after five minutes it seemed to be over, though the sheriff left them hanging in a row for nearly half an hour.

Tom, for his part, forced himself to watch Sarah Good as she hung, her body wiggling at first as she tried to raise her hand or twist her shoulders from the rope, but soon she grew still. His signature had been one of the things that brought her to this. This awful and undeserved death was partly his doing.

But his wife's mother, whose body now twisted slowly on a rope, had said forgive them — commanded that we forgive them — those who put her there. Which was he? Was he not both? Must he forgive and also be forgiven? Did he not believe in one who spoke as Goody Martin from a scaffold -- one who had, in another way, become both parties at once?

The crowd had been there to watch. They were the last crowd to be merely spectators, however. Their reports went out quickly through the colony. Every one of the condemned had died protesting her innocence. Four of them had made clear statements of faith in Christ as Savior. As their last act, all seemed to pray the Lord's Prayer together.

It hardly looked like the behavior of dying witches. Some made much of Sarah Good's malediction toward Reverend Noyes. Others saw subtle diabolical signs. But most went away with doubts they had not when they came, or doubts made deeper. And these were to accompany their reports.

The crowd had dispersed to about half its strength when the sheriff and his men put a movable ladder against the front of the platform and took down the bodies one by one. With a hammer and cold chisel, two of them knocked the bolt from each shackle upon either wrist of the limp bodies on the ground.

The digging of the graves was one among his many responsibilities which the sheriff had delegated to a deputy. That deputy had fallen ill and neglected to get word to him until that morning. Therefore, before he brought his men to the gaol, he had taken them to the back of the hill to hastily dig a shallow, common grave.

Many of the spectators who remained surrounded the officials as they took the bodies down. The sheriff's men were becoming further irritated. They tried dispersing these with officious words, which worked with the more respectable, but had less effect on the unaccompanied servants, laborers and sailors, of whom there were many.

When the men moved the bodies onto the wagon and drove it toward the grave, many followed, which made the five deputies downright angry. They quickly laid the bodies haphazardly in the hole, next to an outcrop of rock, then began to deliberately throw dirt about with their shovels, hitting the crowd. The crowd, joking among themselves, withdrew among the trees, but did not all disperse.

As they piled the last of the dirt back in, nearly thirty blank faces continued to watch. After the officers left, a number of these persons drew close and a few among them began, gingerly at first, to uncover the bodies in the shallow ground.

Late that night, Sam and John Nurse with John Tarbell and Tom Preston drove a wagon half full of hay down the Salem Road. Cutting off near the Quaker burying ground, they made a long loop to the back of the hill and up it from the other side. They knew where the gravesite was, and were grimly determined to do what they came to do, regardless of what opposition might appear.

Near the site they lit a dark-lantern, and sucked in their collective breath when they saw exposed limbs sticking out of the soil. Looking closer they saw what had happened — for there were innumerable footprints and signs of haphazard digging about. Many of the clothes had been removed from the dead.

"What vultures inhabit this country!" Tom choked out.

But it made their task easier, for one of the arms sticking up was their mother's, yet she had been spared any other indignity. They loaded her dear remains in the wagon and took the same path towards home. There, in a copse of trees near their home, they gathered with Francis and their wives to bury her again that night. They read a burial service and prayed together. Then they laid her deeply beneath the warm earth in a cedar coffin under a cover of leaves and brush. They told no one where the grave was, not even their children, until they could be sure her remains would not be again disturbed.

The sheriff upon his return to Salem, got out his quill pen and made careful notation on the reverse side of the death warrant:

Salem July 19th 1692
I caused the within mentioned persons to be executed
according to the tenour of the within warrant.

George Corwin Sheriff

Sheriff George Corwin

Chapter Fifty-Five — Groans Too Deep For Words
(Jul 19-21)

What will be the issue of these troubles, God only knows; I am afraid that ages will not wear off that reproach and those stains which these things will leave behind them upon our land. I pray God pity us, humble us, forgive us, and appear mercifully for us in this our mount of distress: . . .
  --Thomas Brattle, **Letter of Thomas Brattle**, F.R.S. (1692)

Tom Preston bore Rebecca's last message back to the rest of the family. No one could have directed them as she had. No other person on earth could have turned Francis' will toward deliberate forgiveness. Had Rebecca neglected those few words among the many urgencies of her last moments, something more like vengeance would have erupted from the Nurse tribe and prolonged our troubles. Whether in deeds or only in words, it would have been a vengeance of heart quite the opposite of forgiveness.

But her life and her manner of leaving it, her meek and imperious words, diverted and directed Francis to the different battlefront on which he was to fight for years to come. At first he fought it incessantly, then in hourly episodes, eventually but a few times a day, and much later but a few times per week. Nevertheless it was a long and hard-fought war.

Ever since he had married her, he had directed all his powers against her death — the one eventuality at the center of his fears, dread, desires, and prayers. The way it had come was a conjunction of the three worst things he could imagine: being bereft of the greatest source of solace he had known in this world; being unable to protect the one he loved most against anguish and death; and towering over both of these, through monstrous injustice, the wreck of his most certain dogma, the sacred inevitability of righteous reward and due penalty. These were the three pillars of his existence and they had been felled at the same time in one act against his most dearly beloved .

There was mercy in the gargantuan, the colossal and leviathan proportions of this catastrophe, for its suddenness and scale were sufficient to numb him again. Like a great blow, it assaulted and robbed him of senses and calculation.

After he had dropped briefly into bewildered passivity at Rebecca's arrest, and again at her examination (oh so long ago), he had learned to armor himself through months of jarring infamies. But his familiar love for her and his formal love for the God of love kept open the beaver of his helmet and made him susceptible to this final devastation of earthly hope. Yet without that vulnerability, he would not have been anaesthetized and immobilized by the event, and might have embarked immediately on retribution, despite her words.

For his susceptibility to her words and his vulnerability to disaster were both through the doorway of his love. Both her words and his numbness kept him from reacting in swift carnal revenge, and began to make of his sorrow a lasting and fruitful good.

Her words (and the many similar words from most of those executed) were the seed, the germ, the embryo of the greatest — indeed perhaps the only — good to come out of our troubles. His numbness, his near amnesia as it were (which lasted something like the proverbial nine days) were the frosted soil, the shell, and the warm womb within which those words were protected and began to grow. Her love, God's love (for what else is any love but God's), and the undeniable, the burning image of that love on the scaffold, were the rich humus, the yolk and white, the nurturing blood by which he began to grow and to become what he was to be — in obedience to those words.

The other members of the Nurse tribe followed roughly the same development. Some were far ahead of Father Nurse, some more obdurate and far behind. But as her death was the triple destruction of her husband's idolatry, so were those words a triple spell of power to her loved ones — the last words of a loved one; the last words of a martyr; and the benediction of her own last sermon — allowing of no denial.

In them Tom Preston at last found the release from guilt and condemnation which had haunted him since February. Mary noticed it at once. What mystery had her husband beheld at the execution! Never mind what it was, it was clearly of God and good, and she rejoiced that he was beginning to smile again and to play with the children without the preoccupation which had long haunted him.

The Nurse tribe began to remember their early responses to her mention of forgiveness, their slyly superior dismissals of her references to it and not a few exasperated comments. They recalled these and gently reminded each other, with chagrin and humble repentance. From her beginning efforts (so very long ago!) to find forgiveness from God and Sarah Holten to the increasingly difficult struggle to forgive the men called (it now seemed, by oxymoron) ministers and justices, her life had centered about that thing and at the end, that thing alone. To deny forgiveness was to deny her.

The reverberations of that conclusion rang out in every direction. To deny her was to deny forgiveness — to deny forgiveness was to deny Christ. To deny forgiveness was to deny hope, was to deny life and any sort of love. For John Tarbell to deny his mother-in-law, was to deny his wife, was to deny two nieces -- Rebeccas all — was to deny his parents and siblings, his own children and all future generations.

But the first night they wept. They sobbed. And there was wailing up in the lone house after the ninth day, when in the deep of night, Francis was at last able to lament his dearly beloved, the wrinkled old dear who was too much of his life, too much and gone. The daughters and daughters-in-law wept steadily for a few days, and then at odd moments. Their husbands would catch them drying dishes in tears, or trying to see through tears as they were sewing. The younger men choked up only after they had been by themselves for a few hours.

The older children followed a more even course of emotion — intense the first day, less the second, and by the end of the week, some sober cheer.

The little children often wept, too, but mostly in pure emotional sympathy, rather than in great sorrow. Among themselves they said joyfully that Granmer had gone to be with Jesus, and they were going to go there, too, and be with her — forever, which they calculated to be an interminable duration, perhaps exceeding a year.

Many in the village mourned with the Nurses. An unresolved sorrow possessed nearly all of its inhabitants. Some pretended otherwise, especially those for whom admitting it would require the beginning of their own repentances. Yet for those who did admit it, the chiefest symptom became solitary prayer. For those denying the sorrow the chief symptom continued to be a flurry of activity. But almost universal was an unwillingness to discuss the execution of Goodwife Nurse.

The other families bereaved by the July executions reacted according to their own established courses or the dictates and examples of their dying loved ones. There were no overt outbreaks of violence or rebellion.

"Good Will" Good disappeared from the Village and no one saw him for two months. Outwardly, upon his return, he had changed little except to look a bit older and more worn. Benjamin Putnam offered him a permanent home and he, and then his daughter, became members of that household for the rest of their lives. Only in later years did some of us get a few glimpses behind his cheerful exterior, and once Joseph Putnam strolling cross country to visit his cousin heard the sound as of someone pleading an impassioned sermon and was able to hear a bit of William's cry to God, before the latter saw him and fell silent.

"What for would you let it happen! Do you think us but ants for the tormenting of! I would not treat a dog or horse so. What mean you then you love us?"

When Joseph first saw Will he was in the classic stance, his arms raised to heaven. And yet, Joseph said, it had no sound of blasphemy or ill-will. It was a man's heart being poured out to someone he expected to pay attention—like Job on his ash-heap.

Similarly other families and friends of those executed, in Topsfield and Beverly and Amesbury, mourned. But mourning was to be constantly interrupted with further fears and injustices. Our troubles were far from over, and the execution of the innocent was not half begun.

Curiously the leader in the Nurse's new course very gradually seemed to become Sam. He who had been continually active, but always subordinate, in the campaign to prevent further injustice to his mother, went on being active, and even an initiator in the campaign to forgive, and at the same time call her persecutors to repentance. Where Francis' forgiveness remained a more personal and usually a solitary battle, and where Tom's occasional relapses continued to center as much on receiving as giving forgiveness, and where John just seemed to grow gradually weary, Sam outstripped the rest in the peculiar ability to forgive without forgetting, and in bringing his forgiveness to bear in steady, gentle confrontations of those whom it was hardest to forgive.

For the immediate future, that is the two months following his mothers' hanging, Sam continued among the conspirators toward the goal of stopping the witch business. He became the mastermind behind a plan to rescue his two aunts who remained in jail.

Chapter Fifty-Six - The Prayers of Boston
(July 20-31)

Likewise, community of perils calls for extraordinary liberality, and so doth community in some special service for the church. Lastly, when there is no other means whereby our Christian brother may be relieved in this distress, we must help him beyond our ability, rather than tempt God in putting him upon help by miraculous or extraordinary means. -- John Winthrop *A Model of Christian Charity* (1630)

When Judge Nathaniel Saltonstall resigned from the court after Bridget Bishop was hanged, he left behind one man who, though slow in coming to share his reservations, became at last the only judge on the Court of Oyer and Terminer to publicly repent his part in our troubles. That judge was Samuel Sewall. But that repentance was some years coming. Nevertheless, there were early hints of it.

On the afternoon of the Lord's Day, the day after the hanging of the five women, Judge Sewall met in Boston with ministers Samuel Willard, James Allen, and Cotton Mather, and with Captains Hill and Scottow at the home of Captain John Alden, where Captain Alden, on parole, was allowed to join them! They gathered for prayer, Judge Sewall read a sermon and they sang the first part of Psalm 103 together.

Bless the Lord, O my soul: and all that is within me, bless his holy name. Bless the Lord, O my soul, and forget not all his benefits: Who forgiveth all thine iniquities; who healeth all thy diseases; Who redeemeth thy life from destruction; who crowneth thee with lovingkindness and tender mercies; Who satisfieth thy mouth with good things; so that thy youth is renewed like the eagle's. The Lord executeth righteousness and judgment for all that are oppressed. He made known his ways unto Moses, his acts unto the children of Israel. The Lord is merciful and gracious, slow to anger, and plenteous in mercy. He will not always chide: neither will he keep his anger for ever. He hath not dealt with us after our sins; nor rewarded us according to our iniquities. For as the heaven is high above the earth, so great is his mercy toward them that fear him. As far as the east is from the west, so far hath he removed our transgressions from us. Like as a father pitieth his children, so the Lord pitieth them that fear him. For he knoweth our frame; he remembereth that we are dust. As for man, his days are as grass: as a flower of the field, so he flourisheth. For the wind passeth over it, and it is gone; and the place thereof shall know it no more. But the mercy of the Lord is from everlasting to everlasting upon them that fear him, and his righteousness unto children's children; To such as keep his covenant, and to those that remember his commandments to do them.

Then Captain Scottow prayed for some relief from the long drought, and a heavy rain came even before he was finished praying.

Samuel Sewall deplored the accusation and imprisonment of Alden, as did Cotton Mather, but neither of them seemed yet to make the connection between the probability that John Alden was falsely accused, and the possibility that everyone else had been, too. Nevertheless a few leading men did on this occasion risk a public association with an accused "witch," and that was a step forward.

That week is often remembered as the opening of the second great wave of witch arrests, centered in the town of Andover. Martha Carrier of that town had already been accused by the Village girls in May. But now Joseph Ballard of Andover, brother of the constable who arrested Goody Carrier, brought the leading Village accusers there. At the outset, a minister and a magistrate of Andover both blindly cooperated. They gathered a large number of the inhabitants at their meeting house. There the witch-detecting girls were blindfolded and a large number of the inhabitants made to file by and touch them. The girls picked out an astonishing number of witches and a whole new list of complaints was issued.

A young woman, Ann Foster, became a "confessor" and accused many more. Several members of the Lacey family and several more Carriers became cooperative "confessors". Ann Foster mentioned a gathering of witches in which, beside Mr. Burroughs, two other men were prominent, one of them with gray hair.

The governors council met all through that week, but Governor Phips had decided that the best policy to pursue in regard to the high court and Deputy Stoughton, to coin an unkind phrase, was to give them enough rope to hang themselves, which meant in practice, enough rope to hang quite a few other people. The rumors of other reputable people being complained of — some of the stature of Captain Alden — were encouraging to Governor Phips, insofar as he hoped Stoughton's zeal would soon discredit the court, as well as place that bad credit squarely and exclusively on the Deputy's account.

The Essex county assistants brought the general court many tales of "confessing" Andover witches. They retailed stories of diabolical gatherings involving hundreds. The Andover "confessors" were accusing even their own parents and children. Loved ones, husbands, fathers and brothers, began to plead that the accused would "confess" in order that their lives might be spared.

Poor Mary Warren was brought into the midst of it again, with genuine afflictions and false accusations about the agents of them. Anna Putnam and Mercy Walcott continued at the fore.

In the middle of that week, shaken by the recent executions, Thomas Procter sent a letter from Salem Gaol to five Boston ministers whom he thought most sympathetic (Mr. Increase Mather, Mr. Allen, Mr. Moody, Mr. Willard, and Mr. Bailey). He gave a poignant account of the torturing of his sons and a number of other accused men, including the sons of Goody Carrier. He begged them to intercede:

Salem-Prison, July 23, 1692.
Reverend Gentlemen.

The innocency of our case with the enmity of our accusers and our judges, and jury, whom nothing but our innocent blood will serve their turn, having condemned us already before our tryals, being so much incensed and engaged against us by the devil, makes us bold to beg and implore your favourable assistance of this our humble petition to his excellency, that if it be possible our innocent blood may be spared, which undoubtedly otherwise will be shed, if the Lord doth not mercifully step in.

The magistrates, ministers, jewries, and all the people in general, being so much inraged and incensed against us by the delusion of the devil, which we can term no other, by reason we know in our own consciences, we are all innocent persons. Here are five persons who have lately confessed themselves to be witches, and do accuse some of us, of being along with them at a sacrament, since we were committed into close prison, which we know to be lies.

Goodman Procter went on to give the description of the tortures of
several young men , given earlier (*Chapter Twenty-Nine*), then
completed his letter thusly:

> They have already undone us in our estates, and that will
> not serve their turns, without our innocent bloods. If it cannot
> be granted that we can have our trials at Boston, we humbly
> beg that you would endeavour to have these magistrates
> changed, and others in their rooms, begging also and
> beseeching you would be pleased to be here, if not all, some of
> you at our trials, hoping thereby you may be the means of
> saving the shedding our innocent bloods, desiring your prayers
> to the Lord in our behalf, we rest your poor afflicted servants.

> John Procter, etc.

That same day, Constables William Starling, Bartholomew
Heath and Matthew Herman of Andover and Haverhill brought
Martha Emerson to Salem, where she was examined and "confessed,"
naming a number of others. She was later to recant her confessions,
because she said she was in hope of having favor before God, and
could no longer deny Him that kept her from sin. In her recantation,
she repeated those most appropriate Bible words, "Though he slay me
I will trust in Him." In her case, the slaying did not take place, but
there were yet fourteen more whose love of truth would lead directly
to their executions.

The Governor's Council did not yet give much of its formal
time to the witch business, but it continued to be the topic of many
informal conversations. King's Attorney Thomas Newton was
replaced at the beginning of the following week by Anthony
Checkley, a local barrister, who had often been in and out of the
courts at Salem. Various rumors offered explanations for Mr.
Newton's withdrawal, but some at least, indicated that he was
dissatisfied with the conduct of the witnesses and the kind of
evidence that was being allowed. Mr. Checkley had been a fellow
officer with Judge Richards during King Philips War. But he was an
even closer associate of the three Salem magistrates and of much the
same mind as they.

In late July, Reverends Willard and Moody were to visit
Philip English and his wife and invite them to take advantage of their

parole to attend public worship. They did so the day before they were scheduled to return to Salem for trial. The text of Mr. Moody's sermon at South Church that day was Matthew 10:23, in which the Lord speaks to the church of coming tribulation. He says, "But when they persecute you in this city, flee ye into another: for verily I say unto you, Ye shall not have gone over the cities of Israel, till the Son of man be come." After the meeting, the ministers visited the Englishes, and asked them whether they took notice of this discourse.

Mr. Willard exhorted them about the seriousness of their danger and urged them to escape since many in like circumstances had suffered death.

Mr. English replied confidently, "God will not permit them to touch us."

Mrs. English asked, "Do you not think the sufferers innocent?"

Mr. Moody replied that yes, he did so think them.

Mrs. English then asked, "Why may we not suffer also?"

The ministers exhorted them at length about the duty to preserve life and prevent the unjust taking of it.

When Mr. English persisted in saying that God would vindicate them, the ministers suggested that if he would not carry his wife away they would do it themselves.

Apparently the boldness of the ministers moved the Englishes, for they made their escape the next day. Some say Reverend Willard, himself, had a direct hand in it's success.

Nathaniel Cary, after the last round of executions, no longer had any doubts about where to seek justice for his wife. He managed her escape from Cambridge on July 30th. They fled to Rhode Island and then New York, where it is said Governor Fletcher welcomed them with courtesy.

Chapter Fifty-Seven — August Harvest
(August 1-20)

*It is an awful thing which the Lord has done to convince some amongst us of
their error. This then I declared and testify, that to take away the life of any
one, meerly because a spectre or devil in a bewitched or possessed person
does accuse them, will bring the guilt of innocent blood on the land, where
such a thing shall be done. Mercy forbid that it should, (and I trust that as
it has not, it never will be so) in New England. What does such an evidence
amount unto more then this. Either such an one did afflict such an one, or
the devil in his likeness, or his eyes were bewitched.* -- Increase Mather,
Cases of Conscience Concerning Evil Spirits (not published until
1693.)

Enemies make allies. On the first of August, Indians
attacked Billerica west of the Village, and we were reminded we
must hold together in defense. Others had the same response to each
development of the witch trials. They did not all agree, but few
denied we had a common enemy in witches, and only a few as yet
denied we were as certainly under attack by that enemy as by
Indians.

Other sorts of alliances, particularly those of blood and
affection, expanded and maintained the scope of the witch business.
The affection between Increase Mather and his son Cotton was one of
the dams that broadened the flood of our troubles. Had they been
unrelated or at odds with one another at the outset, more differences
might have been displayed in public — not only by them, but by
others, who held back out of loyalty for the older man or out of
desire to keep in his good graces.

As it was, Increase Mather, though probably the most
powerful and respected man in the Bay, was so circumspect in all his
pronouncements, that no statement could be certainly attributed to
him which spoke even mildly against the trials or any element of the
court's procedure, until as late as the beginning of August.

It is generally agreed now that much of the caution expressed
in the minister's letter of June originated with him. But so mild was
that advice that it had no practical effect.

At the beginning of August, another conclave of ministers

met more openly at Cambridge, being "seven elders beside the president of the college". They debated what they regarded as the pivotal issue: whether a demon could afflict someone in the form of an innocent person. The conclusion upon which they concurred was succinctly stated, "That the devil may sometimes have a permission to represent an innocent person as tormenting such as are under diabolical malefications. But that such things are rare and extraordinary, especially when such matters come before civil judicatures."

Why, once more, did they include a qualification that almost canceled the premise? Quite simply, because Increase Mather had three commitments which prevented an unequivocal declaration. First, he was committed to an unbiblical view of spiritual warfare which made much more of the devil than it did of sin. Both parties debating the spectre issue, that is, whether the innocent could be represented by the devil in an apparition, had surrendered to the devil already—in allowing theological and legal status to persons who could miraculously perceive apparitions. The only rational explanation for this is that, while they maintained to a man that miraculous signs were not operative except in extraordinary times during which God affirmed new authority by them (Moses, the prophets, Jesus, the apostles, etc.), they thought <u>ours</u> was such a time!

Second, Mr. Mather was committed to his son, Cotton, and particularly in that thing which both of them found amenable to their natures, the "scientific" pursuit and study of spiritual phenomena. Increase, in the completion and publication of the Davenport manuscript, *Illustrious Providences*, and Cotton in his *Memorable Providences*, had affirmed the spirit of their "science" in which intuition and "wonders" elucidated valuable truths.

Third, Increase Mather had another "child" or perhaps twin children: the Phips government, and the second New England charter. Where a stern warning against injustice would have been natural to him, he could not bring himself to give it to those he had chosen to oversee a government of his own design. The governor and deputy governor, the many assistants, were nearly all men he had recommended to the royal court. The leniency with which the charter was written, nearly restoring self-rule to the colony, was something he had labored and prayed and agonized over. He could not do anything that might threaten it's "life" or appear to do so.

Cotton Mather, on the other hand, had fewer commitments

and somewhat different instincts. He was young and he considered himself thoroughly informed on the most important subject of our times.

He wrote his uncle John Cotton on August 5th:

Our God is working of miracles. Five witches were lately executed impudently demanding of God a miraculous vindication of their innocency. Immediately upon this, our God miraculously sent in five Andover witches, who made a most ample, surprising, amazing, confession of all their villainies and declared the five newly executed to have been of their company; discovering many more; but all agreeing in Burroughs being the ringleader, who, I suppose, this day receives his trial at Salem, whither a vast concourse of people is gone; my father this morning among the rest.

Though Increase Mather was present at the Burroughs trials, and became increasingly reserved and even mildly critical thereafter, he never abandoned his three commitments, which cumulatively one might say amounted to a fourth — an unswerving commitment to what had already been done. This commitment he maintained, in public at least, for the rest of his days.

As the Court of Oyer and Terminer began the next round of trials in Salem, Goodwife Green of Haverhill escaped from Ipswich jail, and gave Sam Nurse the idea he and his kinsmen were to pursue a month later. She was caught within the day, by Constable William Baker, but she was quite determined and attempted another escape later in the month.

The trials of George Jacobs, Sr., Martha Carrier, George Burroughs, John and Elizabeth Proctor, and John Willard went forward during the first week of August. Martha Carrier had spoken for all of them at her examination, ". . . I am wronged. It is a shameful thing that you should mind these folks that are out of their wits."

Inquests were begun for a number of others. Mary Warren, Mary Walcott and Sarah Bibber testified against Mary Easty that week, but as in the earlier round, the paperwork, administration and time spent in trials accumulated and slowed the progress, so that the trials of Sarah Cloyce and Mary Easty were put off with many others to the following month.

On August 9th, 76 year old Robert Pike, magistrate of

Salisbury wrote to Jonathon Corwin expressing his opinion that those conducting the trials handed over the lives of the innocent "to the pleasure and passion of those that are minded to take them away."

Assistant Pike was particularly uneasy with what was going on since the accusation of Mary Bradbury, whom he knew well. Judge Corwin passed the letter on to Chief Stoughton. For the Deputy Governor, the battle orders remained clear, and no opinion to the contrary could sway him. He set the letter aside.

Three days later on the Lord's Day, Reverend Parris asked the church to stay after the congregation was dismissed, and recommended to them that some men be appointed to speak with those from the church who had absented themselves from communion, namely Peter Cloyce, Samuel Nurse, his wife, and John Tarbell. The church voted that Nathaniel Putnam and deacons Putnam and Ingersoll go with the pastor to discourse with these brethren.

The challenges to Rebecca Nurse's last words did not take long in coming!

Toward the end of that week (17 August), Cotton Mather wrote to John Foster, a member of the Council. The tone of this letter was considerably different from that to his uncle, less than two weeks earlier. He continued to be a dedicated supporter of "our honourable judges" and the "excellent judges" "that we are blessed with " who are "so eminent for their justice, wisdom and goodness". And he ended it by entreating Foster, that, "whatever you do, you strengthen the hands of our honourable judges in the great work before them."

Yet he also spoke of the dangers of spectre evidence, and expressed more caution. He seems to have been talking with his father or other men, and beginning to wonder if the "miracles" he had formerly attributed to God, might turn out to be something less.

It was almost as if two strains of thought were traveling parallel through the Mathers' minds—one, the unquestioned support of men in office, and two, a ongoing questioning of the ways and means of the witch trials. But the two strains never seemed to meet, to cross or to influence each other! Rather, at every point where they met, the strain of unquestioning respect fully eclipsed the other.

In this letter Cotton suggested that there may be a middle way—perhaps sending any convicted witches whose guilt the magistrates still find dubious into exile rather than executing them.

He wrote, rather fatuously, that he would be glad to go into exile himself, if he was accused of this crime. But in talking about his alternate method, he made clear the goals of the "wise" are putatively two: that "the land be cleared of witchcraft" and that "no innocent blood be shed."

On August 19th, George Jacobs Sr., Martha Carrier, George Burroughs, John Willard and John Proctor were hanged on Gallows Hill. Elizabeth Proctor was not hanged because she had been found to be pregnant. Her son, whom she would name John, was to be born at the turning of the year.

Reverend Noyes again exhorted the condemned as they stood upon the scaffold. John Procter earnestly requested Reverend Noyes to pray with and for him. The minister told him he could not pray for him if he would not confess, for that must be the priority. But Procter said although he could not own himself a witch, he did not yet feel he was fit to die. Then he asked for a little more time, if not for the minister's prayers, then for his own. He pleaded the same of Cotton Mather, but the young minister supported Mr. Noyes refusal. Procter's pleas were not those of a coward, but of a man in confusion and fear of God. Reverend Burroughs prayed for him in his own prayer, and so at his end John Procter seemed ready.

George Burroughs first gave a speech in which he quoted a great many Bible passages and authorities which showed how wrong these witch proceedings had been. The wise men there scoffed. Some of the afflicted in the crowd said the black man was by his side, dictating the speech that he gave. Nevertheless many of the spectators were so moved by this speech, and by Reverend Burroughs' manner and prayers that there were a few moments when it looked as though they would have hindered the execution.

In a truer show of his views than evidenced in his many books since, Cotton Mather rode before the scaffold on his horse and held up his hands for quiet. Thereupon he delivered an impassioned sermon of his own, calling the crowd to remember that these stood condemned by righteous and godly authority and that the devil often appeared as an angel of light, such that the people of God themselves are almost deceived. He reminded the people that the courts had found Reverend Burroughs, who was not even ordained, to be quite other than a trustworthy man. And that he had been shown to be the diabolical head of the horrible coven among them.

That seemed to appease the people or at least caused the peak of agitation to pass. The hangings went forward.

When they prayed the Lord's Prayer together, John Willard was no longer unsure of the words. Martha Carrier did not rail. Nor was old George Jacobs any longer rough and proud. They stood brave but humble as if they had been chosen for a company of heroes, each shyly doubtful if he (or she) was worthy. This time many in the crowd prayed volubly with them.

As the prayer ended, many in the crowd again cried out, "release them!" And "they are innocent!" and soon a chant went through the crowd, "release them! release them!"

But the sheriff and his deputies put an end to that by a different kind of release.

Judge Sewall wrote in his diary:

> This day George Burrough, John Willard, John Procter, Martha Carrier and George Jacobs were executed at Salem, a very great number of spectators being present. Mr. Cotton Mather was there, Mr. Sims, Hale, Noyes, Cheever, etc. All of them said they were innocent, Carrier and all. Mr. Mather says they all died by a righteous sentence. Mr. Burrough by his speech, prayer, protestation of his innocence, did much move unthinking persons, which occasions their speaking hardly concerning his being executed.

Afterward, when they were all cut down, they were dragged to the same shallow grave (which now was nearly empty, a circumstance that was never officially acknowledged). Reverend Burrough's shirt and breeches were pulled off by the deputies and an old pair of trousers put on his lower parts before they buried him in the same grave with the rest.

In the margin near his description of this event, Judge Sewall wrote "Doleful Witchcraft!" But was he beginning to find something doleful beyond the nominal witches and their purported deeds?

At least some of the "unthinking persons" moved by the "protestations of innocence" were finding other things doleful. Many of them had indeed been unthinking at the earlier executions, but they had done a good deal of thinking since.

Thomas Brattle who had come down from Boston for the executions, was certainly one moved by them. He wrote of those executions:

> In the opinion of many unprejudiced, considerate and

considerable spectators, some of the condemned went out of the world not only with as great protestations, but also with as good show of innocency, as men could do. They said before God they were innocent, and declared their wish that theirs would be the last innocent blood shed. With great affection they begged Cotton Mather to pray with them. They prayed that God would discover what witchcrafts were among them. They forgave their accusers. They further spoke without reflection on jury and judges for bringing them in guilty. They prayed for pardon for all their sins. They seemed to be very sincere, upright and sensible of their circumstances on all accounts; especially Proctor and Willard, whose whole management of themselves, from jail to the gallows, and whilst at the gallows, was very affecting and melting to the hearts of some considerable spectators, whom I could mention to you — but they are executed, and so I leave them.

The next day, in a letter, Margaret Jacobs officially recanted her testimony that contributed to the cases against her grandfather George Jacobs, Sr. and Reverend Burroughs.

The humble declaration of Margaret Jacobs unto the honoured court now sitting at Salem, sheweth That whereas your poor and humble declarant being closely confined here in Salem jail for the crime of witchcraft, which crime, thanks be to the Lord, I am altogether ignorant of, as will appear at the great day of judgment. May it please the honoured court, I was cried out upon by some of the possessed persons, as afflicting of them; whereupon I was brought to my examination, which persons at the sight of me fell down, which did very much startle and affright me. The Lord above knows I knew nothing, in the least measure, how or who afflicted them; they told me, without doubt I did, or else they would not fall down at me; they told me if I would not confess, I should be put down into the dungeon and would be hanged, but if I would confess I should have my life; the which did so affright me, with my own vile wicked heart, to save my life made me make the confession I did, which confession, may it please the honoured court, is altogether false and untrue.

The very first night after I had made my confession, I was in such horror of conscience that I could not sleep, for fear the Devil should carry me away for telling such horrid lies. I was, may it please the honoured court, sworn to my confession, as I understand since, but then, at that time, was ignorant of it, not knowing what an oath did mean. The Lord, I hope, in whom I trust, out of the abundance of his mercy, will forgive me my false forswearing myself. What I said was altogether false, against my grandfather, and Mr. Burroughs, which I did to save my life and to have my liberty; but the Lord, charging it to my conscience, made me in so much horror, that I could not contain myself before I had denied my confession, which I did, though I saw nothing but death before me, choosing rather death with a quiet conscience, than to live in such horror, which I could not suffer. Whereupon my denying my confession, I was committed to close prison, where I have enjoyed more felicity in spirit a thousand times than I did before in my enlargement.

And now, may it please your honours, your poor and humble declarant having, in part, given your honours a description of my condition, do leave it to your honours pious and judicious discretions to take pity and compassion on my young and tender years; to act and do with me as the Lord above and your honours shall see good, having no friend but the Lord to plead my cause for me; not being guilty in the least measure of the crime of witchcraft, nor any other sin that deserves death from man; and your poor and humble declarant shall forever pray, as she is bound in duty, for your honours' happiness in this life, and eternal felicity in the world to come. So prays your honours declarant.

Margaret Jacobs.

And how moved we "unthinking persons" were to hear that she had spoken to her grandfather and Reverend Burroughs in jail two days before the executions, confessing she had lied in her testimony against them and asking their forgiveness. Those who knew the crusty George Jacobs, Sr. were much moved to hear he had fully and gently forgiven her. And Reverend Burroughs was said not only to have fully forgiven her, but also prayed with her that she might persevere in her repentance.

Three days later, Goody Green escaped the second time from

Ipswich jail. Constable William Baker again "pursuing her with hew and cry" caught her on the road through Boxford as she tried to make her way home the following night.

On the last day of the month, Reverend Parris wrote in the Village church record that brother Tarbell proved sick, and so was unable for discourse with the men sent to him by the church. Brother Cloyce, on the other hand, was hard to find at home, being often with his wife in prison at Ipswich. This circumstance was soon to change.

Most remarkable as evidence of how effective Rebecca's dictum had been, the Village pastor records that Brother Nurse and sometimes his wife attended our public meeting — and he the sacrament! What an unearthly thing it was for us to see — a man sitting down and sharing the bread and wine of Christ's great sacrifice and memorial with others who had borne false witness to the condemnation of his mother only a few weeks earlier. What but grace, and that almost of miraculous proportions, could enable one to do it?

Yet that same grace that worked in him the mystery of forgiveness, also enabled Sam to bring together a handful of kinsmen the next week in a bold sally for the rescue of their loved ones.

Chapter Fifty-Eight — Sarah Cloyce Escapes

And ye shall be hated of all men for my name's sake: but he that endureth to the end shall be saved. But when they persecute you in this city, flee ye into another: for verily I say unto you, Ye shall not have gone over the cities of Israel, till the Son of man be come.
   — Jesus speaking, in **Matthew 10:22-23**

In Damascus the governor under Aretas the king kept the city of the Damascenes with a garrison, desirous to apprehend me: And through a window in a basket was I let down by the wall and escaped his hands. — the Apostle Paul in **II Corinthian 11:32-33**

Mary Green of Haverhill had made two brief escapes from Ipswich jail. These had excited considerable interest among the other prisoners there, including Mary Easty and Sarah Cloyce. Through them the escapes had been discussed by many of their relatives. Peter Cloyce, Jr. had been particularly interested. He remembered the resolve of the conspirators to do all that they could, though increasing their own risk where need be, to bring an end to the madness and to help those unjustly charged.

On the occasion of a visit to Ipswich Gaol near the end of August, he spoke with his twenty-three year old cousin, Benjamin Easty, who was there to see his own mother and found him willing to discuss the idea . They both felt the need of other counsel, however, and Peter remembered the Nurse men's discussion along related lines some months earlier.

They went the next evening to the Nurses and found Sam at home. When he learned the subject of their inquiry, Sam encouraged them, at the same time as he warned them about enlisting others.

"If we need another man, I think Tom Preston would be eager for the job, and I know you already have some interests among the Prestons, Peter. (Here he paused and Peter blushed.) But beyond him I don't think I will even tell John, not yet at any rate.

"I assume you are hoping to take the ladies to Eastward, where your Littlefield kindred are."

"Yes, that would make the most sense, particularly since, if we do it in the middle of the night, we can be well on our way from

Ipswich by morning."

"Good, then I think that my part, or perhaps mine and Tom's will only be to facilitate the escape. For the fleeing—you two will have to go with your mothers—and be willing to stay away with them until the end of these things, which could be weeks or years. Are you willing to do that?"

"Of course," said Ben Easty. "We'd do anything now. There is no more hope for us in the court, and both of them are sure to be in the next round of trials."

"All right," said Sam, "The main thing you have to think about is what will follow in the event you are successful. There will be a major 'hew and cry' and any loose end you leave lying about will be picked up and followed.

"How are you thinking of going about it?"

The plan was not a sophisticated one, nor needed it be. At first they talked of taking four horses, which could be obtained among their kindred. But Sam pointed out that while four horses would make better time, a wagon loaded with supplies and hay would allow them to conceal the women, and be less remarked and remembered by witnesses.

They formulated a simple story to explain the two of them going on a trip to Maine—to take supplies to their beleaguered relatives there and look into the possibilities of future prospects among them. They decided to tell this to a few in each family— Cloyces, Eastys, Nurses, and Townes, but also to ask that it be kept close unless anyone official should ask.

The whole plan would have been less likely to succeed if the two women had been kept in Salem jail, which was built of brick through the self-lamented diligence of Daniel Andrews. It was furthermore well-guarded in the midst of peninsular Salem. However, since the two women were being kept at Ipswich where the jail was more flimsy and on the edge of the town, they had a better chance. Further, Ipswich itself was nearer the outskirts of the colony, properly speaking, and by fleeing to eastward, that is on toward the scattered settlers in the territory of Maine, they had a chance of making good their escape.

The Cloyce's had many relatives in Maine—indeed quite a few who were old friends of Reverend Burroughs and thus doubly opposed to the Salem madness. Peter's own natural mother was Hannah Littlefield who died when he was only five. Thus he was taking this risk on behalf of a step-mother. But Sarah Cloyce had raised Peter from the age of eight with a gruff but affectionate care, so that he felt no ambivalence so far as his love for her. And she was also his beloved Mary Preston's great-aunt, her grandmother's sister.

Before the evening was out, they had not only formulated a plan, but settled on a date — Thursday, September 4th — less than a week away!

The plans for his mother's escape brought Peter Cloyce, Jr. to his own Garden of Gethsemane. If he did not sweat great drops of blood, he nevertheless underwent agonies of spirit over the potential cost of his sacrifice. He and Mary Preston were all but betrothed by then, and all their kindred and friends knew it. They had developed that peculiar ability of lovers to anticipate one anothers presence and to see one another a long way off, despite crowds or woods or fog. This, in a way, may have aided their plan for it made Peter's claim a likely one — to be looking for a good prospect where he and Mary might settle to eastward.

But when he and Sam and Ben Easty made their plan specific, it came home to him with a weight almost of despair, that this might well mark the untimely end of his courtship and an abrupt cutting off of his hope of a future with Mary.

Peter Cloyce had enlisted the aid of Daniel at one of their meetings, to write a petition for his mother and aunt, couched in solid legal arguments, and he had taken the finished product to them for signatures a week before. Daniel through Joseph had tried to keep abreast of ongoing discussions in Boston, and Daniel used the arguments he thought most likely to tell.

Unaware of the escape plan, Mary Easty wrote out the petition in her own hand as Daniel had advised, on behalf of Sarah and herself. They finished it and sent it just a few days before:

> The humble request of Mary Esty and Sarah Cloys to the Honoured Court.
>
> Humbly sheweth, that whereas we two sisters Mary Esty & Sarah Cloys stand now before the honoured court charged with suspition of witchcraft, our humble request is first that seing we are neither able to plead our owne cause, nor is councell allowed to those in our condicion; that you who are our judges, would please to be of councell to us, to direct us wherein we may stand in neede.
>
> Secondly that whereas we are not conscious to ourselves of any guilt in the least degree of that crime,

whereof we are now accused (in the presence of the Living God we speake it, before whose awful tribunall we know we shall ere long appeare) nor of any other scandalouse evill, or miscaryage inconsistant with Christianity, those who have had the longest and best knowledge of us, being persons of good report, may be suffered to testifie upon oath what they know concerning each of us, viz Mr. Capen the pastour and those of the Towne & Church of Topsfield, who are ready to say something which we hope may be looked upon, as very considerable in this matter; with the seven children of one of us, viz Mary Esty, and it may be produced of like nature in reference to the wife of Peter Cloys, her sister.

Thirdly that the testimony of witches, or such as are afflicted, as is supposed, by witches may not be improved to condemn us, without other legal evidence concurring, we hope the honoured court & jury will be soe tender of the lives of such as we are who have for many years lived under the unblemished reputation of Christianity, as not to condemne them without a fayre and equall hearing of what may be sayd for us, as well as against us. And your poore supplyants shall be bound always to pray & c.

This proved as ineffectual as all such petitions during our troubles.

Pursuing the escape plan, Sam indeed enlisted Tom Preston, and found him eager. Although both of them had families, the events of our troubles were teaching them one must not cling even to one's family with more than a light grip. The older men's part did not involve taking as great a risk as the two younger men, but their risk was considerable nonetheless.

The night of the 3rd, the four men gathered in Sam's shed, where the wagon was already in place and loaded with various small barrels and boxes of supplies. These they arranged in the center of the wagon, then covered them with a load of hay. It was good hay. Anyone asking would likely believe their story that they had sold it to someone up near Salisbury.

That was the story to cover the first leg of the journey. After the women were rescued, then the supplies would be moved to the periphery of the wagon box and the hay stowed in the middle — with the women hidden beneath it as long as they felt it necessary.

The next night Peter and Ben Easty arrived nervous and sweating. It was a hot, damp night, the kind upon which most people would gratefully sit down to a cold dinner and go to bed early, if they could. Few would be out unless they had to be.

The older men went over the plans with them, and then prayed for courage and calm. They had talked over the extent to which they ought to defend themselves, and decided they would not use violence — even if they were caught in the act. They planned to both appear and to be peaceful about it, for to justify violence against innocent parties would be to surrender to the evil they were opposing.

Peter and Ben drove the wagon out of the yard and onto the Ipswich road an hour or so before dusk, and as they disappeared around the bend, Tom and Sam looked at each other and smiled.

"I can't tell you how good it feels to be doing something like this at last," Tom said.

Tom and Sam rode out on their horses an hour or so later. They had told their wives they were seeing someone about some hay!

Mary Green, according to her own accounts of her escapes, had on the first occasion, figured out a way to pry up the bar on the outside door of the Ipswich jail from the inside. The second time she had found a loose board in a corner and over several days loosened two above it, so that she was able to push them out and crawl through. The failure of her plans had been due to her predictable destination after escaping.

On both occasions, the Fosse's had tightened the security of the building, which was a sort of addition or annex to their house proper. The first time, Thomas Fosse had made the door more secure. He had rigged another bar on the outside, and set a bolt in one end of each bar so that both pivoted down into the sturdy oak catch on the other end. He had further drilled the catches and bars so that he could insert a solid peg to fasten the bars in place each night.

So submissive to the law we were, that no thought was given to the possibility of an escape with outside help!

The wagon drivers arrived well after dark, and took their vehicle a half mile beyond the town on the road eastward, where they drove it off to the side and into a bay of overhanging trees. They rearranged their cargo and the hay. Then they walked back down the road, passing only one man, walking wearily, or perhaps tippsily home from work or inn.

They met the two horsemen near the jail, but did not talk

with them, for the riders passed on a ways, then tied their horses among some trees. Peter and Ben turned, however, and met Sam and Tom as they walked back. The four of them talked quietly, but as naturally as they could, until they drew near the jail.

Peter had told his mother of the plan the previous day. He and Ben had agreed they would let her tell Mary Easty. The two of them were to bring only a change of clothes and to leave all their other possessions behind.

Peter had told her to make sure they both sat as near the door as they could without arousing suspicion — perhaps going to bed first, and only rising well after dark and holding, perhaps, an impromptu prayer meeting near the door.

The agreed signal was three very small taps upon the door, such that no one else would be likely to hear them. The women were to repeat the signal to let them know they were ready.

The older men were posted one near the road and one in sight of the Fosse's front door as lookouts, while the younger two went to the jail door.

There Peter rapped ever so softly with his knuckle and the answering taps came almost at once. He and Ben had already removed the pegs. They swung the bars up and over, and opened the door just wide enough to allow the women through.

However only one emerged. It was Sarah Cloyce. From her face they knew something was wrong, and they feared they had been caught in a trap.

However, she at once told them the trouble in a whisper, "Mary's not here!"

Mary Easty had been unexpectedly taken to Salem that morning by a constable. It seems the magistrates wanted to establish the case against her more firmly and so had arranged another examination with several of the "afflicted".

Ben was crushed by this. Sarah whispered that perhaps it would be better to try the next night, since she might be brought back. But Peter knew the trials were to begin immediately and was at a loss.

Tom came up, sensing some delay, and they whispered the news to him.

"You must go on," he said, after a moment. "If there is another chance, we will do all we can, but we must take this opportunity, for there may not be another."

They slipped the bars back and replaced the pegs, then slid

through the shadows back toward the road. There Sam joined them.

After they had gotten out of sight of the buildings, they began to talk and the others told Sam the situation.

"Tom is right," he said, "we must make the best of this we can.

"We could send Peter alone with Aunt Cloyce. If you want to, Ben, you could stay with us and we will see if your mother is brought back here. Tom and I are willing to try again. But perhaps it would be better if you went ahead to Maine. We will try again in any case."

Ben said nothing until they got to the horses.

"No," he said then, "To have saved Aunt Cloyce is more than any of us expected. I will leave it to you, should a chance come for mother, but I will go with Peter and Aunt. They should not go up among all those Indians without at least one more with them.

"Will you tell father that we tried? And tell. . . tell mother that I love her?"

The two older men mounted their horses with mixed emotions and tears in their eyes.

As the other three trudged on east toward the wagon, and on along road into the wilderness, they turned back, and suddenly thought of another touch of their own.

"Say!" said Sam, "it is a moonless night and we have an opportunity to send all pursuit in the wrong direction. When we get half-way through town, lets break into a gallop! Many are sure to remember hearing it tomorrow morning. If they conclude two horses galloping west were surely the escapee and her companion, so much the better!"

And that they did, with the predicted results.

On September 4th, (Thursday) Thomas Fosse wrote a message to the Ipswich magistrates saying that Sarah had escaped the previous night apparently with the help of an accomplice, and they were thought to have ridden toward Salem on horses. A constable took it to Salem to inform the authorities there. Search was made in Essex county, particularly in the neighborhood of the Cloyce's farm. Some rumor took the constables farther north to the Townes in Topsfield. But although they ransacked the buildings of these and other relatives, Sarah Cloyce was not found.

The Ipswich gaolers, Fosse and his wife Elizabeth, were apparently not too upset about their loss. Nor was any blame directed at Mary Easty. In fact at the request of several Eastys relayed the next day (September 5th) the Fosse's wrote out and signed an affidavit of Mary's good behavior while staying with them. No one asked for a similar affidavit on Sarah Cloyce's behalf! However, a similar affidavit was obtained from the Arnolds for the good behavior of both women while at Boston.

Mary was not returned to Ipswich after that, and no further opportunity for her escape was discovered. Security, predictably, became even tighter at the several jails where the prisoners were being kept.

Mary Green, for instance, had been put in shackles and kept in them until late November.

Chapter Fifty-Nine — Last of The Hellbrands
(5-29 Sep)

Blessed are they which are persecuted for righteousness' sake: for theirs is the kingdom of heaven. Blessed are ye, when men shall revile you, and persecute you, and shall say all manner of evil against you falsely, for my sake. Rejoice, and be exceedingly glad: for great is your reward in heaven: for so persecuted they the prophets which were before you. -- **Matthew 5:10-12**

The next week the Court of Oyer and Terminer forged ahead with another series of trials. The judges had a growing sense of urgency as more and more defendants were being brought from Andover. Among the confessors there were reports of "hundreds" of witches.

The trial court issued summons for witnesses to appear Tuesday. One was sent to the Towne family of Topsfield, requiring the appearance of widow Mary Towne, William and Samuel Towne (her sons), and Rebeckah and Elizabeth Towne (her daughters.)

Mary wrote back to the court that they were in no condition to come being "in a straing condition" so that "most of us can scars git out of our beads we are so wake and not able to reid at all." She said her daughter Rebekah was particularly hard hit: "she hath straing fits sometimes she is knoked downe of a sodain."

The tone of the reply to the summons was apologetic, but no doubt they were wary. Recently their home and farm were searched for their escaped kinswoman. Nor could Mary help but be fearful with three sisters-in-law arrested, one already hanged, one escaped, and one about to be tried.

Two days later the court reissued its summons to the Townes of Topsfield, stipulating that no excuses would be accepted for failure to appear. This time the summons specified they were to testify on indictments exhibited against Mary Easty. Weary Ephraim Wildes, still laboring as a constable of Topsfield, delivered it.

They replied once more that they could not come. Curiously, the Jury of Inquest responded by issuing a "true bill," a further indictment, against the escaped Sarah Cloyce for afflicting her niece, Rebeckah Towne! However, the court took no further action against the delinquent Townes.

That day (the 8th) and the following, Mary Bradbury and five others were tried. Mistress Bradbury was vigorously defended out of court by the aged Major Pike of Salisbury, but as with the others, no attorney for her defense was allowed in the trial. However petitions were presented on her behalf with over 100 signatures.

Despite such efforts, the Court and the Trial Jury found against all six defendants. On September 9th, Martha Corey, Mary Easty, Alice Parker, Ann Pudeator, Dorcas Hoar and Mary Bradbury were pronounced guilty and sentenced to be hung.

For the first time, one of those accused "confessed" subsequent to being convicted in court. Not only did Dorcas Hoar "confess," but in response to her "repentance," the local ministers immediately petitioned on her behalf, asking that she be reprieved at least for the time being. They pointed out that she could be very useful in helping to identify yet more of the great number of witches they now believed to be among them.

Also for the first time, one of the prisoners escaped after she was condemned. Mary Bradbury, daughter of John Perkins of Ipwich and wife of Captain Thomas Bradbury of Salisbury, disappeared from prison before she could be hanged. It is generally thought that she had influential help.

A death warrant was issued for the remaining women.

On the Lord's Day, the Village Church held a solemn meeting before the communion service. Martha Corey, though "a Bible Woman," was excommunicated in absentia. She had been in covenant here since April 1690.

What grace of forgiveness Sam Nurse showed in not only coming to that service, but in taking communion at the Lord's Table that same day! His wife, Rebecca, could not bring herself to it. Perhaps she came intending to partake, but she left as the meeting began to discuss the excommunication of Goodwife Corey. Fortunately the wind wasn't blowing as it had on the occasion her Aunt Cloyce left early, and the door closed very quietly after she joined the departing company of "inhabitants".

The Eastys sent a delegation to the governor the next day, trying to obtain a reprieve. Having learned from the Nurse's bitter experience, they had that and only that as their object. Although Governor Phips was in town and meeting with his council, he would not see them, and their petition was never answered.

On Wednesday (14th) Lieutenant Nathaniel Putnam and the

two Village deacons went with Reverend Parris to Salem prison to deliver the church's sentence to Martha Corey. They found her "very obdurate, justifying herself, and condemning all that had done anything to her just discovery and condemnation. Whereupon, after a little discourse, (for her imperiousness would not suffer much)," wrote Reverend Parris, "and after prayer, -- which she was willing to decline, -- the dreadful sentence of excommunication was pronounced upon her."

Her eighty year old husband, Giles Cory, the most "obdurate" of all the defendants, continued to refuse to plead or throw himself upon the court in any fashion whatever. He was nevertheless indicted. It was forbidden by the Massachusetts Bodies of Liberties to use torture on any person brought before law, except upon a capital felon and then only following his conviction:

> *Torture : It is ordered, decreed, and by this Court declared; that no man shall be forced by torture to confesse any crime against himselfe or any other, unles it be in some Capital case, where he is first fully convicted by clear and sufficient evidence to be guilty. After which, if the Case be of that nature that it is very apparent there be other Conspirators or Confoederates with him; then he may be tortured, yet not with such tortures as be barbarous and inhumane.*
> *-- Laws and Liberties of Massachusetts (1648)*

According to an ancient clause of English law, however, a defendant who refused to place himself "on God and Country," that is submit to the court in its proceedings and conclusions, could be subjected to "peine forte et dure" (which means "pain strong and continuous"). Such a procedure had never been authorized by the colonial courts before this and has never since. But Giles Corey was openly tortured in an effort to get him to confess or at least enter a plea.

On September 17th, Goodman Corey, who had already spent five months in prison, was stripped of his clothes and held upon the ground while deputies placed a heavy door across his body and then piled stones upon it. After an initial great weight, such that Giles could no longer move, the Sheriff periodically lifted more stones onto the heap, exhorting Goodman Corey to speak and save himself further suffering.

Various other persons went to the scene of this torture and begged, reasoned, or exhorted Giles to speak. According to Judge

Samuel Sewall's account, "much pains was used with him two days, one after another, by the court and Captain Gardner of Nantucket who had been of his acquaintance, but all in vain."

The torture was begun on Saturday. On the Lord's Day, the Salem Church where he was in covenant, voted to excommunicate him. Reverends Noyes and Higginson came to him in the afternoon to deliver the church's sentence to him.

But Goodman Corey held his tongue -- held it for twenty-four hours, that is, until it was forced from his mouth by the great pressure on his body. Some say that toward the end, the sheriff tried to stuff his tongue back in with the tip of his staff. Finally he could breath no more and on September 19th, died. Martha did not see him during the last month of their lives. But through the reports of his awful death, she bore an additional burden as she went to the scaffold. Surely the lawless pagans are seldom so cruel.

Sergeant Putnam wrote Judge Sewall a letter retailing an "appearance" which came to Anna -- supposedly that of the deceased Jacob Goodell:

Who told her that Giles Corey had murdered him by pressing him to death with his feet; but that the devil had appeared unto him, and convenented with him, and promised him, he should not be hanged.

Thus Sergeant Putnam perceived dramatic irony and justice, as he thought it, in the death of Giles Corey.

Between their visits to the tormented Corey, the members of the Court pressed forward with yet more trials. They were not satisfied this time to hang so few. With the gradual fading away of his justices (only five were sitting by then) Chief Justice Stoughton was beginning to see the handwriting on the wall. He hoped to rid the colony of as many witches as possible before things ground to a halt.

On September 17th, Margaret Scott of Rowley, Wilmott Redd of Marblehead, Rebecca Eames of Boxford, Abigail Hobbs of Topsfield, and Samuel Wardwell, Mary Parker, Abigail Faulkner, Mary Lacy and Ann Foster, all of Andover, were also condemned.

Mary Easty in her last days on this earth, wrote a petition in her own words and hand, which reflects the spirit of many on the scaffold:

The humbl petition of Mary Eastick unto his excellencyes Sir W'm Phipps, to the honour'd judge and bench now sitting in judicature in Salem, and the reverend ministers, humbly sheweth:

That whereas your poor and humble petitioner being condemned to die doe humbly begg of you to take it into your judicious and pious considerations that your poor and humble petitioner, knowing my own innocencye, blised be the Lord for it, and seeing plainly the wiles and subtility of my accusers, by my selfe can not but judg charitably of others that are going the same way of my selfe, if the Lord stepps not mightily in. I was confined a whole month upon the same account that I am condemed now for, and then cleared by the afflicted persons as some of your honours know, and in two dayes time I was cryed out upon by them, and have been confined and now am condemned to die. The Lord above knows my innocencye then and likewise does now as att the great day will be known to men and angells.

I petition to your honours not for my own life for I know I must die and my appointed time is sett, but the Lord he knowes, it is that if it be possible no more innocentt blood may be shed, which undoubtidly cannot be avoydd in the way and course you goe in. I question not but your honours does to the uttmost of your powers in the discovery and detecting of witchcraft and witches and would not be gulty of innocent blood for the world, but by my own innocencye, I know you are in the wrong way. The Lord in his infinite mercye direct you in this great work, if it be his blessed will that no more innocent blood be shed.

I would humbly begg of you that your honors would be plesed to examine theis aflicted persons strictly and keepe them apart some time and likewise to try some of these confesing wichis : I being confident there is severall of them has belyed themselves and others, as will appeare, if not in this world I am sure in the world to come, whither I am now agoing, and I question not but youle see an alteration of thes things. They say my selfe and others, having made a League with the divel, we cannot confesse. I know and the Lord knowes, as will shortly appeare, they belye me, and so I question not but they doe others. The Lord above who is the searcher of all hearts knowes that as I shall answer it att the tribunall seat, that I know not the least thinge of witchcraft, therfore I cannot I dare not belye my own soule.

I beg your honers not to deny this my humble petition from a poor dying innocent person and I question not but the Lord will give a blesing to yor endevers

Mary's pleas: to have the "afflicted" examined separately and thus catch them in lies — as Reverend Willard had done with Elizabeth Knapp; and to bring some of the "confessors" to trial went unheeded, against all justice but in accordance with what was then "the course of justice." It seemed only the accused could think straight about these matters.

Abigail Faulkner of Andover pleaded pregnancy and her sentence was delayed, but on September 22nd, Martha Cory, Margaret Scott, Mary Easty, Alice Parker, Ann Pudeator, Willmott Redd, Samuel Wardwell, and Mary Parker were hanged.

Some of the condemned were rough women though most conducted themselves upon the scaffold with saintly bearing and words. Again they prayed the Lord's Prayer together, and again they were joined in that prayer by a great chorus from the crowd.

Martha Corey, despite her own suffering and the anguish of mourning her husband, was full of grace and quoted much scripture.

Mary Easty showed a peace exceeding that of the several ministers present. She showed affection and concern for her family during her last moments such that few there could hold back their tears.

After their execution, Mr. Noyes remarked to those near him, "What a sad thing it is to see eight firebrands of hell hanging there."

Nevertheless, these were the last of the twenty persons executed during our troubles. Mary Easty's petition did not save her or her companions, but her greater prayer was answered. It was indeed God's "blessed will that no more innocent blood be shed." With the exception of elderly Lydia Dastin who died the next spring in Cambridge jail, there were to be no more deaths.

Chapter Sixty -- Conspirator Captured
(6 or 7th October)

The punishment of thine iniquity is accomplished, O daughter of Zion; he
will no more carry thee away into captivity: he will visit thine iniquity,
O daughter of Edom; he will discover thy sins.
-- Lamentations 4:22

Not only were the Salem, Boston, and Ipswich jails full of persons accused of witchcraft, with more being examined every day, but the Court of Oyer and Terminer had already condemned a number who had yet to be executed.   No one entertained the hope that the hangings were over.

The conspirators met once more and brought a few hopeful tales of more open objections being raised in Boston. Rumors of letters written by Increase Mather and Thomas Brattle were mildly encouraging. Nevertheless, none but expected more of the same — more heartbreaking judicial murders along the same lines as the previous twenty.

Two weeks after the hanging of Mary Easty, Martha Corey, and the six others, George and Daniel awoke early to the damp cold of a clear day after rain. The cave was relatively dry — the four day spate had once more proved it did not leak — but it was uncomfortable nonetheless. Now in the first week of October, they consoled themselves that they could probably survive the winter there, if that proved necessary. George went out early to make a surreptitious inquiry after the welfare of his children. They had decided it would be unwise for the children to see him, but since they stayed with Daniel's wife, it was no great matter for him to leave a message for her and meet her at the spring where Daniel had rendezvoused with her several times in the last month.

He had been gone no more than an hour when Daniel heard scuffling above the cave, and a loose stone falling. At first he thought it was another episode of Joseph arriving as he had back in June. But then he heard men's voices, as many as three he thought, although they spoke quietly. Only then he realized he had fueled the fire too well in trying to dry out the cave. The smoke was flowing in a thin but steady stream out under the arch of the door, and thence upward in a column.

Daniel had stowed the rope away after George left. He looked out the doorway and saw nothing in sight to further betray them. He smothered the fire carefully with a blanket, and when the flames were dead, poured a thin stream of water on the hotter coals, trying to make as little smoke or sound as possible. He scattered the remains and quickly considered what to do. He decided to assume the worst, that he had been discovered, and would soon be visited at the cave itself. That being the case, he determined to eliminate any signs of George's presence, so that he alone might be suspected of hiding there.

George's distinctive possessions were few: an engraved pistol, his Bible and some writing things, as well as a pair of boots which were too big for Daniel. All of these he bundled in a brown shirt and stuffed far back in the small crack where he had kept his accounts and writings, wrapped in oilskin. He then carried back the largest stone he could lift, at some expense to his back. After setting it before the crack, he scraped up dirt and gravel around its base to give it the appearance of being there some time.

Daniel picked up all George's bedding and rearranged it as part of his own. He looked around anxiously, and saw George's pipe which he had only thrust in his pocket, when he heard further sounds. Looking out he was sobered to see a rope snaking down against the rock at the head of the fissure.

He picked up his own Bible and turned to David's Psalms. How appropriate it seemed to read of a man hidden from his enemies, full of fear of their persecution. He laughed inwardly and found new calm. He sat down, scraped together his scattered fire and began to read just as the sound of boots scraping the wall above told him of his first visitor's imminent arrival.

It was Sergeant Putnam. When he peered into the cave and saw Daniel sitting there, the look of unholy joy radiated across his face.

He shouted up, "It's Andrews! Edmund, you come down, too. Jonathon, cock your musket and stand prepared if need be."

"Save your powder, Thomas," Daniel said, "You might as well save Edmund a trip, too. I'll come along quietly."

"Stay, Edmund! Come out, then, and keep your hands before you!" Thomas ordered. Daniel set down his Bible and complied.

He emerged as Putnam covered him with a fowling piece, for it turned out the three were hunting when they happened upon the clue of his smoke.

"You've kept your neck well for the sake of a rope, " he said, and he was fairly bursting with elation. "Where's Jacobs?" he asked, staring past into the depths of the cave.

"Jacobs? You mean he still lives!" Daniel answered, with all the enthusiasm of the world's best liar. "God be praised! He must be far gone if you have not caught him!"

"Gone when?" he asked.

"Why these four months, I guess, for it's that long or more since I saw him at home. Oh, this is news nearly good enough to make my capture a happy one."

"Oh yes, your capture is a happy one, but it will not prove happy for you, you vile enchanter. We've sent nearly two dozen of your ilk to their eternal damnation, and you'll not be long in following."

"From what I know of those arrested before me, my good Sergeant, I think on the whole I prefer their company to yours." He made this comment, he said later, for the purpose of keeping the Sergeant excited.

"Save your pretty speeches, Mr. Merry Andrew, you will need them all now. Although you have used your tongue overmuch before now, I doubt it will save you again.

"Throw down the other rope, " he called to Edmund Putnam and Jonathon Walcott who stood at the cliff above us. "I'll bind him and you can pull him up."

"Nay, that's more work than they need do," Daniel said. "If I climb the rope as you have descended, they can bind me at the top. Unless you fear I will fly away on a stick, my good Sergeant." In contravention of his official beliefs, Sergeant Putnam did not appear to fear that thing, so Daniel climbed the rope, and stood at the top before the muzzles of two muskets. He looked down and saw that his captor had gone into the cave. Fearing lest the Sergeant make too complete a search or find something he overlooked, Daniel resolved to make a pretense of escape in order to draw him out, but the Sergeant emerged again before he tried it. Quickly Thomas Putnam clambered up to join them.

"Did you find any poppets or other engines of witchery? Daniel asked.

"Nay, laugh, my dear wizard. If you have hidden the outward signs of your witchcraft, you have not hidden the effects, and they will be enough to hang you."

They took Daniel down through the woods directly back to the Village. By the grace of God when they arrived who should they meet but Joseph coming out of Ingersoll's.

"Why, Daniel," said Joseph, "You are not in such good company as I am accustomed to seeing you with!"

"Nay," replied Daniel, "It was not of my own choosing."

"What!," said Joseph, turning to his half-brother, "Thomas, have you been imposing yourself on yet another gentleman! I thought you had learned better by now."

"Keep off, Joseph. This man's wanted by authority and none of your slanging will change the case. He has been hiding out these months in a cave back of Thornton's Hill."

"You mean you interrupted my hospitality and dragged him from it! Why I believe I may go to law against you for it."

"What are you talking about? Did you know he was there!"

"I might have guessed—it is my cave, or rather I should say, it is the cave I discovered many years ago. It is a shame you have not my wits, Thomas, or you might have found it yourself."

"Why, then. That makes you his accomplice. You have aided a fugitive. And are yourself a criminal!"

"Nay, did I aid him? I cannot rightly remember saying that. No indeed. I said it was my cave or rather that I discovered it, always assuming we are talking about the same cave. Where exactly did you say it was?

"Why, behind the northwest end of the ridge on Thorndike's. Down the cliff face in a wide crack there!"

"Yes, that's the one. Definitely mine. But he has my permission. I have no need of it myself. Let him go, Thomas, there's been no trespass."

"But he's wanted. And what do you mean he has your permission. Did you know he was there or not?"

"No, not exactly. I mean he wasn't there all the time was he? Not since you arrested him, and certainly not before he went there. I'm sure there have been many times when he was not there. So I cannot say I did—know that is—that is that he was there. Because on the whole, it would be more accurate to say he wasn't."

"None of your play, Joseph. I haven't time for it. We're taking him to authority and must be on our way."

"But why are you taking him to authority, Thomas. I've already told you there was no trespass—not where I'm concerned. What do you perceive to be his crime?"

"Witchcraft! As you well know. "

"Why, no, quite the contrary. I know for certain he is no witch. Are you, Daniel? Tell him."

Daniel burst out laughing, having restrained himself with difficulty during much of this conversation.

"No," he said, after a few hearty guffaws, "no, I'm no witch, I assure you Thomas. Nor have any of the others been."

"That kind of talk will get you nowhere! The high court has convicted plenty enough and will not be likely to fail with you."

"But Thomas," said Joseph, "I've been wondering seriously. What is a witch, after all? Are you a witch, for instance?"

"Me!" said Thomas, and he drew back as if in physical repulsion, "No, I'm no witch. Far from it! Don't joke, Joseph. Why my own household has been one of the worst afflicted."

"Exactly!" said Joseph, "And wasn't Reverend Burrough's household much afflicted? And wasn't John Procter's household much afflicted? And John Willard — wasn't his household also much afflicted? H-m-mm. I begin to see more clearly. Poor Anne and Anna and Mercy. How long they have suffered. I believe I shall have to go to the magistrates."

"Here!" cried Thomas, "What are you saying! Do not speak so, whether you joke or not. It is no matter for jesting, and particularly not before others." He glanced significantly at his brother, Deacon Edward, and his brother-in-law, Captain Walcott, who had been silently listening to the conversation thus far.

"Am I merely jesting, Thomas? I have been observing you for some months, and have talked to many others. It is clear to me that not only could I credibly accuse you, but also bring five or six witnesses to show that there are many good reasons to suspect you of witchcraft.

"I will give you some examples. Does the Bible not forbid that any should inquire of one who consults with familiar spirits?"

"Certainly it does."

"And have you not called Abigail Williams, Betty Hubbard, and Mary Warren to determine who it was that afflicted Mercy and Anna — particularly on the occasion after Mary Easty was released by authority, having then been found free of witchcraft?"

"Yes, we did — and called the Captain's daughter, Mary, too!" He looked to Jonathon Walcott for support.

"There you see, consulting with those who have familiar spirits!"

"What are you saying! Why these girls are afflicted by witches! You turn things on their heads!"

"Oh, I assure you, not only I but many of our ministers and magistrates are beginning to recognize that what your girls are doing is indeed consulting with familiar spirits. How else is it that they "see" things with their eyes closed, and speak with the dead and see things of the distant past and future? They are just like the Philippian slave girl.

"You then who defend them and seek the destruction of those who contradict them, are just like the masters of that girl, who were angry at the prospect of losing the power and financial advantage they had by her, when Paul cast out the demon that possessed her."

A number of passers-by had begun to gather about the group of men in the center of the Village, and Joseph wisely recognized that the strategic moment would be lost if the crowd grew much larger.

"No, Thomas, I have decided to refrain from bringing these very substantial charges against you and your daughters, (here he glanced at Jonathon Walcott, too) on the condition that you quit bothering Daniel and allow him to go on home to his family, which shows none of the demonic signs that yours does!

"Should the magistrates want him, they know where he lives. For your part, I would look to your own household, and see to it that there is no more consulting with familiars."

And as Thomas stood there red in the face, but apparently speechless between anger and fear, Joseph stepped behind Daniel, untied his hands and led him away up the road toward Topsfield. No one followed.

Chapter Sixty-One — October Reversals

. . .There are several about the Bay, men for understanding, judgment, and piety, inferiour to few, (if any,) in N.E. that do utterly condemn the said proceedings, and do freely deliver their judgment in the case to be this, viz. That these methods will utterly ruine and undoe poor N.E. I shall nominate some of these to you, viz. The hon'ble Simon Bradstreet, Esq. (our late governor); the hon'ble Thomas Danforth, Esq. (our late Deputy Governor); the Rev'd Mr. Increase Mather, and the Rev'd Mr. Samuel Willard. Major N. Saltonstall, Esq. who was one of the judges, has left the court, and is very much dissatisfyed with the proceedings of it. Excepting Mr. Hale, Mr. Noyes, and Mr. Parris, the Rev'd Elders, almost throughout the whole country, are very much dissatisfyed. Several of the late justices, viz. Thomas Graves, Esq., N. Byfield, Esq., Francis Foxcroft, Esq., are much dissatisfyed; also several of the present justices; and in particular, some of the Boston justices, were resolved rather to throw up their commissions than to be active in disturbing the liberty of their Majesties' subjects, merely on the accusations of these afflicted, possessed children.

Finally; the principal Gentlemen in Boston, and thereabout, are generally agreed that irregular and dangerous methods have been taken as to these matters. --Thomas Brattle **Letter of Thomas Brattle**, F.R.S. (October, 1692)

In the first week of October, Reverend Increase Mather, President of Harvard College, denounced the use of spectral evidence in a letter circulated in Boston. This letter was considerably expanded and many signatures added to it the following year when it was published as *Cases of Conscience Concerning Evil Spirits Personating Men*. Not content with the reports of others, Increase had interviewed a number of the Andover "confessors," and found many of them recanting. He learned about the sorts of pressure brought to bear on them by magistrates, ministers, and even spouses, commonly in the form of warnings that "confession" was the only way to escape death and damnation.

Increase Mather's letter emphasized that the devil was capable of deceiving men by fabricating appearances of innocent persons afflicting them. However it also touched on the weightier issues of the admissibility of accounts of "apparitions" in a capital trial. Although he still did not say anything directly casting doubt on the conduct of the court or verdicts in the cases tried, the strength of the arguments showed a change was in the wind.

Also in the first week of October, Samuel Sewall conferred with Thomas Danforth in Cambridge. Danforth was adamant that the court should not continue unless it adopted a procedure that met with the consent of the people and ministers, which is to say, he seriously doubted the present course did. It is ironical that Mr. Danforth himself had been vulnerable to the Salem hysteria, not only during the one occasion when he headed the magistrates conducting examinations there, but as a member of the Court of Oyer and Terminer until July. He had withdrawn after those executions, but without formal resignation, and now, with cooler head, he joined many others in expressing doubts.

With an eye chiefly to justifying his administration before the Royal Court, Governor Phips had earlier asked Cotton Mather to prepare for him a report of the "sufferings brought upon the country by witchcraft". Mather had asked Stephen Sewall for copies of transcripts for several of the trials. But amidst the many other demands placed upon the secretary of the court, he did not complete this task. In the third week of September, Cotton wrote him that it was a matter of some urgency. Governor Phips, however, dropped the idea of publishing. This change in plans was due to a new perspective gained through many discussions since the first execution, and finally through an accusation leveled at his own wife. His new policy, since the Nurse petitions, was to leave credit or blame for the witch business entirely to Deputy Stoughton. He did, however, encourage Cotton Mather to complete the report his own private use.

The project of publishing it more widely was immediately picked up, or carried on, however. The day before the last hangings, Deputy Stoughton met with John Hathorne, Cotton Mather, Captain John Higginson, and Stephen and Samuel Sewall at the house of the last in Boston, where they deliberated over "publishing some trials of the witches."

On October 8th Governor Phips issued an order that spectral evidence no longer be admitted in witchcraft trials. Sensing the sea change, he also issued a ban on publishing any "discourses one way or other, that may increase the needless disputes of people upon this occasion, because [he] saw the likelihood of kindling an inexhausting flame if [he] should admit any public and open contests."

In his "open letter," also dated the 8th, Thomas Brattle rejected spectre evidence, and made a strong statement that he hesitated to think what spiritual tribulation must come upon any magistrate who condemned innocent persons through such means.

Three days later Governor Phips sent a letter to the Royal Court justifying the conduct of judges thus far. In this letter he made use of Cotton Mather's reports on the trials, but he also made clear he knew some accused who were innocent (meaning, no doubt, such as his wife!). He informed their majesties that he had forbidden further arrests or publishing on the subject.

Governor Phips had strong indications of the rift that was coming in his administration. He consolidated his own position as thoroughly as he could, sending out letters to the Dutch Reformed ministers of New York asking their opinions of our trials. He met with the General Court through the next week and on the 18th received his reply from the Dutch ministers, which, although written in Latin, which his more learned assistants had to translate for him, agreed almost entirely with the opinions of Brattle, Simon Willard, and was stronger even than Increase Mather's recent letter. It was coming home to him that his deputy and court had erred and their conduct become a liability to his administration.

That same day two ministers from Andover (Francis Dane and Thomas Barnard) signed a petition with twenty-two others, stating that many of their neighbors were suffering severely as a result of the arrests there, and asking that these hardships be taken into consideration by the governor. They represented their own doubts about the trials, as well:

> Our troubles which hitherto have been great, we foresee are like to continue and increase, if other methods be not taken than as yet have been. For there are more of our neighbors of good reputation and approved integrity, who are still accused, and complaints have been made against them. And we know not who can think himself safe if the accusations of children and others who are under a diabolical influence shall be received against persons of good fame.

The next week, the General Court passed a bill calling for a general fast and a "convocation of ministers that might be led in the right way as to the witchcraft." Judge Samuel Sewall observed that "The season and manner of doing it is such that the Court of Oyer and Terminer count themselves dismissed."

On the 29th the Court of Oyer and Terminer, which had been scheduled to begin another round of trials the first week of November, was officially suspended by Governor Phips, and there was an open breach between him and his deputy over this.

Governor Phips not only prohibited further arrests, but began releasing prisoners on bond or recognizance through their local magistrates.

Dorcas Good was brought home to the Village, having been released into the care of her father under the custody of Benjamin Putnam (son of Lieutenant Thomas).

Chapter Sixty-Two — General Gaol Delivery

Awake, awake, Deborah: awake, awake, utter a song:
arise, Barak, and lead captivity captive, thou son of Abinoam.
  -- Judges 5:12

Wherefore he saith, When he ascended up on high,
he led captivity captive, and gave gifts to men.
  -- Ephesian 4:8

As early as September (although to do so then would still have seemed to invite execution) a number of "confessors" recanted their former "confessions," saying they had been completely false. Notable among these had been Margaret Jacobs, who would then have been executed, had it not been for an "impostume" or abscess on her head, which was strangely found to render her unfit for execution. Increase Mather had interviewed several Andover confessors who recanted, including Mary Bridges, Martha Tyler, Sarah Wilson, and Mary Osgood.

When the court of Oyer and Terminer was suspended, however, more "confessors" began to recant. By mid-November, a number of witnesses, too, were backing away from their former testimonies. One of the strangest recantors was Mary Herrick, an "afflicted" 17 year old, related to many active witnesses and officials in our troubles. She mentioned several startling things, including a "shape" (apparition) of Mrs. Hale, presumably the second wife of Reverend Hale of Beverly. Reverend Hale was one of the more dedicated supporters of the witch business among the ministers, and one of the chief witnesses against Bridget Bishop and Dorcas Hoar. Mary Herrick's testimony, neither fish nor fowl, (accusation nor recantation) was heard by Reverend Hale and Reverend Gerrish of Wenham and recorded by the latter:

An account received from the mouth of Mary Herrick aged about 17 yeares having been afflicted the devill or some of his instruments, about 2 months. She saith she had oft been afflicted and that the shape of Mrs. Hayle had been represented to her, one amongst others, but she knew not what hand afflicted her then, but on the 5th of the 9th [of November] she appeared again with the ghost of Gooddee Easty, and that then Mrs. Hayle did sorely afflict her by pinching, pricking and choaking her. On the 12th of the 9th she came again and Gooddee Easty with her and then Mrs. Hayle did afflict her as formerly. Said Easty made as if she would speake but did not, but on the same night they came again and Mrs. Hayle did sorely afflict her, and asked her if she thought she was a witch. The Girl answered no, you be the devill. Then said Easty said and speake, she came to tell her she had been put to death wrongfully and was innocent of witchcraft, and she came to vindicate her cause and she cryed vengeance, vengeance, and bid her reveal this to Mr. Hayle and Gerish, and then she would rise no more, nor should Mrs. Hayle afflict her any more.

Memorand: that just before said Easty was executed, she appeared to said girl, and said I am going upon the ladder to be hanged for a witch, but I am innocent, and before a 12 Month be past you shall believe it. Said girl said she speake not of this before because she believed she was guilty, till Mrs. Hayle appeared to her and afflicted her, but now she believeth it is all a delusion of the devil.

This before Mr. Hayle and Gerish 14th of the 9th 1692.

Thus one girl found a dramatically ambivalent way to end her performance.

On November 25th the General Court established a Superior Court of Judicature to try the remaining witch cases. The magistrates assigned to the new court were William Stoughton, Samuel Sewall, Wait Winthrop, and John Richards. None of them were from Salem. The new court assured the Governor they would not place the same emphasis on specter evidence that the former court had given it.

The grand juries assigned to the court apparently understood this new approach as well, for they indicted no more defendants.

Another clear sign that our troubles were drawing to an end was the petition sent to the General Court by Marshall George Herrick seeking payment for the many services he had rendered over the previous eight months. He reminded the court that he was a "gentleman" and had given up all other means of livelihood during the witch business to pursue public justice. The Court eventually agreed to pay him twenty-five pounds for his troubles.

Frustrated by what he felt to be a hobbling of justice and dangerous laxness, Judge Stoughton gave orders on January 3rd of the new year for the execution of all those condemned witches who had been exempted for pregnancy and infirmities. Governor Phips immediately countermanded the order, giving a temporary stay of execution. (Elizabeth Procter had given birth to her son at the turning of the year. She named him John.)

The Superior Court made short work of twenty cases in the first half of January, releasing most of those tried. By the end of the month 49 out of 53 surviving defendants were released.

Despite Governor Phips earlier order banning publishing, Cotton Mather went ahead with his project to publish five of the witch cases. Mather wrote that Lieutenant Governor Stoughton had become his firm defender, providing him a shield, "under the umbrage whereof I now dare walk abroad." He picked the cases of those ones he believed to be the most flagrant and indubitable witches, namely Reverend Burroughs, Bridget Bishop, Susannah Martin, Elizabeth Howe and Martha Carrier. In his introduction the author assured his readers that "I represent matters not as an advocate, but as an historian." There were still plenty of delusions among us.

At the end of April the Superior Court was held for the County of Suffolk. The Lieutenant Governor was back at the bench, accompanied by Mr. Danforth, Mr. Richards and Mr. Sewall.

Governor Phips issued a final reprieve for those seven condemned under the Lieutenant Governor 's earlier death warrants. When the Superior Court sitting in Boston heard that the temporary stay had become a reprieve, Deputy Stoughton was so incensed he said, "We were in a way to have cleared the land of these awful wretches! Who it is obstructs the course of justice I know not! May the Lord be merciful to the country."

He then got up and left the bench, serving no more on the court. By May the others had tried all their cases and found none guilty. The Governor pardoned all witch defendants still held in gaol

That month Tituba was also released from gaol. She had been forgotten in the flurry of activity over the previous nine months. The last time she had testified had been as a witness against Rebecca Nurse in July. Like most of the confessors, Tituba had hoped, indeed some said Reverend Parris had promised her, that she would be released and freed for her cooperative testimony. However, she, too, recanted her story when she discovered that others were safely doing so. She said that Samuel Parris had beaten her and that was why she confessed herself a witch. She attributed all she had said and her accusations of others to his threats and beatings. Reverend Parris would have nothing further to do with her. In May of 1693, Tituba was sold to a new master and left the colony.

On June 12, 1693, Judge Samuel Sewall visited Captain Alden and his wife, and told them he deeply regretted their sorrow and temptations by reason of imprisonment, and that he was glad of the captain's restoration.

Elizabeth Emerson, who had been in Boston gaol since May 1691 convicted for the murder of her twins in September that same year, was not hanged until June 1693. She was under the pastoral care of Cotton Mather during much of her last six months, but despite his avocation, she was never charged in connection with witchcraft. (He did persuade her to "confess," however, which has left some doubt about that confession.) Nevertheless she was the all but last in prison connected to the "witches".

The last accused "witch" in prison was a servant, Mary Watkins of Milton, who petitioned from prison in August that she be provided a master to carry her "out of this country into Virginia."

Chapter Sixty-Three -- The Apologists Divide

" . . . If the devil by divine permission may cause supernatural concomitances and consequences to attend the natural actions of men without their allowance, as is manifest in possessed persons, how is it reasonable and just that the impositions of the devil should be imputed unto any man. And (saith he) God forbid that the devil's signs and wonders, nay his truths should become any legal allegations or evidences in law. We may therefore conclude it unjust that the forenamed miraculous effect by the devil wrought and imputed by the bewitched, should be esteemed an infallible mark against any man, as therefore convinced . . . [since] the devil and the bewitched have so decyphered him? " Thus that learned man. [Dr. Cotta]
> -- Increase Mather, *Cases of Conscience Concerning Evil Spirits* 1693

It were a most unchristian and uncivil, yea a most unreasonable thing to imagine that the fitts's of the young woman were but meer impostures: and I believe scarce any, but people of a particular dirtiness, will harbour such an uncharitable censure; . . .
-- Cotton Mather, *Another Brand Pluckt Out of the Burning*: *An Account of the Sufferings of Margaret Rule* (1700)

We have spoken of the divisions that ran between and among us — those of accusers, accused, and silent observer, or in law: prosecution, defense, and witness or jury. But there were also divisions among our leaders and prosecutors — and those on more than one plane.

The dividing issue that was increasingly cited — that of spectre evidence — was not the most foundational issue. Cotton Mather, who claimed later to have advised John Richards against spectre evidence at the very outset of the Court of Oyer and Terminer in June, and Increase Mather, who wrote the vigorous cautions against specter evidence in his *Cases of Conscience . . .*, (published in October) continued to affirm that the court had done nothing but justice — that nobody had been convicted on specter evidence alone. Indeed, Increase Mather in an ill-considered supplement to *Cases of Conscience...* stated that he would have found George Burroughs guilty, too, had he been a judge on the court, so strong was the evidence against him!

But the spectre evidence issue did create a formal division, and perhaps provided the tip of the wedge, so to speak, for the greater and more important division over the question whether there was any legitimacy to the witch trials at all.

On the 9th of August, Robert Pike, the 76 year old magistrate from Salisbury who conducted the early examinations of Susannah Martin, expressed grave doubts after the accusation of Mary Bradbury. He wrote to Jonathon Corwin arguing "humbly" about the dangers of admitting spectre evidence against those pleading innocent "who are of blameless conversation." :

> For as for diabolical visions . . . they are more commonly false . . . than real, and cannot be known when they are real and when feigned but by the devil's riposte; and then not to be believed because he is the father of lies.

He went on to address a more basic question:

> But this case seems to be solved by an assertion of some that affirm that the devil do not or cannot appear in the shape of a godly person to do hurt. Others affirm the contrary . . .
>
> And we see by woeful and undeniable experience, both in afflicted persons and the confessors, some of them, that he torments them at this pleasure, to force them to accuse others. Some are apt to doubt that they do but counterfeit; but, poor souls! I am utterly of another mind, and I lament them with all my heart; but, take which you please, the case is the same as to the main issue. For, if they counterfeit, the wickedness is the greater in them, and the less in the devil; but if they be compelled to it by the devil, against their wills, then the sin is the devil's, and the suffering theirs; but if their testimonies be allowed of, to make persons guilty by, the lives of innocent persons are alike in danger by them, which is the solemn consideration that do disquiet the country.

Major Pike agreed it was the command of God to put witches to death and therefore the "indispensable duty of man". He said there must therefore be such a thing as witches and it must be possible for men to know them, or God's command would be in vain.

But "it must be witches that are put to death and not innocent persons 'thou shalt not condemn the innocent or the righteous (Exodus xxiii.7)' "

Major Pike spoke of how a witch should be known: first, by the mouth of two or three witnesses; and second by their own confessions, "being *compos mentis*, and not under horrid temptation to self murder." Pike says emphatically that the witnesses should not be asked to swear the person is a witch (this had become the regular practice of the high court) because that exposed the lives of everyone:

> to the pleasure or passion of those that are minded to take them away. . . and because. . . in such testimony, the witnesses are not only informers in matter of fact, but sole judges of the crime, which is the proper work of the judges and not of the witnesses.

He says:

> it may be more safe for the present to let a guilty person live . . . than to put an innocent person to death . . . because a guilty person may afterward be discovered and put to death, but an innocent person put to death cannot be brought again to life.

Mr. Pike also cautioned about looking for signs of "imps" in "suckages," "because of . . . diseases that people are incident unto, as the piles, etc."

He spoke of the afflicted persons at Salem Village "before whom people are brought for detection . . . in order to their being apprehended or acquitted." He said he only knew of this by report in which there might be mistakes, but he repeated what he had heard:

> First, that they do tell who are witches,of which some they know and some they do not.
> Secondly, they tell who tormented such and such a person, though they did not [know] the person.
> Thirdly, they are tormented themselves by the looks of those present, and recovered again by touching them.
> Fourthly, that if the accused look at them, they fall down tormented; but if the persons accused look away from

them, they recover.

Fifthly, that they can tell a person is coming before they see them, and what clothes they have on, and some tell what they have done for several years past, including things nobody else ever accused them of, nor thought them guilty of.

Sixthly, that the dead appear to them, and name their murderers, some of which persons are well know to have died natural deaths, and were publicly buried in the sight of all men.

Major Pike suggested all these things were done by the devil:

> ... of his own proper action, without human concurrence ... and thus it follows that the devil is always the doer, but whether abetted in it by anybody is uncertain.

He then asks:

> Are those tormented by him legal witnesses to say that the Devil doth it by the procurement of such a person when as they know nothing about it but what comes to them from the Devil that torment them?

He argued it was contrary to human nature to be at the same time pleading innocent to witchcraft and yet at the same time to be acting witchcraft in the sight of all men, when the defendant knows his life is at stake by doing it. It is also contrary to the devil's interests to accuse witches, since they are part of his kingdom.

All these points would be repeated and magnified, attested to by ancient authorities and so forth, over the next months in the writings of others, including especially Increase Mather and Thomas Brattle.

Increase Mather's *Cases of Conscience* makes reference to a more personal argument for the possibility that spectres of innocent persons have been seen, a reference to the accusation of Reverend Willard during an examination:

> since there is one amongst ourselves whom no man that know him, can think him to be a wizard, whom yet some bewitched persons complained of, that they are in his shape tormented; and the devils have of late accused some eminent

persons.

He also says:

> I bless the Lord it was never the portion allotted to me, nor to any relation of mine to be thus abused; but no man knoweth what may happen to him, since there be just men unto who it happeneth according to the work of the wicked. Eccles. 8. 14.

The great 'hedging of his bets,' occurs when Mr. Mather declares:

> to take away the life of anyone merely because a spector or devil in a bewitched or possessed person does accuse them will bring the guilt of innocent blood on the land . . . . . Mercy forbid that it should (*and I trust that as it has not, it never will be so*), in New England.

Then again, after encouraging skepticism toward reports of extraordinary sights he says:

> . . .If two credible persons shall affirm upon oath that they have seen the accused party speaking such words or doing such things which none but such as have familiarity with the devil ever did or can do, that is sufficient ground for conviction.
> Notwithstanding I will add; it were better that ten suspected witches should escape, than that one innocent person should be condemned. . . It is better that a guilty person should be absolved, than that he should without sufficient ground of conviction be condemned. I had rather judge a witch to be an honest woman, than judge an honest woman as a witch. The word of God directs men not to proceed to the execution of the most capital offenders until such time as upon searching diligently, the matter is found to be a truth and the thing certain. Deut 13. 14. 15.

Reverend Willard wrote in his preface to *Cases of Conscience*:

> In the case of witchcrafts, we know that the devil is the immediate agent. . . the consent or compact of the witch is the thing to be demonstrated. . . Among many arguments to

evidence this, that which is most under present debate, is that
which refers to something vulgarly called specter evidence
and a certain sort of ordeal or trail by the sight and touch.

The preface was signed by ministers William Hubbard,
Samuel Phillips, Charles Morton, James Allen, Michael
Wigglesworth, Samuel Whiting, Sr., Samuel Willard, John Bailey,
Jabez Fox, Joseph Gerrish, Samuel Angier, John Wise, Joseph Capen
and Nehemiah Walter.

Unhappily Mather's postscript to his Cases of Conscience,
added later, explicitly implies he thought Burroughs guilty and
further exonerates the judges," the worthy persons who have been
concerned in the late proceedings at Salem. . . are wise and good
men." He also commends his son's "Breviate of the Trials" (the
summary prepared for Governor Phips and published in *Wonders of
the Invisible World* in 1693) as showing that more than specter
evidence was used to convict those executed.

Though Cotton Mather's letter to John Foster in August did
say that he did not think spectre evidence was by itself sufficient to
convict anyone of witchcraft, yet he also said he thought spectre
evidence very useful:

> Nevertheless, a very great use is to bee made of ye
> spectral impressions upon ye sufferers. They justly introduce,
> and determine, an enquiry into ye circumstances of ye person
> accused; and they strengthen other presumptions.
> When so much use is made of those things, I believe ye
> use for which ye Great god intends them is made. And
> accordingly you see that ye excellent judges have had such an
> encouraging presence of God with them, as that scarce any, if
> at all any, have been tried before them, against whom God
> has not strangely sent in other, & more humane & most
> convincing testimonies.

It is no wonder — either of the invisible or visible worlds —
that the judges, even those open to counsel, were puzzled by all this
advice and analysis, and made few changes in their approach.

But the second and more basic division among us was
whether the judges in their official capacity were "wise and good
men" or not. Were they in fact dispensing justice or something else?
Sadly, until many years after our troubles, none of them admitted

this question publicly, although privately many of them not only came to the darker conclusion, but acted upon it by private withdrawal.

The first to draw back over the line between affirming and denying that the court dispensed justice, was Nathaniel Saltonstall, as has been described. Following him, after the July trials, but without formal resignation, was Thomas Danforth, the old Deputy Governor under Governor Bradford, prior to the new commission of Governor Phips.

Next to draw back, at the strong advice of Samuel Willard, their pastor, were Waitstill Winthrop and John Richards. But again, they made no public statement of resignation, but merely ceased sitting with the court. Like Saltonstall and Danforth, they resided at sufficient distance from Salem to make tenable excuses. Mr. Richards had the best excuse — he had been courting and in September, married Ann Winthrop, sister of Waitstill.

That left five men, the minimum necessary for a quorum: Deputy Governor Stoughton; our three Salem magistrates: Hathorne, Gedney, and Corwin; and Samuel Sewall. Had any one of them withdrawn, the court would have come to a standstill.

That did not happen, however. Indeed the court did not stop, but speeded up its condemnations, and might well have put several hundreds to death if Governor Phips had not at last suspended it in October.

But the governor would not have called the halt but for a third division, what might best be nominated a political division, most distinctly seen or begun between the highest officers, the Governor and the Deputy Governor.

There were many traits of the two men that led to this division. Were they the central characters of our story, a book might easily be written about them and their differences. But briefly said they were men of different temperaments, diverse backgrounds, different interests, and different capabilities — two men contending for the same quantity, so to speak, that is reigning influence and power over the affairs of the colony.

Governor Phips had a colorful history -- a wilderness upbringing, waterfront brawls, treasure-hunting and marine warfare. His wife was a devoted, and highly refined lady. They had a good marriage — made of opposites.

Deputy Stoughton had a much more sober and prosaic life up to the time of our troubles. He was a scholar, a minister, a university fellow, and an administrator. He thought himself eminently qualified to lead men, although he had but briefly done it. Committed to a course with the support of many books and legal precedents, he was temperamentally unable to assess the court, the trials and his part in them in the light of less theoretical and more practical wisdom.

So when the Governor asked the Boston ministers for advice in June and they deliberated and sent their conclusions to Salem, or when various men sent weighty advice to various of the judges and these passed them around among their fellow justices, or when scholars met at Harvard to debate the question of spectre evidence and wrote up their conclusions, also sending these to Salem, -- all of these met with the same reception at Deputy Stoughton's hand. That is, he politely read them, and set them aside as adding nothing to his already considerable knowledge, nor in any way modifying his practice.

When the Governor asked Cotton Mather to compile his summary of the cases, it was because the Governor had truly been so preoccupied with the French and Indian depredations "to eastward" that he knew very little of what went forward in Salem.

Reports began to come to him from many people he respected, however, and by mid-July he was seriously concerned that there might be some fundamental mistakes being made. At that time the only published account available was Deodat Lawson's "Brief and True Account," which only dealt with the earliest five cases at the examination stage. Nor did that work even hint at the potential for deceit and error.

The combination of accusations and arrests and even executions of highly respected persons, the increasingly vocal reservations of ministers and members of government, and finally the obvious fact that Deputy Stoughton was bent on a course of his own which no advice, no matter how strong, seemed likely to modify, finally brought the Governor to suspend the trials and then the court.

Deputy Stoughton then turned his attention to his rivalry with the governor. At first he made no overt statement or action. He proceeded carefully and subtly to make careful note of potential allies. He wrote to England where he had made many friends during nearly a decade at Oxford.

Governor Phips got wind of his deputy's maneuvers, and began to consolidate his own position. He wrote the royal court and acquainted their Majesties with the present difficulties, making it clear that he had been tied up in defending the colony, and had only lately realized what his deputy had been up to. He spoke of suspending the trials, and of banning all publication on the issue to prevent further division.

In fact he knew that a number of the Salem ministers, supporters all of the witch trials and court, had been working on written accounts of the trials.

Curiously, the two Mathers, Increase and Cotton, although they did not articulate it, found themselves on opposite sides of the political division. Increase Mather was more responsible than any other man for the composition of the colonial government. He was firmly and unyieldingly a supporter of Governor Phips. Cotton, on the other hand, at least for a brief period, felt betrayed by the Governor, who forbade the publication of his "Breviate" of the trials. But by January of 1693, Cotton had found a new sponsor, William Stoughton, under whose "umbrage" he felt free and apparently was free to publish that work as "Wonders of the Invisible World." He was by then firmly in Deputy Stoughton's camp. This may be one reason none of his "retractions" or subsequent writings, which tend toward the school of "I told you so," repudiate the court or the justices decisions.

Reverend Hale and Reverend Noyes were both said to have been writing about our troubles, but nothing by Reverend Noyes ever came to light.

Reverend Hale did publish *A Modest Inquiry Into the Nature of Witchcraft* in 1702, a work he began in 1692 after his wife was accused and at the same time excused by Mary Herrick. His work seems to have gone through some permutations. In 1697, Samuel Sewall wrote of Hale "I fear lest he go into the other extream," an intriguing comment on a work the published version of which contributes little or nothing beyond the ambivalence characterizing most accounts by men personally involved.

Probably the strongest statements on both sides of the three divisions: evidential, judicial, and political, were in sermons. But many of the important ones were not recorded, perhaps advisedly, or else the records were lost or destroyed. We know that Reverends Lawson, Noyes and Parris spoke fervently against the witches among us, and of the mercy of God in revealing and eliminating them. We know Reverend Willard and Moody spoke as strongly urging those accused to flee injustice. We know that Increase Mather, later in the year, preached against convictions on spectre evidence. Would that we had more texts of these sermons.

Curiously, among our divines there was not a division along the theological and anthropological divisions declared at the Reformation, upon which we were supposedly founded. Both sides on most issues had become Arminians—doubting not the human heart, but only some of its methods. No one doubted our "science," our ability to observe and analyze according to prevailing theories of physics and medicine. Few raised the vital issue of a Christian jurisprudence, the necessity that false witnesses be subject to the same penalty as those they accuse. Never were those most directly responsible for the great evil held to accountability.

Perhaps this was due to a sense of obedience to such as Rebecca Nurse's injunction to forgive. Perhaps it was due to the loss of that pillar of the gospel—the weightiness of all sin. Or perhaps it was indeed the wisdom of God to avoid a return to the courts for a resolution of the mystery of iniquity.

But it is a fact that no division was ever healed by covering over or by superficial treatment. Certainly in what continued to go forward in Salem Village, it was evident that for lasting resolution there must be a general repentance—as well as active forgiveness.

On the political front, Governor Phips continued to consolidate his influence among the assistants of the colony, but in doing so left himself open to the kinds of innuendos that served Deputy Stoughton well among his courtly connections in England. Within a few years, the Deputy charged Governor Phips with a series of improprieties, the cumulative weight of which swayed royal favor dangerously against him.

By November 1694, Governor Phips had no option but to return to England in order to defend himself and his government.

Chapter Sixty-Four – Schools of Thought

Secondly, Satan hath his devices to ensnare and destroy the learned and the wise: and that, sometimes by working them to pride themselves in their parts and abilities; and sometimes by drawing them to rest upon their parts and abilities; and sometimes by causing them to make light and slight of those that want [i.e. lack] their parts and abilities in those ways and things that make against the honour of Christ, the joy of the Spirit, the advancement of the gospel, and the liberty of the saints.
(Second Device Against the Learned and the Wise)
... By working a sinner to mind more the secret decrees and counsels of God, than his own duty. (Device 5)
-- Thomas Brooks, *Precious Remedies Against Satan's Devices* (1652)

T he "school of thought" supporting spectre evidence, the witch proofs, and other aspects of the "witch business" was indeed composed of "scholars". This office of "scholar," like the allied one of "scientist" was an innovation among us.

Yet education had been important to the colony from the beginning. In 1647 the Council passed what came to be known as "The Old Deluder Act," emphasizing education as a weapon against the devil:

> It being one chief project of that old deluder, Satan, to keep men from the knowledge of the Scriptures, as in former times by keeping them in an unknown tongue, so in these latter times by persuading from the use of tongues, that so that at least the true sense and meaning of the original might be clouded and corrupted with false glosses of saint-seeming deceivers; and to the end that learning may not be buried in the grave of our forefathers, in church and commonwealth, the Lord assisting our endeavors.
>
> It is therefore ordered that every township in this jurisdiction, after the Lord hath increased them to fifty households shall forthwith appoint one within their town to teach all such children as shall resort to him to write and read, whose wages shall be paid either by the parents or masters of

such children, or by the inhabitants in general, by way of
supply, as the major part of those that order the prudentials
of the town shall appoint; provided those that send their
children be not oppressed by paying much more than they
can have them taught for in other towns.

And it is further ordered, that when any town shall
increase to the number of one hundred families or
householders, they shall set up a grammar school, the master
thereof being able to instruct youth so far as they may be
fitted for the university, provided that if any town neglect the
performance hereof above one year that every such town
shall pay 5 pounds to the next school till they shall perform
this order.

The New England Primer was one of the first books printed in
Boston – along with editions of the Bible and *Pilgrim's Progress*.
Salem made more effort to teach its children than many settlements.
We had to pay a subscription for poor children to be taught to read
and a fine was levied against any parents who would not send their
children to school (although in fact many preferred to pay the fine.)
Ezekiel Cheever, learned investigator of Mistress Corey's witchcraft,
was also a schoolteacher — and son of a schoolteacher on his way to
being famous for his Latin books and school in Boston.

We respected an "educated clergy" because we thought they
were better able to explain the Bible to us, having pored over it in the
original languages, and interpreted each part carefully in light of the
whole.

But as "the Old Deluder Act" emphasized, we believed the
scriptures were for everyone and that everyone ought to be able to
read them. John Tarbell's father taught his sons their letters and the
rudiments of reading before John was nine. After the family moved
from Watertown, his younger brother and sisters studied a few years
with their new minister. The Tarbells were further encouraged by
their parents with family Bible reading. On Friday evening they read
other works aloud. *Pilgrim's Progress* and *The Day of Doom* were
favorites, both printed in the colonies and easily available. They had
little sense of need for more, or even that more was to be had. None
of them were inclined to be ministers. They knew no reason for
further study.

It was not until King Phillip's War, when John was thrown
shoulder to shoulder with men who had studied and read

extensively, that it occurred to him a layman might do so. But even those men were not primarily scholars. Nowhere in the colonies was study alone regarded as a path to manhood. There was only one way to become a successful man in our world—and that was to do something well. Speaking well, even for a minister, was generally held subordinate to doing well, believing well, ministering and living well.

We have good schools and scholars in Salem and the Village. Daniel Andrews was a schoolmaster in Salem Village for four or five years after King Philips War—in his ambitious and impecunious youth. Many young husbands and wives of our town received his tutelage, including Sam's wife Mary (then Smith). He held school from November through April in various homes, at first. When the Royalside Schoolhouse was built, he gathered his scholars there, up the road and over the Frost Fish Bridge. Meanwhile he built up his carpentry and bricklaying business, to which he finally turned in full. But like many a village schoolmaster, Daniel was a good teacher. He did not multiply information faster than he taught the means to use it, nor did he magnify rhetoric beyond virtue or virtue beyond faith.

Yet all that was undergoing a sea change. Cotton Mather, with his many books, was becoming the epitome of a new world, a world in which one could be as invisible as a spectre to normal eyes, yet appear vividly familiar to those who read. Such an author may occupy a pulpit larger than South Church is to Boston, larger than Boston to Massachusetts, larger than New England to the world. Indeed, wherever English letters may be deciphered, a Baxter or Mather may have the world for congregation.

That were good, had the world a consistory or church council adequate to direct, and occasionally correct, the wisdom of books. In fact, however, Mr. C. Mather could be a wholesale libertine, living a life of hypocrisy (I do not say he is) for all his British readers know. He could be pure imagination so far as a many of the students of his books are concerned. He might in fact be a popish follower of Thomas Aquinas or a Hindoo devotee, who merely shipped out Christian claptrap as a Salem merchant ships dried cod and barrel staves. It need not be bad claptrap, not bad doctrine or a poor imitation of Christian piety. There is nothing intrinsic to true words that defies imitation. The Apostle Paul says that although there are those who preach out of all wrong motives such as jealousy, yet if they preach the truth, their preaching may have some good effect.

By which we might conclude it is only the subject and the

approximation of truth in its handling that matter, and cease to criticize Mr. C. Mather or any other multiplier of books. But it is not his ineffectiveness nor even a depravity or hypocrisy of his life to be feared—but rather the idea that truth and understanding are manmade and chiefly to be found, communicated, and preserved between book covers. It is the idea that one cannot trust the judgment of men based on the word of God, but must have a scholar's interpretation intervening. It is no longer the leader of men, not even the minister or school teacher who is most respected. It is the wise man who wrote the book—or who has read the most books written by others.

The learning of schools becomes a gobbling up of words and ideas, as a cow does its fodder, to be regurgitated from memory to page, as the cow between stomach and grinders.

Those students who study at Cotton Mather's knee, or rather between the pages of his books, are more likely to identify virtuous rhetoric with virtue, and pious speech with piety. They are apt to think the verbal representation of holiness is its coin or substance.

One may thus think oneself "educated" and remain a perfect fool. One may ingest a wearisome feed-trough-full of books, and be no more made wise by them than the Gadarene demoniac possessed by his legion. It is no great sin to be ignorant or unread, or even manifestly foolish. It is, however, a beginning of danger when one thinks oneself wise because of a capacity to devour written words. It is dangerous indeed, when having learned a little from paper, one believes he has read the pages of life and is thenceforth ready to paste in corrections. In some sense, we make bold to say, Cotton Mather has lived very little. "By their fruits ye shall know them"— his written words and "ideas" has accumulated as much toward death as toward life.

The worst thing about knowledge paraded as wisdom is this: the "author," like the "afflicted" is too much respected in his person. His ideas are submitted to and treated with credulity, although his trustworthiness is not adequately proven. Thus C. Mather, in person, stopped what almost became a popular confrontation of the officials at the hanging of Reverend Burroughs et al. As he sat his horse before the gallows declaiming, he was afforded the respect due a wiser man. His words in support of the sentence were heeded where they should have been ignored.

This view of scholarship, of education, and these concepts of knowledge and wisdom, formed the flimsy nest in which parents and pastors nurtured the egg of our troubles. For the "afflicted girls" were also viewed as "wise" and given respect they had not earned. When the egg teeth of "sports," lies, and malice began to cut through and crack that egg, the parents, ministers and magistrates could but cluck and preen and nervously await the outcome. To cast the cowbird progeny out of the nest or to stifle their cackling was against all the instincts of the scholar or those who revere him.

Scholarship has much in common with witchcraft. Both consist in the accumulation of arcane knowledge, both believe knowledge to be an essential kind of riches, both expect the greatest gnosis to produce the most powerful magus. Words become spells to both scholar and wizard, formulas which, repeated exactly, wrap the speaker in supernatural armor: helmet, buckler, shield, sword, and magic wand.

This is every much as true of the "pure" religious scholar as of the goetic. For is not pure scholarship but another name for being a hearer of the word, but not a doer?

It was the promise of superior scholarship that first drew and bound Adam and Eve. The desire for "knowledge of good and evil," the promise that they should "be like gods" and know like God made them slaves to the greatest scholar creation has ever known. His was a sort of canted integrity—for he brought them along the same path he had taken—toward an imagined state of being "like" God in some way impossible for any creature. Lucifer is said to have been a pure intelligence, and near the apex of the angelic orders—knowing perhaps as much as a created intelligence can possibly know. His fall was in desiring the further knowledge and office of God.

Adam and Eve, on the other hand, were made in God's image in another way—ultimately intended for a place of judgment on angels. Yet they were far from pure intelligences—meant rather, perhaps, to be pure lovers. For them, the temptation was to know without love: to understand good and evil in the abstract - without charity. Satan refused his chief calling, which was to adore, but Adam and Eve refused theirs, too, which was to obey, to enjoy and to worship. They wanted to taste without obedience, without restriction, to taste what they were not meant to taste, and at the same time to refuse what they were meant to enjoy. They wanted to know in a way that led only to self-worship.

These first two human scholars wished to make a full survey of potential experience without the effects intrinsic to that knowledge. Being like God or "like gods" to them, was a fantasy of sitting above the personal, emotional, temporal, and material. How surprised they must have been to find they had no capacity for such knowledge—they were made for only one kind of knowing, that which is linked to temporal existence and reaches its epitome in love. They were not essential spirits as their Creator is, dwelling first in eternity, but everlasting creatures, moving on through time—and only through time, into eternity.

Adam and Eve were indeed the first scholars and first magicians, for they believed a certain act and certain kinds of knowledge would give them a power over the world of spirits, a rein by which to control the greater universe, a harness upon God's back. To that end they were willing to set aside love—for God and for each other.

Our scholars and theologians continued to be subtly tempted—like those first two. Our road to gnostical magic began when we said our ministers ought to know Greek and Hebrew in order to read the one book worth reading. From this we came to the more general conclusion that we needed a formally educated clergy. Then we began to train scholars and soon were refusing to ordain any others. We believe in the power of this clerical order as thoroughly as the papist believes in the apostolic succession of his priests. Our theological order learns the formulas and schools, the signs and the rituals, the apparatus and the spells. These take the coin of the people—not as payment, but courtesy—humble high wizards (although the people must beware when that coin is lacking). They preach and prophesy, bringing dazzling new things out of the Bible in fierce applications that laymen never suspected.

These are the scholars and ministers, "clerks" and "clerics," which two words derive from "inheritor." They are heirs of Adam and the devil, guardians of secret knowledge. The claimants for power through knowledge are the masters of "ideas" among us, as the guildsmen of England are masters of the trades. But unlike the tradesmen, the guild of scholars publishes its books and spreads its cult throughout the earth. So great its hubris, it does not fear to reveal its secrets, resting assured it will discover new ones tomorrow. Setting aside charity to his own neighbor, like the scribe and Levite of the parable, the scholar hastens toward his greater act of charity, that is enlightening the world.

Yet our scholars and clerics are not much different from the rest of us. The fact that they succeed beyond the rest of us in publishing their ideas and capturing the leadership of our institutions does not lessen the degree to which we all turn to magic where we can. We all manipulate "spells" and formulas to our own ends. We pluck and eat forbidden fruits from which we hope to derive special knowledge and power. Minor wizards are we all — even the most pious at those false moments (and they are many) when we think to twist God's arm by a prayer or hard work or when we justify a small self-indulgence by a small charitable sacrifice.

Religion is either magic or faith. Knowledge leads to adoration or damnation. The message of our hands is either worthless or worship. Either God rules us or we try to rule God. These are the choices for the least as well as the greatest — the most illiterate as well as the most respected author. It is not the scholar alone who descends from Adam and Eve, though he becomes the head of our order. We can only oppose the institution of exalted scholar where we concede to putting no confidence in any part or form of flesh.

Even at its best, book learning can only prescribe doing. It is not life and cannot say "be ye imitators of me as I am of Christ." Only a flesh and blood teacher can do that, and he as much a saint as a scholar. The author of books is a spectre; the mere scholar is scarce much more. It is only the man who cannot be two places at a time, nor live two different lives, who is ultimately qualified to make disciples of men. The best teacher is he who does what he teaches. That is one wonder of the Incarnation. We acknowledge the scriptures as God's book, but if all God gave us were a book, we would be no better off. Instead he gave us himself.

Because of what he had done for us beyond its writing, we have great faith in that one book and its author. A chief evil in the multiplication of books, especially religious ones, resides in this: that the plethora of writing obscures the unique, sufficient, and sovereign value of that book.

Increase Mather

Chapter Sixty-Five — Biblical Discipline in Salem Village
(Oct 1692 - Oct 1693)

Moreover if thy brother shall trespass against thee, go and tell him his fault between thee and him alone: if he shall hear thee, thou hast gained thy brother. But if he will not hear thee, then take with thee one or two more, that in the mouth of two or three witnesses every word may be established. And if he shall neglect to hear them, tell it to the church: but if he neglect to hear the church, let him be unto thee as a heathen man and a publican. —
Matthew 18:15-17

T he best sunsets, those which come late in a good dry year at harvest, are one of the wonders of the visible world.   At their peak intensity they are of such burning crimson and glowing gold, so distinct in form and line of cloud and black horizon, that one can scarce take them in.   They are otherworldly — as though one gazed beyond Massachusetts into heaven.   So it was, in a figure, when Rebecca Nurse stood upon the scaffold and offered forgiveness to us all.   The same sort of glory shone in the last light of most with her and many after her.   Indeed, Bridget Bishop, the first hanged, may have been the first to forgive us thus, although she did not articulate the words.   But like the best sunsets in this world, these seemed not of this world, and description inadequate to their glory.

When the Nurse family began to obey their mother's injunction it was less glorious, a sort of afterglow.   Yet there will still wonders in it, as when Sam went to communion on September 11th, and shared the cup and bread with Thomas and Anne Putnam, Sarah Holten, Deacon Edmund Putnam, and Deacon Ingersoll.   If past the peak of sunset, yet there was still cause for awe in the light lingering on the broken loaves of cloud, in the golden and purple.

But as our Troubles, properly speaking, drew to a close, and as the prisoners were released and all the immediate court business brought to an end (related matters continued in the courts many years later), Sam Nurse began the long labor of practical forgiveness — the vestiges of a sunset that was to linger very long upon the horizon.

If one looks to the west in the evening expecting a marvel and instead sees no more than a pathetic pinkening of the sky, one turns away disappointed.   But if one has just watched the miracle of a glorious sunset, one may well stay to gaze upon not only the waning beauties, but far beyond them until the sky remains but faintly tinged where the great orb went out of sight and the dusk fades to night.

It also may happen that one sometimes sees the effects of a fine sunset at the other pole of the compass, although the horizon between, in north and south shows no color. The phenomena in the east are usually milder and less intense, nevertheless a great wonder like a glorious sunset may have contingent effects worth observing.

Such is our excuse for taking our tale circumspectly to its proper end, recounting something of the steady, patient pursuit of justice which continued distinct from and long after the supreme displays of forgiveness and mercy in the midst of extreme injustice and cruelty.

As a further apology for drawing the tale on, we only add that what Reverend Parris and Reverend Noyes failed to do toward Rebecca Nurse and all the others, was now taught to them, not just in the pursuit of justice (which is the human commission of divine vengeance) but in patient mercy (which is the higher human commission of divine love in grace). Not as they had done was it done unto them. The holy fire of Christian discipline truly pursued was heaped upon Reverend Parris' head.

The message of what he ought to have done was drummed upon his door, not by malicious or revengeful persecution, but by the faithful pursuit of brothers who would not let him persist in sin. That took a long time, and may not have been successful in its object. Yet the doing of it and the manner of its doing were as worth watching as the vestiges of a sunset.

In one sense all that followed from the end of the high court to the end of Reverend Parris' ministry could be summarized as a contest in which he fought with the old weapons of the flesh and in which his opponents (principally the Nurses) fought back with older weapons, those of biblical justice.

Yet as this battle went forward, Reverend Parris was driven gradually into retreat and began to desperately modify his tactics, and accordingly the battle might be divided into a number of campaigns.

Rebecca had become the Nurse's general. If precedence had been in doubt before that, her last words to Francis made clear which was finally commander-in-chief. Her last orders called for a radical change in battle plan and thus the front lines shifted quickly to the confusion of the enemy.

After her execution and on into the fall and winter, various members of the Nurse family began again to attend worship at the Village Church. Sam, as we have said, took the Lord's Supper with the "brethren" in September.

John Tarbell and his wife Mary also followed the new battle plans. On the 30th of October they took their son to be baptized in the Village church. As Reverend Parris scooped the water on their son's head and spoke the conventional words of mystery, they thought of the prayers Rebecca had offered for him. That it had not been an easy thing for them to do may be inferred from the fact that Jonathon had been born nine months earlier, in February, at the very onset of our troubles.

Reverend Parris and the church pursued the Nurses and Cloyces back in August because of their nonattendance and withdrawing from the Lord's Table.   But this subsequent involvement of the family seemed to satisfy the church during the fall and winter.

There were other things less satisfactory, however. The day after Christmas the Village church met at the Reverend Parris' request and voted to send a petition to the General Court, which was to begin its Quarter Session meetings in Salem the next day. The church's petition was for:

> Setting forth its grievances and praying that Mr. Joseph Porter, Joseph Hutchinson, Senior, Joseph Putnam, Daniel Andrew, & Francis Nurse may be summoned to appear personally before their honours (or rather with submission before a committee appointed and fully empowered to settle all differences by your honours, which we conceive most suitable to this tedious affair) and give in their reason, if they have any, why the last year, expired 1st July last, was suffered to elapse and their committee-ship to dye totally without making any rate, in such manifest contempt of that law entitled an act for collecting the arrears of town and country rates passed at the session 8 June 1692.

Thus Reverend Parris and his allies in the Village church began a major campaign of their own, a tactical attack on the old basis of contractual and financial obligations, which seemed to them clear and not as complicated or as dangerous as the weightier matters, which were now the core issues of their differences. They reopened battle on the front where they thought they could win.

Two weeks later the church voted Lieutenant Nathaniel Putnam, and Captain John Putnam, as well as the two deacons, Captain Jon Walcott and Ensign Thomas Flint to serve as principal agents in behalf of the church to negotiate respecting the petition to the general court.

On the 17th of January, Stephen Sewall, secretary of the general court, replied to the church's petition. The court's answer was that the former committee and "several principle inhabitants" of the Village requested a meeting of the inhabitants to choose a new committee to attend to the matter, "alledging that otherwise they cannot lawfully be convened together." Constable John Putnam therefore was ordered to warn and give notice to the inhabitants to convene Wednesday, Jan 25, to chose the new committee.

Thus we see that the Nurses and their allies (the church committee et alia), including both old and new opponents of Reverend Parris, were still willing to fight on that old front of church finances and the pastor's pay. They decided to engage strategically, gradually strengthening alliances rather than fighting a pitched battle on ground chosen by their opponents.

When the Village inhabitants met (a much broader and larger body of persons, including not only full members of the church) they elected a new committee comprised of Joseph Pope, Joseph Holten, Jr., John Tarbell, Tom Preston, and James Smith . This committee was every bit as opposed to Reverend Parris as the former one, and included two Nurse kinsmen! Neither was this committee likely to move forward with a church tax, nor Reverend Parris likely to get his back pay soon—not at least until the committee was satisfied on the issues they held to be most important.

The Nurses and their allies also mounted battle on another battlefront—they stopped coming to worship at the Village, frequently going to Lynn or Boxford or Topsfield instead.

Accordingly, Reverend Parris and his allies moved the battlefront back to an earlier earthwork. On the Lord's Day, February 5th, the "brotherhood" (the church members) voted to send three senior men, Nathaniel Putnam, John Putnam and Bray Wilkins to once again "discourse with" Thomas Wilkins, Samuel Nurse and John Tarbell "about their withdrawing of late from the Lord's Table and publick worship of God amongst us."

But two days later, John Tarbell, Samuel Nurse and Thomas

Wilkins, Jr. took the battle back to Reverend Parris, coming to his house to speak with him as per Matthew 18:15, "Moreover if thy brother shall trespass against thee, go and tell him his fault between thee and him alone: if he shall hear thee, thou hast gained thy brother."

Thomas Wilkins, Jr. (approx 23) was the son of Thomas Wilkins, the third son of Bray Wilkins. Not long after the trials came to an end, he married the Nurse cousin, Elizabeth Towne, daughter of Edmund Towne and Mary Browning (she who had been "unable" to appear despite several summons as a witness against Mary Easty and Sarah Cloyce). Though his father and brothers had been strong accusers of John Willard, Thomas, Sr. had not participated in that case, since Willard's wife, Margaret, was his firstborn daughter. (She, Margaret (Wilkins) Willard, widow of John Willard, was to marry again two years later. Her second husband was William Towne, brother of Elizabeth (Towne) Wilkins.) This branch of the Wilkins had stood in opposition to the rest of the family in regard to the witch trials, and that opposition hardened after John Willard was hanged. Thus they were staunch allies of the Nurses in the ensuing battles, both in principle and eventually through two marriages.

When the three men surprised Reverend Parris' at his house on a Tuesday night, he responded by saying he would only speak to them singly in his study, but when John and Sam took almost an hour each, he protested he did not have time to speak with Thomas Wilkins, Jr. that evening. According to Reverend Parris own notes of these conversations:

> John Tarbell said he thought I was guilty of idolatry in asking afflicted persons who they saw upon other afflicted persons. . . Nor did he understand how my oath was safe in court that such and such, by such and such, were knocked down by their looks, and raised up by their touches. And had it not been for me, his mother Nurse might have been still living . . . that I had been the great prosecutor, and that others wise and learned who had been as forward as myself were sorry for what they had done, and saw their error, and 'til I did so too, he could not join. His brother Samuel Nurse for about an hour's time has the same objections.

These men had summoned their courage and swallowed their pride, put to death their condemnation, so far as they could, and come with stern but charitable hearts to confront the minister in his sins. Their stated goal was that he express sorrow over his part in the witch business.

The next day (7th of February), "Brother Peter Cloyce," who had been a founding member of the church with Reverend Parris, "came from Boston to me with the very same objections, whom I answered after the like manner," wrote Reverend Parris. The "like manner," that is the same way he answered John Tarbell and Sam Nurse, was that he did not see yet "sufficient grounds to vary" his opinion. Peter had already moved to Sudbury. He and Sarah were soon to settle permanently in Framingham. She, however, did not return "from eastward" until the advent of better weather in April.

For Reverend Parris, the question was still a matter of "opinion". He did not then, nor some say ever, acknowledge the agony, the disruption, the broken relationships and the awful deaths his sin had caused. He would not or could not face his own responsibility in spilling a great deal of innocent blood upon our land. Like greater men, and Cotton Mather in particular, he seemed to see the conflict in terms of "opinions," not truth; observations and phenomena, not living – or dead – persons.

Nine days later (16th of February) John Tarbell and Sam Nurse, together with Thomas Wilkins, Jr. and William Way, "desiring to speak to me" came to Reverend Parris in the evening and confronted him again in his study. They explained they were there according to the second step of Matthew 18 (verse 16), "But if he will not hear thee, then take with thee one or two more, that in the mouth of two or three witnesses every word may be established."

Reverend Parris fell back on what became a principal tactic as the battle went on – delaying and counter-attacking on the basis of jots and tittles. In this case he averred that since three of them had approached him in the first step, there ought to be two more, at least, and that Peter Cloyce had disqualified himself as one of these by also approaching him singly, that is according to the first step of Matthew 18.

This was a fatal point in time for Samuel Parris, although there were many more – and each potentially a place of return and resurrection. Here he had the opportunity and even, one might say, almost the mildness of heart to hear these four brothers. He might well have expressed great sorrow for his sin and made that great turning of the will, which is so fundamental to the long course of repentance that we call the act itself repentance. The doorway of submission and sorrow is the entrance to freedom and joy. And how whimsically we sometimes refuse it, and how sadly so. It was only, perhaps, his secret delight in pride, the inward comfort of a private smile, that made him take this unnecessary maneuver and casually remind them of his superior knowledge or badge of higher office.

He pointed out there should be two brothers in addition to Peter Cloyce, and that William Way was not sufficient to make the necessary rule of Christ. The Rule of Christ! How strange those words must have sounded from his lips. But the four men departed patiently, apparently without hard words for their hard-hearted minister.

Through much of March the wind blew relentlessly again — relentless, in the figure Rebecca Nurse once gave it, as God's pursuit of one unrepentant.

The 27th of March was the anniversary of the date upon which Reverend Parris had preached his sermon entitled "Christ knows how many devils there are, " the text which caused Sarah Cloyce to walk out through a slammed door, and soon thereafter to be arrested. On that date, Peter Cloyce and John Tarbell went once more to Reverend Parris at his house, together with Joseph Hutchinson, Sr., Joseph Putnam, and William Osborne as witnesses. They told him they had consulted with and taken "the advice of some neighboring elders" to which he replied that he wished they had talked with him first, since this seemed much like taking the third step of Matt 18, before the second had been properly completed.

Sam Nurse read a paper they had prepared listing their grievances. It began:

> To our pastor and minister, Mr. Samuel Parris of Salem Village, and to some others of the plantation. We whose names are underwritten, being deeply sensible that those uncomfortable differences that are amongst us are very dishonourable to God and a scandal to religion, and very uncomfortable to ourselves, and an ill example to those that may come after us. And by our maintaining and upholding differences amongst us, we do but gratify the Devil, that grand adversary of souls. . .

Reverend Parris carefully recorded that this paper of "the disaffected brethren" spoke of:

being grievously offended by reason of the 'unwarrantable actings' of their pastor, Mr. Parris, in the matter of witchcraft. They said they do habitually absent themselves from publick worship and from communion at the Lord's Table, notwithstanding the endeavours of the pastor and the church to enforce their attendance thereupon.

Again he tried to shift the battle line and put his opponents on the defensive. He records "the grounds of their dissatisfaction are these":

1/ The distracting and disturbing tumults and noises made by the persons under diabolical power and delusions, preventing, sometimes, their hearing and understanding and profiting by the word preached.

2/ Their apprehensions of danger of themselves being accused as the Devil's instruments to molest and afflict the persons complaining; they seeing those whom they had reason to esteem better than themselves thus accused, blemished, and of their lives bereaved.

3/ The declared and published principles of their pastor, and his frequent and positive preaching of the same, with respect to the dark and dismal mysteries of iniquity working amongst them, and their molestation from the invisible world; his easy and strong faith and belief of the affirmations and accusations made by those they call the afflicted; his approving and practising unwarrantable methods for discovering what he was desirous to know referring to the bewitched or possessed persons, as in bringing some to others, and by and from them pretending to inform himself and others who were the Devil's instruments to afflict the sick and pained; and his not rendering to the world a fair or true account of what he wrote on examination of the afflicted.

4/ His unsafe and unaccountable oath given by him against sundry of the accused; and his zeal in seeking out the suspected, insomuch that one of the disaffected brethren (John Tarbell by name) tells him to his face that he has been 'the great persecutor and that had it not been for him his Mother Nurse might have still been living, and so freed from execution.'

5/ His persisting in these principles and justifying his

practices, though others, wise and learned, who were as forward as himself, are sorry for what they have done, and see their error therein.

The men asked for "a Councill of elders, mutually chosen, to hear all grievances between their pastor and selves, and to determine where the blameable cause is." Regardless of Reverend Parris's efforts to hinder and divert their pursuit of church discipline, they were going on toward the goal. They hoped a "council" would not only bring their own church to face the enormity of what had been done in our midst, but also involve the other churches in the colony in bringing biblical judgment to bear on the issues of the witch troubles.

They gave a copy of the paper to Reverend Parris, who observed it was "purporting to be in the name of all the plantation,or a great many of them at least, but without either signature or date." He put the paper in his pocket and replied that he would "consider of it." Like the afflicted girls, he continued to play games with matters of life and death.

More than two weeks went by and Reverend Parris gave no response to the "disaffected brethren". Finally on April 14th, John and Sam and Thomas Wilkins, Jr., came again, this time accompanied by two patriarchs: Joseph Hutchinson, Sr. and Francis Nurse.

Hearing who it was who had come, Reverend Parris was perhaps both secretly fearful, and belligerent. He showed only the latter response, however. He kept them waiting, then went down from his study, as he recorded, to ask "if they would speak with me." They said they wanted to discuss the paper they had given him, but he replied that he had no time since he had to preach to a private meeting that evening!

He further told them he would not meet alone, but would agree on a meeting involving other brethren from the church. They agreed on Nathaniel Putnam's house, and the date of April 20th. To that meeting the "the four displeased brethren" brought Joseph Hutchinson and Israel Porter. Reverend Parris, on his side, brought Deacons Edward Putnam and Nathaniel Ingersoll, as well as Ensign Thomas Flint (who had been on the commission that had originally hired Reverend Parris). Nathaniel Putnam was something of a neutral moderator, having been active on Rebecca Nurse's behalf, as well as continuing to support Reverend Parris.

Reverend Parris said that he had come to hear what they had

to offer, to which the others replied they wanted to discuss the paper. Reverend Parris then took his copy of the paper from his pocket and read it aloud to all present. When he finished, he gave his opinion of it. In his own words, "I told them I looked upon it as a libel." He intended to put them on the defensive not on the theological points, but on a legal one. Since his copy of the paper had no signatures, it could be regarded as an effort at anonymous libel.

At this, the others produced a copy of the original paper subscribed with their own and forty-two additional names. Reverend Parris countered again by observing the names all appeared to have been written by the same hand. He asked to see the original. They replied they did not know its exact whereabouts since it was still in circulation among others who wished to sign it.

He asked if all the names shown had signed the original. They answered they had either signed it or had their names written in by their order. He then asked them to sign the copy they gave him at the same time testifying that no names were on it but those who had been consulted on the matter.

"But," the pastor wrote in the record, "None would yield to this." To his mind, he had won a clash of arms, but in fact, they refused to fight on such worthless grounds. For in consultation with other wise men, they now had one goal—and it was not winning small maneuvers of wits.

He then asked if he had to do with "displeased people or displeased brethren," by which he meant, was it the "displeased" people of the community or of the church whom they represented. They replied that they came as brethren.

He said then there should be none present but brethren.

They answered that they had already approached him on that basis, but gotten no satisfaction.

He countered that he had not discoursed with them at the time, because he had not understood their argument at the time, that they came as "such that had taken offence."

This was another diversion, meant to shift focus to the milder passage in II Corinthians 6:3, "giving no offense in anything that the ministry be not blamed," which seems to speak as much to perceived offense as to actual sin—in some contrast to Matthew 18.

Besides, Reverend Parris said, when they came the second time (which shows he understood Matthew 18 to be their basis, for it was not the second time in simple number) they had brought with them only one church member, William Way, and besides him, only non-church members.

Nathaniel Putnam, desiring peace, and hoping for some compromise, pointed out they could deal with the issue then and there by taking any two church members present and thus discourse with the pastor.

But the Nurses and their friends said no. They could see how things would go if that option was taken (the majority of "church members" present would have voted with Reverend Parris) but said they would meet the next morning with the two deacons and two church members, Brother William Way and Brother Aaron Way, for further discussion.

Reverend Parris was becoming conscious that he was not going to win the kind of victory he desired — that is one decisive enough to keep his opponents permanently at bay. In fact, although there was no evidence thus far he even considered he might have sinned or erred against his opponents, he seems to have to realized he would have to fight warily indeed in order to avoid surrender to some such formal conclusion.

The new meeting which had been agreed upon took place the next morning (21 Apr) at Ingersoll's. The pastor led in prayer. Sam Nurse read fifteen articles describing why he, his family, and a number of others had withdrawn from communion.

Reverend Parris, always the teacher, even as he was a poor student, said that seven of the articles were reasons for absenting themselves from publick worship, while the other eight were reasons for separating from his ministry. He fancied this was another technicality of note. He asked for a copy of the "scroll," but despite the urging of the other "indifferent witnesses," (his account) the Nurses refused to give them a copy. During their mother's trial, they had learned the danger of handing over documents prematurely. They promised they would turn over a copy if and when the church was called together to deal with its contents. They had come to the point where they were ready to go to the next step of Matthew 18, to "tell it to the church!"

On the last Lord's Day of April (the 30th), after the "inhabitants" were dismissed, the congregation were asked to stay in order to plan a meeting. Reverend Parris told them, "Brethren you know some of our brethren have for a time withdrawn from us. I do not understand their methods, which seem to me far from right, but they desire to speak with the church."

The 18th of May was agreed upon, and the pastor's house

settled as the site. Benjamin Putnam and Sam Sibley were appointed to tell Sam Nurse and John Tarbell about it. Mr. Parris wrote, "Brother Cloyce being at Boston, where he had lived these many months . . . we sent not to him, supposing the abovesaid kinsmen would." For the purpose of acquainting Thomas Wilkins, Jr. with the time and place of the meeting, Benjamin Wilkins and Aaron Way were appointed.

On the 18th of May, John, Sam, and Thomas Wilkins, Jr. were present, but not Peter Cloyce. Reverend Parris addressed them and said he had asked the church to set up this meeting at their request, and now wanted to hear from them why they desired it. They answered that they wished to tell the church their charges against the pastor. They also said they had witnesses to prove them.

Nathaniel Putnam was chosen "chair" for a vote of the congregation as to whether the "dissendent brethren" had proceeded thus far according to Matthew 18 or not. Parris recorded that the vote in the negative was "general and universal," except for the three brethren.

Parris also wrote "the general deportment of the said three displeased brethren was at this meeting exceeding unchristian, both to the minister and the other brethren, very irreverend towards him and as rough towards them to the great grief of many, if not the whole church. Nor did they stick to affirm that the church could not judge the case. . ."

He also wrote that when they were asked why they said this (about the church not being able to judge) they replied they wanted to bring it to the attention of the church, so there would be no surprise when they brought it to a council (elders from other churches). The church said they would be willing to bring it to a council "in the regular way."

The three were asked if they were offended by anyone in the church beside the pastor. They replied that it was not their present business to answer or pursue that question.

The pastor asked them if they were "all equal" in their offense against him. They said they were.

The pastor then said that he would not meet with them thereafter together, but singly. (Returning to negotiations he had refused earlier.) He said that when he met with them together before he "did not understand their drift, and therefore did not debate with them, and the case required arguing." Sam Nurse replied that they had passed the point where there was any use in speaking with

Reverend Parris alone.

The minister's next feint was a return to the earlier matter of compensation. On 28th May at a general session of the General Court at Ipswich, Nathaniel Putnam and John Putnam entered a complaint on behalf of the Village church against Tom Preston, John Tarbell, Joseph Pope, James Smith, and Joseph Holten, Jr., the five members elected to the new committee, "for not raising their minister's maintenance." James Smith, it was found, had refused the office after his election, but the others paid the moderately small fines which the General Court assessed.

Near midsummer, forty-nine Villagers asked the governor to appoint:

> . . . prudent and impartial persons to take cognizance of our miserable condition and give us what advice they shall in their vision think fit, for the speedy and happy composure of our lamentable differences, that peace and truth (which are now much wanting) may prevail among us . . .

The petition was signed by Sam, Ben and Francis Nurse; Tom Preston, John Tarbell and Peter Cloyce; Thomas Wilkins, Jr., Thomas Wilkins, Sr.; Alexander Osborne (husband of Sarah); Edward Bishop Sr., and Edward Bishop, Jr.; Daniel Andrew and Joseph Putnam; -- as well as Joseph Pope and Joseph Porter, Sr.; Joseph Porter, Jr.; Israel Porter, Benjamin Porter; and Joseph Hutchinson, Jr. All these were opponents of Reverend Parris. A number of them had loved ones among those hanged and several had been arrested themselves. None had seen any reason to believe Reverend Parris was going to repent of his agency in our troubles.

About three months went by and the elders of Salem (Higginson, Noyes, and Hale) received a letter regarding the church in Salem Village from Samuel Willard of Boston, written on behalf of the Boston elders, urging them to do what they could toward a council. Soon after, in October, Reverend Higginson wrote Reverend Parris and the church and advised they join with their complainants in calling a council of neighboring churches.

A year had gone since the last executions, and that sunset was over, but the memory of the extraordinary faithfulness of the martyrs kept their loved ones patient and willing to wait for dawn.

Samuel Sewall

Chapter Sixty-Six — Excuses and Exodus
(Oct 1693 - Dec 1696)

Whither shall I flee from thy Spirit?
Or whither shall I flee from thy presence?
If I ascend up into heaven, thou art there:
if I make my bed in hell, behold, thou art there.
If I take the wings of the morning,
and dwell in the uttermost parts of the sea;
even there shall thy hand lead me
and thy right hand shall hold me.
If I say, Surely the darkness shall cover me;
even the night shall be a light around me.
-- Psalm 139: 7-11

Our Harvard-educated "elders" scarcely ever spoke against one another. Even when they came to disagreeing diametrically toward the end of our troubles, they always added conciliatory language that made it seem as though no one had seriously erred — that all issues were matters of opinion or argument. This "courtesy," even toward the devil, was part of the prolonging of our troubles and a great hindrance to a biblical resolution of them. Reverend Parris of course hoped it would continue. The idea of a council, urged by the Boston and Salem divines, gave him some relief. He expected a council might exonerate him, a fellow elder, obviously himself wronged, and turn the tide back against his opponents.

The tide was certainly tossing on October 19th, a stormy, leaf-blown day in the Village, when the pastor and twelve brethren of the church met to discuss the two letters of the Boston elders and Reverend Higginson. They also read the petitions the complainants had sent to the General Court and several "remote churches".

The twelve brethren voted unanimously to follow Higginson's advice. Therefore about twenty-three church members gathered at a second meeting, this time with the "dissenters" for the purpose of calling a council. The dissenting brethren arrive about 3 in the afternoon, accompanied by several others. After some debate the church members decided to allow at the meeting any such as "were in full communion with other churches". Accordingly though several men were excluded, Israel Porter was brought in.

Reverend Parris began by going back to asking their reasons for wanting to call a council. The Nurses et al repeated that their offense was with him, not the church. They offered to read a paper concerning the matters they thought should be debated at the proposed council. Argument followed over this. Reverend Parris and his allies refused to hear the paper unless the dissenters would leave a copy for him to consider. They refused to give him one, since a council was not yet called. The Nurses et al suggested there would eventually be a council whether the church members voted for it or not. When there seemed to be nothing more either side could agree on the "dissenters" departed.

Reverend Parris wrote a letter the same evening to ministers of churches in Salem and Beverly stating his grievances against the dissenting brethren. He asked for prayer for his "bewildered case".

On November 5th, the deacons were assigned to tell Sam and John of a meeting at pastor's house on the 13th to discuss calling a council "if we cannot issue [agree] among ourselves." Peter Cloyce was to be invited "if not too remote". Thomas Wilkins, Jr. was also to be informed.

At that meeting, Peter Cloyce, Sam Nurse, and John Tarbell arrived, although not as promptly as the minister would have liked. Reverend Parris prayed and encouraged the dissenters to observe "order and meekness". Once more he asked the dissenters to give an account of their accusations, which they refused. They said they would read them, but would not leave a copy unless they could bring in some members of other churches as witnesses they had done so. The minister and the church would not allow any such "innovation".

The Nurse men did, however, leave a copy of a petition for a council of "indifferent persons indifferently chosen, or a council chosen by the General Court," stating that if such a council was set up, they would give Pastor Parris a copy of their grievances in writing thirty days before the council.

Reverend Parris read a statement of thirty grievances he and others had against their opponents. (This list was pared down to 17 grievances by the time the council met.)

On the 26th of November, Reverend Parris with the consent of the brethren addressed a letter to the same three, saying they had found the paper left with them not at all what they expected. He said it was "far other than we hoped for and altogether alien (or strange)" that is, at odds with the advice they had received and accepted from neighboring elders. He further noted that advice was said to be "well approved by the Reverend Elders at Boston, who on your behalf, and as your sureties, occasioned it." Reverend Parris' letter also gave his opponents several long exhortations and lists of scriptures to study admonishing them "that you have a care of destroying the Church of God."

The bone of contention now was that the "disaffected brethren" wished to invite a wider range of elders — from "remote" (ie, Boston, Salisbury and Ipswich) churches as well as from "neighboring" (ie., Salem and Beverly) ones. Reverend Parris knew where his allies were, and hoped for a smaller council including only "neighboring" elders — not all of whom agreed with him, yet a majority had not only agreed, but participated in the witch business during our troubles.

The Nurses and Cloyces and Townes for some weeks had been equally occupied with family matters – some sorrowful and some joyful. They were planning funerals and weddings.

On November 21, thirteen year old Elizabeth Preston died after a few weeks illness. Before our troubles she had been a sometimes playmate of Abigail Williams and Elizabeth Parris. She was buried in a quiet ritual on a blessedly still, though frozen day – in a grave chopped out of the earth near her Grandmother Nurse's.

But her family and two older sisters, despite their mourning, carried forward their plans for weddings. Rebecca, the oldest, was betrothed to one of the Uptons. Mary, of course, was being courted by Peter Cloyce, Jr.

In April, young Peter and Benjamin Towne had returned from Eastward to reunite Sarah Cloyce with her family. Sarah's charges had been set aside in the Governor's general pardon. (In fact she was among the accused who never sought compensation.) Her family swept her into their arms and back into the rebuilding of their lives and enterprises.

Peter, Sr., had decided to turn the farm over to Peter, Jr. at his marriage, and to move with Sarah and the younger children to Framingham, where he was purchasing part-interest in a lumber mill. He had practiced that trade with his Littlefield relatives in Maine during the early days of his first marriage. They dwelt temporarily in Sudbury, but by September, he and Sarah, were building a house in Framingham.

Meanwhile, Peter, Jr., made up for lost time in wooing Mary Preston. He spent every spare moment during the summer down at the Village, helping his prospective father-in-law, or (preferably) sitting or walking with Mary and her mother and sisters. Soon Peter and Mary were formally betrothed, though, at the advice of their fathers and other kinsmen, they waited several months to set a date for their marriage.

At last they set a date for the middle of December, by which time his parents' house in Framingham would be finished.

Although recent legislation authorized the "new" practice of being married in the churches, people were used to our old way, that is marriage by magistrate, which went back to the very first marriage in Plymouth colony. (Up to recent times, marriage in a church was viewed as "papist," since the Roman church treated marriage as a sacrament, to be administered in church by clergy. The "Reformed" churches, Lutheran, Anglican and Presbyterian were regarded by New Englanders as insufficiently reformed in continuing the practice.) Although most marriages were "published" by posting at the local meeting house the requisite three weeks beforehand, the law allowed "publication" at town meetings or lectures, as well.

The next two issues the young couple had to decide, then, were which magistrate to ask to marry them, and where to publish their marriage intentions. In order to give no unnecessary offense, and in the spirit of Rebecca Nurse and Mary Easty, they decided to ask Mr. Gedney to marry them. Although he had been on the court which hung their mother and step-mother, he was least involved of the three Salem magistrates. Furthermore, he had been a friend of the Nurses nearly twenty years earlier when they had purchased the home place.

They also decided to publish their marriage intentions in the most common way, that is, by posting it on the meeting house door in the Village.

The anticipated day, 13 Dec 1693, broke with a brisk morning, but promised to become delightfully mild. Mr. Gedney rode out from Salem, accompanied by Reverend Higginson. The innumerable Townes, Eastys, Cloyces and Nurses were crowded into Francis Nurse's house, chosen for its greater capacity. In addition there were many other guests from all around the Village and Topsfield. Reverend Parris chose not to come, and thus missed another opportunity for an act of repentance and reconciliation. He was occupied in moving his wife and children to Boston to stay with her family there.

The ceremony was very simple. The couple stood before the magistrate and clasped hands, while he asked them if they freely covenanted together in marriage as long as they both should live. The witnesses broke out in many cheers when the covenant was made, no doubt somewhat aided by the wedding punch that had been dispensed from a large bowl—which continued to be replenished and emptied all day long.

Reverend Higginson was asked to pray for God's blessing on Peter and Mary, and when he had done so, the blushing couple spent the next hours receiving the congratulations and best wishes of young and old.

For Francis Nurse it was another step toward joy. Despite the recent death of his granddaughter, the bride's sister, he saw this forging of bonds between this granddaughter and step-grandnephew as a concrete sign of God's restoration and grace.

There was much story-telling and laughing as the family and guests wandered throughout the house and back and forth to the other family homes nearby. A great deal of rich wedding cake and roasted meat was consumed. The children got up games of tag. And though there was an element of mourning for loved ones lost, there was a degree of rejoicing that recalled many other such days before our troubles.

Toward evening, the newlyweds got in Peter's wagon, richly loaded with supplies and condiments, and various gifts, including a magnificent rocking chair Francis had made for them, and a thimble which had belonged to Grandmother Towne. They then departed amidst another burst of cheers and merry cries, and made their way toward their new home on the Cloyce place up the Topsfield Road. Daniel Andrews and his family waited a decent interval, to follow along behind their new neighbors.

Fifteen days later, Mary's sister Rebecca Preston was married in much the same style.

Six months later, on the 14th of June 1694, seven ministers wrote a letter to the Village church. Reverends Higginson, Allen, Hale, Willard, Cheever, Gerrish, and Noyes advised a council of six churches. (Reverend Noyes signed only on the condition that he not be asked to serve on the council.)

On the 10th of September 1694, the same seven wrote more plainly and suggested a council of six churches, "not excepting against any that are chosen on either side." On the 29th of the same month, the Village church agreed to a council and wrote to the dissenters saying they would go ahead with seven churches, if the Village church were allowed to choose four and dissenters three !

When their opponents did not agree to this, fifteen members of the Village church met on the 2nd of November at the pastor's house and debated whether "it was not high time to call our three dissenting brethren to give us in the grounds of their withdrawing from us." They concluded to ask the rest of the church whether it wanted to call John Tarbell to give his reasons in public. The church, with but one opposed vote (Joshua Rea), agreed that John Tarbell be required to give his reasons in public on the next Lord's Day.

But John Tarbell did not appear the next Lord's Day. On behalf of the messengers, Nathaniel Putnam said John indicated "he did not know how to come to us on a Lord's Day," since he was attending worship elsewhere.

Church members by a full vote renewed the call to John to appear next Lord's Day. The following week in the afternoon, John appeared. He was asked the reasons for withdrawing, to which he replied by producing a paper, which he wanted to deliver to the church. Instead he was asked to give a copy to pastor, but he refused. The Nurses had dealt long enough with the pastor, and were not willing to go over that ground another time.

"Who speaks for the church?" John asked.

"The pastor, "said several in the congregation, to which all seemed to agree, including the pastor.

"Then I can not talk with the church, because my offense is with the one you would have speak with me on its behalf." he said.

"Have you any offense against the rest of the church?" the pastor asked.

"No" he replied.

However, John said he would allow the paper to be read by a non-member, which the church "suffered". Joseph Hutchinson then read it.

Afterward Reverend Parris read his own written overtures for peace and reconciliation, which were the closest he ever came to a public statement of repentance. It's points were:

1/That God sometimes permits the devil "(as of late)" to afflict people in the shape not only of innocent but of pious persons, or so to delude the sense of afflicted people that they strongly conceive their hurt is from such persons, when indeed it is not.

2/That it is wrong to use one afflicted to inquire who afflicts others. He admitted this method had been unlawfully used.

3/That his frequent functioning as a court reporter during our troubles was in error at various points—that he was "inexact" at several points in his reports.

4/That he regretted swearing on oath to things which he would not now necessarily think true.

5/That although intending due justice in all his preaching and teaching, "in that sore hour of distress and darkness" he might have sometimes and possibly sundry times, through weakness, unadvisedly expressed himself.

6/That he had known none of the "confessors" himself, although they were known to better men than he, however "seeing God has so amazingly lengthened out Satan's chain in this most formidable outrage" he had been inclined to side with those who give the "confessors" the benefit of the doubt.

7/That he truly sympathized with all those "that have unduly suffered in these matters (either in their persons or relations) through the clouds of human weakness, and Satan's wiles and sophistry ."

8/That he was convinced God allowed the evil angels to doubly delude us, "but how far on the one side or the other is much above me to say. And if we cannot reconcile 'til we come to a full undiscovering of these things, I fear we shall never come to agreement, or, at soonest not in this world."

9/Since therefore, "the matter being so dark and perplexed as that there is no present appearance that all God's servants should be altogether of one mind," he "heartily beseeches pardon of merciful God through the blood of Christ for all his mistakes and trespasses in so weighty a matter; and also all your forgiveness of every offence in this or other affairs, wherein you see or conceive I have erred and offended."

He said he believed he had done his duty, but through weakness or ignorance he may have been mistaken.

He made an eloquent ending in a plea for peace and reconciliation so that "Satan, the devil, the roaring lion, the old dragon, the enemy of all righteousness may no longer be served by us, by our envy and strifes." He desired that they might be covered with a mantle of love and forgive each other.

It was so nearly a "surrender," compared with his former stands, that John was much affected by it, and said that if half of it had been said formerly, things would never have gotten to the present pass. But he added that others beside himself were dissatisfied, and therefore desired opportunity that they might hear it also, which was granted.

At the meeting with the rest of them, on the 26th, the "disaffected brethren" read their objections which were by then divided, as per the church's questions to them, into two categories: 1/Why we attend not on publick prayer and preaching the word (three sub-points) and 2/The reasons why we hold not communion with them at the Lord's Table are we esteem ourselves justly aggrieved and offended with the officer who doth administer, for the reasons following: (eight more points).   It was signed by John, Sam and Thomas Wilkins, Jr.

Reverend Parris asked, again, if they were offended with anyone else besides himself. They answered they were not. He asked if they withdrew from communion because of anyone other than himself. They said no.

Parris then read the same "Meditations for Peace" which he had formerly read to John.

After reading this, he asked dissidents if they were satisfied. Tarbell replied they would like a copy of what he had just read, in order to further consider it. Reverend Parris in turn, requested a copy of their objections, signed by them.

During the meeting or in Parris words, "during this agitation with our dissenting brethren," they and their companions consulted on a number of occasions with others. Reverend Parris made note that he found the communications among them offensive, particularly those of Daniel Andrew and Tom Preston with Israel Porter and Joseph Hutchinson. Although the others had been seldom to the fore, the Nurses were now seen as representatives not only for them, but for a much large contingent in the Village.

On Nov 30th, Sam and John, with Tom Preston and Joseph Putnam, went to a meeting at the Parris house, called to hear the verdict of the dissenters — whether they were satisfied with Reverend Parris' "Meditations" or not. They met with Deacon Edward Putnam, John Putnam, Jr., Benjamin Wilkins, Ezekiel Cheever, and Jonathon Walcott. On this occasion Nathaniel Putnam was conspicuous by his absence. John gave their verdict on Reverend Parris' "Meditations for Peace". They were not satisfied. They desired that the church should call a council.

After lengthy consideration the "dissenting brethren" had concluded the "Meditations" were but another ploy. There was no plain repentance in them — no naming of the central and fundamental sins—murder, lying, false witness, sorcery and going to those who consulted familiar spirits, necromancy, idolatry. Instead there were strings of conditionals—'I'm sorry if you were offended because I was unwise …' or at most, 'It may well be that I was misled and a bit careless about such and such and did so and so which I would know better than to do today.' This was not repentance at all, but a show of it. In fact it was essentially excuse making—hiding from God while trying to cover guilt with self-made coverings as inadequate as fig-leaves. In particular, in his "Meditations," Mr. Parris hid from repentance behind the idea that many things were yet unclear and that there was much disagreement over the facts of what had happened.

For several months after this "the church" went back to dragging its collective feet, huddling over a revised set of grievances against the dissenters.

Debate over churches to be represented at council continued sporadically. The dissenters wanted Rowley (Reverend Phillips), Salisbury and Ipswich (Reverend Hubbard). Reverend Parris objected to Ipswich, but the dissenters held out.

Finally on the 3rd of Apr 1695, a council gathered to meet at Salem Village. It included elders and messengers from the churches of North Boston, Weymouth, Rowley, Old South of Boston and Third of Boston. The council reached several conclusions, the chiefest aim of which was reconciliation. It was unfortunately another mighty effort primarily toward amelioration, which is far from the same thing. The elders suggested everyone should forgive everyone else, which certainly sounded like a proper conclusion, but included little mention of repentance. The disaffected brethren should forgive the pastor; the church should without reservation receive the disaffected. If absolutely necessary, the disaffected brethren should be allowed to join another church. If absolutely necessary, the pastor should be allowed to find another pastorate.

The weakness of the document was that it did not deal with the heart of the issue. Absent was the open recognizance that there had been serious sin. Since Christ did not die for mistakes or errors, but for sin, to forgive as he forgives, at least in mutual forgiveness, involves an admission of sin by one or both parties—calling it by its particular and ugly names. Therefore the conclusions of the council did not signify much more than Reverend Parris' own "Meditations".

A number of these godly men had opposed the witch business fairly early. Were they nevertheless blind to the seriousness of what had happened? Perhaps they still were. Perhaps most of us still were. But in addition they—and we—were weary of the great weight of it, the long bearing of it, and heartily wished to set it aside without having to sort through it anymore. The colony had erred on the side of accusation before, now it recoiled from blaming anyone.

Patient pursuit of righteousness is not put off by obstacles large or small, nor the recalcitrance or weariness of others. The next step for those who pursued purity as well as peace, those who had been called disaffected, and disappointed and worse things, was to suggest outright that Reverend Parris could not remain among them. They hoped this would return the discussion to the issues which could not be ignored—the sins which they had forgiven, insofar as the Lord requires that transaction to be unilateral, but also which needed to be repented, for the benefits of forgiveness to accrue to the perpetrators, and thus to facilitate a fuller and mutual act of forgiveness.

Several score of Villagers signed a petition which they addressed to Increase Mather and eight other elders. This petition dated 6 May 1695, suggested Mr. Parris leave and another pastor be called.

Two weeks later, (20 May), having heard of their opponent's action, the zealous supporters of Reverend Parris sent another petition to the same addressees, this one with 107 signatures.

But Reverend Parris soon after, for the first time, made public that he was considering leaving. He told the congregation that messengers from Suffield had come to him, at the direction of some elders of Boston, and spoken to him about going to minister in Suffield. He suggested he might go, at least for a couple of months, during which the church could try to find another minister for the Village. After several hours' debate the congregation expressed itself averse to this. Whereupon Parris thanked them for their professed love for him, and said he was not free to go without their consent. His supporters wrote to Increase and Cotton Mather saying they were resolved to keep him. Thus things continued into the fall.

On the 5th of October, Peter Cloyce came to Reverend Parris and asked for a letter of recommendation for himself and his wife to the church at Marlborough.

The next Lord's Day, the minister asked the congregation if they would grant a letter of dismission to Brother Cloyce and his wife, and a majority agreed to it. The following day, Reverend Parris put a dismission letter in a sealed envelope and left it at John

Tarbell's, but the day after that Peter Cloyce returned the letter to him, saying "it was a letter of recommendation and not a letter of dismission that he desired." The Cloyces, grown weary themselves, had no more dealings with the Village thereafter.

Francis Nurse had kept back from most of the active efforts in which his sons and sons-in-law still struggled. He had tried to make peace with as many of his former enemies as he could. During the two years previous he had become chiefly a grandfather, spending nearly every day with his numerous grandchildren. He taught the boys something of woodworking, and made dolls and furniture for the girls. But he spent more and more time sitting peacefully and watching them play about the yard and meadows and woods or around the fire in the big house. Francis had blossomed into the sanctity of the sedentary. Although he still had a room there, the big house had been surrendered to Benjamin, who had come back to take on the mantle of householder. Benjamin and Thomasin had moved back from Framingham after a year and half away. Now Benjamin took up the last of Father Nurse's responsibilities on the farm.

Francis officially turned the farm over to his children the next year, no longer finding his fulfillment in accomplishment and hard work, nor any longer looking to the work of his hands for reward.

On the 22nd of November 1695, after a few days during which he was short of breath, Francis died at the age of seventy-seven. There were many dear and sincere mourners from all over the surrounding country. Mourning their father's passing refreshed and completed his children's mourning over their mother. But it also presented the problem of how to conduct themselves in relation to the Village Church under this special circumstance.

Thirteen months earlier, Ruth Swinnerton, daughter of Job, had died in the Village, and the Swinnertons had pointedly carried on her burial service without asking or involving Reverend Parris. They had even conducted their service on Lord's Day and taken the procession through the Village during meeting, so that the singing from the meeting house accompanied them as they passed. Reverend Parris and others of the congregation noted that there were more people gathered for the funeral than there were at meeting.

The Nurses did not want to make such a gesture, nor did they think it right to ask the unrepentant minister to participate, so they neither held the service on Lord's Day nor bore their Father's coffin through the Village, but had the burial service at the house, and in their own small graveyard where the remains of Mother Nurse and her granddaughter lay. Eight months after her death, the men had cleared the trees and brush from the secret grave, and fenced in a little graveyard, where the women had planted flowers and shrubs. There also they had buried her thirteen year old granddaughter. There they buried Francis.

They invited all their acquaintances, including Nathaniel Putnam, Captain John Putnam, and the two deacons of the church. But they did not invite either the minister or Sergeant Thomas Putnam and his wife.

Among the others invited, however, the young widow, Sarah Holten, came, and much to Rebecca (Nurse) Preston's surprise, came up to her after the service, obviously in much consternation and yet upon an errand.

She began in a somewhat thick voice, "My sincere condolences on the death of your father. He was a fine man." Sarah then paused and seemed to lose whatever else she had formulated to say. She seemed to gather herself, and then blurted out, "I'm sorry!" and burst into tears.

Rebecca, who had been very stiff until then, melted and folded her arms about her. "We forgive you. Oh, we forgive you, Sarah. Father and Mother forgave you long ago." And again she murmured, " We forgive you."

Others in similar ways, used the opportunity of grief to offer subtler, but sincere sympathy. A few attempted to ask forgiveness without actually saying anything so clear, and the Nurses returned the transaction in slightly better coin.

Good Will brought Dorcas to the service. Mary Tarbell had her most poignant moment at the funeral with her. After he made sure Dorcas had something to eat, Will wandered off by himself to smell the nostalgiac aromas of the turning shed, and left her sitting alone. Mary came up to Dorcas and said she was glad she came.

"Are you Granmer Nurse's?" Dorcas asked, after gazing intently at her for a few moments.

"Yes" answered Mary.

"We was witches together." Dorcas said. And again after a few moments, during which Mary's eyes began to overflow. "She and Granmer Cory was my granmers."

Mary reached down and lifted the girl in a maternal hug, but Dorcas hardly responded to it at all. She flopped down again when Mary released her.

In spring 1696, Samuel Parris resigned, although he

continued to spar with the Village church over his unpaid salary and the question of the house and property.

In July that summer, the Village received the news of his wife's death with mixed emotions. She had been a friend of many during their first two years here. The strain she had suffered in the midst of our troubles can scarcely be calculated. Elizabeth Parris, Sr., died and was buried in Boston.

By August 1696, Tom Preston and Nathaniel Putnam were united in purpose. They, Joshua Rea, Sr., and Joseph Holten made plans to go to Boston and to ask the advice of the "reverend elders" about getting a new minister.

On the 11th of October, Reverend Parris made his last few entries in the Village church record book. One had to do with the transfer of William and Aaron Way and their wives to Reverend Mr. Lord's congregation of Dorchester, lately moved to South Carolina.

Thus the exodus from the Village continued. While the movement toward our frontiers is often spoken in terms of a desire for opportunity and a desire to escape economic hardship, among us it also took place under the compulsion of fear, anger and broken relationships. While the people of Dorchester had the double motive of severe Indian depredations in Massachusetts and alluring prospects in South Carolina, the Ways, original members of the Salem Village church, had grown exhausted with the conflicts and bitterness that ran through their families and so much of Village life during those years.

We have mentioned Peter and Sarah Cloyce's move to Framingham. Others of the Towne, Cloyce and Bridge relatives moved there during the year after our troubles, including the families of Samuel Barton and Daniel Elliott, those early witnesses to the unreliability of the "afflicted."

The previous year Thomas Haynes, a peacemaker during the pastorate of Reverend Burroughs and a signer of the petition of 1695 in favor of Reverend Parris, also moved. A leader in reconciliations before our troubles, he had been embroiled during them through kinships with Ingersolls, Holtens and Putnams. He moved with a number of neighbors and kin to New Jersey where they settled a new town, also called Salem. Peacemakers grow weary and seek peace elsewhere.

Sam and Mary Abby (of the witchcake, etcetera) sold their home and land in the Village to Zachariah White of Lynn in the spring of 1697 and moved to Windham, Connecticut, near Sam's older brother John, who had moved there from Wenham.

Yet there were many ways Villagers dealt with the residue of our troubles besides forgiving or moving. Some became hard in their judgments toward the families of the afflicted and toward other witnesses. A few among the families of the accused, the condemned, and the executed, had particular ones with whom they would exchange neither greeting nor smile. But many of those who acted thus were several steps removed from the accused. To use biblical language these "took up the offense" and had not grace sufficient to deal with it by forgiveness.

Others, both among the guilty and the angry returned to the anaesthesia of hard work and activity. Some of these had never left off the pursuit of prosperity and now went after it "with a vengeance."

Others, chiefly of the scholarly or philosophical bent, talked about changes in government and law, "systems" with which to prevent future injustices of the sort we had experienced. But the human heart was never at last amenable to inner control by outward structures—not the most elaborate or stringent. After all a "system" of law and scientific principles of witchcraft had contributed much toward our troubles in the first place.

But the forgivers continued to go forward and steadfastly led us as they alone could.

Chapter Sixty-Seven — God Smiled — Public Repentances
(Dec 1696- Oct 1697)

Have mercy upon me, O God,
according to thy loving-kindness:
according unto the multitude of thy tender mercies
blot out my transgressions.
Wash me thoroughly from mine iniquity,
and cleanse me from my sin
For I acknowledge my transgressions:
and my sin is ever before me.
-- Psalm 51: 1-3

O n the 17th of December 1696 , the General Court issued the following proclamation for a Day of Prayer and Fasting. Cotton Mather had submitted a more ambivalent version for the court's consideration, but the court accepted and published one written by Judge Samuel Sewall:

By the Honourable, the Lieutenant Governour, Council and Assembly of his Majesties Province of the Massachusetts Bay, in General Court Assembled.

Whereas the anger of God is not yet turned away, but his hand is still stretched out against his people in manifold judgments, particularly in drawing out to such a length the troubles of Europe, by a perplexing war; and more especially, respecting ourselves in this province, in that God is pleased still to go on in diminishing our substance, cutting short our harvest, blasting our most promising undertakings more ways than one, unsetling of us, and by his more

Immediate hand, snatching away many out of our embraces, by sudden and violent deaths, even at this time when the sword is devouring so many both at home and abroad, and that after many days of publick and solemn addressing of him, and altho considering the many sins prevailing in the midst of us, we cannot but wonder at the patience and mercy moderating these rebukes; yet we cannot but also fear that there is something still wanting to accompany our supplications. And doubtless there are some particular sins, which God is angry with our Israel for, that have not been duly seen and resented by us, about which God expects to be sought, if ever he turn again our captivity.

Wherefore it is commanded and appointed, that Thursday the fourteenth of January next be observed as a day of prayer, with fasting throughout this province, strictly forbidding all servile labour thereon; that so all Gods people may offer up fervent supplications unto him, for the preservation, and prosperity of his Majesty's Royal Person and government, and success to attend his affairs both at home and abroad; that all iniquity may be put away which hath stirred God's holy jealousie against this land; that he would shew us what we know not, and help us wherein we have done amiss to do so no more; and especially that whatever mistakes on either hand have been fallen into, either by the body of this people, or any orders of men, referring to the late tragedy, raised among us by Satan and his instruments, thro the awful judgment of God, he would humble us therefore and pardon all the errors of his servants and people, that desire to love his name and be attoned to his land; that he would remove the rod of the wicked from off the lot of the righteous; that he would bring the American heathen, and cause them to hear and obey his voice.

Given at Boston, Decemb. 17, 1696, in the 8th year of his Majesties reign.

The ending, with it reference to one of the fruits of repentance being a conversion among the Indians, was not simply a recognition that our injustice and violence toward them as toward each other was a hindrance to the gospel going forth, nor simply a return to our central founding principle, but it also gave expression to a particular burden of Judge Sewall's, which he put in more extensive form in his *Phaenomena Quaedam Apocalyptica,* published the next year. In it he suggests that the Indians are the remnants of Israel, and perhaps the "other sheep" mentioned in the gospel of John. America, it seems, is still to be the center of Christ's kingdom, and the scene of the ultimate confrontation between Gog and Magog. But Judge Sewall's soft heart toward the Indians was a sign that he indeed was more deeply repentant than most. He also was to become one of the few men who wrote vigorously against African slavery. At the end of his book he addresses local landmarks as symbols and tokens of spiritual hope:

> As long as Plum Island shall faithfully keep the appointed post, notwithstanding all the hectoring words and hard blows of the proud and boisterous ocean; as long as any salmon or sturgeon, shall swim in the streams of Merrimack,. . . as long as any cattle be fed with the grass growing in the meadows, which do humbly bow themselves down before Turkey Hill; as long as any free and harmless doves shall find a white oak within the township to perch, or feed, or build a careless nest upon . . . as long as nature shall not grow old and dote, but shall constantly remember to give the rows of Indian corn their education, by pairs: -- so long shall Christians be born here; and being first made to meet, shall from thence be translated, to be made partakers of the saints in light.

Three weeks after the proclamation, on the afternoon of the appointed day, at the public service in Boston's Old South Church, Samuel Sewall stood as Reverend Willard read that high court judge's personal confession of guilt. When the Nurses heard of it, they wept, and wished that Father Nurse had lived to see the day.

> Samuel Sewall, sensible of the reiterated strokes of God upon himself and family; and being sensible, that as to the guilt contracted upon the opening of the late Commission of Oyer and Terminer at Salem (to which the order for this day relates) he is, upon many accounts, more concerned than any that he knows of, desires to take the blame and shame of it, asking pardon of men, and especially desiring prayers that God, who has an unlimited authority, would pardon that sin and all other his sins, personal and relative: and according to his infinite benignity, and sovereignty, not visit the sin of him, or of any other, upon himself or any of his, nor upon the land: but that He would powerfully defend him against all temptations to sin, for the future; and vouchsafe him the efficacious, saving conduct of his Word and Spirit.

Many have wondered at the fact Judge Sewall was the only member of the court to publicly confess to sin in his part in our troubles. Some suggest it was partly because his family had undergone such severe hardships in recent years: the loss of children and straitened circumstances. Others have said he was more of a man of conscience than most of the other justices. But perhaps it would be more acute to observe he went through more of a change in his understanding than the others, and was more faithful to his opinions at each point along the way. He had a kind of integrity that is rare.

On the one hand, Deputy Governor Stoughton never admitted to any wrong-doing, although he had been the central mover of the capital court and its most blood-thirsty justice. On the other hand, Justice Saltonstall resigned immediately after Bridget Bishop was hanged. We might say Justice Sewall, was neither blood-thirsty nor quick to withdraw, but merely steady in his progress toward clearer understanding. (Yet even though he shoulders the whole weight of the court's "guilt" in his confession, he did not confess its particular sins. Perhaps he felt they were all too well known by then.)

The Court of Oyer and Terminer had needed but five men for a quorum, and toward the end had but five upon the bench — the three from Salem and Justice Stoughton, plus Justice Sewall. Had he resigned, too, the court might have ceased to function — and to execute.

The Salem magistrates were in too deep — through their own long involvement and the local fervor. Justice Stoughton was that most dangerous of men, a proud idealist. In a sense then, Justice Sewall was the most culpable, because most capable of guilt. But with his public confession, he became a remarkable moral leader.

Perhaps some of the other high court judges refrained from public statements like Sewall's because they thought withdrawing and refusing to further prosecute was equivalent. Those actions so little and so late, nevertheless seemed to them right and sufficient. Since Sewall hadn't withdrawn, they thought it appropriate he should publicly confess his error. In the same way, the Salem ministers admitted errors, albeit in what seemed comparatively muted terms. Beyond that they comforted surviving defendants and the families of those hanged. They, too, felt this was all that was required of them.

There were other good examples. The members of the Salem jury also publicly acknowledged their guilt:

We confess that we our selves were not capable to

understand, nor able to withstand the mysterious delusions of the powers of darkness, and prince of the air; but were for want of knowledge in our selves, and better information from others, prevailed with to take up with such evidence against the accused, as on further consideration, and better information, we justly fear was insufficient for the touching the lives of any, Deut. 17. 6, whereby we fear we have been instrumental with others, tho ignorantly and unwittingly, to bring upon our selves, and this people of the Lord, the guilt of innocent blood; which sin the Lord saith in scripture, he would not pardon, 2 Kings 24. 4, that is we suppose in regard of his temporal judgments.

They went on to ask forgiveness of God and men for their sins against both. Tom Preston told his wife the sweetness and relief in hearing of these confessions lifted his spirits better than a spring thaw after a long hard winter.

Within a few weeks, however, Tom ended his long winter in a more lasting spring, and departed this world full of peace. He came down suddenly with a consumption like that which carried off his father, and though his family grieved a great deal, he was full of encouragement until the last. Another great funeral was held in the Village, and there was only one man who stayed away. Even Sergeant Putnam and his wife were there. Tom was laid in the small plot near his daughter -- and his beloved in-laws, Francis and Rebecca Nurse. As his mother-in-law's death began the great movement toward reconciliation in the Village, the death of this man whose signature stood on the first three complaints, nearly completed that reconciliation, so far as it would be completed in this world.

As encouraging as the public statements of repentance by Judge Sewall and the jury were to many of us in the Village, there were none of our local leaders, judicial or spiritual, who were as open. Their confessions came in small installments, by dribs and drabs — a few sentences in a sermon by Reverend Noyes, a small concession in private conversation from Reverend Hale, and nothing further from the Village pastor, whose private expressions indicated he felt he had gone beyond the required second mile. The Village was still caught up in the latter stages of "negotiation" with Reverend Parris. But from the time of Tom's burial the Village no longer had two "sides".

On the 23rd of Feb 1697, the Villagers chose John Putnam, Israel Porter, and Thomas Flint (captains all) to treat with Mr. Parris concerning "our ministry house". Both sides of the congregation were working together. Reverend Parris had no more supporters.

The next month, a new Village committee was chosen. The committeemen were Nathaniel Putnam, Sergeant Thomas Putnam, Jonathon Putnam, John Buxton, and Sam Nurse! Both "sides" were represented.

This was the first time Sergeant Putnam had been officially involved in Village affairs since the end of our troubles. Since the spring of 1693, he and his wife Anne had acted like hunted people, staying at home and rarely even visiting with their many relatives. They were as much in hiding as Daniel and George had been in their cave. Their faces grew pale and gaunt and on those rare occasions upon which they were seen in public, they glanced about them as though they were pursued. Anna was seen more often than they, gradually becoming the caretaker of her many brothers and sisters. Mercy Lewis went away to live with an uncle in New Hampshire. We saw no more of her.

Sam said little to Thomas Putnam on the few occasions the committee met, and the Sergeant said nothing to him, but Sam for his part found himself feeling more compassion than anger for the man, and was surprised at himself for this. As Sam once told John, it seemed a kind of confession that the Sergeant came to meetings. It was obviously hard for him, and not done in pride. Sam was impatient to be about forgiving him.

As spring came that year, along with birds and flowers, the Salem Village countryside was also rich in suits and countersuits. Joseph Hutchinson, Sr., Daniel Andrews, Thomas Flint, Sr. Joseph Herrick, and Joseph Putnam were appointed agents or attorneys for the inhabitants of the Village, plaintiffs versus Samuel Parris. The plaintiffs lost the case in Salem court (still under the oversight of Judges Hathorne, Gedney, and Corwin) and had to pay costs.

Reverend Parris countersued the inhabitants and won. As a result the Village was ordered to pay him 125 pounds specie plus costs. This was all it took to close any divided ranks in the Village!

On the 13th of April, an official meeting was held at Ipswich for the purpose of settling the contractual obligations of the Village and Reverend Parris. Nathaniel Putnam was the moderator and Stephen Sewall, the clerk of the court.

Nathaniel, Thomas, and Joseph Putnam, Dan Andrew, and

Joseph Herrick, Sr. were there as attorneys for the Village. The chief issues still to be settled continued to be the pastor's salary and the ownership of the minister's home and lands.

In this meeting the Village book of records was read. The controversial vote of October 1689 was debated. The moderators agreed it ought to be set aside as a constitutional change from the prohibition passed in 1681 (which forbad the transfer of the home and lands to any) and therefore requiring more exhaustive procedures to be validated. When an entry made the 18th June 1689 was read which indicated the pastor's compensation would not be settled until he had come among them, Reverend Parris rose and said they were knaves and cheaters who entered it! He said, no doubt in full honesty, that he had never heard anything of it before.

Nathaniel Putnam replied and said "Sir, then there is only proposals on both sides, and no agreement between you and the people." Parris answered heatedly that there was not, "for I am free of the people and the people free from me."

Joseph Porter, Daniel Andrew and Joseph Putnam swore that "there had never been any agreement made with Mr. Parris that we knew of, or ever heard of." It was a remarkable statement, perhaps in the same letter-of-the-law mode as so much of Mr. Parris' own casuistry.

So great were their differences at this point that the parties agreed to ask for outside and "indifferent" arbitration.

The Villagers did not waste much time after that. On the 23rd of April, they voted unanimously that "whereas Mr. Samuel Parris, our late minister, hath for more than nine months past desisted in his stated work of the ministry amongst us, and yet still he doth keep the possession of our ministry house to our great damage. . . " that they would appoint attorneys to arbitrate or otherwise sue Parris for the house and lands. These attorneys were the same as at the Ipswich meeting with the addition of Thomas Flint, Sr.

Three months later on the 21st of July, John, Sam, Joseph Putnam and Daniel Andrew addressed a petition to the "Honourable Wait Winthrop, Elisha Cook, and Samuel Sewall" asking for arbitration between the inhabitants of Salem Village and Mr. Parris.

They stated their need for arbitration had to do with the witch business, giving details of the pastor's involvement, and averred that these had formerly been stated to him in April 1693. They accused him of swearing falsely, departing from charity in accusing and encouraging others to accuse blameless and godly persons, going to those with familiar spirits for divination, and being the beginner and procurer of the sorest afflictions both to the village and the whole country. They ended by asking the arbitrators to determine if they had any legal obligation to honor, respect or support such an instrument of their miseries.

On the 14th of September 1697, a settlement was reached through arbitration: the Village was to raise 78 pounds to be paid to Mr. Parris through Nathaniel, Thomas and Joseph Putnam, Daniel Andrew, and Joseph Herrick in exchange for his giving up claim to ministry house and land. The settlement was signed by Barthomew Gedney.

On the 5th of Oct, a meeting was announced in the Village — for prayer and fasting for a new minister. It was sponsored by Mr. Hale and Mr. Noyes. In the Village record book, a few years later someone wrote of this date and meeting, "from which time God has smiled on ye people."

Chapter Sixty-Eight —The Diligence of Reverend Green
(Nov 1698 - Feb 1699)

*How beautiful upon the mountains are the feet of him that
bringeth good tidings, that publisheth peace; that bringeth good
tidings, that publisheth salvation; that saith unto Zion, Thy
God reigneth!   -- **Isaiah 52:7***

T he signs of God's smile came in many forms. There were
marriages between families of accusers and accused. Within a few
years of our troubles, Henry Kenny's grandson Jonathan married
Samuel Nurse's daughter, Rebecka —Rebecca Nurse's own
granddaughter and second namesake.

Mary Walcott, one of the leading "afflicted," and closely
related to the Sibleys, and Ingersolls as well as the Putnams, married
Isaac Farrar in 1696. He was the grandson of "Old Pharoah,"
Thomas Farrar, one of the accused from Salisbury.

A significant agent of God's smile came in the person of
Reverend Joseph Green. Green was no young idealist or pristine
Harvard philosopher. He graduated from Harvard in 1695 and had
been quite the prodigal for the next few years, gambling at cards,
dancing, hunting, and fishing on the Lord's Day. He continued in
this dissipated style until he was converted through a sermon of
Cotton Mather —and became quite a different man thereafter. When
he shared the testimony of his conversion at small gatherings,
various ministers encouraged him. He was invited to preach at a
number of churches, and soon became known as a warm evangelist.
He proved to have a listening ear and a wise heart, as well.

Reverend Green was ordained by Reverend Hale on Lecture
Day, the 10th of November 1698. Mr. Noyes gave him the right hand
of fellowship. Elders from six churches were present.

Only two weeks later, at John Putnam's house, following
exercises in preparation for the sacrament of communion, Reverend
Green led the congregation in a vote to join together in welcoming
back the "dissenting brethen".

I desired the church to manifest by the usual sign that they
were so cordially satisfied with their brethren Thomas

Wilkins, John Tarbell, and Samuel Nurse that they were heartily desirous that they would join with us in all ordinances, that so we might live lovingly together.

Reverend Green was very explicit about putting past contentions to rest. As part of the vote taken at John Putnam's he asked:

> . . . further that whatever articles they had drawn up against these brethren formerly, they now looked upon them as nothing, but let them fall to the ground, being willing that they should be buried forever.

Chapter Sixty-Nine — It's Over
(February 1699)

Blessed are the pure in heart: for they shall see God.
Blessed are the peacemakers, for they shall be called the children
of God. -- **Matthew 5: 8-9**

Near the top of the gentle rise the angular building stood stark against the blowing snow. They stopped and their hands slipped together as they stood leaning back against the wind.

"**I** never thought to see this day," Mary said.

Sam felt her fingers cold inside his palm. He answered with his eyes still on the old homestead.

"**N**o, we could not expect it. Though we have wanted and worked for it, it comes unlooked for, like so much."

The children were gone ahead. Their dark figures faded into the brown of the bare woods blending into the form of their own smaller home in the distance.

Mary spoke again. "Goody Holten was shaking as we rose to sing. I was almost overwrought myself sitting between those two women. At every moment I felt I must run out of the service. I prayed a desperate prayer. Before I knew what I was doing, I reached out to share my psalter with her. It was then I saw how she shook. Yet she took it, and clung like a leaf in a gale. That was all, but enough. At the last song, in a mystery, I touched Anna Putnam's arm — it did not seem my own hand that did it — and the three of us worshipped together."

She paused as a gust struck the high gable before them and lifted a cloud of loose snow from the roof's peak.

"**I** feel now what I never expected to feel. . ." and just before her voice broke into childlike sobs, "it is over."

Sam reached out to her shoulders, drawing her against him.

Tears ran down his rugged cheeks and over his smile.

"**Y**es, inasmuch as anything in this world can come to an end, it is over."

When they came in out of the cold, they found the girls had already set the table and the boys got the fire ablaze. These saw and wordlessly shared the knowledge that their parents had come from some lofty place. Something new and mysterious had been revealed. An exhilaration passed among them and infected all they did. Each spoon placed rang beside its platter which shone as a talisman. Each placement was a priestly act. Each loaf and porringer became an icon of glory. The slightest word seemed a proverb, every gesture bestowed blessing. Something was over and something new begun.

They sat down and Rebecka asked, as she passed a bowl of hominy, "Mother, did you see that Uncle John sat by John Putnam?"

"Yes, dear," Mary replied, and her joy burned brighter for her daughter's wonder.

"And Mr. (Nathaniel) Putnam was on his other side!" added Thomasin, "And Widow Walcott sat by Aunt Rebecka."

"And Father sat by Sergeant Thomas!" added Ebenezer with an exuberant squeak.

When neither of his parents replied, George answered his younger brother, "You have good eyes in your head, Ebby."

"And Mother sat between Anna Putnam and Goody Holten!" Ebenezer went on.

After the meal, Sam took up the Bible and read from the Sermon on the Mount. When he finished his reading, he said, "If Jesus has no enemies, then neither do we. We have no enemies — only fellow sinners. And tell me, Ebby, is there a friend for sinners?"

"Yes, Father! Jesus is a friend for sinners."

"Amen! " Sam answered, and the others echoed, "Amen."

On the 24th of May 1699, only two and half months after the "reconciliation" service, Sergeant Thomas Putnam died at the age of 47. Three weeks later his wife, Anne, was also laid in her grave, although she was almost a decade younger than he. They left eight children living: Anna; Thomas; Elizabeth; Ebenezer; Deliverance; Abigail; Susanna; and Seth. The name of the last son, after the third son of Adam and Eve, was perhaps meant to indicate his parent's hope that the history of Cain and Abel might be left behind them.

At her parents' death, Anna became "mother" to her younger siblings, although she had considerable help from the older two and from many of her nearby relatives. While it was hard that she, who was never to marry, would be left to care for a large family, it was also a mercy that her parents were called home when they were. For it is doubtful Reverend Green would have been able to minister as he did to her, and she to the rest of us — if they had continued with us.

In keeping with the idea that our troubles are worth hearing about, it would be well to wrap them up, so to speak, with an accounting of some last little episodes in the Village, during which Reverend Green continued to be a wise and welcome healer of wounds and breaches, ever ready to offer careful guidance and prayer, and quick to give thanks.

On 19 Jan 1699/1700, we had a church meeting on the subject of our policy regarding the half-way covenant and baptism. Ever since Increase Mather and Governor Phips arrived in the midst of our troubles with the new commission, the half-way covenant was a source of considerable grumbling, since by it the strict churchmen are no longer the only voters for officers of the colony. Now the franchise extends to all householders such as are of good character and not known to be vicious in their conversation. That puts the onus on the churches to accept these men, too. So the old rigorous standards for a credible profession of faith have been many places relaxed, and our churches have mostly conformed themselves to this "half-way covenant."

We in the Village had not addressed the issue, however, since we had been too busy fighting with each other and Reverend Parris. When the matter came up and a meeting was scheduled, most of us expected the worst. But strange to say, there was not one angry outburst or head-to-head butting match during the whole meeting. People from every "faction" of the church (and as must be clear by now, we had many — remnants of almost every controversy) were courteous and careful. And at the end, we voted on the four points put forward and all carried, without any evidence of rancour.

Reverend Green wrote in the record book: "Blessed be God for such a peaceful meeting" . Such seemed to be the new tenor of our congregation.

In July 1700, Nathaniel Putnam, Sr., died, a stalwart who tried to steer a true course amidst the furious storms and alarms, and who corrected that course wherever he found a better star. With him an epoch seemed to be drawing to a close.

In January 1702, Bray Wilkins, at the age of 92, also departed this world. For ten years he had lived with the knowledge of his own active part in the wrongful death of his kinsman, John Willard, but his own family had achieved some measure of reconciliation among its members, and that was good.

By June, we had grown so confident in our new peace, that we held a Day of Publick Thanksgiving, during which Mr. Noyes and Mr. Pierpoint taught and preached. Mr. Pierpoint's sermon concluded that the reasons for thanksgiving were:

1/that God so far discovered the wiles of the devil which
might have been more hurtful and destructive of us if God
had not in judgment remembered mercy;
2/that when the people were farthest from peace and unity
that God was pleased to hear our prayers and unite us and
especially to hearken to those prayers that were put up here
on a [former] day of publick fasting and prayer by Mr. Hale
and Mr. Noyes, from which day God was pleased to succeed
all publick endeavours for a peaceable settlement;
3/And that God has now for some years continued peace and
prosperity to us; and 4/that he has been carrying on his work
in the midst of us & c.

In October the first published copies of Cotton Mather's
Magnalia Christi... arrived in Boston (he had begun it about 1693,
and finished it in 1697). The work contained no repentance,
nevertheless it reflected more "doubt," "caution," and "regret" about
what was actually done in our troubles than anything he had written
up to that time. Such things were in the wind and he was ever a
good weather vane.

    Daniel Andrew, who came back from Boston feeling ill one
day, came down with smallpox, and departed this world on
December 3rd, after three days of extremity. The former conspirators
gathered after his funeral and made a special memorial which they
presented to his widow. But Sam Nurse and John Tarbell were
shocked to find how sad his passing left them — they who had
endured so many opportunities of mourning before.

    Two weeks before Daniel Andrews died, Sam saw him in
Salem and as they stood on the quay-side, he said, "Sorrow
continues, but at least we have learned evil should be resisted – and
perhaps a few have learned how it ought to be resisted."

    The next month, Daniel's second and third sons, Thomas (24)
and Samuel (19) also died of smallpox. Thus, despite what he once
said about his hopes, the world, in an other sense, did not prove any
'safer' for them than for him.

    That same December, the pastor spoke to the church about
Martha Corey's excommunication:

    ... the generality of the land being sensible of the errors that
    prevailed in that day — some of her friends have moved me

several times to propose to ye church whether it be not our duty to recall that sentence that so it may not stand against her to all generations and I myself being a stranger to her and being ignorant of what was alleged against her — I shall now only leave it to your consideration, and shall determine the matter by a vote ye next convenient opportunity.

The congregation was very wary of touching on the subject again, and little more was said publicly. In January we had a day of prayer and fasting on account of the small pox that was threatening us. During a meeting one or two prayed that we would have wisdom and unity in regard to the matter of Martha Corey.

Reverend Green went forward. At a meeting in mid-February 1702/3, the pastor moved the church to vote on revoking Martha Corey's excommunication. It became clear that some still believed she had been involved in witchery and not only these, but some others were unsure what we were saying in such a vote. Sometimes a whole generation must perish in the wilderness before a people can pass into God's promised land. There was therefore not quite a full or unanimous vote, but the majority of the brethren consented to revoke it thus:

Whereas this church passed a vote Sept 11, 1692 for the excommunication of Martha Cory and that sentence was pronounced against her Sept 14 by Mr. Samuell Parris formerly the pastour of this church; she being before her excomn condemned & afterwards executed for supposed witchcraft . . . we being moved hereunto do freely consent & heartily desire that the same sentence may be revoked, and that it may stand no longer against her for we are thro' Gods mercy to us convinced that we were at that dark day under the power of errours which then prevailed in the land; and we are sensible that we had not sufficient grounds to think her guilty of that crime for which she was condemned & executed; and that her excom — was not according to the mind of God; and therefore we desire that this may be entered in our church book, to take off that odium that is cast on her name and that so God may forgive our sin & may be atoned for the land, & we humbly pray that God will not leave us any more to such errours and sins, but will teach & enable us always to do that which is right in his sight.

Three years later, the church received Anna Putnam in full communion. Reverend Green sat down with her and helped her to write out a confession to be read when she joined. He also brought Sam and Mary Nurse to meet with her and they talked and prayed and cried a little together.

On August 25, 1706, her confession was read as she was received, It said:

> I desire to be humbled before God for that sad and humbling providence that befell my father's family in the year about 92, that I then being in my childhood should by such a providence of God be made an instrument for that accusing of several persons of a grievous crime whereby their lives were taken away from them, whom now I have just grounds and good reason to believe were innocent persons, and that it was a great delusion of Satan that deceived me in that sad time, whereby I justly fear I have been instrumental with others though ignorantly and unwittingly to bring upon myself & this land the guilt of innocent blood through what was said or done by me against any person. I can truly and uprightly say before God & man, I did it not out of any anger, malice, or ill will to any person for I had no such thing against one of them; but what I did was ignorantly being deluded by Satan. And particularly as I was a chief instrument of accusing of Goodwife Nurse and her two sisters, I desire to lye in the dust & to be humbled for it in that I was a cause with others of so sad a calamity to them & their families, for which cause I desire to lye in ye dust & earnestly beg forgiveness of God & from all those unto whom I have given just cause of sorrow & offence, whose relations were taken away or accused.

In the fourteen years after our troubles, there was no statement of repentance or anything approaching an explanation from the "afflicted girls" before Anna Putnam spoke before the church. While one might at first be inclined to ask how it took so long before such a one confessed to the devastation she and her fellows wrought, a more honest and charitable question might be, how could even one of them bring herself to it, when so many wise and respected men never did!

Nevertheless it is strange that the judicial murder of twenty-five precious persons, the terrible wreck made of families, communities and churches, the great accumulation of bitterness and suspicion, took but eight months, while in some ways, fourteen years had only begun to rebuild it again. Perhaps the fallacy lies in the idea that these institutions and associations had an intrinsic integrity to begin with.

No, none of us would like to go back to what we were. Though we are seriously crippled, raddled, riddled and addled by our diseases and distractions — we are humbler. And that is worth a good deal — a great deal.

Thus another "end" was brought to our troubles — not perhaps satisfying our desire for clearer understanding or further evidence with which to reason and understand what befell us. Yet Anna's confession and its wholehearted reception were themselves evidence that forgiveness can cover a multitude of sins until the final day when all mourning shall be turned into dancing.

Chapter Seventy -- The Nurse Trees

And they shall not hurt nor destroy in all my holy mountain: for the earth shall be full of the knowledge of the Lord, as the waters cover the sea. And in that day there shall be a root of Jesse, which shall stand for an ensign to the people; to it shall the Gentiles seek: and his rest shall be glorious. -- **Isaiah 11:9-10**

The fruit of the righteous is a tree of life; and he that winneth souls is wise. — **Proverbs 11:30**

In July 1703, a petition had been delivered to the General Court for reversal of the attainders against those charged during our troubles. It was considered but no definitive action taken.

In March 1709 another such petition was debated. In response to this, a committee of the General Court met at Salem, 13 Sep 1710, and recommended reversal. On 17 Oct 1711, the General Court acted to reverse attainders for those convicted of witchcraft in 1692/3, thus restoring the rights and good names of those accused and granting 600 pounds to be distributed in restitution to their heirs.

On the 2nd of March 1712, the church of Salem met to consider Sam Nurse's request that Rebecca Nurse's excommunication be blotted out. On the 3rd of Jul 1712, exactly twenty years since her excommunication, the elders of the Salem church proposed and the members voted unanimously to revoke and erase Rebecca Nurse's excommunication from their covenant fellowship.

In 1716, Anna Putnam died at thirty-six, leaving her father's land divided among her brothers and her personal effects among her sisters. She had never married.

Reverend Green died four months later.

In the forest where a great catastrophe has struck, be it fire, hurricane, or flood, the devastation of mighty trees is an awful sight to behold, and he who beholds it despairs of ever seeing recovery. How can such a forest rise again.

But let him go away and return five or -- better -- ten years later, and he will be amazed to see a new prospect. Between the decaying wrecks of once mighty trees there will already be other living ones standing fifteen or twenty feet high, green with spreading foliage, and the ground rich among them with grass and shrub.

Looking closer he will see young oaks, maple and beeches springing up again, beneath the protecting shadows of the faster growing trees. These first trees are birches, aspens and poplars, called "nurse trees" by foresters. Their roots stabilize the earth, their leaves mulch it, and their spreading foliage shades it against the ravages of direct sun in summer and freezing wind in winter. Thus they are "nurses" because they protect and nurture the slower growing scions of the departed giants.

The King's trees may be the trees of highest value when they come at last to maturity — but they do not reach their height and strength by themselves. There would be few of the slower-growing and more vulnerable little oaks, pines, maples and beeches without the nurse trees.

Rebecca Nurse, was such a birch — a tree both "pale" and "fast " in the words attributed to Anna Putnam and her spectral sight. She was a spiritual nurturer, a "granmer" not only to little Dorcas Good, but to us all — so it was peculiarly appropriate that Anna had claimed to see her spectre "sitting in her grandmother's seat." Most of those hanged were also "nurse trees," including especially Mary Easty. Thomas Brattle cited Reverend Burroughs, John Procter, and John Willard as noteworthy for their gracious bearing on the scaffold. Martha Corey was also such a one. And we know that there were very few who did not cast a shadow of holiness and humility especially in their last groaning as they were felled.

They were relatively short-lived, as the nurse trees of the forest usually are. But our forest would have become a desert without their gracious self-sacrifice: gracious in the way they accepted unfounded condemnation; self-sacrifice in that they did not take the easy way open to them through the deceit of "confessing".

Without the shadow of these trees, spreading a benevolent charity over the outrage against judicial process and Bible religion, we cannot guess when or how our troubles would have ended. But for that wide and extensive penumbra of pardon, nay incredible forgiveness, the pusillanimous leaves of many "great oaks" in the infancy of their righteousness, would never have begun to stir, and the rapid retarding and then reversal of the general decay would not have come on so soon, if at all.

In men like the Nurses, Daniel Andrews, and Reverend Green, we were privileged to have other "nurse trees" after the devastation of our troubles. These two were also short-lived, yet cast mighty shadows.

As events went rapidly forward after the last hangings, we began to realize we had taken a turn, though for a while it was barely perceptible. As the prospect of a certain end to our troubles became surer, we were apt to forget what those departed did for us. We were apt to think no more of them than one trying to put out the remnants of a forest fire thinks of the dead stumps. Neither does one looking over the new forest fifty years later pay a great deal of attention to the smaller remains, the now-decaying trunks of birches and aspens among the new giants.

But to forget those old trees would be much like forgetting the old oaks that marked the division between Endicott and Nurse land -- it would be a mistake that can only result in further conflicts. The better men and women among us did not allow us to forget. For the nurse trees not only nurtured oaks and maples, but they left us their own young, other birches and aspens ready to spring up wherever other devastations strike our forest. And if the new crop of oaks and maples left more room for the children of their nurses, it was a good sign.

THE END

AFTERWORD

The reader who has finished this story may wish to know what parts and passages are fictional –indeed, I suppose he has earned the right to know. Fully half the tale as told is solid history, but the other half ranges from informed speculation to pure invention. I close then by distinguishing which sections have little or no support in documentary evidence.

The "conspiracy" led by Daniel Andrews, and including Joseph Putnam, John Tarbell, Samuel Nurse, Peter Cloyce and George Jacobs, Jr., is fictional. They were all real people with significant involvement in 1692, but the degree to which they worked together is unknown. All of the documents "gathered" are genuine -- we have the signatures of the many who signed the petitions -- but how they were gathered and by whom is not known. The accusation and flight of Daniel and George is genuine, but their hiding place is not. To the best of my knowledge, no one knows where they hid. The patient pursuit of justice after the "troubles," particularly by John Tarbell and Samuel Nurse, is extensively documented -- much of it by Reverend Parris, himself, in the Village church records.

The origin of the strange behavior of Betty Parris and Abigail Williams -- in imitation of Mary Warren's fits -- is fictional. Mary Warren was indeed subject to fits of distraction before the "troubles," and was indeed drawn in as one of the "afflicted". The back-and-forth of her participation in the accusations and withdrawals is reflected in the records. She was indeed brow-beaten (apparently literally) by the ministers as here told. (That the *New England Primer* was the book the Procters gave her and she "touched" is speculation -- based on her mention of "a mark" like the letter "M" and the fact that book had been printed in the colony.) However, Betty and Abigail were indeed the first girls to manifest the "afflictions," and were the first diagnosed as "bewitched," but there have been many, many speculations about the details of how their behavior began.

Many theories put forth over the years in explanation of the origins of these and the other girls' behavior. Most of these speculations rely on solitary psychological, pharmacological or physiological causes and cannot be made consistent with the facts we know. Another popular explanation -- that the girls themselves had formed a sort of "coven" of their own around Tituba -- is no more credible. Anna Putnam's heartfelt statement in the Village Church in

1706, when she confessed her sorrow over her part in the "troubles," offers little to satisfy our curiosity on this score, but it is certain it contains no hint of any "witchery" on her own part. She explicitly denies that she had any conscious malicious intent, so far as she is able to understand or remember it. I am tempted to mention two or three other theories about the origins of the "afflictions," but will only say here that I have found none that fits the historical facts and human nature as well as the one proposed in this story.

It is documented that near the beginning of the examinations two of the girls (which ones is unknown) admitted their accusation of Goody Procter was a game -- "we must have our games." The depositions of Mary Ingersoll, Daniel Elliott, and William Rayment, Jr., testifying to that statement are genuine. Likewise we have genuine testimony of Mary Easty, Mary English, and Edward and Sarah Bishop to Mary Warren's statements in prison to the effect that the girls were no more to be believed in their "distractions" than Keyser's daughter. The deposition of Samuel Barton and John Houghton is also genuine -- that which tells of hearing Tom and Anne Putnam dictating to Mercy Lewis about whom she saw in her fit.

Although the "yellow birds" did indeed come up again and again during the examinations, Sam's account of seeing Sarah Good and Dorcas feeding the goldfinches is fictional. No explanation of the yellow birds, apparently unique to the Salem witch episode, arises from any primary source of which I am aware.

The account of Sarah Cloyce's escape from Ipswich gaol is fictional. Secondary sources differ on exactly what became of Sarah Cloyce between her indictment and her return to her family after the trials had been stopped. It is possible she remained in prison, however the fact that she was indicted, but not tried, and that the prison records give no account of her, together make an escape the most popular interpretation of her history. The idea that she escaped is also supported by the fact she was one of the few who did not apply for compensation, despite the fact that her husband signed petitions in support of compensation for others. The details of the escapes of Edward and Sarah Bishop are also fictional, although the Bishops are shown to have escaped in the records.

The long discussions among the magistrates and ministers are speculative fiction, as is Cotton Mather's interview with Samuel Willard. The "scientific" basis of the witch proofs in Cartesian physics is referred to by Thomas Brattle in his *Letter*. He also mentions Nicholas Noyes as the chief apologist for it. The salient features of Cartesian physics were those which are discussed in these passages, although we do not have the ministers' actual expositions of how they interpreted and applied them. We do have extensive records of the ways these came to bear in the examinations and trials, however, and what I have portrayed is consonant with those records.

The gaol passages are fictional, although there are quite a few records indicating who was kept in which gaol, and when they were transported. Boston actually built a new stone gaol in 1690, but I preferred the old one – more like the one in *Scarlet Letter*. The deaths and births are a matter of record, although the date of birth for Sarah Good's and Elizabeth Procter's babies (and the date of death of the former) is debated. Cotton Mather reported the episode at Boston gaol in which Mercy Short was "cursed" by Sarah Good after throwing a handful of straw at her in response to a request for tobacco. That Mercy Short and "Mrs. Thacher's maid" are the same person is speculation. (One other possibility is that the obscure Mary Watkins was "Mrs. Thacher's maid".)

The execution scenes and are much expanded beyond the historical accounts, although many of the details are derived from firsthand accounts, including much about the godly demeanor of most of those hanged. The death by crushing of Giles Corey is described in sources with much (but not all) of the detail given here.

A number of the genealogical connections given here are open to question. Genealogy provides many instances of conflicting accounts of relationships in colonial families. The Ingersolls of the Village Ordinary, for instance, are variously represented in different relationships, death dates, and so forth. I have made a few "leaps" to connections for which I have no authority whatever. All the names are historical, except Will Good's nickname "Good Will," an invention I could not resist. I have no doubt given too much information about family relationships, but genealogy is a disease with no known cure.

Apart from the examinations and trials, most of the dialogue is fictional. The extensive records of the examinations give us most of that dialogue verbatim. In light of the fact that the persons "recording" them are known to have misinterpreted things according to their own prejudices, I have occasionally edited the record. (Prejudicing of the records was one of the charges the Nurses brought against Reverend Parris, a principal recorder of the official transcripts we have, and in one of his own later documents, his

"Meditations for Peace," he more or less admits it.) The changes I made in the examination dialogue are slight, but they and the added narrative elements, which are extensive, make the examination sections into fiction, too, strictly speaking.

Few details of the efforts to obtain a pardon for Rebecca Nurse are known. There was a pardon and it was revoked. All documents quoted in that connection are genuine, but I have speculated and fictionalized in those episodes.

The dates of deaths, births, and marriages are as accurate as I could make them, including the marriage of Peter Cloyce, Jr., and Mary Preston. That they were courting during the troubles is reasonably inferred. The descriptions of these events, however, are fictional.

Quite a few of the original legal documents are available. There are very many of them, ranging from arrest records, gaoler's account books, and bills from innkeepers to death warrants from the Court of Oyer and Terminer signed by Deputy Stoughton. Most repositories arrange them according to "case," that is according to the person charged. These have been gathered and collated by various people and institutions over the years, including the Work Projects Administration, the Essex Institute, and the University of Virginia. The New York and Boston Public Libraries have some original documents. New ones pop up every now and then -- from some disused folder in a file drawer or attic. Anyone wishing to study the events in a scholarly way can find transcripts of the original documents in print and on-line. A brief bibliography is included below.

In addition to the primary documents, there are many secondary studies of various aspects of the witch trials, the period, and the Salem community. Quite a number of authors have made an effort to unravel the events in stories, novels and plays.

There have also been some notable forgeries of Salem Witch Trial documents. I hope with this explanation, the reader will at least absolve me from that charge.

James Howard Trott
Philadelphia,   January 2004 / July 2015

BIBLIOGRAPHY

Brooks, Thomas. *Precious Remedies Against Satan's Devices.* (1652)
London: Banner of Truth Trust, 1968.

Calef, Robert. *More Wonders of the Invisible World : Display'd in Five
Parts. . .* London: Nath. Hillar, 1700. (Available online at the
University of Virginia website shown below)

Dow, George Francis. *Every Day Life in the Massachusetts Bay Colony.*
(1935)   Mineola, NY: Dover Publishers, 1988.

Maule, James Edward. *Better That 100 Witches Should Live: The 1698?
Acquittal of Thomas Maule of Salem, Massachusetts on Charges of
Seditious Libel and Its Impact on the Development of First
Amendment Freedoms.* Villanova, PA: Jembook Pub. Co., 1995.

McMillen, Persis W. *Currents of Malice: Mary Towne Esty and Her
Family in Salem Witchcraft.* Portsmouth, NH: Peter E. Randall,
Publishers, 1990.

Miller, Perry (Editor). *The American Puritans : Their Prose and Poetry.*
Garden City, NY: Anchor Books (Doubleday and Co.), 1956.

Morgan, Edmund S. *The Puritan Dilemma: The Story of John Winthrop.*
Boston: Little, Brown and Co., 1958.

Narratives of the Witchcraft Cases, 1648-1706. George L. Burr, Editor.
New York, NY: Barnes and Noble, Inc (1914) 1968.

*Salem Witchcraft Papers, The : Verbatim Transcripts of the Legal
Documents of the Salem Witchcraft Outbreak of 1692. 3 vols.*
Compiled and Transcribed by the Works Progress
Administration, Under the Supervision of Archie N. Frost, 1938.
Edited with an Introduction and Index, Paul Boyer and Stephen
Nissenbaum. New York, NY: Da Capo Press, 1977.

Sloane, Eric. *A Museum of Early American Tools.* NY: Ballantine
Books, (1964) 1974.

*"Some Miscellany Observations On Our Present Debates Respecting
Witchcrafts, in a Dialogue Between S. & B.* [Salem and Boston]. By
P.E. and J.A. Philadelphia: Printed by William Bradford, for
Hezekiah Usher, 1692." (Letter generally attributed to Reverend
Samuel Willard of Boston.) (Available at University of Virginia
website listed below.)

Savage, James. *A Genealogical Dictionary of the First Settlers of New
England,* 4 vols. Boston: Little Brown & Co., 1860-2   Baltimore:
Genealogical Publishing Co, 1965.

Starkey, Marian L. *The Devil In Massachusetts.* NY: Time, Inc., (1949) 1963.

Thomas Hutchinson: The History of the Colony and Province of Massachusetts. (1768) Lawrence Shaw Mayo, Editor. Cambridge, Mass: Harvard U., 1936.

Trask, Richard B. *The Devil Hath Been Raised* . Danvers, Mass: Yeoman Press (1992) 1997

Upham, Charles W. *Salem Witchcraft, (2 vols)* Boston: Wiggins and Lunt, 1867. Williamstown, Mass: Corner House Pubs, 1971.

BIBLIOGRAPHY OF SOURCES FOR EPIGRAPHS, ETC.:
King James Version of the Bible
The Necessity of Reformation, General Court Synod, 1679
Edward Johnson, *Wonder-Working Providence of Sion's Savior*, 1654
Peter Bulkeley, *The Lesson of the Covenant for England and New England*, 1651
Thomas Hooker, *A True Sight of Sin* (1659)
The New England Primer, (1st published in colony circa 1687)
Cotton Mather, "Beelzebub and his Plot," *Wonders of the Invisible World*, 1693
Committee of Salem, arbitrating dispute Village Church vs. Rev. Deodat Lawson, 1687
Second Royal Charter of Massachusetts, 1691
Thomas Brooks, *Precious Remedies Against Satan's Devices*, (1652)
Thomas Shepherd (1605-1649), *Autobiography*, (circa 1647)
John Winthrop (1588-1649), Speech to the General Court, 1645
Deodat Lawson, sermon, *Christ's Fidelity the only Shield Against Satan's Malignity*, 24 March 1692
Laws And Liberties of Massachusetts, 1648
Michael Wigglesworth, *God's Controversy With New England*, 1662
Cotton Mather, *Memorable Providences, Relating to Witchcrafts and Possession*, 1689
Michael Wigglesworth, *Day of Doom*, 1662
Edward Taylor (1645-1729), *Sacramental Meditations*
William Perkins, *A Discourse of the Damned Art of Witchcraft*, 1608.
John Cotton(1585-1652) , *Christian Calling*, 1641
William Bradford, *Of Plymouth Plantation*, 1669
Increase Mather, *Man Knows Not His Time*, 1697
Anne Bradstreet, *Meditations*, 1664
John Winthrop, *Journal*, (1636)

Thomas Shepherd, *A Defense of the Answer made unto the Nine Questions or Positions sent from New-England against the reply thereto by Mr. John Ball*, 1648

Gershom Bulkeley, *Letter to Benjamin Davis*, 15 March 1700

Cotton Mather, *Magnalia Christi Americana*, 1702

John Cotton, *Limitation of Government*, ?date

Urian Oakes, *The Sovereign Efficacy of Divine Providence*, 1677

Some Miscellany Observations On our Present Debates Respecting Witchcrafts, in a Dialogue Between S. & B. by P.E. and J.A. Printed by William Bradford for Hezekiah Usher, Philadelphia, 1692

Cotton Mather, *Another Brand Pluckt Out of the Burning: An Account of the Sufferings of Margaret Rule*, ?date

Robert Calef, *A Warning to the Ministers in More Wonders of the Invisible World*, 1700

Thomas Brattle, *Letter of Thomas Brattle, F.R.S.*, October 1692

John Winthrop, *A Model of Christian Charity*, (Sermon on Arabella), 1630

Full Covenant of the Church at Salem, 1629

Increase Mather, *Cases of Conscience Concerning Evil Spirits*, Boston, 1693

Salem Village *Church Covenant*, 1689

WEBSITES

I consulted several hundred internet sites, and they cannot all be listed here. However searches of individual names will reveal how much information is online concerning the Salem Witch Trials of 1692, as well as related genealogy, and colonial history. I would warn any internet researcher, however, that the amount of misinformation available on this subject is much greater than that of accurate information. Here are several sites I found useful during the year of my research (2002). These are linked to many others :

http://etext.virginia.edu/salem/witchcraft/archives
http://www.ogram.org/17thc/teachermaterials.shtml
http://www.salemwitchtrials.com
http://www.law.umkc.edu/faculty/projects/ftrials/salem/salem.htm

A Gallows Set

www.ingramcontent.com/pod-product-compliance
Lightning Source LLC
Chambersburg PA
CBHW070535030726
47505CB00001B/48